WHEN NIGHT FALLS

THE THREE GIFTS

By Gerald L. Coleman

BOOK ONE

WHEN NIGHT FALLS

By GERALD L. COLEMAN

Copyright © 2014 by Gerald L. Coleman

All rights reserved. No part of this publication may be reproduced, distributed or transmitted in any form or by any means, without prior written permission.

Gerald L. Coleman
Atlanta, Georgia
Geraldlcoleman.co

Publisher's Note: This is a work of fiction. Names, characters, places, and incidents are a product of the author's imagination. Locales and public names are sometimes used for atmospheric purposes. Any resemblance to actual people, living or dead, or to businesses, companies, events, institutions, or locales is completely coincidental.

WHEN NIGHT FALLS

ISBN 9780578474274

Cover art by Edli Akolli
Map Design Gerald L. Coleman
Map Art by Gregory Shipp

For my mother June, for giving me a love of reading and always believing in me, Tim for being the best big brother, and my community of writers, particularly the Affrilachian Poets ...

FOREWORD

This book, well series of books, began as a way of changing the world of literature, which I love immensely. Growing up I read all the great science fiction and epic fantasy I could get my hands on. The house I grew up in was simple, clean, and filled with reading. I have my mother to thank for that. Some of my earliest memories are of her reading to my brother and I. She raised us on her own. One of the greatest gifts she gave us was a love of reading. While we did not have much in the way of material possessions I was still able to travel the universe. I moved through time and space. I rode on the back of horses with heroes. I fought monsters with them, pushed back the Darkness alongside them, wielding a sword, or magical powers. My mind was alive with the wonders of far away realms, distant battles, and magical possibilities. All the while I learned what it meant to make a difference in the world.

While I reveled in dragonriders, wizards, knights, elves, and even hobbits I never really got to see myself reflected in the thousands of pages that passed before my eyes. I appropriated the position of hero as an avid reader but somewhere in the back of my mind I knew these heroes did not look like me. They looked just like most of the square-jawed, white, men I saw on television or at the movies. Even in the comic books I read the same archetypes applied. There was the occasional Luke Cage: Power Man or Black Panther but mostly the prevailing archetype held. So I decided to write an epic fantasy adventure with all the normal facets, which I have loved so much about the genre, but with one simple addition. In my adventure everyone would find a heroic character with whom they could identify. To you, the reader, I say thank you for reading my homage to epic fantasy. I appreciate you taking this journey with me. I hope you enjoy reading this first book in the series as much as I have enjoyed writing it for you.

Gerald L. Coleman
March 2014

CONTENTS

PRELUDE 1

CHAPTER ONE 11
Things fall apart
CHAPTER TWO 27
Keep the home fires burning
CHAPTER THREE 41
Storm a' brewing
CHAPTER FOUR 55
An open door and words between
CHAPTER FIVE 83
A fork in the road
CHAPTER SIX 105
And those who carry on
CHAPTER SEVEN 135
Thoughts of home
CHAPTER EIGHT 159
A change in the weather
CHAPTER NINE 173
A touch from the dark
CHAPTER TEN 185
Holding on and letting go
CHAPTER ELEVEN 209
Someone watching over me
CHAPTER TWELVE 231
Of things past
CHAPTER THIRTEEN 271
Gifts and graces
CHAPTER FOURTEEN 291
Where need takes us
CHAPTER FIFTEEN 315
Around about midnight
CHAPTER SIXTEEN 337
A caution against favors
CHAPTER SEVENTEEN 371
The silent speak

CHAPTER EIGHTEEN 383
    Questions and answers
CHAPTER NINETEEN 401
    Homecoming
CHAPTER TWENTY 413
    Al'akaz
CHAPTER TWENTY-ONE 443
    As deep as the Wadi
CHAPTER TWENTY-TWO 457
    Where women do not tread
CHAPTER TWENTY-THREE 475
    The debt
CHAPTER TWENTY-FOUR 495
    Shadows in the Hall
CHAPTER TWENTY-FIVE 513
    The hallowed place of horrors
CHAPTER TWENTY-SIX 533
    Sidesteps
CHAPTER TWENTY-SEVEN 553
    When visitors come calling
CHAPTER TWENTY-EIGHT 575
    Challenge
CHAPTER TWENTY-NINE 593
    Moh'di'ba
CHAPTER THIRTY 613
    Selene
CHAPTER THIRTY-ONE 625
    Sacrifice

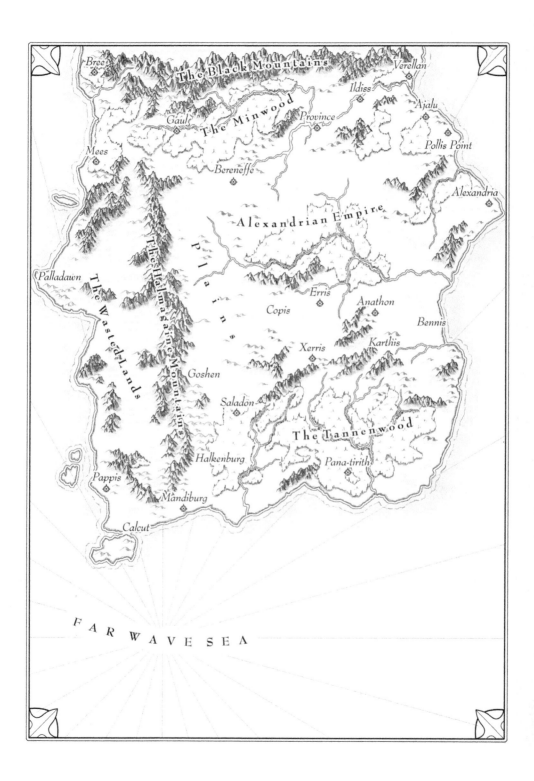

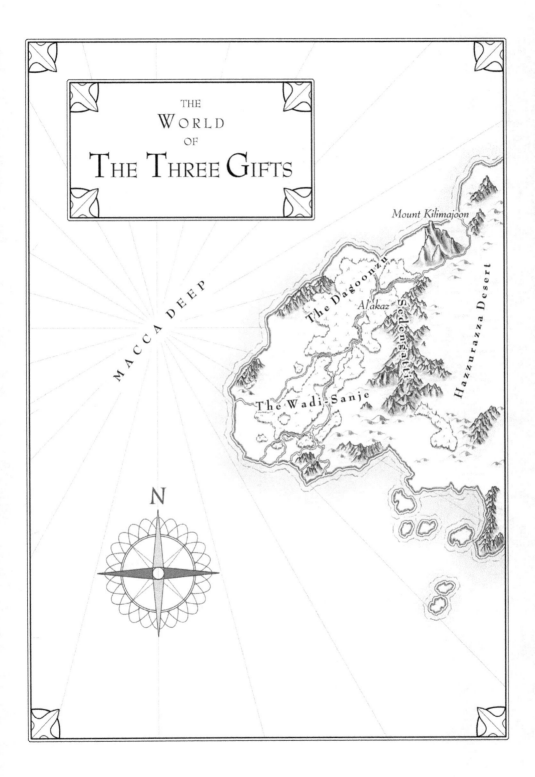

... and they made their bed in darkness, forswearing the light, the sun hid its face from them even as tears fell from the heavens; for to those who pitched their tent beneath the face of the shadow, came great tribulation, bathed in fire, leaving them bereft of hope while they sat among the ruins in sackcloth and ashes crying out for a salvation that would never come ...

                    - Jillis Jossen the Mallibarr
                          Witness to the burning of Chessa Hollabring
                                 at Mandiburg 342 C. E.

PRELUDE

The tea was so hot she had to blow on it before she could sip from the small porcelain cup. Its matching, pale-blue saucer, with tiny, yellow flowers winding around its edge, rested on the tips of the fingers of her right hand. With her left hand she raised the delicate cup to her lips. She sipped lightly. The taste of orange blossoms, with a sweet, subtle hint of honey, filled her mouth. The tea's heat warmed her as it trickled down her throat. She breathed in the fresh, cool, evening air that blew across her face as it brought the smell of mint, mixed with hibiscus, to her. *And maybe*, she thought, *a hint of lilac and honeysuckle?* The fragrances filled her nose causing her to smile brightly. *Peace.* This place, along with the time of day, always brought her comfort. She reclined in the oversized chair, on the veranda, as she gazed out on the lush Valley of O'lukaz. Fully leaved trees intermingled with thick stands of flowers in every conceivable color as they filled the valley below. It made for a breathtaking sight from her vantage point. The house had been built along the rim of the valley to take advantage of the beautiful view.

She loved coming out onto the veranda, leaning over the slatted railing, or just nestling into Azmatthamelle's large chair while reveling in that view. Rocking herself slightly, she mirrored the treetops, as the wind turned, then twisted, down into the valley causing them to sway in the breeze.

"Joy of my heart." His voice was deep, with a rich complexity, as if there were other, fainter, voices echoing behind it, just out of hearing. Caught by surprise, she nearly jumped out of the chair. As it was, she spilled some of her tea on the front of her dress. The too-white, nearly sheer fabric shimmered as the tea drizzled down its front. Then, in a brief twinkle of multi-colored light, the tea disappeared leaving no trace. It was the only thing that kept her from giving him a stern look, even if she would not have meant it.

Setting the cup lightly on its saucer she placed both on the small table nestled against the chair while rising from her seat. Turning, she looked at him as he stood in the open doorway leading from the house out onto the veranda. When her eyes fell on him it happened. He had taught her how to mask the effects of the *presence* so that she would not be so overcome, but sometimes she enjoyed letting herself feel it. He was one of the Glorious Ones. She was only mortal. As he walked onto the veranda, gliding with an unearthly grace that only they possessed, the *presence* washed over her. Joy blossomed in her chest. She had to fight to keep tears from filling her eyes. She let it wash over her. A slight moan escaped her lips as she swayed almost imperceptibly from one foot to the other. A warm hand cupped her chin then lifted it, tilting her head back ever so slightly. Opening her eyes she let her smile stretch across her entire face. By the Ancient, she was giddy!

He shook his head slightly back and forth with a rue smile of his own adorning his face. His voice rumbled from somewhere deep, almost far off. "Aas, I have taught you how to temper the effects of the Presence yet you still allow yourself to be overcome." He was trying to sound stern and failing miserably. She almost laughed at the faint-hearted attempt.

Aas reached up, placing both of her small hands on his, turning them so that she could lay her head in them. She took a deep breath, inhaling him. "I am sorry my love. I only do it when you have been away longer than usual. My heart leaps that you have returned to me." Ducking under his outstretched arm she threw her arms around him. Even on her tiptoes her face nestled against his body just shy of his chest.

He put his arms around her squeezing gently. She felt as if she could stay there forever. It was only when he spoke again that she could hear something different in his voice. "Aas my love, we must move quickly. I do not have time to explain fully but something has happened. I must get you to safety."

Aas tilted her head back to look up at him. It was then that she noticed the tears, unshed, but glistening, in his eyes. Today those eyes, which he normally liked to be light brown or green, were a hard, slate, gray. Her breath caught in her throat. She had never, *ever*, seen Az cry. Pushing back from him she really *looked* at him. If she had not let the *presence* overcome her she would have seen it as soon as he came out onto the veranda. His sleeveless, pale-green robe with blue vines embroidered along the seams was stained with dirt and blood. His long, black, woolly locks hung loose around his shoulders. There were cuts on his arms. She could see bruises that were hard to make out because of his dark brown skin. Her voice caught in her throat as she spoke, "What ... what has happened Azmatthamelle? There has been violence? How is that possible?"

Azmatthamelle put one hand on her slim shoulder while brushing at her hair with the other. The tiny bells tied in among the countless braids of her black hair, which hung to the small of her back, jingled lightly. "*Mnasha nnanda*, my precious." *Be at peace*. He said it in the First Tongue. "Blood stains the steps of Allemdashhar. The Anointed One is dead." His jaw clenched then unclenched as he spoke the words. She knew a rage was building deep within him. His voice trembled lightly as he went on. "We have been betrayed. Even now Palladawn burns. The Glorious Ones shed each other's blood in the Hall of Adoration. I left the fighting at Allemdashar, but I must return. I came to get you to a place that will be safe."

Aas listened in stunned silence. She was so shocked that she barely took notice of how Azmatthamelle's voice grew harder as he spoke. *Palladawn burning? The Anointed One dead?* She realized that she was not breathing and suddenly gulped in air. Before she could speak Azmatthamelle was pulling her, nearly dragging her off the veranda then through the house. Her voice sounded breathless as she raced to keep up, "I must gather some things for us husband." But he was shaking his head as he spoke over his shoulder, "No time my heart. The Betrayer knows that I have a mortal wife. The Twisted Ones might let you live but if their plan is to succeed they cannot let the child you carry survive."

She squeaked at his words then stopped only to be nearly jerked forward as they continued on toward the front door. It had to be very early if she was really with child. In fact it must have been only a few weeks. It did not surprise her that he knew even before she did, after all he was one of the Glorious. While he raced them out of the house and into a sparkling whirlwind of shimmering lights that appeared with the wave of his hand she fought with her fear of what had happened to her world. It warred in her chest with the joy of what was happening inside her body. She was going to have a child.

†

Tellahmaraineth sat on the hilltop looking down on where the Spires of Ell'sithelle'menerith had stood, ancient and resplendent against the skyline, as recently as dawn. Now all she could see was thick, black smoke signaling the presence of the raging fires below. From time to time the earth shook underneath her forcing her to brace herself with her hands to keep from being tossed about. Normally she would have *Spoken* to the clouds to keep the rain at bay until she was gone but she could not afford to attract attention. Some of the *betrayers* were probably still in the city.

Her skin tingled but she did not turn her head. Tellah knew before he arrived exactly who it would be. Azmatthamelle had always liked *Shifting*. He claimed it was easier on the place you left as well as where you arrived. If you questioned it he would launch into a lecture about metaphysics and the nature of movement. The young were always particular about certain things but Tellah was in no mood for lectures. His voice rumbled behind her. "Tellah, I have come."

She continued gazing down on burning Ell'sithelle'menerith. She knew she sounded tired, but she did not care to try to modulate her voice. Tellah spoke without turning to look at him, transfixed by the fires ravaging the city below. Her question was punctuated by the periodic flash of lightning, as dark as the midnight, high in the sky above. "How is Aas?"

"She is safe. She is troubled, but safe. That is all that matters." Tellahmaraineth could feel him scanning the hillside. She knew what he would say next but cut him off as he opened his mouth to ask, "I do not know what is keeping Tutthameldaszar." They both nearly jumped when a third voice spoke from above them.

"The *Thaumaturgis* has arrived. The Awaited One is here. I have come." The voice was rich, melodic, and completely full of itself. Tutthameldaszar had not simply wielded the *Gift* for more than an eon, he had taught its nuances in the Eedris, even debated its complexity on the Pavilion. He always spoke as if he had an audience, whether he had one or not. He was one of the eldest of them all.

Tellahmaraineth looked up to watch him float down out of the sky landing gently, with a flourish, not far from where Az stood. Laughing softly, she watched as Tutthameldaszar bowed deeply with another flourish while Azmatthamelle looked at him as if he were considering what part of him to break. Tutt's robe was smartly cut. It was fitted to his slim frame. The purple, gold, and gray robe was tattered a bit around the edges but somehow his boots shone glossy black while his cloak flapped lightly in the wind. *Had he stopped to polish his boots,* she thought? Though his bronze colored face was lightly smudged, his silvery white hair sparkled as it hung loosely around his shoulders.

Though her heart was pained she could not keep a hint of mirth out of her voice. "Tutt, you can never stop putting on the performance, can you?"

He shook his head at her, making a *tsking* sound with his tongue, as he said, "Tellah, sometimes the performance is all you have, no?" Tutt looked skyward with irritation then absently waved his hand. The rain continued to fall but it did not touch the hilltop. With a brief nod, accompanied by a grim grin, he clasped his hands behind his back as he stepped closer to her.

Tellah took a deep breath. She stood, brushing at the pale-blue gossamer gown she wore as she rose. The sleeves were fitted from shoulder to elbow but flared into bell cuffs. The high collar curved up stopping just below her ears. Her slippers were delicate with sparkling gems covering the sharply curved toes. The gems picked up what little light remained. She towered over mortals, though Az and Tutt were a half-head taller still. While the rest of their brothers and sisters were fighting for their lives, along with what was left of the world, she had been able to contact these two, convincing them to leave the fighting. They waited for her to speak. After all, *she* had contacted *them*. They had come at her call. For that, she was grateful. It could not have been easy for Azmatthamelle to leave his beloved Aas. Tutthameldaszar would have gotten himself killed strolling up to the Hall of Adoration. No doubt he would have called the betrayers out to meet him in formal combat right there on the Great Steps. He would have died. He was the *Thaumaturgis,* so many of the betrayers would have fallen beneath his wrath. The countryside would have been decimated for a thousand miles in every direction, but in the end, they would have taken him with them. Had she not gotten to him first it would have been a waste - a costly, disastrous waste.

Tellah took another deep breath. Finding her voice, she said, "We have lost the day. But, we must not lose eternity. Somehow, something must survive the devastation." Standing very still, she waited. Tutt gazed toward the burning city with his arms across his chest, a single finger tapping his pursed lips. Az looked her in the eye. He did not blink. He did not even move.

It was Tutthameldaszar who spoke first. Low, soft, and with fewer flourishes than his voice normally held he said, "There is blood on the steps at Palladawn. The Anointed One is dead. The Spires of The Ancient City are blackened and crumbling." He turned to look at her then, his eyes ablaze, but his voice stilled like ice as he continued, "What would you have us do Tellahmaraineth, Daughter of Allgashain, Stone of Heaven, Keeper of the Everlasting Flame, She, who stands at the Right Hand of the Presence? What can we do now, that will matter, except take as many of them with us as we can, and hope that the One who sits on the Throne may yet stir?"

Tellah looked from Az to Tutt noticing that their cheeks were not wet because of the rain that still fell from the sky. Tears had begun to fall from their eyes. She blinked fiercely as she realized that she too had begun to cry. She gathered her thoughts, steeling herself for what must be done. She needed these two Glorious Ones to believe one more time, to choose the good in the face of overwhelming, seemingly inevitable evil. The Ancient of Days would not move from the Throne of Heaven to intervene, at least not in the way Tutt wanted, for that was not the Way of Heaven. They would have to act if the world was to be saved. If they failed the world was lost. Tellah spoke the words that she hoped would make all the difference. "Glorious Ones, I have a plan."

As Tellahmaraineth spoke, Azmathamelle nodded slowly, while Tutthameldaszar began to smile. There was no mirth or joy in that smile only grim resolve. As she spoke they both stepped closer to her. She told them her plan. They listened as tears continued to fall from their eyes. All around them the ground shook, the fires raged, as the world they once knew came to an end.

An unlit candle is of little use when night falls.

*~Ana Belle
mother of Junn, overheard at the
Festival of Home Coming
Springs Field, near the Flat Woods
at sunset.*

*Bid the morning
Sweetly come
Bid it ever, sweetly*

*Ask a blessing
Of the day
Ask it ever, so*

*Touch your feet
To earth and smile
Turn your eye
To touch the sky
Stretch your arms
To wind and wave
And chance your
Soul to fly
As the sun
Her rays do kiss
And warm your
Up turned face*

*And bid all sweetly
Meet the dawn
And may it sweetly come
Yes may it sweetly, sweetly come
May it sweetly, come*

~Pascha morning prayer

Wishing for a good morning is like asking a blind man for directions.

~*Kushka the baker,
upon being told good
morning by her first
customer.*

Chapter one

Things fall apart

Onya Onoto eased up along the wall. At the end of the wall she paused, listening intently, as she held her breath. The gray rock of the wall held her weight, roughly, as she leaned against it. The cool touch of its unheated, textured surface brushed against the base of her neck sending a slight chill down her spine. Her left palm brushed across its chiseled grain, feeling its rough-hewn unevenness. Silence seemed to hold the entire area in its grasp. Onya flipped open her round, Tink-made, silver pocket timepiece. She watched the black second-hand tick around the white face for a few seconds. Part one of the operation was complete. Having crept into the compound under the cover of early morning darkness it was time to wait. Insertion had been achieved. Taking in her surroundings, Onya allowed herself to believe that all things were as they should be, at least for the moment. She let herself exhale. Her breath turned to mist in the air. As it drifted off, dissipating in the cool, pre-dawn air she went over the parameters of their mission in her mind.

The key to entering a facility, where you were not wanted, without killing everyone you saw, was not being seen. The secret to remaining unseen was not what most people thought. Yes, stealth was important, but the most valuable asset was patience. Patience was not just one of the great virtues, used correctly it was a potent weapon.

You watched. You waited. And then, you waited some more. When it was time, you moved. When you moved, you did so quickly, with precise, deadly, economy, and absolute silence. All of this was certainly more easily said than done. Onya could almost hear Bantu's voice echoing in her mind relating the price of excellence. *High standards*, he would say. Hard work mixed with high standards combined to create excellence. Onya smiled to herself as she watched the seconds tick away.

The sun would be peaking over the horizon soon. It would be a breathtaking sight. High in the northern hill country of Province with its lush greenery, rolling hills, and thick clouds brushing those hilltops, would make for a beautiful sight. Maybe it would be reddish-gold with a hint of purple or possibly, considering the hour, more yellow with hints of rust. Whichever it turned out to be, it would be worth seeing.

The sky, just before dawn, always brought on a stillness in Onya, which she had found could be had at no other time of the day. Others had said they felt that stillness late at night when most people were in their beds, but for Onya it was early morning, just before the sun came up.

Peering into the distance, she could see what appeared to be two birds of prey circling high above her. They seemed to hardly flap their wings. They just lazily drifted in great intersecting circles. The hazy light of approaching dawn slowly began to pour over the nettletree-covered hilltops. The immense rock outcroppings dotting those hilltops, which momentarily held back the sun's early morning arrival, seemed small when viewed from such a great distance. They reminded her of very old men asleep under thick, green blankets caught as if frozen mid-turn in their beds. The vastness of the view made her seem so small.

The air was refreshingly crisp with a hint of mint on the breeze. The day would warm quickly. The successful outcome of her mission would only be a part of the reason for that warmth. She took a deep breath and held it. Rubbing her fingers, one against another, she felt the texture of her own fingertips. As she watched the horizon, the world seemed to slow down while the greens of the lush hillsides seemed to brighten. The wall against her back, along with the ground beneath her feet, for a moment, seemed to be a part of her. She stretched out her awareness feeling how the wind swirled as it rustled through the trees. It was called the *abundance*. Onya immersed herself in the moment. Exhaling through her left nostril - then inhaling through the right – made her feel like she could almost taste the sweetness of the morning.

The mission's protocols were clicking off, one after another, with the smooth precision of one of Tink's time-pieces. But as her mind drifted back, for a moment, she had to admit to herself that it had been a long couple of days. Those two days had commenced hundreds of miles to the south at Sanctuary, where Bantu had received a visitor from Rulers Hill - an imperial messenger, in point of fact. Almost immediately, he had left for the royal house of Alexandria. The royal house stood atop an imposing rise of land overlooking the entire capital city. *The Hill*, as it was called in the capital, could be seen from miles away as one approached the city from land or sea. The intent of the city's layout was to inspire a sense of awe in all those who came to the capital, especially noble visitors, ambassadors, or envoys coming to conduct the business of state. For most people, it did exactly that.

Looking out a front window of the palace, it would be possible to see, not only, the city stretching out beneath you but much of the surrounding countryside. The rear of the palace looked out onto the clear, blue, sparkling waters of the great sea known as the Macca Deep. Ships, of varying size, could be seen taxiing in, or out, of the harbor from the rear windows of the House of Lilies. Alexandria House, the palace at the heart of the Empire, took its formal name from the title of the House from which the current ruler came. At least that was the tradition before the current occupant's grandfather began turning a single kingdom into an empire. He, his son Alexander, who completed that conquest, along with his granddaughter, who now sat on the imperial throne, Empress Natassha Sobrine, were of the ancient Samosian House of the Lilies. The name Samosata was no longer in use. The Samosian kingdom had been turned into the Empire, while Samosata the city was now Alexandria.

Bantu had been away from Sanctuary most of the morning. When he returned to Sanctuary late in the afternoon he sent for Onya. She was informed that she would command a strike team on a mission of extreme importance, the particulars of which would be discussed on route to her destination. A *Cadet-Third* appeared in the doorway of her quarters, tugging absently at the white coat that marked him a cadet, with a summons to Aerie just as she completed packing her gear.

Aerie was a building several stories high, at the edge of Sanctuary, overlooking the Macca Deep, which had been cut down into the cliffs beneath it. The building, along with that section of the cliffs, housed the air wing of the Peoples Company. Its members were known as *Mountain Feathers*. Upon her arrival at Aerie, she was led briskly through the heart of the building, down into the inner recesses of the cliffs, which opened into the air above the crashing waters of the Deep. As Onya was arriving, two of the enormous birds, called *Pradas,* came in for a landing. The Pradas had circled above the pale, blue, crystal waters of the Deep that crashed thunderously into white foam at the bottom of the cliffs, just before their Mountain Feather pilots gave them the nudge to land. The speed with which they came hurtling into the yawning opening of the caverns in the cliff face was always shocking to Onya. It just did not seem like they should be able to stop so quickly. Amid the bustle of cargo loading, or unloading, bird feeding, and grooming, which had to be done with scaffolding, the sound of birds cawing, mixed with people shouting, echoing off the cavern's roof, Onya found Bantu standing with her crew. The master of Sanctuary had been standing in the midst of all that hectic activity, clad in Company black.

He towered over her. It wasn't just that she was a small woman, it was that he was taller than most. His face was like chiseled stone, with a clean-shaven, strong chin. He had a small, but broad, nose with tiny ears. All of those lovely features were covered in blemish-free skin that was a golden dark-brown. His head was shaved completely smooth. His eyes were hazel but somehow hard like steel. When he looked at you those eyes could be piercing, as if he was seeing right into your very center. Bantu had broad shoulders on a lean frame, but Onya knew that it was hard muscle beneath the close-cut, high-collared, black, wool coat that hugged at the waist, and flared out slightly over the hips as it fell to the top of the thigh. The embroidered, intricate scrollwork, which wound thickly up the coat sleeves, from cuff to elbow, showed up again around the high collar, where it was an even deeper black. The buttons, which ran down the center of the front of the coat, were also a glistening black. The breeches were matching black wool with a thick, raised seam running down the center of the thigh giving them a structured, rakish look. Those breeches were tucked into knee-high, black, leather boots with a wide, round toe, and heavy sole. They had a just-shinned, glossy look with a single, thick, silver buckle slashing across the ankle of each boot.

He held himself in that still way that made you think of the calm before a storm. It was the same sense you got when, though the sky was clear, you could still feel an approaching storm just over the horizon. That anticipation of something powerful or dangerous, just out of sight, seemed to emanate from him. Onya, along with anyone who had served with him, knew it was not just imagination. As she made her way across the Pradas' landing area, to where he had been standing, Bantu was silently supervising her team while they loaded their gear.

At her approach the team's members stopped their various activities, snapping to attention, with their right hands rising respectfully to their foreheads. They had stood there unmoving. Dropping her gear, she had flipped a quick salute in their direction. As Bantu turned from the strike team to face her, she snapped to attention. Without thinking, her hand had risen sharply to her forehead again. Onya Onoto, of the Quiet Blossoms, Captain-Commander of the Peoples Company, stood there, unmoving, with her eyes focused just over his shoulder. She waited for her commanding officer to acknowledge her. The five tiny, circular, silver pips pinned in a row along the right side of his high collar marked him as the Commander-General of the Peoples Company. His name was Ossassande Bantu A' Omorede. Onya, with four full pips, marking her a Captain-Commander, not prone to fear, nevertheless moved very deliberately around Bantu. They had become close friends over time, but she had never really gotten out of the habit of exercising a certain caution around him. After a salute, a half-smile, followed by a quip about him not having to come after her, he turned on his heel. Striding back toward the building she had just come from, he had turned his ear to the several officers rushing alongside him, trying to keep up with his long strides. Onya remembered watching him go, shaking her head while watching him deal with the questions, as well as the papers they handed him, all without slowing. She recalled thinking to herself how much she did not want his responsibilities. With a sigh, she had turned to deal with her own. The Company ran on responsibility. You accepted the burden of your responsibility to the people. It also ran on courage. You summoned the courage necessary to fulfill those responsibilities.

With their gear completely loaded, her team had climbed the rope ladder that allowed them to access the personnel carrier strapped to the back of the Pradas. It was a wooden flight-carriage with an oval design, reinforced by steel. It was flanked by small curved wings just behind the doors, which flared back, tapering off into a small pointed tail at the rear of the carriage. The entire carriage was secured with steel reinforced rigging, as thick as her arm, attached to steel bolts on the carriage. The particular carriage they piled into had been constructed to carry seven people, along with their accompanying gear.

The towering, reddish-brown, feathered bird, whose coloring meant he was male, had a golden, curved beak matched by golden talons. The massive bird rustled his wings while making a low rumbling sound that caused the carrier to vibrate slightly. Their pilot appeared miniscule climbing the rope ladder running from the ground, thirty feet up the height of the great bird, to where his seat awaited him. It was in a second smaller cabin, of similar design to the personnel carrier. The flight cabin sat just behind the Pradas' neck, while the carrier holding them was nestled securely between the bird's wings. The Pradas were enormous, magnificent birds. They looked like the Ancient of Days had taken a hawk and decided to make a version of them the size of a small building. Onya remembered the pilot adjusting his weathered, black, leather jacket just before climbing up to, what the Mountain Feathers called, the Pilot's Nest.

Onya could not have seen it from her seat in the carrier, but she knew what he had done next. He climbed into the Pilot's Nest, which was covered by a steel reinforced glass shield. The Mountain Feather pulled the shield down into place after securing himself in his seat. It protected him from the elements while allowing him complete visibility during flight. The leather reigns came up through the front of the cabin, threaded in by way of leather covered wooden tubes made to let the reigns in but keep the weather out.

The young Lieutenant had taken hold of the reigns. With a nudge of his left heel into the exposed neck of the bird, inside his cabin, beneath his feet, coupled with a cluck of his tongue, the great bird, *Santeju*, Onya recalled, rose to his feet. The massive creature unfurled long, powerful wings. The Mountain Feather's voice command was picked up by his communication gemstone, flaring to glowing, green life on the high collar of his black coat. The gemstone transmitted his voice to the matching stone attached to the inner ear of the great bird. By foot, reign, and voice command the Pradas was trained to understand his pilot's instructions.

The bird's huge wings, flexing with reserved power, had sent uniformed attendants scurrying for cover. Slowly, making his way to the edge of the cavern, at his pilot's urging, Santeju leaped out into the air bearing them all aloft. Hurtling down toward the crashing waters of the Macca Deep, the bird gained neck-breaking speed until suddenly snapping his immense wings downward in powerful strokes. Catching the wind beneath him, Santeju allowed the buffeting wind to push him upward. Soaring, he climbed almost straight up in tight arcs swallowing the sky like a man dying of thirst would have gulped fresh water. The Lieutenant, Onya remembered thinking, was showing off. He urged Santeju upward with some rhythmic chant Onya had heard other pilots use with the birds but could never quite catch. Exhilarating would be the word to describe it, even as her stomach tried to leap into her lap.

Onya watched in silence, from the glass window of the carrier, as Sanctuary, followed by all of Alexandria, had dwindled away beneath her. As they leveled off, thousands of feet in the air, Santeju began to glide on the rising heat thermals, at least that is what she overheard some Mountain Feather call it one night. Slowly, she began to feel normal again. She felt the shift in her stomach as the Mountain Feather turned Santeju northward. That way, she had known, led to Province. With the wind streaming around the flight carrier, its sealed, reinforced, thick glass, and sculpted wood, as usual, made for a quiet, steady ride. Onya waited patiently for the officer seated across from her to get his sky-feet under him so that he could begin the mission briefing. The scabbard for his sword was wrapped with a braided crimson cord. It also had three small feathers tied just below the scabbard's mouth. Those decorative additions, along with the small, red bird in flight, embroidered on his black coat, just over his heart, meant the man was a Red Bird. His name was Brigatt. He was the Information's Officer for their mission.

One hour, as the Pradas flies, outside Alexandria, with the clouds below them as the sun brightly bathed their cabin with warmth, Brigatt opened a small metal box. From its contents he meticulously prepared five cups of steaming choca, its lightened brown coloring indicating it had been mixed with cream. Its sweet taste meant that sugar had also been mixed into the hot liquid. This made serving it during the flight a simple affair. The smell of vanilla filled the flight carrier. It was her favorite. The smell, and somehow the choca, even though it was a stimulant, had relaxed her. With sunlight on her face, the scent of vanilla in her nose, all complimenting the sensation of a warm cup of choca in her hands, calm washed over her.

One of the first things you learned as a member of the Company was, when the opportunity presented itself, you relaxed. Looking around the interior of the carrier Onya noticed the rest of the strike team doing just that. There were the six spans of leggy Orah, with her raven-black hair, which was tied back into a long tail, her bright green eyes, and her overdeveloped trigger-finger. She accepted a cup of choca passed to her from Brigatt. Orah, Rain Catcher that she was, specialized in bodyguard assignments, among other things. Tom-Tom had also been reaching for a cup. His massive, dark-brown, hands engulfed the small, green, porcelain cup, delicately decorated around its lip with pale, cream gardenia blossoms. Tom-Tom leaned back in his seat with a closed-mouth grin as he took his first sip. The first cup of the day was always the best cup.

You didn't really taste the cups after that. His six span-plus frame was heavily muscled. His long legs stretched out into the aisle where he crossed them at the ankles. The sunlight reflected off his black, leather, calf-high boots. A treatise on the problem of evil by Terriss Bymm was in his lap. You made a mistake with Tom-Tom if you equated his size with a lack of intelligence. He specialized in rescue and retrieval. If you needed someone to come get you, you needed Tom-Tom or one of the members of his unruly band of Stone Hands.

Mallic leaned back in his seat, with his feet propped up on the edge of one of the small wooden tables secured to the floor of the cabin. A Far Eye was trained to be a sentry, or scout, along with the skills needed to serve as an occasional spy. Mallic could disappear, like morning mist evaporating at the appearance of the sun, almost right before your eyes. Just shy of six spans, with the slim, but strong, build of a dancer, one of Mallic's sun-darkened hands was behind his head. He had a distant look in his blue eyes. His other hand held his steaming cup of choca. His time had been divided between sipping from his cup and blowing at a stray lock of rumpled, slightly curly, brown hair that had decided to lay, just so, across his forehead. Behind Mallic, to his left, receiving the third cup of choca, was Ving. Ving had been unceremoniously saddled with the name Ving the Merciless. He was a small man with a bright intelligence that twinkled in his gray eyes. He combated the name, ostensibly, by ignoring it. His very light-brownish face would redden slightly as people cried out in fake terror while he passed by, or as he entered a room. The only hair on his face, or head, was a grayish- white, pointed shock of beard on his chin that he kept braided. He was handsome, relatively quiet, and was preoccupied with staring down into the depths of his cup. Ving was a *Maker* from the arm of the Company Bantu called *Solutions*, which fell under the purview of Tinker. Tinker, along with the people from Solutions, performed what Onya could only call miracles. You could not say that in front of Tinker, however, unless you were interested in a tremendously long lecture about how the ignorant perceived advanced knowledge as magic or miracle. Onya had made that mistake only once, blushing bright red as Bantu slid quietly from the room holding back laughter while Tink battered her about the head with a longwinded tirade on the subject. Nevertheless, the things they made, as well as the things they could do, were breathtaking. It was the work of the *Gift* she knew. It was one thing to know what Makers could do but quite another thing to see it up close.

Dreyden had been at the rear of the cabin, lightly snoring, atop the stacked gear. A little taller than Tom-Tom but with a slimmer build, Onya had only been able to see the bottoms of his boots. Those black eyes, though closed, would be ready to snap open at a moment's notice. Dreyden was Team-Second for the mission. If you were in the hot seat, faced with a situation that could go either way at any second, you wanted Dreyden in the thick of it, slashing about with his shoulder-length black hair flipping around, while he flashed that foolish, but bright, smile as if he could not see himself anywhere else but right there. He was in the thick of a snore while Onya sipped her choca. Death Singers were odd in that way. Dreyden was odder than most. They were the rear guard in any action. Death Singers could be heard crying out encouragement to other Singers, in the heat of battle, to hold the line. They called themselves *T'Sima Na Bantu MDo*, in the language of Bantu's homeland meaning, *the line that Bantu draws in the sand.* For Death Singers, once Bantu drew the line, no one crossed it alive. Onya always thought they were insane. But you never said that when there were Death Singers within earshot. Even then you looked over your shoulder just to be sure there were none around.

Onya had reached for her own cup from Brigatt before crossing her legs. She folded them up into the seat beneath her. Taking a sip of the hot liquid, she nodded to Brigatt to begin his recitation. What he had related to her did not so much frightened her as it shocked her. Province, directly to the north of their resident Alexandria, across the Mountains of Marra, had been constructing a weapon. It was a weapon with devastating potential called the *Dragon Orb.* If, or when, it was finished it would dramatically change the balance of power among the nations. The commander of the Empresses secret service, along with the chief military advisors to the crown, had encouraged the Empress to call on the services of the Company.

Unrolling a large piece of parchment, Brigatt revealed to Onya that the empire had supplied them with all of their intelligence reports along with the request for action. The weapon was to be completed within a day. It was to be tested within seven. It was further believed that the first act, after a successful test, would be to use it against the empire. Their mission was to retrieve all the information regarding it's making before destroying it, along with the facility where it was being made. *Seek-and-Destroy*. Brigatt said it matter-of-factly before going quiet. Turning his attention to the view, he lost himself gazing at the visage passing outside the glass. He appeared to be captivated by the large, billowing, clouds, which looked like waves caught frozen as though posing for a portrait. After a moment he began to hum to himself. The tune was called *Many Shades of Blue*.

Reflecting over the particulars of the mission, Onya thought, in those next moments, that Bantu had surely charged the Empire a significant, if not outrageous, amount of coin. Company practice was to charge the wealthy based on what they were worth, others what they could afford, while the poor were charged next to nothing for the Company's services. To compound matters for the wealthy empire, the mission was political. Taking a sip of her choca, Onya smiled to herself. It had occurred to her in that moment, that for the Empire, the job was going to be very expensive.

Santeju, all the while, plied his great wings on the powerful air currents that all Pradas seemed to know intimately. The nearly one hundred spans of reddish-brown, feathered muscle had angled this way, then that, as though he was dancing with the sky as his partner. Santeju carried them aloft over miles of terrain that day. He cut in and out of cloudbanks for cover. The great bird flew well into the night, landing somewhere in Province hours before dawn. A small rise in the woods caught them as they fell from the sky. Santeju's powerful wings had buffeted the landing site with gusts of wind. Their landing was as smooth as their lift off had been. Rustling his wings, the enormous Pradas cooed softly while the team unloaded. They stood silently, black clad haunts on that small rise, as they looked west. The target was three clicks to the west. Onya had instructed the pilot to wait for them until noon. If she had not made contact by then the Mountain Feather was to return to Sanctuary. The young lieutenant had ground his teeth at that, clenching his jaw as if he were forcibly swallowing any objections to her orders. Santeju rustled his wings while making deep rumbling sounds in his chest. None of the Mountain Feathers would admit to it but the rumor was that the birds could sense the emotions of the pilots with whom they were teamed. She made him repeat back to her the orders she had given him to reinforce the fact that it had not been a request. You did not disobey an order in the Company if you wanted to remain in it.

Another of their advantages, courtesy of Tink, was the Strike Suit. The black, woven-cotton bodysuits fit snuggly but gave a little in all the right places. The various straps and belts, which carried their gear, were cinched tightly to silence any jingling or rubbing noises. They would be invisible. They would be silent. It was one of the things that made a strike team so deadly.

The strike team, under her command, had left the wooded rise at a dead run. Floating like a westerly breeze, tinted black as the midnight sky, they made their way through the thick woods. Loaded Tink-specials were in their hands. The black metal of those crossbows did not give off even a hint of reflected light. On they had run. The perimeter of the base was protected with traps, but they swept through them without even a disturbed leaf on the way. As the moon thought of disappearing, just before the sun contemplated rising, the strike team rolled silently into the base like fog off the sea. Three clicks, in record time, Onya had thought as she edged up to the end of the interior, gray, rock wall running her hand over its rough surface. It had been a long, eventful, two days.

Onya was still watching the *tick, tick, ticking*, of the Tink timepiece in her hand as she turned her thoughts from the series of developments that had brought her to the present moment. Her heart beat slowly. This was what she trained for constantly. She was good at it. It would not be long now. Part two of the mission was about to begin. Focusing fully on the present the past few days melted away into the background of her mind. It was time to concentrate on the work ahead. The workday had just begun. Releasing the safe-latch on her crossbow, which kept it from firing accidentally, she listened for the soft click that accompanied the movement. It was a Tink-special, and Tinker *was* special. Awe was a constant when you were in Tinker's company. She had often wondered at Tink's ability to create, especially to create what had never been thought of before. But then, Tinker was a *Maker*. From what she had ever been able to gather Tink was among the gifted even of that enigmatic group. Most were loners or nomads, shunning normal society while remaining cloaked in secrecy. When they came across another of their kind anything could happen from clasping one another as if they were long lost relatives to challenging each other to their version of a duel to the death. Whatever happened, a meeting of Makers was rare but always worth seeing. Tinker had earned a reputation among them over the years. Only rarely did one show up at the gate to Sanctuary demanding to see the Company's chief Maker. Those were always interesting days.

The crossbow she held in her hands was one of those creations. Made from a metal of Tinker's composition it was both incredibly durable and amazingly lightweight. The black finish reflected almost no light. The firing arms were made from a metal that flexed, which gave it more power than its conventional wooden counterparts. They were so powerful there was actually a small kick when you fired one. It was very slim. It was also slightly longer than conventional crossbows. None of these characteristics, however, were the true genius behind the Tink design.

Tinker had constructed a crossbow with a number of truly unheard-of capabilities. The Tink-special did not fire a wooden, feather-fletched bolt from a carved groove down the length of the crossbow shaft. Instead it fired a long, metal spike, three-fourths the length of a normal bolt, from a barrel mounted on top of the crossbow shaft. Two metal cords were attached to the spring arms on one end and a tiny cup inside the barrel on the other. The barrel had slits along both sides to allow the cords to propel the cup along the barrel's length. The spike slid neatly into the cup nestled inside the barrel when loaded. By pulling the trigger you released the metal cord launching the cup forward. The cup propelled the spike it held in place, down the length of the barrel, firing it at an incredible speed from the open end of the barrel. From there it got even better.

The crossbow had a small lever on its right side next to the trigger, which, when rotated, pulled back the metal cord, setting the metal arms for firing. When the first shot was fired, the forward momentum of the firing arms, put into motion an internal set of gears, loaded with springs, which did two things simultaneously. They reset the crossbow to fire again while rotating another spike up into the barrel. The spikes were loaded from a long, slim cartridge, which snapped into the underbelly of the shaft, located in front of the trigger. The crossbow, in a matter of seconds, was ready to be fired again. It was sheer genius. Next to its conventional counterpart the Tink-special was lighter, more durable, easier to load, fired faster, and had ammunition that was by far, easier to carry. It was also more deadly. Each cartridge was designed to hold twelve spikes. When you ran out you simply pulled out the empty cartridge. After inserting a full one you rotated the crank on the crossbow until the cords were pulled completely back. A clicking sound let you know the gears were set. It also indicated that the first spike was loaded into place. In the time it took a normal crossbow to fire twice Onya could fire off an entire cartridge.

Glancing at the timepiece she knew it was almost time. Any moment now Tom-Tom would rejoin her. Looking up from her timepiece she saw him. Just like counting on the fact that one day you would die you could count on Tom-Tom. She laughed to herself at the horrible example her mind had produced. But there he was, right on time, heading toward her in a slow, cautious gait. He seemed to flow like water as he turned the corner joining her as she leaned against the wall. Tom-Tom towered over Onya. While he was above average in height it did not help that her people were known for being small. The folds of their eyes were also a unique trait that distinguished them from others. As large as Tom-Tom was Onya had not heard a sound or even a hint of his approach. Everything was as it should be. It was time for Part Two of the mission. *Acquisition.* She nodded up at Tom-Tom to move out just as a crossbow bolt hit him in the shoulder. That was when things fell apart.

When I have closed my eyes
these pools of what I have seen
have closed them at last

when finally these sound catchers
these halls of what I have heard
echo no more

at the last
sing a song, pull with your hands
on a chiming rope and burn a scent for me

let me hear a song, smell a scent
as I journey upward
outward

let the smoke and the song
and the ringing bell
carry me gently, gently home

-Aras Tu'un
Poet Chief, Anatas Point
Twelfth Age, Common Era 118
Written for the death of King Agrias Aggabar

What isn't supposed to happen often matters more than what is.

~General Gathrobaric

Chapter two

Keep the home fires burning

Even as the crossbow bolt slammed into him Tom-Tom was twisting so that it only grazed his left shoulder. The impact spun him about. The shorter, thicker version of an arrow struck the wall with a thudding sound. As the bolt fell it flung blood against the wall dotting the ground with more as it bounced. Before it stopped rattling, with a hollow clatter at their feet, Onya launched herself out from her position next to Tom-Tom. Her crossbow recoiled lightly against her shoulder with the *thump-crack* of spikes being fired, one after another, down the line of the wall. The projectiles streaked through the air as she side-pedaled, with her legs, while holding her upper-body almost completely still. Her head tilted slightly as she sighted down the length of the crossbow. Three men fell from that barrage while a recovered Tom-Tom took two others down just moments behind Onya's final shot. The last sound was the soft whirring of gears from inside their crossbows as each clicked back into firing position.

This was not good. Onya stepped toward Tom-Tom but he gave her a brief shake of his head. He was fine, it said. But now the clock was running. Any agent worth the name would tell you that the only truly successful mission of this kind was one where no one even knew you had been there. No evidence in or out. Dead bodies were considered evidence the last time she had checked. Onya shook her head in disgust as she looked down the line of the wall at the slumped bodies. Even though they were still on the outskirts of the compound she knew that very soon the uniformed guards, now riddled with long, slim spikes, would be missed. As she turned to go a clock began ticking in her head.

They moved then. With precision, matched by an unmistakably deadly intent, they flowed across the early morning courtyard of the enemy base like wraiths looking for the living to consume. With a determined speed, in silence, they headed for their target as if they were spikes shot from a Tink-special crossbow. They were good. It was not a self-conceit. It was a proven truth. They were probably some of the best at what they did. Bantu believed in training above all else. That focus had fashioned them into a preeminent force. They were sought after. The name, *Peoples Company*, enjoyed a kind of hard-won celebrity. Some of that had certainly come from the telling of tales in taverns, inns, and the like, by those who might exaggerate the facts for effect. But another thing was also quite true. You did not leave Sanctuary on a mission, as a member of the Company, unless you were good at what the Company did. This was a part of what the Company did.

Their movement fell into a familiar pattern. It was a skill that had been honed by many hours of training. Both held their Tink-specials with the butt of the crossbow tucked neatly against the shoulder. Their eyes rested along the sights at the end of the barrel. They moved through the complex like black-clad ghosts floating, from doorway to doorway, corner to corner. The end of a hallway called for one to stop at the corner, aiming down the direction they intended to go, ready to fire at anything that moved, while the other moved further ahead. Entering a room required each to cover the others blind spot, ready to fire at a moment's notice. Moving in tandem they never exchanged a word. The training had taken over. In Onya's head the clock was ticking.

Several times they ducked into side passages, storage rooms, or closets, as a guard paced quickly past them. Onya had chosen just before sunrise because it was normally the weak point in an installation's defense if it used a guard rotation like this one did. The guards who were on duty had been on for most of their watch while those coming on duty would not be arriving for at least another two hours. The consequence was that at the present hour the guards would be bleary-eyed and sluggish. It was the best time for human error to be a factor in the guard's performance. As they paused at the end of a corridor her mind went back for a moment to the last guard who had raced by them. It occurred to her that he should not have been moving so fast. It disturbed something in the back of her mind, but she let it go. Now was no time to be distracted. The clock in the back of her mind was ticking faster.

In minutes they were into the main building of the compound where the object of their mission was reportedly being stored. A few moments more had them slowing from a half-run to a slow walk. They breathed deeply, though, as a consequence of the *gift,* they were not breathing hard. Checking both ends of the hallway they found the chamber where the Orb was being constructed. The room itself was perhaps twenty paces in both directions. The walls were wood, from the floor to about waist high, then glass the rest of the way up to the ceiling. It was mostly furnished with tables. A quick glance showed papers, maps, and drawings strewn about in what seemed to be a haphazard manner. Onya had seen the same kind of mess in one of Tink's workshops. If you went so far as to mention the mess Tink would immediately claim, flinging up a hand in some dismissive gesture, that everything was where it should be. This *maker*, if asked, would probably make the same claim.

There were various liquids bubbling in glass pitchers or flowing through tubes into jars, on their way to other jars, all of which were connected or at least appeared to be. In the center of the room on a circular table sat their objective, the Dragon Orb. It was half her size, pulsing from somewhere deep within, orange to white, to crimson, and back again. Onya exhaled sharply, trying to clear the smell of sulfur from her nose, rubbing at it in an attempt to stop the light burning sensation.

"What in the bloody Pit!" Tom-Tom exclaimed sharply, just above a whisper, as his eyes came to rest on the thing. He straightened from the running crouch he was in while lowering his crossbow.

Whispers tended to attract attention. Even though things were already falling apart they still wanted to be able to thank someone for keeping the home fires burning because they made it back safely. So, they made sure to pitch their voices so as not to attract attention. Onya spoke in normal tones as well.

"It is called a Dragon Orb. A creation based on the manipulation of natural, and not so natural, forces. It's supposed to have enough explosive capacity to destroy an entire city within moments. The upper levels of the explosion are supposed to flare out into what appears to be wings of flame. And so, I would guess, comes the name, Dragon Orb. And we, Tom-Tom-san, are here to see that it is never used. Cover the door. I will see to the materials." She pitched her crossbow through the air to where he stood in the doorway before turning her attention to the rest of the room.

"Aye, Commander." Tom-Tom said with a quick nod as he snatched the bow from the air. He trotted to the door like some large predator filling the open doorway with his mass. The man reminded Onya of one of the great hunter cats she had seen once. They roamed the Aralial plains. Some hunted them for their stripped skins. Tom-Tom moved with the restrained power of one of those graceful cats ready to explode into action in an instant. Onya immediately began collecting papers. In the back of her mind the clock was ticking louder. Time was running out like water from a cracked pot. But you did not become a commander in the Company by losing your nerve when it counted especially when life and death were a matter of splitting hairs.

Onya smiled to herself but did not look up as she turned over a page of diagrams. The person had not moved the entire time they had been in the room. She sensed the presence behind her. Closing her eyes, she recalled the layout of the room in her mind. Scanning over the tables, chairs, and cabinets in her mind's eye she stopped at the mental image of a particular corner. Yes, there it was. A false alcove had been created in the room by the placement of a large file cabinet that stood against one wall by a corner of the room. The person was crouched in the makeshift alcove waiting silently. Onya mentally focused the image, letting her mind reconstruct the form of the person, until she had it.

"I mark you, Rain Catcher." Onya spoke without looking up from the papers she was rummaging through. It was Orah. Her green eyes poked out from behind the cabinet followed by her thin frame. Small, but well-defined muscles stood out beneath the form-fitting, black strike suit in places where there was no padding. Frowning briefly – it was actually a slight pout - Orah joined Onya at the table.

"Commander, how is it that I can never stay hidden from you?" Her voice was smallish as well as a little high. It always led people to the incorrect impression that Orah was delicate. That was a mistake. Sometimes it was a final one.

Orah's normal responsibilities, on any given mission, were as the High Eye. Placed in an elevated position with a Tink Far-shot, an elongated, specially designed version of the Tink-special made with distance in mind, she could hit almost anything, moving or not. Onya looked up from the papers she was stuffing in a bag.

"Orah-san, were you hiding?" Covering a smirk by holding up a page, to veil her face as if examining it closely, she forestalled Orah's reply by continuing on as Orah opened her mouth to speak with a now fully developed pout coupled with a hand on a cocked hip. "Join Tom-Tom at the door Lieutenant. We have encountered some resistance. Time is precious."

Orah closed her mouth, turned on her heel, and walked toward the doorway. Small but well-rounded hips swung slightly as she went. A very amused Tom-Tom was biting his lower lip. He was trying hard to keep focused on looking down the hall. Orah walked directly to him. Stopping in front of him she stared at Tom-Tom for a moment during which he refused to look at her. Nodding to herself, as if deciding something, she punched him in his unwounded shoulder. With a satisfied grin she took up a position opposite him in the doorway. Tom-Tom glared at her but she smiled sweetly back at him as though nothing had happened. After a brief pause Orah pointedly set her gaze down the hallway. Tom-Tom looked at Orah for a moment longer before shaking his head in feigned disgust. He turned his own attention back to the hallway.

Orah had not been in position more than a few moments before turning her head back into the interior of the room toward where Onya stood filling the bag with more papers. Orah's voice was very matter-of-fact when she said, "Heads up Commander. I hope you're hungry. The soup just got thick." Turning back, she took aim with her Tink-special at whatever was coming down the hallway, lowering herself into a half-crouch so that she would be ready to launch herself out of the doorway. Tom-Tom stood on the other side of the doorway with his crossbow half-raised leaning just slightly toward the hallway. Without looking up from her task Onya spoke offhandedly. The sound of rustling papers accompanied her voice across the room to the ears of her team members.

"Tell them we are not prepared for guests, Orah-san, they will have to come back when we have had a chance to prepare a proper breakfast." Orah shook her head at that, grinning grimly, as if Onya's sense of humor was a bit difficult to swallow. Tom-Tom barked out a laugh that stopped short when Orah looked at him pointedly, raising her eyebrows slightly.

Orah moved. She placed her back to one side of the doorframe while wedging her right boot against the other side. Leaning her upper-body out into the hallway she fired a single spike down the corridor. Onya heard the next spike click into place just as a scream erupted from somewhere down the hall. The sounds of cursing, coupled with the muffled thump of boots on hardwood, told her that whoever was in the hallway was now scrambling for cover. She heard more curses amid the shuffling of bodies as a flight of bolts slammed into the floor just outside the Orb room. A few bolts slammed into the doorframe forcing Orah, followed closely by Tom-Tom, to roll away into the room. The quivering thuds of multiple bolt heads sinking deeply into wood followed them.

"They are insistent Commander. They wish to join us immediately!" Orah said as she rolled up fluidly, throwing herself forward, slamming her back against the wall next to the doorway. Whipping her shoulders around the doorframe Orah returned fire. Three successive shots whizzed from her crossbow punctuated by more screams. As she rotated back inside, Tom-Tom joined her, leaning out to speed a triple volley of his own down the hallway. More yelling, emphasized by crossbow bolts, followed him as he spun back into the room.

Onya cursed under her breath so that only she could hear. The guard she had noticed earlier had not been walking like a guard should have been at that hour of the morning. She had seen it but had not paid attention to it. Somehow, they had been prepared for her team's arrival. Onya felt like slapping herself for missing the clue that had been practically shouting at her. Her father had told her long ago that you only got one. If you were perceptive you could catch the one clue that would give you an edge. She had missed it. Now her team, along with the mission, might suffer the consequences. Just then a booming voice echoed from down the hall interrupting her thoughts.

"I am unarmed! Hold your fire! I am approaching so that we may discuss our current predicament with calm reason. I repeat, I am unarmed, do not fire!"

Orah ducked back into the room looking askance at Onya. Onya arched an eyebrow. Orah shrugged her shoulders. Onya gave a short affirmative nod while tightening the straps on the pack, now secured, on her back. Words had passed between them unspoken. *The man was not a threat. He was allowed to enter the room.* It took years to develop the ability to communicate among team members with a handful of gestures, which was why Bantu tended toward fairly set teams. Onya thought it could not hurt to converse with the man who was on his way down the hall.

During the brief exchange Onya had placed several small crystals around the base of the Dragon Orb. The Orb was now, slowly, beginning to brighten as the small crystals pulsed in sequence. One flared to life, then, as it faded, it was followed by another.

Tom-Tom saw Onya motioning, with her hand, toward him. He tossed the second crossbow he was holding to her. Onya snatched it from the air, clicking off the latch that kept it from firing accidentally, as she brought it to the firing position, snuggly against her right shoulder, in one fluid motion. She sighted on the doorway. It was a smooth, practiced, motion. They trained for these moments until the movements were done without thought, until the motions were a part of them.

As Onya sighted on the door Orah began backing away, into the room, opposite Onya's position. Her sights were also leveled on the doorway. Tom-Tom floated two paces backwards completing the triangle that ensured the man would walk into multiple lines of fire.

Slowly, he entered the room. The man was of middle years with a great deal of gray in his hair. A handsome man, in a rough sort of way, he was beginning to spread across the middle. In Onya's mind that named him more of an administrator than soldier though he wore a uniform. It was dark-brown with red piping on the sleeves of the coat. Red also ran up the sides of the baggy pants, which were stuffed into turned down, brown, leather boots. She noticed his thick hands. Sweat was evident on the pale skin of his forehead. His voice had a nasal edge to it.

"I am Caleb Mouring, the Outpost Commander. Of course, you probably already know this." He paused as if to give them an opportunity to acknowledge the truth of his statement. Onya simply stared at him down the length of her Tink-special. Caleb cleared his throat as he looked at each of them in turn. He continued with a slight pause, "Well ... I will not bore you with more mundane details or small talk. I will, however, inform you that this outpost is, at this moment, on full alert. I have forty guards in the hall and more on the way." He shifted his weight from one foot to the other. His eyes shifted along with his weight. Caleb Mouring licked his lips as he continued to sweat. The commander had managed a bit of confidence in his voice, but his body gave away his fear. His shifting weight, along with the constant moving of his hands from his belt, to behind his back, to being clasped in front of him, all said he wanted this over quickly. He was most likely a low-level noble who had been given military rank. As Onya sized up the man in front of her Tom-Tom corrected Caleb Mouring's count.

"No, Outpost Commander." Tom-Tom gave him an easy grin that did not reach his eyes as he continued, "You have twenty-*six* guards in the hall and if you knew who you were dealing with, you would know that is not enough." Tom-Tom's deep voice resonated across the room as he deliberately raised the level of his crossbow to Caleb Mouring's head. Onya stopped herself from smiling at Tom-Tom's statement. His boast was, of course, an exaggeration. It was the kind of bluster that team members, in the Company, had sometimes taken to in dire situations such as this one. They believed that, from time to time, leaning on the legend of the Company was helpful in these kinds of circumstance. She could almost hear Basil's voice as he tried to explain it to her. It inspired an irrational, unfounded fear in the enemy, he would say. In Caleb Mouring's case it seemed to be working. The man appeared to be sweating even more profusely. His voice had a slightly strained quality about it.

"As you say, sir, twenty-six. The point, however, is this. You cannot escape. But if you surrender now I will let you live. Resist, and you will die a very painful and … slow death. That is my only offer." Caleb Mouring folded his arms across his chest while trying to maintain a look of superiority. The problem with the ultimatum, as well as the feigned look of confidence, was the line of sweat that trickled down his forehead to the bridge of his nose. When faced with still further silence from the black-clad intruders aiming at him he added, "Let me add this one minor, yet salient, point. Your compatriots, a Dreyden, Mallic, and Ving, have been captured and summarily executed." He smiled smugly then. "You see, my good *People*, information, particularly secret information, can be purchased on both sides of the street."

Onya lowered her crossbow. There it was, as she had suspected, there was the rest of it. The guard had been moving in the direction of the second half of her strike team. Their job had been to keep the exit point open. Her heart pounded in her chest. She, along with her team, had been sold out.

Onya walked slowly up to Mouring. Her voice was flat. It was devoid of emotion. "I hope you have been having a good morning." She paused. Mouring waited a moment before leaning in with a lop-sided grin.

"And just why, my dear, would you be interested in the kind of day I have been having?"

As he finished the sentence Onya's arm shot out. With her thumb laid against her palm, her fingers held together in a knife-hand, she planted the ridge of her top knuckle in Mouring's left temple. He crumbled to the floor in a heap. Onya's jaw flexed as she ground her teeth together.

Looking down she spoke to the unmoving form at her feet as if he could still hear her.

"I asked because I knew the rest of your day would be decidedly bad." Onya raised her right hand, tapping a small, circular gemstone with the tips of her first two fingers. It was pinned to the high collar of her strike suit's shirt on the right side. The left side of the high collar was always unadorned because they did not wear rank insignias when they wore strike suits. The gemstone flared to green life with a glowing brilliance that radiated from the collar. "Onoto to Lieutenant Raiden. Respond Mountain Feather."

A young voice responded quickly. The disembodied words emanating from the, still glowing, gemstone on her collar.

"Raiden here, Commander."

"Lieutenant, we are Situation Critical. I repeat, Situation Critical. Team members down, exit point compromised. Prepare for *Eagle Skims the Lake*." There was a moment of silence before the voice returned. But this time it was a little shaky.

"Commander, I think I should inform you, ma'am, that I have only performed that manuever with Santeju in drills."

"Well, Lieutenant, that is the reason for drills. So you can make all your mistakes when no one's rear-end is on the line. We'll get one shot at this so make it a good one." Onya paused as a half-grin crossed her face, then she continued, "And Lieutenant, don't call me ma'am. Onoto out!"

Onya tapped the gemstone at her collar again causing the glow to wink out. The Communications Gemstones were another of Tinker's amazing creations. They gave the Company a decided advantage in most situations. She looked back at the Dragon Orb. It was lighting up the entire room now. The humming sound, coming from within it, was passing upward through each note in the musical scale. Onya knew that when that sound became so high that it was about to pass beyond a person's ability to hear it the Orb would explode. It was now or never. The clock in her mind had stopped ticking. Onya glanced over at what remained of her team.

Tapping the *com-gem* on her collar again she spoke as it flared to life.

"Onoto to Dreyden. Respond." She paused but there was only silence. Again, she spoke into the air while the glowing gemstone transferred her words. "Onoto to Mallic. Respond." Nothing.

Onya tapped the still glowing *com-gem* three times in quick succession followed by a brief pause and two more taps. At this, Orah and Tom-Tom's com-gems flared to glowing life. Onya's voice echoed through their gems. The entire team should have been able to hear her voice simultaneously.

"This is Team Leader. All members, I repeat, all members report location and disposition." She waited.

One voice came back along the link. "This is Mountain Feather to Team Leader. We are on route to the ordered destination. Will be in position in five minutes. Response complete." Raiden's voice ended but no others followed it.

Grimly Onya answered. "Acknowledged Mountain Feather. Communication complete."

The room was deathly still with the exception of the increasing intensity of the Orb. Tom-Tom was looking down the hallway where the rest of the outpost's soldiers still awaited a commander who would not return to them. Orah stood with her eyes closed slowly shaking her head from side to side. They all knew. Someone had sold them out. Most likely the transaction had taken place over a quiet cup of tea or choca. Or maybe it was over a glass of wine. They were trapped with half the team dead. Onya tapped her com-gem once more causing its glow to wink out.

Looking across the room at the remainder of her team Onya spoke. She was struggling to keep her voice from breaking. "This is an emergency evacuation folks. We have no time to play nice. Do you understand me?" Her face was stone as she walked slowly toward the door.

Both Orah and Tom-Tom nodded curtly. As Onya came alongside them she stopped. She spoke so softly that the two of them had to lean in to hear her. Her words were punctuated by the click of her Tink-special's firing latch being released. "Emergency Evacuation. That means if anyone else is going to do any dying today it will be them." Onya walked past Tom-Tom and Orah. With deliberate steps she walked out of the Orb room, turned right, and fired her crossbow into the mass of men at the end of the hall.

... and it is perhaps the most ludicrous of assertions to begin with the premise that the Divine does not, in some way or form, dwell among us. Tertossian claimed in his pre-common era treatise on Nature and Being, that it was an act of centrifugal self-actualizing essence which, once harnessed for the creative effort, was then exhausted. I reply to him directly, as well as the Neotertossian school of thought, with this question. If, in point of fact, the Divine no longer exists, what then is love?

> *~Pragic Ome*
> *Holder of the Oswallow*
> *Chair of Philosophy*
> *Alexandria University*
> *Third Age, Common Era 723*
> *The Erris Symposium on*
> *Nature and Being held at*
> *Polis Point*

My friends asked me why I would do something so very foolish. I said love.

~*Courson Scene iii act ii*
Benssil Walkenthread
Poet and Playwright

Chapter Three

Storm a' brewing

They dropped from the sky without warning. Not even a shadow drifting across a patch of grass had signaled their arrival. Like a rain shower that comes suddenly while the sun still shines, causing passersby to gaze up in disbelief while holding out their hand to feel at the raindrops, they fell from the sky. Two things had made it possible for them to appear without a hint that they were coming. First, they had flown in keeping the sun above and behind them. Second, they had waited until they were directly over their target before beginning their descent. They circled down in tight spiraling arcs from the clouds above. It was a maneuver designed to make it seem as though they had appeared out of thin air as well as keeping their position hidden until the very last moment. The Pradas fell from the sky like reddish-brown, feather-covered raindrops. Cold intelligence radiated from saucer-like eyes as the great birds scanned the ground. Leather guidance straps were pulled taut as their helmeted pilots gave the signal to wheel around in a final tight arc, their wings fanning up immense gusts of wind, mixed with dust, from flame-scorched earth. They touched down perfectly, one after another. These were not younglings. They were blooded birds of prey piloted by senior members of the Mountain Feathers. Grim black-swathed faces, revealing only hard eyes above dark cloth, gazed out of the heavy glass windows of the personnel carriers as they landed.

Forty-seven Pradas dropped in from the late afternoon sky. Their wings fluttered as they cawed loudly while settling to the ground where they landed. Ladders unfurled from flight cabins. Personnel carriers disgorged pilots along with black-clad forms in close fitting strike suits. Golden eyes the size of tabletops reflected the wooded landscape as the great birds continued to scan the surrounding terrain. Their eyes could see much further than the *wingless* they now watched over. A sharp cawing would communicate to their pilots any sign of approaching danger from land or air. As the carriers emptied of their human cargo, twelve Pradas, with emptied personnel carriers on their backs, their pilots still strapped in, hurtled back into the air to begin patrolling passes at varying heights. Some would be flying so high they would be nearly invisible. In the span of a few heartbeats their position was secured.

A tall, brown-skinned man exited one of the flight carriers, which had been flown in by the only Pradas with feathers the color of burnt gold. He stepped off the ladder onto the flame-blackened hardpan where the Orb installation had once stood. His clean-shaven head reflected the late afternoon sunshine as he gazed around him from left to right. A slight breeze stirred the dust. He rubbed at his nose to clear the burnt smell from his nostrils. Behind him standing half a head shorter was Tom-Tom followed closely by Orah. Their faces had looks as hard as the ground they walked on. Their black strike suits were tattered. Dried blood had turned the black cloth an indeterminate color in places. Even as Orah followed Tom-Tom she rubbed at her right leg as if trying to rub away the memory of something. Each of them trailed the tall brown-skinned man who strode forward in silence.

All around the three of them, men and women, carrying Tink crossbows, swept the terrain, fanning out before them, like a black wave rolling out to sea as the tide shifted. Black boots kicked up dust as they moved across the hardpan. They were strapped with the unrelieved black of leather belts, which held swords, and small, hardened, leather storage boxes. Rectangular, leather quivers were strapped to their thighs, with a loop securing them to their weaponsbelts. The quivers held spike-filled cartridges for Tink crossbows. An assortment of knives could be seen tucked into boots, in sheaths on hips, nestled behind weaponsbelts at the small of the back, or strapped across chests. Heads were swathed in black cloth. These well-armed apparitions showed only their eyes. They were hunting. It was standard procedure for a Strike Team to remain faceless. Faces could be remembered, so they were concealed.

The tall, brown-skinned man was the only one with his head uncovered. Neither was he wearing a strike suit. He wore the standard black coat and breeches of the Company uniform. He walked straight to a small body that lay on the ground, curled in a fetal position, half-buried in the scorched earth. A slightly curved sword, single-edged, with a simple, circular handguard, and a long ivory hilt, was nestled in the crook of his left arm. It was held, like a mother holds a babe, with a reverse grip so that the hilt pointed forward where he could draw it with his right hand. It was sheathed in a black-lacquered wooden scabbard. Partway down the scabbard was an emblem. There were three intersecting circles, etched in silver. As he reached the prone form, he twirled the sword once in his left hand before passing it to Tom-Tom. Slowly, he knelt next to the unmoving form. Gently, very gently, he turned the body over so that the face was turned up toward him. Lovingly, he laid the head in his lap. Behind him Tom-Tom shifted his weight from one foot to the other. The man motioned to Orah who was holding a small mahogany-stained, wooden box clutched to her chest with both arms as if she were afraid it would be damaged or lost.

Strong, but well-shaped, brown hands reached out for the box. Orah laid the box gently in his hands. Turning it right side up he twisted a copper clasp free, which allowed him to lift the lid. The box was cushioned, lined in purple velvet, with a brass bottle fitted snuggly in its recess. The bottle had a long, slim neck with a large, pear-shaped bottom. Tilting the woman's head back he opened her mouth. Pulling the cork from the bottle he tilted it so he could slowly pour a clear liquid into the woman's mouth. As he was pouring Basil came to stand close by. The brown man looked up from what he was doing. Turning his clean-shaven face up from the woman in his lap his hazel eyes focused on Basil.

The face that gazed up at him was calm. The hazel eyes squinted slightly as he looked into the sun. Instantly Basil knew. He had known Bantu long enough to recognize that look. Underneath that calm exterior a storm was brewing. Basil had known Bantu since they were both barely old enough to call themselves men. At least they had thought they had been old enough. The Company took care to prepare the *People* for what they would have to face in the field. But Basil also knew that Bantu loved the People. Basil had always wondered whether that intense connection had something to do with whatever had happened to bring Bantu across the Macca Deep to the distant shores of a foreign empire. Bantu had odd notions about the way he thought a commander should conduct himself. As a result, he tried to keep his true feelings to himself. Even though the man's face was as hard as the wall surrounding Sanctuary Basil knew that thunder and lightning were brewing just beneath the surface. Bantu did not look at the People of the Company as pieces on a game board. They were his family. He did not take hurting one of them kindly.

The words came again to Basil's mind, like a cloud adrift in an otherwise clear sky, as he looked into Bantu's face. *Thunder,* Basil thought, *thunder and lighting.* The lips on that upturned face began to move. He was speaking to him now not just looking at him. Basil quickly went back in his mind to retrieve what Bantu had just said to him. He forced himself back into the moment.

"Report, Captain-Commander." The voice was flat. It was a strong baritone. On the surface it gave away nothing of what was going on beneath it. It was the Commander-General's battlefield voice.

Basil took a deep breath. They were old friends, yes. But right now, Basil was a Captain-Commander answering to his Commander-General.

"Sir, the perimeter is secured. We were not detected but I wouldn't like to make our stay long." Basil searched the perimeter with his eyes again. They were only a few hundred yards from where the center of the Orb installation had only recently stood. They were also only thirty clicks from Gaul proper. They would not stay undetected for long. Looking down again into the Commander's eyes he doubted that Bantu would mind if they were discovered. The Ancient One help the first ones who attacked if someone managed to make it here from Gaul with a force large enough to make them believe attacking would be a good idea. As Basil let his gaze sweep across the Company detachment, which had, in short order, occupied this now decimated area, he took particular notice of their body language. Shoulders were held taut while hands stroked crossbow triggers or swordhilts. Even the Pradas were on edge reflecting the emotional state of their pilots. Mercy was a part of the People's Way, what Bantu called the *Warring Way*, but Basil would not have bet on whether that would hold sway here, today, in this place. The thought of treachery had even Basil looking to repay someone for what had taken place here. Looking down he noticed he was slowly easing his own sword in and out of its scabbard with his thumb. He forced himself to stop. If they stayed much longer they would probably get more than their fill of killing.

Northwestern Province was on the border. Province was always guarded when it came to its borders even more so than most. They did not like outsiders. News of the destruction of the Orb Installation was surely on the desk of the Chief Minister by now. The man would have an entire battalion on its way to investigate. There would likely be a few *Inquisitors* at its head. Basil's hand drifted again to the hilt of his sword where it hung from his right hip. He clenched his jaw as he thought of those bloodthirsty hounds. They claimed to believe they were entrusted with the search for truth. There had never been any love lost between those inept boot-trailers and the clear-minded methods of the investigative branch of the Company. That Order, to which Basil belonged, was known as the Windchasers. Now his Order knew how to search for the truth. They understood deduction. Windchasers knew how to clarify perception until all that remained was the truth for all time. They were the best. They could chase the wind to its lair and back again. He thought of the words that had, over time, become the motto of his Order. It was always spoken as if it was inevitability itself. Basil smiled to himself. *Chased and caught*, he thought, *chased and caught*. If he, or any Wind Chaser, could chase and catch an Inquisitor they would not hesitate. It was a kind of axiom, a sort of undeniable truth, that true craftsmen detested those who practiced their craft with incompetence. That was the only way a Windchaser could see an Inquisitor. However incompetent they were he knew they would be arriving soon with that legion of troops to back up their idiocy. His commander was looking back down at the woman whose head rested in his lap. That baritone drifted up to Basil's ear again.

"Have the others been retrieved Captain-Commander?" It wasn't really a question it was more of an expectation.

"No sir. Lieutenant-Commander Dreyden, Lieutenant Mallic, and Agent Ving are unaccounted for. They are presumed dead. From what we can ascertain their bodies were destroyed along with the installation when it exploded. We await your command to depart." As Basil spoke his eyes continued their journey around the perimeter. The dust blew about in cool gusts of wind that beat against them from the west. The chill in the northern air did not bother him nor would it affect any other member of the Company. Many would pay to know the how and why of that secret.

The sun was beginning its descent as the day burned away. Overhead, Pradas were drifting on the updrafts, circling the area in wide arcs. The woods were still thick outside of the flattened blast area. They could hide a considerable sized threat. So, the Pradas were acting as their warning system. They would be able to see any large force approaching for miles, but a smaller contingent might be missed. They searched for any sign of movement. Their circuit through the air gave no indication that there was, as of yet, any sign of incoming hostiles.

Bantu, Commander-General of the Peoples Company, was putting the bottle back into its box as Onya stirred to consciousness. He spoke to her softly. "Onya-san. I thought we had lost you little one. You have been healed but go slowly. You know the *okoi* takes almost as much as it gives." Bantu steadied her as she sat up. Basil was always deeply grateful for the *Okoi*. In the First Tongue it meant *water of life*. The *water* had saved many of the People with its healing properties. Basil had drunk that salty, clear liquid a time or two. Absently he rubbed his side, where a long, thick scar should have been. The wound had been healed when a bottle, filled with the *water*, had poured the restorative liquid into his mouth, but the memories of the wound had not been taken away. Onya would remember what had nearly killed her as well.

†

Onya groaned. Opening her eyes, she instinctively held up a hand to block the brightness that flooded in. She blinked several times trying to get her eyes to adjust. As her vision cleared the blurry shape above her resolved into Bantu. Concern shadowed his narrowed, hazel eyes. Over his shoulder she could see Basil grasping reflexively at his swordhilt looking like death on the hunt. Her fellow Captain-Commander was - hovering - yes, hovering would be the proper word for it. Realizing that she was in Bantu's lap, Onya cleared her throat, as she tried to speak, but words would not come out. She hated to be thought of as needing protecting. They all knew that. Basil knew that better than most. *So why*, she thought, *was he hovering!* If she had been strong enough at that moment she would have punched him. She would have punched him hard! She cleared her throat again. For some reason she felt hoarse.

Onya's voice cracked. When she spoke, it sounded more like the croaking of a frog. "Help me up sir. Please." She seemed to be in one piece. She was a dirty, bloodstained, cloth-ripped, mess, but whole nonetheless. With a bit of movement, she could feel that her wounds were gone. But in their place was that familiar weakness, which was the aftermath of using the *okoi*. It would soon pass. The *water of life* had done its work. She was healed. The Commander helped her to stand. Onya wobbled a moment before gently twisting away from his supportive grasp. She knew he would grimace as he watched her sway in the wind like a tree limb in a stiff breeze. Onya swayed in the wind as it whipped at her. Looking around her she quickly surveyed the devastation she had caused by setting off the Dragon Orb. The destruction was stunning. There was nothing left of the buildings except a blackened, yawning, chasm in the earth. Looking at herself as she continued to try to get her feet under her she shook her at the mess. *Dragged through the Xi market at noon by a provincial Legate*, she thought. That is how she looked. Straightening a strap or two she stopped, sighing, as she gave up. It would have to wait. Running her fingers through her hair she pulled out a small twig. Throwing it to the ground she really looked around at her surroundings.

The Company was everywhere. They looked like the Lopar that roamed the mountains of her home in Tachenko province. They resembled those enormous black cats as the Company members prowled over the general area floating in and out of the nearby woods. The Pradas were there as well. Shading her eyes against the late afternoon sun with her right hand Onya looked skyward seeing what she knew would be there. They were magnificent creatures. No matter how often she saw them or was carried by one of them their size and grace still left her in awe. Then her eyes fell on Tom-Tom.

Her smile was warmth mixed with relief. "Tom-Tom! You made it. Thank the Ancient One." She trembled slightly. Tom-Tom walked to her. Softly, as though he was holding something easily broken, he took her into his dusty arms. Onya noticed that he had not changed. Torn cloth tickled her ear at his embrace. Her face rested softly against his chest. He was so big. Her voice was muffled by his hug.

"And Orah?" She went very still in his arms.

That high, gentle, voice answered her. "Yes Commander, I am here." Orah was close to tears as she joined the group embrace. The Company was more than just work. Orah continued, holding back tears, as she attempted to keep her voice from breaking. "When you turned at the last instant to cover our extraction the Pradas scooped us into the air. We wanted to return for you. But as Santeju began his turn, to come around for another pass, the Orb exploded. The entire area went up in flames. The Mountain Feather got tight-lipped. He kept saying that he would deliver us safely to Sanctuary. The Feathers are always stubborn on that point. It offends them to return with fewer passengers than they left with even when it's not their fault. He wouldn't let us return to look for you. I blistered his ears for half the flight back and would have knocked some sense in him if I could have reached him through the flight cabin."

Onya pushed them back then smiling at Orah. "He was correct not to Orah-san. Coming back was not what I had ordered him to do." Onya patted Orah on the shoulder before turning to face the Commander-General of the entire Company. He was looking off toward Gaul as if he could see the city from where he stood. He was a tall man, taller than anyone present, even the massive Tom-Tom. With his sword nestled like a baby in his left arm he stood staring off into the distance as if he were a statue in the Plaza of Getto. He almost looked like he was carved from granite or some such rock like those statues. She had failed him. The notion hit her like an unexpected gust of wind. Without thought she dropped her head while sighing deeply. Their orders had been simple enough. Her team had been experienced yet they had still failed him. Once upon a time he had saved her. It was a distant memory now, but he had saved her. Onya had vowed on that day that she would dedicate the rest of her life to serving him while trying to repay him. Never mind that he had said she owed him nothing. No, she knew deep down that she owed him everything. But he had been forced to come rescue her again. To make matters worse she had lost some of the People on her watch. She had failed. It would have to be faced. In the Company you did not run from the consequences of your actions. You faced them. It was part of what made you one of the People. With a deep breath she came to attention.

"Commander, sir. This was my operation and I failed." Tom-Tom and Orah opened their mouths almost at once. But a quick glare from Onya forestalled whatever they had been about to say. Orah's mouth twisted up like she was sucking on a large wedge of lemon while Tom-Tom grimaced like a caged Lopar. She was still their commanding officer, at least for the moment, and in the Company, you obeyed. She continued, "Regardless of the circumstances, sir, it was a simple operation and we – *I* - should have anticipated and responded to the threat before we had a chance to take such grievous losses."

As Onya spoke, her voice getting stronger, her resolve to face her failure strengthening, Bantu turned from looking off into the distance to gaze directly at her. Onya caught herself thinking, which she did from time to time, about how handsome he was. *Rugged*, she thought. Basil was the pretty one, but Bantu was very handsome. She caught herself. How odd it was to be thinking about that at a time like this.

Bantu's expression was unreadable but there was something there. Onya opened her mouth to continue but his hand came up sharply. This time it was Onya with her words caught in her throat, left to stand silently, working her mouth as if chewing what she had been about to say. He was *her* commanding officer, not to mention, *the* commanding officer of the entire Company. And in the Company, you obeyed.

Bantu's tone was unmistakable. He was a man who wore command like he wore the well-fitted, black, wool coat that glistened slightly in the sunlight. As he spoke he took one step forward. He was looking directly down at her. Years of training unwittingly surfaced in her at the tone in that voice. She stood completely still, at attention, while her eyes gazed just over his right shoulder.

"You were Team Leader." He spoke with a slow reverence. "In the process of performing your duties you did preside over a failed mission while losing People under your command. But you are still getting your bearings after being revived. Because of that I will forgive you your misspeaking. But," he paused pointing his right finger into the air, "– and I emphasize this with my heart aching for what has happened here. *Your* commanding officer is now present." Bantu pointed to her chest for emphasis then let his hand fall back to his side. He continued, his voice warm but very firm, "This is *my* responsibility. This is my company, Captain-Commander. If we were betrayed here I will find the leak and I will plug it with my own hands. If you keep insisting on taking responsibility for what you could not have prevented I will rethink your rank. I am clear Captain-Commander?" It was all spoken levelly but even through her pain Onya saw what he was doing. Bantu was letting everyone in earshot know that she was not at fault for the mission failing. The only problem was that he was doing what he had just accused her of doing in taking the blame for something that he could not have controlled. She would not say anything though. He was doing it for the same reason she had tried to do it. It was not that they were both irrational. But they both understood the cost of command. She could not stop him from taking the responsibility for this as he had stopped her for one simple reason. He outranked her. He outranked everyone actually.

That made her remember that there was something she could do though it would have to wait. Right now, there was protocol. But beyond all the other considerations, the truth was, she could not bring herself to contradict him. Not in public. Though they were longtime friends he would not abide her contradicting him in public. In private, in a limited way, he would allow her to argue with him but not in public.

"Yes sir, Commander. I understand you perfectly." Onya's voice was firm now. She stood there at attention waiting for orders or to be dismissed. He gazed down at her for a moment longer before turning his attention from her. Basil, standing close by, had tapped his com-gem as soon as Bantu moved. It flared to life on his high collar as Bantu strode off. Basil barked the words. He was heard all over the occupied area as everyone's com-gem came to life simultaneously.

"Attention to orders!" he cried, snapping to attention, his boots raising a small cloud of dust, even though Bantu was past him now.

Bantu walked toward the First Pradas who would carry him. She flexed her golden-feathered wings at his approach. She was slightly larger than the other Pradas. Unlike the reddish-brown males the females were gold in color. They were also larger than their male counterparts. Bantu's voice gained volume as it was caught by his com-gem, glowing brightly on the high collar of his black coat, transferring his command to everyone. It was the field commander's voice. It was the one you used to speak over the roar of battle. His right hand formed a fist with only his first finger extended, pointing straight up, as he made a circular motion once over his head.

"Evac. people!"

At the sound of the Commander-General's voice, the outer ring, nearly five hundred yards out, collapsed in upon itself, with crossbows pointed out toward the now shrinking perimeter. Everyone, including Onya, along with Tom-Tom and Orah, loaded into the flight carriages. In seconds the Pradas, with full carriages, were launching themselves into the air. Not a trace was left of their presence. They disappeared into the clouds as silently as they had come.

†

Fifteen miles east of that destroyed outpost, inside a covered wagon that rocked back and forth in the ruts on a narrow, winding road, a man came awake. His hands were tied to his feet. His mouth was gagged. He wore only a pair of short, close-fitting smallclothes. His legs, feet, and chest were bare. He did not know where he was, nor could he see anything other than darkness. The wagon struck something in the road causing it to rock violently jostling him. His head was pounding. The pain stabbed through his head with greater intensity each time the wagon rocked. He realized with horror that not only did he not know where he was or how he had gotten there. He did not know *who* he was.

†

Baquent Hevendere held up a green, suede, gloved hand. The column of soldiers behind him stopped as he stroked his thick black mustache. He had a pointed shortbeard on his chin as an aesthetic counterpoint. He looked over his shoulder past the five junior Inquisitors riding directly behind him at the head of the Twelfth Legion. The blue and red uniforms of the Twelfth stretched as far back as he could see along the road. Gelvin Hastroth had told him, in no uncertain terms, to find out if the outpost had been attacked. If it had been he was to discover by whom. He was then to bring their dead bodies back to hang from the walls of Gaul proper. With a few hand gestures he had the Twelfth Legion, under the command of Terrel McCove, secure the area so that he could get to work. *To shine a light into the darkness* were the words that hung high in the Grand Inquisitor's office, behind his massive desk, in Gaul. That was their appointed duty. It had been for an age. They would do that today. Shine a light on the events that led to the destruction of the Orb outpost. He had his suspicions. Once he had discovered the identity of the culprits then McCove, with his legion, would help him hunt them down. Baquent Hevendere was not going back to Gaul empty handed.

Many things pass between them. Their bond is both, blood and water, both, what is thought good and what is not. From what is spoken to what is heard may span the distance between valley and plain, and a river of understanding flows through it. Though standersby cannot tell, even anger becomes them, deepening their hands in the waters they stir together. So it goes between them.

~The Ethini on friendship

Friendship is more precious than silver and gold, and will cost you more than both.

~Vicar proverb

CHAPTER FOUR

An open door and words between

The choca trailed wisps of steam as it was poured into her cup by a young, delicate, brown hand that tilted the container without a hint of wavering. The choca pot had been carved from a large shell from the distant shores of Maya across the Far Wave Sea. Empress Natassha Sobrine, Daughter of the Morning, Sword of Tallanmoor, High Protector of Allmathon, Prince of Merrideen, and by the Hand of the Ancient of Days, Defender of the Dawn, nodded briefly as a thank you to the young woman. The woman serving her wore the purple livery, trimmed in creamy white, of the Imperial House. Her word was Law. The sun rose because of her. She was divine. At least that was the thinking of the Chancel of Peers. As she went so did the Empire. It had taken the reign of both her father and grandfather to make that so. What they had fought to make real had become the way of things.

The Empress let her thoughts drift where they would. She contemplated the notion that all labor had an innate nobility, while she watched Kemme move gracefully down the length of the thick, cherry-stained, wood table. There was a glimmer of recognition attached to that thought. That idea had been put forward by some scholar, whose work she had read during her days of study, while her father had been busy expanding the Empire. *All work was noble work.*

Small, delicate Kemme with her black, woolen hair tightly braided against her scalp, glistening lightly with scented oil that Natassha only caught a delightful whiff of as Kemme poured freshly brewed choca into white porcelain cups moved with practiced elegance. Those who served the Imperial House did not cringe or shuffle, as some rulers would have it. These were people who went about their duties with a sense of dignity. They were fiercely loyal to her. They were also learned. Natassha had seen to that. They ate from her table. Their meals were prepared in the same kitchen as hers. Her seamstresses made their livery from the finest materials. They had the run of most of the palace. The Chancel of Peers had been offended by those new notions, particularly the fact that Imperial Servants would not bow to them or cringe around them, but none dared say a word. She was the Dawn, the Dusk, and the very Twilight. In their minds the sun came at her bidding and only went by her leave. For many, that worship was not devout but merely lip service. Even so, they would never openly challenge those assertions. She *was* the Empire. Those cultic notions began under her grandfather. He father had solidified them.

In her mind she was *N'thuata ingo v'sulthra*. In the High Cant, a singsong language from a nearly forgotten age, it meant *first among equals*. Very few knew the old language anymore. It was only spoken at high ceremonies. But she had learned it because she was the voice of the people. Not to mention the fact that her father had required it as part of her studies. He had also used it as a way of speaking to her or her mother in public so that no one could tell what the Imperial family was discussing. It allowed them the freedom to speak openly.

A teaspoon of cream, followed by three sugar cubes, disappeared into her small cup. As Natassha stirred in the ingredients she had added to the dark-brown liquid with the tiny spoon it lightened. It was the way she enjoyed it. Unadorned the choca would have been a bit bitter for her tastes though she knew that there were those who enjoyed it that way. It made her grimace slightly at the thought of drinking her choca so plain.

The smell of choca floated up from the table, filtering through the room, carried by a slight draft from open doors at the far end of the room. They opened onto a large balcony from which Natassha would have been able to look out on most of Alexandria including part of the harbor. Lifting the cup, which bore the characteristic lilies of her House Sigil, etched delicately in tiny crimson, mustard, and peach buds, she took her first sip of the morning. The first cup of the day was always the best. Natassha had some advisors, to whom she would not speak, until they had their first cup of the day. They would invariably be grumbling or apt to be short with their comments. Brushing back a stray lock of curly, brilliant-red, hair with her left hand she placed her cup lightly on its delicate saucer with her right.

Natassha's dress was lime green with pale blue roses embroidered randomly across the bodice in good numbers. The dress fit snuggly from her shoulders to just below her chest. Past her waist, it fanned outward falling in a flowing cascade of silk to the top of her feet. It was not a structured dress, so the fabric billowed as she walked or as a breeze might blow. There was, however, enough material that, as she walked, the dress would trail a few feet behind her. She liked the cut. It had been designed by the masterful, Nicolla Tullhemaine. The woman was a virtuoso when it came to clothing. The collar stood tall, curving away from her face into points that curled slightly downward like a falcon's wings. At the base of her slim neck the collar was pinned together by a small rose-shaped broach the size of a large button. It was made of diamonds, green emeralds, and blue sapphires matching the colors of her dress. The slashing neckline, exaggerated by the high collar, was designed to bring the eye to her face. It was severe yet elegant or that was what Nico claimed. Whatever the statement, Natassha loved the look. She had commissioned Nico to make her eleven more in a similar style. Natassha curled her toes inside the matching velvet slippers. Blue eyes turned from gazing into her cup to glance down the length of the table. The heads of her military staff were updating her on the state of affairs.

To her immediate left was the head of her personal guard, Ellom Vam. The Captain of the Imperial Guard was rugged and, to her mind, somewhat attractive, in the way men who had seen much of the world were. That was Ellom Vam. The man was her walking headache as well as a constant reminder of her position, particularly when she wanted privacy. Next to him was Camilla Rodrick, the Minister of Defense. Rodrick was a breathing contradiction. A handsome woman, not beautiful by any stretch of the imagination, she had the regal bearing of any queen Natassha had ever seen, with her black hair highlighted by white streaks. She had sharp, dark eyes with a slender nose that ended in a slight hook giving her the look of a hawk ready for the hunt. Natassha knew that the woman was beloved among even the most common of the empire's soldiers. It was said that she could drink with the best of them. Rodrick's greater distinction among the ranks was that she could tell the dirtiest jokes ever heard in the rowdiest camps. Natassha had fought the urge on several occasions to ask Camilla Rodrick to tell her just one. She was convinced, though, that even the suggestion would embarrass the woman beyond repair.

Further down the left side of that table were Galant-General Axel Dreg and Commodore Onx Mancel. Those two could best be described as an old boot behind the barn and a gnarled stump in an otherwise empty field. Gray heads both, they believed that their time was best spent trying to win their running argument, which concerned whether land or sea forces were the keys to the defense of the empire. They would quote long-dead generals, legendary admirals, military instructors past or present, as well as site historic battles, along with their unending commentary on the virtue of the advantage of an attack from their favored purview or the consequences of not having used their particular military apparatus in this or that engagement. It was often laughable to watch the two become so utterly engrossed that they would eventually irritate one another by espousing a position the other thought completely preposterous. They were both insane. The depth of their compulsion, however, made them incredibly competent. Natassha's father had often had her laughing so hard she cried as he described the two of them actually arguing in the middle of the battlefield with arrows raining down, or flames exploding around them. The imperial family tolerated them because they were brilliant tacticians.

To Natassha's right was the principle military officer of Alexandria, Imperial Marshal Lewin Brahm. Brahm was younger than most at the table with the exception of Natassha. Though only about forty, Brahm was one of the most decorated soldiers in the empire. His tactical mind was first rate. Those who had served with him said that when he looked at a battlefield it was as if he saw a Talss Board. Each piece on that board represented a component of the battle. In his mind he positioned them, piece by piece, until he had victory. Brahm believed you fought the other commander on the field not the army he commanded. There were three members of Brahm's command staff to his right. Two of them were men and one was a woman. They were polished to within an inch of their lives.

At the far end of that line sat Gaiden Colling. Of all the people at the table Gaiden Colling was, in his own way, probably the most dangerous. As the Minister of Secrets, he was entrusted with securing the empire's interests abroad. Some called Colling, along with his command, *Her Majesty's Secret*.

Colling was of average height but above average intelligence. People all over the known world answered to him as he fought to maintain the security of the empire in the name of its Empress, Natassha Sobrine, *blessed ever she be*, he would chant after speaking her name as some did. He had never been a man who cared for pushing papers behind a desk or simply giving orders. Letting her eyes rest on him for the briefest of moments she considered his odd tendencies. Gaiden Colling had been known, on occasion, to take to the field in person. He was dangerous but also very odd. There were secrets there. Secrets, Natassha knew, that he had not even shared with her. Her father had taught her well, however, so there were contingencies in place in case those secrets ever became dangerous ones. It had taken time for Natassha to learn just how ruthless she could be but still manage to be just. It had taken both her parents to help her find that balance. She feared she was still learning.

The man who was her chief eyes and ears sat at the end of the table quietly sipping his choca. As a man who listened more than spoke, it was a consequence of that behavior that, when he finally did speak, people tended to listen. He sat sipping like a man who did not have secrets. But everyone at the immensely long, opulently carved, table knew that secrets were his trade.

Close-clipped was how she would have described his black hair. It was lightly oiled making it shine softly in the light. His face was clean-shaven.

The eyes were a lighter shade of blue than hers. They had an edge to them. He was a man who had seen more than he would be telling anytime soon. They knew more than he might ever tell. Natassha knew that some of what he knew might even go with him to his grave.

Today he was wearing a well-cut coat of blue velvet with blue wool pants. The pants were tucked into black, leather field boots. His coat had a wide, floppy collar. It was buttoned all the way up. The collar of the coat was cut to reveal the shirt he wore underneath. The stiff, white shirt that peeked out at the neck was well-pressed. He wore no jewelry. The man was supposed to be unarmed in her presence. But it would not have surprised her were she to learn that he was carrying at least one knife hidden somewhere on his person. Colling was a proud man who took great pride in his appearance as well as the job he did. He continued to sip his choca quietly as the others around the table talked softly.

Commodore Mancel, a thin, gray-haired man with a slim nose, began a report on the movement of ships in the Macca Deep. His voice was seasoned with the partial cracking of age like the patina of an old painting. Aside from his very dark skin, his singsong accent named him from the Isles of Joon immediately south and east of the capital city. That paradise of a land floated out in the crystal, blue, waters of the Macca Deep. Whenever Mancel could get away from Alexandria he took a ship for the four-day trip to his lush, tropical, home. People learned quickly not to bring up Joon around Mancel, unless they were prepared to be held captive for hours while he extolled the virtues of his homeland. If he had been drinking you could be put in the position of listening to him drone on for so long that you began contemplating taking your life because you believed death was preferable to hearing one more word. Natassha had laughed to herself on a number of occasions while witnessing people, very nearly, running in the opposite direction at an imperial function, when they first caught sight of Mancel with a drink in his hand. They looked as if the Betrayer were behind them. A brief smile crossed her lips just thinking about it. Mancel was speaking in that tone he used when making a report. Natassha forced herself to listen.

Her father would have asked her what good were reports if you did not pay attention to them.

"Her Majesty's *Valiant Sail*, *Blue Spray*, and *Morning Glory* be patrolling northeast. They do be prepared to enforce the trade embargo on Bree should the efforts of the ambassadors fail. Three Harbor Class ships do be on alert in case they be finding themselves needing assistance." He rearranged the papers lying in front of him, took a sip of choca, and prepared to continue in that singsong drawl that echoed off the domed ceiling.

Natassha's seat, at the head of the table, faced the door on the far wall, giving her a clear vantage point of the entire chamber, including the main doors, as they virtually exploded inward. She jumped slightly in her seat as the wood slammed against the stone of the walls. The hinges groaned in protest. Everyone froze with the singular exception of the Captain of the Imperial Guard. Flinging back his chair with one hand, while freeing his blade with the other as the chair rattled along the hardwood floor, Ellom Vam leaped forward, placing himself squarely alongside Natassha. The steel of his longsword glistened, along its well-oiled length, in the sunlight that splashed into the room from the towering windows that ran along the length of the wall opposite the now open doors. All along the wall of the chamber those windows faced east toward the Macca Deep. Vam stood like a cat ready to pounce. His left leg was forward, his knees were bent, while his chest rose and fell slowly. She could hear his breathing change. His shoulders moved with the rhythm of ever-deeper breaths. He was preparing his body for what was to come.

The Imperial Marshal imperceptibly adjusted himself in his seat. Natassha had not seen him take his sword out of his belt. Though still sheathed in its scabbard it now lay across the arms of his chair. The hair on his head was just beginning to gray at the edges but Natassha knew him. He had served her father faithfully. The Marshal was still quite capable of dealing out death like the cards in a game of Campel five. Only the Imperial Marshal and Captain Vam were allowed to be armed in her presence without express permission. The lack of armed guards caused a chill to settle over the room as the professional soldiers around the table, who had instinctively reached for weapons, realized they simply were not there.

The intruders flowed into the chamber. They were an odd mixture of stillness matched by fluidity. Faceless, save for exposed, cold, eyes, each of them was covered in black cloth from head to foot. Wrapped like wraiths, they brought to mind the fabled assassins of Jopo who also only exposed their eyes.

As Natassha watched them enter it only took a moment to realize that something about these intruders was out of place. It was hard to look at them. The air around these cold soldiers seemed to blur with their movement. As she blinked, trying to get her eyes to focus, they were no longer where she had just been looking. It was disconcerting.

Toned muscle stood out beneath the black bodysuits. Natassha could tell the men from the women due to the snug-fitting clothing but nothing else could be discerned. Then it dawned on her that, maybe, just maybe, she was about to die.

The words, *Imperial assassination*, rang in her mind. She had always known in some distant way that it was a possibility. Her grandfather had survived a number of attempts on his life as he began conquering surrounding countries in order to create the Empire. Her father had been faced with fewer attempts. Over time she had begun to believe that she would not really have to face any. It was the kind of thing you thought would never really happen. Had there been only a handful of intruders she would have held out hope that Vam, along with Brahm, might give her time to reach the hidden servants entrance five steps directly behind her seat. But the black-clothed soldiers kept pouring into the room like water spilling from a cracked barrel. Black, knee-high boots made no sound as they floated over waxed hardwood flooring in a low crouch. As they moved they periodically reached out in the direction they were not looking as they briefly touched one of the other members of their dark band. She settled her racing heart as she tried to prepare herself for what was coming. If she were going to die it would be with dignity. *May the Ancient of Days take her soul.*

As Natassha steadied herself she wondered how so many had gotten into the palace, to the hallway outside the chamber, without any alarm being raised? How was that possible? The Chamber of Roses was high in the palace. It was not easily accessible. Then she recognized the crossbows they were carrying. It all suddenly began to make sense. Only one group of people could have gotten this close to her, in such numbers, without even a shout of warning. Her heart leaped in her chest with euphoria. Breathing deeply, she let air come rushing into her lungs, which made her realize she had been holding her breath. *Relief.* Relief washed over her like a wave on the shoreline of the Macca Deep.

It had all happened in a few brief moments. Near panic had given way to relief. As the frenetic pace of Natassha's heartbeat slowed her thoughts stopped racing. She reached for her cup. Slowly, she took a sip of choca. Light wisps of steam still drifted up from the cup. It was gratifying to see her hand remain steady as she raised the cup. With a just-achieved calm, Natassha let her gaze sweep over the entire room with a severe, chastising look on her face. At least that was what she was trying to achieve. Though she was relieved to realize who had invaded the sanctity of the palace there was still something gravely wrong for this to have happened. There could be very nasty repercussions in the aftermath of whatever this turned out to be.

The man Natassha hoped was about to walk through the open doors, behind this *Strike Team*, as he would call it, would not have done something of this magnitude without grave reasons. Holding onto her composure she folded her hands into her lap. This could all still turn out very badly. If Gaiden Colling was the most dangerous man in the room the man who would walk through the doorway was the most dangerous man she had ever met.

The black-swathed soldiers fanned out around the edges of the room. In moments they had the entire chamber covered by loaded crossbows tucked tightly against their shoulders with hard eyes gazing down the sightlines. Those crossbows were the work of a *maker* she knew only as Tinker. That was all she knew because, even though it had been asked on more than one occasion, the offer to purchase those crossbows to arm Imperial soldiers had been refused. She also noted, to her further encouragement, that not even one of those crossbows was aimed at her. Looking more closely she could see that, given the way they were arrayed around the room, some of those crossbows *should* have been aimed at her but were studiously pointed in other directions, even at the floor. It all said to her that something was wrong, terribly wrong in fact, but not irredeemably so.

Glancing around the table, without moving her head, Natassha looked at the faces of her staff. She mostly saw badly covered shock or outrage but there were also a few reddened faces. Camilla Rodrick divided her gaze between her empty hands and the strangers who ringed the room. Rodrick kept looking at her hands as if expecting that the act of looking at them would make a weapon appear. Clenching then unclenching empty hands, she continued to look disgusted, while the only smirk in the room was on the face of Commodore Mancel. Mancel was leaning back with left hand on the arm of his chair, causing his elbow to jut out, as his right forearm rested on the chair's other arm. He looked from the others seated at the table to the intruders. Mancel had the look of a man being entertained who was waiting to see what happened next. Just looking at the Commodore tempted Natassha to smile along with him. Mancel had obviously realized, as she had, who the intruders were. But it was still a dangerous situation, which kept that smile from Natassha's face. This was not entertaining to her. She would have to unravel this situation delicately like a weaver at the loom repairing a priceless rug. *Great care.* The words went through her mind again. Wrapping the thought around her like a cloak Natassha reminded herself that she had not become Empress simply because she was next in line.

Natassha's high alto fell smoothly into the silence of the room as the last of the intruders floated into the chamber like an early morning fog rolling into lower Alexandria off the waters of The Deep. There had to be a *maker's* touch involved that made these people waver so. It was not the air that wavered, *they* wavered, or maybe it was the cloth.

Natassha used the voice of the Empress. It was that tone that said she ruled as far as the falcon could fly before it fell exhausted from the sky, and perhaps, even farther. Her mind's ear could hear the Chancel

Speaker intoning, during one of her entrances into the Assembly, *the Wind from the east, the Rain from the clouds, the Turning of the seasons, these are just some of the things Her hand directs.* She was the Empress of Alexandria. "Kemme, more choca." To her credit, Kemme did not hesitate but came directly, if cautiously, from her place at the copper serving carafe along the wall. She did not make any sudden moves but did everything very deliberately, while constantly darting looks around the room, as she poured. Some of those faces around the table turned toward Natassha now. *Good*, she thought. Let them remember with whom they were seated.

The clicking of twenty-one crossbows, as their firing latches were released, shattered the silence. A small sound normally, but in the stillness of the chamber, at that moment, it sounded like a thunderclap. Captain Vam wavered ever so slightly beside her as if he had nearly launched himself into furious motion. He was a large cat coiled for the attack. Natassha prayed to the Ancient One he would see he was hopelessly outnumbered. Her mind had been racing as she considered the situation. She had begun to think that there was only one reason for there to be so many of them. The man had wanted a contingent of sufficient size to smother any thought of resistance. It was becoming clearer to Natassha, by the moment, that this was not really an attack at all. Something else was going on.

Natassha was not going to embarrass Vam by verbally calling him down. But she also did not want him to make matters worse by dying in some unnecessarily heroic attempt doomed to failure. Her mother had taught her that men would do that if given the chance. They would further infuriate you by dying with a smile on their fool face as if they had done something constructive. Her mother had also told her that understanding men might never be achieved in a lifetime, but she could learn their quirks so that dealing with them would be somewhat easier. As she looked at the table Natassha thanked the Ancient that Vam had been the last to fix his choca. She spoke to him in a voice loud enough for everyone in the room to hear. "Captain Vam, would you be so kind as to pass the sugar so that I might finish mixing my choca to my taste?"

Vam turned his head slowly. His voice came out a little higher than usual, as if he could not believe his ears, "Empress?"

Natassha just looked at him and waited. She ignored the rest of the room as she looked directly at Vam while she waited for him to move. Cautiously, trying to watch everyone in the room at the same time, Vam reached out patting blindly at the tabletop until his hand located the small porcelain container. Passing it slowly to her he turned his attention back to the rest of the room. Natassha immediately busied herself pouring cream into her cup. She stirred the choca as she dropped in several sugar cubes. While her spoon clinked against the inside of her cup she hummed a few bars of, *the farmer to the market has gone*. Out of the corner of her eye she could see Kemme visibly fretting over not being able to keep Natassha from fixing her own choca. But at least she had bought a little more time while keeping Vam from doing something foolish.

When Natassha thought the tension in the room could not last one more moment without erupting *he* walked in. A light breeze blew in off The Deep through the doorway to the enormous balcony that ran the length of the Chamber of Roses. The bottom of the light green, sheer curtains billowed slowly up on the breeze before floating gently back down to brush against the hardwood floor. The room was awash with the smell of the sea. *He* walked into the room with purpose. He did not move too fast. But he was not moving as slow as he did when he strolled alongside her when she invited him on long walks through the palace gardens. *It was him*. It was Bantu.

The Commander-General of the Peoples Company walked into the room as though the ground he walked on was his. It was a steady, flowing, gait like the kind Natassha had seen on other men whose trade was violence. Bantu's was different, in that, there was no swagger to it. When you watched him, you only got a sense of competence, not the puffed-up pride of some. It was one of the things she had always liked about him. There was a quiet certainty about him. Whether among the nobility or the common folk he needed no one to tell him his place in the world. He had a way of making you feel the same way. He made room for himself, without preamble or excuse. His confidence, along with his lack of deference, infuriated many among the Chancel of Peers. But under her father's rule Bantu had become a powerful man, powerful enough that they could only fume, hoping he would make a mistake one day.

Natassha knew that his self-possession had better be justified today or he would be handing those enemies a reason to do what they had wanted to do ever since he had helped her ascend to the throne during the Twelve Days War. That nasty rebellion against her rule had erupted shortly after the death of her father before her coronation. For twelve days civil war ran rampant through the streets of the capital city. A man who had thought himself the rightful *Imperiata* of Alexandria had led that rebellion. Since the end of the rebellion some of the Peers wanted Bantu out of the city proper. He was too dangerous, they said. It was not because they had sided with Calbet Harken and the House of the Raven during the rebellion, but because Bantu, with the Peoples Company behind him, had been powerful enough to make the difference. There were many who did not like that reality. They considered him a mortal threat to the Empire. Some even thought he might one day decide to be emperor himself, which, in their estimation, would be difficult to prevent. Today he might give them more wood for their fire. But she knew this man. Bantu was not hungry with ambition like the members of the Peerage. Somewhere deep within herself Natassha knew he had a very good reason for what he was doing. His methods infuriated her. But she knew there must be a reason for this behavior. She added the thought to the other that she was wearing like someone wrapping a second blanket around them to keep out the cold.

The tall, brown-skinned man took three strides into the room. He was wearing the Company uniform. The coat was of unrelieved, finely woven, black wool with a tall collar. The coat fell to the top of the thigh with thick, black embroidery at the collar, wrist, and hem. It was a beautiful, if simplistic design. The buttons were also black, stopping just shy of where his black, leather swordbelt was strapped around his waist. The coat fit close. It flared out slightly from the hips to the hem. It was a smart looking garment. The breeches were also black, and slim-fitting but not too tight. They were tucked into the top of round-toed, black, leather, knee-high boots.

Bantu was resplendent in unrelieved black. But more than the various points of his well-appointed uniform Natassha took note of the calm expression on his chiseled face. That he was in her presence unannounced, with his armed escort, meant that the palace guard had their hands full. His sword was not hanging from his belt. Instead, it was nestled in the crook of his left arm like a mother holding her baby, as was his custom. The long hilt was pointing across his midriff toward where his right hand hung at his waist. His right thumb was tucked behind his swordbelt. She imagined that the blade could be loosed instantly from that position. At the same moment she was hoping it would not come to that.

Out of all the information she had gleaned from her circumspect perusal of the situation, this was the most important fact, aside from the knowledge that none of the crossbows were pointed at her. That greatsword was still in its housing. The situation was frightening, as well as puzzling, all at the same time. But the man's sword was still in its black lacquered scabbard. He wanted answers, it seemed, not blood. *So what, by the Light of the Dawn, did he want?* Had his goal been blood it would already be staining the hardwood floor. Not to mention that sword would be whirling about him cutting through flesh and air. Natassha had seen him find the need to free that sword from its housing before. The title the best in Alexandria held was, *Karturi-dan* in the High Cant, which meant Swordmaster. It was insufficient to describe what she could only call artistry. He was an artist with the thing. To watch him was to feel as though you were attending a performance by the Imperial Dance Company.

Bantu stood very still. It was like looking out on a pond when there was no breeze. *Complete stillness.* To her right Captain Vam adjusted himself slightly. Though Bantu stood very still you could feel his readiness. He was like a storm gathering itself out on the waters of The Deep before slamming into the shoreline. Or like that moment of perfect stillness as the hunter froze in the high grass just before attacking its prey. Vam looked directly at Bantu. Bantu returned the gaze unwaveringly. The leopard had locked eyes with the wolf. A weighing took place. Then Bantu, as if satisfied at a conclusion having been reached, looked back around the room in silence. Natassha dared not look up at Captain Vam. She was afraid of what she might see reflected in his eyes. Resignation was there, more than likely, but she would not like it if she saw it.

The Empress of Alexandria took a very deliberate sip from her cup of choca. Setting her cup down gently she addressed the Wolf of Sanctuary, which some of her advisors called him privately. They were unaware that she knew of the label. He was more lion than wolf the truth be told. Right now, he was a lion that must be calmed.

Natassha made her voice conversational, as if she were discussing the weather. "Good morning, my long-time friend. Have you come to share a cup of choca with me? If you had alerted me to your visit I would have had them brew your favorite. It is still a dark roast with a hint of vanilla?" Natassha was saying something beyond the words she actually spoke in the way only very old friends could speak to one another. *You must be upset, but tell me what is so important that you could not have simply told me and let me deal with it? Are we not friends? This will not get out of hand!*

Bantu just stood there, for a moment, motionless. *Was he considering what she had not spoken aloud?* His head turned up slightly, at an angle, as though he was picking the unformed words she had not spoken from the air. His voice was as chilly as the first autumn breeze of the year at the end of summer.

"It is still my favorite, ruler of Alexandria. But I have a taste for something different today." Bantu did not look at her directly as he spoke but watched the people seated around the table. He was ready for something. He was ready to move at the slightest provocation. It was as though he were waiting for one of them to do something. The Commander-General was saying to her, *we are still friends Empress, but I have come for answers that you cannot give.* The muscles in his cheeks flexed as his jaw clenched.

Something was happening here that Natassha could not get a grasp on. She desperately needed to know what. If someone died here today the repercussions could be disastrous. Bantu had an incredibly large force along with vast resources. If he was provoked the man could probably wage war against a small country unaided. While the empire would doubtlessly be victorious, the price would be high, too high to risk if it could be avoided. She took a deep breath letting it out slowly.

"Well then, my Lord Commander, speak your peace. Your service to the House of the Lilies and the Imperium has earned you more commendations than most. Imperial Rank has been bestowed upon you though you decline its advantage. But that rank gives you the right to petition the Empress directly, with candor, whether you acknowledge it or not." She gazed directly into his eyes now. Her chin was raised just a fraction. Here was the Empress. The *Empress* required an answer without further delay.

Bantu slowly lowered his still-sheathed sword, placing the tip on the floor between his feet, the black, lacquered, scabbard disappearing against the black backdrop of his uniform. Only the long hilt stood out. He folded his hands over the top of the carved ivory hilt, which stood even with his swordbelt. The ivory hilt had been worked with tiny golden blossoms along its length. There was a single, matching, blossom etched into the circular handguard, which separated the blade from the hilt. The weapon was of the finest craftsmanship. Leaning lightly on the sheathed sword, he spoke. Natassha could almost feel the first winds of winter in his words as his voice hardened. She stopped herself from shivering.

"Yesterday, I took an Evac. Squad into Northern Province, on the far side of Gaul. The purpose was to extract a Strike Team that had been ambushed while on a mission for the illustrious body now seated around this table. Three of the *People* are dead. Three more were seriously wounded. They knew we were coming." With a twirl he returned his sword to the crook of his left arm as he stepped up to the foot of the long table. There was an almost imperceptible growl beneath his words as he continued. "My end is secured," he tapped his finger on the tabletop emphasizing his next words, "- the leak, is here. And so, I, am here." Bantu looked to Vam, then the Imperial Marshal, who had stopped smiling at Bantu's words before finally turning his gaze back to Natassha.

She was startled. Natassha slid her cup and saucer away from her across the table. This was not good. Without turning from Bantu's gaze, she spoke levelly. "Imperial Marshal. Who was in charge of the details for the mission we contracted to the Peoples Company?"

Imperial Marshal Lewin Brahm looked across the table at Camilla Rodrick, the Minister of Defense, with an askance expression. It seemed like the People, ringing the room, with aimed crossbows had been nearly forgotten with the information Bantu had just dropped on them. The First Officer of Alexandria leaned forward in his seat, his voice rumbling lowly, as he spoke.

"Minister, you contracted this particular mission. Who handled the information?"

Rodrick looked nervously around the room.

"Out with it, Camilla!" Natassha spoke sharply.

The Minister of Defense jumped in her seat at the tone the Empress had taken. She stuttered a reply. "It ... it was ... it was Gaiden Colling." Rodrick put her hand to her forehead.

The two men moved like lighting. Gaiden Colling pulled a dagger from his jacket while kicking his chair back from the table. Bantu moved faster than Natassha thought possible. While slapping the dagger from Colling's grip with one hand Bantu laid his sword on the tabletop with his other hand. Colling turned smoothly on his left leg. In one fluid motion he flowed away from Bantu in the direction the dagger had been thrown. At the end of that tight, coiled, spin Colling snapped a kick at Bantu's midsection. Turning slightly, as if he were edging down a narrow hallway, Bantu slid toward Colling. Bantu made one languid move in response. Turning as he did made Colling's kick miss Bantu by less than a finger's width. Partway through his turning motion Bantu froze as the kick flashed by. As Colling's leg snapped past him Bantu flowed into a reverse spin, which carried him into Colling. It left Bantu with his left shoulder just slightly below the level of the now extended leg. Bantu danced. From one position to the next, he moved effortlessly, without ever stopping. Rising up from a crouched position beneath Colling's leg he lifted his left arm sharply, fully extended, with his palm facing the floor. That slim, but well-muscled arm came up sharply beneath Colling's extended leg. Bantu remained rigid as he moved up and slightly forward. The effect of that single move was startling. Bantu's rigid arm made contact with the underside of Colling's leg, just beneath the thigh, as the leg reached the full extension of Colling's missed kick. Colling's forward momentum met Bantu's counter movement as he slid into Colling catching the man with his center of gravity compromised. Natassha watched as Bantu's fluid, singular counter knocked Colling cleanly from his feet. There was a loud, solid, thump as Colling crashed into the hardwood floor. The air left Gaiden Colling's lungs in a rush.

Before he could recover Bantu was moving. Bantu took a handful of Colling's jacket with his left hand while grabbing the man by the throat with his right. In one swift move he hoisted Colling into the air. Three long strides carried them both to the wall opposite the door as Bantu braced Colling, with another crushing sound, against the wood paneling between the windows with a view onto the veranda.

Bantu's face was very still. His hazel eyes and tenor voice were calm. His words were deliberate. "You will tell me who the traitor is. And then, then you will convince me why you should live, where your betters have died."

Captain Vam took a step toward the two men. As he began to move several silently held crossbows came to rest aiming directly at him. The message was clear. This was to be a two-party conversation, with just the two men, no more. Natassha spoke quickly. She pitched her voice low enough so that only he could hear her clearly.

"No, my good Captain, be still a little while yet." She raised her voice to include the entire chamber. "I too should like to hear the answer to at least the first part of the Lord Commander's inquiry."

All eyes shifted from the Empress to Gaiden Colling. Comodore Mancel's eyes had narrowed to angry slits. His hand had gone to the hilt of his sword. Imperial Marshal Brahm had a look of pure disgust on his face as the level of the evident betrayal took shape. Brahm was a man of honor, a warrior of the Old Way. They faced you directly with no pretense as to their motivations or intentions. If the Imperial Marshal were going to kill you he would send you an invitation written on parchment inviting you out to the pavilion or a street square. When you arrived he would salute you before setting about the work of planting his saber firmly in your chest. Brahm had made no pretense that he either liked Gaiden Colling or his methods. But Natassha had needed him, needed his *Shadowwatch*, so Brahm had tolerated them.

Natassha's mind raced. She knew what Brahm would be thinking. What would the Wolf of Sanctuary require in payment for a betrayal of this magnitude? Would he stop with Colling or would all of Alexandria be next? Where enemies abroad could not penetrate the defenses of the Empire the Commander-General already thrived at its heart. One word from him and the Peoples Company could turn the capital city into a burning ember. Brahm had once given her his best guess as to how many people were in Sanctuary at any given time. It was a number large enough to worry her military advisors.

A sneer appeared where pain had been evident on Colling's face. Having caught his wind again his voice had the clipped inflection of indignation.

"I will not answer to this foreign filth!" he said with spittle decorating his lips.

Natassha rose quickly from her seat. She walked to where Bantu held Colling with his polished boots dangling several handspans from the floor. She noted, with relief, that not a single crossbow so much as waivered as she moved across the room. In fact, as she crossed into their line of fire, crossbows were moved keeping her out of harms way. That spurred Natassha on encouraging her boldness.

Natassha walked right up to Bantu laying a gentle hand on his arm. Looking up at him she met his eyes as he turned his head at her touch. She had often kept herself from looking too long into those hazel eyes with their flecks of what she thought was gray. If you looked into them too long you could get lost. There was a depth there that was captivating. Forcing herself to continue looking into their depths, Natassha applied a gentle downward pressure on the rock-hard arm holding Colling aloft.

After a moment's hesitation Bantu lowered Colling to the ground releasing him as he did.

Natassha faced the Prime Agent and Minister of Secrets. *Former Prime Agent*, she thought. She faced him as he tried to adjust his rumpled jacket in short snatches. She grabbed his chin roughly with her right hand. Their eyes met. Her gaze defied him to move. Colling stood still, waiting. She thought she saw in his eyes the briefest of notions but then it was gone. He stood there with a look of disdain on his face. When she felt she had his attention, she spoke, her hand still holding his chin. Natassha added a knife's edge to her voice as her mother had taught her. Her mother had taught her as a child how to control her tone in order to say the things her words did not. An Empress needed that skill.

"Colling, this man, whom you insult as if I were not in the room, has served the empire faithfully. While you may think it safe to disrespect him you do so at your own peril. He is my friend. I will have you answer him. And you *will* answer." Colling's face changed as she finished. She removed her hand. His face darkened as if a shadow had fallen across it.

"You weak, pathetic, little woman." He spat the words with venom. "I have given you the world to conquer at your ease. But you do not have the stomach for what must be done to secure it. That's the difference between children who play at ruling and a true conqueror – a real Prince!" More spittle flew from his mouth. He had a wild look in his narrowed eyes. He pounded his fist against his chest emphasizing each of his points. "I have scaled the walls of Tracdenmoor. Crossed the Dangerwaters at Ogmon. I have infiltrated throne rooms! I have taken life and rescued it. And I did all of it for the glory of Alexandria. But what have you done with what I have given you?" Colling jabbed a manicured finger in the air at Natassha. "Nothing! You have squandered it!" He pointed at Bantu then but even as he did his eyes did not leave Natassha. "And the final insult was that you would call this, this, monkey to do my job? Ha!" Colling twisted his lips, shaking his head as he continued, flicking his wrist as if he were waving off something invisible – a dismissive gesture. "I handed his pathetic little team over to soldiers of the Outpost in Province and they were appreciative." Colling turned his head from left to right looking around the chamber as he breathed heavily. He was a trapped animal.

Bantu's voice was flat. Pity ringed each syllable. "You will die, little man. The turning of the cycle of this life is at an end for you." Bantu's words sounded like the intoning of a ritual litany. It sounded like something said over the dead. Natassha stepped closer to Bantu. Placing her hand on his arm she squeezed lightly.

"No, not like this." She stepped between Bantu and Colling continuing to speak in reassuring tones. This was the delicate part. Natassha knew Bantu, knew he would think he had every right to kill Colling where he stood. "He has served as an Imperial Officer, but more importantly, he is a citizen of the Empire, however guilty. I will punish him accordingly but only after he has been tried by the Imperial Tribunal." No one else could see it because Bantu towered over her as he stood between her and the rest of the chamber, but her eyes pleaded with him to accept her words.

Bantu's face did not show it but his eyes hardened as he weighed her words. Natassha also thought it might well be their friendship being weighed behind those eyes. Societal conventions held little weight with him. No law bound him only the tenants of something he said came from the Ancient of Days. It was something he called *Mdao' Nnanda*, the *Warring Way*. The laws of Alexandria had been fashioned based upon the light of reason. It was one of the central contributions of her family to the empire. She was prouder of that contribution than any other. One need only walk through the halls of the great centers of learning in the empire to hear the great minds of the age discussing the notion, the idea, of what it meant to be a *citizen*. But Natassha did not know how much those laws paralleled what Bantu believed to be true.

Natassha looked firmly into Bantu's eyes. Friendship hung in the balance. It hung in the balance over notions about how a thing ought to be done. Their friendship, Natassha knew, was twisting in a wind, borne aloft by a lifetime of beliefs. Her heartbeat quickened. If Bantu killed Colling now it would likely destroy their friendship, which she might have already done by standing between Bantu and the man who had killed some of the People by betrayal. It would break her heart to lose

Bantu. He had, as surely as her legitimate birthright, placed her squarely on the throne of Alexandria with the might of the Peoples Company, when she had desperately needed it. He had then remained in Alexandria to see that her crown was securely on her head when he could have taken the Company anywhere. *What must he be thinking now*, she wondered? She held onto his gaze with all she had. There was a flicker of movement reflected in his eyes. Before she could react, she was already flying through the air.

It took a moment for Natassha to realize that Bantu had thrown her. Vam, his sword clattering to the floor behind him, had leaped forward in order to snatch her from the air. As Vam's sword rattled to the floor Lewin Brahm's chair followed it. Brahm had also kicked it away from him while leaping forward in order to try to catch her. The Captain of the Imperial Guard had simply beaten him to it. Natassha twisted her head sharply to see what was happening behind her while Vam set her gently on her feet murmuring some apology for having touched the *Person* of the Empress.

In throwing her to safety Bantu had taken the attack meant for Natassha. Colling had struck him as he rotated around to release Natassha into the air keeping her out of harms way. Colling had trained for a lifetime in an empty hand discipline called *Hapka-do*. He was very good. Natassha had seen him in action.

A slashing hand had struck Bantu firmly between his shoulder blades as Bantu released her. Natassha had turned in time to see Bantu dive, rolling forward, in order to put distance between himself and Colling. Colling closed the distance as Bantu rolled back up to his feet. Before Bantu could set himself, Colling was raining savage blows on him from all directions. He came down on Bantu like a rockslide on a crumbling mountain. It was brutal. Natassha looked quickly to those black-clad wraiths ringing the room to see which of them would kill Colling with a shot from one of those crossbows. Not one of them moved to help their Commander. She had often been puzzled by the way the *People* acted. One moment they harassed Bantu like a gaggle of overprotective parents but in the next they were standing idly by while this happened. She wanted to scream at someone in the room to help him, but she could not speak. The only thing she could do was watch as Colling tried to kill her friend. Bantu took two vicious blows to his midsection. Gaiden Colling saw that he had the advantage, so he kept coming. When he realized no one was going to help Bantu a wild smile stretched across his face.

Colling launched himself again at the Commander-General with a flourish of his hands. Natassha's breath caught in her throat as Colling danced around Bantu battering him with a flurry of punches followed by several driving kicks. But something changed as Colling drove vicious blow after blow at Bantu, which caused the smile to fade from the man's face. Bantu began blocking everything that was thrown at him. The advantage Bantu had given to Gaiden Colling, by getting Natassha to safety, evaporated.

Colling paused his attack. He stood there for a moment breathing heavily from the exertion. Bantu drew a thumb down the right corner of his mouth. He raised it to his eyes so he could look at the blood smeared across it. His eyes took on a distant look. Something changed in him that Natassha could not quite describe. But he became *different*.

Gaiden Colling threw himself at Bantu again with an audible growl escaping his lips. He came in low erupting upward, suddenly, into a floating kick. Bantu shifted to his left. With immaculate timing he jabbed his right elbow downward into Colling's rising leg at the thigh. With a painful grunt Colling spun left as he landed. A spinning backfist came hurtling toward Bantu's head in the same instant. But Bantu raised his right arm to block it. As Colling's arm hit the block he snapped his arm downward grabbing Bantu's right wrist. As he continued the spin Colling pulled down on Bantu's arm. Thrusting the palm of his other hand behind Bantu's elbow he pulled his wrist into him as he pushed away from himself with the hand behind the elbow. Colling threw Bantu toward the wall he had been braced against earlier. He flung the larger man, as he released his grip, so that Bantu slammed into the wall while Colling hopped in behind him. The smaller man moved on the balls of his feet like a cat. It all looked to Natassha like a beautiful, deadly dance.

Just as his back hit the wall Bantu launched himself off the hardwood paneling to meet Colling who was moving toward him. Colling brought his left knee up toward Bantu's midsection. Crouching a moment earlier than would have been expected, or should have been possible, Bantu kicked out his left leg in a tight arc that circled outward, gaining speed as it whipped around him. The kick took Colling on the inner thigh of his rising leg. The impact spun him throwing him completely off balance. Colling stumbled as he fought to keep his balance. Bantu hopped to the right so that he could slide in behind Colling. When he did he struck him on the back of his neck with his hand pressed flat into a knifehand. It propelled Colling forward but he rolled with it throwing himself into a head over heels roll. When he came up out of the roll Colling turned quickly lashing out with his left hand.

Sweeping his left arm down, across his body, then up in a tight half-circle, Bantu caught Colling's arm at shoulder level wrapping it up in a single move. The block pushed the punch away from Bantu's face pushing Colling's arm out to Bantu's left. Stepping into Colling with his right foot forward, Natassha would have to say, he *applied* a punch with his right fist directly to the left side of Colling's head, just in front of his ear, slightly above his jaw. The blow was jarring. It made a heavy thumping sound like a bag of grain being thrown into the back of a cart. Colling went limp. He fell to the floor like a dropped sack of meal. He did not move. He slumped so limply to the floor and lay so still that Natassha thought Bantu had killed him.

The room was quiet again. The exchange had only taken seconds though it had seemed to stretch on for much longer. Bantu stood over the unmoving body of Gaiden Colling. He rubbed briefly with his left hand at a spot low on the left side of his waist. It was where he had been hit when he had thrown Natassha across the room. The tall Commander-General turned from where Colling lay adjusting his black coat as he did. A small trickle of blood could be seen in the corner of his mouth. Natassha noted that he was not breathing hard. He was not sweating either. It was something she had noticed before. She wondered again, as she had before, how that was possible. She knew he trained constantly. But even men who trained constantly had to sweat. They did get tired. They even breathed heavily. *Didn't they?*

Bantu looked toward Natassha before letting his gaze sweep over the rest of the room. Natassha noticed the look Captain Vam directed at the man. There was a deep respect in Vam's eyes as the Commander-General met the Captain's gaze before looking beyond him. Vam hovered at Natassha's elbow with that look of respect still directed at the man who had probably saved the life of the woman he was sworn to protect. The dishonor Vam would have carried had Natassha been even slightly injured would have been too much for the man to live with. Bantu had put himself at jeopardy to keep Natassha from harm. Vam would find a way to honor that, Natassha knew, with more than just a look of respect. Natassha noted the wry look on Vam's face as Bantu turned away from him. Vam hated being in anyone's debt.

Natassha turned her attention from Vam to watch the Commander-General. What would he do now? She wondered if the unmoving body on the floor was dead. *If he is dead, what will* I *do*, she thought? She could probably put it off on defense of her life but she would not like it. Still, that could be her lying unmoving on the floor. This time she did shiver, ever so slightly. Vam touched her lightly on her elbow, while murmuring a further apology for touching the Imperial Person, but she waved him off. She was the Empress. She was fine. She turned her eyes from the unmoving body on the floor back to Bantu.

As their eyes met he spoke, breaking the silence that covered the room. "He is not dead ruler of Alexandria." That voice still had a sharp edge to it. He did not like what he had done – what he had *not* done. She knew he could have used the man's attack as justification to kill him, but he had not. He had not and the thought of it was bothering him. As if accentuating the point, a low moan came from the body on the floor. Natassha could see now that Colling's chest was rising and falling. The man was breathing.

Bantu walked back to the table. As he past Lewin Brahm the man nodded briefly at the Wolf of Sanctuary. Brahm seemed to have a renewed respect for the dangerous wolf that lived inside the gates. Bantu retrieved the sword with its beautifully carved ivory hilt placing it back in the crook of his left arm with a single spin. He faced the open doors leading to the hall with his back toward her. After a brief pause he moved toward them. Natassha spoke before he reached the doors. At the sound of her voice he stopped. He turned his head a bit at her words.

"I am saddened by your loss, friend of the Crown." *I am still your loyal friend*, her underlying words said to him. She tried to will him to accept them as she spoke. "Ask what you will in compensation for the loss to the *People* and their families."

Bantu turned his head forward again keeping his back to her as he replied. "What price can be put on the life of one of the People? Pay what you see fit Empress. And as to their family, all of the People are their family."

As he took another step toward the doorway Natassha said, "Rest assured, my Lord Commander, Colling will be punished for his treachery." *Are you still my friend*, her tone said to him.

"See that he is Natassha Sobrine. See that he is." Just as he reached the threshold to the doorway he paused for a final moment. It was as if he was mulling something over. After a few seconds he spoke again without turning his head to look at her. "The Last Rite will take place at sunset. You may come to pay your respects to the fallen." In his way, Natassha knew, he had just said to her *our friendship lives though my friends do not*. And then he was gone. She could not hold back the tempered smile from her face.

Three heartbeats more and the silent, black-clad, people with their crossbows began evaporating away through the doorway behind their Commander-General. They flowed out of the chamber in the same way they had entered. They were clearly covering his exit. A few gave darting looks toward where Colling lay unconscious before disappearing into the hallway. Their eyes seemed to harden for that fleeting moment just before they were gone. The giant double-doors were left hanging open. The words of the Wolf of Sanctuary still seemed to hang between the doorway and the unmoving form laying only a few steps from the velvet-covered feet of Empress Natassha Sobrine. *See that he is*.

Passing out of sight, the course holds, straight off to an unknown trail, standing there, a breeze that is not a breeze catches me, and to all of me, it asks a question I can only hear on the wind – that when, that moment, holds me wavering there. Laid out before me like shimmering doors about to evaporate, one path off to eternity, the other off to a kind of everlasting, and neither tells me its secrets. Another sound approaches, or maybe it was always there, like the sound of voices already passed this way, or dry leaves turned in the hand, a whispering ... a whispering ... a speaking that says unmistakably, you must choose.

~ Jait Hert
Excerpt from a collection of
Essays entitled,
Musings on Restlessness

When fortune smiles, smile back at her.
~*A Pascha saying*

Chapter five

A fork in the road

Onya leaped. With her arms outstretched, like the wings of one of the great birds, she surged forward. In a heartbeat, which seemed to stretch on longer than it should, she was airborne. Soaring momentarily, through the air, she sailed over the space between the last rooftop and the next. For a fleeting few seconds she thought she understood what it must feel like to be one of the Pradas. Landing lightly, and soundlessly on the next rooftop she kept running. There were other, nearly inaudible, sounds behind her. Onya could barely make out the footpads of six other women as they launched themselves into the same sky-grabbing leap. The smell of Alexandria, this part of Alexandria, occupied only part of her attention while the rest of her mind lost itself in the physical movements of her body, making minute adjustments as she ran on the balls of her feet.

Someone, somewhere below, was stewing beans. Onya thought a hint of garlic brushed her nose as she caught the air again. This time she went sailing twenty feet through the air in order to bridge the gap between buildings. Over gabled oak or fired, red clay tile she soared. Terraced brick or stained hardwood met her feet as she landed. Dye, tar, cement, candlewax, and pipe smoke, along with dozens of other smells gave their unique, distinctive contributions to the particular scent that was Alexandria in the early evening.

Ducking under a wire, likely used for hanging clothes out to dry, Onya stretched out her stride. Planting her right foot on a raised brick retaining wall she vaulted into the air. This time the intervening space between each roof was only about twelve feet so she added a full flip, with a half turn, to the jump. Landing on the other side she flowed into a second flip, this one sideways, accompanied by another half twist to right herself. Racing to the center of the roof she turned to watch, smiling with glee, as her sisters took her cue. They performed various twists, flips, and turns of their own as they hurtled across the gap.

Onya continued smiling beneath her face-wrap. These were her sisters. Not by birth, mind you, but sisters nonetheless. Their relationship went just as deep as blood in many ways. Years ago, while the Company was still taking shape, a number of women had come together to form an Order. It was meant as a female counterpoint to *Tsima Na Mdo*. The all-male Order called themselves *the line he draws in the sand*. The *he* referred to Bantu. Tsima Na Mdo translated as *those who sing to death*. The Deathsingers embodied those words. They served as the rearguard. They were always the last ones out. They took pride in the notion that their job was to thumb their noses in the face of death until everyone else was out of danger. They were a kind of dichotomy, at once a hard lot, but given easily to laughter. Their other quirk, which haunted those who had the misfortune of having to face them in battle, was a favorite practice calculated to insight fear. They sang. While arrows flew, and steel clashed, they sang.

So, a group of women had come together to form their own Order. The Commander-General had named them like each of the other Orders when they were ready. He named them *Yoru Battai*. Yoru Battai meant the *Quiet Blossoms*. No men were allowed. The profile of the Order was reconnaissance. They specialized in a number of things. They were known mostly as an advance guard. They also tended to serve as primaries in certain specific operations. Inscribed on the door to the gathering place of their Order were the words *First In*. They brought balance to the Orders. Where the Deathsingers were the last to leave, the Blossoms were the first to arrive, the first to dance the old dance with death.

The Blossoms had not been an active Order for more than a few operations before Deathsingers had taken to calling them *the quiet death*. Onya leaped again tucking her knees tightly to her chest with her hands wrapped around her shins as she sailed through the air. Forming a small ball as she rotated, head over heels, through the air, she came out of the tuck just in time to land softly on the next roof. Looking over her shoulder she flung her head daring her sisters to top it. *Yes,* she thought as she smiled to herself, *the Blossoms were her sisters.*

Upon their return from Northern Province, earlier that day, Bantu selected twenty-one of the People out of the Strike Team that had retrieved her from the destroyed Orb facility. They were going to accompany him to the Imperial Palace on Rulers Hill. He was going to get answers. During the return flight, he had communicated with Sanctuary through the long-range communication gemstone located in the Command-Flight carriage. It was a much larger gemstone that was nearly the size of a person's head. When they landed in Sanctuary, Bantu was met by one of the Far Eyes. The man had given him a report, which had him nodding his head. When Onya had seen his expression, she could have only described it as grim. People were stepping lightly around the Commander-General today.

Bantu chose seven Deathsingers before picking seven Windchasers. Basil's people were investigators. It was said that the Windchasers could catch what was not there and find the truth before the lie was spoken. Bantu had turned toward the place where the Far Eyes were unloading their gear from the flight carriages as if he were about to call the final numbers for the Strike Team from their Order. But before he could speak one of the Quiet Blossoms marched right up to him, planting her small form in front of the towering Commander-General. With her hands on her hips she demanded the right of *Yoru Battai* to be included. *After all*, she said, *Onya had nearly died.* It was the right of her sisters to have an answer from those who had betrayed them.

This led to the ranking officers of each of the Orders, whose members had been a part of the Orb mission, quickly adding themselves to the discussion. Far Eyes spoke up for the loss of Mallic even as Rain Catchers named the wounding of Orah, while Stone Hands vehemently pointed to Tom-Tom. Bantu had been surrounded by the present ranking members of the represented Orders with each adamantly protesting about being represented.

The Commander-General of the Peoples Company listened patiently before finally holding up a hand for silence, which he received immediately. He picked out a second team of twenty-one, containing members of each of the Orders who wished to be included. They were responsible for securing the guards at the Imperial palace. After that was settled they immediately departed for answers on Rulers Hill.

As Onya ran with her sisters across the array of Alexandrian rooftops she knew that below her, on the street, the Commander-General walked alone. After leaving the palace he had given the command for the strike teams to turn *ghost*. That meant they were to be invisible. They were to remain out of sight. Even though they complied all forty-two of them were within shouting distance of the Commander-General as he strolled down Hawker Street. The People were a little overprotective when it came to Bantu sometimes despite his orders to the contrary. They would obey him without question, even in going to their own deaths, but when it came to his protection he sometimes had to fight with them to follow his orders. Onya smiled at that. No one would admit openly that it was being done. They would nonetheless set his orders aside. They would do it but deny it later. It had almost become a game among the Orders. Who could protect the Commander-General? Who could be there when his life was in danger so that they could place themselves between him and death? When someone succeeded they walked a little taller among the People. They kept it all from him. Though Onya suspected that he knew. She thought he knew but was simply accepting what he knew he could not change. Bantu had learned not to bang his head against a brick wall.

He had tried. Oh, Onya knew, he had tried. For a time there had been systematic meetings with the ranking officers from each of the Orders in which Bantu had soundly, loudly, objected to the notion. They would all agree with him wholeheartedly. They were a solemn, sufficiently chastened, group during the meeting. It was all very serious. Then, upon leaving the meetings, they would resume the same activities as if the meetings had not taken place. It had infuriated him for a time. But finally, he did what all great leaders do, which is to accept what cannot be changed. That great leader walked on the street below her with the knowledge that, though his people were following his orders, some of them were probably very close by watching him. Bantu probably had a look of partially hidden disgust on his face as he walked. The look on his face would likely cause others on the walkside of the street to move out of his way. Onya laughed to herself as she sprang across another open space between rooftops.

Onya, along with the other Blossoms, was padding along the top of Alexandria softly. It was her elevated position that allowed her to see the man through a third-floor window. He was crouched behind an overturned desk. Onya stopped at the edge of the roof she was about to leap off. She held up a hand signaling for her sisters to halt. Her hand tapped the com-gem on her collar. It flared to life as she put her right foot on the raised ledge. She leaned forward resting her right forearm on her raised knee for support.

"This is Onoto for the Commander-General." Onya spoke as she watched what was transpiring in that third-floor room. She continued to watch while she waited for a response. She knew the Commander would not answer her until he was in a relatively secure area. He was probably, even as she watched the room, stepping into an alley.

"Go ahead Captain-Commander." The deep tenor of her Commander hummed through her com-gem.

The pitch of Onya's voice drifted lower as she fell into the familiar motions of reconnaissance. Her eyes narrowed in response to what she was seeing.

"Sir, I believe I have a situation."

†

Hiding behind an overturned desk, in a dust covered room, which must have once been the office for the now vacant warehouse, Alec sa' Salassian wondered to himself. *It wasn't supposed to end this way*, he thought. But then he was sure very few people saw their lives end in the way they had planned. In his mind Alec could hear his mother's voice. It was still thick with the sounds of what she called the old country as she pounded dough, rolling it out, into long thin strands for making *possma*. She would be saying to him how one always reaped what one sowed. Olive-skinned, with the ever-present white apron, – she had been right about quite a lot of things as mothers often were, even when sons rarely listened. It seemed she would be right about this as well. But still, he thought, it wasn't supposed to end this way.

Alec ran his hand over the mustache, followed by the beard, which framed his slim olive face in ink-black hair. This was bloody deep stable muck. He didn't think he was going to get out of it this time.

Admittedly, he had done some vicious things in his life. Only hours ago he had been a rising young general in a large criminal enterprise. He had killed as well as given orders to kill. Both of these items would be on his record, if there were in fact some nebulous being keeping track of things, somewhere in the heavens. He had stolen, designed schemes for skimming, and had even been involved in kidnapping. He had always been able to ease his mind by telling himself he had never hurt anyone who did not know the rules of the game or deserve what was happening to them. He had never taken from someone who could be considered an innocent, hard working, citizen. Well, at least, he believed, not directly.

It was, in point of fact, the kidnapping part that had him huddled in the dust of an abandoned warehouse on Hawker Street. What a dismal place to die. Why could it not have been on say, the Glittering Way? That would have been a marvelous street to end things on. Alec looked around the room again, listening intently, but heard nothing of the pursuit he was expecting at any moment. In his mind he continued to go over what had gotten him here. Maybe, he wondered, this was what people had meant when they said your life flashed before your eyes.

As ruthless as he had ever been, Alec noted, it had been with those who understood the stakes as well as the consequences. It was why he was not surprised at what he was now facing. He knew the consequences of what he had done, knew them, down to the very syllable. But with all that he had done this had been more than he was willing to accept. His mother had always taught him that one was shaped by what one allowed as much as by what one did. But this he had not been able to allow.

Kidnapping a minor noble's child for ransom was an old, if reliable, racket presuming it was done right. Hurting the little girl you kidnapped was something else altogether. When Antione came into the room and told him to leave Alec had thought it strange. But Antione was the son of the Boss. So, he had done what he was told. But when Alec had heard the girl scream in terror something in him was wrenched free. Bursting into the room he had found Antione, on top of the girl, trying to restrain her while she screamed. Antione had lifted his right hand preparing to hit the girl. At that moment Alec felt as if the whole world had stopped moving. It was as if it was waiting for him to choose a path – to make a decision. It was almost like a dream. He had moved without having to think. A shocked Antione looked up at him as Alec wrestled him to the floor. And just like that, in the heat of the moment, Alec broke his neck. He had killed before but never the son of a Boss. Then the world that had seemed to stop rushed forward again. It did not just resume spinning normally but seemed to move faster than he could keep up with as if it were making up for the lost time.

Running with the girl in tow they had been just minutes ahead of the pursuit Alec had known would come. Out of the alehouse the Organization used to disguise its unsavory dealings he, carrying the girl in his arms, had fled. A harried, desperate, chase had carried them to the warehouse. Crouching there, out of breath, he felt like life had caught up with him.

A little hand on his cheek, rubbing his beard, which was shaved into a thin line along his jaw, filling out at his chin into a point, pulled him from his thoughts.

She spoke in that way of very young children who could not quite fully form their words, "Chu ave air on da face." She wrinkled her small nose as her little fingers played with Alec's beard. Big brown eyes looked into his, "Tank you, my was scared." The little voice had a pure quality. It was like clear honey.

She huddled there in his lap. Dirt tracks made of dried tears covered her lightly freckled cheeks. It amazed him that this child could give him that tiny smile after what she had been through. Alec found his resolve, in that moment, as he looked into those big brown eyes. That distant feeling, hovering at the edge of his thoughts, came to him again indicating that everything had changed. He was on a road that was foreign to him, but he was on it nevertheless. Everything had changed. What a difference a few hours could make.

Alec heard himself say, "Do not be afraid little one." There was a smile to accompany the words. "I will make sure that you get home safely." A brief hug accompanied that sentiment. He hoped his voice was as soothing as he had tried to make it. He would make sure she got out of this even if he did not. He just didn't know how.

The door to the dusty office was lying discarded in the corner. His pursuers had only to walk into the room once they caught up to him. Alec heard their footsteps echoing up the distant staircase. They walked, almost casually, into the room. Their boots made a scuffing sound on the wooden floor that creaked under their weight as they walked across loose floorboards. He could tell, by the sound, that they were fanning out to completely block the open doorway. Alec thought he could make out eight distinct footsteps. They would be well-armed and highly motivated. He recognized the voice that carried to him over the desk he had hidden behind as belonging to Pezzu. Pezzu was Antione's younger brother.

"Alec." The voice was callous but with the feigned conversational tone the Organization used to reassure people even though they intended to kill them. "Alec, Alec. You have led us on an amusing chase, no? But now my friend, it is done. Due to your years of service to my father, I will make you a preposition, yes?"

Alec shook his head, *its proposition you idiot*, he thought. But he didn't say anything. Over the desk he could hear Pezzu, most likely, pacing by the sound of the floorboards. Pezzu stalked slowly, back and forth, some ten feet from the overturned desk. Alec knew he was trying to remain calm. The way his footsteps seemed to attack the floorboards told Alec he was on the verge of letting his rage loose. This was nothing new to Alec. He knew the moves. Pezzu would try to make him feel like there was a chance for making a deal if he cooperated. It was a lie but that was the move.

The room was spacious. It was almost thirty feet in each direction. Pezzu was still pacing. Alec heard what had to be Pezzu kicking one of the old chairs that was among the broken furniture littering the room. He continued talking when Alec did not respond.

"If you will hand over the girl, Alec, you will only be disciplined. You will not die or lose your position among us, eh? We both know that he was a fool. He got what he deserved." Pezzu paused a brief moment as if waiting for Alec to join the conversation. When Alec did not respond he went on. "Alec. I must have the girl. She is worth a great deal of money, yes? And losing that could not be so easily forgiven. What do you say old friend?" Pezzu's voice ended high.

Someone sneezed from the dust they were all disturbing with their movement. Alec waited a moment before projecting his voice over the desk toward where Pezzu should have been standing.

Alec tried to keep his voice level. "We both know that your father cannot – will not – let the death of his son go whether Antione was a fool or not. He would lose face. And, in his mind, it would make him look weak. So, why don't we cut through the act we normally put on for targets and admit that you are here to kill me."

There, he had said it. They were going to kill him. If he died here today, it would not be as a fool, or a target, begging for his life from those who were going to take it no matter what he said. There was no dignity in that. Alec heard Pezzu take a step toward the desk.

"Alec. I must. Have. The girl! Release her to me or I will come and take her." Pezzu's voice had a ring of finality to it. Knowing Pezzu as he did Alec could picture him with his teeth clenched. The Organization had a special way of using that small tool. With practice you could make a man shiver with just a smile. With a smile you could make him fear you more than the Betrayer. But Pezzu had always been too overly dramatic to pull it off.

Alec heard the unmistakable sound of crossbow bolts being locked into place. He looked around desperately for a way out as if he had not already looked a hundred times. It was with the same result as before. There was no way out. He cursed to himself. By the Good and the Ancient! His eyes fell on the windows opposite the door on the back wall again. They had been a consideration when he had first entered the room, breathing heavily, as he scanned it hurriedly. Out of them, however, was a sheer drop of three stories to the ground below. There was not so much as an exterior ledge to jump from or to use for climbing to the roof above. If he jumped the girl would either be hurt or killed along with him and that was considering the glass did not cut them to pieces. But the risk might be better than what she faced in the hands of the Organization.

Looking down at the girl he spoke to her so that only she could hear. "When I say run I want you to run through the door as fast as you can. Don't look back. Find someone on the street and tell them who you are. Do you understand?" With her big brown eyes wide open she nodded her head yes. It was his only option. He could make room for her to get to the door. He might even be able to give her enough time to get to the street. He would die in the doing of it but she would have a chance to get away. A chance was all his life would buy her. He hoped it would be enough. Alec took a deep breath. Calling back to Pezzu as he loosened his hold on the girl Alec smiled with exuberance at her. There was something freeing about finally choosing a path. Her tiny arms wrapped around his neck as she nestled her face in his chest one last time.

There was a hint of laughter to Alec's voice. "Pezzu, it seems you leave me with no choice. I won't give the girl to you. You have to come and take her. But I think … yes, I think I must also deny you that pleasure, eh!"

Alec rose coiling his legs to spring at the men between the girl and the doorway. He would only have seconds before crossbow bolts began flying his way. That was when he saw a man step into the room behind Pezzu and his men. It stopped Alec dead keeping him from throwing himself forward just long enough for the stranger to speak.

A rich tenor filled the emptiness of the room.

"Today is not the day for the child to die. Release her to me." A sense of authority resonated in the man's words. Alec almost began walking toward him in response to it but caught himself. The man stood very still. There was no fidgeting or nervous energy about the way he filled the doorway. Alec could feel his readiness beneath that still exterior. It took only seconds for Alec to remember where he had seen a stance like that before. The Master that had instructed him in the sword had stood like that. *Danger*, it said. *Be wary of me.*

Alec had not risen in the Organization without becoming a very good judge of people. This man was not to be trifled with unless you thought it unavoidable. But Alec would have needed an exceptional reason. The stranger spoke as if there was no question as to whether his command would be followed. It was not arrogance that sent a chill up Alec's spine. It was certainty. The man radiated it. *Now how does one learn to do that?*

Alec had learned, at some point, how to give off an air of belligerence. He could do deadly intent. He could even do that, don't mess with me, thing. But how, he wondered, does a man give off the sense that reality would bend itself to his will? Learning how to do that was added to his mental list of things to do. *If, that is, he managed to survive.*

Pezzu turned quickly to face the stranger as Alec's mind raced from notion to notion. Pezzu's face turned up in a snarl aimed at the stranger standing just inside the doorway. Some of his men trained their crossbows on him. The stranger just stood there. Standing still, relaxed, with a hint of a smile at Pezzu's expression, the man gave an almost imperceptible shake of his head. It was as if the expression Pezzu had meant to frighten him was somehow amusing him. Pezzu spoke with his snarl migrating from his face to his voice.

"Stranger, you would do well to go on your way, yes? This is not your business. You would be in over your head even if it were. Just move on! I won't say it again." Pezzu stroked the hilt of his sword as punctuation to his words.

Everyone waited. The men with Pezzu looked from him to the stranger. Some of them took Alec in with their sweeping gaze. The stranger slowly, deliberately, reached down to where his sword hung at his hip. He grasped the scabbard just below the circular handguard. With his thumb he pushed up on the round handguard so that he loosened his sword in its scabbard with a faint click. Because the room was so quiet the sound seemed amplified. A small smile crossed the stranger's face. Some of the men looked nervously toward Pezzu for a signal. Alec thought the stranger must be insane. But he gave him points for style. The man had the henchmen thinking he was almost as much a threat to them as they were to him. Alec smiled to himself. That was either courage or foolishness. Sometimes the two were hard to tell apart. The tall, brown-skinned man, his hand resting lightly on his scabbard, spoke again. Alec noted the man's voice was not just playing at calm. It was calm. How did he do it? Maybe he was crazy to be that calm in a situation like this.

"I am Ossassande Bantu A' Omorede. Commander-General of the Peoples Company."

Alec laughed. He laughed loud. He laughed very loud.

Some of Pezzu's men jumped at the sound. Everyone looked at Alec as he took a moment to gather himself. He was sure the laughter had almost brought him a crossbow bolt in the chest, but as he continued laughing, he realized, he did not care. The laughter rang in his voice as he spoke. "Pezzu, when you step in it, you don't just step in dog leavings, you fall into the bloody pile left from the stables being mucked out."

It was clear now. The man wasn't crazy. He was – well, he was who he was. The Commander-General was the number one *don't-mess-with* on every list in Alexandria. Everyone in the Organization steered clear of the People as they called themselves. It was one of the first things you were taught when you joined. The Company was the kind of trouble that superseded even the Empire. From time to time one found a singular odd member of the Imperial Guard who might be bribed but the People would truss you up like cattle before delivering you to the front doorstep of the Magistrate with a note pinned to your jacket. This was divine intervention. Not only was Pezzu confronted with one of the People. It was the Wolf himself. Why they called him the Wolf Alec had never learned. Maybe if he ever ran into a wolf, that was the pack leader, he would understand the analogy. Whatever he was called Alec loved him at that moment more than all the gold in the world. Now how could he turn it to an advantage?

As Alec's mind raced Pezzu looked at him through narrowed eyes. He was clearly not amused by the identity of the man in the doorway. He turned back to the Wolf. His men were shifting nervously on their feet. Some were wiping sweat from their hands onto their shirts or breeches before returning those hands to crossbow stocks or swordhilts. They knew who he was. Pezzu recovered quickly.

"Well, Commander-General. Your reputation precedes you. We are honored that you wish to assist us in this delicate situation, but this is, after all, an internal matter. I am sure you understand about internal matters, eh? We would appreciate your moving on, yes?" Pezzu's face was blank. His voice was low. His hands were spread wide with the palms turned upward.

The Wolf tilted his head slightly to one side as he answered Pezzu.

"As I said, internal matters or not, I will not allow you to hurt the child. Release her to me, now, and I will leave you to your internal matters."

Pezzu nodded his head.

"I see your point Commander. However, we are eight, and you are one, no?" His voice became cold like steel. "And now I suggest that you move on!" The threat in his voice was clear.

The Wolf stepped further into the room. Three of Pezzu's men took an unconscious step back. The Commander kept his right hand resting on his scabbard while his left hand hung at waist level with his thumb hitched behind his swordbelt.

With a well turned, nasty, half smile, the timing of which Alec admired, the Wolf said, "Moments ago you mentioned that my reputation preceded me as if you knew me. You have, I am guessing, taken the child from her home. You have threatened the man who protects her while suggesting that I walk away." Then his voice took on an even colder edge than Pezzu had managed. With eloquent precision, the timing of which Alec could have whistled at in appreciation, the nasty half smile disappeared. With chilling alacrity, the Wolf continued, "You do not. Know me." He paused for a heartbeat before continuing, "You have to the count of three. Disarm yourselves and leave. If you don't I will do it for you."

His clean-shaven head glinted in the fading sunlight flooding into the room from the windows behind Alec. The eyes of the Wolf took in the entire room. Alec watched events unfold while his mind raced – he would have to leave the girl behind the desk and take out the man to his immediate right. Next, without so much as a breath, he would have to get to the next man before he could fire his crossbow. The Commander-General would have to be better than good if they were going to have the slightest hope of surviving. Two against eight were miserable odds no matter who the two were. Alec knew his own skill. He was better than most. But this would not be a one on one fight. Pezzu spat on the floor as he pointed his finger at the towering man. His arm was trembling with anger.

"Listen to me, dark man." he shouted. "I will have the child, I will have Alec's life, and because you stick your nose where it should not be, I will have you gutted and nailed to the door of your precious Sanctuary!"

A lovely female voice floated over Alec's shoulder into the wake of Pezzu's shouting.

"I am Onya Onoto of the Peoples Company. Neither I, nor my companions, would allow that even if it were possible."

Alec jerked around to find seven women, *Seven*, his mind shouted, sitting in the windows, which had been opened without his noticing. A few of the women had one foot on the windowsill with the other on the floor, while others had a leg dangling out a window with their backs leaning against the window frame. They looked as if they were lounging in private quarters. The beautiful eyes, of the woman who had spoken, gazed out over a black face-wrap. The other six women looked on almost casually. The only thing that gave them a threatening air were the strange looking crossbows in their hands. The sunlight, flooding in behind them, seemed to curve around their black garments. It made for an impressive sight. The woman's voice was soft. Her eyes were hard but beautiful. There was something else there as they exchanged looks but then it was gone.

Pezzu, duplicating the response Alec had, jerked around to see the women sitting in the open windows. He seemed to notice what the sunlight did or maybe it would be better to say what it did not do. His mouth fell open. He shut it quickly but opened it again to speak. Before he could say whatever was on the tip of his tongue two of the women in the window opposite the woman who had named herself Onya Onoto chimed in. One of them turned to face the other.

"Erra, I don't understand why people think they have to make such horrendous threats? I mean really - cut open guts? And would it really hurt for him to call the Commander by his name or rank?" The slightly taller woman, who must have been Erra, was already nodding her head before the shorter woman finished speaking. Her voice was pitched like a teacher giving an important lesson to a beloved pupil.

"Yes, yes, Saffra. You are quite correct. The little man's intention is to frighten the Commander into withdrawing from the confrontation." The one lecturing stepped out of the windowsill into the room. "He does not know the Commander very well or else he would know this particular ploy will not work. You see, in order to assert himself, as he attempts to regain control of a situation that is now spiraling completely out of control, he inflates his ability. Then he threatens the Commander's well-being in order to bolster both his own confidence, and the confidence of his men." The woman could talk.

She turned her attention back to the rest of the room, which was not as empty as it had been when Alec had first entered. "Gentlemen, I shall repeat the Commander's instructions once more since we interrupted his count. It will be the last time you will hear them. Place your weapons on the floor at your feet and then exit the building."

As if to add emphasis to what she was saying the other women raised their crossbows to target Pezzu's men. Alec knew he was in love. He could not see her face, but he was in love. She was tall, forceful, and obviously intelligent. She had to be beautiful under that head wrap. If she were not he would have to reconsider his notion of beautiful.

The woman who had called herself Onya had come within two steps of Alec as Erra completed her instructions. Saffra, along with one of the other, as yet unnamed, women flanked her. Alec looked at Pezzu. The man was clearly wondering how this had become so complicated. Alec spoke to him.

"Pezzu, the odds are now better than even in our favor. But if I know you, as I think I do, you will still attempt to fight while you hope for the best." Alec was saying this as much to Pezzu as to these new allies. "I think today is a day for retreat, eh? You do not have to die here. Leave and live to fight another day."

Pezzu looked from Alec to Bantu. His voice was agitated.

"How do I know that I will be allowed to leave if I lay down my weapons? Maybe you will kill me then, eh? Maybe you will kill my men? Maybe you will kill us all where we stand, or shoot us in the back?" He looked at Alec. Alec shrugged as he responded to Pezzu.

"I think the Commander will agree to let you go for the child's sake and because he has given you the option to leave. My understanding of his reputation is that he is a man of his word, yes?" Alec said this looking over at Bantu as he raised an eyebrow.

Bantu nodded once. The woman, who had given her name as Onya, spoke next.

"You may leave. Lay down your arms and exit slowly. Keep your hands where we can see them." While she was speaking Bantu moved away from the doorway making room for them to exit. Slowly Pezzu's men complied. One by one they dropped their weapons before filing out past the Wolf. Pezzu did the same. As he came to the doorway he turned to the Wolf.

"You have interfered with the Atazzi today, dark man. We will not soon forget this." Turning to Alec he said, "You keep looking over your shoulder Alec sa' Salassian. One day I will be there. Mine will be the last face you see, yes?" And with that he was gone.

Alec released a breath he had not known he was holding. He just stood for a moment trying to let it all sink in. The girl immediately wrapped an arm tightly around his leg as she looked at the new strangers. The two Alec now knew to be Erra and Saffra, along with the women he did not know, had begun collecting the weapons now scattered on the floor. The Wolf, with the woman called Onya a step behind him, was walking over to Alec. So, this was the illustrious Commander-General of the Peoples Company. The man was impressive. Alec was tall in his own right, but he had to look up to the man. The color of his clothing was simple, but the cut and materials were both exquisite. Alec knew a little about clothing. In fact, he spent as much time at his tailors as he did anywhere else. Though no orders had been given the room was quickly secured.

Alec wanted to ask the women how they had gotten into those windows without so much as the sound of a boot scuffing against the sheer brick wall. But that would have to wait. Bantu looked down at the girl with a genuine smile. Alec felt her grip loosen on his leg. She darted across the space between Alec and the Wolf. When she reached him she leaped into his waiting arms. He stood there holding her gently. She smiled at the large man before quickly pointing at Alec.

"He help me." After those words she promptly stuck her thumb in her mouth as she looked around the room like she was looking for a toy she might have lain somewhere.

The Wolf spoke to the child in soothing tones. "Yes, little one. I know he helped you. We are very happy that he did. And now we are all going to take you home." He looked up from the child who was still preoccupied with the taste of her thumb. Dirty, as it was, it could not have tasted very good. But that did not seem to matter to her. Looking at Alec, the Commander-General continued. "I take it you know where she lives." Again, it was not a question but a statement of fact.

Alec responded formally. He put his feet together, standing straight, as he assumed soldiers did.

"Alec sa' Salassian, at your service Commander-General. And yes, I know where the girl lives. Though I am not proud of having that knowledge given what it means." The last he spoke as much to himself as anyone else. It was an interesting realization to say the least. Bantu half smiled at him. Alec thought it must have been his attempt at military formality that the man found humorous.

Straightening the green vest, made of fine wool, which he was wearing over a slim-fitted, white, silk shirt - though not quite pressed or completely white anymore - Alec pulled a long, slim, metal container from one of the inner pockets. He retrieved a cigar that was almost twice the length of his smallest finger but as thick as his thumb. Replacing the cigar container in his pocket he removed a tiny metal box from one of the exterior pockets of the vest. It was a silver firebox. Alec opened it. He took the small metal pick from the slot that held it in place. He struck its end across the ribbed surface of the box's lid. This caused sparks to shoot over into the pan of the box containing a clear gel. The gel caught fire. As it burned slowly Alec lowered the end of the cigar into the flame while puffing at the other end. When the cigar was well lit he replaced the metal pick before snapping the lid shut, which snuffed out the lazy flame. He returned the small firebox to his vest pocket. It was a practiced maneuver, so it only took a few seconds to have a lit cigar in the corner of his mouth. Puffing on it several times to assure himself that there was a good burn Alec returned his full attention to the Commander-General. He was thinking of a smooth, yet strong, drink that would accent the taste of his cigar as the smoke began to relax him. He spoke congenially.

"May I ask what exactly brought you to my aid sir?" Alec examined the burning end of the cigar as he blew out a puff of smoke.

The Commander-General looked at him for a moment. His words came in a rhythm like the sound of someone quoting an old saying or the lines of a poem.

"A duty is mine, a road to tread, the Dawn to call, the darkness to shed." He finished with the hint of a smile again.

Turning from Alec he put the girl on her feet. He ruffled her hair playfully with his hand as she stood next to him. With a final smile for her he headed for the doorway. Half of the women went out in front of him while the other half flowed out behind. The only one remaining was the woman who had spoken first. The woman with the beautiful eyes watched the others go. Standing there as she was she appeared to be an apparition. She seemed unreal with the sunlight curving around the black cloth she wore. Alec found his voice as he tried to puzzle out what Bantu had meant.

"Excuse me. Onya Onoto, is it? What, may I ask, did the Wolf mean by that?" Still half-staring out the doorway Alec placed the cigar to his lips again. Thick smoke slowly swirled upward toward the ceiling. He thought he could almost make out a smile beneath the cloth covering her face. That light lovely voice with an odd accent answered him.

"Some people are motivated by gold, others by notoriety, or glory. Still others are motivated by some distorted notion of honor. And then there are the Bantu's of the world. They do what they believe is right. No, wait, let me be clear. They do what they believe will hold back the Darkness." She finished her thought looking at him with a hint of curiosity sparkling in her eyes as if they were the night sky with stars flashing brightly against their backdrop. Alec realized he was still not satisfied.

"And how did he accomplish that today?" His voice had lost some of its volume.

Onya tilted her head at an angle.

She said, "By being ready to give his life so an innocent child would not die. So that you, Alec sa' Salassian, might have a little more time to learn how to live. You have been given a precious thing."

Without thinking Alec responded. "And what might that be?"

"Why, time, Alec sa' Salassian. The most precious thing in the world."

"And why would he do this for me?" Alec stuck the cigar in the corner of his mouth before crossing his arms.

"You ought to ask a better question than why." She stood there, expectantly, with her hip stuck out as she slung her crossbow, an odd-looking crossbow, over her shoulder.

Alec looked at the small woman wrapped in black. Speaking around the cigar in his mouth he decided to take the bait.

"Alright, I'll bite. What question should I ask?"

She turned at his question. As she walked toward the doorway her voice drifted over her shoulder to him. "Ask yourself, what will I do with the opportunity I have been given?" Turning into the hallway she looked back one last time. Her voice had the sound of laughter with a hint of warning in it. "Oh, and Alec sa' Salassian? Never. And I mean ever. Call the Commander-General, Wolf. At least not where he can hear you."

Alec was left standing in the room alone as her laughter faded away. He saw it then, as he stood there alone, with only drifting smoke as his companion. He had heard others talk about it. Most had recalled that it had been during a battle or a fight of some kind. It was a moment not made for the kind of minor decisions you had to make everyday. It was a moment where circumstances conspired to make one of those decisions, just one of them, carry sufficient weight that it would drastically alter the way the rest of your life would turn out. It was as if two great roads stretched out before him in that moment. Alec could almost feel the weight of it as he stood there. He knew he had to choose. What would it be? He puffed on the cigar.

He had missed the small hand tugging at his pants while he was lost in thought. He looked down to see the girl following Onya out of the room. She paused in the doorway.

"You come. You come take me home?" She laughed as she said it. All the fear that had engulfed her was nowhere to be seen. Alec thought it must be at the thought of going home but he wasn't sure.

She trotted out of the room after the others. Alec realized he was smiling in response to the girl's laughter. Blowing smoke, in a wispy trail behind him, he followed after the rest of them. He hitched at his swordbelt as he went. This room would be etched in his memory. Alec knew the little girl would forget it almost immediately. Even the members of the Peoples Company who had come to his aide would only mark it in a minor way in their minds. But Alec would remember this place. In a way he had died here. He actually felt more alive than he had in a very long time. He could not quite put his finger on the why of it. *Maybe*, he thought to himself, *just maybe*. But he didn't let himself finish the thought. It was a dangerous thing to believe. He knew that all too well. He had never been a believer. Letting the thoughts slip to the back of his mind Alec jogged down the hallway to catch up to his rescuers.

†

Pain greeted him as a rough jerking woke him. Looking around he tried to pierce the darkness. It was pitch black. There was a pounding somewhere. It only took a moment for him to realize that it was his head that was pounding. Wooden planks rubbed against his skin as he was tossed about. It dawned on him that he had only his smallclothes on. He tried to move only to discover that he was trussed up like a slain deer after the hunt.

While trying to sit up several things became clear. He was in the back of an enclosed wagon on a road that was in terrible disrepair. He was someone's prisoner. But, remarkably, he was not frightened. In fact, he felt very calm. As the wagon rocked, his mind was busy piecing together, in a calculating way, the nature of his predicament. Without conscious thought he was already working at his bonds with a deep sense of certitude that he would be free of his restraints momentarily. He knew he was a prisoner, in the back of a wagon, in only his smallclothes, and what should be done about it. What he did not know was his name.

*an unfound place
by a stream or ford
where it appears
your steps are the first
a tree, a city street
a village festival
where children laugh
not cry*

*we pass over walking ways
sites where
life is fully in bloom
and if we do not stop
to join in
who can we blame?*

*like bare toes
in summer water
have we mingled with
what lives on all
around us
with what makes having been here worthwhile*

*lived, have we
lived
despite the symphony at play
have we
and in our living
have we
prepared ourselves to die?*

.

*~a poem found in the rubble of the
burned village at Damasc*

Do not cry for those who are gone, but for we who must carry on.

~*A Vicar saying*

Chapter six

And those who carry on

Maria, it turned out, was the little girl's name. They returned her, without further incident, to her parents. Upon exiting the abandoned warehouse Alec had found a hired coach waiting. Erra had flagged it down. She had brought the irritated driver through the winding alleys of the warehouse district to pick them up. The driver droned on about the fact that he was only doing this for The Lord Commander. He claimed they were completely off his normal route, but he was willing to take them where they needed to go as a service to the Peoples Company. He made it a point to declare that he would have told anyone else that they could have gone to the Dark One's Pit for all he cared. His horses were, after all, high strung. They did not appreciate the cramped space of the alleyways they had to trot through. Saffra had given the middle-aged man, with the whining voice, a gold Imperial Mark. While he salivated over it she told him pointedly, but very politely, to shut up. The heavy coin, nearly the size of his palm, was sufficient to hire his coach for an entire week. He had not even creaked in his seat for the rest of the ride.

After extricating himself, along with the women he called the Quiet Blossoms, from the embrace of the overwhelmed, weeping, nobles, the Commander-General Ossassande Bantu A' Omorede kissed the little girl on the cheek before heading for the waiting coach. As he walked toward the coach Maria's father had walked beside him. It turned out that he was the Fifth Earl of Westminister, which made him a member of the Peerage. Alec had watched the Commander-General repeatedly refuse the gold the man wanted to give him. As he stepped up into the coach he told Vester Morganstaff that having the Fifth Earl of Westminister owe him a favor would suffice. Morganstaff had told the Commander-General that whenever he needed him all he had to do was send word. He was adamant that whatever, or whenever, it was he stood ready to honor his debt to the Commander-General. Alec had laughed to himself. He would have rather paid the Commander had it been his daughter. Owing the Commander a favor could end up costing the man much more.

Little Maria waved to Alec from the arms of her mother. Alec returned her wave, with a smile, as the coach pulled away from the immense townhouse. The coach rolled through the front gate. It rolled off the uneven cobblestones of the manor's small courtyard onto the smoother stones of the main thoroughfare called Gatten Pass. Bantu had instructed the driver to take them to Sanctuary. Given where they were Alec knew the ride would take them nearly an hour. Alexandria was not a small city.

Alec rode in silence taking the opportunity to contemplate what he was going to do next. The ride was uneventful. They were rolled to a stop in front of the entrance to the home of the Peoples Company known as *Sanctuary*.

The coach rocked as it emptied. Erra was telling Saffra a variant of a joke concerning a fisherman, a farmer, and a palace guard. Alec had not heard the joke told in that way before, but it was still funny. Two other women were discussing the current theatre troop performing in Troubadour Square in the Old City. Women always seemed to have something to talk about. His father had told him to learn how, at the very least, to look like you were paying attention to them even if you were thinking about sharpening your sword. Alec remembered his mother overhearing one of their conversations. He smiled thinking about the look of his towering father sleeping on a couch on the first floor of their house. It was at least a week before his father had been allowed back into his own bed.

Alec saw the Commander at the head of the group as he moved toward the front gate. One of the women, whom Alec had not yet put a name to, was walking a step behind him. She was speaking to him as they walked. The Commander was nodding his head as he listened. To Alec's surprise an entire host of people in those black bodysuits materialized out of nowhere. They came around the coach from both sides streaming into Sanctuary behind the Commander. The women acted as though they had been there the entire time. The more Alec thought about it the more he thought they may very well have been.

Alec sat in the coach in silence. Somewhere on the way from Maria's house his cigar had burned down to its end. As he sat in the coach watching the People trail into their home he lit another cigar. Only after blowing a few puffs of smoke into the air did he realize that he was not alone. The small woman, with beautiful eyes, was still sitting across from him. She had removed the black facewrap revealing an attractive woman who must have been of Yen-le descent. The door of the coach was still hanging open.

Alec knew if it had not been for that large, gold Imperial Mark the driver would have been haranguing them to get out so he could be on his way. As it was Alec could only hear the driver mumbling something as he sat up front on his high perch. Alec puffed on his newly lit cigar letting the light, nutty flavor of the smoke roll across his tongue. He looked over at Onya. His eyebrows rose expectantly while he waited to see why she had stayed behind. She gazed out the window of the carriage toward the gate to Sanctuary, watching the others walk through its gate, before she spoke.

"I'm Onya Onoto, a Captain-Commander in the Peoples Company." Alec nodded as if he knew what that meant. She turned from watching her companions in order to look at him. "This coach will take you anywhere in the city you wish to go. But if, in our brief time together, you have glimpsed a form of life that intrigues you, you may knock on that door." She pointed to a small wooden door to the left of the much larger gate through which the others had entered Sanctuary. She continued, "If you knock there you will be able to begin your life again. You are welcome here. More welcome than anywhere else save, possibly, in the presence of the Ancient of Days." Her smile was a winning one. It did not stop at her lips, but ran over her entire slim, slightly-rounded face. Strands of long, straight, black hair hung over her eyes. In what seemed a habitual gesture she brushed them back with one hand. Vaulting from the coach to the ground below she turned back to look at Alec.

"You may choose to move on, Alec sa' Salassian, but if you do I would suggest you leave Alexandria. Your former colleagues seemed very serious about concluding their business with you. I think he used words like, impale, and gut? Whatever you do I wish you well. May you outwalk the Shadows and watch for the Dawn."

With that invocation she turned and entered Sanctuary. The enormous gate, followed by the massive metal doors it protected, closed, one after the other, with finality. And then he was alone. Alec sat for a moment more before yelling to the driver to head for Stables Way. He had to leave Alexandria in a hurry.

Anyone standing on the street in front of Sanctuary would have witnessed the coach roll for ten feet before stopping. The door popped open. Alec sa' Salassian, former criminal and all-around rogue, exited the coach trailing cigar smoke. He motioned to the driver to move on. Murmuring about the smell of cigar smoke in the cabin of his coach, the driver snapped the reigns causing the coach to lurch forward. Alec thought to himself, as he watched the coach roll out of sight down the busy street, that he had to know. *It was dangerous to believe.* Those words crossed his mind for the second time today, but he had to know. Alec continued to watch the coach roll away. It was probably heading toward the far side of Alexandria in order to find fares at the docks. There was usually someone getting off a ship who needed a ride somewhere.

Alec watched the street where the coach had rolled away as if it had been carrying the last vestiges of his old life. He puffed smoke. The tip of his cigar flared red as the sun began to dip beneath the horizon in the western sky. He stood very still, the cigar in the corner of his mouth, his thumbs tucked behind his sword belt, while his fingers grasped the belt's bottom edge on either side of his silver buckle. He did not really take notice of anything in particular as he stared down the length of the street. The walls of Sanctuary rose high beside him. Standing as close as he was Alec could not see over the wall. There was foot traffic on the walkside of the street where he stood. People continued to pass him. They stepped around him while he just stood there quietly.

Alec could tell shopkeepers from wives on errands. There were various groups of young people on their way to some merriment. Couples walked arm in arm, likely, on their way to the theatre or the concert hall. With all of the day's excitement Alec had nearly forgotten that Jamila Ayo was performing tonight. Her voice could bring tears to your eyes if you were not carefully on guard against such things. An embarrassing memory of an Ayo performance surfaced in his thoughts. He grinned at himself as he pushed the thought away. The young woman he had been with thought it was quite endearing, but Alec had only hoped none of the men present had taken notice.

Coaches, carrying people, rolled from one end of the street to the other while tarp-covered carts, loaded with various items, did the same. Shop windows brightened with oil lamps or glass covered candles. The evening was upon them. In the distance, at the top of Rulers Hill, in the Old City quarter, the Torch of Alexander roared to life against the darkening sky. Alexander was the man who had first strung the Empire together, like so many pearls on a string, half a century ago. It was said that he had not only been a great general but a great man. Alec had been named after the greatest man in Alexandrian history. He went by Alec because Alexander had become a common name among mothers who dreamed of greatness for their sons. While shaking his head he laughed a little as he watched the Great Flame flare up. He thought about the irony of a criminal being named after a legend.

The Great Flame was lit every evening. It burned on the roof of the Imperial Palace, which was the highest point in Alexandria. It was high enough so that a ship at sea, far out on the Macca Deep, could see it from leagues away. It could also be seen far out into the countryside. The roaring flames represented the light of freedom. It was the symbol of the primacy of Alexandria. The people of the Empire went to sleep each night with the assurance of the flame as comfort. All is well, its light claimed. All is well. Alec left the notions of the flame to the more imperial minded.

The Great Flame, competing with the last moments of the day's sunlight, brought Alec out of his reverie. Taking a deep breath, he dropped his cigar to the ground, stepped on it to put it out, and walked back down the street to the wooden door immediately to the left of the gate to Sanctuary. The gateway was wide enough for two-way traffic, even if there were large supply wagons going both ways, while still managing to have room for foot traffic. In Alec's mind it made sense to have a second, normal sized, entrance for times when the gate did not need to be open.

Alec hitched at his swordbelt as he examined the smaller door. It was plain but well-crafted. It had been made from a single piece of wood, which would mean a stronger door overall. The door was flush to the doorframe. The hinges must have been on the inside. The Commander-General, it seemed, understood quality. Alec was really beginning to like the man. In the center of the door was a carving. A large oval plaque, which took up most of the door face, hung at chest level. Carved into the wooden plaque were three evenly spaced, overlapping circles large enough for him to place his hand inside. To create the symbol, one would likely begin by drawing a triangle. You would draw a circle around each triangle's tip so that they were equal in size while laying over each other. When the triangle was removed all that would remain would be the identical overlapping circles. Though they overlapped one could still see each complete circle.

The plaque was stained dark-brown. The circles were a burnt gold making them seem to glow in the fading light. He ran his hand over the deeply carved lines of the symbol. It was smooth to the touch. The work was that of a master craftsman. As he looked closely he could see that the symbol was beginning to wear in places. He ran his hand over the overlapping circles. When he did it became apparent that the wear must have been the result of hundreds, maybe thousands, of people who had done what he was doing. The wear in the wood reflected the number of people who had stood right where Alec was standing rubbing their hand across the symbol of the Peoples Company. Those three circles had become well known across the empire and beyond. Below the symbol there were, golden stained, words carved into the wood that Alec read slowly:

From what has been

From what is now

From what will be

There is Sanctuary

Knock

Alec ran his hands over the deeply carved words with appreciation. The work was masterful. The wording was simple but in an elegant script. As his fingers brushed the wood he felt as if he could feel all the hands that, caressing the wood, had caused some of the wear on the door. Before he realized what he was doing, he had knocked. His heart began to beat a little faster.

A voice came from the other side. Alec could tell it was a young man. The words came to him in that singsong rhythm of a voice speaking a familiar refrain.

"Have you read the call?" The question came through the door perfunctorily.

"Yes, I have." Alec kept his voice steady.

"Is there trouble on your trail?" Again, the young man's voice sounded as if he already knew the answer.

"Yes, there is." Alec was glad the trouble was not directly behind him or he might be dead by the time the fellow finished with his questions.

The young man said, "Are you willing?"

Alec turned a corner of his mouth up. What kind of a question was that? But he said, "Yes, I am willing."

"Say your name for Sanctuary to hear." The voice lost some of its hard edge. But there was a stillness that filled the place where the young man's voice had been. It was a stillness that was waiting to be spoken into. Alec could feel it.

"Salassian. The name is Alexander sa' Salassian. You may call me Alec." As Alec spoke he thought he heard a distant echo of his words.

A female voice spoke from somewhere that Alec could not pinpoint. It sounded as if there was a chorus of voices speaking along with it. *"Alexander sa' Salassian, enter and find sanctuary."*

The door, to Alec's surprise, did not swing open at all. It slid to the right recessing into the wall. A young man in a smart uniform, made up of a black coat, with matching breeches, made from fine wool, with polished, knee-high boots smiled at him. He waved Alec in. Stepping off the street Alec strolled into, what was ostensibly, a tunnel of stone running the length of the thickness of the wall surrounding Sanctuary. The wall was unimaginably thick. It was at least fifteen paces before he emerged back out into the waning sunlight inside the legendary compound known as Sanctuary. His breath caught momentarily in his throat. *Magnificent.* It was the only word he could call up. A veritable second city spread out before him. All around him buildings stretched into the sky. Redbrick, trimmed in white Sandstone, coupled with stained, cherry wood was everywhere. Clear glass windows, while a rarity elsewhere, were in abundance here. Oil lamps mounted atop tall, black, metal poles one of which was planted every ten paces on either side of a broad thoroughfare, made of large pieces of cut stone, lighted the way. The thoroughfare stretched forward from the gateway he had just entered to an incredibly high tower that rose farther into the sky than every other building Alec could see. It appeared, at a glance, to stand in the very center of Sanctuary. It dawned on him then that the building must be Bantu's Tower. That was what it was called by people in the city. The blue crystal spire sparkling in the last light of the sunset on the building's roof clenched it for him. Popular wisdom was that Bantu had built it just shy of the height of the Imperial Palace out of respect for the Empress, so that Alexander's Torch, the Great Flame of the empire, would remain the highest point in the capital city. Alec knew the Torch maintained that distinction by the merest of margins.

Across the stone thoroughfare, to his right, was what appeared to be a wooded area with cobbled walkways trailing off into the foliage. There were quite a few colorful flowers coupled with trimmed shrubs surrounding the trees. Alec thought it must be an arboretum as he continued walking deeper into the compound. To his immediate left was a barn-like building running down the line of the front wall he had just walked through. Horses were being led in through several large doorways. That, he knew, had to be the stable. Craning his neck back, at movement above his head, he saw enormous birds circling high above. Some spiraled down to pass the top of Bantu's Tower before angling off to land somewhere further inside Sanctuary behind the great tower. Alec had always thought them magnificent but had never seen them from even this relative closeness. He could just make out people in small wooden canopies nestled between the bird's shoulders. A few of them had larger windowed canopies further back between the massive wings. Was it a place for carrying some kind of cargo or were those people in the wooden containers? Alec shook his head in amazement. There seemed to be almost constant traffic everywhere he looked. He began to wonder how many people - that is *People* – were in the Company?

"It is a spectacular site, is it not?" The voice that was swiftly becoming familiar wrested him from his gawking. Color rushed to his face as he thought about the times he had seen some rustic bumpkin fresh from the countryside on the streets of Alexandria about to be run over as their heads swiveled around in awe at the wonders of the empire's capital city. He knew he looked like one of them.

Alec noticed for the first time that not more than ten feet away from him, each of the people – *People* - he thought, mentally correcting himself, who helped save him were waiting. It was Onya who had spoken. She stood to the left of the Commander-General facing Alec with a large smile on her face. In fact, they were all smiling; even the Commander's face was fixed with a small grin.

Onya moved closer to Alec so that no one else could hear. All around them people were turning from wherever they had been going to join the crowd that was gathering nearby. Almost all of them were smiling to one degree or another. Alec must have had a strange look on his face.

"I know all this must feel strange to you." Her voice was musical. The accent was light. The words weren't spoken differently as much as accentuated in a different way. "But the People are always happy to see another person come out of the Darkness into the Light."

Alec looked down at her lovely, slightly-round face. "Is that what I am doing?"

She tilted her head in what he was coming to know as one of her looks. "You are if you … pass." She smiled a smile that said she knew more than she was saying.

"What do you mean pass?" Alec said, unable to keep a creeping concern out of his voice.

Turning away from him Onya motioned to someone in the crowd as she spoke over her shoulder. "Don't worry. As long as you are sincere you have nothing to fear."

He could not resist saying, "And what if I am not, sincere?"

Onya barked a short laugh. "Then you will be … *escorted* from Sanctuary."

Alec did not miss the emphasis she placed on escorted. He stood there watching as a young woman, in the same uniform that he saw everywhere he looked, came over to them carrying a slim box made of wood, stained so dark it was almost black, with what appeared to be a large purple gemstone embedded in its lid. When she got close enough he could see that the box was about the size of a large book with some kind of writing carved all over it. But it was in a language Alec did not know. Onya took the large book-like box, which seemed as heavy as it appeared, from the young woman who snapped Onya a salute as she stepped back. Onya turned to face Alec. She held the box out in front of him. Looking at him again, she spoke. Her tone said that the time for light banter was over.

"Alexander sa' Salassian. Do you renounce the Darkness and all of its ways?" Again, Alec sensed the tone of long-standing ritual in the words. Onya whispered, "Your answer is, 'Yes, the Ancient being my helper'."

A knot began to form in Alec's throat. The walkway had become crowded with onlookers.

"uh." He cleared his throat. "Yes. The Ancient being my helper."

Onya smiled. "Will you obey those who are given charge over you, keeping yourself from all darkness?"

His voice was a little stronger now. "I will. The Ancient being my helper."

"Then place your hand on the *Graendelle* and be judged!" Onya looked at him encouragingly.

Slowly, Alec reached out, placing his hand on the large purple gemstone. He was close enough to it now to see that the wood looked ancient. It, like the door, was worn in places. As he touched it the gemstone came to life. A purple light rose from somewhere within the gemstone's depths becoming so bright it engulfed him. Instinctively he tried to snatch his hand away but found he could not move it. The light was so intense that he had to close his eyes. Then he felt something. Or was it someone? It felt like someone was rummaging around in his head. A voice came to him. *Stop struggling.* Was that Onya? The sensation changed as a feeling of warmth washed over him. He relaxed.

Deeper it went until he began to feel like someone was stripping off his clothes leaving him standing naked for all the world to see. Finally, he surrendered to it completely. Alec watched from inside his own mind as he was turned over until he was finally let go. Stumbling, as the light winked out, he realized that Onya steadying him with her hand was all that had kept him from falling on his face. Alec blinked as his eyes readjusted to normal light. Onya turned to the crowd raising the box to show everyone that the gemstone was still glowing. A cheer rose from the crowd. Turning back to Alec she smiled up at him as she said, "Welcome." Stepping back she made room for the approaching Commander-General. Alec put his hand to his head as he wavered a little. He was still a bit off balance.

The Commander-General walked over, wrapped his arms around Alec, briefly embracing him. It was a strange feeling. Then, holding Alec at arms length, by his shoulders, the Master of Sanctuary spoke.

"Look around you, Alexander sa' Salassian. You are safe. Be honest that we may know you. Be faithful that we may believe in you. Be courageous that we may love you. This is Sanctuary. You are home." With that the Commander-General of the Peoples Company released him. The others crowded in on him, one by one, welcoming him with a hug, a handshake, or a slap on the back. Smiles abounded around him. Voices called him "little brother." It was all strange to Alec, all of it. For a moment, he wondered what would have happened if that purple gemstone had not continued to glow. He was a stranger to them, but, for some reason, they were acting as if he was one of them. They must be crazy.

The crowd grew larger. Passersby stopped as the word spread that someone had *taken sanctuary*. They gathered. Their complexions were a multi-colored tapestry of tribe, clan, and kin, from the darkest brown, which looked raven-black, to a gold so pale as to appear like lightly darkened cream in a bucket, along with a host of shades in between. They wore smiles that made their eyes glisten. Some, who had not yet been able to reach him, called out from the crowd saying, "Little brother! Welcome!"

Still standing to Alec's left Onya began to sing:

Carry me, over terror's hill
Carry me, through the plain before
Lest, I fall upon my knees
Giving o'er to Hollow's thorn

It was a haunting melody. It moved slowly but with a firm pace. Each syllable came deliberately as it carried the tune forward. In a tavern it would have been a slow foot-tapper. The tune had the sailors sound to it. As though it had been used to keep their minds occupied while they worked. It did not have the lewd words of most sailor songs, but the tune would have been welcome in any dockside tavern. The lyric was melancholy. As Onya sang others came close to her picking up the tune. Soon there was an added harmony as other voices took up the stoic rhythm. To his surprise, Alec found himself moving with the sound of it. He noticed that some were holding hands as they sang. Still others had an arm around one or two other people. The crowd sang in a boisterous throng. As they sang they began to make their way along the cobbled walk that ran from the gate to the tower. It had the taste of loss in it. It had the sound of a longing for something unseen or out of reach. The song swelled as more voices blended in:

We have been
touched by the morning
we have been
kissed by the Ancient's song
we have passed beyond the enemy's reach
and we have come running home

As they walked the song rose. The closer they drew to the tower the more people joined in. Some sang the words while others hummed behind them filling the breaks between the words in the melody. Alec smiled broadly as the procession moved. They were singing for him, he realized! They were singing because he had knocked on the door to Sanctuary. The song, like a wave, seemed to carry him to the tower.

When the day
is setting near, again
and the night
falls once more
we will sing
yes, we will sing
til we reach that other shore

For, we have been
touched by the morning
we have been
kissed by the Ancient's song
we have passed beyond the enemy's reach
and we have come running home

for we know
his wrath cannot hold us
nor will our long past sin
when we open the door
so in the darkness
we light a flame
til we reach that other shore

And, we have been
touched by the morning
we have been
kissed by the Ancient's song
we have passed beyond the enemy's reach
to hear you say welcome home
To hear you say welcome home

The last sounds of the melody were haunting. The hair on the back of his neck stood up as if he were hearing something as old as the world itself. When they finished, they roared. The procession came to a raucous halt at the front entrance of the enormous tower. People clapped their hands as cheers went up. The inscription over the door proclaimed it, *The Peoples Tower*. Swords were rattled in their scabbards.

Ossasande Bantu A' Omorede, Commander-General of the Peoples Company, was standing in the open doorway of the Tower of the People. His eyes were bright. His thumbs were hitched behind his swordbelt. The crowd fell silent. Somewhere above them one of the giant birds of prey Alec had seen circling earlier made a loud screeching sound as it passed overhead. Alec could smell honeysuckle coming from somewhere he could not readily see. The air had a salty tang brought inland by the wind blowing off the Macca Deep. He could hear the sound of wood on stone as people opened the windows of the Tower so that they could look down on the gathering.

The Commander-General looked out over the crowd with his gaze sweeping from left to right. His eyes settled on Alec. A space cleared around Alec setting him apart from the rest of the crowd. The Commander-General's voice warmed as he spoke.

"Who stood to the Watch when this one came to us from the dark?" his voice had that ritualistic tone again.

A young man, the young man who had questioned Alec at the door to Sanctuary, stepped from the crowd with a large, leather-bound, book open in his hands. He spoke through a broad smile that was infectious.

"It was I, Commander, Povla Kinis, Lieutenant of the Second Rank." Povla inclined his head as he spoke. The Commander spoke again.

"Give the name of the Called."

Povla looked at the page the large tome was opened to and recited the name. "The one who comes is Alexander sa' Salassian." Povla closed the book and saluted the Commander crisply.

The Commander nodded in acknowledgement. He turned back to Alec. "Alexander sa' Salassian, do you, of your own free will, choose to stand among the People, watching for the Dawn?"

Alec stood a little straighter, putting his feet together, in what he thought was military fashion before answering in a loud voice. "Yes Commander, I do."

Again, the crowd roared. Swords were rattled in their scabbards. Some of them thumped their chests. There were even shouts from the open windows of the tower. Onya eased up beside Alec so she could speak into his ear.

"Now you will be asked to choose where you will stand among the People. If you say, *as the hand that serves*, you will be choosing to serve as an artisan, craftsman, or the like. You will be giving the Company your skill at a trade. You may even be a farmer if you choose. However, if you say you will stand, *as the hand that reaches into the darkness*, you will be choosing to serve as we served you today, as a soldier. If you know very specifically how you will reach into the darkness you may speak it by name." She said most of this without looking directly at him. She had watched the cheering crowd as if they were not talking to each other at all.

Onya did not rejoin the crowd but continued standing next to him. Alec thought quickly about what she had said to him. He tried to remember what he knew of the Company. Being in the Organization, rising to the unspoken rank of lieutenant, he had learned the power of information. During those years he had learned what he could about the Company for the sake of self-preservation. Leaning over he spoke quickly to Onya in the same low tones she had used with him.

"I did enjoy rescuing little Maria." Arching his eyebrows, he made the statement a question.

With that hint of a smile he was getting used to from her Onya leaned over to speak again. She said, "Then, when asked, say *Stone Hands*." She smiled fully then as if she had been expecting him to say exactly that.

Straightening, Alec turned his attention back to the Commander who had been watching their exchange. With a nod from Onya, the Commander continued, causing the crowd to fall silent.

"Alexander sa' Salassian." The crowd became very still as the Master of Sanctuary spoke. "Choose where among the People you are willing to stand."

Alec never really liked speaking in front of crowds. Something about the profession he had spent years perfecting had lent itself to a natural aversion to recognition or notoriety of any kind other than within the Organization. If you were wise you cultivated a reputation within the Organization but shunned all recognition outside of it. Only a few foolish members had prided themselves on being in the daily papers. They thought it glamorous, but it brought the attention of the Magistrate, which was simply foolish. As a consequence of his lack of notoriety Alec had only been accomplished at speaking in front of his people. He could give orders or explain matters to those few people who always seemed to think they could deceive him. Public speaking, however, was never one of his accomplishments. He tried to keep it brief.

Alec cleared his throat. He said, "Lord Commander. I will stand with the hands that reach into the darkness."

There was more sword rattling along with what appeared to be a nod of approval from the Commander, which was repeated by other hardened faces in the crowd.

The Commander met his eyes as he spoke again in that deep tenor. "It is a gift to be where your talents can do the most good. A man must know himself in order to do that." The Commander gave him a smile. It was an easy smile. It was the kind of smile that seemed like it made a regular appearance. He continued. "And in what way will you reach into the darkness?"

Alec ran his hand over the small shock of hair on his chin as he opened his mouth to answer. He was interrupted by voices calling out from the crowd around him.

A man's voice pierced the general rumble of the crowd as he yelled, "Alexander! The Far Eyes! Choose Far Eyes!" Another voice immediately rang out, "No, Cloudwalkers! It should be Cloudwalkers, sa' Salassian!" A host of voices chimed in.

"Red Birds!"

"No! Not those feather heads! Windchasers!"

"Ha! They couldn't find their tails without directions! Mountain Feathers!"

A couple of those names Alec had at least heard before even though he did not know what any of them meant. As the commotion died down some male voice yelled out "Quiet Blossoms" causing everyone to laugh. He would have to ask someone to explain the joke to him later. Maybe Onya would. As he thought about it the Commander raised a hand causing silence to fall on the assembly with the exception of someone in the crowd who was having difficulty stopping himself from laughing. The joke had him in its grasp. It was not letting go easily. It made Alec smile. He almost laughed at the man trying to stop himself from laughing. The sound of half-stifled laughter seemed to be getting farther away indicating to Alec that the man was failing in his attempt to stop so he had chosen to retreat. Alec took a deep breath as he took a step forward.

Forcing his smile from his face he said, "Commander. I choose to stand with the Stone Hands."

The word, *hands,* was hardly across his lips when voices cried out from the crowd again. "Stone Hands! Stone Hands! *En Nmai Yah!*"

As the voices subsided a handful of women and men separated themselves from the rest of the crowd. They were a tough looking bunch. Alec thought about what he had done earlier that day as he drew a conclusion. This hard-nosed group of people looked as if they could go anywhere, and bring anyone back, even from the Pit itself. Forming a half-circle around Alec they faced the Commander. One of them stood next to Alec on his right. It was to him that the Commander addressed himself next.

"Lieutenant, First Rank, Oakton Immiss. Do you speak for the Stone Hands?"

Oakton Immiss was a largish man with clear blue eyes above a square jaw. His golden hair was close-cropped. The man stood a full head taller than Alec with the added weight to match. His voice was the deep bass you would expect to hear coming from his massive frame. But as Alec looked at him he figured the man must have been a few years younger than him.

The man nodded. "Yes sir. I speak for Lieutenant-Commander Nattah and the Stone Hands." As he spoke he looked around the crowd as if he were hoping to see someone who might outrank him. No one stepped forward to indicate that he should stand down, so he just stood there.

The Commander returned Immiss' nod. "Then, Lieutenant, will the Stone Hands allow Alexander sa' Salassian to stand with them?"

Alec realized that he was not breathing. Onya had not told him that he could be rejected by one of the Orders. Immiss' deep bass rumbled into the space left by the question.

"Yes sir. We will accept him."

The crowd erupted again. Some cried out, "Good form, good form!" Others simply cheered. Alec looked over the crowd before letting his gaze slip back to where Onya was standing. He noticed that she seemed tense. Her eyes were locked straight ahead. Alec wondered what was wrong. But before he could even begin to guess he heard the Commander speaking again.

"Who will sponsor him?"

Onya stepped forward as the last note of the question fell from the Commander's lips. Her voice had something in it that Alec could not make out. It was not fear. But there was certainly something else in her tone.

She said, "I will, Commander."

Immiss was right on her heels. Alec had been so caught up watching Onya he had missed Lieutenant Immiss making the same gesture. Immiss barely let Onya finish before he jumped in.

"Sir, I must object. Respectfully, of course, but I must object nonetheless. Sa' Salassian has chosen to stand among us! It should be one of us who sponsor's him. How should a Quiet Blossom be responsible for a Stone Hand?" Alec was looking at Onya, but she would not look at him. Her face looked grim as if she were resigned to something unfortunate.

Alec had not heard any animosity in Immiss' words but he thought there had been something else. He thought he detected a note of concern in the young man's voice. Alec looked at the others gathered around him. There was something going on that he could not see. What was he missing? The cheering was gone now. It had been replaced by an eerie silence. What was wrong? Onya's face reflected only calm giving Alec no clues. Oakton Immiss was stone-faced. Alec looked over at the Commander preparing to ask him what was happening.

But Alec saw that the Commander was staring hard at Oakton along with the other Stone Hands. The scrutiny seemed to be making them uncomfortable. After a moment, the Commander turned his gaze on Onya. Alec thought he saw a flicker of curiosity there but then it was gone. She would not meet the Commander's eyes but kept her focus directly ahead. He let his eyes rest on Immiss once more.

"Lieutenant." The Commander's voice now held a slight edge to it. "It is not unheard of for a member of one Order to sponsor a candidate for another. I admit it's not the normal way of things, but it's not unheard of." The words had a rising inflection that made it a question aimed at Immiss.

Immiss nodded briefly as he licked lips that had begun to dry. His voice had the sound of a man being very careful to sound respectful. "Yes Commander. You are entirely correct. But in the absence of my Order's commanding officer I must answer this request with the *Challenge*. It is our right." Oakton Immiss had a strained look on his face as he addressed the Commander-General. Alec knew it was never a good feeling when you thought you were giving your superior a reason to be displeased with you let alone the person at the very *top* of your particular food chain. The man was being obstinate with the one person who did not have to answer to anyone. It was clearly more than a bit uncomfortable for him. But, Alec smiled as he thought, you had to give him points for the sheer guts, or stupidity, of it depending on your point of view.

The Commander hitched his right thumb behind his swordbelt. He looked from Onya to Oakton as if he were deciding something. After a few seconds he nodded to himself as if he had finished his deliberation. "It is your choice Lieutenant. But be sure this is not merely a matter of pride for the Hands."

Oakton looked as though he was growing ill by the moment, but he put on a good face. "My apologies, sir. The Hands do not defy you in this. But it is our right. To sponsor is a serious matter. It is the honor of the Stone Hands he will carry with him into the Dark. If he is not ready the blood that is spilled will be on our hands." Oakton turned to Onya. "This is not to say that the Captain-Commander is not up to the task. She is honored throughout the Company. But this is something that we should do. In the absence of Commander Nattah I fear I must challenge." His face was set with the haunted look of grim reluctance. In that moment, Alec understood.

Had the Commander of the Stone Hands been present there likely would have been no problem with Onya sponsoring Alec. But Oakton Immiss would have to answer to his superior in the Stone Hands for the oddity of a member of a different Order sponsoring Alec. He was carrying out a duty he would rather be relieved of, but he was, at the moment, the ranking member of his Order. He had calculated that it would be better to Challenge than be accountable for having not. Alec continued to piece it together as he watched people shuffle around repositioning themselves in the crowd. Onya must have known it would happen this way, which was why she had been so tense. Alec wondered, *why hadn't she simply let a Stone Hand sponsor him? And just what did the Challenge entail?* His head was spinning as he tried to catalogue all of the information he was gleaning from the exchange. He realized that there was too much he did not know. The Commander clapped his hands. The crowd began forming a large circle.

Alec stopped just short of letting his mouth fall open. They were going to fight. They were going to fight, right here, right now. Someone, one of the other Stone Hands he thought, took him by the arm. The woman pulled him back to the edge of the circle. She must have known he was going to speak because she whispered, "There is nothing you can do to stop this, so honor them, and the People, by remaining silent." Alec clamped his mouth shut. He continued to watch wide-eyed. The dark-haired woman, who held his arm, nodded after a few seconds of watching him. She released his arm when she turned her attention back to the circle.

The Commander stepped to the center of the circle. To his left Onya stood, small, slim, feet together, hands at her side, with her perfectly straight, black hair draping her shoulders. She was still wearing the black bodysuit that made your eyes look past her. But she was no longer carrying the crossbow she had earlier. To the Commander's right Oakton loomed large, standing just as Onya did, in what had to be the Company uniform. The black coat, with its high collar, was matched by slim-fitted, black breeches of fine wool, that were tucked into polished, black, knee-high boots. He had a black, leather swordbelt, with a silver buckle shaped like three intersecting circles, belted around his waist. It was identical to what the Commander was wearing. There was a stylized brown hand, wrapped around a silver stone, embroidered over his heart on the coat. It was the size of a small coin but stood out on the unrelieved black of the coat.

The Commander looked from one to the other as his head turned from his left to his right. Alec noticed the peculiar way the man was holding his sword in its glossy black scabbard. The sword had an extra long hilt, which was ivory of all things. The ivory had gold etchings in it. One could see the beautiful carving on the ivory even from this distance. It was nestled in the crook of his left arm like he was cradling a baby. The length of the blade did not run under his arm, as one might expect, but along the outside of his forearm curving past his elbow while the base of the hilt rested in his left hand. Standing in front of the Commander one could see the entire sword. Alec noticed the extra long hilt, the circular handguard of worked black steel, along with the slightly curved, black, scabbard. He made a mental note. A man who carried such an obviously well-made blade, which was at once that simple, but also that elegant, knew his business. In some circles swordmasters had markings that named them. In the north, it was the crane in flight emblazoned on the hilt or sometimes etched in the blade itself. To the west it was a tattoo, behind the left ear, of a Boboa tree, to indicate that a Master's Wheel could usually be found beneath the branches of one. To the distant east corded, colored, strips of cloth hung from a steel loop at the end of the hilt. They were intricately woven cords indicating the swordsman's level of training. Alec's *Sabado* had said one did not need such things. Sometimes all you needed to do was look at a man's sword.

As Onya faced Oakton, the Commander pulled that magnificent blade free of its scabbard, holding it high over his head. When he did, Alec was able to see the intricate, flowing, etchings running down the length of the blade along its unsharpened, top edge. What a magnificent blade. Alec was not close enough to make out what the etchings were, but he could tell the craftsmanship was masterful. When the Commander held his naked sword aloft the two combatants pulled their swords free with a slight ringing of steel as they left their scabbards. The blades shone brightly as they reflected the fading sunlight. Onya stood holding a single-edged, slightly-curved sword that was very similar to the Commander's but without the etchings on its blade. Oakton held a straight longsword with a beautiful, basket handguard attached to a two-handed hilt. Alec could tell the longsword was sharp on both its edges. It was quite similar to the sword that hung from Alec's own belt with the exception that Alec's blade was, ever so slightly, curved like the Commander's. The contest would not be decided by the quality of their swords. They were both exceptional. Alec made another mental note – the Commander liked more than quality clothing - it seemed he liked weapons of quality as well.

They were frozen there with naked death, reflecting the last few rays of sunlight, in their hands. Onya stood holding her blade with a two-handed grip, above her head, with that glimmering arc of steel curving away behind her. Onya's held her left leg and shoulder forward leaving only her left side open to Oakton. As Alec watched he took note that the tip of her sword did not waver perceptibly. She was in amazing condition. Alec noted the slim muscles that stood out on her arms under the black cloth of her bodysuit. She was on the balls of her feet like a cat. It was the stance Alec's Sabado would have called *Cat Awaits the Swallow*. Others would have called it position eight. In the *Sol* it was known as *Almeriss*.

Oakton stood in a similar stance. His hands were grasping the hilt lightly as he held it level with his right ear while the blade of his sword pointed toward Onya with its tip pointed downward. He stood in the position called *Thunder Waits in the Cloud* or position seven. Some would also call it *Otumiss*. The forms were rarely fundamentally different from one school to the next, but the names sometimes were. You learned ways of naming the forms based upon what you were taught but you could tell what you were seeing no matter who had taught you. Alec always thought names like *Cat Awaits the Swallow* were the easiest to remember, which was probably why they were more common. Oakton's elbows were in close to his body. He rested easily on the balls of his feet. Like Onya he was as still as a mountain. The two did not even blink. Alec realized their breathing had slowed until one could almost not perceive it.

A thought floated across his mind. Alec wondered if they were going to kill each other over who would sponsor him? It was foolish! The Commander twisted on the balls of his right foot like a dancer. As he spun around he slashed his sword in a straight line between the two still figures. The slashing arc of the blade ended with his sword firmly in its scabbard. As his sword clicked into place the two combatants moved with blinding speed. The Commander's spin took him backward, out of the ring, as Onya and Oakton clashed in its center where he had been standing a split second before. Alec heard the clash of steel as they met. Seemingly, without pause, they passed each other as their blades cut through the air. In that instant *Wind Trims the Sail* met *Threading the Needle*. Both stopped three paces from where they had clashed with their backs to each other. No one moved. Onya crouched with her sword curving out in front of her with her hands, wrapped around the hilt, held at her side. A slight breeze ruffled her long hair. Oakton crouched just as still with both hands grasping his sword as it hung in front of him.

Alec looked from one to the other wondering at the stillness of it all. No one in the crowd made a sound. It took a second for him to notice the small splattering of blood staining the cobblestones where the two had slid past one another at the circle's center. It was fresh blood. Still no one moved. Alec had not even seen which sword dealt the wound nor could he tell which one was hurt.

The wind blew again ruffling their clothes. The two combatants stood slowly, almost in tandem, rising from their crouched positions. They still had their backs to each another. Oakton spoke from where he stood without turning. Alec could not see his expression from where he was standing.

"Commander, permission to step from the circle." Oakton's voice was still strong.

The Commander looked to where Onya was standing. Her hands still grasped her sword.

"The Lieutenant wishes to step from the circle Captain-Commander. Will you allow him to withdraw or do you require another Pass?" Alec thought he noted a hint of something unspoken in the tone that the Commander used. He wanted it to end.

Everyone waited. Oakton had pressed for the Challenge. So, apparently, he could not withdraw without Onya's agreement. She spoke over her shoulder.

"Commander, the Lieutenant may step from the circle with honor as well as my respect." Onya exhaled with her proclamation.

Everyone began to breathe again. People were slapping their scabbards in agreement as the circle dissolved into a crowd again. Alec heard people shouting out, "Good form! Good form!"

As quickly as it had gathered the crowd began to thin. People talked in small groups about what they had just seen. It was not long before only Oakton, with the few Stone Hands that had been present, and Onya, along with the women who had helped her rescue Alec, were left. Alec looked around him in stunned silence. They were crazy. They were all crazy.

Stepping over to Alec, with his sword resting, once again, in the crook of his left arm, the Commander-General of the Peoples Company said, "It is finished. Alexander sa' Salassian, you are commended into the care of Onya Onoto. It is a rare privilege to be sponsored by a Captain-Commander of the People. Be worthy of what you have seen today." He held Alec's gaze for a moment as if to be sure that his words had sunk in. Then, with a brief flicker of a smile, the Commander-General disappeared into the Peoples Tower.

Alec split his gaze between the Stone Hands and the women who had been with Onya earlier. He blinked as he took a second look. The Stone Hands had moved to stand behind Onya. The women who, Alec realized, must be Quiet Blossoms were standing with Oakton Immiss. It was backwards. But before Alec could ask what was going on one of the Stone Hands, standing with Onya, spoke to Oakton.

"Is there peace here brother? We stand with the Blossom in this matter between Orders." The other Hands were nodding as the man spoke. Some had their hands resting on Onya's shoulders.

Oakton looked at the members of his Order standing next to Onya. "Yes brothers, sisters, there is peace between us."

The Quiet Blossoms, who were standing next to Oakton, held onto him. One of the women was examining his side while he grimaced a bit. The other women had comforting hands on him. Erra, the tallest of the Blossoms, spoke from where she stood just behind Oakton with her hand on his shoulder. Her other hand rested lightly on the hilt of her sword. Her words were meant for Onya. "Is there peace here sister? We stand with this Stone Hand in the matter between our Orders." Then she added with a smile, "Dim-witted though he may be." Oakton glared as everyone laughed. Alec looked at all of them still puzzled. *Insanity*, he thought, it was sheer insanity. What had he gotten himself into? But he watched as the tension flew away with the laughter.

Onya replied, "Yes my sisters. There is peace between us. He is a formidable opponent, as a Stone Hand should be."

Smiling broadly Onya was rewarded with a shout from the other Stone Hands as they heard the compliment. "*Alladai* Quiet Blossom!" It was the High Cant from the First Tongue spoken until the rebellion at the Tower of Budaai. *Well met Blossom,* they had said. This was followed by more laughter.

Onya and Oakton slid their swords back in their scabbards before stepping close to embrace one another briefly. Alec shook his head. They had just tried to kill each other but now they were hugging. What *had* he gotten himself into?

As they parted Onya placed her hand gently on Oakton's side, "Please see to this immediately Oakton-san. And let us share a drink tonight?" She looked up at the large man.

He gave her a small smile. "Yes Onya-san. That would be nice."

The Stone Hands gathered up Oakton. They walked off across the compound. They walked very close to him as if they would protect him from any further injury. Someone in the group said something Alec could not make out, but it was punctuated by laughter. Oakton's face began to turn red. Another of the Stone Hands began examining Oakton's wound far too circumspectly. Oakton shoved the fellow away causing even more laughter. They seemed to be a rough lot. Alec watched them go. He thought, for the third time, shaking his head, *what had he gotten into?* He continued to shake his head as he turned his attention back to Onya. He found the Quiet Blossoms fussing over her.

Erra was pawing at her. "Sister, are you alright?"

"Are you sure?" Saffra was right behind Erra looking stern. Her voice was indignant.

Onya pushed away the hands that were trying to get at her. "Yes, yes, you flustered flock of hens! I am fine." She slapped away more hands trying to examine her.

They laughed again before they all turned to face Alec. Hands went to hips even as some arms were crossed over chests. Alec swallowed hard. He had seen this before. It was not good. Somehow this entire episode would become his fault. As they continued looking at him he finally said, "What?"

They laughed at him. Erra turned to Onya.

"Onya I have not cleaned up, or rested, since Gaul. I need to do both. Try not to stay long? You need rest too."

The others chimed in their agreement with Erra. They had to bathe. They needed to rest before the evening meal and Last Rites. She should do the same after getting Alec settled. Onya nodded graciously as she herded them off with a half-terse command. She was, after all, the highest-ranking officer present. They were all still laughing, with their arms around each other's waists or shoulders, as they departed in a bunch. Onya turned to Alec. As she looked up at him she smiled softly.

Alec opened his mouth to ask her to explain what had happened in detail. She held up a hand to forestall his questions. "I know, I know, Alexander. We will have time for all of your questions later. Right now, the girls are right, we need to bathe, and eat. There are certain rites to be seen to tonight. Some of the People have fallen so we must pay our respects. I will show you to your quarters." A hint of what Alec would have called sadness crossed her face momentarily as she mentioned the fallen People. It was gone as quickly as it had appeared. She smiled again as she began walking away from the tower, off to the left, motioning for him to follow.

Alec caught up with her as he cleared his throat.

"Excuse me, uh, ma'am?" Alec saw her laugh to herself, at that, but he continued on. "So, you are having a ceremony for the dead tonight?"

Onya looked over at him as he matched her stride. "No, Alexander. It is a ceremony for the living."

Stepping from the grass onto a wide, stained-wood, walkway that curved like a snake, weaving among several buildings, they walked at a fast pace.

Alec said, "I don't understand. You said some of the People had fallen. I'm guessing that it happened in battle. Are they alive then?"

Onya shook her head as she waved to someone who was waving to her from off to the right. "Alexander, while we may shed tears for those we have lost, the ceremony is really for those of us who must carry on. Put another way, the dead don't care about death. Only the living do."

Onya walked on expecting that he would keep up. She spoke when the people they passed on the walkway spoke to her. There was a constant stream of black uniforms passing them. Alec wondered how about the size of Sanctuary. He began to realize what he had seen in her eyes earlier in the day. When she had come to his aid, he saw something in her eyes he was unable to identify. Now, he understood. A great sorrow, mixed with anger, had been in those dark eyes. It saddened him as he thought about it. He did not want her to be sad when she had risked so much, even though she barely knew him. Then it dawned on him, like sunlight hitting his face when his mother came in his room, when he was a child, and threw back the curtains, forcing him awake on Ancient's Day. Alec hated that. She always said that no matter how late he stayed up, when Ancient's Day was celebrated, he would get up so that he could attend. It dawned on him, smacking him in the face like that sunlight, as he trailed this smallish woman, that he was already fond of her. It was not a passionate desire. No, it was more a familial feeling. He was not quite sure what to do with those feelings, so Alec fell into his own thoughts, letting his body operate automatically.

The words Onya had spoken kept surfacing among Alec's many other thoughts. She had said the celebration was for those who would carry on. Alec had never been big on fate or destiny but something about his being in this place, at this time, felt right. He told himself he was going to help. He was going to help Onya, the Commander, and all the rest. If they were going to carry on he was going to help. His steps fell more smoothly as he stood up in his stride a bit straighter. He felt the tension begin to leave his shoulders. As he relaxed Alec began to pay more attention to his surroundings. There was still so much he did not know about these people - the *People* - he thought. He had a lot to learn if he was going to be useful. Without thinking, he smiled. He smiled one of his rare smiles. It was not forced, or half-hearted, nor affixed to his face to coax someone into doing something for him. He smiled a rare, true smile. There were no words to describe fully why he felt freed at that moment. But he smiled as he walked. He paid attention to the woman in front of him. In one day, all that he had worked for during the better part of his adult life had been destroyed by one decision. That former life was in shambles. It was, irrevocably, lost to him. But he knew he would not cry over it. There would be no tears. He would carry on because there was work to do.

Welcome them then, with arms spread wide
welcome them then, with hearts abeating
with a smile that fills the face and a wave of all arms
welcome them then, to this home
those who have been so long gone

~An excerpt from the fragments found
at Goshien, thought to be from the
Fifth Philosophy a funereal rite
Fragment 17, Codex 2

Home is where you hang your sword.

~Dominic Brimmon
Founder of Brimmon's Brigade
Third Age, Common Era c. 213

Chapter seven

Thoughts of home

Rex snuggled deeper into the overstuffed, brown leather. The chair was large, soft, and doubly cushioned. It was as if it had been made for promoting laziness. A low mahogany table held up his feet, which were crossed at the ankles. With his arms folded over his chest Rex shifted slightly to keep from cutting off the blood flow to his legs. An easy, close-mouthed, smile rested firmly on his face. It was Free Pass. Depending upon whom you asked it was either late afternoon or early evening. Training was completed for the day. Rex was trying to clear his mind of Kardic remnants. Kardic was an ancient scholarly language they were studying in one of his classes. As he rubbed his eyes his mouth stretched open, unexpectedly, into a wide yawn. As he closed his mouth he turned his mind from thoughts of ancient grammar. He tried to relax. It would be time for Common Meal soon but, for the moment, he allowed himself to think of how good it was, sinking even deeper into the chair, to do absolutely nothing.

The plush chair, into which he nestled, looking for the most comfortable position, was in the common room on the fourth floor of Cadet House. A crisp white jacket with a single, shining, silver pip, marked him a Cadet of the First Rank. The pip had a sunburst engraved on its tiny face. It was pinned on the right side of the high collar of his coat. The coat hung, neatly folded, over the large back of the chair.

There was, at the end of the hall, on every floor of Cadet House, a common room just like this one. Large and airy, the room's fourth wall, which was directly opposite the door, was paned glass from floor to ceiling. The glass wall, whose panes had a hint of bluish tint, overlooked their small courtyard, which the cadets called the Square. Along another wall was a smallish cooking alcove where one could find snacks, cold water, juice, or tea - hot or cold. There was also choca. Today there was a blue-veined, white cheese, a heavy, brown bread, and bite-sized pieces of deep-fried fish, along with a tart redsauce for dipping. There were also, always, various kinds of fruit. Rex had eaten a few handfuls of green grapes, which somehow, someone, had managed to grow seedless, before he had made his way to the plush chair.

Wisps of flavorful steam rose from a cup of choca sitting beside his feet on the low table. Rex had made a fresh pot of a Highland brew, which he liked, when he had first entered the Common Room. There had been dregs of a hearty breakfast blend of ground choca beans left in the carafe probably strong enough to straighten a bent swordblade. It had not taken long for him to boil the water while grinding the flavored beans. He had put those grounds in the pot. After he had poured the steaming water he had attached the straining screen. When he had poured himself a fresh cup only the dark-flavored brew passed through the screen leaving the grounds behind in the pot. At present the smell of the choca rising from his cup lulled him. In the early morning that same smell would call Rex to wakefulness but, at the moment, it simply calmed him.

The Common Room was all hardwood. The floor, as well as the wall paneling, was a beautiful cherry wood with a light cherry stain. A few throw rugs adorned the floor in green complemented by shades of sea blue with silver trim. There were chairs, couches, along with an assortment of tables, including one very long mahogany meeting table in the very center of the room. Around the room twenty cadets were in their own various stages of relaxation. You learned in the Company, even as a cadet, to relax when you were able.

Another neck-tightening yawn ripped Rex's mouth open. His eyes watered as his jaws stretched wide. The impulse to sleep had crept up on him like a Quiet Blossom. *Those women moved liked ghosts.* It was a stray thought, but he did not have the mental strength, or inclination, to wonder where it came from. Rex was on the verge of a very deep, all consuming, nap. Another odd thought hit him as his mind drifted. *Naps were wonderful.* He snuggled a shade deeper into the cushy reserves of the chair.

Of the twenty cadets in the room Rex recognized members from six different cadet teams. Cora, a bright-eyed girl, playing cards with Assat, was a member of Mountainflight. Assat was with team Nightfeather. Rex also spotted members of Half-blade, Songbird, Hightower, and of course, his own team, Redhawk.

All cadets belonged to a team. One of the first lessons their teachers wanted them to learn was that you achieved nothing in life alone. Someone has to help you along the way. So, the Company taught you how to work with others. You were supposed to learn how to rely on someone. Most importantly you learned what it meant to have someone rely on you. Outside the gates of Sanctuary, they would be putting their lives at risk. You had to be able to trust that the people around you could be relied on. Most cadet teams consisted of seven members, usually of varying rank. However, Redhawk, at the moment had only four. Three of its members had received the *Call* in the past turn. That had left Rex with seniority, which had made him the Team Leader. He had been promoted last turn from Second to Cadet of the First Rank.

Sophie lounged on a long couch with one leg slung over its arm just a few feet away. Her coat, as crisply white as Rex's, was unbuttoned. It hung open revealing the top of a white, ribbed bodysuit underneath. She held one of the city newspapers in her hands. Those hands were delicate like the hands of a painter or musician. Sophie liked to keep up with the news in the capital, so she tried to read the papers when she could.

Sophie was Team-Second. She was also a Cadet of the Second Rank. Soph was a beauty if Rex had ever seen one. Of course, he would never admit that to her. She was just over five spans tall. She was quick as an eyeblink. Lithe and agile, Sophie walked as if she were floating an inch off the ground. After she was *Called* she was headed for the Quiet Blossoms. Given her gifts she would certainly fit in with that lethal group of women.

Across from Sophie, on the floor with her back against a large chair, sat Tessa. She was almost the opposite of Sophie. Tessa was over six spans in height. Where Sophie was dark-brown skinned, wore her curly, wool-like, black hair in several long, thick braids, Tessa was pale-skinned with a sun-kissed complexion. Though Tessa's golden hair was as long as Sophie's it was perfectly straight. Sophie had black eyes while Tessa's were pale-brown with gray flecks. She was attractive in a quiet way. The one thing Rex loved about Tessa was that when she was at your back you could concentrate on what was in front of you. You did not have to look over your shoulder. It was like resting against a brick wall. You did not worry about whether it would hold you up you just leaned on it. Tessa was one of the toughest people Rex knew. Finally, there was Finn.

Finn was shy of Tessa's six feet plus by at least a span. He was also much broader. The added weight he carried was all muscle. Big eyes, coupled with sharp angled features, gave Finn the kind of face that would look young well into his middle years. If there was a drawback in Finn's makeup it was that he was almost never satisfied. You always had to call Finn to catch up with everyone else because he was still fiddling with the last project or assignment. It drove his instructors mad. Thorough was an insufficient description of him. Finn was obsessive but at the same time uncomplicated. Rex thought the last was his most endearing quality. With Finn, what you saw was what you got. He had a smile for everyone. Rex had seen Finn gladly accept what no one else would endure. The oldest of them by a single year Finn was a believer in the innate goodness of people. He thought that given enough time anyone could show his or her better nature.

Finn was, at present, polishing his boots. He sat in a corner, out of the way, with his lips compressed. His tongue was sticking out of the side of his mouth. His short, dusty brown, spiked hair was sticking up as if it had not been combed. There were polish-stained cloths on the floor around him with a few lying in his lap. With practiced stokes he was brushing his black boots to a glossy shine. Rex smiled knowing they were spare boots whose shine was only surpassed by the shine on the boots Finn was currently wearing. It was a funny scene. But Rex had learned that you did not laugh at Finn unless you enjoyed being wrestled to the ground before being made to say something ridiculous, in order to be released.

That was Redhawk. *His team*, he thought. They were his responsibility. His eyelids' desire to fully close was becoming more persistent by the moment as Rex allowed his mind to drift. As he began to fade into the darkness of slumber in earnest the thought that he was wasting a perfectly good cup of choca briefly surfaced but then faded.

The blue eyes of Rex Aloran closed completely as the door to the Common Room opened. Distantly, he heard the door swing in as he let go of consciousness. Since his eyes were closed he did not see who entered. The sound of white-coated cadets jumping to attention tickled his ears. Through the haze of partial consciousness Rex heard someone bark, "Commander on the floor!"

Fighting his eyes open Rex wondered what the commotion was about. Coming fully awake he heard the sing-song voice of a woman standing at the door.

"I am looking for the members of Redhawk, as for the rest of you, at ease." Her voice was not stern only matter-of-fact.

At that moment, Rex realized who was attached to that distinctive voice. Onya Onoto, Captain-Commander, as well as chief member of the Quiet Blossoms, stood glancing around the room from just inside the doorway. He had heard her name often enough when Sophie would go on, at length, about the Blossoms, cataloguing the accomplishments of Onya Onoto. Rex jostled the cup of choca on the table where his feet had been resting as he jumped up. Choca spilled over the cup's lip into its matching saucer. Realizing that his coat was lying on the back of his chair, he snatched it from where it lay, throwing himself into it with practiced speed. As he opened his mouth to call his team to order he wondered what the chief officer of the Blossoms wanted with Redhawk?

Orders would have come through the Cadet Commander. He would have surely remembered a message or visit from her.

Rex put on his field voice, barking only two words, "Redhawk! Attend!"

He continued buttoning his coat as he carried out his own order. Each of his team members dropped what had occupied them before falling in behind his almost fully composed form. As they reached the area in front of the door where the Captain-Commander stood, with a stranger next to her, they fanned out behind Rex in standard inspection formation. Though Rex could not see them standing behind him he knew they were there. He could even guess what they were doing. Sophie was more than likely smiling like a fanatical fool at this woman whom she worshipped. Tessa was likely looking half-bored while thinking of how many ways she could disarm or take out the stranger if he made a wrong move. Finn was most likely gazing forlornly at his unfinished boots out of the corner of his eye. Rex stopped himself from smiling. He shot off a crisp salute to the Captain-Commander knowing that three other salutes accompanied his from the rest of his team.

Rex barked again, "Attention to orders!"

The team had been standing at Parade Rest, but they snapped to full attention. Squared off, facing forward, directly in front of the commander, Rex addressed her.

"Team Redhawk reporting Captain-Commander." As he spoke Rex kept his eyes focused just over her left shoulder.

Standing with his feet together, his shoulders square, and his back straight, he waited. Behind him, Rex knew, his team was just as spit-shine. Absently, he hoped his coat was not wrinkled.

The commander looked him over before doing the same to the rest of his team. She did not move from where she stood but simply ran her well-trained eyes over them all. Those eyes were examining them to within an inch of their lives. She would not miss anything even without walking around them. Her rank seemed to come with that kind of perception. Rex realized he was holding his breath. His heart was beating a little faster. After a few moments of silence, she nodded to herself. Her voice was warm as she spoke. Rex thought he heard a hint of pride.

"At ease cadets." Stepping forward, a half step, her hand came up slowly. A fingertip touched Rex just under his chin moving slightly. He let his head turn in the direction her fingertip indicated. She brought his eyes in line with her own. He saw there, on her face, a broad, friendly smile. Rex, along with his team, clasped their hands behind their backs at her order. They moved their left leg out until their feet were shoulder-width apart. The commander looked into his eyes.

"You are Rex?" Her eyes were clear, sharp, like a predator, but somehow, they were also friendly.

Rex nodded. "Yes ma'am. Team Leader of Redhawk." He let himself return her warm smile.

She pursed her lips briefly. "Yes, I have been told good things about Redhawk from the Commander of Cadets."

Rex nodded curtly as he said, "Thank you ma'am."

She shook her head. "No, no thanks are necessary. From what I am told you are deserving of the high opinion. You had three of your team receive the *Call* last turn, and Onandra does not exaggerate. The Commander of Cadets did not exaggerate when I was under her care. She still does not to this day."

Rex hoped he kept the surprise from his features. Onandra El' Vallem must be very old. She looked only fifteen or twenty years older than Rex. The Commander of Cadets moved like a young woman. Rex had often thought he would like to see her wield the sword she carried around as though it were an extension of her own body. He focused on the commander as she continued.

"I am not here to cause you to miss your free time. I recall how precious this time can be. But this could not wait." She half-turned indicating the man behind her with a nod. "This is Alexander sa' Salassian. I am his sponsor. He is newly come to the People. At the entrance to the Tower, arbitrated by the Commander-General, I challenged for the right of sponsorship and won. Alexander is a candidate for the Stone Hands. I present him, Rex Aloran, under the authorization of the Commander of Cadets, as a member of your team.

You will square him away. I expect to receive weekly reports on his progress. You are responsible. I am clear Cadet?" Her left eyebrow rose with the question.

"Yes ma'am." Rex replied quickly. "Quite clear ma'am."

She nodded. "Very good. Meet your new teammate, Alexander sa' Salassian." Turning to Alexander sa' Salassian she touched his shoulder gently as she spoke to him. "You know how to reach me, yes?"

The man nodded to her quietly, then said, "Yes Captain-Commander." Rex noted that the words sounded odd on the man's tongue. Alexander, it seemed, was not used to the forms of address used in the Company.

The Captain-Commander laughed a little as she spoke to sa' Salassian again. "*Nsamsahdo*," she pronounced it slowly. "You may call me *Nsamsa*, which means *Sponsor* in the ancient language of the Commander-General's homeland."

The man smiled at the Captain-Commander with an easy smile. He said, "All right then, *Nsamsa*. Thank you … for everything."

She hitched at her swordbelt as she looked at him a moment more like a mother about to leave her only child with relatives for the first time. Then she was gone as quickly as she had come.

Rex stood very still, just for a moment, giving Onya Onoto time to put distance between her and them. He looked at Alexander sa' Salassian who was looking back at him. Rex realized that he was staring quite openly at the new arrival. He cleared his throat.

"Forgive me brother. The Captain-Commander is something of a legend around here. She is a member of First Team, which places her very close to the Commander-General. We rarely get a visit from someone of her standing, especially, in the Common Room of Cadet House."

Alexander sa' Salassian waved it away as though it was not even worth mentioning as he smiled a little at each of them. He was about Rex's height. Rex noted that his clothes were expensive if a bit dirty. Where Rex's hair was a dark brown and curly his was the same shoulder-length but straight and black. Alexander's glittering green eyes were also different from Rex's deep sea blue. Alexander seemed well built without being bulky but the facial hair would have to go. Rex could tell the man was a bit nervous. That feeling was quite reasonable given the circumstance. Rex could recall his first day vividly. It had been several years, three to be exact, since he had knocked on that door feeling that there was no longer hope or a reason to continue living. Nervous was the least of what he had been feeling. Someone had been there for him. His new team had made him feel welcome. Now it was time to return the favor. Exhaling loudly, Rex began unbuttoning his white coat, for the second time today.

Letting out one more deep breath for good measure Rex said, "Alexander, let me introduce you to the rest of the team."

Alexander smiled saying, "You may call me Alec."

Rex nodded in acknowledgement as he turned to point to the others. "This is Sophie, the Team Second. These two are Tessa and Finn. I am Rex."

Alexander, *no*, he thought, *he wanted to be called Alec*. Alec turned to each of them in turn as their name was called offering his hand in a firm, friendly, clasp.

As Alec finished Sophie spoke up. "Alexander. No, sorry, make that, Alec. Alec, have you been taken to be equipped or fitted for your uniform?"

Alec shook his head slightly. "No, I have not." Rex watched as he pulled out a piece of parchment from a vest pocket continuing, "Onya - I mean Captain-Commander Onoto - gave me this requisition for all of that. My *Nsamsa* -" he tried the word on his tongue again, "-said that you would help me with it?" Alec looked from Sophie to Rex.

Rex nodded, smiling warmly, at the new addition to the team. He gave his voice a light-hearted tone. "Yes brother, we will help you get squared away, fear not." Taking a step forward he clapped Alec on the shoulder indicating the rest of the team with an arm sweeping out in a grand theatrical way as if he had an audience. Rex continued, "You are now a member of the most illustrious band of cadets in all of Cadet House. Or at least we think so. Team Redhawk!" As if on cue the rest of the team called out. "Ahh-eee!"

Finn went immediately to get the boots he had been polishing. When he returned, he went to stand by the door. Rex surveyed the room, his hands on his hips, as though he were seeing it for the first time. Turning back to his team he dropped his arms and began to issue orders. The first went to Sophie.

"Team-Second. You will take our new cadet to the weavers for his uniforms." Turning to Tessa he said, "Tess, find him some quarters. Try to get him on our floor. And use his Nsamsa's name if the House Steward gives you a hard time." Finally, he turned to Finn to round out the immediate necessities. "Finn, go sign Alec in with the Recorder. Get his preliminary schedule. Then, meet up with Alec and Sophie at the armory to help them draw weapons." Rex rubbed a hand slowly across his own face. "I am clear?"

They spoke in unison. "You are clear, sir."

Rex nodded curtly. He was going to enjoy the privileges of rank.

"Dismissed," he said.

Rex turned away from his departing team to walk back toward the chair he had been lounging in before the interruption. He heard Sophie's voice, with a sarcastic drawl, following behind him.

"Oh sir? Excuse me ... uh, sir? But what, may I ask, will *you* be doing to contribute to the *team* effort?" Rex noticed the slight emphasis on each of the words in his Second's question.

He laughed a little as he returned the favor of a tone-laden sentence. "Why, Sophie. *I* will be making sure that the Team *Leader* is in top form so that he may help guide the new cadet."

Rex heard the sarcastic tone deepen as she spoke again. "And just how will the *Leader* do that?"

Rex plopped down into the plush chair. He hopped over the arm on his way to the seat cushion. The cushion *whooshed* with the sound of air rushing out. Placing his feet on the low table for support, Rex crossed them, as he had earlier.

Rex shot Sophie a reply while smiling across the room at her. "Team-Second, I am going to take a nap." Closing his eyes, Rex ignored the rest of the snide remarks and abusive jokes that were spoken in his direction.

He ignored them mainly because he had not learned the dialect of Sophie's native tongue, so it would have taken time to translate. As for the rest, he ignored them because he did want that nap. It was early evening. With his team gone to get Alec squared away Rex closed his eyes slipping finally, blissfully, peacefully, into darkness.

†

Only an hour had passed since Alec had been introduced to his new team. With their help, he had been squared away, as his new teammates would say, with dispatch. Despite his normal level of caution, when it came to new people, he had already begun to like them. His first impression was that they were good people, if a bit odd, in their own unique ways. Finn, who reminded Alec of a brick wall, appeared to be something of a perfectionist. The man seemed to have a gift, a singular focus, which allowed him to ignore distractions so that he could concentrate on the task at hand. Sophie, apparently, abhorred any sort of meandering in a person's conversation showing, instead, an appreciation for getting to the point. Alec really liked that about her. It didn't hurt that she was very easy to look at. Absently, he wondered if she were from the same land as the Commander-General given that she had the same brown complexion. That was certainly not conclusive evidence, there were a number of lands whose inhabitants had the same coloring, but she also seemed to speak with the same cadence as the Commander-General. Then there was Tessa.

Tessa was funny. It wasn't just that she had a lovely sense of humor. It didn't take long to discover that she had, in Finn, the perfect foil for her many jabs. While everyone around him laughed Finn just looked puzzled making whatever Tessa had said all the more humorous. After a few hours together, Alec had begun to get a feel for them. Alec liked them – he was still wary of the entire company, but he liked them. There was, however, still Rex. He had been asleep in what they called the Common Room while the others took care of the routine matters that were a consequence of getting him settled. Alec had reserved judgment concerning Rex until he could spend some time with him. Sophie had spoken highly of their Team Leader. Alec had, surprisingly, already begun to feel like he could trust Sophie's judgment. He could see how she would inspire that kind of confidence given her straightforward personality. The woman was incredibly smart.

Alec tugged lightly on the collar that now encircled his neck. It was just shy of a snug fit. They assured him he would get used to it. Alec consoled himself with the notion that if he had to wear a uniform at least it was a well-made one. The longer he examined it the more he appreciated the craftsmanship involved. In the back of his mind he kept thinking that the white coat, identical to the ones worn by the rest of his team, was going to be hard to keep clean. Polishing boots, buckles, belts as well as keeping the actual uniform clean, was going to be time consuming. Alec wondered why it seemed that when it came to those who occupied the bottom tier of any cohesive group of people there was always so much cleaning to be done? When he first joined the Organization, he spent a lot of time washing dishes, wiping down horses, picking up laundry, and the like. He was again faced with cleaning.

The Weavers had given Alec a great deal of advice about how to take care of the uniforms they had given him. Along with the uniforms, they had provided him with several sheets of parchment, wrapped in a leather script that tied closed, with leather cord, detailing various points of protocol as well as how to care for his new garments. It had made his head spin. *So much to learn*, he kept thinking, *he had so much to learn*. While he was contemplating the amount of work that lay ahead he was also recognizing a kind of excitement that came, hand-in-hand, with the newness of everything. *Everything* was new again.

The black breeches fit well. Like the coat, the breeches were made from finely woven wool. They were thicker than most breeches with a heavy seam line down the middle of each leg. But like most upper-end breeches they ended, just above the ankle, with a broad cuff. They were tucked into the top of black, knee-high boots that felt glorious on his feet. The breeches were cut so well that they did not puff out over the boots but fit snuggly around the knee. The boots were wondrous. A padded lining inside of them hugged his feet. The insole sprung back lightly with each step. He could run, jump, or kick in them without fear of wear on his feet. The sole was thick, but well shaped, with a heavy toe. They had a good-sized heel. The leather was thick while remaining supple, with a gorgeous, thick, silver buckle on the outside at calf-level. It would have cost Alec a lot of coin to purchase similar items. All in all, it was a well-made uniform from head to foot. The lines were clean while the material was top quality. Even with all of that Alec still managed to miss his vest.

Raising his right hand, Alec touched the right side of the collar of his white coat. The collar stood high along his neck. The weaver had cut it so that it would stand up straight, unwrinkled, fitting snuggly. The collar nearly encircled the neck completely with the exception of the very front where there was a sliver of space. The two ends of the collar touched lightly. Moving his fingertips along the right side of the collar Alec felt the four, tiny, silver pips spaced evenly in a straight line. They were highly polished with a sunburst etched on their small surfaces. They had also been coated with something that would prevent them from tarnishing. The white coat had been dipped in a solution during the final stages of its creation so that stains could not embed themselves in the fabric. The coat could be cleaned no matter what you got on it. At least that is what the Weavers had told him. Even blood or wine would come out though you still had to scrub. Alec caressed those four evenly spaced pips on his collar. Sophie had given him a brief explanation of the hierarchy in the ranks of the Company beginning with the cadets. He was a Cadet of the Fourth rank, which put him at the very bottom of the barrel. That had been a wonderful piece of news. Sophie claimed that promotion could be earned quickly in the lower ranks. According to her it only slowed after one was *Called* from the ranks of the cadets. Sitting on the edge of his bed, in his new quarters, Alec let it all sink in.

The quarters in Cadet House were like the uniforms. They were nice but simple. He, actually, had two rooms. There was a large, all-purpose room that was about ten paces by ten, connected to a smaller room for meal preparation. The smaller room had running water of all things. Both rooms had hardwood flooring. The larger room had a throw rug that covered most of the central floor space. The rug was a beautiful piece woven with a floral motif in light gray with pale green accents. Whoever had done the decorating seemed to like flowers.

Alec thought it was a lot of room for someone at the bottom of the chain of command. He wondered what kind of quarters his Nsamsa had. She was at the uppermost level of the chain of command. Certainly, if a Cadet of the Fourth rank could have this kind of room Onya must have rooms the size of a small house. Alec got up from where he was seated on the edge of his bed. Walking around his rooms he looked more closely at his accommodations. There was a flattop desk, a bookshelf, a large comfortable couch, along with a few chairs of various sizes spread around the room. There was also a dining table that would normally seat about six. If you didn't mind everyone having a little less room it could be made to seat as many as eight.

The smaller room had a washstand with a large, cherry wood, bowl coupled with a matching water pitcher. There was a food preparation stand, shelves for food storage, along with a waist-high metal box in one of the corners. The food preparation table had a corked spout that, when unplugged, would release water. When Alec lifted the large lid of the metal box he was utterly shocked. It was divided into two sections. One side was a bay for large blocks of ice that kept the entire interior of the box cold. The other side had shelves holding food, cold water, juice, and even chilled wine. A quick glance revealed fruit, vegetables, and various pre-made sauces. It was a wonder to behold. In the corner, opposite the metal box, was a metal table that had an inserted section for a wood-burning grill. Looking up Alec saw a vent for the smoke to float into, presumably, leading out of the building. The final area of the small room contained a station for the preparation of choca. There were cups, choca beans, a wood box with a metal arm on its top that Alec took to be a grinder, as well as canisters for cream, sugar, and other miscellaneous items. A doorway without an actual door separated the two rooms. Standing in that doorway, looking into the small room, one stood directly across from the only window in the quarters.

It was five paces wide. The window nearly covered the entire wall save for a span below the ceiling. The window was actually a collection of small glass panes. Each pane was about the size of a man's head with five sides. They were honeycombed in geometric perfection. The frame of each pane was a length of dark-stained cherry wood. All the glass panes were perfectly clear except for the panes on the very edges of the large composition, which were tinted, alternating between pale green and blue. It was not simply an artifice to look out. It was also a work of art to be viewed for its own beauty. For the fourth or fifth time, in the same hour, Alec's opinion of Bantu – he knew now that no one called him Ossassande - his new Commander-General, climbed another notch. That a Cadet of the Fourth Rank would have rooms like these, appointed in this way, said something about the nature of the Company's Commander.

Alec had looked out of the window when he had first entered the small room. The window faced east. That told him he would get sunlight for most of the first half of the day. Alec had a nice view of the part of Sanctuary where Cadet House stood. Looking off to his right he had been able to see Peoples Tower while a half turn to his left had shown the top half of the next tallest building in Sanctuary. Sophie had called that building Aerie.

Alec stepped through the doorway into the smaller of the two rooms. After pouring himself a cup of choca, from the pot he had made earlier, he slid into the window seat. The designers of the room had not put in a window ledge but instead had gone with a classic, wide, cushioned, window seat. Alec placed his back against one side of the window nook, put his feet up near the other end, then leaned lightly against the paned mosaic of his oversized window. As he sipped choca he let his mind drift while he looked out on the place he would now be calling home. Minutes passed as Alec lost track of time. The sun finally finished setting while he lounged in the window nook taking in the beauty of it. A knock at his door pulled him back into the firm grasp of time. Four easy strides carried him to the doorway between his two rooms. Three more strides took him to the overstuffed couch. It was covered in deep crimson cloth with pale gray stripes matching the colors of the rug in the center of the room. The couch faced the door to his quarters.

Alec sat as he called out, "Come in."

The door swung inward on well-oiled brass hinges admitting his new team. They flowed into the room with that way of moving that people who have trained their bodies possessed.

Sophie's voice was warm with a light chiming sound. "Alec, it's time for Common Meal. It is customary for the entire team to eat together." Her smile was only the slightest of hints on her lips. No teeth, no curving of those full lips, only a vague pulling at the corners of her mouth. It was the tone of her voice that gave the almost-smile life. For the fifth time today, his mind threw up to him the fact that she was incredibly beautiful. He would not let her know he was thinking it though. In his experience, it was a bad idea.

Alec sat his cup on the small, low, table in front of the couch. Standing slowly, he straightened his white coat as he looked at his team.

Smiling an easy smile Alec said, "Now that I think about it, I could eat. Do we go now?" Both of his eyebrows rose slightly with the question.

Tessa walked over. She put her arm around his shoulder. Speaking slowly as if to a little brother who did not quite understand what was going on she said, "Yes Alec. We. Go. Now." She laughed loudly while holding on tightly to him as Alec tried to push her away. It was a half-hearted attempt. Alec was smiling as he moved around the room fending her off while she tried to cling to him. The others joined in the laughter as Tessa began to make kissing sounds. Alec was almost running before Tessa finally gave up the chase. They were all laughing, as they worked on winding down from a long, tense, day. Laughter was always good medicine. Alec remembered his Nana, his mother's mother, saying that when he was little. She would grab him so she could tickle him until he could not breathe. Alec had learned never to pout around Nanna or he would suffer the consequences.

They all stepped into the hall outside Alec's quarters pausing long enough for Alec to close the door behind them. They all fell into step behind Rex. Twenty minutes later they were entering the Peoples Tower with a stream of other members of the Company. There were white and black coats everywhere. The black coats outnumbered the white five to one.

The Peoples Tower was an eight-sided wonder of architecture that reached into the sky as if it were the first finger on the hand of the Ancient directing the movement of the heavens. Alec could only guess at how many stories high it could actually be. It was mostly large burgundy stone blocks with white sandstone as accent around the doors and windows. Stepping through one of the several doorways that let you into the Tower Alec discovered that they opened into tunnels. The exterior wall of the Tower was similar to the wall surrounding Sanctuary. It was several long paces deep. Exiting the tunnel with a stream of other Company members as well as his teammates Alec's mouth fell open, but no words came out. Stopping just past the exit of the tunnel he had just walked through he stared, almost stunned, as people flowed around him like a sea parting.

The words that could adequately describe what Alec was seeing escaped him. He had fancied himself someone who had been exposed to art, but this awed him. He looked up into open space. The view expanded up farther than the eye could see clearly. Alec knew he was gawking like a farmer just in from the countryside, but he could not help but crane his neck back to stare.

There were, in point of fact, not one, but two towers. There was an outer tower, which he had just walked through, which enclosed an open space of at least fifty long strides, followed by the inner tower. Thought after thought wheeled through his head. Before one thought could be fully formed another was already taking its place. *What must it have taken to balance ... how many people were needed to build ... how did they make it so high* ... his thoughts flitted from one idea to another. The tower was not taller than the peak of Ruler's Hill out of respect for the Empress, but it surely surpassed the Imperial Palace in the ambitious nature of its design.

As he turned slowly, continuing to look up, Alec could see walkways stretching from the inner tower to the outer one across the open intervening space. The walkways crossed to each floor for as high as he could see. The interior face of the outer tower was covered by open-faced walkways on each level. The railings, which appeared to be of a polished, dark, wood must have been intended as a restraint to keep people from falling. On every level he could see people moving about, along walkways, some even crossing the walkways that connected the outer tower to the inner one. All of the things he was viewing were doubly amazing because of the knowledge that the outer tower enclosed it all.

"Close your mouth before a fly gets in there and spoils your meal." The voice was Tessa of course followed by the laughter of his team with the exception of Finn who was fiddling with a small piece of something. They were all standing several feet away waiting for Alec to finish gawking.

So, with a sigh, Alec took hold of himself. Pulling his eyes away from the sheer immensity of the structure he fell back into step with his team. Boot soles padded softly on the marble floor beneath their feet. Approaching the inner tower, it dawned on Alec that they could be in for an incredibly long, potentially exhausting, climb up what had to be an interminable number of steps. Grunting to himself, at the thought of all those steps, he began to prepare himself mentally. He guessed it was the price you paid for architectural wonders.

Finn pulled open another door on the face of the inner tower. They all walked into what appeared to be a large closet. Standing alongside one another they waited as Alec filed into the closet behind them. Finn closed the door behind them. Alec opened his mouth to express his puzzlement. *Why were they standing in a closet?* But before he could express his confusion Rex spoke to a large blue sapphire embedded in the front wall to the right of the closed door.

"Fourteenth floor please." Rex spoke in between humming some tune Alec could not make out.

The blue sapphire glowed to an unearthly light. Only that split-second warning kept Alec from jumping as a soft female voice spoke with an odd tone. There were hints of other voices beneath it though they all spoke in unison. Alec thought the other voices were saying other things that he could not make out.

She said, *"Thank you for your request Rex Aloran. Fourteenth floor."*

A soft humming immediately followed the voice. There was a vibration accompanied by the sensation of climbing. Alec's stomach tried to sink to his knees. Before he could say anything, Sophie was answering his unspoken question.

Sophie's voice had an absentminded quality to it like she was thinking about other things while talking to him. "It is called a *Lift*. It was made by Tinker. Tink is our resident, masterful, Maker." She was staring at nothing in particular as she spoke. Finn was rocking from front to back. There was no sign of what he had been working on earlier. Rex was still humming while Tessa was leaning into the corner with her arms folded across her chest. Alec just stared at the blue sapphire that continued to glow. *Fascinating*, he thought. He had heard of what Makers were capable of doing. But hearing and seeing were often two entirely different things.

Alec felt the closet – the *Lift* - slow before coming to a stop. The blue sapphire pulsed again.

"Fourteenth floor. Enjoy Common Meal." The voice sounded as if it knew what it was saying as the other voices echoed at it edges.

Rex stepped from the closet as Finn opened the door. He spoke on his way out.

"Thank you Saza." He said it like it was second nature.

Each of his team said their thanks as they exited the Lift. Alec hesitated for a moment then followed their example.

"Thank you Saza." Alec said as he stepped out of the lift.

Closing the door behind him Alec turned to follow the rest of his team while shaking his head. Just when you thought you had a grasp on what was going on you found that your hand was empty.

What Rex had called the fourteenth floor turned out to be where the dining hall was located. Standing in the large alcove, just a few paces from where he had exited the Lift, Alec looked through its large archway into a vast chamber. It had to be capable of serving a thousand people at one sitting. Tonight, it appeared to be close to capacity. He took in the hall in one sweeping glance. Surprisingly the meal was proceeding quite orderly given the number of people being served. Each wall, with the exception of the one containing the Lifts – there seemed to be more than one - housed a doorway to a kitchen where the food was prepared.

Cooks, along with servers, wearing black linen trimmed in white, floated among the tables serving food to those who were seated. They carried platters as well as various sized bowls with large wooden spoons sticking out of them. As they passed those who were standing about talking they muttered looking at them as if they were in the way.

A low, but rising, rumble erupted in Alec's stomach. Apparently, he was hungry. It dawned on him, at that moment, that he had not eaten all day. The smell of food, coupled with the sound of utensils hitting plates, rushed over him. He was not simply hungry he was starving. Scanning the room Alec quickly located his team. As he spotted them it seemed they were only just realizing that he was not with them. They waved him over to the table they had selected. Walking to the table his nose caught a full whiff of something sweet. His mouth immediately began to water. Something, somewhere, smelled very good. He didn't yet know what he was catching a whiff of but whatever it was it *had* to taste good. Since he was so hungry he imagined it would taste even better than the cook had intended. Hunger had a way of doing just that.

Filling his nose, as he continued toward the table, he tried to inventory the smells that were floating about. He caught the zest of lemon, which he knew right away. Honey, along with the strong scent of garlic, was also fairly easy to identify. By the time he reached the table he had achieved the kind of single-mindedness his swordmaster would have applauded inside the Master's Wheel. So, intent was he that he almost missed the look Sophie gave him. Wide eyes coupled with raised eyebrows said, *what were you doing?* He motioned around the room as if to say, *gawking again.* He took his seat.

The table was an Argonian long table. But instead of the matching long bench that would have normally accompanied such a table there were individual chairs. *That was good*, Alec thought. There was no need to have to worry about someone else's movements disturbing your own. Alec liked to eat with a chair he could lean back in. The floor was Cocan tile while the walls were white with cream trim framed in stained cherry wood. Fresh flowers were arranged in clear, heavy, crystal vases on each table. At that moment, it dawned on Alec that he had been hearing music since stepping from the lift. Turning his head, he searched the hall with his eyes attempting to locate … *there they were.*

In the center of the dining hall was a collection of musicians. The musicians were dressed in shimmering long coats with lace falling from collars or high-necked gowns with bell-sleeves. All of the apparel was in some form of black trimmed in white. Alec counted nine pieces including string, metal, and wind instruments. They were playing in the tradition of the Imperial Symphony, it could have even been a Makran composition, but he was not sure.

Across the length of the hall there were no tables higher or lower than any other, no dais or stage, nor head table. The way the hall was arranged suggested that in this place all were equal. With a lovely melody floating across the hall to delight his ears Alec began to relax. Not only had he been famished he had been wound tight as a drum. Tension that had gone unnoticed began leaking away. His shoulders loosened just as his back began unknotting. He leaned back in his padded, high-back, chair. The aromas, the music, all mixed with jovial conversation, poured in replacing the tension. The darkness that had been pent up in him began to drain away like water from a leaky boat. Leaning back in his chair Alec allowed himself to feel the joy bubbling up in the hall.

"Now that is what I have been waiting to see." Tessa's deep alto carried to Alec from where she loomed over the table in her seat.

Tessa had pulled her long golden hair back, tying it, with a leather cord. Her elbows straddled the table, one hand lying flat, the other propping up her chin. Bright teeth gleamed as her eyes glittered in the light given off by the countless lamps hanging from the walls balanced by those sitting evenly spaced down the center of the tables.

She continued, "He can smile. Wonder of wonders, he is actually relaxing."

She nodded at him. Alec thought she had a very good smile as he nodded back.

Finn interrupted Tessa as she was opening her mouth to continue. "All right Tess, that's enough. You have been harassing our new mate all day. Now let him be." Finn's own smile was infectious taking the bite out of his comments to Tessa. She turned on Finn.

"Well! Wonders never will cease, will they? The mute speaks. What next, will the lame walk, or the dead rise? Has the Anointed come into the world again to bring the Age of Peace?" Forming her face into an exaggerated look of surprise Tessa got everyone laughing again. Finn, who had been leaning back in his chair, lost his balance. He fell back. His chair slammed to the floor. Everyone laughed all the louder. They spent the next few minutes trying to stop laughing. Finn's attempts to get up, coupled with the server's expressions of exasperation as they tried to help him up, kept them all in fits. Just as one calmed down, another person would start up without anyone speaking. It went on like that until the drinks arrived.

Alec continued to let his smile have free reign across his face. It felt good to let his guard down. Everyone had made it clear that he was one of them now. The Commander-General had said that this place was now his home. Alec had to admit that it was beginning to feel that way.

Alec saw Rex reclined in his seat with his eyes closed. The man had his hands behind his head. Sophie had liberated a flower from the vase in front of her. Her nose was resting in its yellow petals while she twirled its stem between her fingers. Finn had regained his seat but reached hesitantly for the table's edge every time one of the servers or some other person passed behind him. Alec told himself, *do not laugh. Do not laugh.* Tessa had turned her attention to the cup of choca that arrived on a platter in the hands of a small, but stout, brown-eyed, woman with sandy brown hair bound in one long braid trailing down her back.

The two women exchanged pleasantries. Alec just listened to the conversation. When a cup was handed to him it came with a welcoming pat on his back from the young woman Tessa had called Megan. Megan placed a cup in front of Alec on the table and poured it just shy of full of fresh, steaming choca. Looking him briefly in the eye she rubbed his back slowly as though comforting someone who was nervous or anxious. Her smile had a familiar curve. It was something in the way she showed her teeth. When he realized it was like his mother's smile he swallowed hard. The fullness of the day tried to wash over him all at once. Alec saw in Megan's eyes that certain something that said she had seen great suffering. They had been present, those eyes, at some private tragedy, which they had recorded leaving indelible images on her mind. The person who now gazed out from those eyes had been changed by it – whatever *it* had been - its remnants were there in those pale brown pools that were looking down at Alec.

She said to him, "Welcome home, it's good to have you with us."

Alec smiled but could not speak. The events of the day swirled around him almost attacking him. The way strangers had come to his aid, how they had fought for him in a way no one had since his parents, came rushing in. In the blink of an eye he had new friends that appeared to be honest and affable. All of that coupled with this moment with the smile he had not seen for some fifteen years. Megan was new to him, but her smile was as old as he was. The tears were there though he did not let them fall. Alec drank some of the choca without adding cream or sugar. His throat was tight with emotion.

The food began to arrive. Alec was thankful that it occupied his teammates. Megan turned to fill other cups with choca leaving Alec without anyone's attention directly on him. The smell of food, the sound of music, the laughter matched only by the smiles, the loss of tension, all added up to one thing. Sipping again at his choca he let one word reverberate in his mind. It wiped away all the dross of the thoughts of the day's events. *Home.* This place was as new as anything he had ever encountered in Alexandria while managing to be as old as the memory of another place, another time, another group of people. He smiled slowly again, fully, recognizing as his plate arrived, that he was, indeed, home.

A tortured knuckle speaks of wind
A worried knee smells rain
An anxious elbow, buffeting clouds adorn
A scornful back, a coming storm
These worries, these aches
Tell the tale of what the sky will make

~Ethini Skywatcher
The Rain rhyme

If you walk in the dark, expect to stub your toe.

~Kalim Barone
Professor of Ethics
Calot school of Thought
Lower Bree

CHAPTER EIGHT

A change in the weather

Consciousness eluded him. It was as if he were trying to hold a handful of water that kept escaping through his fingers. One moment he was awake, trying to get his bearings, but then, without warning, the darkness would reach up to swallow him whole again. He knew it was his head. Though he could not reach up with his hands to touch the wound, the pain was there each time he clawed his way up from that disembodied blackness. Each time he had come awake the throbbing in his head had lessened, but it was always there to take hold of him again.

Finally, like a man tired of a swim, who turned toward the shore, he managed to pull himself out of the unrelenting darkness to remain awake. Time was utterly lost to him, a thing forgotten, while he had fought to remain awake. The pain in his head had finally subsided to a dull murmuring instead of an overpowering, nauseating roar. Something, or someone, had hit him hard.

There was no way of knowing how long he had been slipping in and out of consciousness. The best he could do was guess, based on the ache in his muscles, the growth of hair on his face, as he rubbed his chin against his shoulder. Maybe it had been a day or so since he had been –

been what? Information eluded him. What he wanted to know was there, but he could not reach it, could not pull it to the forefront of his mind. In that moment it dawned on him again that he did not know where he was, or worse, who he was. The enclosure he was in still cloaked him in darkness. It must have been an enclosed wagon because it continued to rock with the motion of turning wheels on uneven ground as it rolled to wherever he was being taken.

Suddenly, he realized that he was working himself free of the ropes that bound him. The way he had worked against his bonds was beginning to ease their grasp on his hands. *Chains on captives* – the thought floated across his mind - though even they could be beaten given enough time. He did not know where the knowledge came from, only that it was there, floating in the great void that was his memory. A few more minutes passed before he had worked his way free of the ropes around his wrists. With his hands unbound he managed to quickly free his legs. Sitting still against one of the walls of the rocking, rattling enclosure he took inventory of his physical condition. Apparently, aside from the lump on his head, which he could now run his fingers over, even as it still pulsed dully with pain, as well as a few abrasions from the ropes, he seemed to be in good shape. Running his hands over the length of his body while working his limbs allowed him to deduce that he was in really good shape. He seemed to be in the kind of shape that came from intense training. In the darkness, he flexed well-developed arms. Feeling at his freed wrists, he realized, that even though he did not remember that training, apparently, his body did. After taking enough time to loosen sore muscles he thought he was ready. Breathing deeply, he felt his body gathering itself in preparation for what he was thinking. He balanced himself easily as the wagon continued to sway, lurching roughly to one side periodically, on what had to be a road in bad disrepair. Running his hands across the wooden walls of the wagon he found what he was looking for. He felt at the seams that told him where a door was located. Feeling the way the wagon moved he concluded that the door was at the rear of the wagon. The fact that the interior of the wagon was hot, leaving him with sweat dripping from his chin and running lazily down his chest, led him to believe that it was relatively warm outside of its confines. At least he was hoping that was the case. Moving around, in the cold, in only his smallclothes was not an appealing thought.

He stood on his bare feet, nearly naked, taking another deep breath as the feeling of a rush of energy ran through his body. Without further thought he lashed out at the door. Twisting sharply, in the narrow space, he threw a viscous, spinning, back-kick that caused the door to fly open. Jumping from the back of the still moving wagon he let his body, which seemed to know what it was doing, go to work.

Rutted, uneven earth greeted his bare feet, but he immediately adjusted, crouching slightly as he landed, maintaining his balance. Without thinking about how his body was shifting beneath him, redistributing his weight, he was already turning, quickly marking potential threats. The road was simple, compacted dirt, which accounted for the deep ruts caused by wagons rolling on it after a heavy rainfall.

The road was wide enough for the wagon he had been in as well as a few horses with room to spare. On either side of the road thick forest stretched for as far as the eye could see. In the distance, to his left, was a mountain range. The rest of the surrounding country was vast wilderness. They were in the middle of nowhere.

On the road behind him, bringing up the rear, were three men, heavily armed, on horseback, wearing leather coupled with the glint of chainmail. On top of the wagon was a man carrying a crossbow. Coming around the side of the wagon as it was rolling to a halt were two other men on foot. He had to assume that there was at least one more man pulling on the wagon team's reigns. He had counted seven. His heart pounded, his blood raced, but there was, at the same time, something very familiar about it all. Even though his mind was racing he was not panicked. He expected to be overwhelmed at any moment by a tidal wave of fear. But for some reason his body was utterly relaxed. He had assumed a stance without thought. He was presenting his left side to the wagon with the horsemen at his back. Listening intently to every sound behind him he let the rest of him focus on the men coming from the wagon. The wave of fear he expected never came.

The man on the roof of the wagon loosed a crossbow bolt at him. Instead of trying to duck, or roll out of the way, his right hand curved around in front of him snatching the bolt from the air. Momentarily stunned by what he had just done he threw the bolt to the ground as he spun in one fluid motion wondering where in the bloody Betrayer's prison he had learned to do that? But there was no time. The two on foot were moving in on him. He could hear the horsemen, behind him, closing fast. The crossbowman was reloading with a flood of curses that would have singed the ears of anyone close enough to hear him.

Putting aside his shock, he tried not to think. He just allowed himself to act, and it was working. The two on foot rushed him with swords drawn. The man to his right was first, pulling up just short of him with a stop-lunge, fully extending himself. An instant before the man would have run him through he twisted to his right. As he slid his body along the length of the sword he rotated his right arm over the passing blade. As the hilt of the man's sword passed him he clamped his right hand around the man's wrist. Twisting the wrist sharply he pulled it in toward his own body. He extended the man's wrist past its normal range of motion. With a sharp scream the man dropped his sword. Stepping into the man, pulling him onto his hip, he wrenched the arm over his shoulder, hurling the man into his partner. It knocked them both to the ground. As the man passed over his shoulder, into the air, the hilt of a long, wide-bladed knife, tucked into the man's swordbelt, rubbed across his right hand. He snatched it free without thought.

He looked down to see that he had caught the hilt of his first attacker's falling sword on his foot just below the handguard. Kicking up with that foot he launched the sword into the air. It floated up in front of him where he snatched it out of the air with his right hand as he flipped the knife to his left. Taking a step forward, as the two men began to get up from the ground, he launched the liberated knife from his left hand with a smooth flick of his wrist. The knife, spinning hilt over blade, sank, with a thick thud, into the chest of the crossbowman atop the wagon. The man had been lining up a second shot as the knife sunk home. It took a second for him to realize that he was dead before he dropped, with a loud clatter, to the roof of the wagon, while the crossbow skidded off the roof.

He continued to spin to his right catching the grounded men as they were rising to their feet. He cut across the first one's midsection with his liberated sword. He did not hesitate. Hesitation in battle is a death sentence. He reversed his motion, stepping to his left, putting the now crouching, disemboweled, man between himself and the second attacker. Feinting, he made as if to turn toward the horsemen who were almost on top of him, which froze the second footman's attack for an instant. As the disemboweled footman fell to the ground screaming he stuck the borrowed sword underneath the second footman's guard catching him in the neck. Blood spurted from the man's neck pouring down the length of his borrowed sword.

As the second footman fell he stabbed the borrowed sword into the ground as he dove over the dying bodies at his feet. He managed to pull two more knives from their belts as he flew over them. Rolling up to his feet, he turned, in one fluid motion, launching the knives at the horsemen. He hit one in the eye while the second knife sunk deep into the second horseman's shoulder. The third horsemen continued forward raising his sword high as he screamed. When the horse was right on top of him he feinted toward the horseman's sword-arm but grabbed the horse's bridle instead. Swinging his body around to the other side of the horse he put himself opposite the horseman's sword-arm while his weight on the bridle caused the horse to pull up hard. The horse lurched to its left as he grabbed the saddle pommel with his right hand. Pulling hard on the pommel he brought himself up into the saddle as he drove his knee into the rider's left side. The result was the horseman flying from the horse's back.

With a second hop he settled fully into the vacant saddle before reining the horse in. He quickly surveyed his surroundings from horseback. The man he had just unsaddled lay unmoving with his head at an odd angle. His first two attackers lay in a heap where he had left them while all that could be seen of the crossbowman was a leg hanging limply from the roof of the wagon. The third horseman, with the knife wound in his shoulder, was nowhere to be seen. Kicking the horse into a slow walk he leaned over in the saddle so he could reach down to the borrowed sword he had stuck in the ground. It came free easily as he passed. With the sword in his hand he rode around to the front of the wagon. The driver's seat was empty. Off to his left he could hear the distant sound of branches breaking in the woods. Suddenly, it was quiet. All he could hear was his own breathing. Though oddly, after all of that exertion, he was not breathing hard.

Though he was still on edge he circled the wagon three more times before deciding that there were no more immediate threats. He dismounted. He patted the horse's shoulder, but it did not seem to need calming. As his feet hit the ground the immensity of what he had done struck him. He was stunned. Who can kill several men and walk away without a scratch? He turned his empty hand over staring at it like it belonged to someone else. He stood there wondering even as something in the back of his mind pushed at him. It was a sense of urgency. Somehow, he knew he was not safe yet. He could not just stand around staring at his hands or wondering who he was. Things needed to be done so that he could get away from this wagon. Shaking himself from his reverie he forced himself to move.

As he stepped around the stallion he ran a hand over him. He was excellent stock. He quickly catalogued the strong legs, deep chest, and good curvature, which was all complemented by a nice arch of the neck. The stallion would serve his purpose.

As he approached the front of the wagon he heard a deep rumbling in the distance. When he looked skyward he saw that dark clouds had begun to gather. He had not noticed, while fighting for his life, that the evening was warm but overcast. Breathing deeply through his nose he caught the musty hint of rain in the air. An errant thought about joints combined with changing weather skirted the edge of his mind but was gone before it could fully form. He turned his thoughts from the weather so he could focus his attention on a quick search. All the while, during his search, he kept an eye out for the man with the knife wound in his shoulder. The missing driver did not concern him as much.

Upon searching the wagon, he found supplies, coin, and clothing in a small chest-like compartment behind the driver's seat. After dressing quickly, he turned to search the dead men. He took a pair of black, leather, riding boots off one of the men who was almost his exact height. They were nearly new, with a large silver buckle adorning the top, along the outside. Remarkably, they fit like they had been made for him. He tucked the cream-colored breeches he had found into the tops of the knee-high boots. He took the same man's vest. It was purple wool, with tan stitching, complemented by black wood buttons. A clean, white, blousy shirt with a large collar was tucked in the back of the compartment. It may have been hidden because of the pearl buttons running down the front.

Lastly, he put all the swords together in a line. One by one he tested each of them. A few cuts at phantom opponents gave him the heft as well as the balance of each. He decided on a long, slightly curved, single-edged saber with a handguard that was like a steel, see-through basket worked in silver. The basket covered the hands as they held the hilt, which was wrapped in good leather, but did not prevent a two-handed grip. The hilt was a full span in length. The metal was a gleaming alloy that would hold a fine edge without becoming bent or otherwise marked. Too bad its owner had not been as skilled as his blade was fine. He walked over to where one of the men lay motionless on the ground. Bending down, he unlatched the black, leather swordbelt that the dead man was wearing around his waist. He pulled it off along with the sword's scabbard. The scabbard was wood, stained with black lacquer, with a polished, steel tip matched by a steel band at the scabbard's mouth. It was a fine piece of craftsmanship. The man should have invested as much time practicing with the sword as he had invested coin to purchase it. Sliding the sword home, he pushed the scabbard through a loop on the swordbelt. He buckled the belt around his waist. It was sliver worked into the shape of three small intertwining circles. While packing the saddlebags with coin, food, and the rest of the supplies he had located he wondered, absently, at what the emblem meant. Finally, after throwing the saddlebags on the horse he threw on a voluminous black cloak. The last thing he confiscated was the crossbow that had been fired at him from the roof of the wagon. It was a thing of steel mixed with wood. That it was light, and made of expensive materials, with pearl inlaid on the stock, lead him to believe it was custom made. He had to climb onto the wagon's roof to retrieve the quiver full of bolts. Once he had climbed back down he quickly strapped both to the back of his saddle.

Equipped, and satisfied that he was not being watched, he mounted the stallion he had taken. As the sky rumbled more loudly, while growing ever darker, he urged the brown stallion away from the mess he had just made at a slow trot. As he rode he decided to call the horse Speckle. The brown stallion had white spots across its chest. While he rode, he watched the horizon. Before he rode too far he decided he needed a name as well. Everyone needed a name even when you could not remember your real one. Looking at the dark clouds rolling in he felt the darkness of his own mood, which was likely a result of what he was leaving behind him. The name Alla'mirridin floated up from the endless darkness of his memory along with its meaning. Somehow, he knew it meant an *approaching storm.*

After trotting a few miles down the road, he turned Speckle off into the woods heading east. Alla'mirridin decided to follow the road the wagon had been traveling on but to do it at an oblique angle. He would crisscross the road working his way toward whatever town, village, or city they may have been heading toward. This would allow him to be sure he was not being followed. He might even pick up the trail of one of the two men who had survived the encounter at the wagon. Someone had wanted him trussed up in the back of that wagon. They had not minded injuring him in the process. *I am going to find out who and why,* he thought. As the darkness of early evening fell so did a light rain. He pulled up the hood of his cloak, which had a light coating of something that made the water bead up before it rolled off. Alla'mirridin wrapped the oversized cloak around him nestling back into the recesses of its oversized hood. As raindrops hit the cloak the elusive thought about storms, followed by joints, came to him fully causing him to laugh softly into the oncoming darkness. Some farmers believed that aching joints meant approaching storms. Speckle tossed his head, snorting, as if in defiance at the rain that was falling on him as he trotted on. Alla'mirridin used that thought for fuel. Whoever they were, whoever had cost him his memory, had trussed him up like a beast going to market, they had best be listening to any aching joints they had. Those joints would be the only warning they would have to tell them the weather was about to change. A storm was rolling in from the east. It was headed directly toward them. Wrapped in the darkness of his black cloak, he road on, shrouded in the cloud-covered darkness of the oncoming night. A storm was coming.

†

Junior Inquisitor Polshem Delver walked across the encampment toward the tent of Baquent Hevendere. The Inquisitor's tent was noticeable for two reasons. The first was that it was the largest tent in the camp. The second was the seal of the Inquisitorem, which flew on its flagpole. Polshem's eyes caught the familiar insignia as the wind pulled the flag taut with a snap. The standard was a stylized eye partially covered by a curtain of twinkling stars. The colors were green, gray and black on a field of midnight blue. Many thought they knew what that standard meant but only the initiated really knew. A small smile crept across his face, as he thought, *in time they will all know*. That time was not now, he knew, as he turned his attention back to the task at hand. As he approached the Inquisitor's tent he was struck by a few errant raindrops. Hitching at his green cloak he halted in front of the entrance.

The two guards, hard looking Legionnaires, recognized him as he came close enough for the two watchfires to bath him in light. The man to Polshem's left nodded curtly before stepping into the tent. Polshem waited while he heard the faint murmur of conversation. The guard, in his Legionnaire red trimmed in blue, stepped back out of the tent motioning for Polshem to enter.

Polshem stepped into the tent. As the heavy flap fell away behind him the heat emanating from a small fire washed over him. That warmth made him realize that there had been a slight chill in the night air. He stood at attention just inside the tent. He waited patiently as protocol dictated. His senior would get to him when he was ready. The Inquisitor's tent was spacious. The ground was covered with a tarp, which was covered, in turn, by two large throw rugs. The tent was large enough to hold twenty men with room to spare.

The Inquisitor liked space but was not overly concerned for things to fill it. The tent had a small, wood burning, stove that was presently being put to use heating the tent. The top of the stove held a pot that must have contained choca. The smell of the dark, ground, bean being brewed was unmistakable. The stove also had a tall pipe, which stuck out of a small hole in the top of the tent venting the smoke it produced. With a quick glance Polshem could see a large circular table covered with papers. There was a cot with a stuffed mattress, two oversized armchairs, as well as various chests spaced around the tent's interior.

Baquent Hevendere looked up from a piece of parchment he was reading. The man flashed Polshem a white-toothed smile. The voice accompanying that smile was as warm as the fire that crackled in the stove's black, cast iron belly.

"Young Delver. Good evening, Alexandria must fall." Hevendere greeted him with what had become the traditional greeting of Province.

Delver bowed slightly at the waist, with a minor nod of the head in respect, the proper amount from junior to senior. As his head came up he returned the traditional greeting, "Good evening sir. Alexandria must fall."

Baquent Hevendere waved a hand absently motioning Polshem to the armchair a few feet from where he was sitting. "Bring that pot of choca from the stove with you my young friend." As he finished speaking he went back to studying the yellowish page in his hand.

Polshem made his way to the stove. Grabbing a thick towel, which hung from a towel bar attached to the stove, he grabbed the pot of choca, wrapping the towel around the hot handle. Walking over to where Hevendere sat he took the measure of the senior Inquisitor again. Hevendere was a man of average height with a matching build. He was actually a half a head shorter than Polshem, but he was not a man to be trifled with. The eyes that studied the page in his hand were black as the night sky. The graying black hair on his head was short, but long enough to style. The sides were trimmed close while the top had been curled just so. The curved mustache, matched by the pointed shortbeard on his chin, gave him a kind of gravity. His skin was the golden complexion of a man used to being in the sun. He had a rugged jaw balanced by a high forehead. It all made for a visage that allowed him to command respect with looks that could make a man tell his darkest secrets.

Thick fingers held the page up as Hevendere continued in thought. His green longcoat was draped over the end of his cot. He sat in a matching green shirt. The gray wool breeches had broad green strips down the outside of each leg. The polish on his rust-brown boots reflected the firelight. Polshem hitched his right shoulder adjusting, unconsciously, the fit of his own green longcoat. The only difference between what he and Hevendere wore were the gold leaves that encircled the cuffs of Hevendere's green shirt. Had he been wearing his longcoat one would have been able to see matching gold leaves embroidered around those cuffs as well. An Inquisitor outranking Hevendere would have golden vines, sprouting golden leaves, running up the length of the sleeves on both shirt and longcoat. *Those embroidered gold leaves would be his, one day.*

Polshem cleared his throat softly. Hevendere looked up, smiling again, showing his gleaming, bright, white teeth. Reaching to the right of his chair Hevendere picked up a cup, with its matching saucer, which had been resting on a small table with several other dishes. Polshem poured the dark-brown liquid into Hevendere's cup before he turned to replace it on the stovetop where it would remain hot.

Hevendere's voice stopped him. "Lad, you may share a cup with me."

Polshem turned back in time to see Hevendere motion at a second cup, with its own matching saucer, sitting on the small table. Polshem quickly poured himself a cup before replacing the pot on the stove. As he returned to his seat, retrieving the proffered cup balanced on its saucer, Hevendere pulled the tops off two small porcelain containers. One held a brown-colored sugar, the other an off-white cream. Cream was rare road fare so Polshem accepted the offer with a broad grin of his own. He did not mind choca without such accompaniments, but it was much nicer with them.

With the contents of his cup mixed, Polshem settled back in the chair he had been directed to, sipping his choca, as he waited for direction from his senior. While pouring the cup of choca he had noticed that Hevendere was looking at a map of the region. But even having seen what Hevendere was studying so intently there was still no way of telling what the man was thinking. Inquisitors did not survive by being easy to read. The *Progression* weeded out such weak candidates for the Inquisitorem. Polshem had practiced that same impervious look. He knew he would need it. After a brief time Hevendere looked up from the map to address him.

"Now, Junior Inquisitor, what pray tell, have you discovered?" He gazed at Polshem with anticipation.

Polshem cleared his throat and began his report. They had found tracks around the burned-out installation but could not tell how a fairly large group had arrived at the site. Further, a wagon accompanied by several men had gone northeast toward Upper Gaul, but they were not believed to be the same people who had left the most recent tracks around the Orb installation.

Hevendere nodded slowly as he listened to the report while continuing to drink his choca. When Polshem was finished Hevendere looked again at the map he had been studying earlier, nodding to himself, as if something had been confirmed in his mind.

Looking up again he said, "Take a detachment toward Upper Gaul. I want to find that group of men. Tell McCove to strike camp. We leave tonight." His voice was matter-of-fact. It had the tone of finality.

Polshem braved a question. "Sir. You have the answer to who we are looking for?"

Hevendere nodded, putting the map down, before looking up at Polshem. His voice took on the tone of instruction. "Note: The surrounding terrain is such that we would have found some sign of a large force marching on the installation. Since we cannot find that evidence there is only one possibility. The large group must have arrived by some method other than over land. There is no access by water so they must have come by some means other than land or water. That leaves one real possibility. Note two: As to the wagon that left to the west it has to be someone independent of the large group or they would have left the same way the larger group did, hence the two groups are not directly related, only indirectly. Conclusion: Find the wagon and you can at least confirm what can only be inferred by the larger group's mode of travel."

Polshem nodded his understanding making the necessary mental notes in case Hevendere later called on him to repeat any part, or all, of the *Notations and Conclusions*. Rising from his seat he placed the cup and saucer on the small table. He came to attention, inclining his head, in salute to the Inquisitor.

Hevendere said, "Seek and Find my young Inquisitor. Seek and Find."

Polshem replied, "I shall look where you have pointed me Inquisitor."

With an absent, almost imperceptible, nod of dismissal Hevendere turned his attention back to other pieces of parchment he was picking up from the table next to his cup of choca. Polshem stepped out into the night air, which seemed colder for his having been in the warmed tent. After a half-hearted nod at the guards he stalked off across the camp. He would find Terrel McCove so that he could issue the proper orders. He would stay in Baquent Hevendere's shadow for now because the man still had his uses. As Polshem approached the area of the camp where he had last seen McCove more erratic drops of rain hit his face. Looking up at the dark clouds he knew it was not just going to be a rainfall. It was going to storm. He put his brown leather gloves on. As he stalked off into the darkness he pulled his green cloak about him more tightly.

*There are three things the wise never do,
Stand between a child and its mother,
A love and their lover,
Or a Watchman and The Watch.*

~An Alexandrian saying

Never cross a person who is better than you in a fight.

~Heeth Bandabain
*Consummate ale drinker, and self styled
Philospher at The Winding Clock tavern,
Brill Street, in Copis*

Chapter nine

A touch from the dark

They never ran. *Well, almost never,* he thought. But this was not a time for the normal way of things. They were not running in the truest sense of the word. At least they were not running *from* something. They were running *toward* something. In Cordovan's mind that was a towering distinction. Even though he held that notion in his mind he still had not been able to shake the feeling that someone, or something, was behind them. Something was chasing them.

The rapid, rhythmic cacophony of thudding reverberated in the back of his mind as the hooves of their horses pounded the ground they hurtled across. Cordovan scanned the terrain in front of them as Swift carried him, unerringly, forward. He held his focus like an archer aiming at a moving target. Night had newly fallen. The darkness shrouded the wooded countryside in shadows. Even though it was dangerous to ride in the dark they could not stop. *If they were too late* - but Cordovan would not even allow himself to complete the thought. When it came to Her *The Watch* could not be late. It wasn't that the notion was just too horrible to contemplate. It was the fact that *Watchmen* were not even allowed to consider failure when it came to Her. It was really simple. If they failed, they were not who they claimed to be. The Great Oath would become just another empty collection of words to be studied at some University or added to the list of other creeds that had been wonderfully idealistic but utterly impractical. Cordovan would not allow the Great Oath, or Her, to fall because of his inability to do what he had spent most of his life preparing to do.

Since *She* had been a child, he knew he had wanted to stand to The Watch. Only the best were accepted. Once they were commissioned, they were allowed to take the Great Oath. He had trained, and studied, with abandon in order to ensure that when he applied he would be accepted. As he urged Swift on, he knew he might be doing irreparable harm to her. She had carried him faithfully for years. She deserved better than to be run to death. Yet Cordovan could not allow the Oath to be shattered on his Watch. He would allow himself to be shattered, along with his mount, but not the Oath.

A low hanging branch slashed across Cordovan's shoulder as Swift thundered down the narrow path that trailed through the Minwood. Swift was well trained. She was a mature mare sired to be fearless. *She* gave the Watch the very best. They had the best training, weapons, and mounts coin could buy.

Chancing a glance behind him Cordovan looked over his purple cloak, which flapped in the wind. He could see Tark, Opus, and Mallory. Fairuk, Assum, followed by Salk would be further back in the trees. Cordovan knew the other three would be spread out, flanking him, but within earshot of the sound of his own horses pounding hooves. They did not have much time. He urged Swift forward. *Faster,* he thought. The Ancient One forgive him if, in his haste to reach Her, he broke Swift with this mad gallop.

The path widened abruptly. The trees seemed further apart up ahead. The treetops kept the path murky at best with the little moonlight there was to be had streaking through the forests canopy like sunshine through breaks in a dark cloud. Cordovan found himself thinking that this small clearing would be a good place for a – he did not get to finish the thought. Fire erupted from the ground in front of him. Swift pulled up short throwing Cordovan clear of her flashing hooves. He hit the ground hard. He exhaled sharply while relaxing his body in an effort to absorb the impact. Rolling with the momentum of his fall he came to his feet in one, smooth, fluid motion freeing his sword from its scabbard. Everything seemed to happen at once.

Tark had been riding directly behind Cordovan. As he came to his feet he saw Tark reining in Cadence. A rope net had ensnared them both. Mallory thundered into the clearing astride Maple. Just as he reached the clearing he took a crossbow bolt to the thigh. Cordovan watched, almost frozen in place, as Mallory fell from the saddle of the large chestnut. Before he could move to help darkness fell all around him.

Cordovan felt as though a cold hand had reached inside his chest. It was as if that hand was gripping his heart in an icy clutch. He could hear horses dashing about while men shouted. The sound of steel on steel, the roar of erupting flames, along with the clamoring voices of men he knew well, all jumbled together in a great, tumultuous, wall of sound. It was pandemonium. But Cordovan could see none of it. Holding up his hand, he waved it in front of his face, but saw nothing. It struck him that he might have known what this could be. He did not like the thought that crept into his mind. *By the dark pit, and the chains binding the Betrayer,* he thought! He knew that fire mixed with shadow meant one thing. There was a Catcher about - a *Soulcatcher*. It was a nasty thing if ever there was one. It was said that they had been made by the Twisted Ones for the war of the *Allgis-sein*. Cordovan only knew about them from the Chronicles of the Watch. There had been a few encounters over the past hundred years that had been reported by Watchmen travelling in the far north, beyond Province, at the edge of the Black Hills. But the prevailing thought was that they were things from a distant, long gone, dark age. They were things you read about. You scared children with the thought of them to make them do their chores. They were not the kind of things you saw walking around in real life. There had been rumors of course, whispers of dark, malevolent things roaming the night. But that was always the case. No one had actually laid eyes on anything out of the ordinary recently. The only thing that made sense was that this walking nightmare was tied to the other information in his possession. But that would mean that things were far worse than he had imagined. *They did not have time for this!*

A shout from a voice he recognized as Opus came to his ears through the liquid-like darkness surrounding him. That mid-range tenor was unmistakable even in the heat of battle. "Cordovan, down! Down man!"

Without hesitation or thought Cordovan hit the ground rolling. Something passed right over him tearing a piece of his cloak away. Rolling to his right, he rolled along the ground until he was out of the area that was cloaked in darkness. Free of the inky shroud, Cordovan could see that all around him the battle had been joined in earnest. The others were in the clearing fighting for their lives. As he rose to his feet the battle cry of the Watchmen of Alexandria tore free of his lips. "To the Watch!" he shouted. He roared the words at the top of his lungs. A growl punctuated the exclamation as he leaped into the thick of the fighting.

They were being smothered by three times their number in men who looked like a nondescript rabble. They had no distinguishing badges or colors naming them soldiers in an army. Nothing marked them as a cohesive unit other than the fact that they fought in a coordinated fashion. Unadorned, drab, clothing accentuated by sharp steel was the extent of their ornamentation. They swarmed around the Watchmen like insects buzzing around a dead thing.

All around the clearing the hard-pressed Watchmen took up the battle cry.

"To the Watch!" Salk shouted, as he cut a man down before turning to another he had been keeping to his right side.

"Yes! To the Watch!" Fairuk yelled, as he ducked under a slashing arc of steel meant to take his head off at the shoulders. He kicked the man in the gut as he straightened turning just in time to meet an overhead cut from his left. He raised his blade, bringing it parallel to the ground, in seventh position, with a two-handed parry that caused steel to ring against steel as blue sparks flew.

Cordovan spun, pivoting hard, on his left foot. He rotated outward as his opponent stop-lunged. Letting his momentum turn him in a full circle he cut at the back of the man's thigh as he came out of the turn. He finished him with a downward stroke while moving on to the next opponent without slowing. The odds were not the best, but the Watchmen were. It was part of what they trained to be.

Fighting several attackers at once was common for Watchmen. They tended to travel alone. Seeing several Watchmen together was a rarity outside the capital. They carried the Empresses Justice to every corner of the empire. They were used to having to fight several enemies at once in some distant village where they had unearthed corruption or had to impose the justice a local functionary had been unwilling, or unable, to despite it being their responsibility. She had always wanted her subjects to have direct access to true justice even if they could not make the journey to the capital to seek an audience. The Watchmen, by her imperial writ, could be judge, jury, and executioner in her stead. She took great care to ensure that they were honorable, beyond reproach, with sound judgement given the power they could wield in Her name. The only reason that Cordovan had been able to bring together this many Watchmen was because of the particular nature of the threat he was trying to stop. *If he wasn't too late*, he thought.

The wind changed direction. Cordovan caught the rank smell of sulfur. He flung himself hard to his left. The man he had been facing erupted in flames. The man dropped to his knees as he burned away without making a sound. It shocked Cordovan that the man did not scream.

Pulling his knees to his chest, Cordovan kicked out with his feet, flipping himself back up to a standing position. He came up to find the thing staring him in the face. Sniffing loudly, he tried to clear the acrid smell from his nose. The thing loomed over him. Standing, at what must have been, nearly nine spans high it looked like a nightscreamer. Nightscreamers were leathery-skinned, winged, mixes between birds and rodents. They were small creatures with fanged teeth, which matched their pointed ears. This twisted thing, vomited up out of the abyss, had those traits as well. Like the flying rodents, it had fanged teeth, and large, pointed ears, which framed bulbous eyes. Its limbs were thin but corded with muscle. Its body was covered in a dark, brownish, leathery skin. What passed for hands and feet ended in claws. All of this was on a warped man-like frame. The thing hissed at Cordovan as its head moved around on an oddly long neck. The only question he had in his mind was would it bleed.

It darted at Cordovan, impossibly quick for something so large, tearing at him with clawed hands. Spinning to his left, in a tight arc, which kept him dangerously close to what he thought was a Soulcatcher, he ended up behind it on its right side. Cordovan cut its hamstring with one strike. He reversed his movement catching it in the throat with a rising cut of his sword. *The Hawk Skims the River.* The Catcher screeched loudly as it leaped backwards. The sound made Cordovan shiver as he stepped toward it. His heart pounded in his chest. He had to grit his teeth while willing himself forward. According to the Chronicles that sound was meant to freeze its prey with fear. Cordovan knew somewhere deep down that he was frightened but he did not have time to think about it. The Catcher jumped sailing over his head in one leap. As Cordovan spun to face it the thing kicked him in his side sending him flailing. Hitting the ground on his left side, he grunted, as he lost his grip on his sword. The Catcher landed on him as he rolled onto his back. He grappled desperately with the thing. But it was incredibly strong. Both his hands were locked with the creature's arms as he tried to fend away the claws that would rend his flesh asunder given the chance. It reared its head back opening its mouth to reveal razor sharp teeth. Cordovan knew that it was only the *gift* that saved him. It had come from the ceremony, which made him a Watchman, imparting to him *the blessing* that had changed him. It was surely the *gift* that made it possible to fight off the fear washing over him. Not to mention that it had imparted to him the physical strength necessary to grapple with the thing. It was so strong that had he faced it before becoming a member of the Watch he would already be dead. Just as its claws were inching close enough to tear at him something heavy hit them both knocking the creature off Cordovan.

Scrambling across the ground to his sword Cordovan snatched it from the dirt. He turned in time to see Mallory on top of the thing struggling to hold it. Had they not been Watchmen they would both be dead. Cordovan walked over and stuck his sword over Mallory's shoulder impaling the Catcher through its left eye. The thing screamed again sending chills through Cordovan. It thrashed about wildly in pain dislodging Mallory who was knocked into Cordovan. Cordovan cursed as he tried to untangle himself from Mallory. He thought he was about to die because the Catcher would not. But as he freed himself he turned toward it again only to see that it lay unmoving.

Pulling his sword free from its ruined eye Cordovan noticed that the sound of battle had died down. Looking around the clearing he saw Fairuk finishing the last of their attackers while the others looked on. Salk was helping Assum up from the ground. Tark was limping slightly. It was only at that moment that Cordovan noticed his own left arm was bleeding. Three vertical claw marks were visible through his tattered gray sleeve. He breathed deeply while he stared at the wound. Wrapping his thoughts around the pain he isolated it in his mind. With another deep breath he tucked it away as he had been trained to do. Exhaling, he let the pain wash away as if it had never been. As his body complied he turned to his companions.

Grim faces, dimly lit by the flickering firelight of two trees that were burning, looked back at Cordovan. As quickly as it had begun it was over. The stench of arid smoke, mixed with burning flesh, hung over the clearing making it difficult to breathe. Stepping over the body of the Catcher he walked over to where the other Watchmen stood. As he walked he felt pain in both his sides. There were certainly bruises but there may have also been a cracked rib, where the Catcher had kicked him in his side, because it hurt like the Great Torment. In a few moments, he would deal with that pain as he had with the other. But first he moved to where he could stand with the others just as Mallory limped into the ragged circle they had formed favoring the leg where the crossbow bolt had lodged in his thigh.

Opus, a tall slender man, was as hard as they came. As he rose from a crouch, where he had been cleaning his sword blade on one of the dead men's cloak, he was shaking his head. Cordovan's light brown eyes met the man's deep green. Opus ran a thick hand through his close-cut black hair. His face was calm, but his eyes were troubled and tired. *Very tired*, Cordovan thought, and so was he.

Standing beside him Mallory rubbed lightly at his thigh. He was a highlander. Mallory was as tall as Opus but a bit thicker. He no longer had his purple cloak, but the chill air did not touch him. He always said the Highlands were cold. It was a cold he loved. Where Opus had trouble reflected in his eyes Mallory carried a hint of it in his low voice. He had not rid himself of the highland cant in his tongue even though he had not been home in many seasons.

"This do be a bad thing we stumbled on. Dark work it is." He did not say a word about the broken shaft that was still in his thigh. Tark joined the ragged group standing around the dead bodies. Firelight made the shadows around them dance. Some of them were searching the bodies. Tark was a small man. He was the only man among them with facial hair. His thick, reddish-brown, mustache covered most of his upper lip. His skin was tanned. His hair was a bushy, sandy red. His eyes were steel gray as they gleamed in the firelight. Tark tended to growl more than speak.

"Cordovan. These Pit-begotten things are *Gaunts*. They are not raiders or brigands they are Gaunts I tell you!" Tark spit on the ground as if the words had left a bad taste in his mouth. Looking back at Cordovan he turned his left-hand palm up pointing his finger down into his left palm to emphasize his point. "Blood and glory, Cordovan! We are facing nightmares walking here. It is said they have no souls. Bloody Gaunts!" Tark walked off growling over his shoulder. He could be heard saying, "No good. This is no good I tell you. This is the touch of the Dark. Has the Barrier failed? The Watch is difficult enough without the failing of the -" The rest was the kind of cursing that would redden faces in the roughest tavern.

Gaunts, like the thing Cordovan thought was a Soulcatcher, were things from another time. They were men without souls. It was said that the Betrayer created them during the war with other Allgis-sein by taking men, lost in their own pernicious schemes, and twisting them until there was nothing human left. They were lost men, bound to the Betrayers will, who became the walking dead. They had been footsoldiers. They were one of the fingers on the hand that reached out from the Darkness. The presence of Gaunts indicated the attention, at least to some degree, of the *Twisted* – if that was possible. It would mean the unimaginable, that dark, evil things were walking the land again. Cordovan's thoughts echoed what had already been said, *this was not good*.

The bodies were gathered together in a pile. When that was finished they set it on fire. The Watchmen whistled at the darkness outside the clearing. In answer the shrubbery parted as Swift, Cadence, Mist, and Maple, along with the other mounts, trotted into the clearing. Looking gravely at one another the Watchmen climbed into their saddles. Most of them were still bleeding but they turned toward the east again. Spurring tired horses, they urged them back to a gallop. There was no time for rest or binding wounds. Like an arrow shot from a bow they launched themselves toward Her. Had anyone been able to see Cordovan's face they would have noted that his eyes had an unnatural cast to them as he took the lead once more. The other Watchmen fanned out through the woods on either side of him.

They tore through the Minwood like a pronged hand sweeping into the night. Emerging from the thick of the wood they rode with the luminescence of a starry night sky softly beaming down on them muting the darkness. Off to the distant north flashes of lightning told of a storm raging.

As they raced onward they stretched out like an opened fan. The Watchmen covered the flat farmland of Exle passing through it on mile-eating hooves. Swift, surging beneath him, courageously galloped on. Cadence, Maple, Mist, Carmel, Ossle, and Bay carried the others as though they raced one another with their riders almost an afterthought. They had been bred to run, to remain calm in the midst of battle, and tonight they ran with the night wind.

Cordovan ripped off the tattered purple cloak that was the symbol of the Watchmen casting it high into the air so that it would sail over the heads of those trailing him. As the night drew on they pushed themselves, defying fatigue, as they hoped to defy time. All the while one thought rang through Cordovan's mind. *Not on my Watch*, he thought. *Not on my Watch.*

None of them spoke of the small, torn, piece of parchment Cordovan had taken off a dead man. It was tucked into the pocket of his coat. At the top and bottom of that small piece of parchment were the unreadable remnants of names. While that bothered him, while the nature of what was apparently a list in the hands of a man who had been unmistakably turned to dark things bothered him, it was the one name on that small piece of parchment that could be read clearly that had him, along with every other Watchmen he had been able to reach, racing through the night. The clearly legible name on that torn piece of parchment tucked in his coat pocket was Natassha Sobrine. *Not on my Watch*, he thought for the hundredth time.

When you say goodbye
say it well
do not speak with
the sound of I will see
you again, on your tongue
do not presume
eternity
or everlasting
for snatches of dribbling
sand are we

When you say goodbye
say it well
do not say it
desperately
or in agony
but rather with hope
fully
on your tongue
do not presume
eternity
or everlasting
for tiny ripples on
deep waters are we

When you must say goodbye
say it well
and if a tear clings
to the edge
of your eye
catch it in its
falling
place it on your lips
and kiss someone near

Hold on
fully
to all that is sacred now
for we are not
eternal
or everlasting
so when we are gone
say goodbye

~Ethini Death Poem

Death here is life somewhere else.

- Aanaxagon IX
Prefect at Emaon Temple

Chapter Ten

Holding on and letting go

The air smelled of freshly crushed mint. Drawing a deep breath, he inhaled slowly, languidly, until his lungs were full. Emptying them just as deliberately, as though he were pouring water from a large pitcher into a small, delicate cup, he let the air flow out of his lungs. The movement of time became palpable, textured, as if he could feel it between his fingers, or hold it like a butterfly sitting on the palm of his hand, which he knew might fly away in an instant. He held onto it, nestled in it, embracing it with his whole being. Bantu wrapped the *abundance* around himself like a thick cloak.

It had taken longer, once upon a time, early in his training, but now he could enter the *abundance* without much thought. The first step was to empty himself, which meant quieting his mind. It happened all at once now. He emptied his mind like a pail of sand being poured into an endless desert. Time seemed to slow until there was no yesterday, no tomorrow, only now. Once he had emptied himself the *abundance* filled him. The sky twinkled with stars inside him. Even the ocean, which Bantu could see from the balcony, ebbed away from him before flowing back to him. Being completely open to the world around him meant that he only distantly recognized his hands grasping the railing on the balcony of his quarters high up in the Peoples Tower. He was *full*.

He stretched out his senses. The *abundance* took hold of him until suddenly he was flying overhead, drifting silently, on the night wind's currents, hunting for mice in the fields surrounding the Great Nest where the *Wingless* lived. His wings plied the winds like a ship's sail at sea.

The *abundance* took him still wider, even farther, filling him up until, all at once, he was among the rocks high up in the distant hills. His hooves clacked against the rocks while he tossed his head displaying his curved horns, which were his crown of authority. This High Place was his. All the Others obeyed him. The *abundance* rushed over him, threatening to wash him away, until he stood towering above the ground, the winds laughing through his leaves as he tickled its breezy belly. Centuries hung on him like an old coat. His roots were the deepest, deeper than any of the short-lived, *Unrooted*, would guess. He was the First Grown here. His bark turned the breeze aside as his branches waved in tune with the music of the night's sounds.

Breathing deeply Bantu pulled back. Narrowing, distilling, what was his self from the area around the city. When he had first learned how to open himself to the *abundance* the process had been difficult. But now even removing himself from it was routine after all these years. In his mind he pictured the Dagoonzu Forest. As he focused he pictured the Balsam tree, which stood in the shadow of Mount Kilimajoon, with its thick, low hanging, blossoming branches. Early in his training he had picked that tree, camping under its bough for seven days, so that he could learn every inch of the forest along with the tree. All so that he could imprint those images on his mind. It was the place where he and his father had first talked about the *form*. His father had spoken to him about emptiness, followed by substance, ending in abundance. He had explained to Bantu the nature of the One True Form that was at the heart of all that the warriors of Al'akaz knew. There, he had learned, as a small boy, the truth behind the movements from which all combat evolved. Bantu had later discovered that there was nothing like the One True Form anywhere else in the known world. Under that tree the seedling of what would become his mastery of combat had begun to blossom. The image of that place, really that tree, became the focal point for opening himself to the *abundance*. It was known by many names in many places. Some called it the emptiness, or the oneness, the center, or the void, but they all described the same sacred merging with the world around you as well as the focus it brought you. As he drifted, he recalled the image of the purple, layered petals, and there he was, like some other person he knew well. It was *him*. Picturing himself there, he reached out with his mind to touch the image sitting there – not the boy, now, but the man – and in a few moments, he was himself again. Clenching, and unclenching, his hands he ran the fingers of his left hand over his thumb. He felt his breathing, his heart beating, slowly. It all let him know that he was back. All at once he let go of the *abundance*.

The danger to the untrained was that you could go so far, so wide, out of yourself that you would not be able to find your way back. His teacher, what they called a *Sabado* on this side of the Deep, had warned him about the true nature of the *abundance*. A Weaponmaster used only a portion of what some called the Outgoing. They had, over an age of practice, come to call it the *abundance*. The danger was that you could get lost. The *abundance* could wash you away. You would not come back.

There had been stories of lost ones who had gone *Out* but not returned. Their bodies would slowly wither away unless someone fed them. They could be kept alive but there was no record of anyone ever coming back. A general practice had evolved over time. It had been practiced slowly at first until it had become commonplace enough to finally be deemed tradition. As more time passed the tradition had become covered in ceremony. The result was that after seven days family, along with friends, would gather together. With music and song, they celebrated the lost one's life, which included a recounting of their deeds. It often lasted through the night. If the lost one had not returned by the following morning, they were given something in their water as the sun rose. In a matter of minutes, they were gone.

Sanctuary stretched out below Bantu as he leaned against the railing that enclosed the balcony. He let his eyes sweep from his far left to his right. There was still a hint of the *abundance* in him so that he could almost feel what was going on below. Flaming lights, on tall lamp poles, flickered in their glass balls while people leisurely walked about in small companionable groups. Most likely the groups were teams or parts of teams. That was not to say that team members did not mingle but it was not a Free Day. Some used free time to handle team issues.

Activity on the grounds had slowed only marginally since sundown. That minor drop in traffic was usually the result of visitors having left the grounds in order to return to the city proper. Sanctuary sparkled brightly in the warm Alexandrine evening. The Empire was far enough south that even with the cooling breeze blowing in off the Macca Deep it was still warm after nightfall. *It was a perfect night for a stroll through the arboretum*, Bantu thought, as he looked on. The arboretum, buildings, along with walkways laid in a winding path through Sanctuary, were all the beneficiaries of the tall polelamps that shed light throughout the grounds. The Makers, under Tinker's direction, had connected the lamps to an underground supply of oil that was somehow pressurized so that it flowed up from reservoirs placed in sections around the entire compound. The reservoirs were large enough so that they only needed refilling a few times a season. Sanctuary beamed brightly in the night.

Bantu knew that those walking below him would be headed to the library, theatre, observatory, or one of the many other diversions in, or around, the Tower as well as Sanctuary at large. There would even be some headed for an evening duty post. Bantu looked up as a dark shadow passed overhead. There always seemed to be Pradas in the sky over Sanctuary.

Voices that had earlier floated around, outside of the *abundance*, now caught his ear as the sound of them drifted out onto the balcony from his quarters. Turning from his twenty-first-floor view on the balcony he looked into his room. Most of First Team was already present while the rest were trickling in. Common Meal was over. Some nights the members of First Team would gather in his quarters for laughter, light fare for late eating, good conversation, or a drink. Like all teams who worked together long enough the group had grown close over the years. They were Bantu's friends as well as his team. Tonight, though, they knew to give him some space.

What was called Bantu's *quarters* was actually one enormous room on the twenty-first floor of Peoples Tower. The room faced east giving him a view of the front gate, the main thoroughfare of Sanctuary, and the arboretum. Just beyond the arboretum Bantu could also see the sparkling waters of the Deep. If he leaned out on the balcony, looking back to the west, he would be able to see a part of the Imperial Palace. Lighting up the night would be Alexander's Flame atop the palace on Ruler's Hill. He smiled. Above him, reaching high into the skyline, was the flame's only competition in Alexandria. At the top of the Peoples Tower the blue crystal sunburst would be glowing bright blue as it caught the light from the flames that would be roaring just beneath it. Bantu thought, not for the first time, of the different statements the shining beacons made. The Flame of Alexander was a burning declaration of supremacy to other nations as well as its own populace while the Peoples Light sent out a glowing, bright blue, beacon that symbolized the availability of sanctuary. It represented hope. Many had stumbled through the night with only the Peoples Light to guide them to safety.

The double doors to the balcony hung wide open. They were directly opposite the front door to Bantu's quarters. To the left of where he was standing on the balcony, in the corner, was a raised dais on which his bed rested. In the center of that wall, halfway to the front door, there was a large fireplace. The opening of the fireplace was close to the height of an average sized man. It was a good three strides across. Flames crackled in it, at the moment, warming the room that, despite the relative warmth outside, still held a slight chill. Encircling the front of the fireplace were several large, cushioned, leather armchairs.

On the same wall, to the right of the fireplace, stood floor-to-ceiling bookcases that stopped a few feet short of the corner. In that corner two more armchairs sat on either side of a table with an oversized game board on top of it. The large, silver, pieces represented soldiers, officers, warlords, kings, and queens. No piece moved the same way even though all of them worked in concert to trap the opponents King in order to win. The game, known as *Toos,* took only a few minutes to learn but a lifetime to master, at least that was the worn out saying about it. Bantu had found that it helped train one in strategy. He had been playing for years. He was currently in the middle of a game with Tink. It was an odd game in that Tink sent moves written on a piece of parchment. Bantu might be engaged in any number of activities throughout the day only to find one of Tink's acolytes standing nearby, patiently waiting, with a piece of folded parchment in hand. Once, Bantu had enquired of one of them where Tink kept his *Toos* board only to be told that Tink did not have one. Tink kept track of the game mentally. When Bantu had learned that fact it had not surprised him. Tink was brilliant so it made an odd kind of sense.

Opposite the raised dais, which held his bed, in the corner, to the right of the balcony doorway was a large washstand. The washstand stood next to a tall mahogany wardrobe that held his clothing. Just up from the wardrobe, on the other long wall, was the door to the staff room. The staff room had a kitchen as well as storage space for food. There were also closets with cleaning supplies, towels, linen, and more clothing. The room itself had been a major point of contention with the Matron of the Tower. Anna, puffing herself up to her full five and a half spans, looking as regal as any queen with her brown hair pulled back in a tight bun – her brown eyes gleaming dangerously - had claimed that a man of his station did not have time to make his own bed, clean his room, or fix food, especially if he had guests. She had insisted that he allow the Makers to add the staff room to the design of the floor where his quarters would be when they were building the Tower. In the midst of arguing with her about fussing over his *station* she had refused to speak to him for a week until he gave in to her demands. He had acquiesced to her design inputs as well as a small contingent of her staff to service his room. The entire experience had been exasperating. Bantu had always tried to insist that he was no more important than the newest cadet but it was an argument he consistently lost especially with those who joined the Company, not as soldiers, but as craftsmen, cooks, or farmers. They had the concept of an aristocracy so engrained in them from their former lives that it was nearly impossible to keep them from transferring that sense of class over to him. Anna had some of that in her. But the real problem with Anna was that Bantu had saved her. She had been a badly battered wife in a small village with no one to tell, or care, until he had, by chance, passed through. Bantu had not tried to hurt her former husband, but the man had pushed things to the point that Bantu had been forced to kill him. Anna had followed Bantu out of the village with nothing but the clothes on her back that night. He had tried giving her enough money to start a new life somewhere else. He had even tried sneaking off in the night while she was asleep but no matter what he had done he had not been able to get away from her. After that Anna had taken to looking after him. When they made camp, she would cook. She took to cleaning his clothes. She made his choca. She had fussed over him like he was a king. The worst part was the few times he had gotten exasperated enough to shout at her. The look on her face, followed by the tears on her cheeks, had been enough to leave him feeling like horse dung. Bantu had finally given in. He let her do as she pleased. She was fierce when it came to his care. She was especially prickly over what she saw as his prerogatives. He had learned that lesson when Anna had produced a knife from somewhere on her person before promptly attacking a village warden who had spoken harshly to Bantu. Had Bantu been a little slower the man would have been dead on the spot. Anna tended to get her way where Bantu was concerned.

After a time, Anna herself had taken to serving his quarters alongside those she had hand picked for the detail. Word had even reached Bantu's ears that the staff of the Tower thought of the duty as a privilege or some kind of honor. They had begun to wear a small patch with the three, silver, intersecting circles of the Company sigil on the sleeve of their black and white linen uniforms. It was all intolerable but when he raised the subject with Anna she became defensive, hurt, and insulted. He ended up having to apologize for suggesting that they not treat him like an effete member of the Peerage. It confounded him. But he had tried to learn to live with it. At least they called him Commander rather than Lord Commander. That fight he had won.

Anna, with a few of her select people dressed in livery, were busy bustling about Bantu's quarters serving things to nibble on. They also circulated with pitchers to pour drinks. They moved unobtrusively from the staff room to main room. The rest of the wall, which also held the door to the staff room, was nothing more than a small library. Its length was dedicated to more floor-to-ceiling bookcases. The bookcases were filled with large tomes, volume sets, maps, scrolls, and books. His collection was small, by library standards, but it was filled with the rarest materials around.

The final corner of the room held a desk that had been a gift to Bantu from the empress. It was a large thing wonderfully carved from wood. The legs were arched ending in golden lions. The top curved inward encircling whoever sat at the desk. There were several small drawers also gilded with gold. The entire thing was embellished with gold appointments. The drawer knobs were tiny, golden lion heads. The entire desk was cherry-stained with a glossy finish. The Empress knew something of him. The desk managed to be elegant as well as simple even given the gold appointments. It had come with a matching chair and bookcase.

The central area of the room stood empty with the singular exception of a long dining table. The table sat fifteen people comfortably. It ran most of the length of the room. It was unadorned except for a large, clear, crystal vase that stood in its center. Anna insisted on always having the vase filled with a fresh flower arrangement even in Bantu's absence. He had soon admitted to himself that he liked it especially the fresh smell the flowers lent the room. Though he admitted this fact freely to himself he never even hinted at the truth of it to Anna. Were she given even that little bit of acknowledgement, Anna would feel empowered by the admission to take further liberties with his quarters, which was the last thing he wanted. But the flowers were a nice touch. Tonight, there was a heaping bundle of purple lilies with white speckles giving off the faintest sweet scent.

Above the dining table was a ceiling relief. Anna had cornered one of the People, a man gifted with a paintbrush, so that she could enlist him – she had actually dragged him - to paint the relief that now glistened there. The painting covered the same area above that the dining table covered on the floor below it. Anna had said that the matching size would give the room balance. An immense sunburst of browns, reds, and burnt gold, in front of billowing, white clouds, on an iridescent blue sky, was the scene the artist had chosen to reproduce. The balance of the sunburst over the dining table had seemed to center the room, breaking up the large, otherwise unadorned, space of the arched ceiling.

Bantu closed his eyes. The small of his back rested on the railing as he folded his arms across his chest. Standing there in the slight evening breeze, with his eyes closed, he let his ears take over. They told him that Wen, Bella, and Gabriel were sitting in front of the fireplace talking about the day's events. Gabriel was mentioning a report he had received on activity in the Esdril sector of the Deep. It had him concerned. Wen reminded him that the time for work was at an end. He needed to relax. After letting a few moments pass Bantu opened his eyes again.

Onya was sitting at the long table staring off into space. On the other side of the table Basil was searching the wall-length bookcase for something, his hands on his hips, his head moving slowly from one side to the other. He stood there scanning the shelves while lightly biting his lower lip.

Essen, followed by Almaldren, was just arriving. Almaldren Shadowcatcher hovered over Essen even in the safety afforded by all of Sanctuary. Bantu's mouth curved into the hint of a sly grin. It was not as though Essen was a harmless old woman. Essen Stormbringer was far from harmless. After a quick glance around the room Essen moved to join Wen, Bella, and Gabriel at the fireplace. They already occupied three of the plush chairs encircling the crackling flames. Essen took one of the two remaining chairs as Almaldren dropped lightly into the other. Almaldren lifted the shoulder strap of his mandolin over of his head. Gripping it lightly, he began to softly pluck out a tune. The mandolin was made of a dark burgundy wood with curving, intricate, silver work around its edges and along the neck. It was a beautiful piece of work. It looked like it could have been a family heirloom that had made its way through several generations. The mandolin had always made Bantu wonder, given that Ki'gadi abandoned family ties when they were taken to Palladawn. Almaldren's playing was as beautiful as the instrument itself. He was strumming something slow. His fingers tickled the strings with a dexterity that they should not have.

Almaldren was not an actual member of the Company. He was present because Essen was there. Bantu had met Essen years before the Company was the Company. While working freelance he had been sitting at a campfire, one late night, preparing for a mission. From out of the surrounding woods she had appeared, with Almaldren in tow, walking right up to his campfire. With her robes twirling around her as she walked, along with her long, windblown hair, the two of them had been a startling contrast. He had stalked out of the darkness right behind her. She was smooth while he was rough. Essen was all soft curves while Almaldren was sharp edges. With light from the fire playing along her features She had gazed across the flames at Bantu with sharp, blue, eyes, while Almaldren looked out from smoldering, gray, ones. There were only two things that were identical about the two of them. The first was that they both moved like flowing water. The second was the startlingly silvery-white hair on their heads. Without a word she had taken a seat at his fire. With a broad smile she had reached out to warm her hands by the flames. Almaldren had watched the darkness at the edge of camp like it was a living thing daring it to move. After a span of about a hundred heartbeats she had begun talking to him as though they were old friends. Essen claimed that they were. She had said that the Ancient One had tied them together. She had made some point about verses in the same immensely old song. The One was, even at that moment, singing it, she had said. It had been sung to begin time itself. It would be sung until all things ended. Bantu still did not know why he had not felt threatened when they had appeared out of the darkness. But Essen, with Almaldren a step behind her, had been with him since. She had lent him her assistance in each of his freelance missions when she was around. She had even been involved in the circumstances that had led him to the Company without ever asking for anything in return.

Over time Bantu had learned pieces of their story. They were *Ki'gadi*. Not much was known about the *Keepers of the Barrier*, the *Watchers of the Flame* - the Ki'gadi. It was said that they were the only thing that stood between the world and the all-consuming darkness of the Twisted Ones. They came from *Palladawn*. They had put the world back together after the war of the Allgis-sein had torn it asunder. They stood apart from nations, political ties, and, depending on whom you asked, were either the protectors of all that was good, or good-for-nothing meddlers who needed to stay behind the high walls of Palladawn. The one thing Bantu knew for certain was that they were handy in a fight – or anywhere else for that matter. Apparently, when it came to the Ki'gadi, there were always two. They did what they thought was right. Usually when people came away from their dealings with the Ki'gadi upset, even downright angry, it was because what the Ki'gadi had thought was right was rarely what those dealing with them thought of as right or appropriate. It could even be that the Ki'gadi had swept in, taking over without so much as a by your leave, expecting to be obeyed without question. It could be maddening. They shared information only sparingly but had proven themselves to Bantu to be somewhat reliable over the years. If there was a downside to dealing with them it was that they might disappear without a word, for months at a time, only to stroll through the front gates of Sanctuary as if they had only been gone for the afternoon. Bantu had learned to trust them, not utterly mind you, they were still Ki'gadi – but to a degree.

Laughter erupted from the fireplace. Gabriel had managed to set aside the business of the day. He was leaning against the left side of the fireplace spinning some humorous tale with a silver cup of chilled wine in his hand. Gabriel was a little shorter than Bantu though still very tall by Alexandrian standards. A native of northwestern Alexandria, Gabriel was in his middle years with the silver strands in his once black hair to prove it, though he had managed to remain slim. The skin on his face was sun-kissed though a bit leathery from exposure. While his silvering hair hung to his shoulders, at present, it was tied back with a leather cord. Gabriel was still in his uniform, but the coat was unbuttoned revealing his white shirt underneath. Almaldren had switched tunes. He was strumming what Bantu thought he recognized as the opening notes of *The Portmaster's Wife*.

Basil, a long pipe with a small bole, trailing thick, sweet smelling, smoke behind him as it hung from the corner of his mouth, was walking toward Bantu. Tucked under his arm was the prize from the bookcase he had been seeking. Basil had an easy, rhythmic, step. With his back straight, his head held high – Basil always had great posture - he managed to look relaxed, but still at attention, all at once. The man was a walking dichotomy. Bantu knew Basil was as much a scholar as he was a soldier.

Standing at just shy of six feet Basil's presentation was, well, impeccable. His woolen hair was cut almost skin-close on the sides while it was left a few inches longer on top. Basil was clean-shaven with a complexion that was a little lighter than Bantu. His slightly broad nose was tiny along with his ears. He had the full lips of most of the people who shared the darker skin of Bantu's ancestry. Basil's parents had discovered Alexandria while traveling abroad. They had liked it so much that they decided to stay. He had been born in Alexandria. Though his family was from somewhere across the Deep Basil had grown up in the capital city.

Basil, like the other Company members, had changed out of his uniform. He was wearing a pressed white shirt with pearl buttons. The breeches were thin, brown, suede with a well-worn look. He had decided on a pair of heavy, calf-high, square-toed, brown, leather boots. A matching brown leather belt was wrapped around his waist. Basil's sword was propped against the wall next to the front door.

Basil mounted the three steps that brought him onto the balcony. Ten strides brought him over to where Bantu stood, leaning against the railing, out in the night air. As Basil came to stand next to him Bantu could see the spine of the book under his arm. It was the account of the fall of Brimmon Pass. *History,* Bantu thought. Basil was an incurable academic. From time to time he even guest-lectured at the University.

The man was a Windchaser. For lack of a better description they were known for finding things. If you needed to locate a particular drop of water in the sea you sent for a Windchaser. It was said, albeit in jest, that they could find a wind that blew over a barn making it confess to the crime and pay for the damage. Basil was puffing absently on his pipe as he gazed over Bantu's shoulder at Sanctuary. The smell of vanilla, with a hint of rum, tickled Bantu's nose as the burning leaf's aroma drifted toward him. Basil's voice was mellow, smoothed by the smoke, as he spoke around the pipe-stem securely lodged in the corner of his mouth.

With a slight nod of his head, Basil said, "Commander. How is the evening?" Basil turned his head, looking off into the distance, with one hand cupping the book under his arm while the other hand adjusted the long-stemmed pipe in his mouth.

Bantu turned his head to the left looking down at Basil. "Basil. You know very well that there's no need for protocol when we're off duty. I'm not the Commander here, in my quarters, just Bantu." Bantu's voice came out relaxed with no trace of his earlier anger.

Basil smiled, pulling the pipe from his mouth, as he turned back from the view. He met Bantu's gaze. "Yes Bantu. I know that. I am just trying to—" turning again to the view below them, Basil seemed to be searching for words. Shrugging his shoulders, he continued. "I … I have been out of sorts all day. Angry even. And part of me still is. And, I dare say, I'm conflicted. I know it comes with the territory. I know we face the possibility of death every time we strap on our swords but by the Ancient and the Pit! It's the *how* that bothers me. Our people did not die because they weren't good enough, or fast enough, or even clever enough, but because they were betrayed!"

His voice had been rising with heated emotion but then Basil clamped down on himself visibly. Taking a deep breath, he adjusted the pipe in his mouth as he puffed furiously. He began to tap the book, now in his hand, on the railing. "They were betrayed. That is the long and short of it. Betrayed into the hands of enemies by people we trusted. They did not know it was coming. And something in me is bloody well crying out for something to be done about it. That part of me wants to take a few Storm Holders with me to the Tower of Alexandria, remove Gaiden Colling from his holding cell, and finish what we started earlier today." Basil said the last of it in a quiet voice. Properly applied that voice would send a chill through the bones. That lesson had come from his Alexandrian *Sabado* who had made sure that Bantu understood that a trained body was no substitute for a trained mind. Bantu had passed that lesson on to the People. Sometimes less is more.

Running both his hands over his clean-shaven head Bantu felt the smoothness of the skin of his scalp along his fingers. Breathing deeply, he exhaled audibly. He knew exactly how Basil felt admitting as much to his longtime friend. "Basil, I feel the same way." Bantu turned to face Sanctuary standing next to his friend. The two men stood there, unmoving, in the night, while the scented smoke from Basil's pipe circled around them in the light breeze. Though he had only lived to see thirty-three turns of the seasons, still too young to lead in the minds of some, Bantu was a commander of people. An entire Company, he reminded himself, of people he had spent twelve of those years building from a small, respected, cadre of warriors of an ancient order, into a formidable force. He had learned along the way that sometimes all they wanted was to be close to their leader. Knowing that he was listening often made the difference. After a few moments had passed Bantu placed his hand on Basil's shoulder. Speaking softly, he said, "I promise you, my friend, I will give the Empress an opportunity to do what she said she would. And if she does not-" he let the sentence trail off into silence. Bantu had wanted to kill the Prime Agent of Alexandria but deep down he had known, even before Natassha had said anything, that if she pushed he would let her have the traitor for *her* justice.

She was trying something unheard of. Natassha Sobrine was attempting to create an empire where real justice prevailed, where every person, noble or commoner, could count on that justice. It was a remarkable vision, particularly given how her grandfather, and to a lesser degree, her father had ruled. They had been hard men. They had been the kind of men that made empires. Though they had bequeathed to the empress an empire Bantu knew that she would be the reason it lasted beyond a few generations. Needless to say there were those, mostly members of the Peerage, who did not care for this new way of doing things. It was quite possible that the empress had made more enemies with her new ways than her father or grandfather ever had. Bantu also knew that if this new vision was going to be realized it needed not just her way of thinking. It needed her. He had not protected her for most of her life, including helping her to the throne, only to damage her chances at realizing that vision. So, he would give her a chance to show that she would keep her word.

Onya appeared in the doorway to the balcony. Bantu and Basil turned together as she came up the steps to join them. Her voice was light with a hint of her homeland on her tongue. She had not rid herself of her accent even given all the years she had lived away from the land of her birth. Bantu had never asked her about it especially given the fact that he still had some of the sounds of Al'akaz on his own tongue. His tendency was to over pronounce words. It was not that Alexandrians underpronounced them, as was the case, the further south you travelled. They simply did not wrap their mouths as completely around words as was his custom. He supposed she, like he, felt it gave her a connection to her distant home.

"I thought I was the one you loved Bantu-san? Yet here you are huddled up with Basil?" She laughed softly as the two of them turned to face her. Her odd jab caused them both to smile. Onya continued, "I always have to make sure my two commanders, especially the one that outranks me-" she winked at Bantu, "-maintain at least a modicum of joviality. It is the least I can do." With those words Onya bowed low. She bowed so low in fact that it became clear it was intended as a mocking gesture.

Basil bent at the waist with his own, overly exaggerated, courtly bow adding a flourish with his hand. It looked so ridiculous that when he rose from his genuflection, looking from Onya to Bantu, they all burst into laughter. Bantu had learned long ago that laughter was one of the best healers especially for the kind of wounds you could not see.

As the laughter trailed off Onya came the rest of the way across the balcony speaking again but with a softer, more somber tone. The laughter faded to a mere hint at the edges of her voice. "It's time to prepare for Last Rites." She looked from one of them to the other.

Bantu and Basil both nodded once. They walked in off the balcony with Onya leading the way. They had all been waiting for the hour to reach one Pass before midnight. Midnight was the hour the ritual would take place. Stepping down the last step into the room Bantu looked at the gathered group as he thought about how he had seen more than his fair share of midnight rituals. The voice of his Sabado came to him. *Hold tightly to the blade in your hand and let go of the rest.*

†

Onya stood on a raised wooden dais. It was used for public addresses as well as ceremonies. The open area was on the western side of Sanctuary between Cadet House and the Peoples Tower. It was also the site of their early morning workouts.

The night sky was clear except for the bright stars high overhead. The dais had been surrounded with large bouquets of white lilies. There were so many that only the very top of the platform could be seen. It looked as though those on the dais were standing on a sea of flowers. The groundskeepers had been busy all evening making the necessary preparations. The area directly in front of the dais had a narrow walkway outlined by two rows of white lilies about twenty paces long. The walkway opened out into a ring about thirty paces across that also encircled the bushels of lilies. These lilies, however, were purple, lavender, pink, and white. Directly opposite the walkway leading to the dais was another walkway identical to the first.

Onya stood alone on the dais, watching, as the rest of the crowd gathered in the open field. They were all there except those who were on duty or away from Sanctuary altogether. Cadets, ranking members, as well as craftsmen of the Company, swelled the gathering. The People were slowly arriving to fill the open area. It was a sea of unrelieved black and white. Cadets were resplendent in their freshly pressed white coats while ranking members matched their polished look with their own black version. The Company uniform was matched by the black and white livery worn by the members of the Company who did things other than carry weapons. From farmers to blacksmiths, cooks to grooms, scribes to healers, and gardeners, they were all there.

Onya gazed out on that sea. They were the People. It was a beautiful sight to behold. Behind her the musicians had taken up their positions wrapped in hoodless, black robes. They sat in the only chairs in the entire setting bringing their instruments to the ready. As an easy breeze blew in from the east, having begun somewhere out over the distant reaches of the Macca Deep, the drummers began to beat a strong, slow cadence. *Long, short-short, long, short-short.* The beating continued.

At the sound of the drums the sea of people parted. In the rear a procession began making its way toward the dais. The corridor made by the parting of people was in a direct line to the opening in the central ring of many-colored lilies connected to the dais by the second walkway lined with white lilies. Onya knew the procession would stop in that center ring.

At the head of the procession the Commander-General of the Peoples Company strode to the beat of the drums. Onya watched Bantu. He carried his sword, as he always did, in the crook of his left elbow with the ivory hilt slanting across his waist, the top of the scabbard in the underhanded grip of his left hand, so that he could draw the blade easily with his right. The scabbard curved out around the front of his left elbow.

Bantu's head was covered by a black headwrap that curved around his head in several folds ending in a small knot at the base of his neck. Tiny white blossoms, the size of a fingernail, were stuck in the folds making small rings around his head. Immediately behind him Onya saw the woman who sat on the Alexandrian Imperial throne. It was Empress Natassha Sobrine. She was wearing a black dress that had long, slim sleeves with a high collar that buttoned at the neck. The dress was cut close around her chest, flaring out from the top of her waistline down to the ankle. The buttons must have been made of black pearl to glisten as they did in the lamplight. There was a tiny flower pattern running throughout the dress, which was a lighter shade of black. Her thickly curled red hair had been put up with pearl tipped pins. A white-gold circlet rested on her brow. The front of the simple circlet was worked in roses made from diamonds. A simple necklace of black pearls rested snug against her neck, like a choker, just above where the collar of the dress buttoned. She looked regal, with a simple elegance, as she maintained a somber, reserved, set to her features.

Behind the Empress, in black waist-jackets with white lace spilling from their collars and sleeves, matched by black, loose-fitting breeches, marched seven members of the Imperial Guard led by Captain Ellom Vam. Following just behind the Imperial Guard was Minister of Defense Camilla Rodrick in a single breasted black longcoat that flared away like a cape with black breeches. Imperial Marshal Lewin Brahm walked beside her in similar garb. Onya knew that Bantu had sent a messenger to Ruler's Hill earlier with a message about what would be appropriate apparel for the ceremony. Onya nodded to herself in appreciation of the taste shown by the Empress. She had ensured that they were dressed appropriately. They carried themselves with the proper demeanor. The Empress had even come with only a handful of the Imperial Guard, which showed a proper sense of decorum. But then, Onya thought, *Natassha Sobrine had always shown good taste.* Onya could even say that she liked the woman, which was something she could not say about most of the so-called nobility. They tended to fall into the category of the pompous, overbearing, and self-centered. The Empress was different. Maybe that was why Bantu did so much for her, why he allowed her to attend a ceremony that was never for outsiders.

Bringing up the rear of the procession were the Last Walkers. Each Order that had lost a member fielded seven of its members to carry the body to its final rest. Since the Company had lost people, but had retrieved no bodies, the woodworkers had carved life-sized replicas of the fallen. The replicas had been carved lying in repose. They looked like fully uniformed members resting on their backs with their arms folded, one hand over the other, on their chests with their legs straight and their feet together. The lost were carried according to the ancient practice of the Free Companies. Six Last Walkers stood shoulder to shoulder with an arm around their opposite's waist. Each set of two stood one pace behind the other. The body was laid on their shoulders, the head between the first two Walkers, the waist between the second two, and the feet between the last two. In front of the six the seventh walked alone with a sword drawn as escort.

Six Far Eyes carried the replica of Mallic with one Far Eye out front looking like he was expecting an attack at any moment. That scene was duplicated with seven Death Singers escorting the replica of Dreyden, even as seven Sky Dancers carried the replica of Ving. They all marched in unison with the slow cadence the drums had set so that the bodies swayed together from one side to the other.

As the procession approached the central ring encircled by the many-colored lilies the drums began beating faster. Onya watched Bantu, along with the Imperial retinue, walk through the center ring, moving along the walkway. Finally, they mounted the steps of the dais to join her. The Last Walkers stopped at the entrance to the center ring of lilies. Those on the raised dais arranged themselves at Bantu's direction. He stood at the front of the dais facing the sea of black and white-clad members of the Company. Onya stood a half-step behind him to his right. To his left the Empress stood, with her delicate hands folded demurely at her waist. She held her chin up just a fraction. She was beautiful in the lamplight. Flanking the Empress, to either side, a full step behind her, were Minister Rodrick and Marshal Brahm. Finally, in a half-circle behind Rodrick and Brahm, stood the members of the Imperial Guard with their leader Captain Vam at their center.

Onya stood there watching silently as Bantu checked to ensure that everyone was where he or she ought to be. When he was satisfied he raised his right hand to shoulder height. At that signal the drumming stopped with a unified *boom*. The sound reverberated across the crowd fading slowly into the silence of the night. Bantu tapped the communications gem at his collar, three times, in quick succession. All across the crowd matching gemstones flared to green, glowing life on countless collars including Onya's. When the master of Sanctuary spoke, his voice resounded through thousands of glowing com-gems. The words echoed though he spoke softly.

"The Ancient gives, and the Ancient takes away. Blessed be the Ancient's name." The word *name* echoed. It faded as Bantu let his gaze sweep across the sea of faces that looked back at him. "We are here to honor our fallen. They served with distinction and, even at the cost of their lives, completed their mission. We hold on to their memories, but we let go of the hope that they will walk among us again in this life. They rest now, awaiting the coming of the Ancient, awaiting the Eternal words, while we who live continue singing the Old Song." Stepping to the edge of the dais at the head of the steps Bantu raised his voice. "There is one needful thing left to those of us who still reach into the Darkness. Let the Guardians come!"

As Bantu made the pronouncement the drummers rattled off a staccato roll. They continued in a slow steady beat. As they drummed, black-clad members of the Company, who had been given the places closest to the ring of lilies, leaped the flowered barrier landing in the open ring. They were the people who had the closest ties of friendship with fallen. All told, twenty-eight people, leaped into the ring. Onya launched herself from the dais, twisting in the air, and landing on the walkway. Rising from the crouched position she had landed in, she strolled into the ring, to stand with the others. Looking around she noticed some of them had tears trickling down their cheeks or eyes swelling with those that were as yet unshed.

As a group they turned to face Bantu who still stood at the edge of the dais. Again, he raised his hand causing the drumming to stop with a resounding *boom*. His voice swelled in the pregnant silence carried by the still glowing com-gems. "The Guardians come to escort our fallen beyond the reach of the hand of the Dark. They carry the entry warrants for our departed. Will they be denied?"

As Bantu ended with his question the crowd roared. Shouts of, "No!" and, "Never!" rose up in a thunderous cacophony. Some even shook their fists in the air. The musicians took up their instruments. The sound of a triumphal march swelled up around them. Drums thumped as the horns swelled. The stringed instruments played a counter melody. While they played the staircase at the front of the dais opened on hidden hinges. From beneath the dais a throng of people came rushing down the walkway toward where Onya was standing in the ring of lilies. They were dressed in white with red sashes hanging diagonally from shoulder to waist. The red sashes had a black sigil embroidered across them from the Old Tongue representing the Lord of Sufferings, the Twisted One, known as the Betrayer. They wore wooden masks with twisted facial features painted in a myriad of colors. Bold strokes of black slashed with red were prominent among the colors on the masks.

The music rose as the Guardians, in their unrelieved black, drew their swords forming a wall of protection between the coming onslaught of masked warriors and the Last Walkers still waiting to enter the ring of lilies.

Waving their swords, the Hand of the Dark, as they were called in the ceremony, rushed into the ring opposite Onya. She raised her sword over her head in the first position of *Twirling the Ribbon*. The two groups faced off as the ceremony began in earnest. In slow choreographed form the two groups merged. They paired off. They slowly struck at one another in mock battle, as form countered form, with steel ringing lightly off steel in expected positions. The music soared as the drums beat, ringing in Onya's ears, even as the masked Hand of the Dark appeared to be gaining the upper hand. But just as it seemed they would overwhelm the Guardians, Bantu leaped from the dais charging into the rear of the Hand of the Dark. His sword held high, his voice amplified by the broadcasting com-gem on his collar, he began to sing. They were words that went with the triumphant tune the musicians were playing. All of the Company joined in with him.

A crown of tears of thorns be laid
For those who cease to roam
We hear their cry we join the throng
And carry them home

So come you Bane
And scorch you barren
And bar our rally on
We'll be reborn
And close our ranks
And then fight on til morn

As the voices of the People rose, the tide of the mock battle turned. Bantu fought his way through the rear of the enemy in choreographed form to join the Guardians. Onya came to his side. Along with the rest they pushed back the masked attackers. The masked People, portraying the Hand of the Dark, began to fall as though mortally wounded. Wherever they fell they lay there unmoving. When they were all *dead* the crowd roared in celebration. With that as their cue, the Last Walkers carried the bodies on their shoulders over the battlefield, past the decimated enemy, down the walkway, and up onto the dais. At the rear of the dais were three low platforms just long enough to lay the bodies.

As the musicians changed the tune to a more somber melody, Onya returned to the dais a step behind Bantu while the Guardians returned to the crowd. Those who had portrayed the Hand of the Dark removed their masks, robes, and sashes to reveal the black coats of the Company. The costumes were dropped into large baskets held by attendants dressed in black and white livery. After that quick change, the former representatives of the Dark also joined the rest of the Company outside the ring.

The three members of the Last Walkers who had been the honor guards had sheathed their swords exchanging them for torches. Bantu spoke a final time as he stood off to the side of the dais with Onya by his side. The Imperial guests stood in a close group a few paces behind him. The three biers holding the bodies were now the center of attention.

His voice was again low but strong coming through Onya's communication gemstone. "They were ours, and they will be missed."

Bantu nodded at the three honor guards. Onya looked from Bantu to the honor guard as, one by one, the torches rose, held high in the air, before falling to rest on the wooden replicas of the fallen People. They immediately caught fire. In moments, the flames reached high into the night sky. Onya could feel the warmth on her face. She closed her eyes. The faces of her lost team members crossed her mind. For a moment it was as if they were with her. Dreyden smiled slyly. Mallic looked as calm as ever. Ving's brow was furrowed as he worked through some problem or other. Her breath caught in her throat as her emotions sought to overwhelm her. Opening her eyes Onya breathed deeply.

Onya listened in silence as Bantu spoke again. "We hold on to their memories, but we let go of their presence among us. May they rest in the hands of the Ancient One."

From high above them, without warning, shadows fell from the sky. Looking up Onya saw the Pradas hurtle down from the sky as they darted over the gathering. There had to be dozens of them with their Mountain Feather pilots in their Pilot's Nests. Each of the Pradas had a flight carriage nestled on their backs. As the great birds passed over the crowd the doors of the flight carriages opened. While the assemblage watched tiny flower blossoms, of nearly every hue, floated down on them like snow. The fragrant blossoms filled the air. It was a sweet-smelling blizzard of color. It was the final act of the Rites.

As the tiny blossoms swirled in the air the drummers beat out another slow cadence. Bantu led the group with him off the dais, down the walkways, and into the crowd. The fire behind them rose higher. It began to consume the wooden dais as Onya trailed Bantu. By the time she reached her quarters there would be nothing left but ashes, a few blossoms in her hair, and tears on her cheeks.

If you would make a difference
Dance in the dark and die
Lay down your life, then live on
Knowing that you have already
Crossed over to the other side
Having died, you may take up life
And living, dance in the dark
Where suffering breathes fully
Meet it there and strike
And bring alive the lost

~Excerpt from the fragment
at Goshien, the Fifth Philosophy
Frag. 23

You do what you can.

~Oldershaw Nerruzenzza
Legendary member of the Watch

CHAPTER ELEVEN

Someone watching over me

An Imperial coach, lacquered, glossy black, with polished silver appointments, being pulled by a team of six white, prancing horses, rolled smoothly through the gates of Sanctuary. Natassha allowed the night sky to occupy her completely. She had only to tilt her head back slightly to see through the small window in the roof of her coach. Resting comfortably on thickly padded, purple, velvet-covered seats Natassha allowed herself to stargaze. The night sky was unendingly black. It looked like a dark sea broken up by an occasional heavenly light flickering in the great expanse. Some of the stars that were grouped together formed the constellations her astronomers busied themselves studying. She thought that one of the stars, which made up *The Crown of Arabellus*, winked at her tonight. Though her face was still a somber mask, she knew her eyes glittered with the remnants of unshed tears. The death rites she had been witness to, left her saddened, though, oddly inspired. She was a jumble of emotions. She rode alone not simply because she was the Empress but because she was not fit company tonight. Natassha had watched her friend, her long-time protector, very closely tonight. Though Bantu hid it well Natassha knew he was hurt deeply by the loss of members of his Company. Her heart ached for her friend.

Tonight, was another reminder that there were many things beyond even the power of an Empress. Yet, somehow, she still felt responsible for the ceremony she had just attended. Bantu had been all too kind in receiving her entourage. But Natassha knew him well enough to know that, not only was he hurting, he was angry. Men never let on that they were in any kind of pain other than the obvious physical kind. They would brave the most horrendous wound claiming, all the while, that they were fine. But if they caught the least little sniffle they were like little boys who had to be waited on hand and foot. That trait made them infinitely useful, completely intolerable, and nearly impossible to understand.

When it came to hurts of the heart it was as though they had some unwritten code. They would not allow themselves to show what was really going on inside. It could be maddening. Still, Natassha knew, Bantu was hurting. What was worse she could not help but feel responsible. One of her people, one of *her* people, she thought, clenching her right hand into a small fist. One of her people had betrayed them causing the deaths of soldiers of the Peoples Company. Though Gaiden Colling would be tried for his crimes it would not bring back the three men who had lost their lives.

Natassha cared for Ossassande Bantu A' Omorede more than she might like to admit – certainly more than she let on. So, knowing that she was the cause of his pain troubled her. She continued turning the situation over in her thoughts as her coach rolled on making its way toward the imperial palace. Natassha continued gazing up at the night sky in silence. Outside the coach the Imperial Guard sat astride their horses riding in a protective ring. They rode with grim faces in utter silence. The only sounds were the jingle of harnesses, the clip-clop of hooves, and the dry sandy sound of coach wheels rolling across cobbled stone.

Most in the empire held some level of respect for the Peoples Company. They had proven to be courageous, honorable, people with a deep, abiding sense of fairness. The members of the Company gave a great deal to the world. When they suffered a loss of life it affected more than just their Company.

The People, as they called themselves, made it easy, by their conduct, to respect them. That respect was even reflected in the Imperial Guard. Tough soldiers, though they were, they had been moved by the ceremony they had witnessed. They guarded the prized possession of the empire with their usual diligence but kept to their own thoughts tonight. It was not a very long journey back to Ruler's Hill but tonight it seemed like the palace was a league away.

†

Swift faltered, but caught herself, as she rounded the bend that brought her to the open field leading to the first gate of Alexandria. The city was alight in the darkness off in the distance. Lather fell from Swift's flank as her powerful muscles fought against exhaustion. Cordovan had pushed his mount past her limits. Swift was running on heart alone. All of the Watchmen rode mounts that were fading fast. But Cordovan knew they could not stop. The Great Oath had to live. They had to be in time. *They just had to*, he kept telling himself.

They must have ridden like madmen for more than a week trying to get to the capital, trying to get to Her. All of them were wounded. They were each close to the end of their physical endurance after fighting through several ambushes with little sleep. It was as if some great hand kept trying to reach up out of the Darkness to drag them into the Abyss. The fragment of parchment, folded up in his pocket, may have had something to do with that.

It was only the *gift*, which came as a result of the Empress laying that ancient talisman on their shoulders, in the ceremony where she made you a Watchman, which fueled them now. Without what that talisman had imparted to each of them, during that ceremony, they would all be dead from either exhaustion or the wounds they had sustained. Seeing the Imperial City, being close enough to feel *her* presence through the connection that came as a part of that gifting, somehow redoubled the fire in them as they hurtled forward. They were close to Her. They had to be in time, they just had to be!

Just as Cordovan, trailed by the other Watchmen, came over the final rise that would spill out of the trees into the quarter mile of open land surrounding the main gates to the city they struck. Pouring out of the trees like something vomited from the Pit they made a barrier between the mounted Watchmen and the city. A number of Gaunts, accompanied by at least two Soulcatchers, barred the way. Without thought Cordovan urged Swift forward. With what must have been nearly the last of her strength she leaped the line of Gaunts. Shouts, matched by exploding fire, accompanied by the sound of steel on steel, erupted behind him but Cordovan did not stop. Swift lurched left as she tried to get her feet under her while they careened down the small rise that spilled into open field. In a clatter of hooves, she lurched upright again haggardly racing for the city gates. Looking over his shoulder Cordovan saw that he was the only one who had gotten through. The others were fighting for their lives, *and may the Ancient One have mercy on them*, he thought. But he could not stop to help them. He was an arrow, in flight, aimed at *Her*.

Traffic was almost nonexistent as the hour closed in on the second Pass after midnight. But, Alexandria kept its gates open. The city was always awake. It was, after all, a major seaport as well as the capital. Cordovan pulled a small hand-held flag from his saddlebag as he galloped toward the front gate. The flag was bright purple, with a brown and gold hawk emblazoned on it, with its wings spread wide. The standard of the Watchmen fluttered in his hand as Cordovan waved it high over his head. The guards were scrambling to defend the gates as Cordovan hurtled through without stopping. Several of the gate guards were taking aim with crossbows while a number of others began mounting waiting horses. As he passed through the gate Cordovan threw his flag toward a group of the guards so that they could identify the emblem. Crossbows were lowered as the guards stood watching him ride on into the city. No one interfered with Watchmen especially when they were in a hurry. Cordovan raced through the streets of Alexandria. He could almost point to Her.

Late night revelers dashed from the street as Cordovan, atop Swift, careened over the cobbled stone. Her hooves clattered out a haphazard rhythm.

At Vester's Court he turned her barreling around the fountain before clattering off down the street. As he drew closer to the Hill the crowd thickened. Cordovan shouted, gesturing for people to move from his path, as he tried not to slow down. Vaulting onto the side walkway, to avoid a group of people leaving the theatre, he steered Swift back into the street, leaping her over a bench in front of a bakery before they raced on. Cordovan could feel time slipping away from him. It was like a blade being pulled too slowly from its scabbard to meet an attack. Gritting his teeth, he hurtled on, with the wind pulling tears from his eyes. Something deep down told him they were out of time.

†

Natassha jerked awake. A tortured squealing pulled her from the darkness of the sleep she had slipped into. It was the sound of a wounded or dying horse. She had drifted off while the coach had continued on toward the palace. Its gentle rocking had lulled her to sleep. But she knew immediately that it was no longer moving. Pulling back a thick, purple, velvet, curtain Natassha looked out the window of the door of the coach. Her eyes widened as she looked out on chaos. Men dressed in dark clothes fought viciously against her Imperial Guard. Horses were down while men were dying on both sides of the fray. Natassha could only guess that her driver was dead, or the coach would have been racing away as the Guard covered her retreat. A man slammed into the door of the coach. His face pushed up against the window. She jumped back startled. Natassha saw then that the men were wearing, what appeared to be, painted masks. The eyes could be seen but the mask covered the rest of the face. He turned, engaging one of her guard, and was gone.

The other door to Natassha's carriage sprang open behind her. Turning, with a surprised jerk, she saw another man wearing a mask carved with an exaggerated square jaw, with an elongated nose. He leaped into the coach. As he grabbed her shoulders she noticed his touch was ice cold. It made her shiver. She also noticed the eyes through the mask. They seemed lifeless.

Natassha did not panic. She remained calm, as she had been taught. She rotated her arms, thrusting her rigid palms, striking the inside of the man's elbows. The move threw his arms wide breaking his grip on her shoulders. Slamming her hands onto the cushioned seat behind her for leverage, Natassha snapped the heel of her right foot into his groin. The man fell back into the other seat of the coach with a muffled grunt. As he bent down, reaching between his legs to cover himself where she had just struck him, she lashed out with the inner-ridge of her left hand. With a perfectly formed knife-hand she struck his throat. There was a snap, followed by a gurgling sound, as the man fell over in a heap on the floor of the coach still trying to breathe through a ruined throat.

Gathering her dress in her right hand, to keep from stepping on it, Natassha climbed over the convulsing form, jumping out of the same coach door the man had leaped in. Stepping into the street she was frozen in place by what she saw. Blood spread slowly over cobbled stone from the motionless bodies littering the street like rag dolls. Horses and men law sprawled in awkward positions from one side of the street to the other. By quick count Natassha confirmed that the masked men in their dark, nondescript, clothing had outnumbered the Guard at least three to one. She began feeling sick as it dawned on her that she was meant to die here. The thought settled on her like a wet blanket. She looked around quickly for any surviving members of her Guard, but no one was moving. The coach rocked as it was jarred roughly. Natasha heard scuffling sounds coming from the other side.

Easing around the coach to its rear Natasha moved slowly to the edge of the left side. With her right shoulder against the rear of the coach she peeked around its lacquered side. Braced with his back against the side of the coach Captain Vam, of the Imperial Guard, was being held roughly by two masked attackers. Blood covered the white lace shirt where it peeked out from his black waistcoat. Natassha could see at least one wound in his thigh through a rip in his black breeches. The Captain struggled with the two holding him as a third rose from the ground approaching him with a sword in hand. Looking around wildly Vam noticed her at the rear of the coach. His eyes narrowed to hardened slits.

His voice was still defiant as he yelled at his assailants. "You have lost vile spawn! The Empress has escaped." His voice seemed to emphasis what came next. "Even if she is on foot, and has run all the way to the palace, you have failed!"

While continuing to struggle, he had told her what he could not say openly without revealing that she was close at hand. He had said to her that she was to run all the way to the palace. She continued to watch as the masked men looked at one another while Vam struggled to free himself. Natassha ducked back, leaning against the rear of the coach for a moment, sick with fear. She knew what she was supposed to do but part of her refused to listen. But what good would it do to die when so many had given their lives so that she would live? She steeled herself, preparing to run, with tears brimming up in her eyes. Just then darkness fell around her as the smell of sulfur filled her nose.

†

Wen was running to catch up. She floated across the rooftops of Alexandria like a wraith. The soles of her knee-high, black, boots thumped softly when she landed, as she flung herself through the air, vaulting from one rooftop to the next. Night Patrol was always fun. At least she thought so. Landing softly, nearly silently, she flipped forward once without the use of her hands. You got to haunt the top of the world that was Alexandria standing above it all. Wen's crimson shirt hugged her body flowing smoothly into fitted black breeches made from soft cotton. They were tucked into her polished boots. A blackwood scabbard was strapped to her back leaving the hilt of her sword, with its small square handguard, peeking over her right shoulder.

Wen breathed deeply as she planted her left foot stretching out her stride. With a hop, her right foot launched her off a brick retaining wall as she leaped the intervening space. Peddling her legs through the open air as she tucked her body in tightly at the top of the arc, she held her arms out like wings. Sailing fifteen feet through the air she touched down on the roof of an Inn adding a handspring with the last of the momentum from the jump. She came up to her feet running.

They should be just ahead, she thought. Wen had given them a head start before leaving Sanctuary. Bantu had wanted to be sure the Empress arrived back at the palace safely. Wen was their invisible escort. The Chief of Orders, Master Chief Maddock, had said no residual presence. The Master Chief liked wordy phrases. Maybe it was because he had served in the army of Bree before joining the Company seven years ago. Most of the Company called it going *ghost* for short. Say to a member of your team, go ghost, and they knew exactly what you meant. If the Commander wanted her ghost she would be ghost.

Crossing two more rooftops Wen slowed to a trot before stopping. Walking over to the edge she ran her fingers through her long, curly, fiery-red hair. Her gray eyes gazed down onto the street below her. A string of curses came unbidden to her lips.

†

Natassha ducked and ran. Something clawed at her back, but she had begun to move as soon as the darkness had fallen over her. Heading back the way the coach had come, the ruler of the greatest empire in the Twelve Nations, hiked up her dress as she went running down the street. Tears waited to erupt from her eyes as she ran. She thought of the fact that Captain Vam was likely dying behind her. Too many people had died in the past few days. Now an entire contingent of her Guard lay in the street dead or dying. Their leader was about to join them but all she could do was run.

Something was behind her. Natassha could feel it closing fast. The clattering of claws on stone followed her, getting closer, the farther she ran. The sound made her skin crawl. It, whatever it was, was almost on top of her. Natassha did not turn to look she just kept running. As tears began rolling down her cheeks they stopped being tears of sorrow. They began to become tears of anger as she realized that, if she died, the men who had protected her would have given their lives for nothing. The smell of sulfur hit her again causing her nostrils to flare at the stench. It made her gag as she ran on. There was a tickle at the nape of her neck like something breathing against it. *This is it*, she thought, for the second time in as many days. A thought struck her like a hand across the face. The Empress of Alexandria realized that she was not going to die running. She might die but it would not be running. Darting to her right Natassha spun around. She balled her hands into fists as she did. Holding them up in her front of her she slid into *Crane Crosses the Lake*. The sight of the creature that stopped in front of her almost tore a scream of terror from her throat, but she clamped down hard on the urge. It had dark-brown, leathery skin with thin, ropy limbs. The thing had claws, fangs, and bulbous eyes. It towered over her. It looked like a man and nightscreamer had been twisted together in a tortuous way. It screamed. Natassha could feel its need. The feeling that washed over her was a need to hurt something or someone. Whatever had been done to it the thing wanted to share its pain.

The intensity of the creature's feelings overwhelmed Natassha. Her hands went limp as they fell to her sides. She stood motionless while sheer, unremitting terror paralyzed her. Death was there, in that scream, looking at her. The thought rang out in her mind. Death was walking the streets tonight. Death had come for her. The creature took a step toward her. But after taking that step it stopped. What was it waiting for? Nothing could possibly stop such a terrible thing. It must have come from the darkest corner of the Lord of Sufferings' mind. The Betrayer, or one of the Dark's generals, must have sent this spawn of the Twisted Ones. Suddenly, Natassha heard what had not registered, moments before, through the haze of terror covering her mind like a heavy quilt. A horse clattered onto the street behind her. A deep voice shouted in her direction.

"By the blade of Oldershaw! By the wind-swept souls at the Glorious Gate and the coming Dawn." The sound of hooves pounding on stone accompanied the man's words. "By the Great Oath, I come! To the Watch! To the Watch!" The words came out shrill as he shouted through a failing voice.

Only one group, in all the Empire, used those words. Had she not been gripped with terror Natassha would have felt him drawing near. With immense effort she managed to turn her head to look behind her. There, like a vision of water conjured by a deluded mind, lost in a desert, grasping for any hope of salvation, was a man on a horse. He came galloping toward her with his sword held high. The creature darted past Natassha toward him. She watched the thing hurl inky blackness mixed with fire from a clawed hand. The man was ready. The horse canted sideways but kept coming forward around the fire. He rode through the darkness. The man leaped from the saddle crashing into the creature. Seconds seemed to stretch out forever as the two struggled in the street. The man was obviously weakened, looking near exhaustion, but Natassha recognized the dark-gray waistcoat and the matching breeches trimmed in black. The purple cloak that should have marked him a Watchman was gone. She should have known he was coming, should have felt him, but she had been too occupied to sense him. As the two struggled Natassha saw a strange light in his eyes. There was a wildness in them as if something feral had been released.

The creature clawed at the Watchman viciously. It caught him once in the chest before hitting him in the head. Her Watchman sprawled to the street like a puppet whose strings had been cut. The creature wove a darkness that enveloped them both. There was scuffling that Natassha could only hear. The Watchman screamed. His body came flying out of the patch of darkness hitting the street like a bail of hay. The huge creature walked – no, it hobbled like a disfigured man – slowly from the darkness. It stopped a few steps from the inky blackness. Natassha saw the long gash across the thing's head. Something green began oozing down the side of its head from just above one of its bulbous eyes. The creature fell like a cut tree crashing to the stone in a heap. The stench of it filled the street. Natassha turned away as she emptied her stomach onto the cobbled stone.

Steadying herself, Natassha pulled a handkerchief from her sleeve, drawing it across her mouth. Able to move again, as the terror that had gripped her began to subside, she rushed over to where her Watchman lay. As she approached him he raised himself shakily to one knee. Natassha stopped short of him staring in amazement. He was battered. Slowly, the man struggled to his feet. Looking at her, he swooned, as she came close to him. When she got close enough to see him clearly her breath caught in her throat. Past the bruises, the unshaven face, and the dried blood she could see that it was Cordovan del Allegressa. Her head spun as thoughts whirled about wildly in her head. He should not have been here. How could he be here? He had been sent to the distant northwestern corner of the Empire to take up the Watch. But somehow, amazingly, here he was saving her life.

Looking past her to where the creature was laying, Allegressa's features changed as pain gave way to desperation. Natassha looked back in time to see the thing move. She watched it rise to its feet. It began slowly making its way toward them. Allegressa could barely stand but he pushed Natassha back behind him. The man stood, barely able to remain on his feet, staying between her and the creature. Its screeching howl promised pain.

Her Watchman looked over his shoulder at Natassha. A crazed, feral, grin appeared through the blood-stained visage of his face. His voice almost cracked as he recited words she knew the Watchmen knew by heart.

If the Darkness comes to call
And every righteous hand does fall
I will stand against them all
To see Her safely home

A growl erupted from his throat as his upper lip curled into a snarl. The creature leaped on him. Natassha watched as its hands moved faster than she could follow but somehow Cordovan del Allegressa was not there. He dropped to the ground flinging himself into the creature's legs. The thing lost its balance as the Watchman used its own forward momentum to trip it. It hit the ground but immediately tried leaping up. But the Watchman was already there. His first cut took the thing's outstretched hand off at the wrist. The return swing of his sword cut across its midsection. As the thing tried to back away the Watchman leaped onto it. With a vicious swing he took its head completely off its shoulders. Its body convulsed a few times before erupting in flames. A sulfurous cloud rose from where the body lay as the thing burned away. Natassha had never seen anything like it.

Shaking her head Natassha came to her senses as she rushed to Allegressa. The Watchman took two steps from where the creature had fallen before he collapsed. Gritting her teeth Natassha grabbed him under his shoulders. With some difficulty she pulled him, out of the street, onto the side walkway. Kneeling beside her Watchman she gently placed his bloodied head in her lap. His blood seeped into her gown, but she did not care. Putting his head in her lap was, she knew, useless but she did not know what else to do. He was still alive but, only, barely. Tearing a piece of her gown off at the hem she began wiping the blood from his face. She tore another pressing it over the wound in his head. The tears she had fought came welling up. Her Guard lay back down the street, lifeless, while this man, her Watchman, who had given all for that silly oath they each took before her, lay dying because they were too far from her healers at the palace. The gifts they received when she made them members of the Watch would have made it possible for him to recover were his wounds not so serious. He had simply been through too much.

Hazel eyes opened as he looked up at her from her lap. A harsh, cracked, voice drifted up to her as he spoke. "My Empress, are you well?" he coughed roughly, blood speckling his lips, as a pained expression crossed his face. He focused his eyes. He looked at her in a hopeful way.

Natassha smiled down at him. "Yes, my Watchman. Your Empress is well, and she thanks you." She fought to keep her voice steady wiping the tears from her cheeks with her forearm. "Where did you come from Cordovan del Allegressa?"

He smiled at that as though the fact that she remembered him was significant. Natassha brushed her hand through his hair like a mother would a fallen son.

"Empress," he began. He stiffened with pain. His eyes watered while he looked as though he wanted to cry. He continued trying to fight the pain. His voice was stiff with the effort as he said, "Empress. We have been twelve days in coming to your side to save the Great Oath." A groan escaped his lips. Natassha stopped trying to wipe away her tears. She let them flow for him to see. He continued, "I have ridden from Merril Lee along with other Watchmen from Coste Din, Merric Bay, and even one who journeyed along the border of Province in Dessils Landing. We knew your life was in danger, so we came. Why are you crying, Majesty?" He coughed causing more blood to stain his lips.

Twelve days he had come, to his death, for her. In that moment Natassha noticed the unkempt hair on his face, the bags under his eyes, the way his cheeks sunk in slightly from lack of food, as well as the tattered, frayed edges of his uniform. She had never been able to get used to the lengths that others went in order to protect her. Were the lives that were lost tonight worth hers? Some would say certainly. Deep down, where it mattered, she did not think so. But she looked down speaking to her Watchman with confidence. She owed him at least that much. He should die with a confident Empress holding him, not a frightened, confused girl.

"Your Empress is only a bit shaken Watchman." As she spoke the imperial tone she had been tutored in came to her like the notes of an old well-worn song. "We must get you to the palace so that my Healers can see to you. You have served me well. The Great Oath is upheld. Now you must be helped."

His hand closed over her wrist as she went to move so that she could help him to his feet. "No, my Empress. Please forgive me for touching your Highness and speaking to your Majesty in such a way." She saw a vague sadness in his eyes. He was giving up. He was letting go. "Please Highness. Go into one of the shops or homes on this street until one of the other Watchmen can arrive. Please." The last word struck her like a blow. The tears flowed freely running down her cheeks.

A light female voice sounded from over Natassha's shoulder.

"Cordovan del Allegressa. I should have known you would try to get yourself killed just so your name can be written on your precious wall at

Watchkeep. You would like nothing better than to be hailed as one who gave his life for the Empress. That's supposed to be a big deal for you people, right?"

Natassha looked up from Cordovan to see a sorely wounded Captain Vam being supported almost completely by a redheaded woman she did not know. Natassha addressed the Captain.

"Captain Vam it is good to see you. Who is this woman who ridicules one of my valiant Watchmen?"

Vam looked from his redheaded Empress to his redheaded supporter. He had a strange look in his eye. His voice was rough around the edges. Pain plainly played across his features. "My Empress. This is Commander Wen Ava Noella of the Peoples Company. She arrived in time to help me dispatch the remaining assassins."

The woman was standing with her left arm around Vam. Her right hand was on her hip. She had a sly grin on her face. At the mention of her name she inclined her head ever so slightly.

Natassha sighed, saying, "It seems, Commander, that I cannot help but indebt myself to your Company more and more with each passing second."

The woman laughed softly smiling at Natassha. "We do what we can Highness. We do what we can."

Natassha returned her smile, if weakly, as she continued, "Please contact your Commander-General. Ask him, on my behalf, for an escort to the palace. We are also in need of a healer with dispatch or I will lose this man to the Collector of Souls."

Just as she finished her request a man landed heavily on the ground next to her. He must have jumped from the rooftop above. Natassha jerked her head to the right looking up from where she sat as the rich tones of his voice resonated over her head.

"I have already seen to it, Ruler of Alexandria. Your escort has arrived."

Relief washed over Natassha, like hot water from a shower, as she looked up into the grim face of Ossassande Bantu A' Omorede. He was still in the standard Company uniform of unrelieved black. The coat was slim-fitting. It was made from a very fine fabric. It fit him closely at the waist flaring out as it flowed down to the top of the thigh. The collar stood straight up. It glinted with the five, silver pips indicating his rank on one side with the glittering, green, gemstone on the other. The back of the coat was double-vented with a center pleat. In the crook of his left arm was his ever-present sword. His face looked like a mask of death. The Commander-General of the Peoples Company was angry. He looked around as if he was searching for someone to take it out on.

As Natassha looked up at him, what must have been thirty or forty of the People, with their special crossbows in hand, landed in the street from the rooftops above. They wore various styles of clothing but most still wore black. There were dashes of red, purple, and silver but black breeches, along with knee-high boots, abounded. Those special crossbows were everywhere. There was no shortage of drawn swords either. The Company, it seemed, had arrived.

Bantu looked around as he issued orders. When he finished speaking the People flowed out in several directions. Some took up guard positions while others roamed the general area in search patterns. Another one of them approached Natassha with a small wooden box.

Bantu reached down, pulling Natassha up gently, he drew her away from Cordovan to give the man room. Bantu held her protectively with his free hand engulfing her shoulder while his eyes scanned the street. Natassha watched as the man knelt next to an unconscious Cordovan who's breathing had grown shallow. He was wearing shiny black breeches, tucked into polished, black, knee-high boots, with a silver shirt. Weapons were evident hanging from a black leather belt at his waist with a silver buckle in the shape of three intersecting circles. The man took out a thick glass decanter with a gem-encrusted cap. Pulling the corked-ended cap out he poured a clear liquid into Cordovan's mouth. The man massaged Cordovan's throat as he poured prompting him to swallow the liquid. Natassha knew it was the *okoi*. Bantu called it the *waters of life*. Slowly color returned to her Watchman's features while the strain on his face eased until it was gone. The wounds she had been able to see were also gone leaving only bloodstains on his uniform. Then, Cordovan's eyes blinked open as he inhaled deeply.

The Company man helped Cordovan to his feet. Once the Watchman was standing the man went to take care of Captain Vam. Cordovan was a little unsteady, but he was alive. He walked slowly over to where Natassha was standing next to Bantu. He stopped in front of them. Once he was steady he looked up at Bantu.

Bantu spoke first. His voice was soft. It was filled with respect. For some reason Bantu had always liked her Watchmen. "Watchman. You have performed a great service today. You have upheld the Great Oath, saving your Empress, which I know was your aim." His voice softened as he continued, "But you have also saved my friend. I will not soon forget that. Now go slow. The *okoi* heals but it takes as much as it gives. You will need a good meal followed by a full night's rest to begin to fully recover."

Cordovan nodded in response to what Bantu said. He turned to look at his Empress. Natassha smiled up at her Watchman. Stepping away from Bantu she turned to face him. Natassha opened her mouth to speak but Bantu stopped her with an upheld hand.

"No, little one." His deep voice rose a little. "Do not speak. The time for talking will come. Right now, we must get you to the palace." Just as he spoke, the Imperial Coach, with a Company member in its driver's seat, clattered into view.

Bantu helped Natassha, Cordovan, and the healed Captain Vam into the coach, closing the door behind them. It was a testament to what they had been through that neither Vam nor Allegressa protested as Bantu took charge of her escort. The coach started rolling toward the palace for the second time that night. This time, however, it rolled forward under the watchful eye of the members of the Peoples Company. Twenty of them vaulted over the rooftops on either side of the street while, what looked like, another thirty encircled the carriage, trotting along in a circle that covered their route including the surrounding streets. Natassha could see through the small window in the roof of the coach. Standing astride the roof, as the Imperial coach rolled onward, was a tall, brown-skinned man in unrelieved black with an ivory-hilted sword in the crook of his left arm. The Commander-General of the Peoples Company watched their progress like an avenging spirit sent from the Ancient to stand guard. As Natassha watched, the People trotted by. She took note of how they managed to watch everywhere at once. They wore a look that said anyone – *anyone* - who barred the way would not survive. Natassha also knew that their look was as fierce as it was because they were not only guarding her but their own prince. Their prince stood astride the roof of her coach fully exposed.

The coach, along with its occupants, arrived at the Imperial Palace without further incident. The only commotion was caused by the palace guard nervously responding to the appearance of fifty or so armed Company members until Captain Vam vaulted from the coach to calm them down. Cordovan exited more slowly. He was greeted by the other Watchmen, who were standing in the courtyard with anxious expressions on their faces. Their tattered look told Natassha that these were the other Watchmen who had accompanied Cordovan.

Surrounded by her faithful Watch, the Captain of the Imperial Guard, and members of the palace guard, Natassha exited the coach. When they saw her unharmed the bedraggled Watchmen shouted. "The Oath! The Oath! *Bell'dagar'i* Allegressa! *Bell'dagar*!" The shout was in the High Cant, *Honor to Allegressa! Honor!* They were saluting Cordovan in the old way of the Watch that even predated the forming of the empire.

As Natassha walked into the palace she looked back in time to see Bantu leap from the roof of the coach. He sailed through the air before landing more lightly than a man of his size should. He strolled calmly through the gates walking back into the city proper without a backward glance. Fifty-one members of the Company padded off into the darkness after him, like a pack of wolves, without a word or a sound.

†

High in the Tower of Alexandria, Gaiden Colling paced in his cell. It was a dark, dreary place. The Tower was reserved for those charged with High crimes. You usually ended up in the Tower by Imperial decree. It was not a place for common criminals. A stay in the Tower usually ended in a public beheading. Gaiden paced across the few feet the cell afforded.

Turning on his heel, he paced in the other direction. His mind raced, as it had most of the night, since he had been brought to the Tower. He kept hearing the ominous screeching of the metal door of his cell, as it had slammed shut, repeating itself over and over in his mind.

Though Gaiden had years of training, as well as a finely-honed strategic sensibility, he could not think of a way out of his present predicament. That was one of the things that made the Tower so ominous. No one had ever escaped. It had housed all of the nobles who had failed to bow to Natassha Sobrine's father and grandfather during the making of the Empire. Kings and Queens, who had been unwilling to become simply Lords and Ladies in the Peerage of Alexandria, had not only forfeited their kingdoms but had also lost their heads as other former rulers watched.

Gaiden continued to pace absently tugging at the collar of his coat as though there was not enough room for his neck. They would let him stew for a while. That would be followed by a brief, but exemplary, trial. Judgment would be sure even as the punishment would be swift. After the roar of a gathered crowd Gaiden's head would be staring back up at his body from the bottom of a wicker basket. He wracked his brain but could think of no way out.

"You cannot think of a way out, can you?"

Gaiden froze. Though he stopped pacing at the sound of the voice he could not decide whether he had stopped himself or the voice had stopped him dead in his tracks. It was a cold, slimy, thing that seemed to crawl, over his shoulder, into his ear. He shivered. His heart beat faster as his throat constricted. All of a sudden, he was wild with fear. Sheer horror took hold of him. He opened his mouth to scream in terror, but nothing came out.

"Yes. Yes." The voice hissed. "You can tell, can't you?" The voice slid up behind him nestling in his ear like the cold finger of a dead man. Gaiden knew now. He was holding himself still. Not daring to move or hardly breathe even as his heart tried to jump out of his chest. Sweat began to form on his brow. Whatever was in the cell with him was a foul, deeply dark, thing. For a moment Gaiden thought he could hear faint screams somewhere off in the distance. The thing spoke again.

"You can stop trembling. I have not come to eat your soul. The Master has a use for you. That is if you want to live. You do want to live, don't you?" Its breath was ice cold on the nape of Gaiden's neck making small bumps rise on his skin. He fought not to spasm in terror as the thing licked the outer edge of his ear.

Gaiden stuttered out his reply. "Yes. I want to live." He swallowed hard. "Who is your Master? What does he want from me?"

A cold hand caressed Gaiden's head as it spoke. "You know who my Master is. The whisper in your dreams, the rustling sound in the back of your thoughts, as you satiated your desires. That is the Master. The things you see out of the corner of your eye that you dare not look at, the sounds in the deep of the night that you convince yourself you do not hear, these are manifestations of the Master. Thoughts of the Great, Glorious Lord have been with you all the while as, little by little, you gave your soul to the Darkness. None of you do it all at once. But, compromise by compromise, you give yourself to the Great, Glorious Dark. You know exactly who my Master is."

An unbidden tear ran down Gaiden's cheek as years of small compromises made in the shadows came to his mind. All the concessions he had made, all the tiny, seemingly acceptable, steps away from the Light he had taken, all came flooding back to him. He had sold his soul, little by little, bit by bit. He had never believed for an instant that one day its buyer would come calling. Gaiden tilted back his head and wailed.

A deep, haunting, cackle erupted behind him accompanying his anguished howl. It took only seconds for his cell door to fly open admitting the guards who rushed in with their swords waving about. But when the thing in his cell was finished Gaiden was splattered with blood that was not his and emptying the contents of his stomach in the corner. Gaiden knew there was horror painted across his features along with tiny flecks of blood.

The thing was tall. It was taller than most men. It had pale gray skin with long white hair that fell to the middle of its back. It eyes glowed in the darkness. It had the features of a man but there was a wild look in its eyes. Its clothes, cloak, and spear with its long curving blade, were all unrelieved black. There was a sizzling stench that rose from the hacked bodies of the dead guards. A murderous cackle came from what Gaiden now knew must have been a *Graelim*. Some called them Darklings. It was a foul thing that was not supposed to exist. It was the twisted spawn of a twisted mind. Mentioned hesitantly in the oldest histories, it had been made to be loosed on mortal men. It had been made to be loosed on those who had sided with the Allgis-sein in the fight against the Betrayer. With Gaunts, Soulcatchers, Guiles, Whisperers, and black-feathered Raken in the sky, Graelim had helped lead the armies of the Betrayer. They had tried to blot out the light of the sun from the sky. Here was one of those ancient things men had come to call *Horrors* in his cell. He shook now, uncontrollably, knowing why they had been called Horrors. The Graelim looked up from its grizzly work. It spoke to him in its icy voice.

"Come, Gaiden Colling. It is time for you to stand in the Great, Glorious Shadow of the Night so that you may pledge your allegiance to the Master. For the Master comes, hallowed be the Name. The Master is coming, and the army must be ready."

Gaiden was still shaking when he walked out of his cell behind the Horror wondering if it was too late to choose death.

There are those who believe that time is a constant. They perceive time as a precise measurement of equitable increments that are easily measurable and hence accessible as a function. But I propose to you today that time is, in fact, malleable. It moves, it even breathes, like a living thing, subject to our perceptions. If I am right, we will have to re-envision the nature of how we understand the past, present, and future. We may even have to start using words like inconvenient, or moral, when describing the nature of the passing of time.

*~Excerpt from the Cosgrove Lecture Series
as given by Lelange dek' Merris
from a work entitled
"The Counterfeiting of Time"*

Why doesn't the past stay there?

~*A widow, upon discovering her husband still alive.*

CHAPTER TWELVE

Of things past

The morning had been nothing but commotion. The palace always reverberated with the hum of activity but today was different. Natassha had finished her morning absolutions, after which, she dressed with the help of her servants. She wore a shimmering, blue gown with tiny, silver cranes in flight along the bodice accented by a slim tiara of diamonds with blue sapphires glittering atop her red curls. As soon as she had exited the imperial quarters she was informed that Gaiden Colling had escaped the Tower. Even as she sat on the Throne of the Morning, with its towering silver back, emblazoned with a soaring crane below a rising sun, made from hundreds of tiny glittering diamonds, Natassha knew that a thunderous look had settled firmly on her face. Though she had tried, several times, she had been unable to erase it from her features. As a result, many of the petitioners, not to mention the imperial functionaries, walked lightly around the throne room. They all bowed a fraction lower than normal this morning. She knew Colling's escape was not their fault but she could not make herself shake the foul mood it had put her in. Her jaw was tight, her teeth clenched, but what made the petitioners nervous was the fact that her eyes were narrowed to hardened slits. A deep frown, crowning her distemper, had replaced the warm smile that would have normally greeted those who approached the throne. The Hall of Lilies was an immense chamber of towering, broad, white columns with a polished marble floor. The marble was emblazoned with intricate mosaics of the flower that gave the hall its name. The Hall was where the ruler of Alexandria often sat in state, receiving petitioners, as well as visiting dignitaries, all while holding court. It was also the place where members of the Peerage were expected to make themselves seen on a regular basis. They were to stand under her gaze so that her preeminence was reinforced as she sat above them on the Throne of the Morning. It was also meant to remind them that they lived by her leave. The aristocracy always needed watching. Sometimes they needed humbling or they began to believe that what was yours should be theirs. It was another of the lessons her father had taught her as they sat in this great hall watching the throngs mingle.

The chamber had been designed to inspire both, awe in the subjects of Alexandria, and fear in its enemies. It represented the center of power of the Imperium. It also served as the backdrop for the ceremonies meant to magnify the image of the ruler of the empire. The Empress was someone to be feared, loved, or simply obeyed – depending on who you were. The vast elegance of the great hall made that statement, most notably, through its architecture. Her father had used it to its full effect, teaching Natassha, as she watched him, how to do the same. One of her father's favorite elements of the Hall's design made it possible for a person to speak normally from the throne yet have their voice carry to its furthest corner. That was impressive in a chamber that could hold several hundred people.

Today her terse words, coupled with her foul mood, also carried to the corners of the grand hall. Everyone knew - the word had spread like a small fire in dry kindling – that the empress was in a mood. Only a handful of people knew why but everyone felt the affects. While her mood did not actually alter what Natassha decided - she was wise enough not to allow her mood to affect her judgment - her mood did affect *how* she handled the people who came before her. The common people, those with legitimate problems, received little of the harsh side of her tongue. But those who came with frivolous concerns, as well as nobles with concerns of any kind, more often than not received adjudication of their situations with an ample application of her ire. Members of the aristocracy, along with frivolous commoners, had left her presence red-faced, stumbling, or stuttering their thanks, with their apologies for taking up her precious time. Men left ducking their heads, shuffling their feet, or with strangleholds on their hats. The women, even ladies of high standing, left with handfuls of skirts clutched tightly, or their curls bobbing against their shoulders, as they nearly ran from the Hall of the Sun. The word had soon spread that today was not a day for frivolity. A line that had stretched the length of the Hall, even out its towering double doors, had conspicuously dwindled, over time, to a handful of brave petitioners, grim-faced but resigned, as others decided their problems were not really all that bad. Natassha had even seen a few people in the antechamber, just outside the great hall, shaking hands while nodding to one another – some exchanging documents or coin, as if they had hastily resolved whatever conflict they had come to have heard. With an anxious glance into the Hall, they had left while looking about, as if they were hoping no one had seen the exchange. They left hastily as if they believed that if they were discovered they might still be hauled before the empress.

Kemme approached Natassha from her place on the dais, just behind the throne, on Natassha's left, with a steaming cup of choca. She made soothing sounds as she served Natassha but was brushed away by her empress. Natassha knew Kemme would be sulking for days after being brushed off in that manner. She would have to smooth Kemme's ruffled feathers when she was in a better mood. But for now, she would have to suffer through Natassha's foul mood along with everyone else. Once again, the thought that kept firing her foul mood crossed her mind again. *What will I tell him? How will I explain?* Natassha was in a deep funk because she had promised Bantu justice but was going to have to tell him that Gaiden Colling, the man that had betrayed them, had escaped!

A low growl escaped her lips just as a General with one golden star on the shoulders of his coat stepped forward to be heard. The man paled visibly at the sound. Natassha watched him swallow hard. He looked around at others in the chamber that were watching him closely. He began to get angry. Natassha knew what he was thinking. He had served in major campaigns, likely having faced death on numerous occasions in service to the empire, yet standing there, he thought, he was being made to feel like a child who had broken his mother's favorite lamp. It was clear he did not like the feeling. Natassha watched him take himself in hand. He managed to speak without the stammering others had displayed today, standing before an Empress in the Hall of the Sun, who was obviously less than pleased.

The man had white streaks in his brown hair. He had a strong, clean-shaven face. Though he was a little wide across the middle he stood up straight. His black boots were polished to a bright luster while the blue and silver of his uniform, the colors of the army of Alexandria, known as the Dawnmarch, seemed freshly pressed. The General had not decided at the last moment to make a report to the empress. Clearing his throat, he bowed, thumping his chest with a fist over his heart. "Grand Lady, your Imperial Majesty. May the sun ever shine on the Empire." It was the kind of remark her soldiers usually added when addressing her. The General continued. His voice gained confidence as he spoke. "I have come today, Majesty, with a petition from a young man seeking to enter service to the empire. Mind you, I am only bringing this before your Imperial Highness because you have made it clear in the past that you wished to be informed when the petition was of a certain nature." With another bow, the General, Natassha still could not remember his name, held out a scroll with both hands, palm up. He kept his head bowed until the Chamberlain of the Hall, in his purple imperial livery, accented in cream, removed the scroll from his hands. The Chamberlain unrolled the scroll. He took a moment to examine it. Satisfied that it contained nothing dangerous he rolled the scroll back up, carrying it up the seven steps to the dais, before copying the way the General had offered the scroll to her, with a bow, in both hands, with his palms up. The Chamberlain stood that way until Natassha reached out to take the scroll. With a flourish, accomplished without looking up, the Chamberlain, a plain-faced man of middle years with curly brown hair, backed away, returning to his place at the foot of the steps.

Natassha unrolled the scroll. As she read her face soften a fraction.

Majesty,

Glorious Daughter of the Morning. May the sun always shine upon you and the Ancient One delight in your ways. I do not expect that these words will actually be read by you. But I do know that you have ever been gracious to those of us who have served in the Dawnmarch. My father was with your grandfather at Kemmen's Pass. I was with your father at the battle of Murrik, and was wounded at Belldune Hill. I am writing to you, Glorious One, may the sun always shine upon you, because my son has come of age. He is a good young man, trustworthy and true. He is our joy and our pride. He is all that my wife and I have so we are sending him to you. His grandfather served your grandfather, his father served your father, and we have sent him to the capital in the hopes that he can serve you. It has been our family's way to live in the service of yours. It is our most humble request that our son be allowed to continue that tradition. Long live the Daughter of the Morning! May she ever reign!

Your humble servant
Osdall Devilwind, Captain – Retired
Third Battalion
Dawnmarch

As Natassha rolled the scroll back up she allowed the lines of her face to soften ever so slightly. Her gaze was still hard but not so much as it had been. And how could she not soften her countenance? Somewhere in the Hall was a young man whose family had served her family faithfully for at least two generations. They were asking to make it three! Natassha remembered the stories concerning the battle at Murrik. It had been a bloody mess. According to most it has also been a close-run thing. Her father had often spoken in hushed tones about that place. Late of an evening, with a few cups of wine behind him, he would stare off into nothing as he spoke of the men who served in the Dawnmarch on the killing fields of Murrik. How many times had he spoken of their sacrifice, their courage? How many times had he said to her that had they shown a hair less bravery, been a shade less constant, that he would have died on that muddy field? It was one of the reasons he had made sure to take care of the veterans who had served. They did not become wealthy men but they wanted for nothing. His faithful soldiers were given some land along with a monthly stipend. Her father had made sure that they had access to the Imperial Healers in their retirement. As an added bonus they paid no tax on whatever they made or grew. He had taught her that it was a ruler's responsibility to take care of the people who had served.

The most personal of her father's commands concerning them was that they were always – *always* - allowed an audience with the ruler of Alexandria – even if it meant they had to wait days for the opportunity. He had drilled it into her. Honor those who served you. They deserved no less. An abiding sense of gratitude was one of the simplest things that human beings often failed to remember. Natassha could almost hear her father's voice in her head. Somewhere in the Hall was a young man whose father had been one of those brave men. His father had been a soldier in the Dawnmarch - a man of middle rank. No doubt his grandfather had served similarly. A thought occurred to Natassha, a way of allowing him to serve while bestowing, what his family would see as a great honor, upon his entire family line. Like her face, Natassha softened the edge on her voice.

"General, I thank you for bringing this to my attention. Is the son of Devilwind among us?"

The General nodded to himself as if what she had said was only right and proper. "Yes, Majesty. May the sun shine upon you always." He seemed to say that with more enthusiasm than he had been able to muster earlier. Natassha noticed that his chest seemed to be sticking out further. The man motioned back at the line of petitioners. At his signal a young man sauntered forward with all the obliviousness of the young casually strolling to where the General was standing at the foot of the steps. Natassha looked him over as he made his way over. He walked forward with the kind of innocence that made him immune to the pretention around him. He looked as if he was impressed by the structures around him but not the people. He was plain while still managing to be handsome. Big, brown eyes adorned a face with a slim nose. A strong chin anchored his features resting under a shaggy brown mop of hair. The young man stood over the General's six spans of height looking down at the older man. He had that rakish slimness young men had with the broad shoulders to match. Natassha could tell that under his plain, but well-made, wool clothes, was strong muscle. As he stood there, next to the General, the old soldier whispered to him. Suddenly, as if it was an afterthought, the young man bowed at the waist thumping his fist to his chest over his heart. He spoke in a clear, high tenor. "May the sun shine on your Majesty. May you ever reign." Then, like a fool at a country festival, he smiled the biggest smile Natassha had seen in days. She had to fight not to break into a fool grin herself.

Clenching her jaw, she pursed her lips, in order to drive off that smile. Natassha leaned forward on the Throne of the Morning. "So, young man. What is your name?"

He made like he was about to step forward but was held in place by the General who nodded for him to speak from where he stood. With that fool of a grin still on his face, the young man answered, "Majesty, I am Aubrey Devilwind."

Natassha cleared her throat as she looked down at the scroll in her lap, which she had unrolled again. She held it in her left hand while straightening her shimmering blue dress, brushing absently at one of the silver cranes embroidered on its bodice, with her right hand. Looking at Aubrey Devilwind again she said, "This letter from your father says that he, along with your mother, wishes for you to serve your empress as your father served the Old Emperor. Is that so?"

Still smiling, but less so since her mention of his father, he responded as if he just remembered why he was present. "Yes, Majesty. It is their hope that I may serve you. You are the world to them. They say that we must do all that we can to support you, Mum." His voice had taken on a solemn note. He had reverted to calling her Mum. It was a way of saying mother that was often used by only the most faithful families. They had called her mother the same thing. Natassha half-smiled to herself. It was partly at the ridiculous notion of a young man, who was probably her age, calling her Mum but also because it was not so ridiculous at all.

Looking down from the throne at the young man Natassha asked him, "And what about you, Aubrey Devilwind? You have said that it is the wish of your parents that you serve me. What do you wish?"

His face blushing slightly at her question, he took a step forward, shrugging off the General's attempt to hold him in place, oblivious to the crossbows that were immediately raised to target him from all around the chamber by members of the Imperial Guard. "Majesty! It is not only what my parents wish; it is my desire as well! It is what I have always wanted, since the days I watched my father ride off to serve the Emperor. I only wanted to ride off in service to you one day." He dropped to one knee, placing his right palm on the floor, in the old way. The words of the Old Oath came rushing from him. "For a single day, or a thousand dawns, with a single limb, or my very life, I will serve until I displease you or death comes to call." As the last of his words echoed off the walls he continued to kneel. He waited. The General's eyes were wide with either shock or amazement as he stared down at the young man. The Hall, which had been filled with whispering voices, was now stilled in stunned silence. No one swore the Old Oath anymore. It was seen as antiquated, a relic of an era that many thought long past, most for good reason. Most thought the days of swearing personal fealty were over in Alexandria.

Natassha stood. As she rose from the throne the throng of people filling the Hall of the Sun knelt, almost in unison, with the exception of the Guard. With the train of her shimmering blue gown trailing behind her, Natassha floated down the steps, on her slipped feet, to stand before the young man as he continued to kneel. The Chamberlain of the Hall had come to hover at her right hand, albeit at a customary three paces away, while Kemme was so close to her left side she nearly brushed against Natassha's arm. Kemme was the only member of the entire Imperial Staff, aside from Captain Vam, who could stand that close to her in public. Twenty of the Guard had crowded in to stand within a few steps of them all, pushing everywhere else back to what they thought was a modest distance. Natassha ignored everyone except Aubrey Devilwind. It was rare. It was considered one of the highest honors a subject could ever receive. Natassha leaned over. She cupped his strong chin in her tiny hand. Lifting his head up, so that she could look into his eyes, she spoke to the young man. "Aubrey Devilwind, will you serve wherever I place you?"

Without hesitating, his gaze steady, he replied, "Yes Majesty, wherever and however."

Without releasing his chin Natassha looked over at the General who, though he knelt with his head down, had his mouth hanging open. "General, has he been tested?"

Clicking his mouth shut, the General gathered himself, and without raising his head, nodded as he responded, "Yes Majesty. We put him through his paces. His father served under me so it was no surprise that his father had trained him well. He has exceptional skills in horsemanship, crossbow, and sword, especially to be so young. His mind is quick. He even seems to be able to keep his wits about him. I would accept him in the Dawnmarch without hesitation, nor would it surprise me to be putting knots of rank on his shoulders before long, Majesty."

Natassha nodded to herself knowing, after such a glowing report, that she could go ahead with what she had planned. Raising her voice - what she would say now was for the benefit of everyone still kneeling in the hall - she addressed the young man directly. "Very well. You have taken the Old Oath, Aubrey Devilwind. I will repay you in kind." Her voice took on the tone of one speaking old, well-worn verses. "For all the passing moons of your faith, this I pledge, that I will use the strength of your arm honorably, that I will not sell your life unjustly, nor give you cause to mourn your vow. This I swear." Taking her hand off his chin she laid it lightly on his head. "Aubrey Devilwind, you are to be taken from this hall and escorted, without delay, to Watchtower. Once there you will kneel before the Gallant Master of the Gate, informing him that the Empress has sent you to stand to the Watch. May the Ancient shelter you and have mercy on your soul."

With that she turned on her slippered heel. With a deliberate pace she mounted the seven steps back up to the Throne of the Morning. In her wake, murmurs became a boisterous cacophony of voices as people rose to their feet commenting on what they had just witnessed. It was, after all, a thing rarely seen. Though it had been a stressful morning for them, dealing with an empress in a foul mood, they would be telling their children how they were present to see a man set to the Watch. As Natassha resumed her seat, on the Throne of the Morning, she could see some of the people who had been near the young man patting him on his shoulder. He was tall enough that most had to reach up to do it. The General was beaming brightly as though the young man were his own son. Aubrey Devilwind just stood there, speechless, staring up at her like she was something from an old story. Natassha nearly smiled at him but it would have ruined the effect. She knew that neither he, nor his family, had ever imagined that when he set off for the capital, carrying a letter of introduction from his father, he would be chosen to become a Watchman. They were handpicked, by her, from hundreds of candidates after being put through a rigorous examination of their abilities. Many came seeking entry to Watchtower but only a handful ever entered its gates. Devilwind was stunned. As the General led him out of the Hall Natassha had the sense that she had chosen well. There was still one more thing to do before he would be a true Watchman but that would be done later, in private, at Watchtower. For now, she settled back into her seat. She waited for the next petition as she thought about what she was going to tell Bantu. She tried not to go back to sulking.

†

The sun was up. It was another beautifully temperate Alexandrian day. He was trying his best to enjoy it as he walked toward the front gate. It was early morning - Bantu's favorite time of the day. He felt fully alive even though he had only had a few hours of sleep. Macrina had awakened him at Sixth Pass. There she had been, his ever-present shadow, looming over his bed in the predawn darkness like some ancient spirit waiting to moan enigmatic words from undead lips. He had squinted, rubbing at his eyes, trying to clear them, until he could visually identify her. In her delicate hand, his personal scribe had been holding a steaming cup of choca, while she looked fresh as a newly pressed gown, apparently unaffected by the early hour.

Macrina was the only person allowed in his quarters without so much as a knock. Even Anna, the Matron of the Tower, knocked, but not Macrina. It was not because that was the way Bantu had planned it but because she had taken the liberty early on and he had not been able to convince her that it was inappropriate. Occasionally, unbidden memories of the first time Macrina walked in on him, as he was drying off after a bath, would float up to the surface of Bantu's mind. He would become embarrassed all over again at the memory of leaping back into the tepid water followed by Macrina's indignant, dismissive snort as she laid out clothes for him to put on. She seemed to think that his personal scribe was entitled to know even the most intimate details concerning him. Though she allowed no one else to see him indisposed she would watch him get out of bed with only his smallclothes on seeming to think nothing of it. Since he was too embarrassed to admit that *he* was embarrassed, by her watching him, Bantu never said anything. He had grown used to Macrina always being around. He had even grown accustomed to how she hovered – not that he liked the hovering.

Macrina had given him his choca while fussing about the small amount of sleep he had allowed himself before launching into his schedule for the day. While she read from a large journal, held with one hand, propped against her waist, she had absently touched his head with the other to see if she needed to shave it before continuing on with their morning routine. Macrina had a nutty-brown complexion. Her hair was black as midnight, but perfectly straight, hanging all the way to her waist. She was small all the way around with a tiny nose, ears, hands, and little feet. The only thing big about her was her eyes. They were black as midnight. She came from a land even farther east than his ancestral homeland out across the Deep. Her hands and feet were tattooed with delicate script in a tongue he did not know. There were small complex patterns matched by even smaller flowers around that unknown script. When Macrina spoke it was in a slightly halting, lilting fashion that Bantu had always found lovely to hear. There were times when she reverted to an older tongue that Bantu did not understand. It was usually when she was murmuring under her breath or speaking heatedly about something that displeased her. Macrina would never admit that she was cursing but the tone was clear enough to let you know that was exactly what she had been doing. When asked about it Macrina would protest that a woman of her standing did not curse. That explanation was normally accompanied by a sharp nod with a diffident sniff to punctuate the point.

The top she wore was tight, long-sleeved, in pale lavender with a plunging neckline. She wore a long wraparound skirt of an even paler gray. She was barefoot - she always went barefoot – but somehow managed to have the nicest looking feet, with tiny bells, on a leather cord, wrapped around her ankles. Bantu had thought it would have been a waste to have the tattoos but wear shoes to cover them though he knew that was not her reason for always being barefoot. Apparently, only married women among her people covered their feet or went without the tiny bells around their ankles. Once, when Bantu had asked what unmarried women in her homeland did when the weather turned cold, Macrina claimed that it never got cold in the land of her birth. Big dark eyes had gazed at him from her small, narrow face while he sipped from his cup of choca sitting on the edge of his bed in his smallclothes. She had lit all the lamps in his room and opened the double doors to the balcony, letting the warm breeze in, before waking him.

There had been hot water in a pitcher on the stand in the corner ready for his use. Bantu washed his face first. He cleaned his teeth while Macrina crooned on in the background. He had finished quickly knowing he would wash up in a more thorough fashion after the morning workout. Turning to the wardrobe he had pulled out a black, short-sleeved, shirt of tight woven cotton with three tiny intersected circles, in silver, embroidered over the heart. The shirt was double-breasted. The left side lay over the right. The right flap tied underneath the left, at the waist, holding it in place. The left flap tied off with a bow that remained visible where the chest met the right shoulder. Macrina had stood in front of him, reaching up to take the ties in her hands, making the knot at the shoulder of his shirt. Bantu had also grabbed a pair of black breeches that fit loosely. They tied at both the ankles and waist. A pair of black sandals, which laced up to the knee, had completely his attire. Finishing his choca, Bantu had set the cup on the table at the center of his quarters on his way out with Macrina right behind him.

Looking to the east toward the Macca Deep, Bantu had watched the sky lighten in anticipation of the sun breaking over the horizon to announce a new day. Ahead of him people had streamed out of buildings heading toward the Training Grounds. He remembered thinking that it was going to be a beautiful day. The air had already warmed, sweetening, as the breeze brought the scent of the various flowers planted around Sanctuary to his nose. He could smell the scent of gardenia blossoms that were always planted in greater numbers than any other flowering plant in the compound.

Stepping off the walkway onto the well-packed earth of the grounds, Bantu had walked over to his place at what would become the front of the gathering with Macrina jingling from the ankles a few steps behind him. There were no traces of the stage from the Last Rites or any of the other items that made up the arrangement for the procession of the previous night. The grounds were clear for the morning workout.

This was mostly an informal gathering with the exception of the opening form. As the sun broke the horizon Bantu had clapped his hands together three times. The crowd that had gathered formed themselves into straight parallel lines. Facing what had to be several hundred of the People Bantu began the First Form. The First Form was simple, but it demanded concentration. Dressed in identical attire to his, the ranking members of the Company who were not on duty, just coming off duty, or on a mission outside of Sanctuary, had focused on the Form following the movements of the Master of Sanctuary.

Pressing his palms together, with his fingertips pointed up, and the backs of his thumbs against his chest, Bantu had bowed to the gathering. His slight bow had been echoed by a deeper, more formal, one from the ranks lined up in front of him. Returning his hands to his sides he had stood straight. What had come next had the appearance of a dance rendered in slow motion.

The People had flowed in unison from one stance to another. Arms rotated as legs rose and fell. Hands had shifted, flowing, first fists, and then knife-hands, followed by hammer-fists. Drifting slowly in between movements, it was as if they had been encased in some thick liquid that made moving a deliberate process. While ranking members had been unaffected, a sheen of sweat had broken out on the faces of cadets, as they moved. They had been clothed identically to Bantu with the exception that their clothing was white. Their muscles had been taut, flexing, with each transition. One moment the moves had been as slow as falling snow but in the next became a darting strike that ended with a delicate move of the hand or another slowly developing turn.

Bantu had always thought the Form was the perfect balance between the deadly and the beautiful. The positions seemed to mimic a dance, but they were decidedly strikes, blocks, or transitions between the two. Still, it was a thing of beauty to behold. There was no better way to warm up the body or focus the mind for the rest of the morning ritual.

The First Form had ended with a flourish borrowed from the stilt-legged, white-feathered crane. Right leg suspended forward, bent at the knee, Bantu had balanced there unmoving. His left arm had arched away from his body like a wing while he pushed his right fist forward as taut muscles rippled along his forearm. Suddenly he had leaped, spinning once, the fist turning into a knife-hand strike while planting the left leg as he landed. Bantu had matched the knife-hand strike with a right sidekick. Bantu had let the leg hang suspended at the end of the kick for a few moments while he inhaled deeply. After a few seconds he had returned to the beginning position with his legs together. His hands had returned to his side.

The ranks had followed his movements precisely. They were standing at first position with him. Bantu had taken in the moment feeling his body loosen. His mind had been clear. He had been able to sense where everyone around him was standing. He had known he would have still felt them even if he had closed his eyes. They had been ready for the rest of the morning ritual. Pressing his hands together, palm against palm, as he held them at chest level with the backs of his thumbs touching at the center of his chest Bantu had bowed slightly. The lined up ranks had bowed low before breaking formation. With the Form completed they had grouped themselves according to ability and type of training.

New members of the Company, recently *Called* from the ranks of the Cadets, had carried practice weapons onto the grounds. All over the training area groups of people holding practice weapons had engaged one another while those of greater skill watched as well as taught. Turning from the rest of the field Bantu had faced Macrina who was standing behind him with his practice sword in one hand and a small bundle of parchment under her other arm. She walked over to where Bantu had stood handing him his weapon. They had worked so closely together, for so long, that it was as if Macrina could read his mind.

The basic practice sword was several lengths of thin, flexible, wood bound together with cord in several places along its length. The tip was covered in a padded, leather sheath to prevent injury when stabbing. The hilt was covered with sweat-stained leather. There was a small, round, wooden guard to protect the hands at the base of the hilt. Most practice swords of the type were straight, but Bantu had the Company's made with slightly curved wooden lathes lashed together to represent the slightly curved sword favored by most of the People. Bantu had swung the weapon through the air loosening his shoulders in the process. Turning from Macrina he had faced the group that stood waiting for him.

The people standing in a loose group waiting for Bantu had consisted of some of the best swordmasters in the Company. Practicing with Bantu was a privilege accorded only to the very best. This was the Master Class. Among the group this morning had been Onya, Basil, Almaldren, and Wen to name a few. The master class had consisted of a total of twenty-two. Assuming an opening stance, his right leg slightly out front, his body turned almost perpendicular to the group, Bantu had steadied his breathing. He had smiled again, broadly, as the group stepped back a few paces to allow eight of its members to move forward slowly raising their weapons to the ready. *So, it would be eight today,* he had thought to himself.

The first order of business for Bantu's training group was always an attack on its leader. The People had strange, competing notions about their leader. They were overly protective in general but would attempt to brutally assault him every morning, even though they considered it training. With his practice weapon tucked in the crook of his left arm, his left hand cupping the hilt in a reverse grip, Bantu had raised his right hand into the air. His hand had hung out in front of him with his palm turned toward the sky. Curling his fingers back toward himself Bantu had motioned with a wave that said, *come*.

They had come. They came swiftly and fiercely. Like a pack of wolves that had cornered their prey after a long chase, they had come. Swords clattered together as Bantu had met his attackers, his sword twirling in his hands, its hilt passing through his fingers. A stiff *thwacking* sound accompanied each crossing of wooden blades. The key to defending against multiple opponents was to use their numbers against them. They would not come at you one at a time, as enemies did in some of the plays Bantu had seen performed in the theatre. The world was not a stage. In the real world, enemies attacked simultaneously from several directions. You needed to keep moving unless you could put your back against something that would force them to come at you from only one direction. On the training field he had no such accommodation, so Bantu had to keep moving. While moving you had to remain unpredictable. Attacking out of sequence or in the least expected quarter was a good tactic. It all sounded very mechanical, but it could only succeed when the technique had become so deeply embedded it was in your very bones. The body had to know how to move without thought. Bantu had seamlessly entered the *abundance*. Reaching out with his consciousness he had emptied himself as the sun made a full appearance in the sky. *There was no need to avoid being hit* - it had poured from him like sand running through spread fingers. *No desire to win* - the thought had funneled away like air from his lungs. *No fear of failure* - he had laid it down like flowers on a grave. He had let it all go, all of it. In letting it go he had freed himself to enter the present moment fully. His focus had narrowed to the world around him as everything else faded away. The world had been present with him. He had known what they would do. When one fully realized what the masters in his homeland called the *Warring Way*, one could enter a place where you could almost see what was going to happen a split second before it did.

To his right a sword had thrust in at him. He twisted to his right sliding his body along the blade length. Making the twist into a full turn he had leaned back hard on Almaldren. Laying his weight against Almaldren had forced him have to support Bantu or fall to the ground with him. Two others drifted in at him with well-aimed attacks. Bantu had waited until the last moment before throwing himself to his right while letting Neri's thrust-strike, to his left, impale Almaldren in the back. He caught the overhead slice that had come in on his right on his blade, at the seventh position, above his left shoulder. His parry had been strong enough to send Kellive's blade slashing down at Neri, to his left, catching her in the neck. Bantu had cut across Kellive's waist when he lunged forward. It would have opened his belly were the sword truly steel. Touching the ground with one hand, as he past Kellive, Bantu had tucked his legs into his body rolling up several feet from Almaldren, Neri, and Kellive. But as he rolled to his feet three more had been on him. He had known what they would do. *He* was not there. Bantu had emptied himself filling the space with everything else. He had been lost in the rapture of the *abundance*.

Bantu had blocked Almaldren's overhead cut high. As Wen came in at his left side, at the same moment, he had slapped her blade away with his left hand. Isabelle had come in between Almaldren and Wen hoping they would occupy him so that she could make a touch. Immediately after slapping away Wen's blade with his left hand Bantu had brought the same hand up to catch the wrist of Isabelle's swordhand. A simple hook-kick had caught Isabelle behind her forward knee knocking her leg out from under her. While still holding her wrist, Bantu had turned her blade to block a cut-strike from Wen who had still been on his left. A twist on her wrist, after the parry, had made Isabelle relinquish her grip on her sword. As Isabelle's sword hit the ground Bantu had struck to his right with a block-thrust. Almaldren was re-engaging with a mid-line attack at fifth position. The block had stopped the arching cut while forcing Almaldren's blade out of its attack line to the far right. Bantu's thrust had come in immediately behind the block catching Almaldren in his ribcage. Anyone watching could have listed the forms from one move to the next. *Sweeping the Hall* had become *Hopping the Broom,* which had turned into

Falling Crane. *Falling Crane* had been replaced by *Dragon Folds its Wing*. In a blink *Farmer Fells the Grain* had met *Hawk Splits the Clouds*. Bantu had moved like lightning.

Stepping forward Bantu had shouldered Isabelle into Wen, to his left, and then kicked Isabelle's grounded sword out of the combat area. A quick side-step-hop to his left allowed him to launch into a side-flip clearing the space he had been standing in for too long. Isabelle had stalked from the combat area swordless, massaging her wrist, leaving Wen and two others. While he had been held in place for precious seconds Wen had regained her balance. Along with the other two she had formed a circle around him. As he landed they closed on him. He had known what they would do.

Bantu had rushed Wen, still to his far left, in the space he had just vacated. Just as he had come within her striking range he danced to his right meeting her attack blade on blade. They had closed chest to chest. Locking his grip on her sword hand Bantu had danced left with her as she tried to pull away from him. Bantu had not let go. Instead, he had turned Wen putting her between him and the other two. Pippa, to his right, had been the closest. Spinning Wen to his left Bantu had engaged Pippa, striking once, with vicious precision as he came around. The man had barely blocked the angled strike. It had not been meant to score a touch only to freeze Pippa momentarily making Wen, whom he had just released, believe she could score a touch to his back. As Pippa had blocked his cut Bantu reversed his blade. Without looking, he had stabbed backward, hearing the reassuring curse while feeling the pressure of Wen's body connect with his blade. A startled Pippa had hesitated. Bantu feigned a cross-body cut, from right to left, twirling his sword around to a two-handed forward grip. Mid-cut, Bantu had performed a reverse spin with a stop-thrust impaling Pippa in his mid-section. There had only been one person left.

Onya had glided forward with a smile, shaking her head, while twirling her sword with ease. The thought, easily read on her face, had been, *Why me?* But then it had disappeared as the glide became a hop-lunge. She had nearly scored a touch. Her sword had been held two-handed. She brought it from first position, swinging upward toward the waist, as she lunged. *Serpent Strikes the Wind.* Bantu had cut downward causing the wood of their blades to smack together loudly. Onya used his parry as a pivot position spinning left to her rear as her blade floated up over her shoulders during her turn. She had cut downward as she completed her turn. *Scorpion Lashes its Tail.* He had met her at position six with his hands turned up. His swordblade had been held parallel to the ground. Onya was relentless. Bantu remembered thinking how masterfully she moved. A snap front-kick had forced him to hop backward. She followed him with a stop-thrust that flowed into another spinning reverse cut rising to lunge at his neck. *Willow Waves at the Moon.* Blade to blade they had met as the wood resounded thickly. The group had gathered closer, urging them on, calling out in appreciation of each move. Onya had been flawless. The thought had passed through his mind, but he had not grasped it. He had seen her face between their flashing lengths of wood. His mind had been as still as a mountain pond. They had begun moving at a blinding speed as they danced the dance of death together.

Unthinking, the two had flowed from one position to the next, a mastery of the sword shown in the brilliance of their technique. Bantu had known he was smiling broadly. He had seen Onya's eyes reflect a hint of sparkling glee in their depths. As it had begun to appear that the two were evenly matched Bantu had done what only masters of the *Warring Way* could do, he had stepped out of the *Seeming.* He was no longer breathing. Inside a moment the body did not need air. Things around him had slowed to a crawl. Onya's next strike had come at him like a leaf floating on a slow spring breeze. Her blade had drifted lazily toward him. Bantu struck, and the world had returned to normal.

A roar had erupted in his ears as he stepped back into the *Seeming.* They knew he was the best among them. But knowing and seeing were, of course, two different things. Awe had been written like poetry on the faces around them. Though Onya had been rubbing at her midsection she was smiling. Bantu had heard someone remark that it had happened so fast they had not seen the actual touch. While the group talked about what they had, or had not, seen Bantu had stepped closer to Onya. The small woman had looked up at him with a lopsided grin. It was an expression that said she was smarting from the blow.

Bantu spoke softly enough that his words had reached only her ears as he smiled down at her. "Onya-san. I don't know what to say other than … impressive." Onya had the skill of a master. One day that skill would carry her to a place she did not even believe possible. Bantu would not, could not, tell her. At a certain stage of development along the *Warring Way* the teacher had to step back. The student had to make the rest of the journey on their own. He had no doubt that Onya would get there.

Resting her practice blade on her right shoulder Onya had inclined her head briefly. "Thank you, sir. Both, for the complement, and the lesson. I did not even see the strike coming. I would give much to have you face the Blademasters of my homeland. It would be a humbling, much needed, lesson for them. A defeat at your hands might help open their eyes. Some of the *Kobukku-do* believe that they are unbeatable. But the world is too large for that to be true, no?"

Bantu had hugged her briefly before turning back to the class. They had been going over, in stages, some of the techniques displayed in the engagement. Taking up stances, they had touched blades lightly, progressing from one form to the next in slow, exaggerated motions. Periodically they stopped to talk about a certain sequence. They had discussed the relative strengths or weaknesses of the attack lines that were or were not taken. Bantu, followed by Onya, had joined in. Training had gone on for another Pass before it became necessary to attend to the other duties of the day.

Bantu returned to his quarters for a bath, during which Macrina had shoved several pieces of parchment at him to sign, while asking a hundred questions about Company matters that needed his attention. Bantu had been ready to get to the thing he had been looking forward to for weeks. He had thrown on his uniform quickly, apologizing to Macrina on his way out for those questions he had left unanswered. He was at that moment, leisurely, making his way down the street that ran along the front of Sanctuary toward the docks. There was a winding path at the rear of Sanctuary that circled down along the side of the cliffs. But he enjoyed taking this longer way to the docks because it afforded him the infrequent opportunity to get out of Sanctuary while seeing a little of Alexandria proper on the way. Bantu was back in the Company uniform with his sword in the crook of his left arm. The uniform, along with the silver buckle of his belt, made in the shape of three intersecting circles, was enough to identify him as one of the Company to the people he passed on the street. Most waved, or smiled, at him as he walked by while only a few stopped him to ask about some kind of help. None of it was so serious that it was cause for his immediate attention, for which he was grateful. He was able to direct them to Sanctuary with assurances that they would get the help they needed. Macrina would normally have been half a step behind him but there had been some pressing orders that he had needed her to deliver to certain officers leaving Bantu, blissfully unaccompanied. While there would normally be upwards of twenty Company members, somewhere nearby, trailing him for protection, he had managed to pre-empt even that by hurrying out of Sanctuary unannounced. After a few minutes, he had realized, to his disappointment, that he had not utterly escaped. Using the com-gem, at his collar, he had forced the four Company members, who had managed to follow him, to identify themselves. Somewhere above him Wen, Bella, Orah, and Isabelle were playing bodyguard. After a moment's consideration Bantu had decided to allow them to continue to follow him. Had he sent them away he would have had to contend with fifty, or more, of the Company pouring out of Sanctuary looking for him. He was not going to let this moment be spoiled. Bantu had been looking forward to it for too long. He was on his way to the docks to do something he very much liked to do. He had decided he was going to enjoy every minute of it, even the walk.

It took about an hour to make that pleasant walk to the docks. Kinsington Pass was a long, winding, street. Though it was a long walk the street ultimately only descended some four or five hundred spans from top to bottom. It took time to walk its length because it wound around like it was alive but not sure where it was going. Some thought it had begun as a goat path, along a high pass, long before Alexandria was carved out of the landscape, when the land was just a collection of hills along the shoreline. Bantu liked walking along Kinsington because he was treated to an open, unobstructed, view of the Macca Deep. Kinsington Pass just happened to skirt the easternmost part of Alexandria, which meant that parts of it ran along the spine of the cliffs overlooking the Deep. The city planners had fervently guarded against allowing anyone to build on the left side of Kinsington. As a result, after passing Sanctuary's high wall, you were treated to the breathtaking sight of the Macca Deep off in the distance. The light breeze, from off the Deep, blew into Bantu's face bringing with it the lightest spray of water. The sight of the sparkling blue waters made him smile all the more. It was late in the morning, but noon was still a couple of hours away, so while traffic was constant it was not oppressively so. Bantu enjoyed his walk as he alternated between looking out at the Deep and watching the traffic roll by on the smooth cobblestones of the street. He passed a candlemaker's shop, a bakery – where he stopped to purchase a small piece of sweet, creamy-cheese, loaf with a bit of raspberry preserve filling – and a florist, from whose shop delightful scents floated. The street teemed with coaches, carriages, and carts as well as people astride horses. Thankfully, Alexandria was a city that had gone out of its way to lay down stone for the streets. Its planners had also taken pains to create walkways on either side of the street for those who were walking rather than riding. As Kinsington Pass leveled out, Bantu passed into the warehouse district bordering the docks where the traffic picked up. Here, it was mostly coaches or large wagons. The coaches carried passengers who were either going to take passage on a ship or returning from a voyage, while the wagons carried cargo doing the same. As Bantu left the large warehouses he finally came to the actual docks. Turning back to his left he headed to the docks northernmost section.

Walking along the gangplank, which jutted out into the lapping, shallow waters of the Deep, Bantu moved around men with bulging sacks on their backs. He also passed people who were obviously passengers disembarking from small launches or larger crafts tied to the dock. Halfway to the ships docked at the end of the gangplank Bantu turned left again walking toward a more isolated section of the docks.

This section of the docks was large enough to hold thirty or more large vessels. The entire dock of Alexandria could hold nearly a hundred vessels themselves while another few hundred could be moored out in the bay. As Bantu looked out on that bay he could almost see that many ships lying at anchor with smaller launches ferrying people, along with cargo, to and from those ships. Alexandria was a major port of call. Business was always brisk. The empire made a tremendous amount on trade. As a consequence, they made sure that the harbor of Alexandria was run with impeccable proficiency as well as courtesy so that ships *wanted* to land at Alexandria instead of further north in Province or the Fierrenen Islands. Bantu knew it cost more for a ship to actually dock in the harbor than to lie at anchor in the bay, so many used smaller boats to tie up at the dock, especially for ferrying passengers. It was one of the smaller launches that Bantu was after. However, unlike the rest of the passengers or owners of cargo he would not be paying to hire a launch. With his boots echoing on the gangplank Bantu came to a halt at the end of the northernmost section of the docks. This was the section of the docks, which belonged to the Company. Men and women who were at work among the launches, small boats, and mid-sized ships docked here began snapping to attention as they took notice of the man who had just entered the Peoples Dock.

With the kind of work the Company did there were as many non-Company people on the dock as there were members of the Company. Many of them stood looking around apprehensively, or puzzled, with expressions that plainly said they were wondering what was happening. A few of them, seeing the People around them at attention, went to a knee as if they were in the presence of nobility. They continued to kneel until one of the People pulled them back to their feet whispering a brief explanation as they did. The Commander-General of the Peoples Company was standing on the gangplank. He did not require an acknowledgement of any kind from those who were not of the People.

Most of the members of the Company, who were on the docks, were a part of one of the sea going Orders of the People. They were likely either Waveriders or Gray Fins. While there were some in the regular uniform of the Company, even a few white-coated Cadets, the sea going

People wore black vests instead of coats. The rest of the uniform was unchanged. They wore black boots that stopped at the knee, slim-fitting, black breeches tucked into the top of the boots, white shirts with close-fitting sleeves, and black vests with high collars. The vests were actually a kind of double-breasted waistcoat without sleeves. The high collar was still there holding a com-gem on one side with rank insignia on the other. They wore black belts with the same silver buckles in the shape of three intersecting circles. Most of those belts had swords hanging from them.

A middle-aged man with close-cut, lightly golden hair and sea-blue eyes, wearing that vest, walked up to Bantu snapping off a crisp salute. His voice was deep with the raspy sound that came from shouting over the noise of the sea. "Commander-General. I am Lieutenant Jissle D'brec'd, Dock Master. Forgive us, sir. We did not know you were coming. If you will give me a moment I will have the dock cleared!"

Bantu smiled at the man. "At ease, Lieutenant. This is a surprise I have been waiting to spring for some time. All I need you to do is get me a launch."

Jissle D'brec'd nodded smartly. He turned to bellow down the length of the dock. "Neille Orggos!" A young man, in the Company vest, jumped, nearly dropping a package he had been removing from a launch tied to the dock. Looking around wildly he tried to locate who had yelled at him. "Over here man! Yes, you! I am talking to you! Get that launch squared away for the Commander. Now, man! We don't have all day!"

Bantu spoke again while Orggos was scrambling to get the launch ready, this time so that only D'brec'd could hear him. "Lieutenant, calm yourself. There is no need to give young Orggos a heart attack. He has a few minutes. My escort will take that long to reach us here on the dock."

With a slight reddening of the face, Jissle D'brec'd nodded to Bantu. "Yes sir. My apologies, sir."

Bantu nodded patting D'brec'd lightly on the shoulder. "Get back to your duties D'brec'd, I will take it from here."

Jissle D'brec'd snapped off another salute before turning squarely on his heel. He walked back down the gangplank barking orders. Apparently, ropes were not tied off properly, packages were in the wrong places, and some people could not stow a launch properly if their lives depended on it. Exhaling slowly, Bantu realized that no matter what he said D'brec'd was not going to take it easy, on himself, or anyone else, until Bantu was well out of sight. As he turned to look back up the gangplank he could see Wen, Bella, Orah, and Isabelle gliding down the walkway. Wen stopped next to him, straightening her coat, as she said, "So, Commander, are we going for a ride?"

Bantu smiled down at her. "Yes Wen, we are going for a ride."

It only took another minute before the launch was ready. Bantu, along with his escort, were soon on their way out into the harbor. Another thirty minutes passed as they were carried between ships at anchor passing out of the harbor altogether. Bantu sat in the bow of the boat letting himself relax as he listened to the steady rhythm of oars striking the water in syncopated unison. Just the other side of the harbor's inlet, a little further to the north, was a small island. Though the island was large enough for much more the Company had only erected one building on it. On the far side of the island they had also built a deep-sea dock. It was used for the construction of the Company's ships. It took another ten minutes for the launch to get them to the Peoples Shipyard.

As the launch nestled up to the shipyard's dock Bantu leaped from the boat to the gangplank. He headed for the singular building nestled among the island's thick foliage, stretching skyward, at the end of the dock. It was twelve stories high. The building had been made large enough to house the ship builders, their work areas, along with their materials. Today was special because he had gotten word that the first of the newest line of ships for deep-sea travel was ready. Its construction had been completed a month ago. Three days ago, it had finished its maiden cruise. Now it was ready to be launched in earnest. Bantu was excited.

Striding through the double doors of the building he entered the reception area with the four Quiet Blossoms following. Bantu stopped in front of a small woman in black and white livery who had been standing off to the side of the entrance. When she saw Bantu, she smiled as she walked up to him. Her hair was reddish-brown. It had been pulled back into a long ponytail. She was about Bantu's age with a warm receptive face. She looked up at him with big brown eyes. Her voice was high, almost girlish. It seemed out of place coming from the womanly face. "Commander, I am Jailo Murrat, the Grounds Steward. We are so glad you are here on Proving Isle. If I may say so, it has been too long since the Peoples Shipyard had the pleasure of your presence. I hope everything meets with your approval. Everything is ready, just as you requested. If you will come with me I will see you to the sitting room where you can await the arrival of Nessera ela bin Stormcloud."

Bantu smiled as he nodded at the Grounds Steward. He followed her through another set of doors, down a long hallway. As they walked he expressed his thanks for the reception. He knew how hard she worked to keep the Shipyard on schedule. He told her that he was sure everything was as it should be. Jailo Murrat beamed as he spoke. She stood a little straighter as she walked. Bantu was glad that he was able to compliment her in such a way. The People worked hard. He always tried to make sure they knew he appreciated them. They finally came to an enormous room filled with plush chairs. They were also a few tables. The walls were filled by a number of bookshelves matched by a number of wall hangings. The room was mostly deep mahogany wood with a giant, sea green rug, accented in gray, covering most of the floor. The chairs were large, dark, overstuffed leather. Along one wall was a serving table with food, chilled wine, sweet punch, along with what was unmistakably a pot of choca. Fixing himself a strong cup of choca, Bantu sat in one of the overstuffed leather chairs leaning back into its deep softness. Sipping from the white porcelain cup, with a leaping fish emblazoned along its rim, he looked around the room once again noticing the small model ships that were perched around the room accompanied by sketches of plans for ships hanging in gilded frames on the walls. It was a comfortable room meant for relaxing between the hours of work for those who designed, built, and repaired the ships in the shipyard.

Wen, Bella, Orah, and Isabelle had gotten something to drink. A couple of them were nibbling on some of the food that was available. They only had to wait a few minutes. Just as Bantu's mind had begun to wander, almost without warning, the door to the sitting room opened emitting Nessera ela bin Stormcloud.

Stormcloud was a woman about a decade older than Bantu. Her face was, sun-weathered, almost bronze. Her hair was naturally light brown but had been lightened even more in places, by exposure to the sun, making it a soft golden hue. It hung loosely about her shoulders, windblown with the faintest hint of soft, longish curls. There were fine lines around the edges of her pale blue eyes from constant squinting, but the rest of her skin was smooth. She had a strong jaw with a nearly too-small nose. Brilliant white teeth showed from behind full lips. All told Nessera ela bin Stormcloud was an attractive woman.

After a few long strides into the room Nessera ela bin Stormcloud came to rest at attention. She wore the vest of the sea-going Company, breeches, knee-high boots, all in black, along with a white shirt. She was one of the Wave Riders, the Order of the Company's sailors. As such a tiny stylized ship with sail, in blue, white, and silver thread was embroidered over the heart of her black vest. The sleeves of her white shirt were billowy, a captain's prerogative. The high collar of the black vest held a com-gem on one side with three full silver pips on the other. On land those pips would have named her a Commander in the Company but on the deck of a ship they named her Captain. She opened her mouth to speak. The sound of her voice was deeper than one would have expected from a woman while still remaining decidedly feminine. "Captain Nessera ela bin Stormcloud, reporting as ordered, sir."

Bantu rose from his seat setting his cup on a nearby table. As he walked over to Nessera he fought to keep the smile off his face. He had decided to have a little fun with the situation. A fool-eating grin would give him away. Nessera was a tall woman but he still had to look down at her. "Captain, while you have shown exemplary service to the People as Commander of the Peoples Sea Ship, *Justice*, I regret to inform you that I am relieving you of command, effective immediately."

Bantu watched her as his words hit home. To her credit Nessera ela bin Stormcloud barely flinched. *Barely*. Because he had been looking for it Bantu saw the minute movement, followed by the immediate recovery, as Nessera heard that she was losing command of her ship. To her further credit her voice was even when she responded, "With all due respect sir. May I ask why?" Nessera's eyes were focused just over Bantu's shoulder.

She stood as still as a statue. The woman was proud, used to the chain of command. She would take her apparent removal with dignity. But she did want to know why.

Bantu had never been prouder of her than at that moment though they had history together. Nessera had served the Company faithfully at sea for more than ten years. It was time for that service to be rewarded. Bantu had to fight to keep from smiling or letting his plan spill out. He said to her, "No, Captain, you may not ask why. What you will do is follow me." Bantu walked past Nessera heading for the door. He heard her turn on her heel behind him, falling in, with the Blossoms a few steps behind her. Bantu knew Nessera's mind would be spinning as she tried to determine what was happening. She was a tough woman, so she would not let on that she was troubled at being relieved of her command. Yet, as they walked, Bantu knew she had to be troubled. He fought to keep from telling her what he was really about.

They exited the building to the rear walking down another gangplank to a large dock jutting out into the waters of the Deep. There were a number of ships under construction. This part of the island was used for mooring the ships because the island shelf fell off steeply here. A few steps out from land the water went from a few spans deep to hundreds. It was a sheer drop. Consequently, it was perfect for building the largest ships of the fleet. One could build right next to the edge of the shelf. There would be no problem launching a ship that would have been too large to launch from shallower water without great difficulty. It was here that the Peoples Sea Ship *Leviathan* had been constructed. She was massive. Leviathan was the largest ship ever built for the Peoples Fleet. In fact, it was larger than anything else in the water anywhere. She was built for the deepest, roughest seas and the longest voyages. She was state of the art in shipbuilding with some of the most sophisticated additions that Tink and the shipwrights could come up with. When the plans had been brought to him, as soon as he had approved them, Bantu had immediately decided what he wanted to do with Leviathan.

As they made their way down the gangplank to where Leviathan was docked people moved out of their way murmuring among themselves as they recognized Bantu. When they reached the place where Leviathan was birthed, Bantu climbed the ladder that led to the walkway, which hung between the dock and the main deck of the ship. As he stepped aboard another officer met him. The man snapped to attention saying, "Welcome aboard sir. I am Lieutenant Commander Hallew el mic' Ban. *Leviathan* is ready for your inspection." As Nessera stepped down from the walkway onto the main deck of the ship mic' Ban saw her. He turned to her saying, "Welcome aboard Captain Stormcloud. It is a pleasure to have you here ma'am."

Nessera ela bin Stormcloud smiled politely as she looked from one end of the main deck to the other trying to take it all in at once. "Thank you, Lieutenant Commander. I have only glanced at the plans for the new Deep Sea Class of ships, but she seems a fine vessel from what I can see. A very fine vessel."

As they stood on the main deck Bantu gave his com-gem a series of taps so that it, along with anyone else's com-gem who was on Leviathan, flared to glowing life. He said, "This is the Commander-General. All hands, to the main deck. I repeat, all hands to the main deck."

It took only a few moments. Men and women, in close fitting white shirts, with black vests, poured out of doors or hatches until the main deck was full. It took a few more minutes for them to line up across the deck in straight, evenly-spaced lines. When Bantu was satisfied that everyone was present he continued with the com-gems amplifying his voice across the entire ship. Even those who were below on the dock, or on other nearby ships, could hear him.

"Attention to Orders!" As his voice echoed across the deck they all snapped to attention with a resounding thump. He continued, "Many of you know the name, Nessera ela bin Stormcloud. Once, when I was a very young man, I crossed the great Deep on a small deep-sea vessel. I was headed from my homeland to a distant country I knew nothing about. She stood at that ship's helm as her Captain. With a crew of thirty and a ship as old as I was she rode the vast waves of the Deep bringing me safely to the shores of Alexandria. When the Peoples Company came into being and its fleet was being built I could think of no one better suited to Captain one of our ships. With a great deal of negotiating I was able to convince her to serve in the Company. Since then, Nessera ela bin Stormcloud has distinguished herself on the high seas as a Captain among captains. Today it is my pleasure to relieve her of command of the Peoples Sea Ship *Justice*, and appoint her to Captain the first of this new Class of Deep Sea ships, and the flagship of the Peoples Fleet, the Peoples Sea Ship *Leviathan*."

As a deafening roar went up from the people gathered on deck Bantu turned to look at Nessera ela bin Stormcloud. A rare smile lit his face as he stopped holding back his feeling of immense pleasure at this occasion. Shock was written across her's. Then slowly, as the fullness of what was happening began to sink in, the shock faded while a broad smile began stretching across her sun-weathered face. Bright white teeth shone in the sunlight. Her eyes began to sparkle as she tried to speak, stopped, opened her mouth again, before finally stammering out, "Sir. I … I don't know what to say?"

Bantu smiled back at her as the crowd of sailors continued to shout. "There is nothing *to* say, Captain. You are the woman for the job. Make the People proud." Bantu reached out, clasping her forearm with his hand, while smiling down at her.

"I will sir. I most certainly will. You can count on me!" She clasped his forearm fervently. Leaning forward she spoke low, hoping only he would hear what she had to say. "Sir. If I may ask, what about my crew on the *Justice*?"

Bantu leaned in to respond. "You may bring them with you Captain. But remember, the *Justice* is only crewed by one hundred and twenty. Leviathan will need twice that. I will expect to see a list of the other one hundred and twenty you would like on your crew for my approval within the week."

Nodding sharply Nessera said, "Yes sir. I will begin immediately."

Bantu shook his head as he laughed. "No, Nessera. You will not. You will relax. You will enjoy this day. You will let it all sink in. You will eat a fine meal in good company of your choosing, and you will drink a little too much wine. And then tomorrow, tomorrow mind you-" here Bantu paused as if to let his sentiment sink in fully before continuing, "-you will move from your quarters on the *Justice* to your quarters on the *Leviathan*. Only then will you get to work. And that is an order. I am clear, Captain?"

Nessera smiled even more broadly at him. Snapping to attention to punctuate her answer, she said, "Aye, aye sir."

Looking back at the still milling group on the main deck Bantu tapped his com-gem. His voice echoed out over the throng. "Dismissed!" Another cheer rang out as the people on deck crowded in slapping Nessera ela bin Stormcloud on the back or shoulders congratulating her on the appointment to *Leviathan*. Bantu stepped back making room for them. As he stood watching the display with a broad smile painting his own face he noticed Wen Ava Noella had sidled up next to him. She also had a large smile playing across her features.

"You thoroughly enjoyed that didn't you sir." She said looking up at him.

"Yes, Wen. It was the most fun I have had in months." Wen nodded up at him smiling all the more as if the fact that this had been fun for Bantu made it all the more an occasion for rejoicing. Bantu looked at Wen again, saying, "Well, there are other things to do. I think we can leave the Captain to be the center of the rest of the celebration." Without another word Bantu made his way to the walkway. He crossed it before climbing quickly down the latter. Dropping the final feet with a soft thud on the gangplank as he landed he turned on his heel making his way back the way they had come.

It only took a few minutes to go back through the building. In moments Bantu, along with his Quiet Blossom escort, were back in the launch on their way across to the inlet, into the harbor, finally making their way back to the Peoples Dock. When they arrived Jissle D'brec'd launched into another tirade, barking orders while Bantu made his way up the gangplank. At the end he turned off into the warehouse district. Bantu decided to take the long way back to Sanctuary, which meant a meandering walk through the warehouse district. It was a slow climb up winding streets until he could turn north to head in the right direction. As he walked Wen, Bella, Orah, and Isabelle gave him some space, blending into their surroundings to follow him at a discreet distance.

Filled with the pleasant afterglow of appointing Nessera ela bin Stormcloud to the *Leviathan* Bantu paid little heed to the warehouses as he strode happily through the district. It was that happy oblivion that kept him from noticing them before they had him surrounded.

Bantu froze as the men floated out from two alleys on either side of the street. There were only a handful of people about their business in this part of the warehouse district, but they fled into open warehouses or down other streets as they saw the men surround him. In seconds the street was empty with the exception of Bantu and the men who had encircled him. It only took a glance for him to realize who they were. Once he had recognized them a thought bubbled to the surface of his mind – *So today is the day*. Another distant thought in the back of his mind answered the first – *Am I ready?*

Bantu could not have told anyone what their names were, but he knew their *Bojun*, he knew the – *what* - that they were. They were *Mfundade*, which in the tongue of his people meant *Weaponmasters*. It was as though the past had just stepped out of a drifting mist into clear, full-blown life right in front of him. Yes, he knew, the nine men were of the Mfundade. They were from home. Standing in a large circle, surrounding him on the empty street, most had open disdain written on their faces.

Most people, on this side of the Macca Deep, would have thought of Bantu as incredibly tall. But among his people he was just slightly above average in height. These men were tall. Six of them, the younger ones with the bad dispositions, were well-muscled, if slim, while standing close to seven full spans tall. The other three men were older, if still on the young side. The older men were a little wider as well as a few measures shorter than the younger men. The younger men had heads full of the shoulder-length braids that marked them *Mfunde*. The six of them were not yet *Mfundishi*.

The older men, whom Bantu knew led them, were. Their clean-shaven heads glistened lightly with oil in the morning sunlight. They must have each seen at least forty turns of the seasons. Yes, Bantu thought again, they were certainly Mfundishi. Their stillness, the way they seemed to see everything all at once, along with the look in their eyes, which said they were men who feared nothing because they had mastered themselves, all marked them for what they were. Confidence flowed from them like water down the side of a great mountain. The three older men were Mfundishi. The other distinction, which separated the three older men from the six younger, was color. The young Mfunde were wearing a brilliant, blood-red under-robe that Bantu knew was sleeveless coupled with a matching outer-robe of red with white trim that had full, bell-shaped sleeves with an oversized hood. The older men wore identical robes with the exception that their robes, both inner and outer, were black. Their outer robes were trimmed in gold. All the robes were made from finely woven linen. They were so long they brushed the ground. Each of the men wore black sandals with leather straps that, Bantu knew without seeing, laced up their ankles to the top of their calves. If there had been any doubt as to whether they really were who Bantu knew they were there was the *Yari* that each of the Mfundade held in their hands.

To the casual observer the Yari looked to be a slightly curved short staff, or walking stick, made of a black wood, standing chest high when its tip was on the ground. But a sharp twist, followed by a pull, would reveal that two-thirds of its length was a slightly curved blade of steel. It was an ancient blending of sword with staff. While the blade was a fraction shorter than a traditional sword blade, the hilt was a hand longer. The Yari was the ancient weapon of the Mfundade. What made it dangerous was the way it could be used. At first it was a short staff that, in the blink of an eye, could become bared steel, handled as a sword would be. One could easily forget the leftover shaft that had housed the blade end, like a scabbard, but had become, in the other hand, a long fighting stick. The Yari was three weapons in one. Each of the nine Mfundade encircling Bantu held one, easily in hand, leaning on them as if they were only long walking sticks.

The men were all just a shade darker than Bantu, but their facial features were relatively similar. They had well shaped noses, balanced by full lips, as well as high cheekbones. Their black woolen hair, along with dark eyes, in addition to their other features, named them from the distant shores of Al'akaz, which meant *The Land of Beauty* or *The Beautiful Land* in the long dead tongue of the ancients.

Bantu forced himself to relax. *Let it come*, the fraction of a remembered lesson echoing distantly in his mind. *Let it come as it would and be ready*, he told himself. His Sabado had taught that one kept the hand open until the last instant before the strike. Only then, at the last instant, was the fist made. A fist formed too soon, he had said, could force a confrontation that may have been avoided. Watch but wait, he had continued, be ready but not hasty. Bantu breathed deeply as he stilled himself for what would come next.

Thoughts of his Sabado, the old dark-skinned, wrinkling, bald adept, always lightened Bantu's mood. He had admired the old man tremendously. There had been a kind of open defiance about him that had angered some in the Mfundade. Zalakazam had been called *Ta' Ballanjoo* - The Defiant One. It was of note that they never called him that to his face. Nevertheless, he had taken a pernicious delight in the name. Zalakazam had followed the *Warring Way* faithfully. He had been so gifted that he had been one of the youngest men ever to be raised to the Mfundishim. Those were the reasons he had gotten away with being as defiant as he had been. Much of Zalakazam's defiance had rubbed off on his youngest pupil. That defiance rose up in Bantu, as he stood there relaxed, watching, but ready. It even threatened to overwhelm his ability to stay centered.

The black-robed Mfundishi had been examining Bantu as though he were a horse being sold at auction. They seemed undecided, if their expressions were a true indication of their feelings. When they finally realized he was not going to speak first the three older men looked at one another. They did not keep deep smiles from spreading across their smooth dark faces. Not smiles of joy but rueful, considering, smiles. After a few more moments they nodded to one another. What must have been the older of the Mfundishi, standing to Bantu's far right, had a look that seemed to say – *so, you have not forgotten all our ways*. Bantu maintained a look of utter calm as the *abundance* washed over him like an ocean wave. He was the wind, the distant sound of the waves, the small bird that circled above the rooftops of the warehouses. In an instant he was full. He could feel each of the men who surrounded him, feel them breathing, sense those who were anxious to move. He did not smile, nor did he frown, he simply raised his eyebrows a fraction. His expression said to the Mfundishi – *I am who I have always been.*

Again, the oldest of the Mfundishi nodded to himself. Straightening formally, he stepped forward into the large circle created by the others. His voice was a bit deeper than Bantu would have thought but it did have the studied ring of one of the grandmasters of the Corral. "Ossassande Bantu, of the Great House Omorede, I present myself." A slight bow from the waist accompanied his words, as he continued, "I am Nentan Yasadande A' Yaah. I also present," here a flourish of the hand, causing the ivory bracelets at his wrist to click together, took in the other grandmasters in black, "of the Mfundishim, Oba Mtumbaba A' N'kosi, Ampah Oturede A' Gamba, and of the Mfundem; Mtoomba, Neric, Kandii, Ayo, Sulda and Beye. We are of the Mfundade of Al'akaz." Bringing both hands together with the palms pressed against one another, Nentan pressed the backs of his thumbs against his forehead, making another slight bow. Looking at Bantu he brought his hands back down to his waist. He was handed his Yari by one of the other grandmasters.

Bantu looked at each of them in turn. The quiet was thunderous as they stood waiting. Just as Bantu was about to speak the Quiet Blossoms dropped to the ground from above. They had leaped, no doubt, from the roof of one of the warehouses, landing inside the large circle of men, with their backs to Bantu, facing the Mfundade. Bantu spoke sharply as the Blossoms pulled their swords free from their scabbards. "As you were Blossoms! Do not move, that is an order!"

The Mfundade were disciplined. They had not moved as the Blossoms fell among them. The Blossoms froze, where they had landed, in a tight ring around Bantu. Though Wen, Bella, Orah, and Isabelle were not small women the Mfundade towered over them. Bantu knew that if it came to a fight, however, the Mfundade would be in for a surprise. The Blossoms would defend his life at the cost of their own but it was not going to come to that. He had known this day was coming. He had prepared himself for it. Another thought drifted in the back of his mind, *I hope I am ready.* Taking a long step forward, Bantu moved out of the small circle the Blossoms had made placing himself directly in front of the black-clad Mfundishi. Wen hissed violently as he stepped in front of her, but she did not move. His voice was unwavering. He was ready.

"I am Ossassande Bantu A' Omorede, Commander-General of the Peoples Company. I am *Karshoon Deshar*." It meant *The Man Who is a Mountain*. He continued, "I know why you are here, Mfundishi. I have only one question." Bantu took another step, which brought him almost eye to eye with the senior Mfindishi, the one who had spoken for the others, though Bantu had to look down at the older man. "Will you follow the *Warring Way* in this matter? Or are you outlaws operating outside the Law of the Corral?"

The older Mfundishi grimaced looking levelly at Bantu. "We are men of honor, *Karshoon Deshar*. But you, you claim a *Name of Honor*?" The Mfundishi twisted his mouth as though he was tasting something bitter. Bantu had, by naming himself Karshoon Deshar, claimed the right to an honored place in the Corral. It would mean that his case would have to be heard in the Corral itself. To take a name of honor that you had not earned was a serious matter. The Mfundishi, sour look in place, continued, "You will have to answer for the truth of that in the Corral of the Mfundade, but until then you have the protection of the *K'si*, the Challenged." There were grunts of deep displeasure from some of the young Mfunde around the circle, but no one spoke. Nentan continued, "Must I speak the Challenge in full, here and now, or shall we dispense with further formalities and go?"

Bantu nodded once at Nentan. "We may leave momentarily, Mfundishi." Turning his back on Nentan, which pulled another hiss from Wen, Bantu looked at the Blossoms who were looking around perplexed, but unmoving, barred blades in hand like a group of lionesses with their teeth showing. "Attend me," he said. Quickly the four of them sheathed their swords as they lined up in front of Bantu. Speaking in a low voice Bantu said, "Orah, you will return to Sanctuary and tell Basil what has happened here. He will know what to do. The rest of you will travel with me to Al'akaz under one condition." Bantu paused. He knew that if he had tried to send all of them back there would have been the Betrayer vomited from the Abyss to pay, followed by blood staining the ground. They would not give him up without a fight. But this was going to be a delicate situation at best. He needed them to understand. Wen, Bella, and Isabelle looked at him expectantly. "You will accompany me, but you will ask no questions." Before he had finished Wen opened her mouth to speak but Bantu held up a hand sharply. "No questions, Commander! Not a single one!" Snapping her mouth shut, Wen stood in front of Bantu with her face flushing red to match her curly locks. Looking at the other Blossoms, he saw the same frustration running to anger on their faces. They were stunned, edging toward infuriated, that he was leaving, apparently as a captive, and they could not even object. Bantu continued once he was sure he had their full attention. "I cannot explain right now so you will have to trust that I have my reasons for allowing this. I always thought that when this day came I would go alone. Circumstances have conspired to force me into allowing you to accompany me. That will have to be enough of a compromise for you. But you will do exactly, and I mean *exactly*, what I tell you to do." He paused a moment to let it sink in before he continued, "Without exception. I am Clear?"

It seemed that they had begun to comprehend the serious nature of the situation. The three of them looked at one another, and slowly, with a grim certitude, spoke in unison. "Yes, sir." Their affirmation came through faces that could make one of the Twisted think twice, but it came.

Bantu hesitated only a moment, as he looked each of them in the eye. "Orah, leave now. Deliver my message to Basil. The rest of you, on me."

Orah looked cautiously at the circle of towering men, robed in red and white, as if she was memorizing every stitch, every nuance of their appearance, before she slowly walked between two of them. The men moved aside, letting her through. In moments, she was sprinting away down the street moving faster than a person should be able to move. Bantu nearly smiled as he watched her go, noting that, in their arrogance, not a single one of the Mfundade watched her. Had they seen how fast she was moving they might have looked more closely at the other women in their midst. They had three lionesses by the tail but did not know it. That underestimation had been one of the deadliest weapons in the Quiet

Blossom's arsenal. They had been given the *gift*, which made them more than a match for any man in strength or endurance. All their opponents ever saw were women, until it was too late. The other Blossoms, still grim-faced, lined up behind Bantu as he turned back to Nentan. "We are ready."

The older man nodded. He motioned toward one of the alleys. When a small man walked out of the alley, into the street, Bantu nodded to himself. He had thought they might have a *Griot* with them. How else would they be able to leave without being run down by the Company? Bantu wondered how they had convinced the *Grammat* to lend them one of their own. The man was a half-measure smaller than even the Blossoms. He wore sandals matched only by a small, many-colored cloth wrapped around his mid-section. His hair was long, woolly, and sprouting wildly from his head like a bundle of cotton. The Griot was thin except for his small protruding belly. His skin was as dark as night. His expression said he was bored. There were tatoo's up his arms as well as down his back. Their meaning was a secret known only to other Griot of the Grammat. But it was not the tatoo's that made the Griot special. It was their *Bojun*.

When the little man cleared the alley, his hand was nestled in the wild locks on his head scratching absently at his scalp. When he was far enough into the street he pulled out a long cord with a small rectangular piece of fluted wood on the end. Making sure he had plenty of room the Griot began to twirl the long rope over his head. As it whirled, faster and faster, the fluted piece of wood on the rope's end began to make a deep humming moan that vibrated the air. As the speed increased the tone of the sound fluctuated up and down. In moments small forks of lightning began to form shooting off into the air. A large circle of light erupted along the path of the fluted piece of wood as it spun. The sound grew deeper, fuller, and louder until suddenly the space around the Griot *changed*. Dust flew up from the street while small pieces of debris were thrown into the air. The area around the Griot, outlined in light, surrounded by crackling lightning, was suddenly someplace else. Right there in the middle of the street one could see that a single step would take you from the cobblestone of Alexandria to some other place. Bantu knew where that other place was. Without a word, with the Blossoms close behind him, Bantu walked across the street, stepping off cobblestone onto dark brown earth, moving past the Griot who continued spinning his rope overhead. Within minutes he, the Blossoms, along with the Mfundade, disappeared from the street in the warehouse district, swallowed up by a small whirling of wind mixed with lightning, as the Griot stopped his spinning. His image, outlined in light, pulsed brightly, before it faded into a dust cloud that finally settled before disappearing altogether. The only sign that remained was a slight breeze, a few errant, fading, crackles of lighting, and the dissipating aftermath of an odd hum.

There is no more astounding puzzle than that of the Ki'gadi. An ancient, mystical, Order of quasi-mortal creatures with unnatural abilities; they drift through the world on the most tenuous of mortal threads. Ephemeral, with their white flowing manes and distant demeanors, one is never quite sure whether their presence is a gift to be celebrated or a burden to be suffered. While they are born of almost every nation under the heavens, their allegiance is surely, indelibly, and solely to, that most ancient assemblage of golden streets and eldritch structures, known as Palladawn. It is whispered softly, in dark corners, that they fear nothing, that they are only haunted by a singular thought. They fear a star, trailing fire across the heavens, that is said will be the harbinger of the end of all things. [This author reserves judgment concerning such a prophecy seeing that it is outside of the purview of my expertise.]

> *- Excerpt from A Brief History of Palladawn*
> *by Gallein Gal*
> *Herferth Institute, Halkenburg*

Sing, song, sing and sing
Ring, ring, bells to ring
See the flame, hear the sound
And we all fall down

~Verse from a children's play song

CHAPTER THIRTEEN

Gifts and graces

Alla'mirridin had traveled undisturbed. He had made camp the night before, deep in the forest, without a fire. Though the lack of a fire had meant eating cold food, he had eaten wrapped only in his cloak, though it was cool enough that he could see his breath. He had awakened fully rested. It had taken only a moment to realize his head was no longer throbbing even though his memory had still not returned. The morning, like the night before, was uneventful as he continued making his way east, before turning north, in search of a village, small town, or city. Any of them would allow him to get his bearings. A village or city would also offer the possibility of getting some information that would help him figure out what he had gotten mixed up in. He might even find a clue to his identity.

The morning was blessedly dry. It began warming up as soon as the sun rose. The woods had come to life with the breaking of day. Insects buzzed about merrily on their way to wherever insects went. Birds chirped softly in the distance. A slight breeze blew through the leaves making a faint rustling sound. As he had stirred to life, breathing deeply as he stretched momentarily, he noticed how the air was fresh.

Alla'mirridin had eaten his breakfast in the saddle, cold again, keeping Speckle to a fast walk, which slowly ate up the miles that lay before him. What he would have given for a steaming cup of choca, even badly made choca.

The forest continued to be thickly wooded but with trees staggered so that it could still be easily traversed. He found that he could nearly ride in a straight line. From time to time, the woods thinned, breaking abruptly into a flowery meadow or sunbathed clearing. He could see the mountains just off to the north from those clearings. It was beautiful, breathtaking country. It was lush, green, and seemingly unspoiled.

The ground had begun rising upward, in a gentle slope, which spoke of a hill ahead coupled with the possibility of rolling landscape beyond. The trees, along with the shrubbery, became denser the higher the ground rose. Alla'mirridin reined Speckle in as he crested the hill. Looking down into the narrow gulley he could see that it was formed by the hill he sat atop nestling against another. The gulley ran north to south. It was wide enough to ride along as well as level enough, at its bottom, to make camp. While patting Speckle's neck softly, to keep him quiet, Alla'mirridin focused his attention on a small camp at the foot of the next hill. The fire had been made in a small, but relatively deep, pit with a brush-guard of shrub-covered branches making a roof over the flames to break up what little smoke there might have been coming from the burning wood. He made a note of it. He tucked it away in his mind as the reason he had not known there was a camp here. It was actually rather smart. Remaining very still, trusting the thick foliage on the hilltop to hide him, he continued to watch the camp below.

There were only two people in it. Alla'mirridin thought he could see a man and a woman. Sitting calmly, on bits of a fallen tree, in front of the fire, they seemed to be having breakfast. There were two horses hobbled several feet away along with one medium-sized tent. As Alla'mirridin tried to decide whether to ride down or turn around in order to skirt the camp entirely, the man looked up from where he was sitting. His gaze came to rest right on Alla'mirridin's position among the trees. After looking directly at the spot where Alla'mirridin sat atop Speckle for a few more moments, the man began waving his arm, motioning for him to join them in their camp.

The woman, whose position on the tree bole meant that her back was to Alla'mirridin, did not even flinch. Alla'mirridin grinned wryly. They had known he was there. They may have even known from the moment he had crested the hill even though he knew he had hardly made a sound. As nonchalantly as he could, he rode Speckle down the slope to the bottom of the gulley where the two had made their camp. As he reigned Speckle in, Alla'mirridin lifted his left leg over the front of the saddle while pulling his right foot from the stirrup. Sliding smoothly from his mount's back he landed lightly on his feet. He allowed Speckle's reins to drop to the ground. Without thinking he stepped on them with one foot. He had discovered the day before that Speckle seemed well trained. Immediately he knew that stepping on the reins in that manner would keep Speckle rooted to that spot even though he was tied to nothing. Alla'mirridin's mind, unbidden, produced the words *ground hitched*. Patting Speckle's neck, Alla'mirridin left his horse standing there. Telling himself to be calm, he walked over to where the strangers were seated. He tucked the thumb of his swordhand behind his buckle to keep it from straying toward the hilt of his sword. As he approached the woman, the young woman – he could tell, now that he was closer - rose from her seat while the, much older, man remained seated sipping something hot from a cup.

The woman was very handsome. It was not the pampered kind of beauty one might see in a nobleman's house or in some king's court. Her's was an attractiveness washed in living in the real world. It was a more enduring beauty to his mind. She was almost as tall as he was. She was slim but, clearly, not frail. She stood straight but with an ease that sent up a warning flag in his mind, which said she could handle herself. Her hand rested on a longsword that hung at her hip on a brown, leather belt with a large, silver sunburst for a buckle. Alla'mirridin immediately noted, with a growing respect, that the sword did not have a handguard. The hilt was separated from the blade by a decorative band of steel with unreadable etchings. Her boots were knee-high, and dark-brown, with several small, silver buckles, running up the outside. Her tight breeches, which were tucked into her boots, were powder blue. The waistcoat she wore was a matching blue, close-fitted in the bodice, and slim along the sleeves, with a high, straight collar. The coat had sliver scrollwork along the sleeves matched by similar embroidery along its high collar. The buttons of her waistcoat, which were made of white pearl, ran up to the base of the collar in a single row. She wore no robe or cloak. She stood there looking like a drawn blade of steel waiting to be used.

As Alla'mirridin came to stand in front of the fire she watched him with clear, deep-green, eyes gazing out of a face with sun-kissed, olive skin. Her thin lips were pressed together neutrally, neither smiling a friendly welcome nor frowning dismissively, but making her mouth seem even smaller than it was. She was watching him. Her hands hung easily at her sides but Alla'mirridin knew that she could have that longsword clear of its scabbard in a single movement. As he turned to look at the older man, who was still seated on the log, Alla'mirridin realized a thought had been nudging at him from the back of his mind. The man tilted his head back emptying his cup. The motion caused his hood to fall back onto his shoulders. In an instant the thought, which has been unformed at the back of his mind, came into focus. Both the woman and the older man had heads full of silvery-white hair. The woman's hair hung in two long, thick braids, with one behind each ear, while the man's hung loose around his shoulders. Had there been only one with that hair, had the woman not had a sword, had the man not noticed him in the trees from so far away, it might not have dawned on him, but it was clear now. A single word floated up from the darkness that was his shrouded memory. "*Ki'gadi.*" He whispered it before he could stop himself.

The young woman did not react but her right hand rose to rest on a rounded hip just above the hilt of her sword. The older man looked up from staring into his empty cup. With a half-laugh running under his words he said, "Pray tell, what gave us away?" A broad smile spread across his lips. His eyes were bright gray with flecks of blue while his skin was only slightly darkened from being in the sun often. He was a thin man shrouded in an oversized, brown, robe. His boots were also brown leather. His breeches, along with his shirt, were a dark forest-green. His longsword was leaning next to him against the log in a brown scabbard that, like the young woman's, had no cross-guard. A sharp, experienced eye would notice that little fact, expecting that the owner of that kind of sword was either a fool or very, very good. Seeing as it had just become apparent that the two were Ki'gadi, Alla'mirridin decided to assume they were not fools.

Looking from the woman to the older man, Alla'mirridin said, "You will have to excuse me Master Sage, I am not, quite, myself. The truth is, I do not ... know myself."

At Alla'mirridin's words the older Ki'gadi set down his cup. The man stood up from his seat on the fallen log. Slowly, he took the three steps that separated him from Alla'mirridin. He looked into his eyes as if searching for something. After a moment he turned, nodding to himself, as he returned to his seat in front of the fire.

"You have been injured? A blow of some kind to the head?" The man spoke with a warm tone full of sympathy as he continued looking at Alla'mirridin.

"Yes, Master Sage. Yesterday I awoke bound in the back of an enclosed wagon. I did not know who, or where, I was." Alla'mirridin grimaced as he said it while his mind flashed back briefly to that moment. "I managed to escape and have been looking for a village, town, or city where I could begin searching for answers."

The young woman chimed in. Her voice was like the sound of small bells. "You escaped from that without help?" Her tone said that she found it hard to believe.

The older man laughed softly. "My young *Had'wadai*. You look but you do not see. I think that this young man probably did exactly that." The woman grunted as if she was still skeptical, but she inclined her head briefly to the older Ki'gadi saying, "Yes, *Shad'ha'dai*."

Alla'mirridin looked from the woman back to the man. He said, "May I ask, Master Sage, what you mean by that?"

The male Ki'gadi waved a hand as if to say it was inconsequential before saying, "Excuse me, young man. I am merely fulfilling my responsibility to my student. You see, I am charged with her training."

Alla'mirridin thought he had seen the man nod in his direction when he had spoken to the female Ki'gadi. He seemed to be covering over something he had noticed. Now that he had recognized them for what they were his mind opened up on the subject. The Ki'gadi, as a rule, never gave information easily. They were the bearers of secrets, shrouded in silence, wrapped up in mystery with a bow on top. You could make a stone give you information sooner than a member of the ancient Sages of Palladawn. The Ki'gadi continued, "But you must excuse us. We are not used to company and, I am sorry to say, we have been rude." The man stood laying a hand on his chest. "I am Mino din' Darksbane. This is my *Had'wadai,* Zezza din' Nightblinder. As you have guessed we are Ki'gadi." Motioning toward a piece of broken log, near the small fire, Mino din' Darksbane concluded, "Please sit, we have been too rude for too long."

Alla'mirridin spoke up as he took the few steps that carried him to the place offered to him on the log. "I am Alla'mirridin."

Zezza din' Nightblinder responded to his pronouncement saying, "If you do not know who you are, how is it that you have a name?" The sweet sound of her voice, like small bells being rung in syncopated succession, moderated the accusatory nature of her question.

Alla'mirridin gazed across the fire, watching her as she took her seat. Once she had he said, "It is what I decided to call myself. I thought it better than telling strangers that I didn't know my name. It means," but before Alla'mirridin could finish Mino din' Darksbane said, from his seat next to Zezza, "*An approaching storm.* It is from the old High Cant."

Alla'mirridin nodded slowly, as much to himself as to the Ki'gadi. He had not been aware of the derivation of the name. It had simply popped into his head. Mino continued, "You will have to excuse Zezza, sometimes she is slow to learn her lessons. And since this one is taking you some time to learn, my Had'wadai, why don't you see to Alla'mirridin's horse while I see to feeding him."

The young woman blanched visibly at the words from the senior Ki'gadi. With a softly murmured apology for her continued rudeness she jumped up from her seat. She stalked off to go see to Speckle.

"Ah, youth." Mino muttered, with a barely audible sigh, as he watched Zezza stalk off. "You must excuse her, Alla'mirridin. She is overly cautious at times but her heart is in the right place. She is a good student. One day she will be a powerful Ki'gadi. She does me credit."

The aged Ki'gadi paused for a moment, his eyes moving off to the left, as if he were remembering something, seeing it in his mind. He continued, as if not realizing he was speaking aloud, "Pestered me, she did. Hounded me, following me all around the Crystal Citadel for more than a month, until I agreed to be her Shad'ha'dai. I had thought I was finished with all of this running about in the world. But ..." As if only just realizing he was speaking aloud he stopped. The elder Sage turned from watching the young Ki'gadi to look at Alla'mirridin. "Now, let us see to a light lunch. Maybe some freshly brewed choca for you?"

As Alla'mirridin opened his mouth to say only the choca, one of the horses reared, whinnying, eyes wide, followed almost simultaneously by Zezza din' Nightblinder shouting something that was gobbled up in the sound of the other horses joining in. Looking around him Alla'mirridin saw dark-clad men drifting silently down both hillsides. Something tall, shrouded in black, with long white hair, looking vaguely human, moved among them. Moving faster than Alla'mirridin would have thought possible, Mino din' Darksbane leaped over the log. The old man was halfway up the hillside in the blink of an eye meeting the white-haired thing with steel ringing on steel. Bluish flashes of light burst into the air as Mino din' Darksbane's ornate blade met the black steel of the shrouded thing's long spear tip. It towered over him but Mino din' Darksbane danced with it, not giving an inch of ground. Zezza din' Nightblinder's voice shook Alla'mirridin from his stupor. "Don't. Just. Sit there. *Approaching Storm!*" Before he realized it he was moving.

The darkly garbed men had not stopped to intercept Mino but had left him to their pale leader, whatever it was. Some of them had nearly surrounded Zezza, moving to keep her hemmed in, while the rest of their number came down the opposite hillside seeking to close the circle on her. They had ignored Alla'mirridin as though he did not matter or even exist. Without thought he had risen from his seat, sliding his saber free as he stood, pulled from his reverie by Zezza's calm, yet firm, voice. He floated up the hill, cutting the second group off as they sought to close Zezza in. It took a second for him to realize he had begun to hum. No words came to mind, but the tune, the tune was familiar. Though it was an odd thing to do in the middle of a battle, he did not stop himself. It seemed natural, even calming, as he raised his blade to first position. In an instant he was among them like a storm sweeping in over the horizon.

Zezza's face was still, unmoving, but her lips were pressed lightly together as her silvery-white braids whipped one way, and then another. Her blade cut a path through the men who made no sound as they fought or died as if it did not matter to them. She was brilliant. Slim yet powerful, she cut a path through them as she danced among the men that swarmed around her like an angry hoard of bees. They did not get the chance to close their circle around her because, as they tried to converge on the spot, Alla'mirridin confounded them. Humming a little more loudly, he held his thoughts at bay, his mind becoming a still pond reflecting its surroundings like a mirror. Lost in the moment, with the tune vibrating in his throat, he relaxed, letting his body do what it wanted. His saber slashed upward, cutting a man from waist to shoulder. As his blade slid free, he twirled about in a short, rotating hop. Sliding backward up the hill, he let his saber swing down with the momentum of his falling arms taking another man's head off at the shoulders. As he danced among them, phrases floated up from the darkness that was his memory, drifting across the surface of the still pond that was his mind. *Hawk Splits the Clouds. Cat Crosses the Roof. Wave Crashes the Shore. Crane Skims the Pond.*

Ducking under a high-line attack, meant to part his own head from his shoulders, Alla'mirridin slammed his right shoulder into the man's left side, knocking him off balance. Reversing his grip, he twirled his blade so that it pointed behind him. Stepping back, he impaled the man who was just over his shoulder. Kicking the man off his blade Alla'mirridin spun, bringing his blade to fourth position, only to realize it was over. Well, it was almost over. He looked around for Zezza. He found her pulling her sword from a crumpled form at her feet several steps to his left. Bending down, she wiped her blade on the coat of one of the dead men. As he watched her Alla'mirridin heard the ringing clash of steel. Turning, he saw Mino still engaging the towering creature that seemed like it was cloaked in darkness. Twirling his sword once, above his head, Alla'mirridin began moving to help Mino only to find Zezza's hand firmly on his arm. Looking away from the fray, back at her, Alla'mirridin opened his mouth to explain that he was going to help, but she spoke first. "I know what you would say. But that," she pointed to the creature swirling around Mino, trailing inky darkness, with its darting black spear, "is a *Graelim*. It is not one of these listless, soulless, creatures we call *Gaunts*, which lay lifeless at our feet. It is what some call a *Horror*, and for good reason. Gaunts are relatively easy to kill because they have no will of their own. Though they were men once, they are no longer, having been twisted by the Dark. Graelim, on the other hand, are not so easy to kill."

Pulling his arm slowly from her grasp, Alla'mirridin lowered his sword as he turned to face her. He kept his voice neutral. He did not want to be angry with her. "I am not afraid. Horror or not, it is trying to kill a man who offered me a place at his fire."

Zezza held up a hand in mock surrender. "I apologize if you thought I was questioning your courage. It is obvious," she gestured at what Alla'mirridin now knew were Gaunts, lying all around them, "that you are a man of skill and courage. But you must understand that this thing is dangerous because it was made for one thing." She paused, looking to where Mino was fighting for his life, before turning back to Alla'mirridin. It was as if she was deciding how much to tell him. She continued, "It was made to kill Ki'gadi. Its kind were created thousands of years ago during the war of the Allgis-sein to hunt those who had joined the Glorious Ones to fight on the side of the Light. Some of those who fought for the light were given gifts by the Glorious to enable them to combat the power of the Twisted. The Betrayers also created *Once-men* with dark gifts to hunt and kill those who had been blessed by the Light."

Alla'mirridin turned back to watch Mino dance, the dance of death, with the Graelim. He was stunned. If what Zezza was saying was true he was watching an ancient battle being fought right in front of him. In that moment Alla'mirridin saw what few men had in a lifetime. Twisting back, stepping out of Mino's sword range, the Graelim reached out with its left hand toward the Ki'gadi. What Alla'mirridin could only describe as black, inky, lightning leapt from its hand, slashing jaggedly through the air, leaving the sharp smell of sulfur in its wake. Mino threw up his left hand. The lightning struck something a fingers-width in front of his palm, which Alla'mirridin could not see, causing a splash of white light to leap up as the black lightning was reflected away. The ground exploded where the deflected lightning hit. Just as Mino recovered the Graelim reached out again. It was as if something grabbed Mino by his neck. It lifted him off the ground. Reaching back, as though he was grabbing something to throw, Mino thrust his left hand forward flinging the Graelim through the air. Mino fell to the ground as the invisible force released him. He grasped at his throat for a single heartbeat before leaping to his feet. Without a moment's hesitation he was moving to his left as more black lightning ripped through the ground where he had been a split-second before. Alla'mirridin was stunned at how the old man moved. As the Graelim staggered to its feet Mino was there. With a violent cut of his blade the Graelim's head went flying. It bounced three times before coming to rest. The headless Graelim still reached out for Mino as he turned his back to it. Mino walked toward Alla'mirridin and Zezza. The thing took four steps before it collapsed. It convulsed for several minutes before it stopped moving. Black blood oozed from its neck making a sizzling sound as it hit the ground. Alla'mirridin swallowed hard. He watched the thing die.

Mino found a loose piece of cloth from among the dead to clean his sword being careful not to touch the black blood with his hand. He tossed the bloodstained rag to the ground as he joined them. When he spoke, it was as if they were out for a quiet walk in a garden. "I see you did not have much trouble, thank the Ancient."

Zezza inclined her head. She said, "No, Shad'ha'dai. The stranger did well once he woke, although his humming was foolhardy."

Mino smiled at Alla'mirridin. "High praise. My Had'wadai has difficulty with compliments, either giving or receiving them."

Zezza grunted but remained silent. Alla'mirridin replied with a smile, "It seems as though your *Had'wadai* has a great many difficulties."

Mino laughed ruefully as Zezza's eyes narrowed to unhappy slits. She looked at Alla'mirridin like he was a heartbeat away from something unpleasant. Mino said, "You may be right, my young friend, though that would make me a terrible teacher. But enough of that, we must break camp. It would be good for us to be far away from here before any of the friends of our attackers, who may be nearby, decide to come looking."

Both Zezza and Mino turned their attention to gathering their things but Alla'mirridin hesitated. "Just a moment. You need to tell me what just happened. Why were you attacked? And where did these things come from? I thought they were old wives tales, things meant to scare children into doing their chores or minding their parents, not real!"

Both of the Ki'gadi stopped but only Mino spoke. "You are right Alla'mirridin, we owe you an explanation, but not here. As I said, they may have friends. Let us put some distance between us and this carnage. Then I will answer what questions I may."

They both looked at him. To their credit, they waited. Looking around at the bodies littering the ground, as he reflected on what he had seen, for a moment, Alla'mirridin thought that maybe he should let these two go their own way. Their attackers had ignored him until he got involved. It was apparent that it was the Ki'gadi they had been after. Not to mention the fact that he had his own problems to sort out. But something told him that these two Ki'gadi, however powerful they may be, were in the middle of something very dangerous. Something deep within told him they probably needed help. It made something in him stir to life. There was an echo of something familiar there. Sliding his sword into its scabbard, he stuck his thumbs behind the buckle of his swordbelt. Without realizing it he began playing with the three, silver, intersecting circles of his buckle with the fingers of his right hand. Something inside of him would not let him leave them. He cleared his throat softly. "You are right, Master Sage. Let's evacuate the area with dispatch."

Mino arched an eyebrow. "Evacuate indeed, Alla'mirridin. Call me Mino. I am glad you have decided to join us. Where we are going, your gifts and graces will be a great ... *help*." Alla'mirridin did not miss the way Mino emphasized the word help, as if he had chosen the word with particular care.

Within moments they were in the saddle. Soon, they were deep into the forest. As they headed north Alla'mirridin told himself that he had been imagining the way Mino had said the word help.

†

Alec was running. It seemed like he had been running all day. They had nearly run him to death, earlier that morning, during what they called the Morning Ritual. It had consisted of general exercise followed by more specific training in weapons before finally turning to unarmed combat. After cleaning up, followed by a quick bit of breakfast, it was off to classrooms for study. His first classes had been in Military Tactics, History, followed by a general introduction to the Company, which covered rank, rules, rituals, and the like. As the sun approached its zenith in the sky Alec had been carted off by some of the Stone Hands to begin learning what they called his *Tradecraft*. After spending some time going over basic floor plans for building construction he was introduced to a training form, which they called *The Escape*. Placed in a guarded building, blindfolded and bound, it was his job to escape. Applying the techniques, they had begun to teach him Alec had flexed his arms at the wrists creating the smallest amount of slack in the leather straps, giving him room to begin working them loose. It took a little time but soon he was free of his bonds, running down a long hallway, with shouts reverberating behind him. By the Pox and the Pit! He was running again.

Had his mother heard him cursing like that she would have, at the very least, raised an eyebrow at him. Reaching the end of the hall, Alec slowed for an instant, so he could look both ways. Flipping hurriedly through his memory he searched for the layout of the building. *Which way?* The question reverberated in his mind as the sound of boots pounding on floorboards echoed behind him insistently. He could almost feel time slipping away from him like it was sand pouring out of his clenched fist. He had been told that the keys to escape were knowledge and timing. One of the Stone Hands had been adamant that knowledge and time were either his allies or his enemies depending upon how he used them. *Know where you are*, they had drilled into his head all afternoon. *Waste no time getting to where you needed to be.* It was as if he could still hear their voices.

Right, Alec thought. It had to be right. Darting to his right, Alec tried to move fast while remaining silent. He had immediately learned how difficult it was to do them simultaneously. Normally, you either moved fast noisily or slow quietly. His instructors claimed you could do both but Alec was struggling with the concept. For the hundredth time today, he reached up tugging at the high collar of the white coat he wore. It was not that it was too tight, the Seamstresses had made sure it fit perfectly, it was simply that Alec was not used to uniforms. As he padded down the long, narrow, hallway the layout of the building came into focus in his mind. He finally knew where he was. As he skidded to a halt, he cursed. *The wrong way*, he thought. *By the forlorn abyss!* He thought a few other things that would have made faces red to hear them aloud. Turning back, he thought, *to the pit with quiet*! Launching himself back down the dark paneled hallway, causing the rug to slide under his feet a bit, Alec ran full tilt. If he could make it to the other end of the hallway there should be stairs leading to a rear entrance two floors down. If he hurried, he could be out before the guards were onto him.

Just as he made it to the place where the two halls intersected he slammed headlong into the three men who had been chasing him. They all landed in a sprawl of arms, legs, and curses. Alec struggled quickly to his feet but so did his pursuers. He was instantly fighting for his life. Knives came out, since the men could not use swords in the narrow hallway. Hands, feet, and knife blades came flying at Alec from all directions. He danced. He danced for his life. Sweat beaded up on his forehead as he snapped an arm just below the elbow. The heavy knife the man had been holding clattered loudly to the floor. Spinning to his left Alec planted a side-kick into the second fellow's mid-section. The man bent over with a *whoosh* of air leaving his lungs. Suddenly a bright light flashed before Alec's eyes. His legs wobbled beneath him. A sharp pain made him realize that the third man had hit him over the head with the butt of his knife. Dropping to his knees, as if he was going down, Alec punched the guard in the groin. He knelt there, holding his head, as the guard doubled over, groaning, before finally collapsing in front of him.

Standing slowly, while rubbing the back of his head, Alec steadied himself before lurching down the hall toward the stairwell. Holding tightly to the rail, he took the steps two at a time. At the bottom of the stairwell he ran into a woman with a white apron on over a blue dress that screamed as she dropped her tray. Without a word, Alec slid past her out the back door. Twenty more steps took him across the street to the safe zone where he stopped. He tried to catch his breath while he continued to rub his head as if it would make the pain go away.

"End session." A deep baritone rumbled. The street Alec was standing on, the three-story house he had just escaped from, along with everything else around him wavered, became blurry, and vanished. What remained was a large, empty, open space, like the inside of a warehouse that held no cargo. At either end of the enormous chamber was a large, egg-shaped crystal sitting on a stand that was about three spans high. The egg-like crystal pulsed from blue to white and back to blue again. Hessle Drake was removing his hand from the crystal, which sat off to Alec's right.

Drake was the lieutenant who had been put in charge of this particular session with Alec. He was also a Stone Hand. Drake was Alec's height, though a little heavier, but with an easy smile. He had hard, gray eyes like granite. His black hair was cut short though it was still an array of thick curls. His nose seemed like it was just a bit too long for his narrow face. His deep baritone made his clipped accent sound even odder to Alec's ear. But it did not take Alec long to discover that Drake knew his business. After each of Alec's three failed attempts at escape, Drake had spoken to him about where he had made his mistakes, pointing out how he could improve on his next attempt. As Hessle Drake crossed the empty space to where Alec stood rubbing his head he could see that the man was smiling.

"Very good, Alec. Very good, indeed. It usually takes a new recruit weeks to make their first escape, yet you have managed it in one day." There was no mockery in his tone as he complemented Alec. In the short time Alec had known Hessle Drake he had come across as a man who did not dissemble.

Alec said, "Thank you ... sir." The pause was audible. He still had to remind himself to say that word. *Sir.* Drake smirked briefly at the hesitation but otherwise acted as if he had not noticed. Alec continued, "I would have preferred to do it without the bump on the head. And though I escaped, it seemed ... messy." He grimaced as he continued rubbing at the spot where the small knot throbbed on the back of his head as if he was trying to massage the pain away.

The musical voice of the other occupant of the training hall echoed across the empty space to Alec from the doorway of the chamber, "Next time duck." Onya Onoto spoke with an undercurrent of laughter running beneath her words. As his *Nsamsa*, Onya was entitled to be present at most of his training sessions, with the exception of those that would reveal what the Stone Hands wished to keep secret. With a half-laugh of his own, sprinkled with a tinge of mockery, Alec responded, "Yes, Nsamsa. Next time I will remember that invaluable bit of wisdom."

Hessle Drake patted him briefly on the shoulder. "All joking aside, Alec. Messy or not, you did well. But you must remember that when this is for real you will have the person you are trying to rescue in tow. Getting into a confrontation is time consuming. It endangers the primary while it gives the guards time to find you. Now, what did you learn?"

Alec took a deep breath. He closed his eyes as he had been taught earlier that morning. Bringing up the image of the hallway in his mind he began. "I did not make allowances for the fact that those trailing me would have time to reach the hallway's intersection. Accepting the fact that my *First Mean* was compromised I should have turned to my *Second Mean.*" Moving his lips as though counting, Alec said, "Last room on the left, out the window to the roof next door, down to the balcony at the rear, short drop to the ground below." Opening his eyes, Alec nodded to Drake.

Hessle Drake returned the nod, "Right, very good. You learn fast, which is an asset. Now let's talk about other strategies for a hard target escape. Remember we enter no *Catch* without at least three *Means* to escape." Alec had spent much of his first days as a new member of the

Company and the Stone Hands learning the language. Stone Hands never called a place that held someone they wanted to retrieve a house, building, or even a prison. They called them all a *Catch*. The way out was called a *Mean*. As Drake began to go over strategies Alec noticed a young woman in a Company uniform entering the training room. She saluted Onya who was still leaning on the wall by the door with her arms crossed. After Onya stood away from the wall, returning the salute, the young woman handed her a slip of parchment, which she opened. After scanning quickly through the note, she crumpled the parchment in her hand. Onya said something Alec could not hear to the young woman. They were too far away for Alec to make out what was being said. Nodding to Alec once, Onya turned on her heel. She disappeared through the door with the young woman in tow. As the door closed behind the young woman Alec briefly wondered what the message had been. But turning his full attention back to Hessle Drake he fell in behind the man as he walked across the chamber to the crystal that was still pulsing softly.

Drake reached out to touch the crystal saying, "Now, Alec, this time try to avoid any kind of confrontation. No residual presence."

Alec moved to the center of the chamber. He readied himself. *More running*, he thought. No wonder these people were in such good shape. They ran all the time. But what he said to Lieutenant Drake was, "Yes sir. I will do my best."

Drake nodded at the sentiment as well as the fact that the sir seemed to have come a bit easier to Alec's lips. His teacher said, "That is all we require in the Company, Alec. Remember that. We do our best according to the gifts and graces we have been given." As if he were intoning an old incantation, Drake said again, "According to our gifts and graces."

Touching the crystal with his hand Drake spoke the instructions for, what he called, *the next evolution*. The crystal pulsed from white to blue, causing the chamber to flicker, as the light from the crystal came pouring out, washing over the Tactical Training Room, like a wave of water. In moments Alec was in what he thought was the underground chamber of a tower. He was running.

†

Polshem Delver sat on his brown mare waiting. Without thought, he repeatedly slapped the leather gloves he had clenched in his right hand into the palm of his left hand. They had finally come across what they had been seeking for days. The wagon sat abandoned in the center of the road. Dead bodies littered the ground around it. The rear door hung limply from one hinge. The horses, which the dead men had presumably been riding, stood around listlessly waiting to be taken in hand. Delver sat patiently as his detachment of soldiers searched the wagon as well as the surrounding area to ensure that they were alone.

Delver hissed to himself. He barked at men who came too close to the sensitive areas of the wagon. The area immediately surrounding the wagon was vital. He had only allowed one man to peek into the wagon at Delver's close direction. He was trying to keep the evidence of what had occurred here from being tainted. The recent storm that had swept through the area would have done enough damage by sweeping away vital clues.

Soon the men returned from the woods giving the all-clear sign. The man Delver had allowed close to the wagon indicated it was also empty. Calling all of them back to where he had stopped the detachment on the road, Delver dismounted, handing his reins to a nearby soldier. Without pause he began his work. Every scene of this kind, if viewed correctly, could tell you what you needed to know, if you knew how to seek it out. This was part of what an Inquisitor did.

The soldiers sat in silence watching him work. Delver examined muddy hoof, as well as foot, prints. He looked closely at the dead bodies. He took particular interest in their wounds. He noted where, along with how, they had fallen. Meticulously, he crept around the wagon, before climbing on the wagon, until finally, he climbed in the wagon. It was all very puzzling. He was seeing what the remaining evidence was saying but it was hard to believe. Maybe the storm had washed away enough of the evidence that what was left would not make sense. It was only when the lieutenant in charge of the detachment of legionnaires spoke that Delver realized he had been standing by the hanging door at the rear of the wagon with a deep frown on his face, a hand on one hip, with a finger pressed to his lips.

"Sir. Is something wrong? Shall I have the men search the woods again?" The man's voice was matter-of-fact. It was not a questioning of Delver's ability, only the soldiers need to be about it. Soldiers hated waiting even though they knew it was what they spent most of their time doing.

Without looking at the lieutenant or raising his head from the clues on the ground Delver slowly straightened his arm pointing northeast. "As difficult as it is for me to believe that this is the work of a single man, he or they, went that way Lieutenant. And that is the direction we are going." Still deep in thought, turning the evidence over in his mind as he walked to his horse, Delver took the reins pulling himself back into the saddle.

The lieutenant said, "And what should we do about the wagon, bodies, and horses, sir?" Again, it was a matter-of-fact question. The man cared little about what was to be done he just wanted orders to follow.

"Leave it all, Lieutenant. We are not after wagons or horses." Without another word, Polshem Delver, having put his gloves on again, spurred his horse northward. The detachment of legionnaires urged their horses on behind him. As the sun climbed higher in the sky he began to wonder if they could catch the kind of person who could have escaped the wagon with the resources Delver had at hand. The legionnaires were hard men but for the first time he began to think he might need another kind of help, a darker kind. He would wait and see. Soldiers were not good at waiting, but Inquisitors were.

Let this be chief among the rules that guide us; we go where we are needed.

> *- The Second Precept*
> *From the rules governing the conduct of the*
> *members of the Watch known as The Discipline.*

Live long enough and you will discover that you usually go where you need to go not where you want.

*- Anvill Westmarch
Founding member of The Watch*

Chapter Fourteen

Where need takes us

Onya stepped off the lift walking briskly, down the hall, on the top floor, of the Peoples Tower. For the third time, since leaving Alec's training session, she realized she was gritting her teeth. Onya forced herself to take a deep breath. She *had* to relax! The hallway was on the top floor of the inner tower though it was decorated as if it were on the first. Wall hangings, depicting pastoral scenes, hung on the walls. Small, darkwood, tables with glass vases, containing fresh floral arrangements, stood along the wall on both sides of the hallway. The smell of lilac hung in the air. Evenly spaced wall sconces, with flickering glass globes atop them, kept it well lit. Onya smiled. Anna was meticulous in carrying out her duties as Matron of the Tower.

Onya walked on, trying to remain calm, as she attempted to steer her thoughts away from what was scribbled on the crumpled note in her hand. She knew that if she kept going over the message in her mind she would only fan the flames of her smoldering fury. *How could he!* He just let them take him. It made her stomach turn over just thinking about it. He let them take him with only three of the Company to back him up. If he got himself killed Onya would take his body to the Isle of Joon to see if the Oracle could bring him back so she could kill him with her own two hands! A low growl escaped her lips. She took another deep breath.

It must have looked like death was sweeping down on them. As Onya approached the entrance to the Mission Room at the end of the hallway the two *Stone Hands* who were on guard duty stiffened visibly. She knew they were Stone Hands with just a glance at their black coats. Embroidered in silver and brown thread, over their hearts, was a small, stylized, hand grasping a stone. Her coat had a tiny blossom with a missing petal, embroidered in purple and silver thread, over her heart. That singular addition to the otherwise unrelieved black of the Company uniform made it easy to identify a person's Order. These two Stone Hands had not been drifting off or less than attentive at their post but somehow managed to straighten even further as Onya barreled toward the door. The two large men, in their black uniforms, snapped off crisp salutes as she passed. It was a testament to how upset Onya was that she did not return their salutes but simply leaned into the double doors heavily. Shoving them open, she stalked into the *Mission Room*. She entered so fast that two junior officers had to practically leap out of her way to avoid being run over. Several other heads shot up looking toward the doorway.

The Mission Room was full of people. The room was longer than it was wide but was by no means small. It would easily hold forty or fifty people comfortably. However, most of the space in the Mission Room was dedicated to Tinkcraft. The walls held large rectangular pieces of glass, the size of tabletops, with pulsing gemstones embedded around their edges. Each glass glowed with maps made of light. Various small icons, which noted everything from Pradas in flight to ships at sail, could be seen blinking on them. There were people attending to each of the panels making notations. Some were touching the glass panels, which changed the orientation of the images, as they received written reports from other officers. Those reports came by com-gem or hand-delivered scrolls that would have arrived in Sanctuary, a number of ways. In this way, the Company was able to track most of the movements, of its own members as well as its adversaries, which affected how the Company used its resources. A massive table took up the center of the room. It had maps strewn all over it. There were large leather chairs around it. Sitting in the chair at the head of the table, opposite the entrance, was Captain-Commander Basil Noruba Mandraggan. He sat upright in the chair with his back straight. His black coat glistened in the light as the silver pips of his rank insignia glinted with polish on his collar. The small monocle, trailing a thin chain, embroidered in silver and red thread over his heart, was the symbol of the Windchasers. Basil was pouring over unrolled scrolls that appeared to be haphazardly strewn, in random piles, on the table in front of him. Several officers were hovering over him waiting to make reports or receive orders. He held a partially unrolled piece of parchment in his left hand. There was a cup of choca in his right.

Onya stalked over to where Basil was seated laying the crumpled piece of parchment on top of the pile in front of him. As she threw herself into the heavy leather chair to his left a junior officer approached with a cup, precariously perched on a matching saucer, accompanied by a pot of choca, on a black lacquered tray. The cup, saucer, pot and tray were painted with yellow lilies. Onya looked up at the young man as she asked, "Is it fresh?" She must have still had a hard look on her face because the young man, with one silver pip on his collar, licked his lips before he answered.

"Yes Ma'am. I only just poured a cup for Captain-Commander Mandraggan before you entered." The young man had a tiny, red bird in flight embroidered over his heart. He was a Red Bird. It made sense for him to be in the Mission Room since Red Birds specialized in information. They often served as negotiators, information gatherers, and advisors.

Onya forced herself to smile at the young Red Bird while he poured her choca. It took only a moment before she was sipping from her cup. She tried to force herself to relax. It almost helped her mood when she heard Basil slam his hand, which now clutched the note, down on the table with a few choice, pointed, curses for punctuation. Onya looked over at him from behind her raised cup. He raised the note in his hand, uncrumpling it, as he read it again. The room had grown quiet at the sound of Basil's outburst. Looking up from the note he motioned for people to get back to work. Looking over at Onya he made a quick shooing gesture in the air. The officers, who had been standing behind him, dispersed. They went to stand in other parts of the room. Basil leaned back in the heavy chair with his elbows perched on its arms. He raised a thoughtful hand to his chin. When he finally spoke, he did not say what Onya was expecting to hear.

"So, it has finally happened." He shook his head slowly from side to side as if he were saying no to some unasked questioned.

Onya leaned forward in her chair with her cup halfway between the table and her lips. She could feel the look of incredulity spreading across her face. Her voice very nearly cracked. "What, by the Pit and the Seal, do you mean finally?" Her eyes narrowed as she looked at Basil who now had a growing look of discomfort on his face. Onya continued, "Do you mean to tell me that you knew something like this was going to happen and you never told me!" Onya only realized that her voice had slowly gained volume with each word she spoke when she noticed the looks that other officers in the room were directing toward the table. The room had grown still for a moment, with an absence of activity, but as Onya let her gaze sweep around the room people turned back to their duties. Returning her attention to Basil she watched as he took a deep breath before raising his hands in mock surrender. His voice was level but low enough that it did not carry beyond the table. Basil did not lose his temper quickly or easily. Onya had always liked that about him.

"You must understand, Onya-san, that even Bantu puts his foot down. You know as well as I, that when he does, you would be a fool to disobey. And this ... this was, and is, about the very thing that brought him to Alexandria in the first place, all those years ago. It is a family matter. His instructions, regarding what was to happen when this day came, were very explicit."

Onya sat back, with her lips twisted in dissatisfaction, knowing that what Basil had said was true. The People played fast and loose with some of what Bantu ordered when it came to his personal safety. In every other instance his orders were followed to the letter or else there was the Pit and the Betrayer to pay. So, even though she wanted to stay angry, to have someone to direct that anger towards, she let it begin to fade. It did not help that it was always hard for her to stay angry with either Basil or Bantu. She would never let them know it but it was true. With Basil, in particular, there was something about his voice. There was also something in the way he looked at her. It was as if he could see all that she was down to her toes. That discomfited her. It made her feel messy. She looked away, clearing her throat as she did, hoping he could not read her in that moment. Why was she always disarmed around him?

They both sat in silence for a few minutes as the reality of the situation hit home. Bantu had been taken from them, had, in fact, gone with his abductors with only three of the Company to guard him. The only question that remained was what they were going to do about it.

"I'll tell you what we are going to do." Onya nearly jumped out of her chair when Basil spoke. She realized that she must have been thinking aloud. "We actually have more than one problem. I am glad you are already here because it saves me the trouble of sending for you. But we need to wait a few moments because I sent for Gabriel."

It must have been serious. Onya, along with Basil, were the only Captain-Commanders in Sanctuary at the moment. There was only a handful more in the entire Company. Captain-Commander was the highest rank you could achieve. There were few who had been given the honor of that rank by Bantu. Gabriel was a Commander, the next step down the chain of command from Captain-Commander, and that rank, though more held it, was still not as numerous as one might think. If Basil needed both of them there were very serious matters to be dealt with.

As Onya reached the bottom of her cup the doors to the Mission Room opened. Gabriel walked in with a confident stride. Gabriel Morgan was an Alexandrian native. He was from the western part of the empire. Slim, as well as tall, he was a distinguished looking man of almost middle years. His black hair was shoulder length with just a bit of silver running through it. Presently, it was pulled back into a tail with a black leather cord. His uniform looked freshly pressed. There was a small, golden lightning bolt held in two brown hands, sewn with shimmering thread, over his heart. Gabriel was a member of the Storm Holders. His boots did not seem to have a speck of dust on them. His walk, coupled with the way he held himself, said that he was a man accustomed to being followed. But as he approached the end of the table he stopped. He gave a crisp salute to both his superiors who were seated in front of him. Basil said, "At ease Gabriel. Have a seat. We have serious matters to discuss."

With a smile that showed bright teeth the older man plopped down in the chair across the table from Onya. He was seated to Basil's right. It only took a moment for a young officer to bring the commander a cup of choca, which he began to sip without adding anything. The young officer refilled Onya's cup as well. By the time she had added the proper amount of cream and sugar Basil's was raising a fresh cup to his own lips.

Resting his cup on its saucer, Basil launched into an explanation of the major matters before them. It was startling. Apparently, while Bantu was allowing himself to be abducted word had come from the palace that Gaiden Colling had escaped. The anger that Onya had begun to get a grip on threatened to rekindle into a conflagration, which would end in her marching to the palace to do very bad things to whomever she could get her hands on. But as the anger began to surge in her Basil's next words doused that flame in ice-cold water.

"First things first. It seems an *Arbiter* has come bearing a message." With that, Basil raised his voice so he could be heard from one end of the room to the other. It was a tone of voice that expected obedience. "I need the room." Basil spoke four short words. In moments the room had emptied. As much as some played loosely with Bantu's orders when it came to his safety the truth was that the Company was not the place for people who could not obey orders.

Once the room had emptied, with the exception of Onya, Gabriel, and a lieutenant manning the door, Basil signaled to the young woman with the single silver pip on her collar. With a sharp nod the young woman stepped outside. She had that, all too serious, look on her slim face that the young, with burgeoning responsibilities, often displayed. Onya hoped that over time the young woman would learn to be a little less serious. The Company taught you that you did not have to carry the weight of the entire world on your shoulders. You shared that responsibility with others.

In a few seconds she returned, still looking very serious, with a man trailing her. Once he was in the room the young lieutenant left. She closed the door behind her as she went. The visitor approached the table. Basil rose from his seat. Onya, followed by Gabriel, were only a second behind him as they stood. Onya tried not to be impressed by the knowledge that an Arbiter stood before them in the flesh. She failed. It was very impressive.

The man pulled back the hood of his red robe, which was trimmed in gold leaf around the edge of the hood, bell sleeves, and hem. Onya could see that he was young. He did not look much older than the young lieutenant who had seen him in. His fresh face looked as if he had only been shaving for a few years. It was likely that he still did not shave everyday. Shaggy brown hair, which was cut mid-length, hung down the front of his face to just above his brown eyes. Though he seemed very young, his eyes had that grave, sober, look of those who have seen things. The young man bowed slowly. He spoke with a graveness that matched his gaze if not his years.

"Please, noble warriors, take your seats. I am honored at the reception. I must admit that it does not surprise me. Though I have not been outside of Saladon in some time the Elders assured me I would be well received by any of the Free Companies. When the other members of the Embassy found out my assignment was to Tal' Algain I was told to expect the best treatment. I am glad to say that they were correct."

Tal' Algain, Onya thought, letting the words roll over in her mind. She knew that was the name used by the Arbiters of Saladon for the Company. The Company was part of a loose confederation of small armies that had long been known as the Free Companies. It was taught in the class on the history of the Company that every Cadet had to complete during their training.

The Free Companies had been formed from bands of people who had sided with the Light in the War of the Allgis-sein. Unused to violence of any kind, they had been forced to learn the art of war through a horribly bloody experience. The Glorious Ones armed them. They even led them into battle until they became vital assets during the war. When the war ended many of those bands pledged to continue to guard against the return of the Darkness. Those loosely formed bands of people became the Free Companies. As nations rose from the ashes of the war the Companies kept their allegiance to the Covenant they had made with the Glorious Ones. As several thousand years passed the Companies changed. Sometimes their composition changed. At other points in history only their names changed. They even began to hire out for short terms of service to countries at war, wealthy merchants with trade or supply line problems, or aristocrats with ambitions.

What had never changed was the Covenant or what came to be called the Compact. In order to insure the Covenant went unbroken the Compact was created. The Compact put certain rules in place governing the eventuality of one Free Company going to battle against another as they hired themselves out in service. The other thing that had not changed was the ancient Order that superintended Saladon. The Order of the Arbitrage was almost as old as the Free Companies. Though things about the companies had changed the Arbiters, along with Saladon, had not. Onya wondered what would have prompted the Order to send out an Embassy to the Free Companies. What had happened?

Motioning for them all to take their seats Basil said, "Please, Arbiter, join us. Tell us what Tal' Algain may do for you."

The young man sat at the other end of the table letting his folded hands rest on the tabletop. He looked thoughtful. At least that is how he seemed to Onya. He looked as if he did not want to say the words he held on the tip of his tongue. After a moment more of thought, he took a deep breath. His shoulders moved as if to say, *there is no way to say this except to say it right out*.

Looking up from his hands the young Arbiter looked down the table at them opening his mouth to speak. But just as he was about to say what was on the tip of his tongue his face changed as if something had just occurred to him. His tone said as much, "Begging your pardon, but where is the *Great Captain*?"

The Arbiters called the leaders of each of the Free Companies, *Great Captain*. As a group they were referred to as *The Captains Great*. The Arbiter was wondering about Bantu. It was not a surprise. He must have been instructed to deliver his message to the Great Captain of Tal' Algain himself. Onya watched Basil nod his head. He leaned forward intently. "You are right Arbiter. I understand that you must have been instructed to deliver your message to the Commander-General, but I regret to inform you that he is unavailable. Please accept my sincere apology for this lapse in protocol. I pray you do not hold it against us. I know that the Commander would not want us to offend you in any way."

The young man listened intently to Basil. He sat back in his chair as if weighing the words, he had just heard. After a moment, he leaned forward again with that look in his eyes. It struck Onya again that those eyes really did belong to a man twice his age. His voice, young but grave, had the sound of a man working through something he was recalling while he spoke. "I am to understand that the Great Captain is not in Sanctuary or the city proper?"

Basil nodded, "That is correct Arbiter. If he were we would have made you comfortable until he could be brought to meet with you himself."

The Arbiter nodded as though he were checking something off a list. "Am I to understand that one of you, by the laws that govern Tal' Algain, is in command in the Great Captain's absence?"

Basil nodded again, "Yes, Arbiter. According to the laws of Tal' Algain, I am in command until the Commander-General returns. In my absence, Captain-Commander Onya Yurishimi Onoto leads Tal' Algain."

After a moment's reflection, looking from Basil to Onya, the Arbiter nodded to himself as if to say all the protocols had been observed. He began speaking with urgency, saying, "Very well, *Grand Captain*." Onya noted the lesser title with which the Arbiter addressed Basil as Bantu's proxy. The young man continued, "The Compact has been called. You are hereby requested, and required, Grand Captain, according to the articles set forth in the Compact, to attend Saladon in your very person, to sit in the Summoned Seat, to hear the Petition. According to the Constraints of the Accord you may be attended by no more than one hundred and thirteen of Tal' Algain. You are required to attend your Seat within thirty days. I, myself, will certify before the Compact, the day and time you received the summons. Attend and be heard. May the Ancient shelter us until the Day of Rest comes."

While the last of his words still hung in the air the young Arbiter rose from his seat pulling up his hood. It swallowed his head whole leaving his face in deep shadow. With his hands pressed together he bowed at the waist, turned, and with deliberate steps made his way to the door. In a few seconds he was on the other side of the door being led off down the hall by the young lieutenant that had brought him into the room. The door closed softly but the lack of sound in the room seemed deafening.

Onya looked over at Basil. She also spared a glance for Gabriel. Both men sat with distant looks in their eyes. Basil's arms were crossed with his right hand holding his chin as he tapped a finger across his lips. Gabriel had both elbows on the table. The fingers of his hands were spread wide alternating between being intertwined and being tapped together at their tips. Onya realized that she had sat back, crossed her legs, while steepling her own fingers together. Her elbows rested on the arms of her chair as she tapped her fingertips together. *A Compact?* Her thoughts flittered about. Gaiden Colling had escaped, Bantu had been abducted, and the Arbiters had called a Compact! She let a short, utterly profane, word float across her mind.

Basil said, "Onya! You really need to get a hold of your tongue. I agree that things are not ideal but that is no excuse for cursing like a sailor on the docks."

Onya looked up at Basil realizing she had said the word aloud. Across the table from her Gabriel had a hand over his mouth trying hard not to laugh. Onya felt her face flushing as she cleared her throat. "My apologies, Basil-san, but you have to admit that this is not a time for soft words."

Basil breathed deeply, letting his shoulders drop, as he nodded. "Yes Onya-san, that is as it may be, but we need less cursing, more decision-making."

Matching his nod Onya said, "So what are we going to do about the-" Onya swallowed another choice word before continuing, "-*blessed* sky falling around our heads? Someone has to go after Colling, you have to go to the Compact, and someone has to run Sanctuary."

Basil grinned. It was his sly, *you-are-not-going-to-like-this*, grin. "I am not going to the Compact, *Grand Captain*. You are." Basil held up a hand stopping her short as she opened her mouth. "And before you say a single word, curse or not, that is an order. I'm going after Bantu."

Onya's jaw clenched as she swallowed what she was about to say. Though she and Basil held the same rank, the chain-of-command, as Bantu had laid it out, made Basil second in command. Onya was third. Bantu did not believe in leaving command up for grabs or allowing chaos to reign. So even though she was looking at another Captain-Commander his orders were just that. They were orders. "Very well, Commander. And who is going after Gaiden Colling?"

Basil shook his head. "Onya, I know that's important to you. I'm as furious as you are. But as much as I want to gather a handful of Windchasers and Deathsingers to hunt him down, we do not have that luxury. Besides, in the message, the Empress herself assured me, that he would be found. And I'm not inclined to argue with *her* without the Commander nearby."

Onya grunted. Today was not a good day. She began a quick breathing exercise because she was going to make herself sick if she did not get a hold of herself. "If I'm going to the Compact and you are going after Bantu then I guess you are going to leave Gabriel in charge of Sanctuary?"

As the words left her mouth Onya looked directly at Gabriel. He had been so busy watching the interaction between the two of them that he had not taken the time to do the count. As her eyes came to rest on Gabriel's his eyes widened slightly. His face turned just a bit pale. Licking his lips lightly Gabriel turned to look at Basil.

Basil still had that sly grin on his face. "That is correct Onya. Gabriel, you will be in charge of the Company until I, Onya, or Bantu returns."

Gabriel stood slowly, adjusting his coat, pulling sharply at its hem. His voice was level but only just. "But sir, there are at least three other

Captain-Commanders in Sanctuary as we speak. Shouldn't one of them be in command?"

Basil stood motioning for Onya to stand as well. Smiling at Gabriel, Basil said, "Gabriel, they have other matters to attend to." Tapping his com-gem in a distinct series made it flare to glowing, green, life on his collar. As it sparkled, pulsing as if it were alive, the gem on Gabriel's collar matched its brilliance. Without looking down at her own collar she knew that her gem had pulsed to life. Onya was familiar with that sequence of taps. Any command level officer would know that series well. It activated the com-gem of every officer in Sanctuary from the rank of Lieutenant Commander on up.

Basil spoke. His voice echoed across Sanctuary. "Attention to orders." Onya knew that at that moment command level officers, all over Sanctuary, were rising to stand at attention wherever they were. They would wait quietly at attention until Basil was finished. Conversations were being halted mid-sentence, lunches were being put down, while various other activities were paused as those officers, wherever they happened to be all around Sanctuary, awaited what Basil would say next. Basil continued after a brief pause, "By the authority given me by the Commander-General, I, Captain-Commander Basil Noruba Mandraggan, do hereby promote Commander Gabriel Morgan to the rank of Captain-Commander, with all the rights and privileges therein. Until further notice, he is in command of Sanctuary. Mandraggan out!" After a quick succession of taps to his com-gem every gem that had been lit up around Sanctuary winked out.

Basil reached across the corner of the table taking Gabriel by his forearm. He gave the man's forearm a firm shake as he said, "Congratulations Captain-Commander, I know you will do well. Now if the two of you will excuse me, I have a ship to catch." With that, Basil stepped around Gabriel and left the room. In the wake of Basil walking through the doorway, exiting the Mission Room, the officers that had been excused, began filing back into the room. They went back to attending to the glass panels on the walls. Gabriel still stood unmoving by his seat.

Onya walked around the table. Grasping him by the forearm she said, "Captain-Commander, congratulations. Be sure that when Basil brings the Commander-General back there is a Sanctuary to bring him back to. Now, if you will excuse me, I have a delegation to put together." With that she copied Basil's pointed exit. There was work to do. Looking over her shoulder she could not help but grin, just at one corner of her mouth, as she saw Gabriel surrounded by junior officers waiting for orders. The older you got the more you discovered that you never really got to do what you wanted. You usually ended up doing what you had to do. *Yes*, she thought, as she made her way to the lift. She would rather be out chasing down Gaiden Colling if she could but there was work to do.

†

It did not take Basil long to get to his floor in the Tower. While he packed his things for the trip he continued issuing orders through his Communications Gem, which glowed brightly on his collar. Soon he was back on the lift as it carried him from the twelfth floor to the first. A few minutes later he was in one of the Company's black-lacquered coaches rolling toward the docks.

Basil rocked gently with the motion of the coach as he sat on the plush, purple, velvet seat. Though he was finally sitting his mind continued to race. Could he get to Bantu in time? Was his friend already dead? If he was still alive, and Basil reached him in time, would Bantu even allow him to help? Was he bringing enough of a force to make a difference? Basil did not know a lot about the warrior tribes that spawned Bantu. He only knew what he had gleaned from the times Bantu had been willing to talk of home. The warrior tribes were organized into what they called Great Houses. There was no king or queen, or empress for that matter. Al'akaz functioned as a society through the almost ruthless application of power. It was power that was only blunted by a competing, but equally influential, notion of honor. Even if Basil got to Bantu in time, even if Bantu allowed him to help, even if he had managed to bring enough assets, Basil wondered if he could pull it off without going to war with all of Al'akaz?

As the coach rolled to a stop at the Company's section of the docks Basil hopped out. His mind raced as he thought to himself that he was relying on a great many ifs. *Maybe too many.* Looking across the docks, Basil tried to take his mind off those troubling thoughts. When his eyes came to rest on a small contingent standing off to the side, out of the way of the hustle and bustle of the docks, Basil grunted without realizing it.

Taking a deep breath, Basil braced himself as he walked over to them. He planted himself in front of the small group. They had apparently been awaiting his arrival. Looking over the small group he shook his head. Somehow, though it did not surprise him, these women had gotten wind of secret information, namely that Bantu was gone along with the fact that Basil was going after him. Macrina, Bantu's personal scribe, stood with her small arms crossed looking like she was about to go for an afternoon sail around the harbor. She looked at Basil, giving him a half-smile, even as her eyes narrowed. The look in her eyes said she was not even going to discuss it. Next to her, Anna, the Matron of the Tower, was standing with both hands on her hips. She was staring, defiantly, at Basil. Behind the two of them were a handful of Anna's people, in the black and white livery of the Company, tending to a pile of travel bags. Basil opened his mouth but before he could get a word out Anna was speaking hurriedly.

"Not a single word Captain-Commander. Not a single. Solitary. Word. Especially, if it has anything to do with us not going. Do you hear me Windchaser?" Anna stepped closer to Basil as he tried to say something again, but she rushed over it. "I have taken care of him-" she paused for only a fraction of a second as she looked over at Macrina, "-*we* have taken care of him every day for years. Years, mind you!" She pointed a finger at Basil jabbing the air with it as if she were poking him in the chest. "And don't you think for a moment that you are going to go harrying off across the Great Bloody Deep without us! Why, the man can't keep himself fed or clothed without us women around to keep him upright and turned in the right direction. So, don't you try, don't you even try, to keep us from handling our responsibilities!" Throwing her hands up as if she had been trying to convince him for hours but had failed miserably she spun on her heels. She took the four steps that separated her from Macrina bringing her back to where she had been standing before Basil arrived but with her back to him. "You would think that the only People around here that mattered were these fools with their swords, crossbows, and the Ancient knows what else." She raised her voice speaking over her shoulder in Basil's general direction. "But I have some news for them. If it weren't for the likes of us cooks, seamstresses, leatherworkers and shipwrights, they couldn't so much as make a cup of choca in the morning." Turning back around to face him, Anna crossed her arms over her chest, nodding her head once, sharply, as if to say, *and that was that.*

Basil realized his mouth was still hanging open. He shut it summarily swallowing what he had been about to say. Without a word he turned on his heel. He walked past the women, down the dock, looking for the launch that would take him to the small island where the Leviathan was birthed out past the harbor. Basil was still a relatively young man by most standards, but he was old enough to know to leave that entire conversation alone. As he walked briskly down the dock he heard a flurry of activity behind him along with a faint shout from Anna. "Don't you think you are going to leave us behind Basil Mandraggan!" With a grimace, Basil kept walking.

In short order, all the while ignoring Anna, Basil was on Proving Isle being escorted by Jailo Murrat, the Grounds Steward. Behind them Anna and Macrina followed with their contingent of Anna's people. Anna talked the entire way but was ignored by Murrat as if she was not even there. This made her face blush bright red, infuriating the tower Matron, but left Basil struggling to stifle the laughter that kept trying to burst forth. Anna ruled the Tower like a queen, but this was Murrat's fiefdom.

Murrat took Basil through the facility leading him out to where the Leviathan was docked. There was a swarm of activity on the ship as well as all along the dock. Basil nodded as he saw that his orders were being carried out. Murrat left Basil at the dock. He wove his way through the throng of people loading cargo onto the ship. Climbing the gangplank, he stopped at the top, standing at its end, while he scanned the crowd of moving people for the Captain. It was a few moments before his eyes fell on her. He realized that she must have been looking for him because she was already strolling across the deck headed directly to him. With a man who must have been her Second standing just behind her left shoulder, she came to a halt in front of Basil standing at attention. Basil said, "Permission to come aboard Captain."

With a broad smile Nessera ela bin Stormcloud responded with a voice that was just a bit deeper than one might expect from a woman. "Of course, sir, the ship is yours." She inclined her head holding it there unmoving. Basil stepped off the end of the gangplank onto the deck of the massive ship. He took three steps, which brought him to stand directly in front of the captain. She was a tallish woman standing just a fraction taller than Basil. Her light, sun-bleached hair was pulled back into one intricate braid, which fell down her back. The captain's skin was light brown from being in the sun often. But for some reason her face was younger looking than her actual age should have dictated. She was a handsome woman, not breathtakingly beautiful, but very handsome. Basil touched her on the shoulder briefly. He had a great respect for this woman. She was a seasoned sailor. "No, Captain. Leviathan is still yours to command. I can think of no one better equipped to get me where I need to be." At that her head came up. Basil noticed her Second relax a bit as he stood behind her. He was a very tall, brooding, man with pips on the collar of his black vest marking him a Lieutenant-Commander. A small, stylized ship, with sail, in blue, silver, and white thread was embroidered over the heart of his black vest. The sailors of the Company were known as *Wave Riders*. The man was two, large steps below Basil in rank so he had held his displeasure at the prospect of his Captain being relieved of her command to a tensing in his shoulders matched by a hardened look on his face. But he had remained silent. Basil continued, "Captain, time is against us, so I hope you are close to being ready to cast off."

Nessera nodded her head. "Yes sir. I have had to speed up the process of selecting people to fill the crew, but everyone has reported for duty." Without looking behind her, she held out her left hand. Her

Second placed a piece of rolled parchment in her hand. Rolling it open, she looked it over as she continued speaking. "We are currently loading the last of the supplies while giving the ship a final once-over. We should be underway shortly."

Basil nodded his head to show that he was satisfied with what he had heard. "Very well, Captain. Now, if you will have someone show me to my quarters, I will settle in while we prepare for our departure." Nessera pointed at a young woman who was hurrying passed them in the blousy white shirt and black vest that was the standard uniform for the sea going People. "Lieutenant. Show the Captain-Commander to his quarters. C-deck, Command Quarters."

The young woman stopped. She caught herself when her eyes started to widen as she looked from Basil to Nessera. To her credit that was the only indication that she had been caught off guard by the company she had just found herself in. The lieutenant snapped to attention saying, "Aye Captain, right away." Turning to Basil she said, "If you will follow me, sir, I will see to it that you get squared away. May I take your bags?" Basil smiled warmly at the young woman. "Thank you, Lieutenant, but I will carry my own bags. After you."

The woman started off toward a door that was halfway across deck. As she walked she bellowed at the top of her lungs that the Captain-Commander was coming through. According to the young lieutenant people needed to make way or she would do unspeakable things to them. Basil tried to ignore the unspeakable things she described as sailors hurried to get out of her way. Basil was tempted to tell the woman to stop but he did not want to embarrass her. So, he followed behind her accepting the fact that she was shouting at the top of her lungs. She even came close to cuffing a few people on the head who did not move out of the way as fast as she thought they should.

Basil was thankful when, not much later, he was safely in his cabin waiting for the ship to cast off. When he had awakened that morning, he had planned on going to the theatre that night. Mansuura Ollivera was going to be reading from his latest work entitled, *Being and the Lightness of the Soul*. But sometimes you did not get to do what you wanted. You learned in the Company that most of the time you had to do what needed to be done however inconvenient that turned out to be. Basil looked around the cabin until he located a wooden tray with short, handle-less, silver cups next to heavy crystal decanters. He poured a glass of what must have been very old *soch* from one of the decanters. It was a light brown, very strong drink but with a remarkably smooth taste. *Soch* ranged from the very cheap, hard to swallow, variety all the way up to the kind he was currently drinking. Any of it would leave you debilitated if you drank too much. Sitting in one of the oversized leather chairs that decorated the large room, he sipped from his cup. With really good *soch*, you sipped it. The cheap stuff you threw to the back of your throat, swallowing quickly, while hopefully having a mug of mead at hand to wash it down. As he sipped, Basil tried to calm his mind but no matter how he tried it was not long before the *ifs* returned to trouble his mind. *Would he be in time? What if he were too late?* He pulled out his pipe, which allowed him to focus on lighting it rather than on the answer to those questions.

†

Cordovan woke wondering where he was. It took a moment for his eyes to focus. Sitting up in the bed he took in his surroundings. Judging from the angle of the light pouring in through the, floor-to-ceiling, window it must have been early afternoon. A quick inventory of the room told him he must be in Watchtower. Swinging his legs over the side of the large bed, Cordovan pushed himself up to a seated position. The bed's heavy mahogany frame did not move as he shifted his weight. Leaning forward, he put his hands on his knees and breathed. He let his head hang.

The previous night, as well as the last few days, was a bit of a blur. He allowed himself a deep sigh as he reflected on the fact that She was safe. Thanks to the Ancient they had averted disaster though it had cost them. Though the price had been high he, along with every other Watchman, would pay that price a dozen times over if it kept Her safe. They had succeeded. The thought washed over him like a refreshing breeze.

For the first time in days he had been able to sleep. Throwing back the blanket that covered him Cordovan stood. Cool air hit him reminding him that he had no clothes on. He looked around the room but did not immediately see anything to put on. Walking over to a large wardrobe he pulled open its double doors only to discover that it was empty. Without warning a sudden urge to stretch overwhelmed him. It was as if his body was acting on its own. He arched his back deeply as he stretched his arms wide. It was a long, deep stretch accompanied by a full-mouthed yawn that made his eyes water. Clearly, he had used himself roughly. While the process that had made him a Watchman left him with certain gifts, even a Watchman could push himself past the point of recovering. As Cordovan walked slowly around the room he realized that he had come very close to that limit. Still somewhat weakened, without thinking, he made his way back to the bed.

Just as he crawled back onto the soft, feather mattress, pulling up the heavy blanket as he did, the door to the room opened slowly. Cordovan watched as a woman poked her head around the door. After seeing him in the bed looking back at her she pushed the door open the rest of the way hustling in two other women. With brief smiles, accompanied by short bows, the women, all in Imperial Livery, with their hair pulled up demurely into buns or braids, carried in folded clothes, along with a tray of food. Two young men, barely more than boys, entered closely behind them carrying a large copper tub. After placing it in the center of the room they quickly exited. In moments the boys returned with buckets of steaming hot water. They emptied them into the copper tub until it was nearly full. While they were filling the tub, the slightly older woman, who had stuck her head in the door, bowed her head to Cordovan again. She said, "Master Watchman, young Janni, who I had waiting outside your room, said she heard you up and about. So I thought you would be ready for a bath, some lunch, and your clothes. Is that acceptable Master Watchman?"

Cordovan sat up in the bed giving the woman a warm smile. He made sure his voice was pleasant. "Yes. Thank you, Mistress. And you may call me Cordovan."

The woman blushed slightly at his smile, and probably at the impropriety of the suggestion that she call him by his name. She bobbed her head with a curtsey. "Yes, Master Watchman. It is a privilege to serve." Shooing the other servants out the woman backed to the door with a bow as she went.

Cordovan watched her back out. Just as she reached the door he said, "No, Mistress. The privilege is mine." Bowing for the third or fourth time the woman pulled the oversized mahogany door closed softly. Jumping from the bed Cordovan almost landed flat on his face. He had to remind himself that he was still weak from his ordeal. Steadying himself on the post of the bed, he looked from the tray of food to the steaming water in the copper tub, and back again. Finally, he chose to totter to the tub. Climbing in, he eased himself down into the steaming water. It was just shy of too hot. His muscles soaked up the heat without protest. For a time, he simply sat in the water soaking. As the water began to change from hot to warm, he grabbed a cloth, along with the large piece of soap, which they had left for him. After a good, lathery wash he rinsed. The rinse was basically him dunking himself under the water several times. Easing out of the tub he dried himself with a large, white, fluffy towel wrapping it around his waist when he was done. He turned his attention to the tray of food. Taking it to the bed he laid on his side to eat. There was a heavy, dark bread, some sharp, yellow cheese, fruit, and a too-large bowl of thick soup. He washed it down with a sweet, dark, red wine that was just a hair colder than the room. It all tasted wonderful on the tongue. Only when he was scraping the last of the soup from the bowl did he notice the small envelope, with the purple seal, on the edge of the tray. The seal identified it as a message from the empress.

Breaking the seal, which held an impression of a lily in bloom, Cordovan unfolded the parchment. The elegant, flowing, script in which the note was written was Her own hand:

My dear Watchman,

I have sent this note with instructions that you not receive it until after you have awakened from your slumber. I am grateful for your assistance as well as your diligence in the performance of your duty. It is clear to me that you saved my very life and that you, along with the other Watchmen who accompanied you, paid a heavy price so that you could be where I needed you last night. Rest assured that the names of the fallen Watch will be honored according to our pact and traditions. I carry them in my heart even as I am writing to you. Take your rest. When you are able, come to me. While I know you should have more time to recover, we are never truly able to do what we wish. Too often our actions are dictated by events beyond our control that force our hand. There is work yet to be done.

Daughter of the Morning,
Sword of Tallanmoor,
Prince of Allmathon,
Keeper of the Watch,
Empress Natassha Sobrine

Folding the letter up gently, Cordovan laid it on the edge of the bed. He was still weak but She was calling for him. He would die before he let Her down. Slowly he made his way to the chair where his clothes had been carefully laid. The bundle turned out to be a fresh uniform. Cordovan pulled on the gray breeches of fine wool, slid his feet into thick gray stockings, before pushing them into the long, black, leather boots that had been standing against the wall. Running a light hand over the boot's fresh polish he cinched the three silver buckles that ran down the outside of them. Standing, he slowly put on the white, silk shirt. The gray waistcoat matched the breeches perfectly. The piping, which ran down the side of the breeches, matched the three bands along the front of the waistcoat. They were all black silk. As he buttoned up the black, pearl buttons of the waistcoat he saw his longsword leaning in one of the corners of the room near the door. The black scabbard glistened, as did the round, steel handguard at the base of the hilt. Someone had polished it. Cordovan walked to the corner to retrieve it. Buckling its black leather belt around his waist he secured the silver buckle that had been made in the shape of a lily in bloom. The last thing he did was to throw on his new purple cloak, fastening the small, circular, silver clasp with its own lily embossed upon its face. All over the empire Alexandrians knew that purple cloak as the unofficial emblem of the Watchmen. Straightening his waistcoat Cordovan thought for a moment about how it felt to be clean again. The empress spared no expense when it came to outfitting the Watch. The wool was the finest. The silk was unrivaled. The black pearl, which served as buttons on his waistcoat, were expensive. The leather for his boots had come from Corsica. Cordovan steadied himself as he opened the door. He strode from the room with purpose startling a handful of servants who were milling around in the hall.

The young servants parted like a wave before him. Looking over his shoulder he saw them go into the room he had just left to begin cleaning up after him. He stopped, spun on his heel, but had to touch one of the walls of the hallway to steady himself. With a deliberate gait, which allowed him to remain upright, he walked back into the room causing servants to scatter again. Crossing the room, he plucked the letter from the empress off the edge of the bed. Securing it in a small pocket in the lining of his cloak he strode from the room again as servants bowed before going back to cleaning. Moving with a slow, but steady, gait Cordovan headed for the stairs calling up the memory of the way to the rooms in the Watchtower that held high chairs. There would be men with razors there who could give him the shave he needed so that he would be presentable to the *Daughter of the Morning*. As he walked he felt the worst of the weakness beginning to pass. He smiled a grim smile as he turned into the stairwell. That was a good sign. There was work to do.

Their making is cloaked in secrecy. Very few know what transpires in the creation of these virtuous paragons whose purple cloaks ripple in their wake. All that is known, all that can be said with certainty, is that men enter Watchtower, and giants leave.

> *~From the opening monologue of Precipai's play**
> *entitled, <u>Call To Arms</u>*
> **It made its debut to critical acclaim at the*
> *Meric Theatre in Lower Alexandria*

It was not his family name,
nor the value of his garments,
it was not the length of his stride,
nor the curve of his chin,
that made him great.
It was his willingness to answer,
when he was called.

~Padiss Bandabon
Primminger of Graden Abbey
From the inscription
on his Gravemark

CHAPTER FIFTEEN

Around about midnight

Cordovan had gone to the palace in answer to *Her* summons. After entering the palace proper he made his way to the Hall of Lilies, where he expected to find Her in an afternoon session, holding court. Sure enough, as he arrived, he was informed by one of the Imperial Secretaries to wait in one of the antechambers. After waiting several minutes, in which he fended off three different servants carrying refreshments, Cordovan turned his attention to the woman who returned with word that he was to attend the empress at the entrance to Watchtower at midnight. While no one besides the empress, and the Watch, knew what that meant, Cordovan understood immediately.

With a shallow bow, to the imperial functionary, Cordovan turned on his heel. He strode from the palace at a leisurely pace. As he passed the black, wrought-iron gates he looked up at a sun barely passed its zenith.

So, Cordovan considered how best to pass the time before his midnight appointment. He began with checking on Swift. It was another half hour of brisk walking before the imperial stables came into view. The uniform of a Watchman got everyone's attention as he strode into the stables. It was an unavoidable consequence of the purple cloak in Alexandria. Grooms leaped to stand stiffly in, what they imagined was, an approximation of standing at attention. Buckets, along with brooms, rattled to the ground next to unmoving feet. The distinct smell of a stable filled Cordovan's nose. It was a clean smell unlike many of the stables he had been forced to frequent. There was no stable kept better that he had ever seen. The stalls were manned by a veritable army of groomsmen. There was fresh straw everywhere. Horses either had glistening clean coats or were on their way to having them. Just beneath the clean scent of horse were leatheroil, straw, and even liniment. All around him, tack was being oiled, while metals were polished. As Cordovan moved into the heart of the stables, walking along the lengthy row of stalls, an older man fell in beside him.

"Master Watchman. My name is Halburke. I am at your service. Are you in need of a mount?" The man's balding head, with wisps of gray strands of hair clinging hopelessly to it, remained half-bowed the entire time he spoke. The man's tone was just shy of obsequious. Cordovan reached out, giving the man a pat on the shoulder, as they continued to walk. "Thank you, Master Halburke, but I am here to inquire after my mount Swift. She's a mare, nearly the size of a stallion? She's a gray with a white spot on her shoulder?"

The man nodded. "Ah, yes sir. And a fine mare she is. She was in a way when they brought her in last night, mind you, but we have tended her around the clock, yes, we have sir. Though if I may say sir, it will be many days afore she be ready for riding again. But give us some time. She'll be right as rain, she will."

Cordovan shook his head as he said, "I am sure you are right Master Halburke. And I thank you for your care of her. I am only here to see her."

The man, who must have been the Head Groomsman, turned right. After four strides around a corner he turned left. He had that ambling way of walking that must have come from constantly avoiding muck. The older man continued down another stretch of stalls, saying a word here, making a noise there, as he passed horses in their stalls, until he came to the last stall in that particular row. It was next to two huge doors that had been opened wide allowing sunlight, mixed with fresh air, in. There, in an oversized stall, was Swift. Her coat glistened with oil as she stood there slowly making her way through a feeding bag, attached to her head, filled with oats. When she saw Cordovan, she tossed her head with a loud snort. Pulling back the gate to the stall, Cordovan smiled as he stepped in. Making soft, soothing, sounds that amounted to nothing coherent - it was the tone that mattered - he ran a hand down her neck, and along her spine, until he reached her hindquarter. Patting her softly Cordovan said, "We did it girl. We made it. Thanks be to the Ancient, and to you, we made it." He stepped over to where the tools hung on the wall of the stall. Retrieving a heavy brush, he began to make smooth strokes from her shoulder to her rear haunch, making his way around to Swift's other side as he did. "There is more work to do but you take your rest for now. I am sure I will see you soon."

Cordovan finished brushing her. After a few more minutes of checking her over he stepped out of the stall closing the gate behind him. Retracing the way he had come with Halburke, he caught sight of the man near the entrance to the stables. A few questions got him the names of the grooms who had been tending to Swift. Before he left Cordovan found both of the young boys. As their eyes spread wide at the sight of the Watchman towering over them he placed a gold imperial mark in each of their hands. It was more than the two of them would make over an entire season. When he thanked them for their services they flashed big smiles back at him ducking their heads several times as if not quite sure if they had already bowed to him or whether they had bowed enough. Cordovan forced himself not to frown at their behavior. He knew the trepidation the boys displayed was a holdover from the days when nobles would have a man's head removed from his shoulders for the smallest lack of deference displayed by what those they thought of as commoners. Thank the Ancient the empress did not tolerate that kind of behavior. He smiled broadly as he thought of how the empress would have the noble's head removed for even thinking about treating the people in such a way. Some of the Peerage hated her for changing the world in that way. But Watchmen would die to protect her because of the way she had changed things.

Cordovan placed a mark in Halburke's hand on his way out. He very nearly had to run to keep the man from returning it. Walking on, Cordovan heard the man shout his intention to watch Swift around the clock, protesting that he would not rest, nay not even sleep, until she was as right as the day she was born.

As he walked away from the stables Cordovan decided he wanted another meal. The thought of another brief nap, before midnight, had begun to sound like a good idea. It was a side effect of how he had used himself in the past fortnight. He would be more hungry than normal for the next few days needing as much rest as he could get.

†

The afternoon, followed by the entire evening, passed with Cordovan blissfully unaware. Had he not left instructions to be awakened he might have slept through the night. The young woman, dressed in imperial livery, was standing just inside his door with a small brass gong in one hand, which was still reverberating from being struck by the small mallet she held in the other. He sat up in bed, rubbing his eyes, as he turned to look at her. She curtsied deeply and tried not to blush as she hurriedly backed out of the doorway. The young woman closed the door softly behind her but not before Cordovan heard her giggling something to another woman in the hall. Wiping his hand slowly over his face, he moved to the edge of the large four-post bed. He pushed himself to his feet.

It took nearly eight strides to reach the oversized leather chair that sat near the window. Dropping into its softness, with a *whoosh* of air leaving its cushion, Cordovan pulled his boots around to the foot of the chair.

He had dropped them in the corner on his way to falling face first into bed several hours earlier. They still had the sheen of fresh polish. He had pulled off his cloak, waistcoat, and boots, just before falling into oblivion. He realized, as he pulled on his boots, he was feeling a bit steadier. The walk must have done him some good. The additional sleep had not hurt.

As Cordovan finished pulling on his second boot there was a light knock at the door. After a brief pause the door swung open a bit. A head poked in around the door. The young woman, who had awakened him, looked around the room. When she saw him in the chair, she pushed the door the rest of the way open allowing a second woman to enter. The second woman - girl really - looking even younger than the first, was carrying a white bowl with a matching pitcher. Both were adorned with small lavender flowers around their edges. Placing the set on a small washstand, opposite the chair he sat in, she upended the pitcher. Cordovan watched her fill the bowl with hot water. Setting the empty pitcher next to the bowl on the stand, the woman - make that girl - turned, curtsied, and hurried out of the room with her hands clutching at the front of her skirt. He watched her go, letting his gaze rest on the young woman who had ushered the second woman in. She caught his eye. She curtsied, speaking to him for the first time. Her voice was airy as if she were almost out of breath, "Is there anything else you require, Master Watchman?" She continued to remain crouched halfway through her curtsy while waiting for his response.

"Yes, little mistress. I require your name." He let his voice make it a request rather than a command.

Her head bobbed even lower. He could almost hear the blood rushing to her face in the sound of her voice. "It ... it is Chelsa, my Lord. Have I displeased you in some way?"

Cordovan shook his head slightly. He was away from the imperial court so often, for such extended lengths of time, that he often forgot to observe its subtleties. A servant's name was rarely requested. When it was it usually involved the servant being disciplined. Rising from his chair Cordovan walked to the door where the woman waited. She was diminutive. He towered over her. He reached down placing a hand gently under her chin. He raised her head until he was looking directly into her eyes. She was pretty. She would not make a man stop in his tracks from twenty paces away just to watch her pass but if the same man took a moment to look more closely he would see that she was worth stopping. She stared up at him with big brown eyes as Cordovan spoke warmly, "Do not worry, little mistress. I simply wanted to know who to thank for waking me according to my instructions." He smiled at her. He held onto her chin so that he could watch as the fear melted away from her expression. Her furrowed brow gave way to a smile, which blossomed on her face like a flower opening to the first rays of the morning sun. Realizing that he was still holding her chin he took a full step back after gently releasing her.

"Now, Chelsa, if you would be so kind as to bring me something to eat, I need to freshen up."

The young woman stood, frozen in place, for another moment. She flinched as if she just realized he had given her more instructions. Bowing her head nearly to the floor she spoke, breathlessly saying, "Yes, Master Watchman." Chelsa rose, backing from the room. The door closed softly behind her.

Cordovan washed up at the washstand. He put on a fresh, white, shirt. This one had tiny purple blossoms running up the sleeves, down the bodice, and around the collar. By the time he was buttoning the last white, pearl, button on his shirt, Chelsa had returned with a tray of food. The repast of roasted duck, covered in a blackberry sauce, with grilled vegetables, and more dark bread, was accompanied by a light wine that had an amber cast to it. It was cold, fruity, and refreshing. He ate like a man who had not seen food for weeks. Once his tray was empty he noticed the hour was growing late. Pulling on his waistcoat he fastened his cloak at the neck on his way out of his room. The quarters he had been assigned were on the third floor of Watchtower. It only took him a few minutes to make his way to the stairwell. He went down two flights to the first floor. Another few minutes saw him in the main hallway walking on plush, purple carpet.

The walls were covered with intricately woven tapestries. There were paintings depicting either famous battles or great warriors. Some were historic members of the Watch. The aged patina of the paintings said that they were very old. Their age could also be deduced by some of their characteristics. In the portrait of Ambic Dross the man was wearing a *red* cloak while Pim Deven was pictured with no cloak at all. Their portraits hung on either side of a tapestry depicting the battle of Elgon Pass. The battle for the Pass had been bloody. According to the histories it had also been a closely run thing. The Watchmen had actually taken to the field as a unified division, a rare thing, under the command of another legend, Gamble Hark. The day had been so bloody that thereafter Hark had forgone his red cloak in favor of a purple one. Watchmen had followed suit for the last two hundred years. Hark had been a Watchman when Alexandria was still Samosata and Samosata had a King, not an Imperial line. To walk down the Hall of Memories in Watchtower was to take a stroll through time itself. Cordovan guessed that the Hall did what it was intended to do because by the time he made it to the antechamber at the entrance to Watchtower he was standing a little taller.

Stepping into the antechamber was like arriving at a reunion. It was filled with crisp gray uniforms, trimmed in black silk, adorned by purple cloaks. He stopped just inside the chamber so that he could look around. It was as if it was his first time seeing so many of the Watch in one place. The men who stood around in the antechamber were tall, short, or inbetween. They were rapier slim as well as thick with muscle. There were men with braided hair above brown faces from Eastend, tied back tails on faces tanned by the sun from Soliss to the west, as well as short styled cuts on olive-skinned faces from Hyden Pann to the north. There must have been seventy or more Watchmen standing in the antechamber murmuring, laughing, and slapping backs. The precious few occasions they got together were always a time for celebrating, even with only a handful of the Watch, because they rarely got an opportunity to see each other. If there were ever a time when every member of the Watch was in the same place, at the same time, it would mean that the world must have been coming to an end, or at the very least an empire.

"Cordovan, you bloody darkhound!" Cordovan turned in time to see Galleden Ip as the man slapped him on the back. Cordovan had to take a step forward to keep from being knocked over. Galleden was the kind of man who drained every drop from life. He also meant for everyone around him to do the same. Some took his jocularity for frivolity, meant to be ignored, but Cordovan would wade through a pack of Spitjacks, fresh from the Pit, with Galleden at his side. He was a bit shorter than Cordovan. His black hair showed a little white in small patches like bits of snow nestled on the tiny leaves of a bush. He was clean-shaven, as was most of the Watch. His black eyes were sharp as a hawk's. His complexion normally tended towards the pale but there was a hint of color in it tonight from being in the sun for an extended period. Cordovan reached out, clasping his hand, meeting a strong, rough grip.

"Galleden, you old dog. Still have all your teeth I see. I thought they would have put you out to pasture by now." Galleden barked a full-throated laugh, nearly choking, while slapping Cordovan on the back again. This time he was ready bracing himself against the strength of the man's arm. Galleden stopped a young man who was moving through the crowd of Watchmen with a tray so that he could grab two tall, slender, silver cups, handing one to Cordovan. They were filled with a tangleberry punch that was sweet, tart, and a bit stronger than wine. It was a dangerous drink. The punch was served ice cold but had no hint of the taste of alcohol. Tangleberry punch had led to many a bad decision.

Galleden raised his cup with solemnity saying, "Courage and Wisdom." He said it while showing all of his teeth. It was the ancient creed of the Watch, the two things that every Watchman needed in abundance. Cordovan raised his cup, with an equal soberness, "Courage and Wisdom."

They both drank. When they lowered their cups, Galleden stepped a little closer to Cordovan. Bringing his voice down he said, "So, a real piece of work that was last night lad. Your name is being spoken around here with as much respect as they used to use when they talked about Valem, or Faldrith. We don't really get to actually save her life, do we?" The older man nodded, with respect, taking another drink as he looked around the room. Cordovan sipped from his cup to cover the fact that his throat had gotten tight all of a sudden. He had a deep respect for Galleden Ip. The man was on his way to legend in the Archives.

Thoughts of the bandits at Corren, or the invasion of Mirrid, not to mention the time Ip had come harrowing across the Midden Mor to arrive just in time to aid a young Watchman in trouble. That, newly minted, Watchman had been pinned down by the Men-at-Arms of a traitorous member of the Peerage. He had uncovered the noble's plot to poison a rival. The rival happened to be a supporter of the empress. Cordovan opened his mouth, but Galleden cut him off.

"No, no. I know you lad - straight as an arrow and humble to boot. So don't try to diminish what you did last night. I know we carry Her justice to the corners of the empire but what you did last night is the reason we put on the purple cloak these days. When these other men realize you are in the room you can expect more of what I gave you. Don't let it swell your head, but accept your due, lad. Every Watchman in the city has the name Allegressa on their tongues today. That is something to be acknowledged." With that he turned his head to look out on the crowd as he continued sipping his punch. Cordovan did the same. A gathering of this many Watchmen was rare. He just stood there allowing himself to enjoy it. Though it was still a while before midnight he had come early, as he knew the other men had, in order to enjoy the rare opportunity of this gathering.

A high tenor reached Cordovan's ear from a few feet away. Turning his head, he saw Ulrich san Ogssell, a head above the other Watchmen around him, walking toward Cordovan. Ulrich was of an age with Cordovan, a fraction taller, and one of the few Watchmen with facial hair. He had a thin, black mustache with a small, pointed chin-beard. He had a thin face with a longish nose. His long arms wrapped Cordovan up in a brief bear hug. After squeezing him tightly the man held him back at arm's length to look at him. "Cordovan del Allegressa!" There was an excitement in his voice. The last time Cordovan had seen Ulrich the man had been headed for the southern tip of the empire. But that had been some three years earlier. Cordovan patted the man on his arm.

"Ulrich. It is nice to see you again. How long has it been?" But Ulrich waved the question off as unimportant. "How long? Inconsequential! You, sir, are an inspiration. Does the rest of the Watch know you are here?" Cordovan's heart began to beat faster. He said, "Ulrich. Wait-" but his words fell on deaf ears.

Ulrich had already turned to the rest of the gathering. He raised his voice so that he would be heard above the din of the other conversations being held around the chamber. "Gentleman, soldiers! Warriors of the First Rank! Let me have your esteemed attention!" Ulrich had always had a way with words but sadly only a casual acquaintance with brevity. He would rather use five words where one would do. The antechamber grew quiet. Men stood with their tall, slender, silver cups in hand as heads turned in Ulrich's direction. Ulrich swelled with the attention. Looking over the gathering he pointed at one of the servants, a young man with an empty tray, on his way to fill it again. "You there, bring me that chair."

Ducking his head in a half-bow the young man, in imperial livery, darted to the wall, snatched up the article in question, and quickly carried the chair over to Ulrich, who promptly leaped onto it. Towering over the assemblage, he raised his voice to reach every part of the chamber. "Gentlemen, I thank you for your illustrious, magnanimous attention. I am grateful, even humbled, by this opportunity to be with so many of my brothers-at-arms. I am pleased, as well as thankful, to be able to take this auspicious moment to raise a cup to one of our esteemed number. While any of us would have done the same, in similar circumstances, it was, in truth, only one of us who had the Ancient smile down upon him providing him with the opportunity to fulfill the purpose for which he donned the purple cloak. So, raise your drinks men, raise them high that you might help me salute, Cordovan del Allegressa!" Ulrich added a flourish of his arm as he raised his cup in Cordovan's direction.

At the mention of his name a raucous cheer went up. Men turned or twisted, some craning their necks, to get a look at him. Others, who had been close by, pointed as if only just seeing him. They began chanting his name. Before Cordovan knew it Ulrich was down out of the chair as three or four of the Watch, including Ulrich, were pushing him up onto it, so that everyone in the antechamber could see him. For the next few minutes men chanted as, one by one, they squeezed forward to clasp his forearm. Many said to him, "Courage and Wisdom." with intense looks on their faces. Others merely said, "Honor, Allegressa! Honor." Some raised their cup to drink with him until his was emptied. But as soon as his cup was empty someone was thrusting a full one into his hand.

The place was close to becoming raucous. Even the servants, who had a moment away from chores, stood along the edge of the crowd clapping or whistling. As Cordovan looked down at Galleden, the man could only lift his hands, shrugging his shoulders, as if to say he had warned Cordovan that this was coming. Looking back over the crowd of Watchmen, as they celebrated him for saving the empress, Cordovan's eyes drifted past the massive double doors at the entrance to Watchtower. It took him a second to realize that they hung wide open with a tiny woman standing in the doorway. Behind her, just outside of the doorway, since by tradition they did not enter the Watchtower, the Imperial Guard stood, ringing her protectively, with Captain Ellom Vam at their head. The doorway was filled with the cream shirts and plum breeches of the Imperial Guard. They crowded as close as they could to the entrance. But the brilliant center of the scene was *Her*. She stood calmly, quietly, in the doorway to Watchtower, which stood at the heart of Watchkeep, resplendent in a lilac gown that left her shoulders bare. It glittered with tiny purple stones along the bodice that caught the light. It was so long that you could not see her feet as the gown's train gobbled them up on its way to trailing several feet behind her. Her red curls spilled down her back from beneath a sparkling tiara of diamonds, surrounded by amethyst, resting lightly on her brow. She was stunning, even from a distance.

Wondering how long she had been standing there, Cordovan found his voice. Speaking loud enough to be heard above the other Watchmen Cordovan said, "The Daughter of the Morning, Sword of Tallanmoor, Prince of Allmathon, Her Majesty, Empress Natassha Sobrine!" When he finished he hopped down from the chair. Along with every other person in the antechamber, he went to one knee. The Watchmen pulled their scabbarded swords from their belts, as they knelt, placing them on the ground before them with their hands still gripping them. The room went still. Cordovan could no longer see her because, like his fellows, his head was inclined, but he could clearly hear the light, musical voice that belonged to Her.

"My Watchmen. I am gratified to see you celebrating Cordovan del Allegressa. He is deserving of your praise, and mine. It is right that we honor him tonight. But I think we have certain customs to observe, do we not? Rise, my Watch."

With that the Watchmen rose as one. Scabbards slid home on swordbelts as Nell Berringer, the Gallant Master of the Gate, stepped forward into the intervening space between the empress and the rest of the Watch. The only member of the Imperial Guard allowed, by custom, to enter the Watchtower - only him, only here, and only now - Captain Ellom Vam, stepped forward to meet him. The two men stood across from one another with only a few feet between them. Standing tall, nearly eye to eye with the Gallant Master of the Gate, Ellom Vam spoke in a resonant voice that carried across the antechamber. "Do you accept responsibility for the safety of the One who is the Dawn?"

With a brief nod Berringer spoke the words that had the sound of having been spoken for hundreds of years, "It is the Watchtower. She is safe here even when she is safe no where else."

Ellom Vam nodded saying, "So be it."

The Gallant Master of the Gate replied, "So be it."

The Captain of the Imperial Guard turned on his heel. He took the four steps that brought him to stand in front of the empress. With words that still flowed from custom he said, "Majesty, we await the Dawn." With a bow of his head to her, his hand on the hilt of his sword, Vam walked from the antechamber. The double doors were closed behind him. Cordovan, along with every other Watchman, knew that outside the doors of Watchtower, where custom allowed them to stand, the Imperial Guard was ringing the building. The show of strength would be impressive. More than a hundred men, in the Guards cream and plum, would be surrounding the tower. Ellom Vam would be marching tirelessly around that ring seeing to it that no one entered or left until the doors opened and the empress was returned to his care. Vam was a dangerous man who took his responsibility for Her safety with a deadly seriousness. Watchtower was the only place in the world he would allow Her to be out of his reach. It was not that he wanted it to be the case, but custom allowed for nothing less. Everyone knew She walked Watchkeep without a care. While the Imperial Guard was charged with Her safety even the Twisted Ones with a dark horde at their backs would be hard pressed to place a hand near Her in Watchkeep. Every member of the Guard, even Vam, knew that they had to give way to a member of the Watch. Nevertheless, the man had won the respect of the Watch for the way he handled the Guard. Vam was respected. Tonight, however, he had to settle for securing the ground outside the Tower.

With the doors closed, *She* turned back to the Watchmen as they stood silently before her. Time honored words passed her lips. "I have come to adjoin the Watch." They were ready, having removed their scabbards from their belts again. Her words were accompanied by the sound of seventy or so scabbard tips thumping against the hardwood floor of the antechamber. A few voices called out. "Is he worthy, Madame?"

Cordovan smiled to himself. In the Watchtower, away from prying eyes, there was a lesser formality She allowed with them. She was still the Empress, but she was also the great lady, the mother, their mistress, and a certain amount of light chiding was allowed. He saw a similar smile spread across Her face. Her voice was spirited, even playful, here. "Yes, my darlings. He is worthy, else I would not have brought him." Again, scabbard tips thumped against hardwood.

Another man shouted from the back. "May we see him, Mistress?" It was not a question or a request, but part of a verbal dance that had been worked out between the Watch and the nobility they had served for more than five hundred years. Cordovan always wondered at these times what set of circumstances had created the need for the different parts of the custom. Was there a time when the nobility they served had needed to provide proof to a more roguish gathering of Watchmen that the man who was offered was worthy of their secrets? That was certainly not the present dynamic. Her word was inviolate here. If she said a man was worthy, that was that. She had earned that level of trust over the years. They trusted her more than they had trusted her father.

A wave of her hand signaled a door to be opened. A tall, young, man was led in by two Watchmen. He was blindfolded but walked with an easy stride holding his shoulders back. He was unafraid. It was apparent that he had not filled out into full manhood just yet, but his shoulders were broad. He showed some of the musculature that would be his full inheritance in another year or two. Cordovan watched him walk, sizing him up, as he was sure other Watchmen were doing. There had clearly been training. The gait that was just shy of the swagger of a man who had been taught to handle himself was there. There was an easy balance as well as a grace in his movement.

The two Watchmen led the young man to a place equal distance between the empress and the rest of the Watchmen. They pulled at him to stop. He was pushed to his knees. Once he was kneeling they removed the blindfold. The young man had short, curly, brown hair, brown eyes, a strong chin, and a calm look about him. He did not stare defiantly at the crowd of Watchmen as some did, nor was there a look of caution, trepidation, or even awe. He knelt calmly as if it was completely natural to be there. Cordovan nodded to himself. The young man had been raised well. If he had the skills to match his demeanor he would make a very good Watchman.

The Gallant Master of the Gate stepped up to the kneeling young man. He said, "What is your name?"

The young man looked up at Berringer. He had a slightly lower tenor. "I am Aubrey Devilwind." After saying his name, he continued to kneel. The young man showed that he had himself well in hand. He made no attempt at listing accolades or accomplishments. He simply spoke his name. *Good*, Cordovan thought, *very good*.

After a pause, the Gallant Master of the Gate nodded to himself. He continued, "Who brings you to the Gates of the Tower? Who opens the way that is shut?"

That light, musical, voice washed over them as She stepped up behind the young man. She placed Her hands on his shoulders. "I do, the Ancient being my guide." Cordovan knew that there was not a Watchman in the chamber who had come to the Watch during Her reign that was not affected. There was not a one of them who was not at that moment reflecting on the day they felt those delicate hands on their shoulders remembering how Her touch had made them feel. He remembered how Her speaking for him had made him ready to march into the Abyss for Her with nothing but his sword matched only by the certainty that he would stop the hordes spilling from the Pit for Her. He saw the young man's jaw clench when she vouched for him. Cordovan knew in that moment they would have to kill him to prevent him from becoming what She wanted him to be. Cordovan had seen enough.

The Gallant Master of the Gate turned to the crowd of Watchmen behind him saying, "And who will walk him through the way that is shut?"

There was a moment of silence as many of them looked around to see who would take on the task of training the young man. Most Watchmen did not like to serve as a teacher. It was time consuming. It could sometimes keep you from extremely hazardous assignments if it was felt that your apprentice was not yet up to the task. But a Watchman had taught each of them. A Watchman had shown each of them the way. It had to, ultimately, be a gratifying experience. Her eyes swept the assemblage searching for a volunteer. Just as her gaze settled on him Cordovan found his voice. He spoke the ancient words, "I will, the Ancient being my guide."

Scabbards thumped against the floorboards as Cordovan made his way through the crowd of Watchmen. As he passed some of them they tapped him on his shoulder or patted his back.

When he emerged at the front of the crowd the Gallant Master of the Gate nodded at him with respect. Turning to the empress, Berringer said, "Mistress, is it acceptable that Cordovan del Allegressa finish what you begin this night?"

The empress smiled the smile that made Watchmen shift from one foot to the other like little boys pinned to the floor by their mother's gaze. Cordovan was close enough now to look into Her eyes. They seemed a deeper blue tonight. They sparkled. He realized he was smiling like an idiot but he did not seem to care. Looking into his eyes she said,

"Allegressa has always been acceptable. He is even more so in this matter."

Scabbards continued to thump against the floor as voices cried out, "Here, here!" and "Well said, Madame!"

Looking around the room the Gallant Master of the Gate thumped his own scabbard on the floor. He shouted, "It begins!"

The crowd of Watchmen surged forward like storm water over a ship's side. They grabbed the young man hoisting him into the air. They carried him deeper into the Tower while the empress, the Gallant Master, and Cordovan followed. They tossed him around, over their heads, jostling him as they went. Aubrey Devilwind, to his credit, maintained his composure while he was tossed around like a rag doll. He did not fight as they carried him aloft. He had been brought in fully dressed. But by the time they had climbed the stairs to the top floor of the tower, entering its central chamber, the crowd had stripped him down to his smallclothes.

The central chamber, at the top of the tower, was bare. It was a room that one might have expected to be lavishly decorated. But since it had been reserved for this particular purpose, the singular addition was a giant, plush, purple rug covering most of the floor. Lying in the center of the room the rug was decorated with a large ornate circle of gold in which the emblem of the Watch had been woven. A brown and gold hawk, with its wings spread, as if in flight, adorned the center of the golden circle.

When Cordovan, the Gallant Master of the Gate, and the empress entered, the crowd of Watchmen carried the young man aloft inside the circle tossing him high into the air. They were yelling with each toss. Closing the door behind them, Berringer strode to the circle, crying out with a booming voice, "Prepare!"

The crowd lowered the young man to the floor. They formed a ring around the edge of the woven, golden, circle in the carpet. Shaking his head, as if to regain his balance, the young man rose to his feet. Standing there, in nothing but his small clothes, he tried holding himself steady while grinning like a plumb fool. He swayed just a little letting Cordovan know he was still dizzy. But it was worth noting that he could stand at all.

Cordovan remembered that he had stumbled briefly before being able to stand after that whirlwind trip from the first floor to the top of the tower.

Joining the Gallant Master at the edge of the circle with the other Watchmen he began to thump the tip of his scabbard against the floor in unison with the others. They all began to hum. The lights were doused with the exception of a single lantern burning brightly in the hand of the Gallant Master of the Gate. He followed the empress into the circle, with the light, as they made their way to where Devilwind stood, nearly naked, at its center.

Cordovan could recall the excitement he had felt in that chamber, in the near darkness, surrounded by some of the greatest warriors of the age, with the most beautiful woman - She was a girl back then - standing over him, speaking with a too-high voice.

Without being told, the young man knelt as she approached him, illuminated by the light from that single lantern. She sparkled as the stones in her dress caught the small amount of light. In her hand she held *Adeladora*. It was also known as the Sword of Destiny. It was made of wood. The wood was stained deep red. Adeladora was older than both the empire and the kingdom that had spawned it. No one knew its exact age. There were whispers. There was conjecture. What was known, by everyone in the chamber, was that wherever it had come from it was a wonder. It was as sharp as a sword made of steel even though it was wood. It also, somehow, managed to be as strong as steel. As miraculous as that was it was not as startling a fact as why it was to be used in this ceremony. Somehow it had been discovered that *Adeladora* had other properties. While no one knew what it had been originally made for another purpose had been discovered. It had been in the Watch's possession for as long as the Watch had been in existence.

With the rhythmic thumping of scabbards against the floor along with the humming of an ancient tune, whose words had been lost somewhere in time, the empress approached the young man with *Adeladora* in her hands. As she reached him she spoke. "Bow your head Aubrey Devilwind." Leaning forward to place his hands on the floor the young man bowed his head. The empress continued, "This is your last chance.

After this there is no turning back. You will either leave this room a Watchman or you will not leave this room. What say you?"

Cordovan remembered when he had been cautioned several years ago. He knew the Gallant Master of the Gate had told him, as he was being prepared for the ceremony, that if he were found unworthy during the rite he would be killed on the spot. He had been given the day to contemplate whether he would chance death. Cordovan knew the young man would have had to say yes to be here. What no one outside of the empress and the Watch knew was what *Adeladora* did. The young man spoke with a resolute voice. "I am ready Majesty." His agreement was accompanied by the sound of the Watchmen's swords sliding from their scabbards. That sound, at his own ceremony, had made Cordovan's heart race.

With an almost triumphant voice the empress raised *Adeladora* over her head. She shouted, "Then be judged!"

As she struck him on the head the room erupted with light that burst from *Adeladora*. Waves of white light, mixed with blue, shifting to green, followed by white again bathed the room in sparkling iridescence. It was like staring into the sun. Having been through the rite and carrying in them the gifts that had been bestowed upon them the Watchmen did not need to fully shield their eyes. They all stood there squinting into the brilliant, colorful, cascade of light emanating from *Adeladora*. Cordovan knew, as did every Watchman in the room, what was happening at the center of that pulsing light. Aubrey Devilwind was being stripped. A force that could not be named was peeling back the layers of his soul laying it bare. It was revealing what he was at the very core of his being to the one holding *Adeladora* in Her hand. Once stripped, if he was found acceptable, those layers of his being were replaced but with a few things added. It would be Cordovan's job to help the young man understand what that would mean.

As the light intensified, bathing the room in a myriad of colors, so did the thumping of empty scabbards. That sound was accompanied by humming from the throats of the men who crowded the circle. The steel in their hands reflected the light of *Adeladora*. She would be speaking to him now. She would be making secret promises, which he would be answering with the Great Oath. They were establishing a covenant between them, a cherished promise about life tempered by truth extracted from each, woven into their bones by the power that engulfed them both. Cordovan watched as the white light pulsed brightly one final time before it stopped changing. It became completely blue. Those gifts, which made them what they were, would be added to him now. As if signaling his thoughts, the young man screamed. It was painful. That pain had shaken Cordovan to his core when it had been his turn. But in a brief moment, one that Cordovan knew young Devilwind would believe took an eon, it was over. The light from *Adeladora* winked out. The young man slumped to the floor. The thumping along with the humming ceased. No one moved save the empress. Kneeling next to Aubrey Devilwind she stroked his head while whispering to him. After a few seconds he stirred. At her bidding he began to rise.

The lamps on the walls of the chamber were lit as Devilwind came unsteadily to his feet. He was drenched in sweat. The empress turned from him to the crowd of Watchmen saying, "He is Aubrey Devilwind. He stands to the Watch!" With those words the crowd of Watchmen shoved their swords back into their scabbards. They roared loud enough to shake the rafters. Cordovan found himself shouting with the rest as if the rite had rekindled something in him. Shouts rang out as the crowd of Watchmen stepped into the circle. "To the Watch! To the Watch!"

Cordovan crowded in with the rest. Berringer appeared next to him with a folded purple cloak. He passed it to Cordovan. Stepping into the small space that remained clear for the empress and the new Watchman, Cordovan draped the purple cloak around his shoulders saying, "Welcome, Aubrey Devilwind, to the Watch. May the Great Oath never fail."

With a voice that only shook a hair the young man said, "May the Great Oath never fail."

The room continued to resound with cheers. Cordovan looked down at Her. He said, "With your permission Mistress?"

The empress smiled as she nodded at Cordovan. Smiling back Cordovan turned back to Devilwind. "Come, Aubrey. There are quarters for you on my floor. While you may think you want to celebrate, in a few minutes you will be ready to pass out."

Looking around the room the young man solidified Cordovan's opinion of him. "As you say, sir. Lead the way. I will follow."

The two of them walked out of the chamber with Aubrey Devilwind leaning on Cordovan. Behind them the cheers rose. "To the Watch! To the Watch!" A few minutes later, a little past midnight, Aubrey Devilwind was in his new quarters in Watchtower fast asleep. Across the hall Cordovan was only a few minutes behind him.

*He who gives, beware,
He that receives, doubly so.*

*~Inscription on the Weeping Wall at Goss
Found at the excavation site of the ruins of
Orceer'eden. Thought to be the home of the
Ceers of Esk.
Dated circa 13 B.F.E. (before first era)*

A favor is nothing more than a debt disguised as a gift.

~Haldor Fann
Advocate of the First Order
Magistracy of Ildiss

Chapter sixteen

A caution against favors

Cordovan sat quietly on the edge of the large bed. It was covered in fluffy, silk-wrapped pillows done in light blue. The comforter was brown with matching blue bands across its length. The luxurious bed coverings made for a wonderfully soft place to find blissful sleep. In each hand he held a strong, steaming, cup of choca. Cordovan had learned to drink it plain while on the road, but, when he could, he liked it sweet with a bit of cream. As he sat, sipping from the cup in his right hand, he watched the young man in the bed. He was blissfully unaware that there was someone else in his room. While Cordovan understood that Aubrey was oblivious as a result of what he had been through the night before, he would, nevertheless, have to be prevented from making it a habit. Sleeping that deeply, even when guarded, was dangerous. Cordovan sighed deeply. He knew what it was like to have his own sleep interrupted. He rose from where he had been sitting on the edge of Aubrey's bed. Though it was still early there was work to do.

Stepping to the head of the large, four-poster bed, Cordovan leaned down to stick one of the cups of choca beneath the young man's nose.

After a few deep breaths, the young man's eyes popped open. He sat up in the bed, without hesitation, rubbing at his eyes. After looking around the room he looked at Cordovan. It looked like he was just beginning to realize where he was as well as what was happening. Cordovan stood still, sipping from his own cup of choca, giving him time to get his bearings. Smooth, with a hint of spicy-sweetness, the choca in both cups was made from a blend of ground beans from the Yaca mountain region to the south. The inhabitants of the small mountain village grew, harvested, and roasted, their beans, producing a dark bean with an oily glossiness that, when brewed, made for a delicious, though strong, cup of choca. It was a major export for them. It was brought out of the mountains on pack mules in coarse bags before being placed on large pallets in the holds of ships that came up the Macca Deep to Alexandria Harbor.

Cordovan took another sip from his cup as he watched the young man come fully awake. Once he took his hands away from rubbing his eyes, Aubrey Devilwind smiled that fool grin of his. It was the smile that the young, having experienced little or no horror, were still able to smile. Cordovan's own smile no longer looked that way. The young man reached out so that Cordovan could pass him the cup he had been waving under his nose only moments before. After handing over the cup he walked over to the large chair that was almost identical to the one in his own room across the hall. Cordovan plopped down in it being careful not to spill his drink. From his vantage point, in the large leather chair, he watched Aubrey Devilwind.

The newest addition to the Watch was tall. He had shoulders as broad as a tent pole was long. He was well muscled, though not with the broad weight that would come to him in a few seasons. The young man's mid-length, curly, brown hair was all over his head, at the moment, though he somehow managed to appear fresh-faced. Running a hand through his disheveled hair Aubrey Devilwind leaned back against the blue, silk, pillows that were piled up behind him as he sipped his choca. Clearing his throat, he spoke, though his voice still had a hint of morning in it. "So, you are going to be my teacher."

Cordovan smiled from behind his cup as he tilted it back for another sip. The words were matter-of-fact, not a question, without a hint of trepidation. He wanted to meet this young man's parents. They had done an extraordinary job raising him. If what Cordovan had seen thus far was an indication of the young man's future he was going to be a formidable member of the Watch, which was a good thing. If things were about to get as bad as he thought, they would need every sword they could find. Though Aubrey Devilwind's future seemed bright, he did have things to learn. Lowering his cup, Cordovan said, "According to custom, for a year and a day. Then you will be on your own, unless, for some unforeseen reason your training period is extended, or you turn out to be wholly incapable of doing the work. And if the latter turns out to be the case-" he shrugged his shoulders as he let the incomplete statement float in the air. Those who had been given the gift, who later turned out to be unworthy of it, were gotten rid of to prevent them from exploiting those gifts. It was rare, but it had happened. Hardly anyone in the Watch ever spoke of it but it had happened.

While Cordovan had been speaking, the young man got out of bed. The servants had stripped him to his smallclothes before putting him to bed. He cast about with his eyes presumably looking for something to put on. While he looked, he said, "Yes sir. A year, and a day. May I ask, why the day?"

"There is some speculation concerning that, but the truth is no one really knows for certain. Those who could have told us are long dead. Some believe that early on the reason was thought to be so obvious that no one bothered to write it down or make it a point to pass on until it was lost to the fog of time. For now, just accept that it is so." Cordovan's voice had, without thought, taken on a lecturing tone. There was a soft knock at the door. Before the young man could speak Cordovan said, "Enter."

The door opened emitting the young woman who had been taking care of Cordovan along with several other liveried servants. In just a few moments, with the women sneaking bashful glances at Aubrey as he stood unabashedly, nearly naked, before them, they had carted in a copper tub. It was followed by a small, folded, pile of clothes. The last thing they brought in was food, two trays of food in fact. As they were bowing their way out the door Cordovan said, "Thank you Chelsa. Your service has been exemplary." The young woman curtsied deeply at his words, leaving with a broad smile on her face. She shooed her companions out in front of her. Cordovan thought he would have to reward her before they left. The imperial servants were well provided for, even in their retirement, but showing them a bit of gratitude for their efforts with a few coins had become custom. He, like every other Watchman, had more than most. He had always tried to share it where he thought it would do the most good. Watching the door close softly, he thought Chelsa would know how to make the most of some extra coin. Cordovan made a mental note about the coins as he turned his attention to the tray of food. Aubrey sloshed around in the copper tub across the room.

There was cold fruit juice, hot oats with honey, topped with a dash of cinnamon, some cured, sliced ham with a sugary glaze, dark bread and a sharp cheese. They had also left a pitcher of very cold water. Gulping down a tall silver cup of water, Cordovan dug into the food, not looking up until his tray was empty. Leaning back, sipping fruit juice, he looked up to see Aubrey had finished bathing. He was eating in snatches as he tried to button his waistcoat.

Cordovan set his empty tray on a sidetable, near the door, on his way over to Aubrey. Pushing Aubrey's hands aside, he showed him how to button the coat properly. When he was done he stepped back. Cordovan looked him over. Aubrey pulled at the hem of the coat to straighten it. Aubrey Devilwind cut an impressive figure. When he had first reported to Watchkeep Cordovan knew he would have been gone over with a fine-tooth comb by the seamstresses who sewed for the Watch. They would have spent the day preparing his garments so that they would be ready this morning. Now, Aubrey stood there, resplendent, in the uniform of the Watch. His black boots shone with fresh polish. His gray pants, of fine wool, with a black, silk stripe down the outside of the breeches, complemented the matching waistcoat. They were freshly pressed. A hint of the white shirt peeked out at the collar and cuffs of the coat. All that was left for him to do was don the emblem of the Watch. Cordovan walked over to the chair that had held the folded pile of clothes to retrieve it. Walking back to Aubrey he draped the long, purple cloak across his shoulders letting him click the silver lily, which was its clasp, in place at the neck.

Cordovan saw the moment Aubrey set his shoulders. He stood straight in his boots rising to his full height. The young man was actually half a span taller than Cordovan. The purple cloak had a way of doing that to you. Standing back a step from Aubrey, he looked him over saying, "Now, you almost have the look of a Watchman. But there are still a few things missing. Come." Turning on his heel, Cordovan walked to the door of Aubrey's new quarters. He sat his cup down on the empty tray that rested on the sidetable. Retrieving his own purple cloak, he fastened it at the neck before walking out the door. As he made his way down the hall it took only a moment for Aubrey to catch up. The young Watchman fell into step beside him. Aubrey kept silent while they walked. Cordovan liked the fact that the young man seemed to know how to hold his tongue.

They walked nearly the same route through the Tower Cordovan had taken the night before. When they hit the Hall of Memories they turned left, walking along the corridor, until they found an exit to the rear of the Tower. There was a goodly amount of activity in Watchkeep this morning. Most of the people they passed were servants dressed in the purple and cream of the imperial livery. Women curtsied, while the men ducked their heads, when they noticed the purple cloaks. Here Aubrey did speak. He nodded at the servants as they passed. While they heard his greeting, none of the servants saw his nods given their own bowed heads. Had they seen it their faces would have likely registered shock or embarrassment. But Cordovan did not stop Aubrey from trying. He rather liked the display of humility from his new pupil. So, Cordovan remained silent on the subject as he walked on with a small smile on his face.

They stayed on the cobblestone paths that wove through the grass, flowers beds, and sculpted shrubbery until they came to a long, low, building that ran along the outer wall of Watchkeep. Pushing open the door, Cordovan stepped into the dimly lit room with Aubrey a step behind him. The young man had to duck his head as he entered. Heat struck them as they entered along with the sound of the loud clanging of forge hammers striking metal. All around them men in heavy leather aprons, with sweat dripping or pouring from their brows, worked at metal meant for various ends. It was the smithy of Watchkeep. Standing just inside the doorway, they watched men pumping bellows for the enormous furnace, while others carried stock rods from one place to another. The smell assaulted Cordovan's nose. It was hard to name it beyond calling it a mixture of sweat, leather oil, and something burning, though he knew it to be more complex. All over the smithy older men were directing younger. It did not take long for one of the young men to approach them. He stepped up to Cordovan bowing deeply. His face was dirty but, when he raised his head, Cordovan noticed his teeth were bright white as he smiled. "Master Watchmen. It is always an honor to have you in The Brace. How may we serve?"

Cordovan smiled back at the young man nodding toward Aubrey. "Devilwind here is in need of a sword."

With a hint of disbelief Cordovan watched as the young man's smile seemed to broaden. He looked from side to side speaking quickly with a hesitant hint of caution. "Yes, yes … of course … Master Watchman. May I … serve you in this matter? I know I am come recently to the title of Mastersmith, but I … I assure you, I am capable."

Cordovan held up his hand to calm the young smith as he spoke to him in a soothing tone. "Mastersmith, I know that it takes great skill to earn your place in The Brace. I am sure that Devilwind is in good hands."

The young mastersmith bowed his head again. When he lifted his head he said, "I thank you sir. While it is an honor to prepare whatever we are asked for *Proving* a blade intended to carry the Empress' Justice to the corners of the Empire is a special honor." Still half-crouched, with his hands held together in front of his chest, the young smith unclasped his hands, placing the right one on his chest while making a flourish with his left. "Now, if you will follow me, we will see to your request."

As they turned in the direction the young mastersmith had indicated, he ran a few steps to get ahead of them setting a fast pace as he slowed to a brisk walk. They followed him through the main chamber passing through a swinging set of double doors. Once they pushed through the heat began to dissipate immediately along with the smell. The newly minted mastersmith continued down a long sparse hall. He turned left around a corner continuing on down the length of a second hall. The second hall was even more sparsely decorated than the first. He walked on until they entered a chamber nearly identical to the main one, with the exception that it was much smaller. It had an open area with a smaller forge at the rear of the chamber. Off to the right was another door. Pushing it open, the young mastersmith stepped through the doorway first holding it open for Cordovan and Aubrey. Closing the door behind them, he turned to the task of lighting extra lamps around the room until it was bright with a warm glow. Glancing around the room, the young mastersmith nodded as if to say the room was bright enough.

The mastersmith walked to a walnut cabinet on the far wall. Pulling out two, tall, silver cups he sat them on the sidetable sitting directly beneath the cabinet. Lifting a silver pitcher that had been sitting on that sidetable he poured a dark red wine into both cups. Returning hastily to where they stood the mastersmith offered them the cups. He bowed again as they accepted. It took Cordovan one sip to know that it was one of the best wines the capital had to offer. He nodded to the mastersmith raising his cup in appreciation. The man nearly jumped with glee without moving from the spot where he stood. Cordovan had only found it necessary to come to The Brace a few times while in Alexandria. But every member of the Watch knew to extend them every courtesy. The equipment they made might one day be vital to your survival. So he stood in what was undoubtedly the newly minted mastersmith's personal workshop where the young smith was expected to dream metal dreams, test those visions, and create the glistening artifacts that would show his worth as a craftsman. Cordovan had been in one of these workshops before as a much older mastersmith had presented him with new rigging for his mount. The craftsmanship had been exquisite though the wine he had offered had been less so. That had probably been due to the fact that the man had been supporting a family whereas this young man was trying to make his mark as a new mastersmith.

Finally, the young man spoke up saying, "My name is Blandis Alland. And it is my pleasure, today, to present you with the evidence of my craft for your perusal." This was followed by another bow. He walked across the room to fling open the doors of a tall, freestanding wardrobe made from a dark, brown wood. Standing back from the open doors, he bowed with one hand over his stomach while the other pointed to the contents of the wardrobe. Before Cordovan could move or speak Aubrey walked over to the open doors. He handed Blandis his half-empty cup as he passed the mastersmith. One by one Aubrey pulled the artifacts that were Blandis' work from the wardrobe. A thick saber came out first followed by a lithe longsword. Next, he pulled out a double-edged straight sword with a crossbar handguard. One after another Aubrey tested their edges, heft, and balance, taking swipes at non-existent targets. Cordovan watched with interest but held his tongue as it became apparent that the young man knew his metal. Cordovan watched Aubrey swing the blades until he got a true feel for each weapon. When he felt he had the measure of a particular sword he grabbed another beginning the process all over again. As Aubrey put Blandis' work to the test, Cordovan caught Blandis' eye. He saluted the mastersmith by raising his cup. The man hurried to the pitcher. He carried it to Cordovan so that he could fill his cup again. Looking down at him, Cordovan said, "Master Alland, your nose for wine is impeccable."

The man smiled at the compliment. "Thank you, Master Watchman. I have been saving it for an occasion such as this. It is very expensive, you know, that is - if you don't mind me saying so, but well worth celebrating this moment."

Returning the man's smile Cordovan let his voice take on a causal tone. "I wonder, Master Alland. Might you have something else of an equally special vintage? Maybe something that you were saving to be sold for a special price?" While the treasury provided for the smiths they were not paid by the item but rather for their service. As a result, a practice had arisen among them that was overlooked by those who handed out the monthly stipends. It was widely known that the smiths made special items, using the best materials, coupled with their meticulously applied skill, in order to supplement their pay. The items were often sold for hefty prices to members of the peerage, or merchants, looking for a showpiece. Though what the smith was showing Aubrey was exceptional, Cordovan thought the man might have something extraordinary on hand.

When Blandis failed to meet his eye, Cordovan knew he had struck a chord. Without looking at the man he continued to focus his attention on Aubrey who still leaped about. While watching Aubrey he said, "Now, mind you, I would not take it as an insult if there was something, say, very dear to you, that you were holding onto in order to secure your welfare. I just thought that if you had something like that laying about we might be able to come to some mutually beneficial arrangement."

Slowly, Blandis looked up at Cordovan. Turning his head sideways he said, "And, you would not fault me for having something like that around without having shown it to you, Master Watchman?"

Cordovan paused to take a sip from his silver cup. Lowering his cup, he said, "Blandis, I know that you are simply planning for your future. Who wouldn't? I would certainly not be insulted."

Blandis looked from Cordovan to Aubrey who had stopped testing blades. Aubrey was watching them both having turned his attention from the steel in his hand to the conversation he had been ignoring. The mastersmith licked his lips. They all stood there for a few seconds until Blandis nodded as if deciding something. He walked over to the wall beside the freestanding wardrobe. Placing his hands against the wall at about chest-height, he arranged his fingers in an odd configuration. Leaning forward, he pushed at the wall. Small plates in the wall, which Cordovan had not seen, but knew he would not have found even if he knew where to look, sunk into the wall. As Blandis pulled his hands back, a man-sized panel slid back into the wall revealing an alcove with a hidden closet. Blandis looked back over his shoulder at Cordovan with a mischievous grin on his face. Reaching into the shadowed recess, Blandis retrieved something wrapped in red silk. Touching another spot on the wall with a single finger, Blandis stepped back. It slid back into place with the sound of stone rubbing on stone. He walked over to Aubrey with the item cradled in his arms as though he were carrying a baby. Aubrey laid aside the sword he was holding when Blandis held out the bundle to him.

Aubrey slowly unwrapped the bundle revealing a longsword as the folds of red silk fell away. Cordovan's breath caught in his throat when the lamplight reflected off the weapon. Even from where he stood he could tell it was a thing of beauty. It reminded him of his own single-edged longsword with its three-handed hilt. A Highmaster of The Brace had made his sword. Cordovan rested his hand briefly on the intricately wrapped purple cord covering his sword's hilt. He fingered the wide circular handguard while wondering how this young mastersmith had the skill to create such a thing. Aubrey was running his hand along the longsword's hilt. Extra long, wrapped in a rust-colored skin, the hilt ended in a small, steel crossguard that curved back toward the blade at its ends and was accented with etched filigree. The blade was perfectly straight. It was slightly wider than most longswords. Cordovan could tell that both edges were sharpened. There was a shallow groove down the center of the blade on both sides. The steel gleamed in the lamplight. Cordovan was sure it had been made with the same high-quality steel all blades in The Brace were made from. It was as much the technique employed in The Brace as the quality of the steel that made the blades tempered here nearly unbreakable. The blades of The Brace were made from steel that was folded hundreds of times before the final shape emerged. The steel was heated, beaten out, folded in on itself, reheated, and beaten out again. The process was completed hundreds of times while powders made of secret additives were sprinkled on the blade before being pounded into the hot metal. When the blade was finally shaped it was stronger than anything produced in any forge in the Twelve Nations. Cordovan had only seen blades made better in the hands of the Peoples Company or the Ki'gadi. Awe spread over Aubrey's face as he twirled the blade in the air. He darted forward into a perfect stop-lunge before hopping back with a smile on his face. Looking at Blandis, Aubrey said, "It is magnificent, Mastersmith. I have never held such a thing! You are truly a master!"

"Oh." Blandis said, as he walked to a large dresser pulling open its middle drawer. Reaching in he pulled out a hardwood scabbard covered in the same rust-colored Corsican skin as the hilt with a matching swordbelt. The belts heavy silver buckle had a hawk in flight etched in the face. Closing the drawer with his hip he carried the scabbard, with its matching swordbelt, over to Aubrey who took it. With a final twirl he slid the sword home in the scabbard with a soft click. Cordovan thought again that it was a work of art that must have taken every ounce of Blandis' skill as well as a monstrous amount of his time.

Looking from Cordovan to Aubrey, Blandis said, "Master Watchmen, that-" he pointed to the sword Aubrey held in his hand as he continued, "-was shown to the Highmasters of The Brace, in secret. It was studied end to end. It was the piece of work that earned me my place among the masters. That blade is very dear to me. My plan was to sell it one day so that I could buy some land somewhere west. A place to retire. It has been my cherished secret until today." He stood there with worry painting his features. To take the sword for little or nothing was their right as Watchmen but would leave him no secret treasure trove to secure his future. Cordovan knew the man's worry sprang from the knowledge that were they to take the weapon there would be no one to whom he could carry a complaint. As Blandis continued to look from the sword to Aubrey worry began to win the battle for outright possession of his features.

Aubrey spoke up. "Master Alland. As I said, it is a magnificent weapon. But I cannot rob you of your dream. I know enough to know that you could take this to a sellsword where you would receive more than enough for a comfortable retirement. Allow me a few moments to look through your other work. I will choose from them."

Cordovan drained his cup. Handing the cup back to Blandis he said, "Stand still young Watchman. I see we have some work to do on your tongue." Looking at Blandis he said, "I require writing materials."

Blandis shuffled around the room looking like he expected the worst. But after digging through various drawers he came up with a quill, bottle of ink, piece of parchment, and a piece of wax for sealing. Pulling up a chair to one of the small desks in the workroom, Cordovan scribbled out a note, signing it at the bottom. When he stood he held the note out to Blandis who bowed his head as he took the note. Quickly scanning the lines of flowing script his eyebrows crept up his forehead as he reached the end of the note. When he opened his mouth to speak he struggled to find words. "But, Master," Blandis made a sound deep in his throat as though he were trying to clear it.

Cordovan smiled at the man. He spoke warmly to him. "Do not worry Mastersmith. I would not have robbed you of your hopes for a pleasant retirement. Take this note to the Treasury. You will receive payment. But mind you, I have written instructions that the amount be given to you in increments over the next ten years. Your gifts are exemplary. They are needed here. So, while I am giving you more than enough for the land you dream of, as well as a comfortable living well into your old age, I am not giving it to you all at once. That is, if that is acceptable to you?"

Blandis fell over himself to shake Cordovan's forearm with both his hands as he promised profusely to work diligently on behalf of the Watch. Cordovan grasped the man's forearm in return while trying to calm him. He assured him that he knew Blandis appreciated the remuneration but since they had come to an agreement they had work to get to. After extricating his arm from the man's grip, Cordovan went back to the desk. Folding the parchment over, he held the piece of wax over a candle flame until he could drip a small amount on the parchment over the fold. Just as the wax was hardening he impressed it with his great ring imbedding the emblem of the Watch into the red wax. Handing the Treasury Note to Blandis, he pushed the still jabbering man ahead of them to the door to get him started leading them out of the smithy. In minutes they were saying their goodbyes to him again, in the main chamber, with promises that if they ever needed anything - *anything at all* - in the way of smithing, that they should look him up. As they exited the building, making one final wave to Blandis, who stood in the door watching them go, Cordovan noticed Aubrey looking at him from the corner of his eye.

Without looking back at him Cordovan said, "What is it young Watchman?" Aubrey paused a moment. He said. "I know you gave him an enormous amount. Was it your own coin?"

Cordovan waited a moment, letting the question settle. It dawned on him that the young man was thinking he might owe Cordovan if it was his own coin that had been spent to secure Aubrey's sword. As they continued walking Cordovan said, "First Lesson. As a Watchman you will have great resources at your command including the wealth of the imperial treasury. With the seal from the great ring on your finger, along with your signature, you will have access to that wealth. The Empress has gone to great lengths to empower us to bring Her justice to the Empire. Sometimes that will mean putting coin to good use. Blandis Alland was not out to rob anyone or to enrich himself at someone's expense. Nor was he a greedy man. He is just an honest craftsman of great skill trying to make his way in the world. The world needs talented men like him. So to answer your question, it was not my coin, it was Her coin. But here is the full part of the first lesson. Be sure, Aubrey Devilwind, be very sure, that when you send a request to the treasury with your signature and the seal of the Watch on it that She will be pleased with how you have spent the coin. Because occasionally, when that Note reaches The Steward of the Treasury, he takes it and places it in Her hand."

Cordovan walked on looking sideways to see Aubrey in deep thought. *Good*, he thought, let him realize that every copper he spends is Her's. It would make him cautious. In all of his time as a Watchman, Cordovan had never been called to task for the coin that he had spent in Her name, but some had. It was good for Aubrey to get in the habit of making good decisions when it came to spending imperial coin.

They walked on in silence, past the Tower, out the front entrance of Watchkeep. Cordovan continued in silence as they made their way through the streets of Alexandria with Aubrey a pace behind him. They walked along Primmon Path, over Berrington Street, past the Crimson Gate. The further they got from Watchkeep the more the side walkway became crowded with people. When some of them noticed the purple cloaks, they began stepping off the walk, into the street, letting them pass. Some bowed or curtsied, while others solemnly wished them a good day. At one point they were stopped in Merchants Square by Meldim, the baker, who forced sweetbread on them declaring that he would die before he saw the standard bearers of the Empress' Justice go hungry. Cordovan had hurried on, with Aubrey in tow, as the baker's wife appeared in the doorway of the bakery. She was stirring a pot while telling them she had bowls in the kitchen.

The walk was pleasant. The streets were only just beginning to fill with traffic. Fresh bread was the only smell in the air. Soon the morning would be in full swing, but it was still early. Cordovan allowed himself to enjoy it. He did not get back to the capital as often as he would have liked. When he did he liked to enjoy a few simple pleasures like a quiet walk through the streets. It was only when they turned onto Imperial Way, where one could see the imperial palace in the distance, that he heard Aubrey's voice catch. The young man had finally realized where they were going. Cordovan laughed quietly to himself as Aubrey held his head a little higher while squaring his shoulders. His hand fell to his hip coming to rest on the hilt of his new sword as if it had hung there forever.

The traffic, as little as there was at this hour, began thinning until it was non-existent as they came to within earshot of the palace. They could have ridden but Cordovan enjoyed the walk from the keep to the palace. When they approached the gate he absently fingered the note that still rested in a pocket in his cloak. It was Her note. It was a rare thing, even for the Watch, to receive a letter from Her, written in Her hand. It was usually a messenger like the one who had awakened him earlier that morning with a piece of parchment that said She wanted to see him as soon as he had squared Aubrey away. So here they were approaching the gate to the palace.

As a Watchman, Cordovan had been in all manner of grand houses on all kinds of estates. He had even had cause to visit some foreign royal courts. Nothing he had ever experienced was a match for the House on Ruler's Hill. The Imperial Palace was the work of Her father. While Alexander Sobrine had been away expanding the borders of the empire by conquest his builders had been creating the symbol of that imperial power in the heart of the capital. The old Samosatian palace had been gutted in order to transform it into something new. The gates were thick, black, wrought-iron, which swung wide enough for several wagons to enter at once. When sealed against attack they were strong enough to stop a battering ram. Due to their size they had to be opened by large cranks housed on either side of the gates in stone gatehouses. If the palace were ever attacked an enormous iron wall, nestled in its housing above the entrance, would fall into place behind the iron gate, making it nearly impossible to breach. To the right was a small doorway that served as an entrance or exit when the gates were closed. This morning they were still closed. That door, covered by its own iron gate, swung open as they approached. Only their purple cloaks, or the black uniform of the Peoples Company could open that door without so much as a hail. When they walked through the door the Imperial Guardsmen on duty saluted. Cordovan returned the salute as they passed. The two Watchmen continued on deeper into the palace grounds unmolested. There had only been one time that Cordovan could remember someone masquerading as a member of the Watch to gain entry to the palace. He had managed to escape when it was discovered that he was a fraud. But the Watch had hunted the man down overturning half of the southern district of Alexandria to do it. By the time they had finished the people of that part of the city had brought the man out to the Watch on their own. When the Watch was done with him word of what had happened spread. Though it was not a crime to wear a purple cloak, after that day, not a single person even considered wearing one.

Once the two of them left the cobblestone of the courtyard they passed through the imperial gardens. The scene was breathtaking. Even this early in the morning there were gardeners out working to keep it in perfect condition. Everyone knew that She liked her flowers. It took only a few more minutes to reach an actual entrance to the palace itself. They had taken only a few steps into the palace proper, onto priceless purple carpeting, when an Imperial Secretary met them. Cordovan could only think that there must have been several of them stationed at the various entrances he might have had access to awaiting his arrival. This one was a tall, slender woman though not as tall as either of them. Her face was severe, with a hauntingly serious look. Her hair was pulled back into a tight, glistening bun. Though she was a high-ranking imperial functionary she still showed deference to Cordovan. Everyone knew where the Watchmen stood in Her graces. The woman bowed low. In a voice awash with deference she said, "Good morning, Good Masters of the Watch. If you will follow me, her Imperial Majesty will see you now."

She stood still, looking directly at Cordovan, until he realized she was waiting for him to acknowledge her. Nodding graciously to the woman Cordovan said, "And a good morning to you, Good Mistress. Please, show us into the Presence."

With a relieved smile, followed by a quick nod, the woman started off toward the palace interior. The walls were paneled with a deep burgundy-stained wood stretching up to a high ceiling. There was delicate colorful porcelain perched on heavy darkwood sidetables. Giant paintings hung alongside plush tapestries on the walls providing lavish scenery as one moved through the palace. Flowers were placed strategically in curving, fluted, heavy, glass vases. Here and there, imperial servants walked quietly as they went about their various duties. There were even members of the Peerage walking about dressed in ridiculously expensive finery. The men had lace spilling out of high collars while the women sparkled with feathery, lacey, gem encrusted gowns that blossomed from the hip spilling onto the floor like small waterfalls of brocaded silk.

The peerage was made up of two distinct groups. There were the indigenous members of Alexandria, most of whom traced their lineage to the former kingdom of Samosata, out of which the Sobrines themselves had come. Then there was the royalty of conquered kingdoms, including a few former kings and queens along with their heirs or other relatives, now known only as Lord or Lady. Regardless of who they used to be they all served the present imperial family. The Sobrines ruled it all.

The imperial palace, as it had been recreated, was vast. The hallways of the palace were so wide that you could walk past someone but still be so far away that proper etiquette did not require you to speak. It was the kind of place where even royalty would feel humbled. That had been the Sobrines intention. When Her father had conquered a kingdom he often brought the deposed kings or queens back to the finished palace so that they might bask in his glory. The conquered royals were brought into his presence in the Hall of Lilies where he sat on the Throne of the Morning. Then, in the presence of the Peerage, assembled for this very purpose, they were made to bow before him to swear the oath of allegiance. It had worked. You could not walk through this vast place with its priceless artifacts, built on such a massive scale, without feeling a sense of the grandeur of it all. Shortly after those audiences those royals would be informed that they were no longer allowed their former titles. They were no longer rulers only members of the Peerage of Empire. Some had thought that a dangerous practice. From time to time a Sobrine had been forced to have a former ruler beheaded, very publicly, in order to make it clear that even discussing rebellion would not be tolerated. Often, once the deposed saw the Dawnmarch, Watchmen, and the other emblems of the empire's power up close they tucked away their ambitions somewhere deep where they faded away. It helped that they lived lavish lives as members of the Peerage.

It took some time, but the Imperial Secretary walked on unerringly toward their destination. She must have known the palace from top to bottom because Cordovan could see getting lost in the vastness of the place. But she walked on, prim and proper in her stride with her hands clasped, just so, in front of her. As they walked Cordovan entertained himself by watching the various servants as they passed one another. They had their own hierarchy. He delighted in seeing which one curtsied or bowed, even to what degree, to the woman who guided them, as they past. Even more interesting was to whom their escort curtsied. One young woman, though in imperial livery herself, with skin brown as burnished leather, caused their escort to fall all over herself as she leaped to curtsy. When the young woman passed them, she inclined her head respectfully in Cordovan's direction ignoring their escort altogether. As soon as their escort popped back up, nearly breathless, she looked down the hall at the back of the young woman. Blood had rushed to her face. Cordovan did her the courtesy of not asking who the young woman was, but she must have been close to the empress to garner that much deference.

One more turn brought them to a room on one of the higher floors in the palace. Cordovan had lost track of where they were almost as soon as they had climbed a flight of stairs. He had gotten caught up in the interplay between servants. Pausing a moment before the door, the woman took a few deep breaths to calm herself, before knocking ever so softly. Slowly the door opened. She curtsied deeply to an older woman in imperial livery. When she stood again she whispered while motioning to the two Watchmen she had in tow. With a nod from the older woman she stood aside taking up a station beside the door right there in the hallway. The older woman opened the door completely, bowing to Cordovan and Aubrey, before ushering them past her with a ceremonial wave of her left hand. Stepping past her, Cordovan entered the room with Aubrey a step behind him.

The chamber was large enough to be a great hall in a smaller palace. It was appointed much the same as the rest of the imperial palace. Here there were a number of servants moving around among high-ranking officers of Dawnmarch as well as members of the Peerage. The Imperial Guard stood at their posts at even intervals around the chamber. They were in the Rose Room. It was a place where the empress held a more informal court. It was also the place where she handled much of the business of the empire. It was a large hall with little furniture save a small throne on a small dais at the room's opposite end. It took its name from the fact that all along the walls were large, hanging, glass vases filled with dozens of roses arranged in large overflowing bunches. Today the roses were yellow with white ones mixed in. There were twenty or thirty different conversations taking place but none of it seemed social. The business of governing the empire was underway.

With the older woman now in the lead, after closing the door behind them, they made their way slowly through the mingling groups. Some of them stopped talking long enough to recognize Watchmen in their midst. When they did they moved out of the way. Even the Peerage walked lightly around the Watch. When they passed one of the high-ranking officers of the Dawnmarch they received a smart nod. Cordovan returned the informal salute with one of his own. Everyone who carried a sword in the service of the empire knew the worth of the Watch. They also knew that no matter their rank the Watch did not take orders from them. The Watch took orders only from the Gallant Master of the Gate or the Empress. After weaving their way through the small crowd, they reached the other end of the hall where the small throne sat. The ten or twelve people who crowded around the foot of the raised dais moved back at their approach. As the crowd parted Cordovan saw Her. This morning she wore sky blue, which sparkled in the morning light. The dress had full sleeves with a tall collar. Her fiery red curls covered her shoulders while her eyes glistened bright blue. No matter how many times he saw Her Cordovan was always taken aback by her beauty. He would die for Her. Standing behind her to her left was Ellom Vam, resplendent, in his cream shirt and plum breeches. He took a pause from scanning the room with his eyes long enough to nod at Cordovan. In a heartbeat he was back to watching everything. The man was competent. There was an appreciation for Ellom Vam among the Watch. Had he been less than impressive the Watch would not have suffered him to watch over Her.

Looking back at the empress Cordovan dropped to his knee. He bowed his head. When his knee touched the floor, he pulled his scabbarded sword free from his belt with one fluid motion. Leaning forward on his knee, he extended his right arm with his sword in his right fist. He placed it in front of him on the carpeted floor. He could see behind him that Aubrey had copied his example. The ancient words rolled off his tongue. "I yet Watch, Empress."

Behind him he heard the slightly higher tenor of Aubrey Devilwind saying, "I yet Watch, Empress."

Cordovan did not move. He let the words settle. He waited for them to dissipate in the air while he remained motionless. He would not move until She bid him to rise. He was at Her service awaiting Her command. Nothing else in the world mattered. Were She to leave he would still be there kneeling whenever She chose to return.

He flinched a bit, catching himself, when he felt delicate hands on his chin and shoulder. The entire hall had gone quiet.

A musical voice spoke loud enough for everyone to hear. "And should I suffer the Watchman, who saved my life, to bend his knee so low? Some will undoubtedly say yes. But I say no. Rise, my valiant one."

All of a sudden Cordovan's knees were weak. He stood, but with a bit of effort. Something caught in Her voice as she spoke. "Ah. I see you are still weakened from your ordeal. And yet you are here at my summons to throw yourself headlong into the fire again. How have I come to deserve such dedication?"

Cordovan did not have the wherewithal to correct Her. He was not his full self yet, but he was far from weak any longer. After he stood he realized that everyone else in the hall was still on their knees with their heads bowed. She had stepped down from the throne. It was custom that no head would be higher than hers save the Guard on duty or those heads She raised herself.

Stepping past Cordovan for a moment she reached down raising Aubrey from his knees. Cordovan turned to see Her looking up into Aubrey's eyes as the blood rushed to the young man's face. "And you, my newly forged champion. Have you recovered?" She stopped short of saying more about the night before, but Aubrey knew what She was saying. He guarded his own response. "I am fine Majesty. I am ready to serve you in whatever way you desire. Send me to my death and I will go with a smile."

Cordovan stood taller at Aubrey's words. He clenched his jaw. By the Pit and the Pendulum, but the young man had the heart of the Watch though he was only a few hours old! Cordovan liked Aubrey more with each passing moment. Her voice washed over Cordovan as She walked past him back up the dais to the small throne. "I am humbled by your dedication, my Watchmen." She settled back on the throne. The Imperial Guard, lining the walls, thumped the but-ends of their halberds against the floor. At the sound the others in the hall rose from their prone positions.

The empress lowered her voice back to a normal level as the other conversations around the hall started up again, albeit at a lower level. Some stole glances toward the throne where the Watchmen stood. The looks on their faces said they were wondering what the empress might be saying. Smiling down at them she continued, "I am glad to see you both well. If you are truly ready to serve me further, there is work to do."

Cordovan, having slid his scabbard back onto his swordbelt as he stood, placed his thumbs behind it on either side of the lily-shaped silver buckle. His voice was steady. "We are ready Highness. Command us."

She looked from Cordovan to Aubrey. After a moment she nodded. "I made a promise to a dear friend. As things stands I am in jeopardy of not being able to keep that promise. Gaiden Colling has disgraced me. He has managed to escape the Tower and my Justice. I need him brought back."

Cordovan saw her jaw clench as she spoke Colling's name. A cool anger began to simmer inside him as he listened to the disappointment in Her voice. He felt, more than heard, Aubrey shift behind him, but the young man had sense enough to keep quiet. Cordovan said, "Majesty, we will bring him to justice. May I ask one question, Highness?"

She smiled at him, "Yes, my valiant one. What would you like to know?"

Cordovan licked his lips, "What if we cannot return him alive?"

She smiled a grim smile then. In that moment he saw a hint of her father in her face. There was a moment's consideration before she leaned forward on the throne and simply said, "Do what you must."

With a deep bow Cordovan said, "Then if that is all Highness we will stand to the Watch."

Looking down at him with a sigh she said, "That will be all my valiant ones. Be careful, Colling has proved to be more dangerous than any of us gave him credit for, and I would not lose another of the Watch to this. Do what must be done and return to me. May the Ancient keep you safe."

With another bow Cordovan said, "I yet Watch, Majesty." Behind him he heard a young voice filled with determination say, "I yet Watch, Majesty."

With that, Cordovan turned on his heel. He made his way toward the door. Where he had entered the hall earlier, approaching the throne of state by a circuitous route, he now marched in a straight line. With

Aubrey a step behind him, the two of them must have looked like they were on the trail of the Betrayer just from the Abyss because people gave way without a word. The older woman who had escorted them through the hall to the throne nearly ran alongside them trying to get in front of them. By the time she caught up Cordovan had thrown the door open startling the young woman who had escorted them through the palace. He stalked past her as she opened her mouth to speak. They did not stop so she raced ahead to try to lead them back. Several times Cordovan almost ran the woman over as she slowed. When she turned to say something, she caught another glimpse of his face before deciding that the best thing to do was to move fast enough so that she could remain in front of the Watchmen. *Gaiden Colling*. That name kept turning over in Cordovan's mind. The more he thought about what She had said the angrier he became. Cordovan knew to whom the empress had made that promise. If it killed him, he would see that she was not shamed in the eyes of the Peoples Company. There was not a single member of the Watch who did not know how much she owed the Company. He would not allow Her to lose face.

Cordovan did not notice when the young woman, breathing heavily, waved them on alone as they came to the door they had entered the palace by. Stalking out of the palace he headed for the front gate. In moments he, with Aubrey in tow, was out in the street in front of the palace. He stopped to look up the street.

Aubrey stepped up next to him. His voice still heated with the same anger Cordovan was feeling. "What do we do first sir? If I may ask?"

Cordovan patted Aubrey on the shoulder. "Right. Yes, yes. We go right." He looked over at Aubrey as he continued, "What first?" He paused as a nasty grin spread across his face. "We have to find Colling. And you are wondering how we begin? I will tell you my young friend. We find a certain man who owes me a favor."

†

They had walked for about five minutes when Cordovan spotted a coach. Flagging it down, he flipped the driver a coin as the coach rolled to a stop next to them. The man took a look at the coin before briefly biting it. Cordovan waited for the driver to tuck the coin away into his gray coat before giving him instructions. The man doffed his tall, pipe-like, gray hat acknowledging that he understood the instructions. Cordovan ducked into the black-lacquered coach with Aubrey right behind him. Once Aubrey pulled the small door closed the coach lurched forward. They heard the driver snap the reigns as he whistled at his team of horses. They rode in silence. Cordovan fought off a smile when he noticed Aubrey absently stroking the hilt of his new sword. After approximately twenty minutes the coach rolled to a halt. Cordovan heard the driver climb down from his seat atop the coach. Aubrey leaned over to open the door, but Cordovan motioned for him to sit still. After a brief interlude the door opened. The driver bowed, sweeping back his gray coat while doffing his tall, round, gray hat. When he straightened, he passed Cordovan a package. Cordovan took the package, a bundle, wrapped in brown parchment, tied with white twine, from the small man, nodding to Aubrey to pull the door closed. He settled back into his seat. A few seconds later he felt the coach rock slightly as the driver climbed back into his seat. In another moment the coach was rolling again.

It must have been half an hour before the coach rolled to a halt. Cordovan heard the thump on the roof of the coach announcing that they had reached their destination. Untying the twine bound package he pulled the folded bundle apart revealing two black cloaks. He handed one to Aubrey. Aubrey sat with the cloak in his hands watching Cordovan unbuckle his purple cloak before draping the black one around his shoulders. After a moment, Aubrey copied him. The two stepped from the coach wrapped in black. The hooded cloaks were large enough to cover their uniforms. Anyone but the closest observer would be unable to distinguish them from others on the street.

Cordovan had brought them to the western part of the city. This section of town was known as the theatre district. If not for the constant presence of the Guard, it could have been a very dangerous part of Alexandria. Even with the Guard's conscientiousness there were still problems from time to time. It took a tremendous effort to maintain order in a city the size of Alexandria. There was a decidedly dark element that made the city dirty around its edges. The theatre district got its name from the three, once brilliant, now rundown, Concert Houses that stood on the broad way. Various eateries, and taverns, filled the rest of the view on either side of the street. The traffic was heavy though most of it was foot traffic since this was a part of town where horse owners were rare. The theatre district was not known for its wealth. Displays of wealth, though infrequent, could nevertheless be dangerous. Moving to the edge of an alley Cordovan scanned the street for a particular sign. After looking along one side he moved across the street to search the other. It was on the other side of the street that he found what he was looking for. At the end of the block, on the side of the street where they had initially stood, was a sign that read, *The Golden Bread Basket*. Beneath the weathered gold letters was a faded picture of an overturned basket spilling loaves of bread.

Motioning for Aubrey to follow, Cordovan walked slowly down the side walkway, careful not to bump into any of the people walking past. In a few moments they were walking into the front door of the *Basket*. On a stool, next to the door, sat a bear of a man with two days growth of stubble on his face. When he smiled at them he revealed several missing teeth. The man wore a leather jerkin complemented by forearm braces. When Cordovan nodded at the man he noticed a heavy stick leaning against the wall next to his seat. It appeared to be a nice, clean, respectable establishment. It surprised Cordovan given its location. The floor was swept. It also appeared that the tables were well kept. There were no mismatched pieces of furniture or uneven floorboards. The main room was fully lit. The crowd, though small, was impressive for the hour. Women bustled about in red aprons wiping empty tables. Others carried trays of food or drink. To his left was a long, high, bar with tall chairs along its length. Another burly man stood behind it studiously wiping its counter with a white towel. He smiled at Cordovan. Cordovan returned the smile with a nod. The room had the wonderful smell of baking bread reminding him he had not eaten.

Before Cordovan could finish scanning the room a small woman materialized in front of him. She stood about as high as his chest, but it took only one look at how she stood for Cordovan to realize she was a woman used to being in charge. Her red apron was spotless. It looked freshly pressed. It even matched her red dress, which was made of good wool. She was just shy of skinny with long, straight, black hair pulled back into a braid. Her black eyes sparkled with intelligence. She looked through him as if she were weighing his purse along with his character. Her voice was just a little deeper than one expected from a woman, but it was strong. Smiling up at him she said, "Welcome, my lords, to the Basket." She inclined her head slightly as she spoke in a lilting accent that sounded like the distant Northeast, more specifically, the highlands above the foothills of Lochlinn. "My name is Meris, and the Basket, she be my establishment. May I show my lords to a table?"

Cordovan smiled down at the little woman copying her accent with a humorous tone so that she would know he was not making fun of her. "You do have the sound of the *Linn* in your voice, lass. Do you not?" She tilted her head to the left with a rueful twist in her lips. There was laughter in the back of her throat. "Well now, my lord has come into my establishment with a taste for humor this morning, has he now?"

Cordovan held up his hands as he saw hers headed for her hips. Switching to his normal voice he said, "No, mistress. I am merely remarking on the pleasant sound of your voice. I have had occasion to be in the highlands. I know you come from an honorable people with a healthy sense of humor."

Meris nodded smartly at that as she waved off the bearish man at the door who had risen from his seat. She beamed a full smile at Cordovan. "I thank my lord, I do, for the compliment. And bid you welcome again to the Basket. Now, may I see my lord to a table?" With that she held one arm out toward the tables.

Cordovan bent in toward her, leaning conspiratorially, as if he did not want to be overheard. "Mistress, if I may beg your further indulgence. I am actually looking for a friend who is known to frequent your establishment."

Raising an eyebrow, but leaning in with a mischievous smile of her own, she said, "I trust you do not intend harm to my patron, do you my lord?"

Cordovan placed a hand lightly on her shoulder. "By no means, Mistress. I simply have some important business to discuss with him. He is a finicky, portly, little fellow who likes things arranged just so. He has a profound love of food and wine in great quantities."

Before he could finish the description Meris began nodding her head. The smile turned to half-frown as she spoke. "I do be knowing the character you speak of. And were it not for the coin he leaves I would have hit him over the head with one of me good rolling pins and had Derrin there, by the door, throw him out on his arse. He runs me girls ragged with his requests and has me in the kitchen dealing with his special orders, he do." Without seeming to be aware of it she flexed her hand into a fist as she spoke about him. "He is lucky, he do be my lord, that his coin is good and he be generous with it. Come, I will take you to him."

With that the little matron of the Basket led them to the end of the bar. They walked around it to the right where the main room extended beyond it. Had they merely walked on into the main room they would have seen him off to the left. Cordovan followed behind the little woman, with Aubrey in tow, as she walked over to the table in the corner. As they approached, the little man was working meticulously at a hard-boiled egg with a knife and fork, as though the slightest wrong move would cause the world to come crashing down around his head. With great care, he lifted the small slice to his mouth. Leaning back against the booth the man savored the taste. Dabbing at the corners of his mouth, he wiped away non-existent bits of food with a pristinely white cloth.

Walking up to the end of the booth Meris said, "Dain Du'urdin, my food do no be that good that you need to chew on it as if it be your last meal. These men do be here to see you."

As Dain Du'urdin turned to look up he said, "My dear Mistress Meris, while your cooking is quite exquisite I always eat as if it were my last meal." Turning his head fully he looked past the small woman until he could see Cordovan. Cordovan had to give Du'urdin credit. He barely missed a beat when he saw him. Sitting up, he cleared his throat. Dain Du'urdin said, "Why, yes, yes, Mistress. I thank you. These are indeed my friends. I am thankful that you have shown them to my table. Please have one of your young ladies bring another pot of choca." With that, punctuated by a deep *harrumph* in her throat, the matron of the Basket went stalking off toward the kitchen. Cordovan motioned for Aubrey to slide into the seat opposite Dain Du'urdin while he slid in beside him. As they settled into the seats Dain looked over at Cordovan with a guarded look.

"Well, well. I see you are wearing a black cloak. So I will simply call you Master Allegressa. Furthermore, I will, with great respect, say to you that I cannot help you. I hope you understand."

Cordovan looked across the table at Dain Du'urdin. The man was of middle years. His hair was trimmed short, dyed black, with each strand brushed meticulously into place. It glistened with the sheen of a light oil. So did his slim mustache, which turned up at its ends. The mustache was complimented by a pointed chin-beard that likely shone with the same oil. His small head was round as was his middle. He wore a fine, dark blue, silk coat, with matching breeches. Cordovan would have given all the coin in the treasury against the fact that under the table his calf-high boots were rich, reddish-brown, Corsican leather with a polished gloss. Dain Du'urdin was a Truthseeker. It was a self-styled titled the man had created to hire himself out to *look into things*. If you wanted to know who broke into your house, what had torn through your crops, how your son had died in an alley, as long as you had the coin, Dain Du'urdin was the man to bring you the answers. What most people did not know was that he had once been an Inquisitor of Province. After falling out with his compatriots some years ago he had found his way to Alexandria before taking up his tradecraft under a different title. As a matter of fact Cordovan had always doubted that Dain Du'urdin was the man's actual name. He had run into Du'urdin, from time to time, while carrying out his duties as a Watchman. On some of those occasions, when needed, Cordovan had found a use for the man's services. It turned out that he needed Du'urdin again. Though, apparently, the man was reluctant to help.

"What do you mean you cannot help me? You don't even know what I want." Cordovan sat with his hands folded together as his elbows rested easily on the table.

Dain Du'urdin barked a funny, nasally, laugh across the table holding up his fork to use as a pointer. "That is quite humorous Master Allegressa. But you forget what it is I do for a living. First: It is known to me that Gaiden Colling has disappeared under unusual circumstances. Second: It is further known to me that the man had run afoul of the Empress' closest ally, one Lord Commander-General? Finally: Here you are at my breakfast table. So what could you possibly want except my help finding Gaiden Colling, or should we say, the former Prime-Agent of Alexandria?"

With that, Dain Du'urdin speared another piece of sliced egg with his fork, plopping it into his mouth. But as he began to chew he inhaled sharply nearly choking. Cordovan turned to look over his shoulder at what had caught Du'urdin's eye. It took only an instant to spot them. Standing in the middle of the main room was a handful of hard looking men with road dust still on them. Grim looks painted their faces. When they caught sight of Dain Du'urdin they made a straight line for the booth. Cordovan turned back to Du'urdin saying, "You are right Dain. It seems you are going to be too occupied to help me with my problem, so we will leave you to the rest of your breakfast."

Cordovan stood, stepping out of the booth, followed by Aubrey, who was watching the hard men intently as they crossed the room. Du'urdin leaned forward, hissing, "Wait! Wait man! I ... I have reconsidered. I will help you with your problem if you can see your way to helping me with mine?"

Du'urdin smiled weakly at Cordovan with a pleading look on his plump little face. Smiling, Cordovan looked down at him, "I will help you, Truthseeker. Then you will help me ... for free." Du'urdin's face blanched when Cordovan added the last. For a moment he looked as if he was going to protest. The man liked coin. His services had always been expensive for Cordovan to use but this time he was going to help Cordovan for free. Looking over at the men who had just stepped up to the booth, Dain Du'urdin turned back to look weakly at Cordovan. With a bit of exasperation in his voice he said, "Deal."

Smiling down at him, Cordovan turned from the edge of the booth. He stepped between Du'urdin and the men who crowded around them. They were a motley bunch. There were five of them. They were clearly brigands. It was very likely that they were used to living off unsuspecting travelers. But now they were in Alexandria. Only one of them came close to Cordovan's height but he stood in the back. They all had weapons hanging from their belts or sticking up over their shoulders. Each man wore an assortment of leather, chainmail, or mix-matched pieces of plate armor, no doubt stolen or scavenged. The one in front looked up at Cordovan as if he were a fly buzzing around his head. His voice was gravelly but with a tone that said he was in charge. "Move along fellow. We got ourselves some business with this Pit-forsaken maggot."

Cordovan smiled his brightest smile. "Why, forgive me good sir. But I am going to be needing the said maggot's services, so I will have to ask you to beg off." Behind him Du'urdin hissed as Cordovan called him a maggot in passing.

It was then that the lead brigand really looked at Cordovan. He gave Cordovan a hard stare as the other brigands spread out behind their leader. Cordovan caught Aubrey out of the corner of his eye. But the young man did not move perceptibly. Had anyone with skill looked closely they would have seen the subtle shift in Aubrey's stance, which was the telltale sign that he was ready. The lead brigand said, "I don't care what you think you need, we have been looking for him for weeks. We are going to repay him for interfering in our business."

As he finished, the man reached out to grab a handful of Cordovan's coat. That was a mistake. Catching the man's wrist Cordovan twisted. When he felt the joint lock he pushed. *Hard.* The man flew backward only managing to stay on his feet because his fellows caught him. With a curse, the man pushed the others off him, pulling his sword free. The others followed. As the brigands stepped forward, Cordovan pulled the black cloak he had been wearing off flinging it aside. A flicker at the corner of his eye told him Aubrey had followed suit. Cordovan did not draw his sword but just stood there. It took another full step by the brigands before they realized who they were facing. Their eyes took in the gray, black-trimmed uniforms. Suddenly it dawned on them that they were advancing on two Watchmen.

Stopping his advance, the lead brigand began to babble. "Uh ... uh. Forgive us, Master Watchman. We did not know." Hastily they began putting away their swords. Slowly, as a group, they began backing toward the door.

While they backed up Cordovan began walking forward. Raising his voice, he said, "I have in my custody, Dain Du'urdin, who can identify each of you by name. You are no doubt brigands guilty of crimes against the Imperium. You will report to the Guard and confess to your crimes, including your attempt at harming a citizen of the Empire. You will do that right now. If I do not get word from the Guard, within the hour, that you have turned yourself in, I will bring the entire Watch down around your ears." The smile was gone. Cordovan had begun to growl. He had a dark look on his face. It was a look that said they did not want him to get his hands on them.

It began with the tallest in the rear. He turned, dashing from the Basket, turning over a chair as he went. In seconds the others had followed him out the door. Cordovan had no doubt the men were looking for the nearest member of the Imperial Guard. No one wanted the Watch on their trail. As the door swung shut behind the fleeing brigands Cordovan looked around the room, twisting his mouth, as if he had just tasted something sour. The side effect of the encounter was that now everyone in the room knew they were Watchmen. All around the room patrons, as well as servers, had fallen to their knees. They held themselves there, with their heads bowed, unmoving. The Basket was deathly still. No one uttered so much as a whisper. Even the bearish men from the door and behind the bar tried to sink back into themselves as they hovered close to the floor on their knees.

The Watch had a reputation for being just as well as honorable. But all across the empire people knew that their justice was swift. They also knew it could be severe. They represented the empress Herself. They brought Her justice to the high and low. People had learned to give them a wide berth unless you had need of their justice. A chill had settled over the room. No doubt people were wondering who was next. Who had acted in such a way that warranted the presence of the Watch? They shivered at the prospect.

Slowly, Cordovan made his way to where Meris, the little matron of the Basket, knelt. She was trembling as he stood over her. Kneeling in front of her, he put his hand under her chin, lifting it, until he could look into her eyes. Her voice quivered as she spoke. "Forgive, Master Watchman. Do forgive Meris. I do be a loyal citizen of the Empire. And I do apologize for any offense I may have given earlier. Please do not take Meris to the Tower, my lord, please?" Her voice had risen, cracking slightly, as she spoke. Cordovan caressed her cheek softly as he reached into a pocket in the lining of his cloak. He pulled out a white square of cloth. He dabbed at her cheeks, tenderly, drying the tears that had begun to trickle from her eyes. He flashed her a warm smile.

"As I said when I entered, little Mistress, I was only here to find Dain Du'urdin. We did not expect the other men. You are a loyal citizen and I thank you for your assistance in this matter. Now rise matron, you have nothing to fear from the Watch or me. Please, dry your tears." Cordovan stood. When he did he lifted Meris to her feet. Looking around the main room he raised his voice, "Please, everyone, rise."

Slowly, cautiously, heads lifted. Seeing Cordovan motioning for them to rise they began to stand one after another. Carefully, they returned to their tables. After guarded looks at Cordovan the servers went back to their work. Though it could not have been possible they tried to look as though they were working even harder than they had been. Looking down at Meris, Cordovan noticed she was still trembling slightly. Sounding as warm as he knew how he said, "What is the matter little Mistress?"

The matron of the Basket ventured a small smile as she stared up at him in wonder. Her voice was still a little rocky but beginning to steady.

"Nothing be the matter, my lord. It is just that I have never had Watchmen in the Basket. It is an honor to have you here. It is like having the Empress, may the Ancient shine upon Her, come to visit! Please, you must let me take you to my best private dining room so that I may serve you myself!"

The matron turned to clap her hands for servants, but Cordovan grabbed her wrists to forestall her. Still smiling warmly, he said, "No, little Mistress. I am afraid we have much work to do before the day grows old. But I promise you this; when we return to Alexandria we will come to the Basket for the best meal in all of the Empire."

Nodding her head Meris smiled deeply. "Yes, my lord. Of course, my lord. The Basket will be ready for your return. She will be ready for your return."

Patting her on the shoulder Cordovan turned to see Aubrey standing next to Dain Du'urdin with a hand on the man's shoulder. Nodding, Cordovan headed for the door. When they reached the exit the bearish man stood with his shoulders stooped knuckling his forehead as they passed. Pushing open the door Cordovan stepped onto the side walkway with Aubrey right behind him. When people noticed their uniforms, they began to remember other places they needed to be. Wherever those places were they, apparently, needed to be there immediately. The coach they had arrived in was still waiting a ways back down the street. Cordovan whistled for it. He stepped into the street as it rolled to a stop in front of them. Opening the door, he stepped aside for Aubrey who pushed Dain Du'urdin in ahead of him following the little man in.

Cordovan turned to step up into the coach but was stopped by a young man running toward him shouting. Stepping back from the coach door Cordovan waited for him. When he ran up to Cordovan he realized it was a junior officer of the Imperial Guard. The young man was out of breath but saluted sharply as he snapped to attention. Cordovan raised a quizzical eyebrow saying, "Yes?"

The young man barked, as young officers were apt to do. "Sir! I am here to report, as per your request, that we have five brigands in custody for an assortment of crimes against the Imperium. They turned themselves in to my command post with word from you that their interment was to be reported to you immediately. I almost did not believe that rabble, sir, but I thought it best to be sure."

Cordovan nodded at the young officer, "Thank you, Guardsman, for your diligence. Please see to it that they are brought before the Magistrate."

The young officer barked again. "Yes, sir!"

Stepping up, into the coach, Cordovan thumped the roof indicating to the driver to pull off. The young officer stood in the middle of the street at attention until they rolled away. Settling back into his seat he looked over at Aubrey, "Tell the driver to take us to the Tower of Alexandria. We have work to do."

As the sea raged, and the sky cried
As the sun fled, and the moon died
As the earth howled, and the heavens mourned
Only then were my eyes opened

~from the third verse of the Prophecy of the Dawn

Most look, a few see.

~*Grand Inquisitor Halvik Dessim*
The Inquistorem, Province

Chapter Seventeen

The silent speak

Cordovan, with Aubrey hovering at his shoulder, stood near the door, just inside a vacant cell in the Tower of Alexandria. There was a single wall sconce, holding a solitary lamp, which cast flickering shadows across a straw strewn floor. Even the air was cooler here. A single cot, along with a plain, wooden desk set, was the extent to which the cell was furnished. The only additional light came flooding in from the hall. There were no windows in the tower. The cells were kept clean so that there would be none of the usual odors one might expect, but there was, what Cordovan could only call, the faint smell of death. The residue from the trauma of waiting for an impending execution seemed to have leeched into the very walls. What horror there must have been for the former occupants who had watched time pour out, like water through a sieve, until the sound of boots, stomping in heart-pounding rhythm, came to take them to the headsman or the gallows.

Cordovan waited quietly as he watched Dain Du'urdin at work. Cordovan had not had much experience with the Inquisitors of Province, but he had seen Du'urdin work before. He had also had occasion to see the Windchasers, of the Peoples Company, exercising their particular skills. The things they were able to do seemed otherworldly. Du'urdin practiced, what appeared to be, the same art. Cordovan knew that what was needed was silence. So he stood just inside the doorway of the cell that had held Gaiden Colling, with Aubrey at his side, watching Dain Du'urdin go over the room with a meticulous kind of grace.

The man moved around oddly with little regard for how it made him look, which was unusual for him. Dain Du'urdin was nothing if not vain. He earned enough coin to keep himself in relative luxury. Yet the moment he set himself to practicing his particular craft all self-consciousness fell away. Cordovan had seen the man dirty a beautiful cape lying in the mud while in search of a single coin he had thought was at the heart of solving a particular mystery. Stepping on his toes, Du'urdin moved backwards over one area, before changing direction to move forward toward another spot in the chamber. All the while he mumbled to himself. Periodically he would pick up a tiny something-or-other or run a fingertip over something else that Cordovan could not see. Some of it ended with Du'urdin rubbing the substance or item between his fingers while sniffing at it. Other things ended on the tip of his tongue, as he held it on his smallest finger, causing Cordovan's stomach some minor discomfort as he watched. After each sampling Du'urdin wiped his fingers on a small white cloth, which he held in his other hand continuing with his examination of the cell seemingly oblivious to what his hands were up to. From time to time he got down on his knees, with a small magnifying glass in hand, studying something closely – again which Cordovan could not see from where he stood by the door. After going over the entire cell in that manner the man stood only to move around the cell gesturing or pointing. Cordovan wanted to interrupt him, to ask what he was doing, until it became apparent that Du'urdin was reenacting what he thought had happened. After a few moments Du'urdin stopped, standing in the middle of the cell tapping his foot with his arms crossed over his chest, while tapping his finger on his lip in time with his foot. Cordovan opened his mouth to speak only to have Du'urdin wave him off. Apparently, he was thinking. How many times had he told Cordovan just that? He was thinking. The mind, he would say, had to do its work so that Dain Du'urdin could do his. There had even been times when Cordovan had witnessed Du'urdin wrapped up in some other endeavor but, when asked, responded that he was giving his mind time to work. Only when its work was done, he would declare, would he have something to report. The man's methods were sometimes baffling to Cordovan, but he always got results.

So, Cordovan took a deep breath. Leaning back against the wall, he continued to wait quietly while Du'urdin stood very still in the center of the cell, thinking. Time passed as they stood there waiting with little to do besides watch Dain Du'urdin. Cordovan could feel the minutes piling up as though large swaths of time were washing away into mind numbing oblivion. Just as his patience was about to wear thin Dain Du'urdin came out of his reverie.

Dashing to the corner of the cell, he fell to his knees digging at something in the floor. Standing, while brushing absently at his breeches with one hand, he turned, holding his prize in the other. The man was smiling his knowing smile – the one that showed every tooth in his mouth. Cordovan had seen that smile before. When Du'urdin had solved some conundrum or unwound the thread entwined around some convoluted mystery he flashed that particular smile.

Walking over to Cordovan, Dain Du'urdin stopped right in front of him. With a self-satisfied nod he placed a small twig in Cordovan's palm. It seemed simple, unassuming even, but not the great clue Du'urdin apparently thought. The man was smiling that smile though – the one that says, *I am a genius! The world has never seen my like!* So Cordovan looked from the twig to Du'urdin. With a raised eyebrow he said, "I assume this means something?"

Du'urdin sniffed loudly, feigning insult, before saying, "Why, of course my good man, of course. Do you think I root around in cells for the enjoyment of it? Of course, it means something. In fact, it means everything."

Du'urdin stood there with a broad grin on his face, as if it was the clearest thing in the world, looking from Cordovan to Aubrey. When neither spoke, he rolled his eyes exhaling with moderate exasperation. Plucking the twig from Cordovan's hand he said, "This is a piece of a branch, of a shrub, called *Lapis Ladillia*, or Lapis for short. It is a living thing, yet it has no voice. Though it is silent it speaks to me! It gives me its secrets. It tells me what I need to know. Do you hear it?"

Du'urdin paused again, with his hand to his ear, as if waiting for the inevitable to be spoken. Cordovan looked at Aubrey, who shrugged, before he turned back to Du'urdin who shook his head, as if to say he was burdened by the presence of lesser beings. "You must ask it where it grows, man! And when it tells you it does not grow in Alexandria you must ask, where then? The twig of Lapis, my good fellows, will answer you. It will tell you that it grows in Northern Province. And before you say anything, it does not simply grow in Northern Province, it actually grows in a specific part of Northern Province. In fact, it grows in only one valley, east of Marragen, along the Black Hills. The twig is silent, yet it speaks, it speaks!"

Wrapping the twig, delicately, in a square of white cloth, he slipped it into a pocket in his waistcoat. Dain Du'urdin stood there looking at them with that smile. The man was remarkable, but he was also difficult to deal with because he knew he was remarkable. With a sigh Cordovan said, "So I am assuming that you are saying that whoever helped Gaiden Colling came from this valley, in the Black Hills, in Northern Province?"

Du'urdin shook a finger in the air saying, "No, no. You are not listening to all of the things in this cell that, though they have no voice, are speaking to us. They tell us the story of what happened here! I am saying that *whatever took* Gaiden Colling came from the Black Hills, east of Marragen, and can most likely be found there. You see, Colling did not go of his own accord. Whatever took him was not a man."

Cordovan blinked. *Took him? Not a man?* Cordovan nearly cursed. He heard Aubrey hiss. Cordovan had seen enough of walking nightmares recently. Du'urdin seemed to be saying he was likely to see more. The fact that Colling had not escaped by himself meant there was more going on than Cordovan had initially thought. It troubled him. He did not like to fumble around in the dark. That was how people got killed. But that was exactly what they were doing. Cordovan consoled himself with the thought that if they were stumbling around in the darkness at least Dain Du'urdin was walking in front of them.

Taking a deep breath Cordovan said, "Very well. It is Northern Province then." He walked out of the cell with Aubrey and Dain

Du'urdin in tow. *Northern Province*. He had not expected that. It was going to be a long, tough, journey, but at least they had something to go on. Besides, he thought, long and difficult was a Watchman's specialty.

†

Alec woke to the sound of the large bell in the courtyard of Cadet House as it rang loudly. Stifling a low moan, he rolled over in his bed. His body ached. Though he had always thought of himself as having been in good shape, apparently, according to the Company standard, he had some work to do. He sat up, pulling back a heavy blanket, thinking that at least he was not tired. Each of the last few nights when he had gotten into his bed, in the Cadet quarters, he had fallen asleep as soon as his head hit the pillow. Though he was being pushed, pressed, poked and prodded, he was learning more than he had ever learned in his life.

Slowly, he slid out of bed. Alec walked across the main room of his quarters to a cabinet that held some of the softest towels he had ever felt. After pulling one out he wrapped it around his waist. Grabbing a hand towel, he closed the cabinet behind him before he headed out. The hall was full of other Cadets in various stages of their morning routine. Some, like Alec, were wrapped in towels, while others were already in their uniforms. Alec went down to the end of the hall where the washroom for the entire floor was located. As he pulled open the door, he was greeted by steam, the sounds of others washing up, but not much talking. It was early yet. The floor was white marble. The ceiling was high. Along either wall were what the People called washstalls. They were dark wood stalls with a stained finish that seemed to repel water. There were bright metal spouts protruding from the wall. There were also drains in the floor.

Alec hung his towel on a peg protruding from the end of one side of the stall before stepping in. Reaching out to the wall, he moved the lever that read hot, pushing it three slots to the right. Then he moved the lever that read cold one slot. He had learned that this arrangement of levers would give him water that was very hot but that fell short of being too hot. With the levers set, Alec reached up and pulled on the chain that hung from the overhead spout. With a soft click, which he felt in the chain more than heard, the spout opened allowing hot water to rain down on Alec. It was a wondrous thing! Alec had never seen anything quite like it. He doubted if even members of the Peerage had such a thing in their grand manors. There was approximately one stall for every three rooms on the floor. The same arrangement could be found on each floor of Cadet House. Alec stood under the hot water letting the heat soak into his bones. After a few minutes the soreness in his muscles began to ease as he reached for a large bar of soap. Grabbing his hand towel, he worked up a heavy lather that smelled of beeswax with a hint of lilac. With his hand towel foaming up with soap Alec began to wash. After a thorough cleaning he stood directly under the hot water for another few minutes allowing it to wash away the soap along with the rest of the aches in his muscles.

Pulling on the chain until he felt a click again, Alec stepped out of the stall as the water stopped pouring out of the spout. Grabbing his towel, which was warm from the steam, he dried himself. Wrapping it around his waist he made his way back to his room. He shaved, while still warm from bathing, cleaned his teeth, and put on his uniform. Soon it would be time to assemble in the courtyard below for morning inspection after which it would be off to study. But, thankfully, he had time for a cup of choca. Walking into the second room in his quarters, which was mainly for food preparation, Alec began brewing a pot. He poured beans into the grinder. Turning the crank, he ground them until they were the right consistency. After opening the door in the middle of the small potbelly stove he stoked its fire with an iron poker. The flames flared to life. Alec threw in a few more pieces of wood. He put the pot, filled with water, on top. Sliding into the window seat, he looked out on the early morning while waiting for the water to boil. He took the opportunity to pull his hair back, weaving it, into one large braid. Sitting in the blissful quiet of the morning he almost missed the soft knock at his door. It must have been one of his team members come to make sure he was up.

Alec left the small kitchen, crossed the main room, and pulled open the door to see Onya Onoto looking up at him. He stood there blinking for a moment. Getting a hold of himself he said, "Nsamsa?" She was resplendent in her crisp, black uniform. The four, glittering, silver pips of a Captain-Commander winked at him from the high collar of her fitted coat. Her straight black hair was laced into two, heavy braids, one behind each ear. There was no sign of the puffiness of early morning around her eyes. She was smiling brightly.

"Good morning, Nsamsahdo." After a moment of standing in the doorway, she raised her eyebrows. It was only then that he realized he had not invited her in.

"Oh. Forgive me, Nsamsa. Please, come in." Stepping back, Alec pulled the door all the way open motioning for Onya to enter. The smallish woman strolled in past him moving like a cat. It was as though she was coiled to leap into action at a moment's notice. But there was also a seemingly incongruent calm about her, which made it seem she was about to curl up and purr. Closing the door behind him, Alec turned in time to hear the sound of boiling water hissing from the pot on the stove. Walking toward his small kitchen he said, "Nsamsa, would you like some choca?"

Onya said, "Alec, you may call me Onya in private, but yes, I would like a cup. I like it creamy with sugar."

Alec went into the small kitchen. He pulled the hissing pot off the small stovetop. Removing the top from the empty, choca pot, which sat on the counter, he emptied the ground beans from the grinder into it followed by the hot water from the, still steaming, pot. Replacing the top on the full choca pot Alec retrieved a couple of cups from the cupboard along with two, small, wooden containers. One was filled with cream, the other with sugar. Placing everything on a silver tray, he carried it back into the main room where he sat it on his sidetable near the room's two leather chairs. Onya had sat in one of the chairs pulling her legs up under her. She had also slid her sword free of her belt, leaning it against the side of the chair. Sliding the sidetable closer to the chairs he poured them each a cup. Onya poured in cream followed by sugar. After she was finished Alec fixed his own cup before sitting back to enjoy it. The first one, he thought, was always the best cup.

They sat in silence for a few moments, enjoying their choca. It was that precious time of the morning. Alec had never considered himself a person who enjoyed getting up early but he did have an appreciation for that time of the day when it was still silent, just before the problems of the day came crashing in. This part of the day, though silent, spoke to him. The silence of the early morning calmed him. It spoke in an encouraging rhythm to him, which prepared him for what was to come. He looked over his cup at the little woman in black. She was looking back at him.

Lowering her cup to her lap she said, "So, Alexander. How have your first days among the People been?"

A slow grin spread over his face, "Tiring."

They both laughed softly. Onya said, "Yes, yes. I remember my first days, even now. I slept more soundly in those first days than I had before and maybe since. But it will get better."

Alec nodded at her in agreement. "I am sure it will. I must admit, though, that I am learning a great deal. I am beginning to understand why you are so good at what you do."

She held up a finger, "How *we,* are so good, at what *we* do."

Alec nodded again. "Yes, ma'am. You are right. How we are so good. That too, is taking a little time. I know I belonged to the Organization before this but that was never actually a real kind of belonging." He stared down into his cup allowing what he had just said to sink in. *A real kind of belonging.*

Onya's light, musical voice changed to a more serious note. "I know what you are feeling, Alec. It is what we all had to come to grips with early on in becoming a part of the People. It was the realization that we had found a place where real belonging was possible. Some of us, depending on what we had gone through before finding the Company, took longer than others to accept that we had *been* accepted. So hear me when I say, there is no rush. You will come to it in your own time."

Alec looked up from his cup. As he gazed into those tilted black eyes, he smiled at the sparkle he saw there. She was quite beautiful. She seemed exotic, otherworldly, even delicate, but he knew, quite well in fact, that underneath that delicate look was steel.

Taking a final sip from her cup Onya placed it on the sidetable. Turning back to Alec she said, "Now, I did not drop by just to see how you were but to tell you to pack."

He raised an eyebrow. "Pack?"

This time her smile had an edge of ruthlessness to it. She absently twirled her hand around the end of one of her thick braids. "Yes, Pack. I am leaving on a special assignment, so I am taking you, and your team, with me. Have no fear about your training. You will all continue that as we travel."

Alec set his own cup down on the sidetable. "May I ask where we are going? Why you are taking Cadet's with you?"

Onya uncrossed her legs. When she stood she let go of her braid. "Not really. You will find out where we are going soon enough. As to why? I will admit that I had not made up my mind until I was sitting here with a cup of choca in my hand. So inform your team. Then pack. We leave at noon."

With that she turned, grabbed her sword, and walked to the door while sliding it back in its belt loop. The black-lacquered, wood scabbard reflected the light as it hung there matching her knee-high boots, shine for shine. As she pulled the door open two of his team spilled in almost on top of her as if they had just been about to knock. When they saw Onya they backed up quickly snapping to attention. It was Sophie, the team-second, with Tessa towering over her. As Onya passed them she said, "At ease girls, at ease. I suggest you go pack." With that Onya strolled off down the hall toward the stairwell.

After quick glances back down the hall his two teammates ducked back into Alec's room closing the door behind them. They both walked over to the sidetable in search of cups for choca. Before they could say anything, Alec rose from his seat. He went to the kitchen to retrieve two more cups. Returning, he handed each young woman a cup. He sat down in his chair again while they made themselves choca. Sophie plopped down in the chair Onya had been sitting in. Tessa stretched out on the one couch in the room. Both were resplendent in their freshly pressed, black, breeches with their matching white coats. Their black boots caught the light from the lamps gleaming with fresh polish. Untidy uniforms made for long days of assigned chores for punishment he had been told.

Sophie looked over at Alec shaking her head. "I don't think I will ever get used to the fact that the Captain-Commander is your Nsamsa. It is kind of eerie."

Tessa grunted from her place on the couch. "Yeah, it is kind of creepy, not knowing when she is going to be about. Coming to your room first thing only to find her here, well - I nearly strained a muscle snapping to attention after we almost fell over her at the door. I mean, a little warning would be nice."

Alec just shrugged, picking up his cup to sip at its nearly empty contents. "Ladies, I don't know what to tell you. I have no control over when she comes or goes. I am caught off guard as much as you when she shows up."

Tessa sat up quickly nearly spilling her choca on her white coat. Cursing would have followed had that happened. The coats were not the easiest things to keep clean. Nothing put a cadet in a bad mood faster than getting their coat dirty first thing in the morning. Shaking her hand to get some of the choca that had sloshed over onto it off Tessa said, "By the by? What did the Captain-Commander mean by pack?"

Both women leaned forward in their seats as Sophie said, "Yeah, what was that about?"

Alec sat his cup down again. His choca was starting to cool off, never mind that it was almost gone. "All I can tell you is that she is going somewhere, and we are going with her. That is all I know."

Both of them sat back simultaneously as if they were somehow connected by a string. They each had thoughtful looks on their faces but neither of them said anything. Alec took his cup to the kitchen. Pouring out the small amount of cool choca left in the bottom of his cup he returned to his seat. He promptly poured himself a fresh cup. He took a moment to stirr in a bit of sugar, followed by cream. He thought to himself that they did not need to speak. The fact that both women were silent spoke volumes. They were captivated by what Onya had said, maybe more so by what she had not. Where were they going? Why was she taking them with her? Alec sipped from his cup. He let himself get lost in thought too. While the sounds in the hall increased, with the other cadets on his floor starting their day, the only sound in his quarters was the sipping of choca, echoed by the unheard cacophony of unspoken questions.

To ask about another person's journey is, in truth, to ask about your own.

~Fragment *Cep Illimatticus*
Site III, The Pappis dig
Correl Gamul, Chief Archeologist
*translated by Yim k'tan

Sometimes, you wish you hadn't.

~*Talliss Omell*
Upon the occasion of winning the argument with her husband over taking ship rather than travel overland to Calcut, as she was sicking up over the ship's rail.

CHAPTER EIGHTEEN

Questions and answers

The full moon hung low in the sky. It took up so much of the skyline it seemed you could reach out and rest your hand on it. The midnight hour was lit with an eerie glow as slender shafts of moonlight slipped through the canopy of the forest's treetops. Alla'mirridin stared at the moon through those treetops. His eyelids were creeping closed slowly. Having taken the first watch, he was now free to sleep through the rest of the night if he could. Nestled in-between two thick branches, high in a heavily leaved tree, with his back against the tree-trunk, Alla'mirridin allowed himself to relax a little, hoping sleep would soon come. Below him, several yards off to his right in a small clearing, was their actual campsite. Mino din' Darksbane was wrapped in his voluminous, brown, cloak, propped up against a large rock, asleep in front of a dwindling fire. Somewhere out in the darkness Zezza din' Nightblinder kept watch.

They had been on the move for nearly two days. Early, on the previous day, they had picked up a trail. While tracking did not seem to be a skill that mysteriously drifted up to the surface of his mind from the dark abyss that was his memory even Alla'mirridin knew that the trail they had crossed was an odd one. There were things in the group ahead of them. The Ki'gadi had pointed out something else mixed in among the footprints of men. Lead by an undaunted Master Sage of the Ki'gadi, Mino din' Darksbane, they had turned northward to follow whatever was ahead of them.

While they had been acting as hunters on the trail of their prey, Alla'mirridin had not been able to shake the feeling that they were also being hunted. He had spent much of the previous day looking over his shoulder. On two occasions Zezza had grown so irritated by this that, with a growl, she had yanked on the reins of her golden stallion spurring him off into the thick wood. Circling back, both times, she had checked their backtrail in order to insure they were not being followed. Her mount, its golden mane and tail braided intricately, which she called Salla'von, meaning Sunchild, thundered off each time only to reappear minutes later carrying a quizzical Zezza who was furtively glancing back over her shoulder. After the second trip to check their backtrail, followed by a few whispered words with Mino upon her return, her looks went from irritated to interested. But whenever he looked directly at her she quickly turned away. Women were a puzzle that you could never quite solve. With a shrug he tried to forget about the way she watched him.

The following day had gone much the same. They tracked a small group ahead of them while checking to see if they were being tracked. They ate cold food in the saddle, only stopping to camp when the moon hung fully in the night sky. Alla'mirridin let his eyelids droop closed with the hope of deep sleep. Wrapping his black cloak around him tightly, he shifted his weight testing his balance among the large limbs. He was nestled between two that were as big as his waist. Though his breath misted in the night air each time he exhaled he did not feel cold. *Sleep*, he thought. What he must have needed was sleep. Yet after two long days he did not seem to be as tired as he should have been.

There was no telling how long Alla'mirridin had been out when his eyes suddenly snapped wide open. The moon hung a little lower than he remembered so he assumed that a few hours had passed. Looking down to his right he noticed that the small campfire, which had been dwindling to a few flickering flames, was now completely out. But what got his attention was the thick mist that had rolled in covering the ground in a heavy white blanket. As he squinted in the darkness, trying to get a glimpse of Mino, Alla'mirridin felt his heart beating faster, thudding against the inside of his chest as if it were trying to communicate something important to him. It hit him like a splash of cold water in the face, sending a shiver up his spine, when he realized that there were no sounds coming from the forest. It was as still as a graveyard. While the forest was often a peaceful place at night it was never a totally silent one. The fact that there were no small *nightingbirds* calling to one another, *whowills* hooting in the night, or even insects buzzing about set off alarms in the back of his mind. Tiny bumps beaded up on his arms while his hair tried to stand on its end. Something was very wrong. Then he saw them.

Moving slowly through the trees, the shadows came. Alla'mirridin saw shapes creeping through the thick white blanket of mist. They were not yet close enough to make out who or what they were, but they were coming. They were quietly creeping from one tree to the next. That meant that they likely were not friendly. Grabbing the rope that he had secured to the trunk for this very purpose, Alla'mirridin lowered himself, silently, from his perch in the branches to the forest floor below. Keeping to the thickest part of the woods, he moved slowly to his left away from the oncoming shapes. Zezza had to be out there somewhere. He needed to find her fast.

There were two problems with finding her, which Alla'mirridin considered as he moved through the night. The oncoming shapes would stumble across a sleeping Mino soon. The second problem was that the Ki'gadi had an odd notion of what keeping watch meant. Most people picked a spot that seemed secure. They settled in to watch the night from there. The Ki'gadi roamed. They did not pick a single spot but rather stood at the appointed time and, without preamble, simply trotted off into the night. You did not hear them or see them again until, without warning, they strolled back into the firelight of the campsite either to sit before the flames or go to their bedroll. It took some getting used to.

Since they roamed the night during their watch Alla'mirridin had no idea where Zezza might be at the moment. With time pulling at him insistently he swung wide through the woods, counting his heartbeats, while scanning the darkness for the other Ki'gadi. Floating silently through the brush, wading in darkness, he avoided shafts of moonlight, which streamed down through the trees. He decided that if he could not find her before his count reached one hundred he would have to hurry back to Mino before the shapes creeping through the night were right on top of him.

If Alla'mirridin had not been moving so deliberately he would have missed her. In fact, he almost stepped on her. Just over a small, moss covered, rise in the forest floor, which turned out to be a rotting tree trunk, next to a collection of berry bushes, shrouded deeply in white mist, lay a sprawled body. Stepping over the mottled trunk, Alla'mirridin knelt beside her, lightly placing a hand on her chest. After a flash of fear, relief washed over him as he felt her chest slowly rise. An unbidden smile crossed his lips. But why was she unconscious? Zezza was not sleeping. Her body lay at an odd angle. There did not seem to be any sign of a struggle on her or around her. Alla'mirridin yawned widely, causing his eyes to water up, as it occurred to him, all of a sudden, that he desperately wanted to sleep. The fatigue he had been wondering about must have finally begun to catch up to him. But he told himself he could not sleep now. Shaking off the urge to lay down, to close his eyes, to fall into blissful slumber, he reached down, gently shaking Zezza. Mumbling something indecipherable she made as if to roll over until he shook her harder. Slowly, her eyelids fluttered until they opened fully. Big green orbs, reflecting the moonlight, stared up at him as if she did not know who he was. Alla'mirridin watched as those big, beautiful, eyes began to reflect dim awareness until it finally became understanding. Zezza bolted upright to a seated position putting a hand immediately to her head. Her eyes narrowed, her forehead furrowed, until a low feral hiss left her lips. Her reaction told him that her head was throbbing.

Leaning in next to her ear, Alla'mirridin kept his voice low. "Are you well?"

The low hiss was gone, replaced by a growl, which answered the question for him. Her naturally sweet voice turned to the raspy sound of impending death mixed with the continued mocking of his name as she spoke into his ear. "I am, *Approaching Storm*, but someone else soon will not be. By the Ancient and the spires of Palladawn!" She snarled in his ear. "What happened?"

Shrugging his shoulders, he said, "I don't know. I woke to find this fog on the ground. There were also shapes creeping through the woods toward our campsite. I came looking for you only to find you lying here unconscious."

Zezza looked around waving her hand through the fog as she cursed to herself. It almost made Alla'mirridin's face flush to hear her speak so. Seeing the question on his face she said, "This is no natural fog. It is a thing from the cesspool of the Pit. We call it the *Malignatta* or the *Mists of Making*. This is the reason I fell asleep. The *Mists* have the ability to paralyze a person or even render them unconscious depending on the relative strength of the person calling it up."

Looking him over, from head to toe, Zezza's eyes grew wide before suddenly narrowing. Tilting her head, she said, "How is it that you are not unconscious? Or paralyzed?"

Shrugging again Alla'mirridin said, "It must be because I was in the treetop when it came rolling in."

Shaking her head Zezza said, "That probably did protect you while you were in the tree, but you must have been walking through the *Mists* to find me. You should be laying paralyzed three steps from the tree you climbed out of." Looking at him more closely now she said, "Help me up."

Alla'mirridin helped Zezza to her feet. She wavered a moment before steading herself. A grim look crossed the face of Zezza din' Nightblinder. Though her voice was still low the tones were unmistakable. She was angry. Someone was going to pay for it. She took one step before a broad yawn stretched her mouth wide. Blinking her eyes rapidly she cursed again but this time Alla'mirridin did feel a slight flush in his face as the foul words poured out of Zezza's mouth. She emphasized each word pointedly. With a wave of her hand a subdued blue glow sprung up around her. With another wave the glow winked out. Nodding her head as if to say all was now as it should be she pulled her sword free of its scabbard before flowing off into the night. It was like a piece of art. Its steel gave off a slight blue hue in the moonlight. Alla'mirridin followed behind her pulling his own sword free.

Alla'mirridin knew, even with the dark shroud across his memory, that the Ki'gadi were extraordinary. However, seeing it in person, up close, was altogether different. Zezza was frighteningly good. It was all Alla'mirridin could do to keep up with her without making any noise. Like a wraith, she floated through the darkness, white hair loose, trailing over her shoulders, bouncing as she moved. The young, female, Ki'gadi darted among the pools of darkness. She was the briefest flash of white slashing through the shafts of moonlight that fell around them. She was like a Kotti-dancer who was in complete control of every movement of her slim body. In moments they were within view of the campsite. Her hand came up, signaling a halt, as she stopped behind a large tree. Alla'mirridin slid up beside her. He noticed, with wonder, that she was not even breathing hard. Looking over her shoulder she gazed at him for a moment. She whispered, "How is it that you do not breathe hard?"

Alla'mirridin's eyebrows climbed up his forehead. Working his mouth for a moment, he found he was unable to come up with an answer. He was shocked by the realization that he was not, in fact, finding it difficult to breathe. Shaking her head in amazement she hissed, "Never mind. Questions, along with their answers, must wait." Zezza turned back to look at the campsite. The white fog still lay thickly on the ground. It also looked as though Mino was still wrapped in its spell. Just on the other side of the dead campfire, he lay wrapped in his brown cloak, his chest slowly rising and falling. Just then Alla'mirridin caught sight of movement, off to his right, from the corner of his eye. They had discovered the campsite. Shapes began to materialize out of the darkness from among the trees, stepping into the diffused moonlight from the depths of the shadowy gloom of the forest.

Alla'mirridin's breath caught in his throat. There were men there, dark-clad men, but men looking somehow odd, seeming somehow twisted. But they were not what grabbed his attention. Two Graelim stepped from the deepest part of the darkness. Towering, black-clothed, white-haired creatures with cold eyes took in the campsite with sweeping gazes while their fanged teeth hung from sneering mouths. The men moved aside at their approach. It was as if the Graelim radiated a malevolent aura that pushed them back. Alla'mirridin could feel his neck constricting, unable to pull his eyes away from the dark things. He began feeling the sensation of hands gripping his neck. His legs felt stuck to the ground while his heart tried pounding its way out of his chest. Then he heard the melodic voice of Zezza speaking in his ear.

"It is why they are called *Horrors*. The Betrayers weaved a twisted piece of the *Presence* into their making. Somehow, as Mino thought, you are different from other men. For some reason the Mists did not affect you. Even now, though you feel the distant effect of the Graelim, you still have control of yourself." There was something different in her voice that Alla'mirridin could not quite identify but it made him want to prove her right. Taking a deep breath, he turned his head nodding to her that she was right.

Nodding back, she said, "Good. If we are to survive this night, we'll need your help. Thanks be to the Ancient that you were here." Zezza's voice turned to steel, "I will not let my Shad'ha'dai be killed tonight. I will not."

While Alla'mirridin was making a quick count, he realized that he liked hearing Zezza say she was glad he was around. There were fifteen men and two Graelim. As the graveness of the situation was becoming clear a series of thoughts came to him in rapid succession, from deep within the darkness that was his memory, affecting him before he could even fully grasp them. His breathing slowed as it deepened. Echoes of a tune came to the tip of his tongue accompanied by the image of a line being drawn in sand. Something akin to rage began building from deep within him as he looked at the Graelim. They were twisted things that stood in opposition to the beauty that was the world the Ancient had made. The intense feelings were sparked by something even deeper inside him. In a flash the image of a woman swept across his mind, hair to her ankles, skin like the darkest night sky, an elegant hand reaching out to touch him.

But as quickly as it had come the image was gone. Calm enveloped him. It was as if a partition had dropped in his mind separating him from the rage he had been feeling, leaving a singular thought. *Death. Death to twisted things!*

Raising his arm, with a rotation of his wrist, Alla'mirridin twirled his sword. The world around him blurred as his focus narrowed. The fog was gone. The forest receded into the background of his vision. The world shrank until it contained only the campsite. It continued to dwindle until all that seemed to exist were the few feet around Mino. He had not heard Zezza hiss at him. He had not felt her grab at his cloak. He had not even realized that he was moving until he was standing by Mino's resting figure. He had barely registered the presence of the dark-clad men because they were not close enough yet. For Alla'mirridin, the whole world was the few feet around Mino din' Darksbane. Alla'mirridin was unaware that he was humming softly, from the bottom of his throat, or that his face was a still, calm, mask. He did not realize that he had locked gazes with the two Graelim who were gliding toward him with a deadly economy in their movements. There was only the slightest awareness of the sound of ringing steel on steel around him as Zezza danced among the dark-clad men trying to fight her way to him. He did not hear her cry out his name. The world was only the few feet around him, a tune in his throat, and the Graelim that would soon enter it.

Words floated up out of the darkness in his mind. *This far, no farther.* Alla'mirridin was so focused on the few feet that constituted his world that he was unaware that he had spoken. The tune in his throat had stopped while those bracing words rang out from him. He saw the Graelim pause for a moment. He saw one of them raise a hand as though reaching out for him. Something hit him, hard. For a moment he felt his strength flowing out of him as his legs began to buckle. A white light suddenly flashed around him, before immediately disappearing, taking the weakness along with it. *This far, no farther.* The Graelim looked at one another, both pausing for some reason. Black-bladed spears twirled in their hands as they started forward again. But Alla'mirridin did not move because they had not entered his world yet. He thought he heard his own voice then, "This far, no farther!"

Glancing down Alla'mirridin noticed a line in the dirt in front of him that he did not remember drawing with the tip of his sword. Then they were there, in his world. He cried out, "This far, no farther, Pit-spawn!"

They came at him from both sides but Alla'mirridin was unafraid. They were in his world now, in his hands. In his hands he held death like it was his to rain down on the heads of whomever he saw fit. Now they had come too close to avoid it. He did not think. He just danced. Black steel echoed against his sword as he danced. He danced in a circle, around Mino din' Darksbane, which was only the circumference of a few feet of forest floor. But that small circle was his world. Nothing was allowed to enter it. He danced with death in his hands while words floated up from the darkness of his mind where his memories should have been; *Crow Shakes the Branches, Hawk Skims the River, Cloud Kisses the Earth, Swan Greets the Morning, Cat Crosses the Roof.*

Alla'mirridin's blade twirled in his hands, sweeping upward to meet blackened steel. He twisted his body leaping over Mino's unmoving form. Powerful, arm shaking, blows rained down on him as the Graelim darted in at him. But for some reason they could not stop him, could not eradicate him like their eyes said they desired. With conscious thought become a distant memory, Alla'mirridin danced with sharp-edged death in his hands. He swept the world away before him with his sword. Bending low, he slid his right leg out along the ground, with both arms stretched out like a bird in flight. Then he spun with his sword, passing it behind his back, sweeping it upward, holding it with his arms over his head as he deflected a spear blade that sought to split him in two. An instant later he was leaping through the air to slash at the other Graelim with a two-handed, overhead, chopping cut, which flung the twisted thing back several steps.

Then Zezza was there. Though blood spattered her face, and one of her arms was hanging limply at her side, she slammed into one of the Graelim causing the two to tumble away into the darkness. Without a moment's hesitation, Alla'mirridin leaped on the other one raining down blow after blow upon it. Distantly he knew he was shouting at the thing, but he was unaware of what he was saying. High-line attack followed low, in a continuous onslaught. He hammered at it mercilessly. All of a sudden there was nothing in front of him but dark forest. He stood there, crouching, sword in hand, staring at the forest in front of him. Looking down he noticed a black substance coating his blade. It took another second to realize that a headless body lay a few feet away thrashing about. Alla'mirridin watched the thing dissolve into the air in flame even as it still fought to stand up. A sulfurous stink wafted up from the ground where it had been.

Turning on his heel, Alla'mirridin slowly walked the thirty steps it took him to get back to the center of the campsite. When he saw the carnage, the world came flooding back in on him. He stuck his sword in the ground so that he could lean on it to steady himself. Oddly, he was not tired, just a little disoriented. Steadying himself he remembered Zezza. Turning to leap in the direction in which she had tumbled off into the darkness he saw her stumble back into the moonlight with her sword tucked away in her scabbard. She held one of her arms close to her body. He stepped toward her but stopped as she raised her hand as if to say he should not bother. Alla'mirridin watched her take a deep breath. With some effort, she stood up straight. Both of them came the rest of the way into the campsite stepping over bodies as they went.

Alla'mirridin looked around him at the carnage. While he had been busy with the Graelim, Zezza had seen to the dark-clad men. All fifteen lay sprawled around the campsite unmoving. He shook his head in wonder at how she had managed that. *One woman against fifteen men?* But she was Ki'gadi. Wondrous things happened when Ki'gadi were about. Looking at her he said, "You are amazing. Fifteen? You killed all of them by yourself?" But she only shook her head looking at him with that different look still in her big, green eyes.

Zezza's voice had a tinge of disbelief in it when she said, "That was nothing compared to what you just did. I tried to stop you, to keep you from getting yourself killed. To tell you there was a plan. But you just walked right out in front of them. You just stood over Mino. Then, as they surrounded you, you began shouting *this far, no farther*. I saw what I never thought I would ever see. A man, who was not Ki'gadi, stood against *two* Graelim and lived. You drew a line in the ground with the tip of your sword. I thought surely you would die quickly, even horribly, but my Shad'ha'dai was right. There is something different about you. You let no one past the line you drew. It was pure insanity. I'm amazed you are still alive."

Alla'mirridin swallowed hard as her words washed over him. It all came flooding back to him. He *had* strolled out in the middle of the camp standing there like an idiot, baiting them. Yelling at them that they could go no farther. What had he been thinking? He stood there in stunned silence watching Zezza wake Mino from his mist-induced stupor. The Master Sage shook himself as he looked around the campsite. After a moment he was on his feet viewing the carnage with disbelief in his eyes. Zezza dutifully recounted what had happened. When she did that look was turned on Alla'mirridin. But the more Zezza talked the more the look of disbelief faded away, replaced by a different one.

When Zezza finished, Mino nodded. Walking quickly to his horse, a gray stallion with a white mane and tail, Mino pulled a small leather pouch from his saddlebags. Returning to where he had left Zezza standing, he untied the small pouch. Dipping a finger in it, Mino pulled out a bit of clear ointment on its tip, which he stuck through the bloody tear in her sleeve, applying it to Zezza's arm. In moments her narrowed eyes widened even as her clenched jaw relaxed. She began to move her arm as if it had never been hurt. With a voice that was still a bit thick with sleep Mino said, "Check the area. We leave as soon as you return." Zezza nodded once before disappearing into the darkness, flexing her newly healed arm as she went. Alla'mirridin watched her go. He noticed that the mist had dissipated. Looking at Mino he said, "I have questions. I have seen nightmares walking, fables that live." Pointing after Zeeza he continued, "Wounded arms healed in a few seconds. We have been attacked by things, out of myth and legend, twice now. While I am willing to help you, I will not continue to do so without answers."

After a moment Mino nodded to himself, exhaling heavily. Looking at Alla'mirridin with the first haunted look he had seen in Mino's eyes since they met he said, "You are right, Alla'mirridin. You deserve what answers

I may give. May I suggest that we move down the road when Zezza returns? We can find a place where we can talk in relative safety."

Alla'mirridin nodded, "Yes, Master Sage. That is acceptable."

The old man ran a hand through his silvery-white hair while he looked around the campsite. "Good. When Zezza returns we will go. But I must warn you. After I have told you what I may, you might wish you had not asked." Without another word Mino din' Darksbane began packing up the campsite. Alla'mirridin bent to help. When he finished retrieving his rope from the tree where he had been asleep he immediately turned his attention to saddling his horse. Mino's last words continued to linger in his mind. *You might wish you had not asked.*

†

They managed to cover several miles in the shrouded darkness of the thickly wooded forest with the dawn still a few hours away. Alla'mirridin rode in a silence that was the byproduct of brooding over unanswered questions. A few feet ahead of him, the two Ki'gadi rode alongside one another. They were close enough that their horses brushed against each other. From time to time Zezza leaned over to speak in hushed tones with Mino listening. Periodically, the older Ki'gadi shook his head until finally Zezza reined her stallion a few feet to Mino's right. She rode on sitting in her saddle with a slight hunch to her shoulders. It seemed to Alla'mirridin that she had been trying to convince Mino of something but had failed. Now, she sulked over the failure. Mino glanced briefly in her direction, shook his head once, before turning his attention back to watching the way ahead. When Mino found a place that satisfied him they stopped for what remained of the night. They did not hobble the horses, put up tents, or start a fire, but simply sat at the base of an enormous tree with their horses ground tethered.

After a bit of sitting still, while Mino listened to the forest around them, Zezza rose from where she crouched. At a nod from him she trotted off into the darkness. For some reason Alla'mirridin immediately felt safer knowing that she was out roaming the night. Even given what had occurred earlier, maybe because of it, somehow, he knew Zezza would not allow herself to be caught by surprise again.

Alla'mirridin sat quietly listening to the forest around them. Periodically, a nightwho called out in the darkness, waiting for a response from a perspective mate. The buzzing chirp of chemicks, which would normally drive him crazy, was a comforting signal that all was well. Mino rummaged through a saddlebag. He soon came up with two, small, silver cups along with a beautifully shaped heavy, glass, bottle that was curved delicately. It was filled with what appeared to be Highland whiskey. He poured each of them a cup as he said, "This will have to do since we don't have a fire to keep us warm."

With a nod of thanks, Alla'mirridin tilted back the cup, bracing himself for the harshness of the fermented brew, only to have it lightly run across his tongue, before smoothly trickling down his throat with the slightest kick. It was a very good Highland whiskey. After a few moments a warm glow started up in his midriff. Looking over at Mino he said, "You have very good taste in whiskey."

Mino smiled in the darkness, "We Ki'gadi do not live the kind of life that lends itself to collecting much. But we do occasionally stumble across something worth having." His long, silvery-white hair caught bits of moonlight causing it to shimmer. Light-gray eyes caught pieces of that light as well making Mino din' Darksbane look like the otherworldly creature most thought the Ki'gadi to be. But, sitting there sipping very old whiskey with him made Mino seem somehow more like a normal man to Alla'mirridin. What he wanted was a pipe, but something told him that the smell of pipe smoke would drift incredibly far pointing anyone in the forest straight to where they were camping. So Alla'mirridin leaned back against the tree trunk, which would have taken twenty steps to walk around, and sipped from his cup of whiskey. After a moment Mino began to speak.

Mino's voice was low, hushed, almost breathy, as if the words he was speaking were carved with sharp edges that would cut his tongue if he were not careful. "We have spent thousands of years guarding the world against the Darkness. We encouraged the Good, where we found it, cutting out evil where it festered. It was our hope that the source that fed the Darkness, man's excesses and moral failures, would dry up leaving the Dark powerless to turn men to their own ends. While that seemed simple enough, it has been an uphill battle fought by every generation of Ki'gadi." Mino tilted back his cup, emptying it in a single gulp. Picking up the bottle from where it sat next to him looking like a piece of art, he filled his cup again. Passing the bottle to Alla'mirridin, so that he could fill his own, Mino sat back swirling his cup in his hand as if the whiskey needed mixing. Mino continued as though there had not been a pause in his recitation, "In all of that time, across all of those centuries, as the names of kingdoms changed, as the borders of those kingdoms shifted or were erased altogether, we watched, and waited, all the while guarding the Good. Sometimes we succeeded, but many times we failed, though not for a lack of trying." Turning, he looked directly at Alla'mirridin, "You see, no matter how you present goodness, no matter how correct or appropriate it may be, a person has to choose it. You cannot force them to walk along the path the Ancient One laid out for them. They must choose it for themselves. It is because of that freedom to choose, given to every mortal by the Ancient of Days, that we have not been as successful as we would have hoped." Looking off into the forest again, Mino sipped from his silver cup. He laughed then, but it was a wry, dry, laugh devoid of mirth. "We carried on. Even in the face of catastrophic failures. You see, Alla'mirridin, we knew a day might come when all of our efforts might not keep the worst from happening. From the time the first of us walked the world we have carried with us the terrible, sure, knowledge that one day a certain star would appear in the heavens and it would herald the end of all things."

As Mino spoke, something in the back of Alla'mirridin's fog-shrouded mind broke loose. He began speaking without thought, *"When a shadow crosses the sun, When a trail of fire streaks across the heavens, When nightmares walk, and children cry for arms that will not comfort them, Know that the time of the Beast is again come, These are the signs that will herald the coming of the End."*

Alla'mirridin licked his lips as the words he had just spoken began sinking in. He looked at Mino who still gazed off into the depths of the forest. After a moment Mino nodded his head. Alla'mirridin said, "But that is just a myth, a fable, just so many dust-covered words that have been uttered by a hundred voices for a hundred generations."

Mino nodded his head again. "Ah, is it now? Just a bunch of dust-covered words? Myth? Fable? Let me tell you about your myth. For the better part of a year now the star that those dust-covered words speak of has hung in the heavens. We have known that this day was coming for more than an Age. And soon, maybe too soon, the world will know that this fable is all-too real. The star is not close enough yet, but soon people will look up into the sky and see not only the star but the trail of fire that follows it. You wanted to know why nightmares are walking. You wanted to know why dark things are hunting us. The Beast that Betrayed, the One that was Twisted, comes. When that Soulless thing falls to the earth from the heavens we had best be ready, or else we will wish for a death that will not come."

Alla'mirridin looked down at his empty cup wondering when he had drained it. Maybe if he had not seen Gaunts. Maybe if he had not fought Graelim. Maybe if he had not been in the company of Ki'gadi for the past several days he could dismiss what Mino din' Darksbane was saying. But he had seen too much now. Something deep within him told him that what the Ki'gadi was saying was true. For the briefest of instants, the image of a woman reaching out toward him, her skin dark as the night, her hair, long and shimmering, flashed across his mind. But just as he tried to hold onto the image it was gone. Shaking his head to clear it, he took a deep breath before he said, "If it is inevitable that the Betrayer comes, what are you and Zezza doing out here in the middle of nowhere, on the edge of Province no less? And why would these dark things be after you?"

Mino nodded, "Yes. Yes." As he spoke he waved his own empty cup around as if it were an extension of his hand. "The Betrayer's coming is inevitable but the victory the Darkness seeks is not. If we can marshal the forces of the nations, we may still be able to survive the coming of the Beast. You only recited part of the prophecy. The next part says, *When these things come to past, that which is needed most will appear, You will find him among you, a man bless'd, yes blessed, and bless'd again, and he will lead you against the Darkness, that the Light may not fail.* There is more, but you get the picture. Though the star comes, all is not lost."

Alla'mirridin found himself filling his cup again. Oddly, momentarily, he wondered why he was not feeling the effects of so much whiskey. When he sat the bottle down he said, "So you are out here looking for this blessed man?"

Mino shook his head, "No, no. The prophecy, or what we call the *Legacy*, seems to indicate that the *Twice-Blessed Man* will be found in or around Palladawn when the time comes. No, Zezza and I are out here looking for something else. Since I discovered the star of which the Legacy speaks, distant, dimly shining in the heavens, I have been looking for the place where the armies of the Dark are gathering. It is my hope that we can catch them while they are building their strength so that we may deal them such a severe blow as to make them useless to the Betrayer. I believe we are close since we continue to run into the creatures of the Dark."

Alla'mirridin nodded to himself. The plan had merit. As powerful as the Betrayer must be, that twisted thing would still need an army at its back if it intended to conquer the whole world. With the very stuff of nightmares standing before them in the flesh even the most stoic, unbelieving nation would be forced to rise to meet the Twisted on the battlefield. If the Lord of Sufferings' army could be severely damaged it would go a long way in helping to defeat the Darkness.

Looking at Mino, Alla'mirridin said, "Thank you for telling me the truth." After a moment of thought he said, "I will help you."

Alla'mirridin barely heard it when Mino replied, "I expected no less, Tal' Algain." But when Alla'mirridin opened his mouth Mino forestalled him by saying, "Enough of questions and answers. Soon enough Zezza will return. I will need to take the watch. Unlike you, *Approaching Storm*, I need to rest." With that, Mino pulled up his large hood, wrapping his brown cloak more closely about him. Alla'mirridin was left with his own thoughts. The sounds of the forest kept him company. For a while, after Mino fell asleep, Alla'mirridin went over what the Ki'gadi had revealed to him. Apparently, things that had once been looked on as myth, maybe even legend, turned out to be very real. He had apparently put himself right in the middle of it. He should have wanted to leap on his horse so he could get as far away as possible from the legendary Ki'gadi, the Keepers of the Barrier, Watchers of the Flame, Bearers of the Light. But something, in the very core of his being, held him there. Though he did not know himself, his true name, or where he had come from, he did know that helping people in trouble was important to him. He also knew that if he had ever met people in trouble, these Ki'gadi were deep in it. With thoughts of a star in the heavens that he could not see, trailing fire, which heralded the coming of The Berayer, he settled back against the tree trunk in search of a sleep that had evaded him. For soon, after Mino had roamed the dark recesses of the surrounding woods and returned, it would be his time to take the watch. Closing his eyes, he tried to calm his mind, which was running over the answers he had been given. The last thing he thought as he drifted down into the darkness of sleep was that he almost wished he had not asked.

*come, come home
come home and let us
show you where you first stood
on two legs
come home*

*come, come home
come home and let us
take you to where you first laughed
come home*

*come, come home
come home and let us
let us ask you what you have seen
come home*

*come, come home
come home and do not leave us again*

*~From Callu's collection of poetry
Poet Emeritus, Upper Ajalu
Entitled, The Possibility of Home*

The deepest pains are found at home.

~Bremllet, Act II, Scene iii
Salkin Playwright
Arkliss Academy of Arts

CHAPTER NINETEEN

Homecoming

The swirling vortex of wind, mixed with flashes of lightning, died away leaving the small *Griot* in its place. The diminutive, dark-skinned man looked around the clearing while winding up the cord of his *Woedom*. Sliding the artifact into a brown, suede pouch, which hung at his waist, he nodded to himself as if he were satisfied with something. Absently scratching in his wild, woolly shock of hair, he walked to the edge of the clearing where the forest began to thicken. Bantu turned from watching the small Griot in order to take in his surroundings, breathing in the warm air as he did. It was air he had not breathed in more than fifteen years. He had forgotten how warm it was here. A heavy breeze brought the lively, complex, scents of the forest to his attention. Bantu caught a hint of mint, mixed with gloryfire, lilac, and gardenia. Turning his head toward what he thought was the east Bantu looked for a particular landmark. There, in the distance, rising high along the horizon, were the snowcapped peaks of Mount Killimajoon. Judging from the distance to those high peaks they must have been standing in the thick woods of the

Dagoonzu. They were half a world away. Though they had stepped through the rift, created by the spinning of the Griot's *Woedom*, in Alexandria's late morning, they were standing in Al'akaz with the sun setting in the west. For a brief moment his vision blurred. A small throbbing began in the back of his head. With a grimace, Bantu remembered that from the time he was a small child the headaches had been a constant ailment, which had become stronger the older he had become. Now, a malady that had not afflicted him since he left the shores of Al'akaz was back. Was he, somehow, so adversely affected by his homeland that he had a physical response to his return? Bantu tried to push the throbbing away from the forefront of his thoughts. Just as he began to focus he heard the telltale clicking of Yari sliding free of their housings. He quickly barked, "Ghost, Blossoms!"

Instantly, the three women leaped into the surrounding woods. Just like that, the women, in their black uniforms, faded into the deep green brush of the Dagoonzu. As fast as the Mfundade were they had not been prepared for the speed at which the Quiet Blossoms moved. Bantu turned to face the three Mfundishi draped in their black robes. Behind him, the six, young Mfunde, in their red and white robes with the blades of their Yari glinting in the last light of the setting sun, spread out around him. A grim look of disdain spread across his features as Bantu looked at the three men in their black robes trimmed in gold. "So, you follow the *Warring Way* do you?" Bantu did not stop his contempt for these men from clinging to his every word.

Nentan Yasadande A' Yaah spat on the ground near Bantu's feet. The calm look he had worn while confronting Bantu in Alexandria was gone. It had been replaced by open derision. "You, who are outlawed! *Borjunai*, a coward who runs, you do not deserve the considerations of the *Way*. You deserve only what you are about to get. Were it up to me you would have been taken to the Weeping Tree so that you could be hung there for all to see. They could watch you suffer as they passed by, laughing, or spitting at you. And when you were close to death your body would have been carried out to the Sedengatti for the jackdaws to eat. As it stands there will still be no death rites, no gloryfires to ring your body, no sacred flame to consume you, no recitation by the Griot in the Corral, no honor for you at all. You will die here. Alone, without honor."

Looking around him, as the young Mfunde eased closer, Bantu said, "I should have known you were without honor since you came with Mfunde from only one of the Great Houses." Bantu noticed the young Mfunde stop. They exchanged brief looks. He continued, "Yes, I have not been away from home so long that I have forgotten the red and white of the N'kosi. Nor have I forgotten the N'kosi's First Son, Nduma. Too bad he did not have the courage to come face me. But then, as gifted as he was in the Warring Way, that was never his style. Even when we were children, in his heart he was a coward, willing to let others do his dirty work." Some of the young Mfunde from House N'kosi hissed while others cursed openly. They all had open hatred painted on their faces. *Good*, Bantu thought, *be angry. Be very angry, so angry that you will lose focus.*

As the Mfunde resumed closing in on him, Bantu noticed the slightest movement in the brush off to his right. A branch shifted the tiniest fraction. Glancing around him he realized that the Mfundade were so focused on him they had not noticed. So he called out. "You will not move! You will do nothing!" Off to his left, opposite from where he saw the movement, a faint curse drifted up from a thicket of flowering bushes. It almost made Bantu laugh. The Blossoms were surely fuming by now. They had moved into advantageous positions, likely surrounding the Mfunde. But they were almost certainly at their wit's end over not being able to do anything more. Bantu had known this day was coming. He had been preparing for it since the day he had been forced to leave Al'akaz. It had been the middle of the night. His parents had hustled him aboard a longboat manned by servants of the House that took him directly to a deepsea ship. He had only the clothes on his back, a Yari wrapped in cloth, and a bag of gemstones worth a fortune. His mother had been in tears as his father had told him to be brave. He had said they would come for him when it was safe for him to return home. But when the longboat was safely out onto the river he had watched in horror as his parents were attacked. They had never come for him. He knew they had not survived. On the deck of that deepsea ship he had begun his preparations with tears pouring down his cheeks. Moving slowly in the moonlight through the forms his father, and Zalakazam, had taught him he had tried not to sob. Every day he had trained in preparation for this. In that moment rage surfaced in him, a rage that he had all but forgotten. A deep, boiling, anger that bubbled up seeking to overwhelm him. It pushed through the throbbing at the back of his head. One of the young Mfunde faltered a step as he met Bantu's gaze. The look of disdain, on Bantu's face, had been replaced by something else, something cold, something darker, something Bantu knew spoke of death in the offing. The look was magnified by how the pain in his head added a haunted look to his eyes. Thoughts of his loss, of how they had come for him, of their present betrayal, of the pain in his head, all came together in a cool, biting focus. He had waited all these years for vengeance. It was surely one House, one man, who was responsible for the death of his parents. The expression on his face said his vengeance would begin here, today, right now.

They moved, all at once. They were going to kill him quickly if they could. Bantu pulled his sword free with a reverberating ring as the blade left his scabbard. He turned into them, twirling his sword around his back, as he prepared to meet the first attacker.

He turned into the first position of *Servant Catches the Cup*. Flowing into that beautifully elegant posture, with his sword grasped in both hands, pointing upward, he looked up to see a tall, shockingly beautiful, woman in green robes, trimmed in sea-blue. She strolled right into the middle of the fray like she was out for a walk in her garden. She was unarmed but, as she stepped past the young Mfunde moving toward him, they recoiled in horror. Blocking two quick thrusts, from one of the grandmasters Yari's, Bantu stepped back hastily as she stepped between him and the Mfundishi. The grandmaster also hastily stepped back. One of the other two grandmasters fell over himself to stop a thrust that would have taken off the woman's arm. Their faces were all painted with shock. Bantu wondered if his was any different. Was she insane?

She looked at Bantu, flashing him one of the loveliest smiles he had ever seen, but filled with mischief, as she said, in a soft voice, "You will stop." That was it. It was not a question, or plea, it was a simple command. She was beautiful. Only a half-span short of Bantu's height, her black hair was braided close to her scalp on the top. It was sectioned into four, large braids, which were somehow woven into a single larger braid that fell to the small of her back. Nestled in the thick braids were tiny white flowers. She was close enough that Bantu caught the scent of sandalwood. Her face was slender, her features small, but with the distinctive broadness of an Al'akazian. Full lips, which had a hint of something glossy painted on them, were pulled back revealing perfectly straight, bright white teeth. Her skin was a shade lighter than Bantu's but managed to be flawless. Her eyes were dark green with a sinister sparkle lighting them. She wore an outer robe that hung open revealing an inner robe that hugged her body. She had full hips, matched by a small waist. The woman was beautiful. Then it dawned on Bantu why the members of the Mfundade had recoiled, falling over themselves in order to back away from her.

The green of her robes, which were trimmed in blue, named her a member of the greatest of the Great Houses, House Aassam. Had even a hair on her head been touched by one of these men the Houses they represented would have been raised to the ground by Aassam. Given the fact that N'kosi was the second largest of the Great Houses, Aassam would have inadvertently plunged all the Houses into civil war with their retaliation. As Bantu stood there, still crouched with his sword barred, his head throbbing, he nearly whistled a low, long, cool note. She had taken a terrible risk. If there had been one misstep, one man who was a fraction too slow, she would have been lying on the ground bleeding out. As word of how she died reached the Houses they would have been preparing for all out war. *Yes*, he thought, *beautiful, but insane.*

Bantu watched her. She winked at him where only he could see it while letting the smile she had flashed him disappear. Turning to face the Mfundade, who were looking around themselves like cornered cats seeking an escape route, she said, "I am Jamila. First Born of Aassam. May I ask why men of the Corral, honored Mfundade, are out in the middle of the Dagoonzu, behaving in such a manner? If there is a dispute among you, why is it not being handled in the Corral, according to the tenets of the Way?" Bantu had swallowed hard when she spoke her name. How she had grown.

Nentan Yasadande A' Yaah, having returned his Yari to its wooden housing, twisting it in place with a soft click, bowed low to Jamila saying, "Begging your pardon, First Born. This man is a traitor to the People. We captured him and were bringing him to the Corral to face the Challenge when he attacked. We merely sought to defend ourselves."

"Lie!" Wen shouted as she walked out of the woods into the clearing. Her sword was out. Bella and Isabelle followed closely behind her. All three looked ready to carve up whomever they could get their hands on.

The three Mfundishi whispered among themselves as the Blossoms came to stand around Bantu. Jamila looked from the Blossoms to Bantu. She glanced back at the Blossoms again as her eyebrows climbed her forehead. Bantu watched her as she took in their uniforms, even the way the women stood close to him. Looking at Wen again, tilting her head up, Jamila spoke in a soft alto that tickled Bantu's ear. The woman stood there like a queen, speaking as if she should be obeyed like one. "Introduce yourself."

Wen stood straight up, taught as a wire, ready to snap. Her voice was strong with a hint of defiance. Looking around the clearing, taking in all of the people who stood in it, she let her voice wash over them. "I am Commander Wen Ava Noella of the Peoples Company." Holding her sword out she moved it so that it pointed at the Mfundade as they stood around the clearing. She let her swordtip point at each of them briefly. "And the next one of you that even breathes hard in the Commander-General's direction, I will kill where you stand."

The woman looked from Wen back to Bantu. She smiled briefly at him again. Speaking so low that, were it not for the gift, Bantu would have missed it, she said, "So the son of Omorede has some honor among the outlanders." Speaking up, Jamila turned to face the Mfundishi. She said, "It seems, Mfundishi, that your words are called into question. And since when do the Mfundade attack like a pack of jackdaws trying to take down a great cat?"

Nentan, along with the other two Mfundishi, had finished whispering among themselves. The man stepped closer. Looking him over, Bantu realized what he was seeing in Nentan's eyes. They had decided to try to kill them all, even the daughter of House Aassam in the hopes that no one would ever know what had happened here. As Nentan opened his mouth there was a commotion at the back of the clearing along the treeline. Bantu looked behind the Mfunde in red and white to see a number of men, in blue robes, trimmed in white, come pouring into the clearing following the Griot who had brought Bantu to Al'akaz. Bantu had been so busy with the Mfundade that he had not even noticed when the Griot had slipped away. The little man looked harried, almost harassed, as if when this was all over someone was going to get an earful. But, as he stepped aside, the other men rushed into the clearing. The Griot flashed Jamila a big grin giving her a single nod. Bantu barked a brief laugh as the men in blue robes surrounded the Mfunde in red. Wen, who was still standing close by his left side, whispered, "Who are they Commander?"

Bantu leaned over as he said, "They are the Mfundade of House Omorede. In short, she brought my family with her." He laughed again as he counted twenty young, towering, Mfunde in blue robes with the telltale head full of braids spilling across their shoulders, accompanied by two Mfundishi in black robes, their heads shaved clean, who were pushing their way forward to where Jamila stood. The two Omorede Mfundishi jostled the young N'kosi Mfunde in red, glancing at them with undisguised contempt, as they passed. With a glance at Bantu, the older of the two Omorede Mfundishi bowed his head to Jamila as he spoke. "My Lady Aassam. We thank you for the invitation to join you on your hunt in the Dagoonzu. But we are surprised by what we find here." The man turned, looking at Nentan, along with the other Mfundishi, while he spoke though he continued to direct his words to Jamila. "How is it that the Mfundade of Yaah, Gamba, and N'kosi are here? And who is this standing among them with naked steel in his hands?"

Jamila shook her head. "Of all of this, Mandisa Ga A' Omorede, I am unsure. I believe it is a dispute that must be dealt with in the confines of the Corral rather than the distant woods of the Dagoonzu. But I am, after all, only a woman and matters concerning the Corral are beyond me."

Mandisa bowed low when she finished. "Great Lady, you do us a disservice to speak to us so. In this place, so far from our Houses and the Corral, we are all aware that your word is law. You are Aassam. If you say this matter is to be settled in the Corral, then so be it." Mandisa looked pointedly at Nentan who looked around him, back at the other two Mfundishi, before slowly nodding his agreement. As he nodded, licking his lips, he said, "Mandisa Mfundishi is correct, Great Lady. Your word is law here." Looking at Bantu he said, "We will bring the petition to the Corral upon our arrival. Until then son of Omorede." Those last words were tinged with scorn but Nentan, with the other Mfundade who had come with him, trotted off into the woods, their long strides carrying them away quickly. Bantu slid his sword back in its scabbard. He twirled it once, before placing it in the crook of his left arm, as he watched them go. They would be even more dangerous now. Having been caught trying to kill Bantu outside the Corral meant they could be made subject to the justice of the Corral. Men like that would do dark things before letting it come to that. There was no doubt in Bantu's mind that, had Mandisa not shown up with enough Mfunde to outnumber the ones who had brought him home, people would be dead by now.

Turning back to Jamila he opened his mouth to thank her just as bright lights exploded before his eyes. Bringing his hand up he rubbed at his jaw where she had smacked him. He had not even seen her hand move. Had he not still been on his guard the open-handed slap she had delivered might have staggered him. As it was the slap added an extra edge to the throbbing in his head. Blinking his eyes to clear the bright spots from his vision, while mentally asking the pulsing in his head to please stop, he looked down at Jamila who was standing in front of him with her hands on her hips. Her lips were pursed. "What, by the Pit, was that for?" he asked.

Jabbing a single finger at his chest to emphasize her words she said, "You know very well what that was for Ossassande! You have not been gone so long, nor grown so much, that I do not recognize you. Where have you been! Do you think you can just up and disappear without a word then stroll back into the Beautiful Land, after the turning of fifteen seasons, like everything is fine? Fifteen, mind you! Well you can't! Just you be glad those brainless fools chose a Griot who deals with my House to go retrieve you, so that I was able to get word they had found you, so I could get here in time to keep your head on your shoulders until your kin could come for you. Now what do you have to say for yourself?" She said it all in a rush as if she did not need to breathe.

Bantu opened his mouth to attempt an answer, but she cut him off. "And where do you get off placing these women in harms way? You men are all the same wherever you come from. You make nothing but trouble. It is we women who always have to clean up after you. You have some explaining to do Son of Omorede." Jamila continued to speak, seemingly to herself, in the same disgruntled tones, as she walked around behind the Blossoms. She began herding them along in front of her. She continued fussing while they walked off in the direction that the Mfundade of House Omorede had come. When Jamila reached the edge of the clearing she collected the Griot before walking on into the woods. Bantu could still hear her fussing as she disappeared through the head-high brush.

Rubbing his jaw, he gingerly shook his head as he watched her go. Bantu looked at Mandisa, "So, cousin, what kind of welcome am I to receive from you?"

Mandisa jumped as if he had forgotten Bantu was there. He had been watching Jamila too. Turning to face Bantu he spoke in a deep, rich, tenor. The man was a few inches taller than Bantu, as were the rest of the Mfundade with him. "So, it is true then. You are the First Born we lost so long ago?"

Bantu looked around him at them. The men draped in blue robes, trimmed in white, were looking at him as if he were something out of a dream. They were all of a similar complexion, which matched his own. Though they were all younger than him, with the exception of the two in black robes, they all had a similar look about the face. They were clearly his family. Bantu could not, in the moment, get a handle on what it felt like to look at them, but he opened his mouth, marshaling his voice to say, "I am Ossassande Bantu As' Omorede."

Bantu watched as Mandisa swallowed hard, nodding his head slowly, as if taking it in. Opening his mouth, the man said, "There is but one way to greet the lost son of Omorede. Welcome home First Born, we stand ready to serve." With those words, Mandisa knelt on one knee, holding his Yari above his head, cupped in both hands. All around the clearing the other Mfundade, in their blue robes, knelt, holding their Yari up as well.

Bantu leaned over, placing a hand on Mandisa's shoulder, as he said, "Stand, cousin. Such gestures are unnecessary."

Mandisa stood, giving a low yelp over his shoulder, which caused the other Mfundade to stand. Gazing at Bantu with a broad grin, looking like Bantu's father, around the eyes at least, he said, "Begging your pardon First Born but such gestures *are* necessary when the First Born of the House, who was lost to us, returns." Raising his Yari high above his head in one hand, the man let out a high trilling yelp, which was answered by twenty-one more from the other men.

Smiling briefly at Mandisa, Bantu simply said, "Take me home cousin. Take me home."

Turning to face the other members of the Mfundade, Mandisa cried out, "We take the First Born home. Jussma! Tadenda! Ossallusa! Run ahead. Let the House know that we come with the Son."

Ahead of them, three of the Mfunde in blue darted off through the trees in the direction Jamila had herded the Blossoms. Through the trees Bantu could see wind whipping violently in a tight swirling vortex accompanied by flashing lights. The Griot had opened another rift, no doubt to the ancestral lands of the Omorede. With Mandisa, followed by the other Mfundishi in black, in the lead flanked by the remaining Mfunde in blue, they left the clearing heading to a place Bantu had not seen since he was a boy. He was coming home. Now, if he could just get his head to stop throbbing.

And they raised their heads at the end of the wasting destruction
And saw that they had been brought to a land of plenty
And when the twenty-four had searched it and returned
They showed the evidence of what they had found
So the people rejoiced and they called the place Bedi Al'akaz,
For they had been blessed with a land of overflowing beauty.

~A passage from the Medi-Namdi

Enemies never forgive, friends never forget.

~*Allhelenides*

CHAPTER TWENTY

Al'akaz

Wen knew she was staring but she couldn't help herself. As a member of the Peoples Company she had been fortunate enough to see much of the known world. From the impossibly high, bluish-gray peaks of the Halmagaine, which cut the west in half, to the unbelievable fire-gouts of Pana-tirith, in the deep south, where the earth spat fire according to some ancient underground clock, she had seen it – seen enough to think she could not be surprised anymore. She had even seen that world in ways most people never would. When she had passed over the Halmagaine it had been on the back of a Pradas. When she had walked through the fire-gouts it had been hunting marauders with a swarm of black-swath Blossoms in strike-suits surrounding her. But what she had heard about distant Al'akaz had not prepared her for what she was seeing. The men were giants.

Bantu had been one of the tallest men she had ever known. There were men almost as tall as the Commander in the company, even the rare one or two who were taller. But what she was seeing now left her speechless. From the Mfundade who had come to rescue them, to the people who dotted the landscape as they passed by, they were all giants. Even the women were taller than she was used to. They were smaller than the men, but in Alexandria, as well as all of the other nations across the Macca Deep, they would tower over the women.

Not only were the people like giants they were proud. Wen could see it in the way they moved, even in the way they held their heads. Even as she studied those who were working in the finely manicured, lush fields of grain, corn, or grapes, she could see it. As the party passed along the stone road winding alongside the vast fields she could see dignity written all over them, even from a distance. Wen walked at the front of their small party. They had stepped from the whirling rift the odd little, mostly naked, man had made with his twirling rope, into a veritable paradise. That was the other thing Wen had been wholly unprepared for, the sheer beauty of the place. Once she had thought, as did many of those living there, that Alexandria was the most beautiful place in the world. But what she was seeing, as she walked along the curving stone path, was changing her opinion. The woods were lush, brimming with color, with air that was warm, pristine, and sweet. The waters they passed, though mostly small ponds or streams, were somehow crystal clear. The landscape rolled gently, rising slightly, before falling almost imperceptibly. It was as if the land knew when you were about to tire of climbing upward. Just when you might begin to think about the rising ground beneath your feet it would give way to a gentle downward slope. Bright shocks of flowers dotted the landscape. The trees were as big as houses, rising higher into the sky than you could see. In the distance was a breathtaking horizon with mountains climbing into the sky. All of this she watched by the last light of day. While the sun sank below the horizon it began to look as if the night would be as gorgeous as the day had been. Even the land, with its wide-open spaces, towering trees, and vast fields nestled alongside teeming forests, framed by enormous mountains, seemed to be made for giants.

The rift had apparently opened on the edge of territory that belonged to Bantu's family. The further they walked the more people they began to see. There were men in aprons carrying tools in their large hands. Wen saw women with large baskets balanced atop their braided heads, no doubt full of what had come from the fields. Though everyone wore different clothing it was all in blue with accents of white. Their party walked past fields that had begun emptying of workers who poured out onto the stone road. They passed low, sprawling, houses of an architecture that was strange to Wen's eye yet breathtaking at the same time. Lights could be seen, illuminating windows or doorways, as people came out to look toward the winding sandstone road. Some began silently lining the road to watch them pass. Mothers stood with their hands on children's shoulders watching the procession go by. The longer they walked the less land there was between houses.

The men who had gone on before them must have made a ruckus as they passed because people seemed to have an idea of who was coming. The crowds lining the road became larger. People began to point at Bantu as the procession passed by. Wen heard the word *son* more than once. Not only did the houses get closer together, while the crowds grew larger, but ornate lanterns with blue flags appeared, stuck in the ground, on either side of the road at even intervals. The closer they came to the center of the land of Bantu's family the more the last light of the day dissipated allowing the night to grow. People leaned in trying to get a better look at Bantu. In the distance, Wen began to hear music. Drums thumped. Pipes piped.

It took nearly two hours of walking before the ground began to rise steadily. Looking off in the distance Wen saw what might have been called a village except that the houses were neither rustic nor was the scene pastoral, in fact the word would more likely be opulent. Stretching into the early evening sky were structures made from white sandstone with blue domed rooftops. They were nestled together so as to appear to be one grand building but there actually appeared to be several. Together they dwarfed the palace in Alexandria. There was no wall, no gate, or even a moat. The only thing that stood between the road and the cluster of buildings was beautiful landscaping. Everywhere Wen looked there were flowers, trees, or cultivated shrubbery. As the moon began to rise into a clear sky, torches, stuck in the ground in intervals of a few feet, lit up the road. Wen looked ahead of her at hundreds of towering men in blue robes. Once again, she was struck by awe. No wonder they called it the Beautiful Land. *It was.*

When they came within earshot of the men who were strung out in a line extending to the edge of her vision on either side of the road, a hand rested on her shoulder gently bringing her to a halt. It was the woman named Jamila. She looked down at Wen with a warm smile. In a husky voice that only Wen could hear she said, "There are things to be said, female Mfundade of the Outland, things that we are not a party to. So we must wait here."

Without thinking Wen smiled back at the woman saying, "Yes, Lady Aassam."

Jamila, still smiling broadly at her, shook her head slowly as though only just then realizing something, "No, no. You must call me Jamila. I ... I know it is forward of me to ask. But I have this - a feeling really, that is to say, I think, given time, we will be great friends. You, your sisters, and I. I have seen how the three of you stood up to the Mfundade without fear, ready to fight for Ossassande. You must be women of honor. So please, I give you the saying of my name."

Wen leaned forward so that the two women could hug briefly. As they hugged Wen was able to see Bella and Isabelle over Jamila's shoulder, but the women were too busy looking everywhere at once, with their hands on their sword hilts, to pay attention to Jamila and Wen. Stepping back Wen said, "Then you must call me Wen, Jamila." The tall, strikingly beautiful, woman looked at her as if waiting for Wen to say more before nodding to herself. Wen said quickly, "I give you, the saying of my name."

Jamila nodded again, smiling even more broadly. She stepped up to stand next to Wen. They stood there, watching the men, with Bantu in their midst, approach the wall of the Mfundade who stood between them and the majestic buildings behind them. Wen leaned toward Jamila, "If I may ask Lady - I mean Jamila. What is happening?"

They both watched the scene in front of them as they spoke. Jamila said, "The Mfundade who came to retrieve the First Born of Omorede must now present him to those who lead the Great House."

Wen grabbed a bit of her bottom lip with her teeth. While she chewed her lip she said, "And what if they do not *accept* him?"

Jamila paused long enough in responding that Wen turned her head to look up at the woman. Jamila was trying to smooth away a worried look from her features but after a moment she said, "Then, according to custom, the Mfundade will strip him then beat him to the edge of Omorede territory. Or they will kill him in the attempt if he fights it. While I was able to intervene back in the Dagoonzu I do not think, here, in the heart of Omorede, that I would be able to keep them from beating him badly or possibly killing him."

Wen cursed. It was a strong, solid, singular, face-blushing, curse. When she looked back at Jamila, the woman was trying to look off as if she had not heard Wen. But Wen caught the tail end of a brief flash of surprise as it flitted across Jamila's face. It must not have been an honorable thing to say.

Wen turned back to watch the scene in front of them play out as the towering man in the black robes with gold trim, whom Jamila had called Mandisa, stepped out in front of the gathering with Bantu a few steps behind him. They came to a halt in front of the crowd. A man and a woman, resplendent in blue robes of fine linen, with gray in their hair, but faces that seemed too young for that gray, stepped from behind the line of grim-faced giants, who, Wen noted, all held Yari in their hands. There were a lot of them. She swallowed hard as she watched.

When the older couple came to stand in front of Mandisa, he bowed low, remaining in that position while he spoke. Wen was close enough that she could still hear what was being said. "Pardon, First. Pardon, Great Lady. I have come with glad tidings of great joy."

The older woman spoke first. "Rise, Mfundishi. We are always pleased when the Yari of the House come with news of joy rather than bloodshed."

Mandisa rose from his deep bow. When he did the older man spoke. His voice rose so that it could be heard from a distance. It was strong, with the sound of many years coloring its tones. Wen looked at the man more closely. She could see some of Bantu in his features. The older man, whom Mandisa had called *First*, said, "Long ago, the House suffered a great tragedy. In the span of a single night we lost the entire treasure of the House. The only First Born was taken from us for his own safety. A few hours later we lost his parents, the First, along with the Lady of the House. My brother, and his wife, served the House with honor. We have waited, praying that the Ancient One would see fit to smile on Omorede again. Am I to understand, Mandisa Mfundishi, that the day we have waited for is upon us?"

With another shallow bow, followed by a flourish of his hand, Mandisa stepped back while saying, "Gisa Adantu As' Omorede, Sellena Juntu Na' Omorede. I present to you, Ossassande Bantu As' Omorede, First Born of the House."

Silence sat over the gathering like clouds on the mountains. Wen heard nothing. It was not the welcome she had expected. If one of the storytellers in the taverns of Alexandria had been telling it, upon the pronouncement of his name, the people would have rushed forward to welcome Bantu home as a hero. But all she heard was silence. Nervously she stroked the hilt of her sword. Maybe they could outrun them. Maybe she, Bella, and Isabelle could give Bantu a head start. *Maybe,* she thought. Looking around she opened her mouth to say something, but Jamila touched her wrist lightly making a quick, almost imperceptible, shushing sound that only Wen caught.

Riveted to the scene in front of her Jamila nodded her head, ever so slightly, so that Wen turned her attention back to where Mandisa had been standing with the older couple. She watched as Bantu stepped forward. Though not quite as tall as the rest who ringed him, he moved with all the dignity Wen had grown accustomed to seeing her Commander display. Even here, in this strangely beautiful place, surrounded by danger – even here he was all self-possession. There was a gravity about him as he planted the tip of his scabbard in the ground, standing with his hands resting on the top of the hilt, one over the other. Standing there, so still yet graceful, he looked like a man come to take on an army single-handedly. The older couple stepped closer to him. Wen had to lean forward to hear what came next. The older man, Gisa she had heard Mandisa call him, said, "Do you know us, young man?"

So, it was a test. Bantu had been gone so long that, even though he had their look about him, they were unsure that he was who he claimed to be. Bantu smiled a slow half-smile, looking from the man to the woman, down the long line of the Mfundade. His head turned up and a bit left. A distant look crossed his eyes as he said, "Uncle, my father used to punish me by sending me to bed without the fruit I loved to have after evening meal. You would sneak me a piece of jojobatte, late in the evening, when you thought no one was looking. It is why you were always my favorite."

The old man's eyes welled up with tears as he fell on Bantu, wrapping him up in his arms. The older woman was right behind her husband. They both held onto Bantu as if he were a lifeline thrown to them in the deep waters of the sea. Stepping back from the embrace, the old man turned to the throng of Mfundade in blue strung out in an immense line behind him. He shouted so that everyone could hear him when he said, "The Son has returned!"

With those words Mandisa let loose a bloodcurdling yelp that was answered by hundreds of other trilling tongues. Jamila slapped Wen so hard on the back, with a broad grin painting her face, that Wen had to take a step forward to keep from falling over. All along the road people began to celebrate. The sound of drums filled the air. They were soon joined by other instruments. The long line of the Mfundade that had blocked the way to the cluster of buildings on the rise collapsed as the young men crowded close to get a better look at Bantu. The people who had lined the road crowded in with parents hoisting small children onto their shoulders, so they could get a glimpse of the First Born. Looking around her, Wen knew what came next without having to ask Jamila. The people crowded together as they swept up the rise to the cluster of buildings, which were the center of the land of the Great House Omorede. As they were carried up by the rushing throng Wen heard some of them shout, "A House again! We are a House again!"

†

Bantu stood on the broad, long, veranda of white sandstone with its lightly faded blue railing winding along the edge. A soft breeze, smelling of mint, and honeysuckle, mixed with what seemed a bit like gardenia, blew across his face. Looking out to the east, above the gardens lazily stretching out from the Seat of the House, above the towering trees of the lush countryside, toward mount Killimajoon, Bantu watched the sun creep over the horizon. He had not been able to manage much sleep before restlessness pulled him from the bed he had been given. But thanks to the *gift* he was neither tired nor hung over. Omorede had celebrated long into the morning hours with a veritable feast overflowing with very strong drink. Mfunde had stood in large circles challenging one another to see who could leap the highest, while the women danced in provocative circles around the enormous bonfires that were still smoldering heaps in the morning sun. Children had run in packs around the edges of milling adults until they collapsed from exhaustion. They had been carried off to bed by parents or older siblings. Omorede's lack of restraint had not been helped by the fact that his Uncle Gisa had called a three-day holiday, for the entire House, in honor of Bantu's return. While Bantu had allowed a small dash of hope to live in his heart, tucked away deeply, that his people would accept him, he knew that the difficult part of his return had not even begun. If he remembered anything clearly it was that, when it came to the Mfundade, it would not be long before it began. The main question was whether he was ready followed closely by whether he could keep his parent's House from being pulled into war.

Bantu turned at the sound of soft footfalls behind him. A young woman, in the colors of the House, her feet bare, her head slightly bowed, with thick, intricate braids, glistening with fragrant oil, walked over to him with a steaming cup of what had to be Juma, balanced on a polished silver tray with delicate ivory handles. Juma was a strong, spiced tea similar to choca. It would wake a person just as well as the dark brew he had grown so accustomed to in Alexandria. In fact, juma was a bit stronger than choca in that respect. With a bow of his head he accepted the cup. "Thank you, cousin."

The young woman bowed lower when he spoke, managing to whisper, "You honor me, First Born. My family stands far from the center of the House, yet it is my honor to serve in the Seat of Omorede."

Bantu had been gone so long that he was only just beginning to remember the many shades of propriety that held sway in Al'akaz. To call someone *cousin* was to share a kind of intimacy with them. Though everyone in Omorede was technically related, the lines of the family were so old, ran so broadly, that the claim of relation for most was a tenuous one. The woman might well be his cousin some twenty times removed, which in Alexandria would not have made them related at all. So, in her eyes being called cousin by him was an honor. Bantu smiled, mostly to himself, as he stared into his cup. "Nevertheless, cousin, I give you thanks for serving me. I am sure you would much rather be sleeping. So, I give my first command as Son of this House. Back to bed with you. And if anyone asks, tell them I sent you to it."

Breathlessly, the young woman bowed deeply, saying, "Again, I thank you First Born. As you have commanded, so shall it be." When the woman moved Bantu was reminded of another of the eccentricities of his people. The young woman lifted her robes out of the way of her feet, turned on her heel, and ran. When the First members of a House gave a command, the lesser members ran to obey it, often literally. Before Bantu could open his mouth, to tell the young woman she could walk, she was already through the open entryway leading back into the House. He would have to be more careful with his words.

The juma had been sweetened. There was a natural hint of orange to its taste. It was delicious. Bantu blew on it to cool the liquid a bit. It was just what he needed. Taking a sip, he turned back to the sunrise. His head was still throbbing this morning, but it was less of a hindrance. Absently, he wondered why the gift had not affected it. Ignoring the pain, pushing it to the back of his mind, Bantu gazed on a sky filled with shades of purple, matched by an explosion of blues. There was even orange, which faded into reddish-gold as the sun climbed fully into view. When he noticed his cup was empty, he began walking along the railing, which enclosed the veranda. He followed it as it wound its way along the outside of the cluster of buildings that made up the Seat of House

Omorede. Bantu took in the smells, along with the sights, reacquainting himself with the place he had grown up in. For a time, he lost himself in those senses even as he faintly recalled some of the sounds of the place. He was able to forget, momentarily, what had brought him back to the Beautiful Land. Though no one came out onto the veranda to disturb him he knew the House had begun to rise from its brief slumber. Through floor-to-ceiling glass windows, which dotted the exterior wall of the house, he could see activity as sunrise gave way to early morning. Bantu leaned forward placing his free hand on the blue railing. He turned a deaf ear to the sounds coming from the inside. All he wanted to do was enjoy the peace of the morning, accentuated by his cup of juma, before the day invaded.

Bantu lost himself in the early morning. He was so unaware of the passage of time that, unbeknownst to him, early morning became full morning. Only when he heard more footsteps behind him did he focus his eyes on the horizon to check the height of the sun in the sky. He did not turn even as the sound of the footfalls made it clear that it was a large man behind him. While he continued to look out at the view, the man stepped up next to him. He stood quietly looking out in the same direction as Bantu. It took a moment for Bantu to realize that he was waiting for permission to speak. Turning his head Bantu saw that it was Mandisa standing next to him, waiting patiently. The man's head was freshly shaved just like his own. The black robes that Mandisa wore were freshly pressed. There was a hint of musk, which Bantu had not smelled since he was a boy. He had no Yari in his hand, as weapons were not carried in the House proper. But even weaponless the man would be deadly. The very word, Mfunde, meant *weapon* in the First Tongue. Men were the weapons a House wielded while women were its heart. Mfundishi meant *great weapon*, while Mfundade meant *weaponmasters*. These men were deadly with or without other weapons in their hands.

Bantu turned back to the scenery he had been gazing at as he said, "The peace of the Ancient be upon you, Mfundishi." It was the old greeting.

The man responded in his deep, resonant, baritone. "And also you, First Born."

Bantu continued, "I take it you have something that needs saying?"

Mandisa shifted his stance before saying, "Forgive the intrusion, First Born, but there is something that you should see."

Bantu sighed heavily. At least he had been blissfully undisturbed for a few hours before the madness began. But he had no doubt that what he had worried over, even more importantly, prepared for, was already underway. Turning toward the house, Bantu motioned for Mandisa to lead the way. The two walked back the way Bantu had traveled earlier along the veranda until they reached the entryway, which opened onto the veranda from the interior of the House. Turning into the House they strolled along the many hallways covered in dark, hardwood, flooring decorated lavishly with thick rugs, and multicolored cloth hangings on the paneled walls. They were accented with ivory carvings, complimented by painted mosaics. Here and there, clusters of bright, bundled, flowers burst from serpentine glass or polished silver vases with inlaid gems. The House was immaculate. The floors seemed clean enough to eat off while the air held a just polished scent. As they passed other members of the House the people stopped to bow to Bantu. It was just an inclination of the head rather than the full bow that was the custom back across the Macca Deep. Bantu gave one of the young women his empty cup along with a broad smile causing her to bow even more deeply than the rest. It was difficult to tell who stood where in the family line since no one wore what could have been considered livery, only robes in the colors of the House. This was only one of the eccentricities of Al'akaz.

Eventually Bantu, with Mandisa at his side, arrived at the entryway in the very front of the House. Standing there in the open air of the high-ceilinged entrance were the Blossoms standing in front of three men in black robes with gold trim. *So*, Bantu thought, *it begins*. But as Bantu and Mandisa came to stand in front of the black-robed visitors Bantu noticed that something was wrong. Isabelle and Bella stood off to the side grinning like the cat that ate the mouse. One of them had her arms folded across her chest while the other, with one hip jutting out, had her hand propped on it. Wen was looking straight ahead refusing to make eye contact. Just then Bantu noticed that one of the visiting Mfundishi looked like he had been attacked. The man's left eye was starting to swell. Blood trickled from his nose. When Bantu looked closer he could see that his lower lip was cut. The man stood tall, with his chest out, trying to look like nothing had happened. Bantu grunted to himself, sticking his thumbs behind his buckle, he hitched at his belt. Neither he, nor the Blossoms, had changed from their Company black. When he had risen from his sleep he had found his uniform cleaned, pressed, and neatly folded on the seat of a chair in his room. Looking at the Blossoms' uniforms, he noted that it appeared theirs had received the same treatment.

Bantu ignored the Mfundishi standing before him who, by custom, could not speak to him until he had spoken to them first. Instead he turned his attention to the Quiet Blossoms. Adding a slight edge to his voice he said, "Blossoms, attend me." At that word, the smiles that had been pulling at Isabelle and Bella's mouths disappeared. The three of them stalked across the marble floor of the entryway like lionesses. They lined up in front of Bantu, standing at attention. Each of them picked a spot just over Bantu's left shoulder to stare at. Bantu looked down the small line at each of the women in turn. While none of them had a mark on her it was clear who had been in the altercation. Without calling her name, Bantu said, "Explain."

Taking a single deep breath, with the other two women looking more like accomplices who had been caught than cats who had just had a treat, Wen began to speak in a slow laborious voice. "Sir, when we rose this morning, after bathing, and dressing, we ran into Jamila, who was leaving for her House. She told us that someone would come to the entrance of the House this morning, looking for you, in order to accuse you of something. She said we had the right to defend your honor since the Company could rightly be considered an outlanders Corral and we its Mfundishi. She said that if we wished we could guard the entrance in anticipation of their arrival." Wen looked over toward the visitors for a brief instant before going back to looking at the imaginary spot over Bantu's left shoulder. "These Mfundishi arrived an hour past demanding to see you. I did not think they were speaking about you with proper respect. When I told them so, they waved us away as though we were a nuisance. They then attempted to enter the House. That one," here she pointed to the man with the bruised face, "tried to put his hands on me as I stepped between them and the entryway. I showed him the error of his ways. It was at that point that Mandisa showed up with a handful of Omorede Mfunde. They escorted the Mfundishi into the entryway."

Jamila. Bantu could have shaken the woman, would have shaken her, had she still been around. She had put the fool notion into the heads of the Blossoms that they should act like members of a Corral guarding *The Way*. Likely the Mfunde, who should have been at the door, had given way to these women who were dressed like the First Born wearing the black of the Mfundishi. Jamila was gone so he would have to deal with her at another time. While he had words to say to the Blossoms he would not do it in front of others. Looking at each woman in turn Bantu said, "You will return to the quarters you have been assigned. Await me there. Dismissed."

The three women looked directly at Bantu then. They would have spoken had they not seen the look on his face. As it was they only mustered a sorry sounding, "Yes sir, Commander," before making their way down one of the halls off the main hallway. When the three women disappeared around the corner Bantu turned back to where the visiting Mfundishi stood waiting, trying to look as dignified as they could.

"I think that maybe, in the future, you will remember your training in the Corral. You will not underestimate an opponent, regardless of how they look." Mandisa snorted derisively as Bantu spoke. The visiting Mfundishi stiffened as though they had been physically hit. In Al'akaz honor was everything — at least to most. Had they not been in the heart of Omorede, Bantu's words would have been cause for Challenge. As it was the men simply stifled their tongues albeit with tremendous effort.

Bantu continued with his less than gracious tone. For years he had determined that when he came home to face this he would do it without any attempt at courtesy toward his adversaries. Besides, they had insulted the Blossoms, which was cause for him to handle them roughly. "So, you have come running on the end of N'duma's leash. Let me guess, to tell me I am summoned to the Corral."

They were not really questions, nor were they polite. Bantu wondered if the men had been as fair-skinned as the Alexandrians he had lived among for so many years if their faces would be bright red. All three had looks of barely contained outrage on their faces. It was not helped by the fact that Mandisa stood off to the side grinning at them like an idiot. They were being embarrassed in front of witnesses. In Al'akaz, that was dangerous. It was as dangerous as slapping a man in the face in any other land.

One of the men, the one Wen had battered, opened his mouth to speak but Bantu cut him off. "I have neither given you the ritual greeting, nor permission to speak! I know what you scurrilous jackdaws have come for. Go and tell your cowardly master that the Son of Omorede will attend the Corral, today. I will not be summoned, nor escorted, like a prisoner. I will come as I am. Now go, before I have the Mfundade of the House beat you to the edge of Omorede!"

The three men looked as if they would explode standing there in the entryway swaying with outrage. When they did not move immediately, Mandisa took a step toward them hissing through his teeth. He whistled loudly. Down the various hallways that split from the head of the entryway Bantu saw heads pop out of doorways. When they did they turned to look quickly in the direction of the whistling. In seconds those halls began to fill with Mfunde in flowing blue and white robes. Bantu saw two Mfundishi of the House, who had been strolling by, outside the front entrance, stop at the sound of Mandisa's whistle. They walked slowly through the entryway. Since they were not fully in the heart of the House they still held their yari. Mandisa looked at the three visitors. He spoke with a voice full of scorn. "It would be my pleasure to *escort* you N'kosi lapdogs to the edge of Omorede. So please, be so kind as to disregard the command the First of the House has just given you, for just a few seconds more, so that I may feel justified in doing so."

Looking around them, as the entryway filled with Mfunde and Mfundishi of the House, all of whom were looking expectantly from

Bantu to Mandisa, to the visitors, the men considered their position. The visiting Mfundishi snapped out of their rage-fueled stupor. Slowly, they began edging toward the entryway. When one of them opened his mouth to say something Mandisa cut him off sharply. "If you utter a single syllable that dishonors the First Born of this House, Odujuba, you will not make it back to House Gamba alive." The man snapped his mouth shut. The three of them turned toward the entrance trying not to look like they were hurrying.

Mandisa caught the eye of the two Mfundishi, of Omorede, who had come through the front entrance. "Calduma, Issadada, please gather a Hand of Mfunde. Follow those sniveling excuses for Mfundishi until they have left Omorede." The two, tall, older men bowed their shaven heads to Mandisa. Pointing to five Mfunde, who fell in behind them, they trotted through the entrance heading in the direction the visitors had gone. When the seven Mfundade exited the House the rest of the Mfundade of Omorede went back to whatever they had been doing before Mandisa's whistle had brought them to the entryway. Watching them go Bantu took a deep breath to calm himself. When he turned back from looking down one of the hallways he saw Mandisa looking at him with a hint of concern in his eyes.

Bantu said, "Speak, Mfundishi."

Mandisa spoke in a low voice that did not carry past Bantu. "Forgive, First Born. But is it wise to go to the Corral? They are surely waiting to hatch some scheme meant to ensnare you. I am sorry to say that the Corral is not what it was when your father sat in the Hall of Masters. N'duma has become the Baba'funde. Much has changed. Maybe we should wait until we can gather enough strength around Omorede to take on the N'kosi and their allies?"

Bantu reached out to place his hand on Mandisa's shoulder. He had only known Bantu for a day but was ready to fight a war for him. "No, cousin. I would not plunge Omorede, along with its allies, into such a conflict. It would cripple most of the Houses. Who knows who would benefit from that? No, I have prepared for this since the night my parents placed me in that boat. I will either be up to the task or I will not.

What you can do is pick an appropriate Honor Guard to accompany me to the Corral. We leave within the hour."

With a bow of his head Mandisa said, "As you command, First Born. Within the hour. My honor is to serve." The man turned from Bantu to stroll down one of the halls. His black robes flowed behind him as their hem skirted the floor. He went to gather the guard Bantu had asked for. He moved with the ease of a man who knew how to handle himself. Bantu watched him go. It struck him how much Mandisa looked like him. The man was a cousin but must have been from a near line of the family. As Mandisa disappeared around a corner Bantu rubbed at the bridge of his nose with the thumb and forefinger of his right hand trying to coax away the dull throbbing in his head. If this kept up he would need to try to find some kind of remedy. His problem was that he could not afford to tell anyone about the headaches. They would certainly try to stop him from going forward with the *Challenge*. He could not afford to give his enemies more time to organize. If he was going to be successful, while keeping Omorede out of a conflagration that would engulf all of the Great Houses, he would have to go forward now. Sighing heavily, he turned back toward the inner recesses of the House. There were a few things to do before he could leave for the Corral. Turning down the hall he thought would lead him to the sleeping quarters he spoke to the throbbing in his head while he walked. *Please go away.*

†

A trip that should have taken weeks by horseback had taken only hours. Cordovan had been able to call on the assistance of the Peoples Company given the prey they were chasing. He, Aubrey, and Dain Du'urdin had been dropped off in the deep woods, a few miles south of Gaul, by one of the Pradas. While the reddish-brown colored creatures were breathtaking to look at, they were also a bit scary. But the colossal mass of feathers, talons, and avian muscle had carried them hundreds of miles in only a few hours. For that, Cordovan was grateful. He had told the Mountain Feather as much. The woman had flashed him a lovely smile before scampering nimbly up the rope ladder to her perch behind the giant bird's neck. They had watched the glorious creature crouch, coiling powerful muscles, before leaping into the air, buffeting them with a rush of wind mixed with loose debris blown up from the ground. Flying nearly straight up in tight, sky-grabbing circles the great bird angled sharply, this way and that, before it finally turned south just moments before disappearing into the clouds.

The rest of the journey to Gaul was quite uneventful. The terrain was rolling hill country. The trees were mostly Alwaysgreens matched by Thatchnettle, while the grasses ran to knee-high. The towns in the northcountry of Province were often nestled in the hills surrounded by dense forest. They had been built in the difficult to reach regions as a way of making them more secure. While the towns could be reached by horseback it was more than a notion to try bringing siege equipment into those guarded recesses. The hills became part of the defensive structure of many of the towns. Gaul was one of those cities on the northernmost border of Province. It seemed to sprout from the ground in those foothills. Gaul sat on a rise where several hilltops met surrounded by a thick forest of Alwaysgreens. The landscape was beautiful. The walk to Gaul was not. It was almost entirely uphill for several miles from their landing site. When they reached the city, they located lodging in one of its taverns, a place called the *Lucky Cock*. It had a wooden sign hanging above the door with a rooster painted on it that was still mostly red albeit faded.

After putting their things away in their rooms, the three of them met in the tavern's mainroom to discuss their strategy. Cordovan had decided that they needed to get as much information as they could about the area surrounding the valley, which was located to the north of the city, before attempting to find Gaiden Colling. Dain Du'urdin was convinced that the three of them should troll the many taverns that Gaul held seeking that information. Given that they had planned to stop off in Gaul, which was a major city in Province, Cordovan and Aubrey had changed out of their Watchmen uniforms on the flight over. They were dressed as any other well-to-do travelers. Cordovan wore light blue breeches with a matching blue vest, along with a brown shirt, boots, and cloak. Aubrey wore black boots, a matching cloak, and dark, green breeches, with a bright, white shirt. Dain Du'urdin was the only one wearing what he had worn when they left Alexandria.

It was several hours past midnight when the three returned to the Cock. They took a table in the far corner of the mainroom near the roaring fireplace. Province was a good deal further north. It was also colder than Alexandria. The clothing they had changed into was mostly wool. Their hooded cloaks were lined with fur but the warmth from the fireplace was still delicious. Most of the customers had left. But there were still a few waitresses about serving the few remaining occupied tables. They were clearly preparing to close down for the night. Yet the place still managed to smell like baking bread with a hint of garlic butter. The women were wiping tables or mopping the floor. One of them dropped her hand towel in a sudsy bucket before making her way to their table. She dried her hands on the hem of her apron as she crossed the room. Cordovan gave her his winning smile. He ordered wine for the three of them. The young girl smiled back at him. She added a bit of swing to her hips as she went to the bar to get their order. After watching her go Cordovan turned his attention to Dain Du'urdin who was sitting across from him. Aubrey brooded in silence where he sat on Cordovan's left.

Dain Du'urdin was near to seething in his seat. His lips were pressed together tightly. He kept glancing over his shoulder at the door as if expecting someone to burst in at any moment. Aubrey, whom Cordovan had sent with Du'urdin to keep an eye on him, looked put upon. The young man sat with his back straight. He assiduously avoided the cool looks Du'urdin cast his way between glances at the door. Something had obviously happened between the two of them. While they had other more pressing matters Cordovan knew he would have to smooth over whatever had the two men's feathers ruffled if they were going to get anything else done. Taking a deep breath, he looked over at Dain Du'urdin opening his mouth to ask him about whatever had happened.

Before he could get a single word out Dain Du'urdin launched into a hushed explanation.

"You Watchmen are fools! No, no, don't try to take issue with what I am saying. I understand what motivates you but sometimes you have to be able to overlook the immediate problem so that you can affect the larger one." Du'urdin glanced again, nervously, at the door to the tavern.

Cordovan spoke into the pause Du'urdin had taken. "I haven't a clue what you are talking about man. Calm yourself and spit it out." His nervous gesticulating was beginning to rub off on Cordovan. He did not like it.

Du'urdin jabbed a stubby, singular, finger at Aubrey saying, "That hot-headed, half-baked excuse for a Watchman there forgot he was not in Alexandria. That is what I am talking about!"

As Du'urdin's words washed over Cordovan he had a sinking feeling in his gut. What had the newly minted Watchman done? With a quick sidelong glance at Aubrey, who was looking at his hands while twiddling his thumbs, Cordovan turned back to Dain Du'urdin. "What happened? Quickly, man!"

Du'urdin detailed a brief account of a woman being attacked in an alley they had been passing. He described how he had tried to dissuade Aubrey from getting involved but Aubrey had waded into the thick of it anyway. The consequence was that there were three dead men, a grateful shopkeeper, along with a tremendous racket, which they had left behind them. When he finished recounting the events that had him on edge he glanced at the door again.

Cordovan rubbed his hand across his chin while his mind raced. Were there witnesses? Were they followed? Did the woman report the attack? How long did they have before someone came calling, looking for two men who fit Du'urdin and Aubrey's description? The problem was that Du'urdin was a man with a distinctive look, thanks to his prodigious vanity, his well-cut clothes, and his odd little mustache. Aubrey was an additional, if different, problem. In Alexandria, he was tall but not unusually so. In Gaul, where men were generally smaller, he stood out as rare, even exceptional. If there had been a witness, or the city guard had questioned the woman, it would not be too difficult to find them.

Cordovan nearly cursed. To compound the problem there were the less than stellar results from their information gathering.

Shaking his head, with a sigh, Cordovan lean forward, placing his folded arms on the table. Quietly, he said, "While that is lamentable, and the subject of a later discussion between Aubrey and I, it would not be so much of a problem if it were not for the fact that I found nothing." He had gone in one direction while Aubrey, with Du'urdin in tow, had gone in another. They had all followed the same plan in each establishment they had entered. They found seats near the largest crowds. Slowly, they eased their way into buying people drinks. Over the course of the evening they were to steer the conversation toward talk of the best routes for travel to the north while surreptitiously inquiring after any trouble they might need to avoid. Cordovan had heard about everything from brigands, to poison ivy, but not a single word about anything unusual or out of the ordinary.

Du'urdin nodded sympathetically but said nothing as he continued to snatch quick looks at the door. Cordovan's mind raced. They would have to travel north blind. Given what had happened they would almost certainly need to leave immediately. Aubrey would need a good talking to. While his instincts could not be argued with his decision-making would need some scrutiny. Although, the more Cordovan thought about it the more he realized he might very well – no, scratch that - *would* have very likely made the same decision Aubrey had made. Though Cordovan would have made sure to send Du'urdin away so that he could have spent time being seen in another part of the city before returning to their lodging. These were things he would be covering with Aubrey. Nevertheless, it was a problem they would deal with when they had more time.

Turning his mind back to the information they did not have he thought that if they were very careful as they traveled north they could spot any surprises before they walked into them. As he thought the problem through the young woman returned with three cups and a bottle of wine. Filling each cup, she placed the bottle, with a bright smile, in front of Cordovan. Digging in his pouch he flipped her a gold piece.

Snatching it from the air with a practiced deftness she quickly deposited it in her blouse. Had Cordovan been other than who he was he would have had some company warming his bed tonight. But Watchmen did not conduct themselves in that way. Not that they were forbidden love, or the company of a woman, but they were very careful about the way in which they went about such things. It could never be a case in which it even appeared that the woman was being used. Cordovan would not have been able to be sure if the woman was in his bed because she wanted to be or because of the coin. Still, he was a man, so he watched her admiringly for a moment as she walked away, her hips still swaying a little more than they needed to.

While Cordovan considered their problem Dain Du'urdin was busy considering his cup of wine followed by the door. Aubrey, who had been quiet until now spoke. In a few years, his voice would deepen subtly taking on a more sonorous texture but for now it was a high, if strong, tenor. He had apparently been thinking over his own quandary. "There is actually another problem that needs to be discussed. Where are the vagrants?"

At first Cordovan was confused by the question. Turning to his left to look more directly at his charge he said, "What do you mean Aubrey?"

The young man leaned forward steepling his fingers together with his elbows on the table. His forehead was slightly furrowed. He spoke as if his subject was the most important of the issues they were confronting tonight. "I mean, I have had the opportunity to visit some decent sized cities with my father as I was growing up. Everywhere we went there were always people on the streets. Some of them were without a single copper to their name. They slept in doorways. Then there were others, who were passing through on their way to other places but were just as indigent. There were always parentless children, women selling their bodies, former soldiers who had been so severely wounded that they were left to beg for a meal. That last always made my father so angry he could burst. But my point is that we have walked through the streets of Gaul for hours, in the middle of the night, but with the singular exception of the woman I saved there were no signs of any people at all living in the streets."

Aubrey looked from Cordovan to Du'urdin and back to Cordovan again. Dain Du'urdin, still pursing his lips, said it before Cordovan could. "Master Watchman, your young pupil, while troubled by a lack of wisdom is some matters, is, in this respect, quite perceptive. I must grudgingly admit that I had wondered at that same state of affairs but seeing as he and I only visited one establishment tonight I felt I did not have enough evidence to draw a conclusion."

Cordovan looked at Du'urdin pointedly making note of the fact that the man had just said they had only visited one tavern while Cordovan had been to more than he could remember. But what he said was, "Now that I think about it Aubrey, you are right. It is very odd. I don't ever recall any reports on Province that mentioned a renewed concern for the poor. That may mean that something else is happening here. The problem is that it is not, at present, *our* problem. At another time we might be able to investigate it but as it is we have more pressing concerns like the fact that we have nothing in the way of information. It may also be the case that someone is looking for the two of you even as we speak."

Cordovan forgot about the other problems they were currently facing when Dain Du'urdin said, "I think we may have something."

Cordovan looked across the table at him. Du'urdin was sniffing lightly at his cup, spinning it around in his hand as he looked over at the door, ignoring the rest of the wine tasting ritual that he knew the man normally took pleasure in. He watched Du'urdin absently take a sip of the wine before placing the cup on the table in front of him. Du'urdin looked slowly around the room in a causal way, calculated not to draw attention, in order to ensure that none of the handful of people remaining in the mainroom were paying them any particular attention. Then, in a normal voice, sitting with a regular posture he shared the information he had gathered from the one stop he and Aubrey had made. He did not whisper, nor did he lean forward conspiratorially, since both of those things tended to shout to other people that something of interest was being said. But he did keep his voice low. While sitting near the fireplace in a bar called the Rugged Roost, Du'urdin had overheard a handful of rough looking men who had been run out of the woods to the north by what they had referred to as *strange, dark creatures*. They were doubtless brigands who made their living attacking unguarded travelers but had been unable to ply their trade for months because of dark things that had taken up residence in the wood around Gaul. Du'urdin had waited for an opportune moment to buy them a round of drinks under the pretense of being a merchant who needed to know the safest routes through the northcountry. In this way he had been able to determine the general area where the, so-called, dark things haunted the night.

Taking another drink from his cup of wine Du'urdin said, "As far as I can determine, the area the men were talking about seems to be in close proximity to the valley. I think we can safely say that we are on the right track."

With his hand covering the mouth of his cup, Cordovan swirled it around slowly as he considered what Du'urdin had said. It was at that moment he heard a man, who had just entered the tavern with four soldiers in tow, say, "I have never been much of a fan of serendipity but tonight may make me change my mind. Well, well, well if it isn't Dain Du'urdin. It has been far, far, too long Inquisitor. I am so glad to see you again."

Cordovan looked at Du'urdin who had stopped his cup halfway to his mouth at the sound of the man's voice. He watched Du'urdin sigh heavily, place the cup back on the table, and turn to face the man by the door who had just spoken his name. Cordovan did not move but looked the man over. He was average height for the men of Gaul, which made him a few ticks short of six feet. His hair was brown with a hint of gray, his eyes were steel blue, and his skin wind-weathered. His nose was large, though sharply curved, complementing his oversized square jaw. But what Cordovan took note of was the green longcoat he wore. There were gold leaves embroidered around the cuffs. Cordovan knew precisely what that meant. *Inquisitors.*

The man strolled leisurely over stopping to stand just a few feet from their table. The four, slightly larger, men in the blue and red of Province's Legion, spread out behind him. One of them held a loaded crossbow at the ready. The others had hands on the swords hanging from their belts.

The man aiming the crossbow was a problem. Cordovan was fast but not that fast. The Inquisitor pulled off green suede gloves, slapping them together in his hand. He slid them behind his rust-brown leather belt. The large, gold buckle was shaped like an eye with a curtain of stars hanging across it. The sound of the man's voice said he was full of himself. He had caught a prize, so he wanted to gloat. He must have dismissed Cordovan and Aubrey as hired help because his full attention was on Dain Du'urdin.

The voice was an oily baritone. He over pronounced each word, which placed him from Glauchshire not Gaul. The man spoke as if he were in love with the sound of his own voice. Cordovan almost laughed because it was the same way Dain Du'urdin spoke. The Inquisitor said, "I am shocked but delighted." He pointed an accusatory finger at Du'urdin. "What happened to you? Has your mind gone to mush? Have you drunk yourself into a fool's stupor? Ha!" The man gestured with his hand, brushing aside the thoughts as if they were immaterial. Stepping closer he continued, "The Dain Du'urdin who walked the heights of the Inquistorim would never be so clumsy as this! I am almost disappointed. Almost." His voice dropped slightly becoming cooler. What he said next had the sound of an oft repeated formula being spoken, "Note: You came back to Province. Note two: You got involved in a street dispute that you knew would be reported to the city guard. Note three: You did not shave off that ridiculous mustache. You see I was preparing to go home for the night when a report came across my desk with the description of a couple of strangers who had saved a shopkeeper on her way home from being attacked. I might have left it until morning but the description of one of the men caught my eye. His voice, his mannerisms, matched with the ridiculous mustache that the woman described. Conclusion: While I thought it highly unlikely that the man was who I hoped he was I had to see for myself. And wonder of wonders, here we are! You, like a fool, anywhere near Province again, and me with you in my grasp!"

The man was rubbing his hands together with glee as he looked at Dain Du'urdin. Cordovan had only known the overall arch of Du'urdin's story. He had never asked the man what had actually happened that prompted him to leave off being an Inquisitor. Or why he chose to come to Alexandria. Apparently, it had been something very serious if his former colleagues wanted to get their hands on him this badly. To his credit, while he had looked at the door nervously earlier, Du'urdin now looked at the Inquisitor with a kind of contempt. His voice was firm, tinged with a hint of disdain, as he spoke. "Keril Alcotovish. I am shocked, even amazed, that the Inquisitorim promoted you. That you have been given the *Golden Leaves* is an affirmation of my decision to remove the Green Coat. I am further reassured of the rightness of my decision given that you, like so many of my former colleagues, still lack the gift of observation essential to a real truth seeker."

Keril Alcotovish laughed at Du'urdin's words. But Cordovan noted that the laughter rang a bit hollow. The man began, surreptitiously, looking around him trying to assertain what he had missed. Unlike Keril Alcotovish, Dain Du'urdin's chuckle was quite convincing. Du'urdin said, "Keril, my grandmother had a saying, *if it had been a snake, it would have bitten you.* You came believing that a handful of the Legion would be sufficient to bring me to justice. But if you saw the world, as an Inquisitor should, if you thought things through, you might have asked the right questions. Note: Would Dain Du'urdin return to Province unprotected? Note two: Why would he not be in disguise? Note three: Why would two men be a sufficient guard? Conclusion?"

Du'urdin finished, leaving what was undoubtedly an Inquisitor's formula incomplete with one eyebrow arched, daring Alcotovish to finish it. Keril Alcotovish looked pointedly at Cordovan and Aubrey. Dain Du'urdin laughed, a full-bellied laugh, as he said, "You came too lightly Keril. You came thinking you had kittens in your grasp. But instead you have grabbed tigers by the tail. And as usual, you will not work this out without help, so I will tell you what your eyes are too cloudy, and your mind too dull, to reveal to you. They are Watchmen." Cordovan cursed while Dain Du'urdin leaned back in his chair laughing even louder. It all happened at once. Cordovan thought it would begin with a crossbow bolt in either his chest or Aubrey's. Keril Alcotovish's eyes widened. Cordovan shoved Aubrey, who tried to throw himself out of the booth so that Cordovan could rise from his seat, while both of them watched the legionnaire with the crossbow steady his aim as he prepared to fire. But just before the man could pull the trigger the loud clanging sound of a pot rang out. The man holding the crossbow crumpled to floor revealing the tiny barmaid behind him smiling brightly with a heavy, black skillet in her hands. Looking at Cordovan she winked. The Inquisitor shouted at the legionnaires behind him, but Cordovan and Aubrey were already among them.

They had their swords drawn before they cleared their seats but that wasn't enough. The gift that was imparted during the rite that made them Watchmen made them stronger and faster than other men. Before they could fall on the Watchmen, Cordovan and Aubrey were out of their seats with their own swords drawn. After that it was almost academic. The problem with everyday soldiers was that they were not really given the time or access to training that would allow them to become truly competent swordsmen. Most were only ever given enough instruction to be adequate. They usually had enough skill to take on local ruffians or an opposing army when it came to a full-scale battle with thousands of other barely trained men across from them. But when they had to face men who had the luxury of real training with a sword they were usually outmatched. In those instances, they had to rely on numbers. Faced with the skill level of Watchmen they lasted only seconds.

Turning from the bodies at his feet Cordovan saw Dain Du'urdin standing over Keril Alcotovish. He was wiping blood off a very large knife onto the Inquisitor's green coat. With a flourish he made the knife disappear beneath his coat. While Cordovan did not know everything about Dain Du'urdin, he had always known that the man was not as helpless as he let on. Cordovan cleaned his own sword before sliding it back into its scabbard. He heard Dain Du'urdin say, as if repeating some ancient quote, "Enemies never forgive, friends never forget."

Cordovan stood there for a few seconds allowing Dain Du'urdin his moment. After a few breaths the former Inquisitor looked up from the body at his feet. "I think it would be judicious of us to find our night's sleep outside the city walls."

Cordovan nodded his agreement. Sending the other two men up the stairs to recover their things Cordovan watched the street from the door. While they were gone he had time to thank the barmaid. She had sauntered over to him when the other two had made their way up the stairs. Smiling down at her, Cordovan said, "And just what were you thinking little miss? You could have gotten yourself hurt."

Shaking her head, she said, "No, my lord. You were not going to let anything happen to Maylelle. Is it true that you and the young master be Watchmen?"

With a deep sigh, against his better judgment, Cordovan said, "Yes little miss. We are members of the Watch. But you still have not answered my question. Why did you do it?"

The little woman laughed brightly as she said, "There do be too few men who know how to tip well. I was not about to let them hurt my best customer of the week."

Cordovan could not stop himself from laughing along with the woman. After a moment he spoke soberly to Maylelle. "Listen carefully Maylelle." Cordovan placed several more gold coins in her hand. It probably added up to more than the woman would see in a year. "I would prefer that you take this coin and leave. I would not want you to be hurt because of what you did here tonight."

Maylelle nodded soberly as Cordovan spoke. She whistled low when she saw the amount of coin he had placed in her hand. Then she smiled that bright smile at him again saying, "Not to worry my lord. Alls I have to do is give some of this to the other girls that were working tonight. They will forget that Maylelle had anything to do with it. Not to worry!"

Cordovan touched her lightly on the tip of her nose with his finger. "I hope you are right Maylelle. The Inquisitor's will want answers when they arrive. Tell them everything about us that they wish to know. We will be out of their reach, so it will not matter." She nodded solemnly before hurrying to the kitchen where the other barmaids had retreated when the soldiers had entered the mainroom. Cordovan smiled after her as she went. It was that kind of courage, often found in the most unlikely places, which inspired him to keep standing to the Watch in the face of so much of the ugliness in the world. He hoped she would be all right.

When the two men returned with their things Cordovan hurried them all out the back of the tavern. He left the establishment's patron with some extra coin for any damages. While they made their way out into the darkness Cordovan considered how they would get the city guard to open the gate. He also thought about the words Dain Du'urdin had spoken over his former colleague. He had never heard the man speak truer words.

To live, we first must die.

~*Inscription above the entrance to the Corral of Al'akaz.*

Anger brings war, serenity victory.

- Shamansara Amandala A' Omorede

CHAPTER TWENTY-ONE

As deep as the Wadi

Standing in the hall outside the room the Quiet Blossoms had been given Bantu paused for a moment. He looked down the hall to be sure he was in the right place before rapping his knuckles on the door. A voice, muffled by the door, responded, "Come in." Lifting the slender, gilded, silver door handle, which curved downward from the center of the door like an arched finger, Bantu listened for the telltale click of the latch releasing. He pushed the heavy door open. The darkwood door, which was likely stained mahogany, swung open on well-oiled silver hinges. Stepping into the room Bantu looked around at the spacious sleeping quarters. The room was rectangular with three large, oval windows opposite the door. Each of them had a view facing east. Sunlight poured into the room brightening its furthest recesses. Heavy, plush rugs in blue, green, and silver covered the hardwood floors. *More mahogany, or teak?* Thick tapestries decorated the walls where there were no windows. To Bantu's left were three medium-sized beds arranged like an opening fan. One of them had Bella reclining on it, with her hands behind her head, and her eyes closed, though Bantu knew she was not asleep. She had the same coloring as her older sister Wen, but her temperament was completely different. Where Wen had gray eyes, Bella had deep green. She was also a few inches taller than Wen.

There was a large table to his right. It had several comfy chairs covered in blue silk with tiny, white blossoms budding from curving vines running along their edges. Isabelle occupied one of those chairs. She sat there sipping the heavy spiced tea called juma. Lieutenant Isabelle Erinelle Lelange was the tallest of the three women not to mention the youngest. Isabelle was willowy without being frail. She curved slightly in all the right places. Isabelle turned a head or two even in her Company uniform. The problem was, here Bantu smiled, while love was not prohibited among the ranks it took a man of exemplary courage to court a Quiet Blossom. It did not help matters that Isabelle moved like a Morsasa dancer. The Morsasa were scandalous by most standards. Only the traveling Borsas, in their rickety wagons, with their aimless lifestyle, thought the Morsasa relatively tame. Isabelle was one of those rare women who, in Bantu's opinion, looked just as beautiful with short hair as she would with long. It was a little less than the length of a finger. It was a glossy raven-black. The layered curls looked like feathers. Today she wore it, as she did most days, brushed back until it was flat on the sides but still wavy, sticking up in spiked curls on top. It was striking. Her eyes were just as black as her hair giving her an intensity when she was concentrating. The oddity was that Isabelle had a very quiet, unassuming, demeanor. She was a natural with the longsword. Underestimating her, given her demeanor, could get you killed. There was a reason she was a member of his Master Class.

Directly across from Bantu, Wen was leaning forward with both hands resting on the windowsill of one of the large oval windows, gazing out on the scenery below. Wen was the senior officer among the three. Though not short, by most women's standards, she was the smallest of the three. Her fiery-red hair was pulled back into two large braids that hung behind each ear to just below her shoulders. Wen was excitable. There was a fiery temper underneath that fiery hair. She had broader hips than the other women but moved with the same deadly economy. With a smattering of freckles across the top of her nose most men would have thought her more than handsome enough. Though not the overtly pretty type, she was surely more than handsome. You had to look at Wen for a moment to realize that she was beautiful. While that is all most men would see, what Bantu liked most about her was the fact that she was extremely smart. There was a reason for the three silver pips shining brightly on her collar.

The room was aptly decorated with a few vases filled to overflowing with bouquets of pink flowers, accented by white ones, placed judiciously among them. The smell of hibiscus mixed with lilac filled the space. As the door clicked softly closed behind him Bantu strolled to the table where Isabelle was sitting, pulled back a chair with one hand, while motioning for a cup of juma with the other. Isabelle turned over a clean cup with her long, well-shaped fingers. She poured steaming juma from a delicate black-lacquered pot, which had a Balsam tree, in bloom, painted on its side. The cups matched the pot. When his cup was full Isabelle handed it to him with a warm smile on her slender face. For whatever reason, which Bantu had never been able to fully fathom, they loved waiting on him. He rarely gave them the chance but when he did allow it they seemed to relish it.

The chairs sitting around the large, heavy, wood table were actually large enough, plush enough, and designed well enough, so that one could either sit up straight at the table or recline back into the chair's recesses, which is what Bantu did as he sipped at his cup of juma. The quarters were emblematic of his House. They were extravagant while seeming somehow simple. They were elegant while quietly highlighting the beauty of things. Lounging in the chair, Bantu stretched his legs out under the table, crossing his ankles. After a long silence Wen turned from looking out the window. She put her hands on her ample hips as she spoke.

"Alright, alright. So maybe I should not have roughed him up. But I swear, Commander, he deserved every single hand I laid on him." She stood there looking at him with a slight slump to her shoulders mirrored by a pout on her slender lips. The People were rarely disobedient. Bantu only had trouble out of them when it came to judgments about his own safety. That being the case, it was usually difficult for him to stay angry with them for long. Craning his neck, to look around the room without moving in his seat, Bantu took note that both Bella and Isabelle were looking at him to see what his reaction would be. Turning back to Wen, he slowly allowed a smile to spread across his face as he said, "Ok. So maybe he deserved it. And *maybe* I enjoyed seeing that pitiful excuse for an Mfundishi embarrassed. But each of you needs to understand that in Al'akaz the rules are different. This is neither Alexandria nor any of the nations you are used to visiting. In the Beautiful Land, the wrong move, the wrong word, even a look, could thrust you waist deep into a blood feud or cause my family's House serious problems. So I need you to be very careful."

The women were all smiling now. Behind him Isabelle giggled like a little girl. Though she was usually quiet all of the Blossoms knew how to laugh. "Commander, you should have seen it! Wen was like lightning." Isabelle jumped around in her seat, throwing imaginary punches, as she reenacted the scuffle. She continued, "It was everything the man could do to keep from being thoroughly trounced. As it was she smacked him around so until I thought we were going to have to kill the lot of them. Luckily they had not come with those yari or it might have come to that."

Bantu sat there listening while sipping his tea. He did not move though he raised one eyebrow at Wen who at least had the decency to blush. When she opened her mouth, Bantu waved her off with his empty hand. Lowering his cup from his mouth he said, "I am glad you ladies could find some trouble to get into so soon. Now, in less than an hour I will be going to the Corral. You will accompany me as part of my honor guard. But I want to be clear that under no circumstances are you to so much as rub your nose without my express permission. We will be walking across the Abyss on a spiderweb. I do not intend to plunge Omorede into a war. Am I clear?"

With a single voice the women answered, "Yes sir."

Putting down his cup Bantu rose from his seat. "Good. Meet me in the entryway." With that he left the Blossom's guest quarters. Two turns along the hallway followed by a quick jaunt up one flight of stairs brought him to his own room. He closed the door behind him. It stirred the air in the room bringing the smell of lavender to his nose. Someone had put fresh flowers in his room. A pitcher, with ice floating in a dark red punch, sat on a side table. He walked to a small desk, nestled against the far wall, in front of one of the windows. The window opened onto a view of the gardens running along the northern side of the House. Someone, probably the servant who had brought in the punch, had opened that window allowing the smell of lavender to float up from the gardens below. The sight, accompanying the smell, was calm inducing. It helped him overlook the throbbing in his head. Sitting at the desk, Bantu pulled open a drawer. He found parchment, a curved metal quill, a bottle of blue ink, and a finger-length of blue wax. It took him a few minutes to write the three letters he needed but in short order they were finished, folded, and sealed. Unfastening the top buttons of his coat, he slid the three sealed letters into an inner pocket over his heart. Smiling to himself, at the appropriateness of that, he buttoned his coat up again. Looking over at the flowers decorating his room, breathing in the light aroma of lavender, he ran through the list in his head, checking off items. There was only one more thing left to do.

Rising from his seat at the desk he strolled quickly to the door. Bantu walked down three flights of stairs. Taking two rights along the main hallway he came to the *Hallowed Well* of the House. The door opened easily when Bantu pushed on it. He walked into what was essentially a gallery that lay at the very center of the House. It held the treasures of Omorede. The Hallowed Well ran half the length of the central building in the clustered structures that made up the House. The gallery was filled with glass cases holding scrolls, gemstones set in necklaces, assorted jewelry, and weapons resting on pedestals. Huge shelves contained books, maps, or large tomes, which held the genealogies of all of Omorede. Around the walls were body-shaped stands with the robes of historical figures of the family draped on them. Along one wall were racks, or stands, holding various valuable weapons. There was the blackwood bow wielded by Shallara Ada N' Omorede when the House was invaded by the Gamba a thousand years earlier. A few steps down the same wall was the knife used by Lalamadan Osa A' Omorede, in the game the people of Al'akaz called Yasa, in which he won back the honor of the House from Galla Ba A' Umbara five hundred years before that.

Just a few more steps down that wall was the item Bantu had come to find.

The case was chest high. It was a blackwood frame holding glass, trimmed in silver, adorned with filigree, just like all the others. Gently, Bantu opened it, pushing its glass lid up, until it leaned gently against the wall. Reaching down into the case he took a long, slim, black-lacquered, wood box in his hands. He lifted it out of the case as if it were fragile. Tucking it under one arm he lowered the glass lid back down until it was closed. Turning from the case he walked to the single empty table that stood in the center of the room placing the black-lacquered wood box on it. Running his fingers along its top he closed his eyes. Sitting there for a moment, he just let himself breathe. He ran his hand along the box. It was almost as if he could feel history there, in the gallery, with him. There were echoes of the past, what felt like the whispers of the long dead, floating around in the room. After a few more seconds he opened his eyes. Easily, gently, lovingly, Bantu pulled the lid of the box open. The black-lacquered container was lined with purple silk. There, nestled in a deep groove, made for the purpose of holding it, was the yari of his father.

Bantu let his fingers trace lightly over the weapon's lines. The blackwood, which came from the Balsam tree, was smooth to the touch. It glistened as if it had been polished. There was a slight curve to it, which he allowed his fingertips to trace. Some liked their yari carved with emblems, or writing in the ancient tongue, but this yari had none of those things. Its beauty came from the coloring of the wood, the delicacy of its curves, and the excellence of the craftsmanship, which had created it. When Bantu was a boy his father had shown him the weapon. All those many years ago Shamansara had told him that the yari was the oldest in the entire House. Some believed it was one of the first made thousands of years ago. It had been made with wood treated with an ancient craft, a way that had been lost to the passage of time. The steel of its blade had been made from *Skyrock*. Over the thousands of years of the existence of Al'akaz, from time to time, great rocks, in streaks of flame, fell from the heavens. When they could be located they were harvested to make tools or weapons that never broke or lost their edge.

Lifting the ancient yari from its case, Bantu twirled it, letting himself feel its perfect weight, which was only matched by its balance. With a twist and a pull, he slid the blade free. A pure, single, ringing note accompanied the metal slipping free of its housing. The blackwood was smooth but did not slip in his grasp. The blade curved, ever so gently, like his sword's blade. Bantu knew it was just as sharp. A few slashes through the air with a twirl of his wrist ended with him slamming the blade home in its housing. He secured it with a single twist. Pulling his sword from his belt Bantu placed it in the long, slender, box that had held the yari before returning it to the glass case. After one more look around the *Well*, he headed for the door. Twirling the yari once more, he nestled it in the crook of his left arm in the same way he was used to carrying his sword. Exiting the room, he made his way to the main entryway to the House. Now, he was ready.

The hallway was alive with activity. It was as if word had been passed to everyone in the House that something very important was about to occur. Bantu doubted that was actually the case, it just seemed like it. He passed barefooted servants in their blue and white robes. When he did they stopped what they were doing in order to bow. He was going to have to do something about that no matter how many generations it had been the way of things. It did not occur each time he passed a servant but periodically they exhaled sharply as their eyes caught the yari in the crook of his left arm. Some even whispered the *Blessing* while never lifting their head. *And the House, be a House again.* One young woman said it so softly that had he not been looking directly at her he would not have seen her lips move. For his part Bantu smiled to each of them as he walked on. He had always thought that the way members of the Company acted around him was difficult to deal with. But the way the members of the House were acting was even worse.

Bantu was relieved when the entryway finally came into view. He stopped by the entryway. He looked around at those who were waiting for him. Just to the right of the entrance the three Blossoms stood patiently. You would have thought they were bored if you did not know them. Isabelle leaned against the wall with her arms folded across her chest. Wen was busy examining the nails on her right hand as if the world would end if they did not look right. Bella was leaning against Isabelle. She looked like she was taking a nap while standing up. In the center of the entryway was the rest of the honor guard. Mandisa was standing straight as a pole with three other Mfundishi swathed in black behind him. Each of the older grandmasters had looks that said they were on their way to the Pit but planned to give as good as they got. Three steps behind them were twenty young Mfunde. Not as experienced as the Mfundishi, the younger men all looked restless but eager. All of the Mfundade that Mandisa had gathered seemed some of the tallest of the House. Their robes were freshly pressed. They also looked as if they were made of the finest linen. Though they were in the House proper they all carried their yari. Once Bantu finished counting he turned to Mandisa opening his mouth to speak. Mandisa darted into the opening, "Forgive, First. I know you would have fewer accompany you to the Corral. But you must know something." When Bantu closed his mouth without speaking Mandisa took it as permission to continue. "Word has spread, First Born. News of your presence in the House has run like wildfire through Omorede. Men who had laid aside the yari years ago began arriving this morning in the freshly pressed robes of the Mfundade. Many of them, still very able, mind you, but with a look in their eye that said they would not be denied. The women, it seems, have begun to stockpile the House, string their bows, even going so far as to put on their knives. You have not been gone so long that you do not know what that means. The truth, First Born, is that I nearly had to loosen my yari to keep your escort to this number. As it was I still had to make a concession for honor's sake."

Bantu was shaking his head slowly as Mandisa spoke. Many knew the story behind his parents having to place Bantu on a ship in the middle of the night. They knew how the First family had been lost on that terrible night. Only now was Bantu beginning to understand how much more Omorede had lost beyond the Firsts of the House. They had lost their sense that they were a Great House. Nevermind the fact that there had been members of the House to take over, Omorede knew that the First Born was out in the world somewhere, alive, alone, and most importantly, lost to them. Now that he was back Omorede was preparing for war. Bantu had miscalculated. He nearly cursed. Sure, he had waited for the day that he could return to finish what had begun that night, but he had hoped he could do it on his own terms, without plunging all of Al'akaz, especially Omorede, into chaos in the process.

Mandisa had been watching Bantu closely as though reading each word as it crossed his mind. When Bantu looked around at those gathered in the entryway again Mandisa whispered, "Please First Born, do not forget, that *to live, we must die.*" The words struck Bantu so hard he nearly took a step back. Every member of the Mfundade knew the words inscribed above the entrance to the Corral. Even the young boys who one day aspired to join the Corral on behalf of their House knew those words. They were an ever-present reminder of the nature of the life of a weapon. To pass through the training of the Corral, to come out as Mfunde, maybe even one day Mfundishi, one had to learn to let go of life, to become unattached to it. Only then could they be the weapons they were meant to be. Only then could they serve their respective House, unafraid, with honor. Mandisa was reminding Bantu that every member of the House knew that if Omorede perished, *then it perished*. But until that moment they would live as what they were. He should not dishonor that. Memories from his childhood sprang to the forefront of his thoughts. Bantu remembered his time in the Corral. Along with the lessons his father had taught him. In that moment he remembered what he had almost forgotten. Nodding his head, he reached out, patting Mandisa on the shoulder as he said, "So shall it be." The smile that lit up Mandisa's face was infectious. Bantu found himself smiling. Then, raising his voice, Bantu said, "It is time."

Bantu walked to the arched opening in the entryway with Mandisa a step behind him. There were not very many actual doors in Al'akaz. When he came abreast of where they were waiting by the opening in the entryway the Blossom's floated from the corner to fall in step behind him. The other three Mfundishi trailed behind the Blossoms. Behind the Mfundishi stalked the Mfunde. The entire procession left the House, stepping into the open air of the late morning. It immediately became apparent to Bantu what Mandisa had meant about making a concession. Bantu stopped, a few steps outside the House, looking around in awe. For as far as he could see there were members of the Mfundade of Omorede. The first several rows were made up of very old men in the black robes of the Mfundishi. A number of the heads of the very old Mfundishi looked freshly shaven. Bantu had no doubt that had they not been shaven they would have shown a great deal of gray. Behind those sage, dangerous looking men, was rank upon rank of younger men in the blue robes of the Mfunde of Omorede. What was startling about the display was the absence of sound. Bantu had rarely seen so many people in one place without so much as a whisper. The men stood there unmoving. Only their robes moved with the breeze.

After a few moments of gazing on such an extraordinary display Mandisa whispered to him, "Nothing need be said, First Born. The concession was that they be allowed to escort you to the outskirts of the Corral. Once there they will return home. But what they wish is to have the Corral see that to trifle with you is to trifle with all of Omorede. They would settle for nothing less. And if I may say so, with respect, First Born. I agree. Let them know that we are a House again, that though you have been gone from us for many seasons, you still command the House. All of it."

Bantu did not speak. He simply nodded. It was not that he had nothing to say. Rather, it was, that he did not believe he could say it without his voice breaking. How could he have miscalculated so? How could he have forgotten how deeply pride ran in Al'akaz? There was an old saying concerning the pride of the people that came to mind as he stood there gazing out on an ocean of Omorede warriors, *as deep as the Wadi*. The pride of the people of Al'akaz ran as deep as the Great River. With a deep breath, as he fought to keep a straight face, Bantu started forward again. When he approached the front line of the Mfundade it parted like the Great River as it flows around either side of the island on which the Corral sits. Once Bantu passed them the men waited for his official honor guard to go by before they fell in behind them. With a sea of warriors following him, Bantu began his journey to the Corral.

The plan had been to walk to the edge of the main compound of the House in order to meet with a Griot who would transport them to the edge of Omorede. As they came down the rise from the main compound Bantu spotted the small man sitting on the side of the road eating an oval-shaped piece of green fruit. He wore the standard many-colored swath of cloth around his mid-section but nothing else, other than the black sandals, with their leather straps winding up his legs to his knees. His wildly woolly hair was all over his head. His tattoos were more prolific than the ones the other Griot, who had carried him to Al'akaz, had. This Griot was of a higher rank. He had the same disaffected look on his face as if he would rather be somewhere else. Bantu seemed to remember that all the Griot looked that way. When Bantu came to stand in front of the small man he bowed briefly. The Griot smelled of sweet musk. His voice was high but with the timbre of time seasoning it. "Greetings from the Grammat, First Born. I am Tetasealle. It is with joy and glad tidings that the Grammat hears of your return. It is my honor to serve the House of Omorede again."

Bantu bowed to the Griot. He had not forgotten everything. "Greetings from Omorede, Tetasealle Griot. It is with respect and thanksgiving that Omorede receives a member of the Grammat. We thank you for your service." The small man nodded satisfactorily when Bantu finished the ancestral greeting. Looking around him quizzically he asked Bantu, "How many will be going, First Born?"

Bantu grimaced as he said, "All of them *Baba*."

Tossing the remains of his fruit aside the man rubbed his hands together saying, "No need to flatter First, we had best begin." In moments he had his woedom in hand twirling it over his head. With his eyes closed he mumbled words that Bantu could not make out. It was not that he could not hear them. The words seemed to slide off his ear as he tried to decipher them. Slowly, the deep humming of the woedom, as it spun over the Griot's head, grew more intense. It was as if the instrument sounded like several voices humming together from one note to the next. Then the lightning began to flash as the wind rushed up.

Before Bantu could think about what was happening the whirlwind had engulfed him. He had to snap his eyes closed to protect them from the swirling gusts and flashing lights but before he could raise his hands to cover his face it was over. Blinking his eyes Bantu opened them tentatively. Miraculously, they were miles away from where they had been standing. They were in the deep woods of the Dagoonzu.

The Mfundade, loose in the Dagoonzu, are like children loose in a playpen.

~Any First of any Great House

Our honor is as precious as the air we breathe.

*~A well known saying of members
of the Great House Allaka*

Sometimes the nature of your army's strength should not be a secret.

~Amandala Shandu's,
The Warring Way

CHAPTER TWENTY-TWO

Where women do not tread

Wen could almost physically touch it. Walking along behind Bantu, with the other Blossoms, she was awash in the excitement of the warriors of Bantu's clan. What they called their *House*. Much of what had occurred, as well as the why of what had occurred, since leaving Alexandria, was shrouded in the fog that was the mystery of the Commander's past. The uncertainty of it all had been troubling to Wen, especially since she felt responsible for Bantu's safety. What would they say if they made it back to the Company without him? What *could* they say? Yet, as she walked, she thought with some relief that they finally had a small reason to hope it would be possible to get him back safely. While she had wondered yesterday if his family would even accept him, today she was relieved, even excited. The Omorede had not only accepted him but had apparently rallied to his, as yet undisclosed, cause. According to the few words she had been able to exchange with Mandisa before leaving the main compound of the Great House, Omorede was preparing for war. If she had needed further proof of their commitment to the Commander, it stretched out behind her.

Another of those small, wild-haired men, Bantu's people called Griots, had conjured up a swirling *rift* by twirling a length of cord. While Wen had no idea how the man did what he did, after seeing the things Tink could do, she was not shocked by the swirling wind or flashing lightning that somehow moved you from one place to another in the blink of an eye. The rift had disgorged them in the thick of the forest, on the edge of Omorede land, at least that is what Wen had overheard.

Behind Wen marched a small army of linen wrapped giants. The first few ranks of towering men were swathed in black robes with gold scrollwork embroidered around the edge of their robes at the end of the sleeves and hems. The linen from which the robes were made was the finest Wen had seen. She had learned that the color of their robes, along with their clean-shaven heads, meant that they were *Mfundishi*. Walking behind them, while they strolled along talking with one another like they hadn't a care in the world, was a larger, more serious looking, contingent of what they called *Mfunde*. The Mfunde wore a light shade of blue. Their robes had white accents. That group of tall men, they were *all* so very tall, was made up of mostly younger men with long coiled clusters of woolly braids hanging at least to their shoulders. Some of the older men, in their ranks, had never attained the rank of *Mfundishi,* so they still wore the colors of their House. While their official escort was some twenty or so of the *Mfundade*, the Great House of Omorede had decided to do what, back home, would have been called - *showing the flag*. They were making a statement. The plan was for the majority of them to turn back at the edge of the Corral but not before letting themselves be seen following the Commander. The occupants of the Corral were to be shown that the Commander had the support, no – *make that the allegiance* – of his Great House. They wanted to declare, without speaking a single word, that - *if you harm him, you do so at your peril*. So, while there was clearly danger ahead for the Commander, the Blossoms could rely on his family for help to keep him safe.

Once everyone had exited the rift, called forth by the Griot, Wen watched the Commander thank the little man who, repeating some formulaic farewell, bowed, before opening another rift into which he promptly disappeared. Wen turned her attention, from the spot where the Griot had vanished into the rift, to their surroundings. While she had been watching Bantu with the Griot, Bella and Isabelle had been cautiously watching their surroundings. This part of the forest, the *Dagoonzu* they called it, was *deep* forest. There must not have been another person, building, or road, within an hour's ride. The first thing that caught Wen's attention was the sweet smell of honeysuckle. Just to her right she noticed the tiny white blossoms as they attempted to engulf a thick stand of jasmine. The two plants were one of the reason's the forest had a clean, bright, smell. The next things she noticed were the trees. They had thick trunks with heavy branches that began low, sprouting sparsely up the length of the tall trunks as far as she could see, until finally erupting into a thick, leafy canopy that diffused the sunlight. The sky scraping, many-leaved giants were everywhere. Were they some form of redwood she was unaware of? While Alexandria had thick forest all through the countryside, adding to its own unique beauty, its trees were often not the most numerous part of its flora. Though these trees were numerous they were spaced far enough apart that it was still relatively easy to move along the forest floor. Moments after the Griot disappeared into the rift that was exactly what they were doing.

Bantu began walking west while looking around as if getting his bearings. After a minute or so he nodded. Wen thought she caught the briefest hint of a smile cross his face. She could almost hear him thinking - *I know where I am*. Immediately, he picked up the pace. Moving through the trees, across the sparse forest floor, his fast walk became a slow trot. Wen, followed by the other Blossoms, was right behind him. She watched as Mandisa looked over his shoulder shooting them a broad smile. Wen was not sure what was happening but the Commander and Mandisa were sharing some inside joke to which she was not privy. A few seconds later, she understood what they were smiling about.

Bantu moved from a slow trot to a full stride. Wen heard a soft rustling of leaves above her. Stopping herself from drawing her sword, she tilted her head back so that she could look up into the tree branches. Gazing up she caught sight of something that brought a smile to her own face. When she looked back over her shoulder Wen noticed that nearly half the men who had been following them were no longer running along the forest floor. They were in the trees. As she ran on laughter erupted from deep in her throat. But she did not restrain herself. Looking up again, she saw the younger men of the Mfundade, some Mfundishi, others Mfunde, leaping effortlessly from branch to branch. Their robes fluttered around them in the wind, making them look like enormous, diaphanous, wraiths floating through the treetops. Their arms were outstretched as though they had wings. Wen had wondered earlier why the Griot had not brought them directly to the edge of Omorede. That would have placed them almost all the way to the Corral. Now she knew. They wanted to arrive this way. With a final look over his shoulder, revealing a broad smile firmly in place on his face, the Commander winked at Wen, turned his head, and leaped. Up into the trees he went without so much as a grunt of effort.

Bantu soared up into the branches as if an unseen force had flung him skyward. Landing lightly on a heavy branch, he threw himself forward, leaping through the trees alongside his family. The thick branches bent slightly but the members of the Mfundade landed so gently that the leaves on those branches barely rustled at their passing. Looking at the other Blossoms, who were wearing their own infectious smiles as they ran, Wen laughed. She did not wait another second before she leaped. It was like being back in Alexandria running through the night along the great city's rooftops. Landing on a branch that was as thick as the tree trunks back home Wen threw herself to her right. She flew through the air. At the apex of her jump her feet landed on the side of a tree trunk. She used it as a spring launching herself twenty feet through the air to another branch ahead of her. It took a little more concentration than they would have needed running across Alexandrian rooftops. But it wasn't long before she, Bella, and Isabelle were floating through the forest canopy, just behind Bantu, as if they had been doing it for years.

While leaping through the treetops was a pure delight she thought it was the look on the faces of the Mfundade they leaped past, or floated through the air alongside, which Wen enjoyed the most. They must have thought they would be sailing through the air overhead while the women ran along the forest floor. To see them leaping from branch to branch, sometimes soaring twenty or thirty feet through empty space, took the Mfundade by surprise. One poor young man was so surprised to see Wen sail past him that he missed the branch he had aimed at. He fell almost twenty feet before he managed to kick off a tree trunk. He landed on a lower hanging branch. Had his skin been a few shades lighter Wen was sure she would have seen the blood rush to his cheeks as his face flushed with embarrassment. As it was, she had to settle for the way he pressed his lips together to match the agitated look he had in his eyes once he hurtled back up to higher branches.

They ran on like that for the better part of an hour, soaring through the branches of the Dagoonzu, like an army with wings. Wen was impressed. While she had the benefit of the *gift* the Mfundade, as far as she knew, did not. They matched her by sheer physical prowess coupled with an uncanny agility, which wasn't just frightening. It was impressive. Bantu's people were a sight to behold. While she wondered where they had come by such prowess Wen let the knowledge of their ability rest in the forefront of her mind so that she would never underestimate them. Watching them leap through the treetops made her realize that underestimating one of them could be the last thing she ever did.

Abruptly, almost without warning, there were no more branches ahead. Wen leaped into open air, turned in a twisting flip, before dropping some forty feet to the ground below. She landed lightly on a rise just behind the Commander. Walking forward, followed by the Blossoms who had also dropped from the treetops beside her, she made room for those who were bursting dramatically from the thick forest canopy above into open air. They were hurtling down to land behind them. Wen shook her head. Ordinary men should not be able to do such a thing. Laughing to herself, she realized that the Mfundade were probably thinking the same thing about her. Walking to the edge of the rise, where Bantu had stopped, with Mandisa at his side, Wen looked down below them. Her breath caught in her throat. It was not what she had been expecting. Isabelle and Bella came to stand beside her. Bella let out a low, appreciative, whistle while Isabelle stood gazing down on what lay below them as if she were a General gauging the strength of the enemy. For her part, Wen thought, *so that is a Corral.*

†

Bantu stopped on the edge of the rise overlooking the Corral. Down the hill, half a mile from where they stood, was a bridge marking the edge of Omorede. The bridge spanned the gap between the edge of Omorede and the island on which stood the Corral. Beneath the bridge was the rushing, blue water of the Great River, the *Wadi-sanje*. The Wadi-sanje was a massive, meandering, sometimes raging river nearly three miles across in most places. It wound its way through all of Al'akaz for hundreds of miles with some of the most fertile land in the region along its banks. It passed through the land of every Great House giving everyone equal access to its waters. The bridge that ran from the edge of Omorede land, over the Wadi-sanje, to the island on which sat the Corral was not the only bridge that Bantu could see from his vantage point. In fact, though he could not see each of them, he knew there were twenty-four such bridges. They were all spaced equally apart, running from the banks of the *Wadi* to the island that stood at the center of the rushing, crystal clear, blue waters. Each bridge sprouted from the edge of territory that belonged to one of the Great Houses even if that territory was only a token sliver of land on the edge of that particular Great House's territory. While the size and disposition of the various Great Houses had changed over a few thousand years, due to feuding, the land around the edge of the Wadi, holding the twenty-four bridges, had always been sacrosanct. It was said that at the heart of Al'akaz lay the Corral. Though it was geographically true, the old saying meant much more than that. If his memory served him, to Bantu's immediate left would be the bridge of the Seseke, while off to his right stood the bridge for Zulumdebe. Leaning easily on the yari that had once belonged to his father, as he crouched on his heels, Bantu steadied himself. His hands rested on the yari where he had planted it between his feet. With his elbows tucked against his sides, helping him maintain his balance, he looked down on the Corral. He did not have to look at the Blossoms standing behind him to know that they were impressed. Their silence, along with the low whistle that had come from Bella, was enough.

"It has not changed much, First." Mandisa's deep tenor rumbled beside Bantu.

"No, cousin. It does not seem like it has. I remember the day my father first brought me to this very spot. It was on that first day he told me the story of Kal'ada'abassa. I was only nine. He towered over me like some giant out of a story. I wore the white robes of a *Sek* with blue bands around their hems so that all in Kal'ada would know I was Omorede. There were bands of gold around the blue so that they would know I was the First Born. He stood next to me, with his hand on my shoulder, telling me what I would find inside the *Seven Walls*. He told me to hold my head high, my honor higher, but to remember that a warrior's true power did not reside in his arm but in his heart. And then he walked me down this hill to the Sacred Isle." Bantu let his voice trail off as he continued to stare down at Kal'ada'abassa. It was the formal name of the place the Mfundade called the Corral. Old emotions washed over him. For a brief moment it almost seemed like his father was standing there next to him.

Mandisa spoke in hushed tones, "Forgive, First. But we miss Shamansara too."

Bantu, with his eyes closed, breathed deeply, taking in the smells of the Dagoonzu mingled with the Wadi-sanje. He breathed in the smells of his home allowing the distant sounds of the rushing waters below to sweep over him. He let a moment, or two, pass. Without turning to look at Mandisa, Bantu simply nodded his head. Mandisa continued, "First Born, I must warn you. While Kal'ada does not look much changed from this height it has changed significantly. Nduma is a man who loves his own shadow more than the people of the Beautiful Land. He is without honor yet has managed to stay in power. Though he is a coward at heart, he remains one of the most impressive fighters the Corral has produced. The only man among the Baba's who could likely defeat him in ritual combat will not challenge him, though we have urged him to do so. I beg you to be careful, First Born. A shadow has fallen over Kal'ada'abassa."

Bantu opened his eyes as he turned to look at Mandisa. The man's face was unreadable. It was still as stone. Catching his eye, Bantu said, "None to challenge him, eh? We shall see Mandisa Mfundishi. We shall see." Bantu stood. Without another word he began strolling down the hill to the bridge that marked the edge of Omorede. Though the Dagoonzu was dense forest the half-mile walk to the Omorede Bridge was not. It was an open plain. Each House had ensured that the half-mile stretch leading up to their bridge to the Sacred Isle was cleared land. It meant that anyone approaching Kal'ada'abassa could be seen long before they reached its walls. Bantu was glad of it. He wanted his escort to be seen. He walked toward Omorede Bridge with his focus on the entrance to Kal'ada'abassa, the Sacred Isle, The City of the Seven Walls. A small, silent army followed behind him. Bantu walked slowly toward the bridge - one did not hurry toward the Corral - especially with so many of the Mfundade at your back. Those inside the Corral would be interested enough in the size of his escort without being prompted to think that Omorede was about to try assailing the Seven Walls.

The Blossoms had duly impressed expressions on their faces because Kal'ada'abassa was impressive. It was the size of a small to midsize city. The first of its seven, circular, walls climbed some fifty feet into the sky. It was also about twenty feet thick. As one moved closer to the city's center, each wall, though just as thick as the first, stood a bit higher than its predecessor. This gave the illusion, from a distance, that the Seven Walls formed a single massive structure. From where Bantu had squatted on the rise behind him one could see the tops of all seven walls glowing golden in the morning sun. They were decorated only by the colorful banners of each of the Great Houses snapping in the stiff breeze along their tops. The Blossoms would be even more startled when they got close enough to the walls to notice that there were no mortar grooves or any other break in the walls smooth surface. Run your hand over every inch of each of the Seven Walls and you would not be able to find a mark that spoke of cut stone laid atop cut stone. It was as if the ancient builders of the Corral had quarried the walls whole from the ground, dropping them from the sky directly on the spots where they now stood.

But the walls had been made. It was an art that had been lost to the ages. Though the builders of Al'akaz were some of the finest, anywhere, they could not duplicate the techniques that had been employed to build the Seven Walls.

As they drew closer to the Bridge of Omorede the message the Mfundade of Omorede had desired to send began to take effect. The attendants on the island side of the several bridges with a view of Omorede went sprinting through the entrance in the outer wall. In minutes heads began appearing along the top of the outer wall. Mfundade, in robes of various colors, began to pour out of the entrance to Kal'ada'abassa. By the time Bantu arrived at Omorede's bridge to the Sacred Isle a fair crowd of towering men, with boys in white robes interspersed in their midst, milled about outside of the Corral watching them. When Bantu reached the bridge, he turned to face the Mfundade of Omorede. The men had come down the hill in precise ranks and total silence. The Mfundade were notorious for looking as if they were unorganized even when they went to war. They often looked like they were milling about up until the moment they struck. Those who had faced the Mfundade of Al'akaz knew the notion that they were disorganized was far from the truth. Omorede had a reputation for being more disciplined than most.

Raising his yari above his head Bantu shouted a single word, "Omorede!" The chorus of voices that answered washed over him, echoing across the Wadi, all the way up to the Corral. The Mfundade of Omorede responded, "Omorede!" The shout was punctuated by the utter silence that followed it. Bantu stood at the entrance to the bridge, while one by one, the crowd of Mfundade from Omorede walked past him, inclining their heads briefly toward him, before walking back up the rise to the Dagoonzu. When they had all personally saluted him, Bantu, with his remaining escort, stood at the edge of the bridge watching them go. When they crested the rise, he watched the last of them vanished back into the Dagoonzu. Then he turned and stepped onto the bridge.

Crossing the Wadi-sanje, by way of the Bridge of Omorede, Bantu noticed the blue flags of his House, hanging in even intervals from the top of the bridge, as they waved in the breeze. No one, except a member of Omorede, could cross the Wadi here without creating a blood feud. Every bridge to the Isle was considered the sovereign territory of the Great House whose flag hung from its heights. The bridge was several paces wide. Its broad-beamed side-rails stood twenty feet high. The entire bridge was made of steel with blackwood accents. From one end to the other it rose some forty feet in the air making a beautiful arc as it crossed over the Wadi. Around the edge of the isle were twenty-three other exact duplicates. The only difference in each House's bridge was what flag flew from it.

It only took a few minutes for Bantu, with his escort in tow, to reach the other side of the bridge. The ground outside the Corral was unremarkable. It had been left that way to ensure that no one could get to the Seven Walls unseen. Attending to the island side of the Bridge of Omorede, as was the custom, was a young man in white robes. Actually, young man was generous. The boy must have been ten or eleven. Already, as was the case with his people, Bantu marked the boy at five spans tall. He was mostly arms and legs, but with that, all-too-serious, look that boys of his age often had. He was a *Sek*, a novice of the Warring Way. At nine years of age boys, who would eventually become members of the Mfundade, were brought to the Corral for training. From the age of nine, until they were twelve, they would spend half the year at Kal'ada. The rest of the year they were allowed to spend at home. But from the age of thirteen on, until they turned nineteen, they lived solely at the Corral. When they turned nineteen they were subjected to the *Trials*. If they failed they were sent from Kal'ada, denied the robes of the Mfunde, never to return. But if they passed they were named Mfunde. Once they were raised to the Mfunde they were allowed to return home to serve their House. As a *Wearer of the Robes* they were given the *Right of Kal'ada'abassa*. They could come or go as they pleased as members of the Mfundade.

The boy, standing as tall as he could, with his narrow chest stuck out, brushed at the white robes he wore, which named him a *Sek*. Bantu could not help but notice that the robes were a coarse grade of cotton, though still well made. The purple bands around the hem of the outer robe, which were trimmed in brown, were the colors of the Great House Allaka.

Bantu looked down at the boy. He waited patiently. Eyeing the men around him, as though he were trying to decide who he should speak to, the boy absently twirled one of the two long, woolly braids that fell behind his ears. Every Sek had those two, thick braids. They would not be allowed the full head of slender braids until they had become Mfunde. Do something foolish and brightly colored ribbons would be tied to those two, thick braids, to the unyielding shame of the boy who had to walk around Kal'ada in such a way. The part down the middle of his head was neatly made. His long, thick hair had been separated with that part to make the two braids. If one's transgression was great enough, that long, thick, hair would be cut to the scalp, adding the time it took to grow it back to the length of time you remained in the white robes. He took in Bantu's freshly pressed, black Company uniform with his big, brown eyes. Bantu, undoubtedly, appeared odd to him. To the boy's mind he surely looked like an outsider. The young Allaka twisted his thick lips into a frown as he turned to Mandisa. Twitching his oversized nose, a trait of the Allaka, he sighed deeply, opening his mouth to speak to the Mfundishi standing before him. But Mandisa shook his head nodding toward Bantu. The boy's brown eyes widened briefly, before narrowing in confusion, as he realized he had made the wrong choice. Looking from Bantu to Mandisa, his expression said he was wondering whether he was being toyed with. When neither man changed his expression, the boy cleared his throat, bowed his head to Bantu, and with a high squeaky voice said, "I am Garu Haldada As' Allaka. How am I to say that you come to Kal'ada'abassa?"

It was tradition to announce your intentions when crossing the bridge to Kal'ada. There were many reasons for Mfundade to enter *The City of the Seven Walls*. At some point in Kal'ada's history it had apparently become necessary for those entering to state their intentions. The origin of that particular custom was the kind of subject that Mfundade debated at the end of the day when they had something strong to drink in their hand. It was also tradition that someone from a different House attended the island side of your bridge in order to hear those intentions. At some point it had become commonplace for that person to be one of the Sek. Today, it seemed, a member of House Allaka attended the island side of the Omorede Bridge. Allaka was substantially smaller than Omorede but, Bantu recalled, it was just as honorable. Though, if his memory served, the Allaka were more prickly when it came to guarding their pride.

Inclining his head, ever so slightly, to the boy Bantu said, "I greet you Garu of the Allaka, honor to your House. I am Ossassande Bantu A' Omorede. This is my bridge." When Bantu finished the boy's mouth fell open. Bantu had used the traditional form of identifying himself. The article *A,* instead of *As,* in front of the name of his House identified him as part of the first family of the House. By telling the boy that the Omorede Bridge was *his* bridge he let the boy know he was not only a part of the first family but, in fact, was the First Born of the House. Bantu waited a few seconds, allowing that knowledge to sink in. Then he said, "I come to Challenge." The boy's mouth fell open even further if that was possible.

After a few more seconds of waiting patiently Mandisa said, "Get a hold of yourself little one. Omorede has business inside the *Shining Walls.* Or must I report to the *Baba'a'sek* that a certain Garu of the Allaka would be well served to have ribbons in his hair?"

At the mention of ribbons, the boy snapped out of his stupor. Looking at Bantu as if he was something out of one of the tails spun by the Griot for small children he said, "Hon- ... Honor, to your House, First Born. I will escort you to the First Wall."

Bantu smiled down at him, "As you wish Garu of the Allaka."

The boy smiled back. Omorede and Allaka had always had good relations. The two Houses had never had cause to feud as far back as memories among the Houses ran. Bantu remembered that he had run with some of the Allaka when he had been in the Corral as a Sek. The boy gave Mandisa a quick sidelong look to see if he still had ribbons on his mind before quickly leading them toward the outer wall of the Corral. His back was straight. With the way he held his shoulders square, as he strode purposefully ahead, you would have thought that he was escorting the *Baba'a'funde*. Bantu understood the boy's reaction. It was rare that the attendants got to escort one of the First Born. All too often watching the bridges was a long, dull, exercise in futility.

It was several hundred paces across flat unadorned grass from the bridge to the First Wall. It was another one of the things that made it difficult to sneak up on the Corral. The area around the banks of the Wadi-sanje had also been cleared. The bridges themselves were out in the open while the area around the outer wall remained uncultivated. Standing atop the outer wall you had an unobstructed view for several miles in every direction. As they approached the outer wall the boy began to shout, pushing at people as though he was twice his size, "Make way! Make way! The First Born of Omorede comes to Challenge. Make way!" The small crowd of Mfundade who stood milling around the entrance of the outer wall parted as the boy pushed through the crowd. Bantu could see A'umbari in purple and white, Fulani in gray and gold, Seseke in silver and bronze, and Adari in brown and black. There were also a number of Mfundishi in black, but he did not recognize any to know which House they were from. What he did recognize was the look of puzzlement that came with a glance at his uniform. There was also the grudging respect that came from a glance at his escort. Bantu forced himself not to smile. The message that the Mfundade of Omorede had sent to the members of the Corral had been fully delivered. They knew that the long lost First of Omorede was present and that, if need be, all of Omorede would come calling.

With the young Allaka, Garu, coming close to creating feuds with other Houses, by shoving Mfundade out of the way, the crowd parted allowing the entryway through the First Wall to come into view. As they made their way through the crowd Bantu noticed angry faces turning to see who was doing the shoving. He watched as they prepared to take umbrage at the boy's behavior, to call for an Mfunde or Mfundishi from the Sek's House to answer a Challenge until, that is, they saw the purple and brown bands of color around the boy's hem. Invariably they turned back to their conversations, or whatever they had been doing, muttering angrily under their breath.

They would let it pass, saying to themselves that it was, after all, a minor offense, that the boy was young. But the truth was that the Great

House Allaka was notorious for its prickly pride. You did not enter into a feud with them lightly. For the most minor of offenses Allaka would feud with your House for a generation. Much larger, more powerful Houses, had been known to capitulate to Allaka, making the peace, because they had simply grown tired of a feud with Allaka that had gone on, a generation too long, with no end in sight. So while Garu barked in his high squeaky voice, pushing at men twice his size, they grudgingly moved out of the way of the diminutive Allaka. When the boy bumped into a Fulani the man almost fell over himself disappearing into the crowd in the opposite direction. That had been a particularly messy feud. Though they had been named the victor, the Fulani studiously avoided Allaka except, in the rare instances, when avoiding them would have been insult enough to fan the dead embers of the feud bringing them back to life. Bantu chuckled softly as he watched the grown man come close to running from the small boy who had not even taken notice of the way people were responding to him.

No door, or gate, adorned the outer wall of Kal'ada'abassa, as was the case in most of Al'akaz. There was a tall, arching, tunnel cut into the sandstone, running the length of the twenty-foot thick wall. The passage was narrow enough that a handful of the Mfundade could hold it indefinitely against a significantly larger force. Al'akazian architecture had always been forced to contend with the Al'akazian philosophy of war found encapsulated in the Warring Way. The Mfundade fought up close. They were not fond of weapons that functioned from a distance nor did they rely on architecture to protect themselves. They defended themselves by combat. That was why no Great House was guarded by walls, moats, or gates. The Mfundade were probably the most skilled warriors in the world. They relied on that to protect them.

Standing in that archway was an Mfunde assigned to *Keep the Way*. Walking right up to the towering Mfunde, who wore the red and white of the N'kosi, Garu planted himself before the man as though the two were equals. "I present the First of Omorede, Ossassande Bantu. He has come, as is the Right of all Mfundade, to *Challenge*." Turning back to Bantu the boy bowed at the waist. When he straightened from his bow he flashed Bantu a bright smile as he spoke, "Honor to your House Omorede."

Bantu nearly laughed. The boy, by rights, should be taken to task for speaking to him as though they were equals. Bantu had truly forgotten how brash his people could be. He had certainly forgotten how much more prideful the Allaka were beyond the rest of Al'akaz. The boy was a true manifestation of the wild, sometimes reckless, nature of the men of Al'akaz. The troubling part was that he was not even a man yet. Rather than take the boy to task Bantu merely inclined his head as he said, "And to yours Allaka." With that the boy disappeared into the crowd behind them presumably making his way back to the dull task of Keeping the Way at Omorede's bridge. Bantu also knew that Garu would likely be boasting among his fellows as soon as he was freed from his duty at the bridge to rejoin the other Seks.

Turning back to the Keeper at the entrance to the arched passage Bantu started toward the First Wall. He watched as the man decided not to try to stop him. With his Honor Guard in tow Bantu walked down the length of the tunnel carved into the First Wall. He stepped out into sunlight again on the other side. Along with the rays of the sun shining down on him the sounds of the *First Way* hit him. The spaces between the walls of Kal'ada, known as *Ways*, were where the life of the Corral happened. Inside the First Way was where much of the marketplace was located. It was also the only place where outlanders were allowed inside the Seven Walls. All around him Bantu could see the stalls, tents, or carts of various merchants selling a little bit of everything. While the ground outside the Corral was kept trimmed down for visibility that practice was not necessary inside Kal'ada. Along the walls, even around the places where the merchants had set up their stalls, there were collections of flowers growing, in a myriad of shapes and colors. Butterflies fluttered their purple, diaphanous wings here and there. Overhead, bluebirds, larks, along with smaller snitchtails, streaked through the air in the manner of small birds fluttering their wings on the morning breeze. Bantu smiled, allowing the beauty of the day to soak in, thankful that the vision of Kal'ada's beauty helped to push the throbbing in his head to the back of his mind. While he drank in his surroundings he continued on to the Second Wall.

Packs of white-robed Seks, obviously out of training for the rest of the morning, ran underfoot, laughing, as they pushed at one another. Men and women in various styles of garb, marking them as Outlanders, passed as he walked. Bantu saw people with the sharp, angular features and fair skin of Herric'dem. Others wore the large hats that were a pandemic in Lellwellyn. There were even the dark-skinned people of Pak'den'bar with their incongruously straight hair. As he passed a stall where Al'akazian wine was sold, he heard a man with the heavy accents of Province. Bantu tried not to look too closely at the fellow. It took more than a few minutes to cross the length of the First Way but they finally reached the entrance at the Second Wall.

The Mfunde who kept the Way at the entrance to the Second Wall wore the dark blue and silver of the Ossessi. He had their long, narrow features along with their deliberate speech patterns. Some made the mistake of thinking the Ossessi were slow-witted, but they simply liked to think at length about what they were going to say. After a few quick words from Mandisa, followed by a number of slower words from the Ossessi, the man let them pass. Bantu ignored the way the man stared at him. He already had enough to deal with without adding a dispute with the Ossessi. Besides, it was probably the fact that Bantu wore the Company uniform that had the man puzzled. Was he an Outlander? Surely, he wasn't because Outlanders were not allowed inside the Second Wall. Mandisa had told the man that Bantu was the First of Omorede. They walked another twenty feet before exiting the passage into the Second Way. The Second Way was less crowded. There were still white-robed boys running around with various colors along their hems. The Seks would be everywhere until they reached the Sixth Wall. There were men and women, from a number of Great Houses, going about their business. The Mfundade were everywhere. The Second Way had actual buildings along it so that it looked like a street in almost any major city. Bantu knew that these buildings held goods in storage. The Second Way also teemed with smithies, weavers, bakers, painters, and every other trade that you could imagine. The smell of bread made Bantu think of the breakfast he had not eaten.

Again, they came to a passageway. This one was in the Third Wall. With Mandisa taking the lead they passed from the Second Way into the Third, which held, almost exclusively, sleeping quarters. There were landscaped areas designed for leisure. They moved quickly to the Fourth Wall. It was at the entrance to the Fourth Wall that they had their first problem. Bantu had expected it. He was surprised that it had not happened sooner. He had even spent the trip from Omorede to Kal'ada'abassa thinking of how to deal with the problem. Maybe it was the nature of the first three walls coupled with the effect of his Honor Guard. Or maybe it was the surreptitious way that Honor Guard had encircled him. Or it could have been the fact that the Blossoms were so small in relation to the Mfundade around them that no one had really noticed them. But the entrance to the Fourth Wall was the line that marked the place where only Mfundade, or Seks on errands, might pass. Since it was a line of demarcation, the Way was kept by several Mfunde led by an Mfundishi who paid close attention to every member of their party as they approached. When the Mfundishi's eyes landed on the Blossoms he simply said the words that Bantu knew as well as any Mfundade. "I am sorry Mandisa Mfundishi, beyond the Fourth Wall women do not tread."

One is best known by the kind of enemies he makes.

*- Zalakazam Kaz A' Aassam
Mfundishi*

Desire is destiny.

~*A Griot saying*

CHAPTER TWENTY-THREE

The debt

Bantu, encircled by his Honor Guard, stood before the opening in the Fourth Wall. Blocking the way into the passage, which would empty out into the Fourth Way, was a sharp-eyed Mfundishi. His black robes, trimmed in gold embroidery, seemed to shimmer in the late-morning sun. Standing behind him were a handful of Mfunde. Bantu noted the red and white of the N'kosi, the pale green and cream of the Bakari, and the purple, accented with gray, of the Gamba. The man, who seemed young to be wearing the black robes, had spoken a refrain well known in the Corral. Women were not allowed beyond the Fourth Wall. The young looking Mfundishi had spoken those old words, that ancient prohibition, because Bantu had three women in his Honor Guard. While they had made their way from Omorede to Kal'ada'abassa, Bantu had been wrestling with two problems. The first was the throbbing in his head that had been with him since returning home. The second was the prohibition against women beyond the Fourth Wall. He had tried to think of a way around the prohibition because he knew that the Blossoms were not going to accept being left behind. It had occurred to him, as they had entered Kal'ada, that there just might be a way to solve at least the problem of the prohibition. His head, however, continued to throb unabated. He had no ideas about how to make it stop or even why it had begun again since he stepped through the Griot's portal.

Mandisa started moving toward his black-robed counterpart but Bantu waved him off. Moving forward himself, so as to stand directly in front of the Mfundishi who was Keeping the Fourth Way, he said, "I am Ossassande Bantu A' Omorede. I have come to bring the Challenge."

The Mfundishi, a relatively handsome man, who seemed to be of an age with Bantu, pressed his lips together into a thin line as he looked from one side of Bantu's escort to the other. His shaven head glistened lightly in the sun as he drew a slow, smooth, breath. Bantu half-smiled as he recognized the beginning steps of the *abundance*. The man was tasting the moment. He was savoring the experience in the way the Mfundade were taught. The people of the Beautiful Land taught their children that it was necessary, especially for those who might face death at any moment, to savor the time they were given. It was common practice among the Mfundade especially when they thought a conflict was imminent. After a few seconds, in which the man seemed to rub the moment across his fingertips, he sighed, shaking his head almost imperceptibly as he spoke. "I am Lazda'ah Mubuzu As' Gamba." Somehow, he managed to incline his head briefly while still shaking it. He continued, "Honor to your House, First Born. Word has come through the Ways that the Son of Omorede has returned to Kal'ada. It is also said that he comes with *Cause*. Though you have been gone from us for some time First, and though I do not wish to stand in your way, you know as well as I that I cannot allow these women, Outlanders even, to pass. If this offends, I regretfully stand ready."

Bantu had been watching the man closely while he spoke. The Mfundishi's hand had tightened almost imperceptibly on his yari. The Gamba knew that, according to custom, Bantu could respond to the questioning of his Honor Guard by challenging him personally. Even though a Challenge, won or lost, would not change the prohibition, there were those who would think that defeating the man, who had invoked it, in combat, would save face. That could mean wounding him seriously enough that he acknowledged defeat or killing him outright if he would not. For some reason the notion that Bantu might invoke the Challenge disturbed this Mfundishi of the Gamba. Finally, after having looked at the man unwittingly for the past few minutes while he explained his position, it struck Bantu. Maybe it was the voice that cinched it. The voice was just a little too deep for the face. There was also the way the man held himself with a dignity that was not put on but worn easily, evenly, somehow gracefully. He had always been that way, even as a child. A full smile creased Bantu's face as recognition dawned on him. He took a step closer to the Mfundishi saying, "So Mubuzu, the Gamba have finally figured out that your talents are best suited to leaning against walls to hold them up?"

Mubuzu smiled his own broad smile then as he replied, "It is a far sight better than trying to undo several thousand years of tradition when you have only been back long enough for the Omorede to wipe your nose before sending you off to have your head separated from your shoulders, First Born."

There was a pause as both men looked one another over. After a breath they both burst into laughter. At once they caught each other up in a full hug. Taking a half step back the two men held one another at arms length. Bantu said, "Honor to your House Mubuzu. You look well. I should have known you would ascend to the black robes quickly. You were always a fast study." Looking him over again, with a more sober look on his face, Bantu continued, "You wear them well."

Mubuzu inclined his head, briefly, acknowledging the compliment. "You flatter me too much Bantu. Even when we were boys, running together in the Seks, I knew you would outstrip me one day. Had you stayed in Kal'ada you would have been the youngest man since Amandala to don the black robes. Your name would be a terror among the Houses, of that I am certain. No doubt you would be the Baba'a'funde by now. Though you were forced to leave us, the rumor is that you have set up a Corral of your own. The word is that you command thousands of outland Mfundade? Is this true?"

They had indeed been Seks together. They had also been close friends. As Seks they had fed off one another's accomplishments. It had been the kind of rivalry that only very close friends could have. The kind that was real but empty of any malice. Bantu knew he was smiling like a plumb fool, but he did not care. He had found an old friend again, which brought him joy. Reaching out he gripped Mubuzu's shoulder, squeezing it gently. "My friend, it is good to see you – to find you again, and to find you well. I would not call the Peoples Company a Corral, but they are my very great joy. We help those who cannot help themselves. They are something we did not think existed in the Outlands, people of honor. Now, while it is a joy to see you again, I must warn you that you are on the verge of insulting three of the members of that Company. May I present Commander Wen Ava Noella, Lieutenant Commander Bella Novilla Noella, and Lieutenant Isabelle Erinelle Lelange. They are officers in the Peoples Company."

As Bantu introduced each of the Blossoms, they stepped forward to stand alongside him. Mubuzu looked at each woman in turn. He seemed to take note of her crisp, fitted, black uniform. He paused briefly on each woman's sword before finally settling on her face. After giving each woman the once over he said, "Honor to your Houses, my ladies."

Before the women could respond Bantu spoke up. "There is your problem, I think, Mubuzu. Yes, they are women, but they are also *weapons*. Wen and Bella might be considered Mfundishi, while Isabelle, due only to her age, might be one of the Mfunde. They have faced death, drawn blood, and I have trusted each at my side in battle."

Mubuzu cleared his throat uneasily. Looking from the Blossoms back to Bantu he finally said, "Forgive me. I do not intend to insult you. But you must understand that in Al'akaz women do not join the Mfundade. So, we have a problem. While I am an old friend of Bantu's and do not wish to offend, there are prohibitions – very old prohibitions - which constrain me in this matter. I have my instructions. I am responsible for Keeping the Fourth Way." He looked back at Bantu as his smile faded. It was replaced by a look of resignation as he continued, "I do not relish what comes next Bantu, but we have our honor." The last was spoken with a shrug, as if to say, what came next could not be helped.

Mubuzu took a step back giving him more room to maneuver. Bantu could see his posture change slightly, so slight in fact, that the untrained eye would have missed the minor adjustments. It would have missed the slight bending of the knees, the loosening of the shoulders, even the forward tilt to the waist. It would have missed the deepening of Mubuzu's breathing. While that untrained eye might have noticed the narrowing of his eyes it would not have caught how those eyes shifted to focus on Bantu's midsection. One of the secrets of the Mfundade was the way the billowing robes they wore could hide most of those changes in posture so that an enemy, who did not know what to look for, would never know that the warrior standing across from him had gone from standing casually to being ready for battle. The Mfundishi was ready for whatever came next. If Bantu, according to custom, took offense, Mubuzu knew that Bantu could exercise his right to challenge him right there on the spot. Bantu knew he needed to make the man understand before bloodshed became unavoidable. He did not want to injure his childhood friend.

To his left, out of the corner of his eye, Bantu saw Mandisa shift his own weight no more than a fraction. Without taking his eyes off Mubuzu Bantu said, "Easy, Mandisa, take it easy. That goes for everyone." Focusing again on Mubuzu he said, "With respect, Mubuzu. You have not heard me out. You see it is my position that the Blossoms are not simply women. They are Mfundade in the formal sense of the word – they are *weapons*. Look to the prohibition of the Fourth Wall closely. I believe you will see that it is not women that are barred from entry it is *nonweapons*. The reason we have named women as *those who are barred* is for the very reason you mentioned a moment ago. In Al'akaz, women do not become weapons. *In Al'akaz,* Mubuzu. But in the Outlands, they do. Seeing as these women are of the Outland, and are in fact weapons, it is my position that they are not subject to the Prohibition of the Fourth Wall."

What Bantu did not say, what he conveniently left out, was that in most of the outland's women did not become weapons either. But that fact would not have helped his cause at the moment. He watched as Mubuzu pondered what he had said. After a long pause that seemed to stretch on interminably in which Bantu could hear only the breathing of those around him in contrast to the distant sounds of people moving past them along the Third Way, Mubuzu breathed a sigh of relief. Standing straight he said, "First of Omorede. I believe you have enough Cause to be Heard. Will a Hearing here at the Wall suffice or would you prefer to wait until you have reached the Hall?"

Bantu nodded, "Here will suffice Mfundishi."

With that Mubuzu turned to one of the Mfunde behind him saying, "I require two more Mfundishi to Hear a Cause. Go quickly."

Without a word the young man darted off down the passage leading into the Fourth Way. The tail ends of his green robes, with their cream-colored trim, fluttered behind him. Mubuzu stepped closer to Bantu. He lowered his voice so that only the two of them could hear what was being said. "You were ever the rebel, Bantu. It is why we called you *Shai' yadam*, while we were Seks, you were always *the one who goes his own way*. I am glad you have finally come home. I know that you have a Cause to place before the Masters of the Hall, so I want you to know that however things go, even if they go badly and N'duma calls for war among the Houses, I will bring Gamba to the Omorede myself. Having risen to the black robes so young I have gained some small honor for Gamba among the Houses. They will hear me in this matter. And it helps that there is no love lost for N'duma and the N'kosi among most of Gamba. He does have a few friends in my House, but their objections can be overcome." After speaking N'duma's name, Mubuzu spat on the ground as if there had been a bad taste in his mouth.

Bantu clasped Mubuzu's arm as he said, "Thank you brother. But it is my hope that I may keep Omorede from going to war over this. When this business is finished you and I will sit beneath one of the Balsam trees along the Seventh Way so that we may drink some strong *Oosh* together. We will speak of better times."

As Bantu finished he saw the young Mfunde, over Mubuzu's shoulder, on his way back up the passage with two Mfundishi in tow. When the men exited the passage in the Wall they came directly to where Mubuzu was waiting. Mubuzu was the youngest of the three but since he was Keeping the Way it made him the senior Mfundishi in the matter. The first Mfundishi was a much older man with hard eyes who moved like silk billowing in the wind. Nearly as dark as his robes, he had small, but broad, facial features. The wrinkles at the corner of his eyes along with his slim build spoke of his advanced age. Yet he did not stoop but stood straight. He stood above Bantu by several inches. His voice was as hard as his black eyes. "I am Kari Gamalla As' Fulani. I have come to Hear a Cause." Like all Fulani the man was succinct. House Fulani did not mince words. The other man was younger than the Fulani but still older than Bantu or Mubuzu. He bowed formally, speaking with a warm, rich, baritone he said, "I am Pash Umadda As' Adari. Honor to your Houses. I have also come in order to Hear. I believe someone has Cause?"

The Adari were warm, hospitable, as well as fair to a fault. The Adari tended to be generous when it came to hearing a Cause. One had to have done something egregious in order to earn their enmity. In fact, as Bantu remembered it, only the Adari had ever been able to exasperate the prickly Allaka. Most avoided the Allaka. It could be disastrous to end up in a feud with their House. Not because you were certain to lose the feud but because the feud would never end. The Allaka often won by attrition. They would feud until the other House couldn't stand the countless, endless fights that sprung up over, literally, nothing. The only House the Allaka avoided, assiduously, was Adari. The Adari were the only ones who could make an Allaka walk away after having thrown their hands in the air in exasperation. One generally had to act so badly to offend the Adari that you usually ended up embarrassing only yourself.

This particular Adari was nearly as tall as the Fulani. He moved with the same deadly economy. The men were very different from each another, but both were undoubtedly deadly. You did not come to the black robes merely by time spent among the Mfunde. The acquisition of skill was central. The Adari smiled as if that was the only way he knew to hold his mouth showing off remarkably white teeth. His big, dark-brown eyes were bracketed by the tiny lines one got from laughing often. He had a very light complexion. Everything about Pash Umadda was large. He planted his yari in the ground between his feet with both oversized hands wrapped easily around its top end. He leaned congenially on it. "Come brothers, let us reason together. As Amandala once said, *there is no darkness so deep that a single light cannot illuminate.* I believe that we can come to an equitable agreement that will prevent any need for loosing the yari. What say you?"

At this the Fulani rolled his eyes heavenward. Bantu had to force himself not to laugh in spite of the seriousness of the situation. It was not that the Fulani disagreed with the Adari, but the man's proliferation of words was obviously grating on his Fulani ears. The Fulani hated to hear twenty words when four would do. Bantu thought he had best state his case before the Adari aggravated the Fulani to the point that the man would Challenge. It would not be the first time a Fulani had loosed his yari in the face of one word too many. Bantu bowed to the two Mfundishi as he introduced himself. "Honor to your Houses Mfundishi. I thank you for Hearing my Cause." After the formal greeting Bantu launched into a brief statement of his position that the prohibition was not specifically against women but against those who were not weapons according to the ancient traditions of Kal'ada'abassa. Furthermore, he pointed out that the Blossoms were in fact weapons, entitling them to passage beyond the Fourth Wall. When he finished he stood silently watching the Mfundishi who would adjudicate the rightness of his position.

While the Fulani brooded, with a sour look on his narrow face, the Adari began speaking as soon as Bantu fell silent. "Well, well now, First Born. You present an interesting argument. While it breaks with standing tradition I think there may just be a hint of merit in your auspicious, albeit succinct, argument." The Adari were always agreeable, which, for Bantu's purposes, was good. But Bantu had been watching the Fulani. The man had been turning Bantu's argument over in his mind, examining it carefully. While the Fulani were sparse with their commentary they were usually thoughtful, not to mention, disposed to upholding not only the letter of the Warring Way but its spirit - what it was meant to convey. His mouth was twisted as though he tasted something that did not agree with him. As Pash Umadda continued to assure everyone that they could come to a solution that was communally agreeable, the Fulani spoke.

"While it is distasteful to consider, I too think that the First Born has a position with the potential for merit. But I have one question." The Fulani was old, but he was still Mfundishi. Before Bantu could ask the man what his question was the Fulani fell on Isabelle, who stood closest to him, like a lightning strike. Had she been one hair's breadth less skilled, a fraction slower, she would have died in that instant. It was only through the benefit of the *gift* that she had the speed necessary to survive the first strike. The Fulani had loosed his yari while striking in the same motion. The blade of his yari would have taken Isabelle's head clean from her shoulders had she not been who, but more importantly, what she was. Isabelle was not the best in the Company with a sword, not by a longshot, but she was good. As she spun away, pirouetting like a dancer on her toes, she drew her sword in one fluid motion. She smiled back at the Fulani who, though she was a tall woman, stood head and shoulders over her. Bantu realized he was holding his breath. It dawned on him, just then, in that moment, that if the man killed her Bantu would kill him in short order, without hesitation. The man's death at Bantu's hand would almost certainly cause a feud to erupt between the Fulani and Omorede. But as he watched the man attack Isabelle it occurred to him that he did not care. Anyone who hurt one of the Blossoms would pay dearly. *To the Pit with the consequences.* Those feelings flew in the face of everything he had planned. But it was only in that moment that he realized, as utterly insane as it would be, that he would jeopardize it all if Isabelle died.

The Fulani was masterful. He was water flowing down a mountainside, silk spilling to the floor from a weaver's table, but there was steel attached. Black robes swirled as he came at Isabelle from every angle. He was fast as a final heartbeat with death following after. Bantu was leaning forward, watching closely. His own hand tightened on the yari nestled in the crook of his left arm. Isabelle, however, was Isabelle. For some, learning the art of the sword was hard, repetitive, work. But once in a while a teacher ran across a student for whom swordplay seemed a natural thing. In that student's hands what was a hard, fought for skill could be elevated to an art. The student still had to be taught. But as you poured knowledge into them it was as if you were only stirring up what was already there. That was Isabelle. She was in Bantu's master class. Right here, right now, at the entrance to the Fourth Wall in Kal'ada'abassa, half way around the world, in a strange land, she showed the Mfundade why. Her face was calm. She looked untroubled. Tranquility exuded from her as she moved. *Good,* Bantu thought, *stay calm.*

There was no strain in Isabelle's eyes, no furrowed brow, though the Fulani reigned down blows on her that would have shaken the arms of other outlanders as steel rang against steel. But Isabelle was a full-fledged member of the Peoples Company. She too wore the black. It was not the black robes of the Mfundishi but the black coat of the People. For members of the Company that meant they had been through the *Call* - that they had been given the *gift*. She was faster than she should have been. She was stronger than she otherwise would have been. So her arms did not shake at the power of the Mfundishi's blows. While steel rang against steel, she did not sweat, did not breathe heavily, nor was there fear on her face. If anyone was anxious it was Bantu. Even the other two Blossoms whom Bantu had reached out to restrain when Isabelle was first attacked only seemed angry, not fearful.

The two of them danced. They twirled this way, spinning that way, each, so very different, as they danced a dance of pure skill. But death seemed to be standing by watching. Bantu shook himself out of his mesmerized state to notice the crowd that had gathered. Mfundishi, with Mfunde standing respectfully behind them, stood in rapt attention at the display. Some with blatant surprise on their faces, others shock, while a few showed distaste, but all watching every stroke. Some watched the two, with their arms folded, like a gemstone trader studied a stone he was considering purchasing. Peeking out from among the many-colored robes were the small, double-braided heads of Seks, who stood wide-eyed, with mouths hanging open as they watched the spectacle.

The Fulani's eyes had narrowed. He had noticed the gathering crowd. Bantu smiled to himself noting that Isabelle's eyes had never left the Mfundishi. The two closed again, steel ringing against steel. Incredibly it seemed as if the Fulani moved even faster than before. Something had changed. Looking around him again Bantu realized that the Mfundishi had initially intended only to test Isabelle but now felt that his honor was somehow at stake. Turning back to the combatants Bantu started forward but a hand grabbed his arm. This time it was Wen stopping him. There was worry in her eyes, but she said, "I see it too Commander. And if you step in she will certainly stop, but will he?"

Wen was right. Isabelle would stop on the head of a copper if Bantu called for it but the Fulani might not. There was nothing else to do except watch. Round and round they went. As the Fulani pressed, Isabelle fell back. At times she came close to being overwhelmed but then she would pivot, or spin, with her teeth barred, turning the attack back on the Fulani. She was a natural. Nevertheless, the longer they went on the more it became apparent that the Mfundishi was simply better. She had managed to surprise him, to keep him off balance, but he was a man born to the Yari, raised in the Corral, who had worn the black robes for as long as Isabelle had been alive. He began to press her.

The longer the confrontation lasted the more Isabelle was forced into the position of using all her skill just to fend off the Fulani's attack. He began to bear down on her closing off her avenues of escape. It was a truly masterful performance. The Fulani reigned down three blows in quick succession that came so fast Bantu nearly missed them. Then his heart sank as Isabelle pitched back, stumbling, off balance. In that instant time seemed to slow. Bantu drew in breath like he was sucking air through a reed. A purple butterfly floated up across his line of vision like it was stuck in thick molasses. Its wings seemed to wave slowly rather than flutter. It was as if the world had slowed to a crawl.

Bantu knew immediately that he would be too late. They were too far away. She was going to die. Isabelle had thrown out a hand to try to steady herself. The Fulani was there. His yari slashed in at her aiming at the gaping opening Isabelle had left in her guard. Bantu leaped forward vainly as the Fulani's blade slashed downward. Steel rang loudly against steel as the Fulani's blade met the barred blade of another yari. Then time rushed forward, all at once, as if catching up to itself. Isabelle bounced back two steps, regaining her balance, and stood, pale-faced, looking at the two men across from her. The Fulani hopped back quickly looking around him before turning back to the man who had stopped his deathblow. All around the impromptu circle, made by the gathered crowd, there was startled silence.

In the center of the circle a man in the black robes of the Mfundishi twirled his yari above his head. The sunlight glinted off the polished steel of his yari before he slammed the blade home in its blackwood housing. With a quick twist, to secure its handle, he rose from the crouched position he had held. He spoke with a resonant tenor that commanded attention. His voice filled the space created by the haphazard ring of the crowd. "I am Alazzmakaz Kandar A' Aassam. And I would know why one of the Mfundade attacks a woman. Speak quickly Mfundishi, before I cut you down where you stand." He was Aassam, so his mouth pronounced every syllable of every word in that pompous dialect of his House.

Before the Fulani could respond Mubuzu stepped into the makeshift circle. "Honor to your House, First Born. I am Keeping the Way here at the Fourth Wall. There was a Cause that needed Hearing of which Mfundishi Kari Gamalla is a party to. If you will give us a moment we will explain." The Aassam's face was tight with anger. He looked at the older Fulani with death in his eyes like a slowly fading shadow. In Al'akaz a woman's safety was sacrosanct. A man could lose his head if he hurt one. Women could walk alone at any hour of the day or night without a worry or care. They could even cross into the territory of other Houses without fear of being attacked unless it was by another woman. The women of Al'akaz had their own rules concerning the conduct of women. The men stayed out of it, mostly. A man who tried to interfere would often be pointedly told to stay out of women's business. Bantu watched as the newly arrived Mfundishi took a moment to consider what Mubuzu had said. He nodded his head briefly in that way that said, *be quick about it*. Mubuzu stepped closer to the Aassam so the two men could speak in hushed tones.

While they spoke, Bantu turned his attention from them to Isabelle. He walked over to where she stood. Sheathing her sword, she came to attention as Bantu drew close to her. He did not have to look over his shoulder to know that Wen and Bella were right behind him. As soon as he was close enough Bantu caught her up in a full hug. He had only meant to place his hands on her shoulders, but he could not stop himself as relief washed over him. After a moment he put her back down on her feet holding her at arms length. Her face flushed with rising color while he looked her over. Smiling, he said, "I'm glad you're not hurt. You did well. I'm very proud of you." You would have thought he had promised her guaranteed passage to paradise when she died the way her face lit up as she looked up at him. When Bantu stepped back Wen and Bella fell on her. They hugged her tightly before beginning to fuss over her, checking every inch of her for the slightest scratch. Isabelle managed to look put upon. But Bantu could tell she was glad of the attention from her Blossom sisters. They fussed over her. Each woman periodically looked over at the Fulani Mfundishi. If looks could end a man's life the Fulani would have fallen over where he stood. The Fulani had won for himself some very dangerous enemies today. You did not threaten the Blossoms without reprisals. Even if Bantu ordered them to let it go, he knew he would be wasting his breath. They would not go against his orders directly but if they could find a way around them without actually breaking them they would. The Blossoms had a knack for that kind of thing. They would be found standing over the Fulani's dead body like lionesses at the end of the hunt, with fresh blood on their swords, looking Bantu directly in his eyes while their own faces were painted with looks of pure innocence. They would spend the next several minutes explaining how they had not *actually* disobeyed his orders.

When Bantu turned to look at the discussion between Mubuzu and the newly arrived Mfundishi he found the two men standing quietly, a few strides away, looking directly at him. Apparently, they had been waiting for him to finish seeing to Isabelle. They had been waiting at a respectful distance. When they caught his eye Mubuzu motioned for him to join them. Bantu had spent many nights thinking about what his demeanor should be when the day came that he returned home. He had always pictured himself as calm, even reserved. He had envisioned himself walking through the Beautiful Land with an air of distinguished detachment even as he sought out his family's enemies in order to satisfy the honor of Omorede in a disciplined, sober way. But he had just watched Isabelle be nearly killed. That brief instant, the lightning fast flicker of steel, replayed itself in his mind again. The more he thought about it the more he felt as thought it was time for a bit of temper. Twirling his father's yari once before letting it rest again in the crook of his left arm, Bantu set his mouth in a firm line as he walked the several steps that brought him to where the two Mfundishi stood.

Mubuzu spoke up hastily. He seemed to sense Bantu's changed mood, "May I present Alazzmakaz Kandar A' Aassam, First Born of House Aassam." Turning to Alazzmakaz, Mubuzu introduced Bantu. "And may I present to you Alazzmakaz, the First Born of House Omorede, Ossassande Bantu A' Omorede."

The Son of Aassam looked Bantu up and down, pausing briefly, apparently puzzled by the Company uniform that Bantu was wearing. When his eyes fell on the yari nestled in Bantu's left arm he nodded to himself. Looking Bantu in the eye he said, "Welcome back, Son of Omorede, I greet you on behalf of Aassam. I declare that there is no grievance between us and I humbly acknowledge the *Debt* we owe. Great honor to your House."

Though Bantu was vexed he breathed deeply before he spoke. The rituals between two First Borns of the Great Houses were different than other ritual greetings. Son or Daughter was used rather than names, any standing feuds were acknowledged, or, as in this case, the lack thereof. Finally, any debts that existed between Houses were recognized. What made Bantu breath deeply was the naming of this particular debt by the Son of House Aassam. It was a complex matter that went back more generations than most could count but that Aassam had never forgotten nor allowed Omorede to forget. The problem had always been that it was the kind of debt that could never really be repaid, though Aassam had insisted on trying in every generation. Omorede had tried to be circumspect in dealing with the matter mostly by never mentioning it. This sometimes aggravated the Aassam. The other way Omorede had chosen to deal with it was by never calling on the debt to be repaid.

"Greetings, Son of Aassam. I thank you for the welcome. I agree that no grievance exists between us. Great Honor to your House."

Alazzmakaz exhaled sharply at Bantu's failure to acknowledge the debt in the traditional greeting. But that had been the way of things between Bantu's father and Alazzmakaz's father, as well as their Grand Fathers, extending even for generations beyond. The Aassam always mentioned the debt while the Omorede always avoided acknowledging it. While it troubled Aassam to no end it did not stop them from trying to repay the debt in every successive generation. Some said that it had become a thing that was trumpeted in the House of Aassam, as each generation claimed that theirs would be the one to finally repay the debt. Alazzmakaz, fighting a sour look, said, while dismissively waving his hand, "That is as it may be though we both know that there is a Debt between us. At the moment we seem to have something of a quandary that needs disposing of? According to Mfundishi Lazda'ah of the Gamba you have questioned the prohibition of the Fourth Wall?"

Bantu nodded. "Mubuzu has the right of it. It is my position that the prohibition is against nonweapons, not, in point of fact, against women. We have spoken in such a way as to make the prohibition seem to be against women since, in Al'akaz, women are not weapons, but rather the heartbeat of the Great House. But in the Outlands, where I have lived since leaving the Beautiful Land, some women do become weapons. There are three of them with me today. Each of them is a part of my Honor Guard. As weapons, vouched for by Omorede, they have a right to discharge that duty." Here Bantu let his voice drop while adding a bit of steel to his tone. "And while it is good to see my old friend Mubuzu, as well as the son of my old teacher Zalakazam, I am on the verge of spilling blood. It is true that I have not been in the Corral for many years. But do not make the mistake of thinking that means I have returned with a dull blade."

Alazzmakaz held up a hand as if to say peace. "I understand your irritation Son of Omorede. If you will allow me to address the matter?"

Bantu looked closely at Alazzmakaz. He recognized the look he saw in the man's eye, not to mention the crook of a, not so nice, smile at the right corner of his mouth. It was the same look Alazzmakaz's father used to get before he did something that would enrage the Hall of Masters. It seemed that the son of the *Defiant One* had grown up to become just like his father. Bantu nodded his assent.

Alazzmakaz turned back to the two Mfundishi who had been brought to Hear the Cause. The Adari, Pash Umadda, and the Fulani, Kari Gamalla, stood several feet apart. The Adari was trying his best to make it appear that the Fulani had been acting on his own. Alazzmakaz spoke with enough volume to be heard by the entire impromptu gathering. "So Fulani, I take it you thought that you would test the premise that these women, accompanying the First of Omorede, were truly weapons? That this is why you thought it appropriate to raise your hand, let alone a blade, to a woman inside the Beautiful Land, especially within the confines of the Shining Walls?"

The Fulani, a man of many more years than Alazzmakaz, responded with an unusual amount of respect to Alazzmakaz, "Yes, First Born. That was my intention."

Bantu took note of the fact that Alazzmakaz must have been almost as good as his father. If an Mfundishi of Kari Gamalla's age and ability spoke to him with such deference it meant something. It was not so much the words but rather the tone of the man's voice. It was soft, even humble. While the man was an inch taller than Alazzmakaz, who was several inches taller than Bantu, the Fulani managed to stoop a bit as he spoke to Alazzmakaz. Nodding at the Fulani's words the Son of Aassam turned to the gathered crowd of the Mfundade. "Is there even one among you who doubts this woman's skill or who would question the other two?"

Bantu nearly burst out laughing as Alazzmakaz stood in the center of the circle holding his yari like his father Zalakazam used to hold it. He stood there with both hands behind his back, held close together at the yari's midpoint, the yari slanted across his body from the back of his right thigh to his left shoulder blade. He looked as if he were going to pace while lecturing the gathered crowd on some tenet of the Warring Way. It was clear that Bantu was not the only man carrying his father's yari. What had nearly made Bantu laugh was the way Alazzmakaz was handling the situation. If no one objected to the claim that the women were, in fact, weapons, then Alazzmakaz could name them so by acclamation, without any particular Mfundishi being responsible for the ruling. There were several Mfundishi in the crowd, which made that possible. But the genius that lay at the heart of doing it that way was the reality that not a single man in the crowd would have dared to say no because Alazzmakaz had made himself the arbiter of the matter. That put him in a position to Challenge any man who objected. As Bantu listened to the silence that followed it was apparent that Alazzmakaz was, in fact, as good as his father had been. Not a single man Challenged. Alazzmakaz turned slowly in a circle looking at each man who stood at the front of the crowd. It was as if he were daring them to say something. After he had made a complete turn he nodded to himself. "I therefore declare the matter closed in favor of the one who brings the Cause. Seeing that these women are in fact weapons, they may pass, and the prohibition stands! This Hearing is at an end, go in peace!" With those words the crowd began to disburse.

As the members of the Mfundade began to move off, many shooing wide-eyed Seks ahead of them, Alazzmakaz made his way back to where Bantu stood. Mubuzu joined them. Alazzmakaz was smiling broadly now, looking like a younger version of his father, with the smallish facial features of the Aassam, the slightly lighter complexion, matched by eyes like the great cats that roam the Sedengatti. He was tall like his father had been standing nearly a full seven spans. While it was not a bulky seven, it was a solid seven. His deep voice still had the lightness of youth to it. "Well, Omorede, I know that does not pay the debt, but it was fun nevertheless. In minutes, someone will have whispered these events into N'duma's ear. He will be outraged. He is a traditionalist, so it will offend his sensibility. Maybe it will offend him enough that he will loose his yari against me."

Mubuzu, who was also smiling broadly, interjected, "Not likely, First Born. He knows that he is no match for the Son of Zalakazam. It is why he avoids insulting you directly in the Hall. He is very careful not to give you cause to be offended. But -" Mubuzu caught himself pulling up short of what he had been about to say. Alazzmakaz looked at Mubuzu expectantly, waiting for the man to finish. But Mubuzu swallowed the rest of what he was going to say. Then it dawned on Bantu why he stopped himself. This was the man Mandisa was referring to when he said that the one man who could have Challenged N'duma would not. While it might have been interesting to find out why Alazzmakaz would not Bantu had other things to deal with. He said, "While I would like to stay and catch up, I have another Cause to be Heard in the Hall of Masters. It has waited many years. It must not wait longer." The two men nodded solemnly. Looking directly at Alazzmakaz, Bantu said, "By the way, how did you know I would be here?"

Alazzmakaz said, "Word has spread throughout the Beautiful Land, like a running fire through the Great Wood, that the Son of Omorede has returned and that Omorede prepares for war. I knew that you would be here for two reasons. First, you are driven to right a very old wrong. Do not the Griot say, *Desire is destiny*? Where else would you be? Besides, my sister thought that I should be here to make sure your head remains on your shoulders."

Bantu looked at the man as he laughed softly with an amused smile on his face. *Jamila*. The single word that described the second headache he could not seem to get rid of. Bantu gritted his teeth. Part of him wanted to strangle the woman. But when he thought about Isabelle, he realized that he probably would do better to thank her for sending her brother to Kal'ada'abassa. Bantu sighed with resignation. Motioning for his Honor Guard, he introduced them to Alazzmakaz. When Bantu came to Mandisa, Alazzmakaz inclined his head slightly. He said, "Yes, yes. I know of the man who has guarded the honor of Omorede in the absence of its First. Mandisa, it is an honor."

Mandisa inclined his head with respect saying, "No, First Born of Aassam, it is my honor to serve. Omorede rejoices at the return of its Son."

Alazzmakaz patted Mandisa on the shoulder with a smile. Bantu nodded to himself, the son *was* very much like the father. Turning to Mubuzu, Bantu said, "Now, may we pass my old friend?"

With an exaggerated bow, coupled with an overly embellished gesture of welcome made with his right arm, like some outland courtier, Mubuzu said, "It is my pleasure to offer you passage through the Fourth Wall." Both men laughed as Mubuzu straightened from his bow. Bantu lead his Honor Guard, accompanied by Alazzmakaz, through the Fourth Wall into the Fourth Way.

The Darkness tempts men with what they desire most, but tortures them by giving it to them twisted beyond recognition.

~Griot saying

The Lion leads.

~Inscription in the Hall of Masters

CHAPTER TWENTY-FOUR

Shadows in the Hall

Wen tried to reign in her emotions as she followed Bantu through the long, shadowed passage in the Fourth Wall. There was a slight echo. The sound of their footfalls bounced off the walls of the tunnel-like passageway. Watching Isabelle come so close to being killed by the Fulani Mfundishi had put Wen on edge. Her mood was turning decidedly dark. It had been headed that way since their arrival in the Beautiful Land due mostly to the ever-present danger that surrounded the Commander. In order to combat that feeling she had tried to put her mind on other things, like the stunning architecture of Kal'ada'abassa. The passage through the Fourth Wall was like all the others. It was unadorned, with a light, cooling breeze, which carried hints of the smells from the next street ahead, which the Al'akazian's called a Way. As they exited the passage into the Fourth Way Wen looked up, marveling again, at the scale of the architecture of Al'akaz. Each time she thought she had begun to adjust to wonders of the place she was introduced to something else that nearly took her breath away. Wen had heard someone call the city the *Shining Walls*. It was deserving of the name. Having gotten a closer look at the outer wall of Kal'ada'abassa as they entered the city, Wen had come away baffled by the fact that there were no grooves in what appeared to be a golden sandstone. When she ran her hand over it she had found that it was smooth as glass. The sun reflected off that golden-colored stone causing it to gleam brightly in the daylight. As they went from one Wall to the next Wen was amazed by their thickness. They must have been some thirty paces thick while each wall climbed higher into the sky than its predecessor. The skill needed to create such a structure was beyond her comprehension. Wen had seen buildings that struck her with awe, the Peoples Tower being one, but what she had seen in Al'akaz was enough to dwarf the imagination.

While there had been a number of circumstances slowing their party's progression through the Walls of Kal'ada'abassa their pace had quickened once they were through the Fourth Wall. Wen barely got an opportunity to see what was contained in the next few Ways. Bantu hurried them along. He paused for a few minutes in the Fifth Way when their party was accosted by a small mob of boys with blue bands of color around the hem of their white robes. It did not take long to realize they were from the House of Omorede. Wen thought it was the cutest thing in the world. She would not have said as much out loud knowing that boys did not take to that kind of praise. Nevertheless, there they were, thronging the long lost First Born of their House, with light brown faces turned up in pride, mixed with awe, jockeying for position as they called out to him. Bantu did his best to speak to as many of them as he could, reaching out to touch them as they crowded in on him. He tried to answer as many of the high-voiced questions as he could make out, telling them that yes, he had come home, that no, they were not going to war, and yes, they were to remain in the Corral to finish their training. Before they relented the crowd of boys even extracted the promise from him that he would come to visit them when he could. When it looked as if the diminutive throng of double braided heads, swath in white robes, would overrun Bantu, Mandisa waded into the crowd. They were called

Seks. Mandisa loudly promised them all red ribbons in their hair if they did not get back to their chores at once. The other Mfundade of Omorede, making up Bantu's honor guard, laughed softly to themselves at the speed with which the Seks of Omorede disbursed. It had only taken a blink of an eye for them to tally the cost of N'Kosi colored ribbons entwined in their braids against speaking a few more minutes with the newly returned First Born of their House. One of the Mfundade standing nearby explained the threat to Wen. She nearly giggled herself as she watched them all decide the ribbons would be too high a price to pay for more time with the First Born of their House.

After that brief interlude, there was nothing else that delayed their journey to the heart of Kal'ada'abassa. In quick succession, their party made its way through each Wall, into each Way. Finally, they stepped out of the last passage through the Seventh Wall into the Seventh Way. It was the last Way. It was located at the very center of Kal'ada'abassa. Wen stepped out into the sunlight of the Seventh Way. Her breath caught in her throat. Unlike the other Ways, they were not immediately met by people headed to their various bits of business. They did not run into the sights or sounds of a busy city street. Rather, as they stepped into the open air of the Seventh Way, they were met by what Wen could only call stillness. Where the other Ways had been populated by people the Seventh Way was filled with trees.

Purple and white blossoms floated through the air as a light breeze lifted the most tenuous of them from thin tree limbs. All around their party, low standing, wide blackwood trees stood as far as the eye could see. There must have been hundreds of them. Each tree had a host of black limbs filled with those tiny, purple or white blossoms. The ground was covered in bright green, ankle deep grass. Surprisingly, that was all there was to what Wen could initially see of the Seventh Way. Nothing distracted from the vision that was the beautiful collection of trees. It was part forest, part orchard.

Wen inhaled deeply taking in a scent that was, almost cherry blossom, almost honeysuckle. It was something she had never smelled before, but it opened her nose fully. She watched Bantu, along with the other men of Al'akaz, walk through the grove with a studied reverence. They moved with a reserved silence. The faint rustle of cloth was the only evidence anyone was passing this way. Wen, and the other Blossoms, followed suit. They walked without speaking. Instead, they took in the simple beauty of the place. After walking for some time through row after row of trees they finally came to the only building in the Seventh Way. By the look of things, it must have been standing at the exact center of the Seventh Way. It was a tower of sheer black stone. Wen's mouth hung open. She had never seen anything like it. As they approached, a single man in black robes rose from his haunches. After a few quiet words with Alazzmakaz he pushed open the broad, black-lacquered doubledoors. He stood aside allowing them to enter.

They stepped into an antechamber of unadorned walls covered in gray marble, with streaks of white running through it, lit by silver-colored lamps hanging at equal intervals. The only decorations were the flowing lines of color in the center of the gray, marble, floor. Wen fell in line behind Bantu. He trailed Mandisa, who followed Alazzmakaz, as they made their way down the hallway. The rest of the Honor Guard, including the other Blossoms, followed. There were no doors only the winding hallway of cool gray marble. The further they walked the more Wen realized that the swirling lines of color in the marble floor were actually the colors of two of the Great Houses, namely the Omorede and Aassam. It took a bit of walking but eventually they came to another set of double doors. This set was similar to the first, with its thick, black-lacquered, wood hanging on golden hinges. The difference was that this set of doors was intricately carved with a colorful lion on each side. There were precious gemstones precisely placed as parts of the great cats. They sparkled in the lamplight bringing the cats to life. The men who stood on either side of the doubledoors ignored them. Wen guessed that if you got this far it must mean that you belonged here. Without pausing Alazzmakaz stepped forward pushing the doubledoors open. He did not wait for them to follow but walked into the chamber.

Wen followed Bantu into an enormous hall with a ceiling that stretched up into darkness. The chamber was lit by a series of lamps hanging along the wall. They cast a dim light, which gave the hall a sinister feel. The flickering lamplight left shadows everywhere. Wen began to get the unshakeable feeling that she was being watched. What she did not expect, but what should have been indicated from the way the hallway was adorned, was that the chamber would be so empty of ornamentation.

In the very center of the hall was a broad circle of simple, blackwood, backless chairs. There was a single chair in that circle, which did have a back. It was also larger than the others. It was decorated in some way that Wen could not make out from where she stood. It did not sit on a platform or dais but was separated from the others by its sheer size. But what really caught her eye was not the blank, gray walls, unadorned ceiling, or even the circle of chairs. It was the floor. The floor was the same gray marble that had been in the hallway but, the colors that had swirled along the center of the floor as they approached the hall, also curled along the edge of the expansive chamber. They picked up other strands of color from other doorways as the curling, twisting pattern swirled around the floor's edge. Wen quickly counted a total of twelve sets of doors. Those swirling lines of vibrant color circled around the outer wall like a rushing river picking up other colors, from each doorway it passed, as if they were tributaries flowing into one great stream, until they finally poured into the hall's center coalescing into a single pattern. Wen followed Bantu to one of the chairs, which sat halfway around the circle from the larger chair. When they got to that spot in the chamber she noticed the nature of the pattern. The swirl of colors formed an intricate border, like detailed lace, ringing the circle of chairs. Inside that border was something else altogether, which Wen was finally close enough to make out in detail. A mosaic in the form of a roaring lion in gold, brown, red, and green was embedded in the floor. It was a stylized representation, which was larger than any lion ever could be, done in colors that stretched the imagination. But it was done with an artistry that took Wen's breath away. The skin was burnt gold. Its eyes were green emeralds sparkling in the faint lamplight. Its mane was made from flowing strands of gold, brown, and red. The teeth, matched by its claws, were made of glittering diamonds. It was a masterpiece. Below its feet were golden words written in a language Wen did not understand. *Moh'di a' juda.* A quick question put to one of the members of the Honor Guard standing next to her told her that the inscription meant, *The Lion Leads*.

Wen was so enraptured by the mosaic that she missed the moment other double doors around the room swung open admitting Mfundishi who strolled into the hall with the gait of men who brought death with them. Looking up from the mosaic she saw them filling the hall, a small army of tall, grim, hard looking men in black robes. Heads shaven, with cleancut faces, each man wore the look of men who were not to be trifled with. They poured out of open doorways making their way to various sections of the chamber. Each of them came to stand behind particular chairs around the circle while the flickering lamplight cast shadows all around them. With her hand tightening on the hilt of her sword Wen saw a detail she had not noticed until now. It was highlighted by where the Mfundishi chose to stand. Looking down at her own feet she realized her eyes were not deceiving her. Part of the intricate pattern formed by the colors in the floor were triangular sections whose points lined up just behind each chair around the circle. Those lines extended back forming a curved border a few feet shy of the wall. Wen counted twenty-four chairs matched by twenty-four triangular sections around the hall. There were patterns within the patterns on the floor. Wen could see ever increasing circles with other forms. There were even patterns within each band. As the men entered they made their way to particular areas behind particulars chairs. Wen should not have been surprised. Apparently, each House had a seat around the circle with a section for its members behind that seat. While one might have thought, at a glance, that the hall represented a kind of unity for Bantu's people, it was quite the opposite.

She watched as the areas behind each chair began to fill with hardened men in black robes. All around the hall the low buzz of conversation began as they settled into the sections of their respective Houses. There was not much attention paid to the men of other Houses except in a few rare cases. In some areas of the hall men stood along the edges of their sections talking to men who stood on the other side of the line in their own section as if an invisible wall separated them. Wen looked around beginning to really see things she had missed as they passed through Kal'ada'abassa. Some of the men, like Alazzmakaz, had robes made of a fine, lightweight silk. Others like Mandisa wore robes made of fine linen that glistened in the lamplight. Still others around the hall wore cotton. Apparently, the Houses were not equal in either strength or wealth. While on the surface the Mfundishi looked to be a single entity, upon closer examination, it was becoming clear that they were not. Wen also picked up on one other thing as she studied her surroundings. Some of the men from different sections of the hall were looking at one another as if they would be very happy to kill each other given half a chance. She wondered what was keeping them from doing just that? Was there a prohibition against fighting in this hall? Why would that be the case when they seemed ready to kill each other at the drop of a hat in every other part of Al'akaz?

Soon, each section in the hall held a number of Mfundishi, though the chairs remained empty. The men in Omorede's section stood very still. They were also quiet. The few attempts to engage them in idle conversation by men on either side of their section had fallen on deaf ears. The Omorede were focused. Wen began to rethink the possibility that fighting in the hall was prohibited. The men of Omorede were on edge. Wen remembered that they were Bantu's Honor Guard. But who needed an Honor Guard if there was not the possibility of being attacked? Unconsciously Wen loosened her sword in its scabbard. *Easy*, she told herself. *Take it easy Wen*. She calmed herself. She also realized that the men who wore blue and white robes in Bantu's Honor Guard were not with them anymore. When had that happened? Only the Omorede in black robes were present.

Just as Wen was about to ask one of the black-robed Omorede what had happened to the others, the double doors directly behind the large chair opened. A procession of black-robed men entered. They came directly to the section behind the large chair. Wen got a good look at them. A chill ran down her spine. When they made their way to the section behind the large chair Wen noticed that the triangle on the floor beneath their feet was the red and white of the N'kosi. The men who had come for the Commander had worn those colors. The ones who had tried to kill him had worn those colors. It dawned on her that these same men were somehow in charge here. *Breathe Wen*, she told herself, *breathe*. She felt her grip tightening again on her swordhilt. She looked from one set of shadows to another. The sensation of being watched intensified for a moment before subsiding. *They will not kill him*, she kept telling herself. Prohibition or not, if they tried to lay a hand on him there would be blood staining that beautiful mosaic in the center of the floor.

When the newly arrived men had filled their section, a gong sounded from somewhere in the shadows. The sound reverberated around the hall as a giant of a man entered from the same doorway. Wen had begun to get used to the size of the men of Bantu's homeland, but this man stood above even them. He must have been nearly seven and a half spans. It was a solid seven too. His robes were the same black, embroidered in gold thread around the hem, just like the other Mfundishi, with one exception. The gold embroidery around the cuffs and hem of his outer robe were not the simple scrollwork found on the robes of the others. His was woven in the shape of lions standing on their hind legs with their front legs lashing out. Their mouths were open as though roaring. His gait had more strut to it than the other men. Though he moved with the same economy that spoke of a man in full control of his body. His head and face were clean-shaven. His skin was as dark as midnight. The man had broad features to match his size. He did not bother to look around the room but walked directly to the large chair. He sat down without preamble or ceremony. It occurred to Wen that he moved like someone else she knew. He moved like Bantu. So, he was not only gifted with size but skill. His voice was as deep as one would imagine coming from that body. He bellowed, "Masters of the Hall, please be seated."

Upon hearing those words, a man from each House stepped forward to take the seat at the head of their section. Wen was not surprised when Mandisa stepped forward to sit in the chair for Omorede. She was even less surprised to see Alazzmakaz step from the ranks of the Aassam to take the seat to the immediate right of the large chair. When he sat the man in the large chair turned to him. "Son of Aassam, we are honored to have you join this session of the Hall of Masters. There must be pressing matters before us today to call you from Aassam."

Without looking at the man in the large chair Alazzmakaz said in his own deep tenor, "Why Baba'a'funde, I did not think you cared."

There was a smattering of laughter around the chamber as Alazzmakaz leaned forward in his seat, not the least of which came from the Aassam behind him. The *Baba'a'funde*, as Alazzmakaz had called him, did not look amused. But he said nothing to Alazzmakaz. Once the Hall settled, the man looked around him as he said, "I understand that one of the Houses has an announcement of joy to share with the rest of us?" Looking over at Mandisa the man nodded his head. Mandisa stood, looking around him at each man seated along the arc of the circle. A deathly stillness descended on the hall. Some, along the Ways, had said that word of what was coming had spread. Mandisa took a moment before he spoke. It was as if he was savoring something he had waited a long time to see. When he did speak his voice was hard but not harsh. "It is the joy of Omorede to announce to the Hall of Masters that the Son of Omorede has returned." With those words a number of the men around the chamber thumped the ends of their yari on the floor. The sound was louder than Wen would have expected. Wen settled in for a speech of some kind but Mandisa sat as if all that needed to be said had been.

The man in the large chair steepled his fingertips together, while looking at the Omorede section of the hall. Wen did not fail to note the dark light in his eyes. She even noticed their slight narrowing. The man managed to keep his voice neutral, but Wen knew the signs of someone who was troubled. This man was bothered by the fact that Bantu had returned. Wen revised that assessment in her mind almost immediately. He was probably not bothered that Bantu had returned but that Bantu was still alive. His voice remained level. The *Baba'a'funde*, as they called him, managed to maintain a noncommittal neutral tone to his voice as he spoke over steepled fingertips. "Let the First Born of the Omorede come forward to be recognized."

With those words the grave-faced, silent Omorede parted. Bantu, in his crisp, well-cut Company uniform, took several steps forward, stopping as he came alongside the seat that Mandisa now occupied. The yari he carried, in place of his sword, which was an interesting kind of part-sword, part-staff as Wen understood it, was nestled in the crook of his left arm. He looked around him at the circle of seasoned men. They all looked the part of lions ready to feast. Something welled up in Wen. She felt like she was seeing the Commander more clearly than she ever had. With these other men as a backdrop she saw him, maybe for the first time, as he was meant to be seen. She saw where he had really come from. She saw why he stood so tall, walked so confidently, and seemed so deadly. He was a lion. He was a hunter born of hunters. Seeing him among the people he was born of made her wonder, *what were they born to hunt?* While Wen allowed herself to see him as he was she watched him look around at his surroundings. He did not seem to be prey for their consumption. In that moment Wen's bottled up trepidation evaporated. He stood there, undaunted, and unafraid, showing her, by his posture, that there was nothing to fear. Pride swelled up in her as she watched her Commander stand in the midst of a throng of predators and show his own teeth. Wen smiled wickedly. Let them challenge him. There would be the Pit to pay.

Bantu's voice was as clear as it was unwavering. He did not raise it, but somehow it carried across the entire hall. "I have come to Challenge."

The Baba'a'funde leaned forward at Bantu's words as if surprised. His deep bass reverberated with shock that Wen found unconvincing. "Why, Son of Omorede, what could have given you cause to Challenge? Has someone offended you or your House since your return? Point them out, or if they are not here, speak their name and I will personally see to it that they are dealt with."

Before the man had finished Bantu was already shaking his head. "No, Son of N'kosi, you mistake me. It is not a new offense that brings me here. It is a very old one. On the night that I was spirited away from Al'akaz my parents were killed. Earlier that day I had fought with another of the Seks over a girl, a girl who had spurned his advances. The young boy came to me believing I was the reason." As Bantu spoke Wen saw the Baba'a'funde lean further back in his seat. His face became darker by the moment. Bantu continued, with a dangerous edge creeping into his voice, "The truth was that she didn't want him. But she was the First Daughter of the First House. So his relentless, boundless, ambition would not allow him to be dissuaded. You see, winning her hand would have catapulted him to the very heights of Al'akaz. Harsh words passed between us in the Warren of the Seks. There, without witness, we loosed our Yari. I defeated him without much effort. But later I came to realize that he could not live with that either. That night his father, followed by others of the N'kosi, came for me in the darkness. My parents got me to safety, but not without losing their own lives. I have not come for some other member of the Mfundade, Son of N'kosi. I have come for you Nduma." Bantu's voice turned to ice as he barred his teeth, "I Challenge!"

At those words a host of voices went up around the room in a roar like thunder, "Challenge! Challenge!" The voices echoed off the chamber walls while the butt-end of yari clattered against the floor. When the noise began to die down Nduma rose from his seat. His voice was cooler than it had been. The giant of a man spoke around clenched teeth. "I … have sympathy, for what the Son of Omorede has suffered. And while I would not call him a liar, I believe he has been misled concerning the facts of those days. But before I can answer the Challenge there is another matter that must be dealt with. According to the tenets of the Warring Way, as well as the mandates of the Rights to the Corral, the Son of Omorede, while having the Right of the Hall to address the Masters as First Born of his House, has not been through the Rites of Passage. He does not wear the black robes and, as such, is not entitled to Challenge in this place."

The Hall erupted at the man's words. There were some men yelling that it did not matter while others shouted that the tenets must be upheld. The men who had been sitting in the chairs were standing as they tried to restore order. Bantu did not move, nor was he yelling. He simply stood there with a face like stone. Wen looked over at Nduma who was smiling sardonically at Bantu as if to mock him. After allowing the uproar to continue for several moments the large man made an absent motion with his left hand. A gong sounded loudly. The sound caused the men around the hall to settle down.

Once the Hall returned to some semblance of order Alazzmakaz stood from the chair at the head of the section holding the members of House Aassam, "The House of Aassam would be heard." After a moment Nduma nodded his assent. Alazzmakaz continued, "The Baba is correct." Around the Hall men began shouting again but the gong sounded immediately. Silence returned more quickly. Alazzmakaz continued, "If the Hall will allow me to finish?" This time the Son of Aassam looked pointedly around the hall daring someone to interrupt him again. After assuring himself that silence would reign during the rest of his comments he went on, "As I said. The Baba'a'funde is correct in that the Son of Omorede has not been through the Rites of Passage. As such, he is not truly entitled to bring Challenge, against a Master, in the Hall of Masters. But, I would hear the minds of the Masters of the Houses. I would know if any of them are aware of the ancient Way of the Hall as it relates to the raising of Mfundishi?"

Wen looked around the Hall. The men in their chairs were looking at one another seemingly as puzzled as she found herself. What, by the Pit, was he talking about? A low murmuring rose in the Hall. Undoubtedly, it was the sound of men wondering, like Wen, what Alazzmakaz was getting at. Then, at the opposite side of the circle, almost directly across from Nduma's large seat, a much older Mfundishi stood slowly from his chair. He had one of the lightest complexions in the Hall as well as being the thinest. Though his head and face were shaven, Wen could see time hanging on him like a well-worn cloak. His face had the look of a mountain weathered by the wind. When he raised his arm to get the attention of the Hall she could see that there were spots on the back of his hand. The murmuring around the chamber fell away when the man began to speak. "I am Gesi Aman A' Solowetu." Wen noticed that his robes were slightly wrinkled. They seemed to be made of some coarsely woven cloth. There were only a handful of Mfundishi standing behind him. Apparently, Solowetu was a small, undistinguished House but that seemed immaterial at the moment. Gesi Aman was still given the floor.

The sage looking man leaned on his yari, not for effect but to steady himself. He took his time in the manner of the very old. After his first words, which did not carry above the murmuring, a hush fell on the Hall. His voice had the soft timber of time in its tone. But without competing sounds it still managed to echo around the large chamber. "I would be pleased to share my mind with the young Son of Aassam on the matter he has eluded to. According to the records of the Hall, in ancient times, there was more than one way to gain the Right of Kal'ada. Yes, there were the Rites, but there was also the Will of the Hall." The aged Mfundishi paused, licking his lips before he continued. "Since I do not have many sunrises remaining I will not waste what time I have left on a long drawn out explanation of the origins of it. It is there for any of you who would take the time to read about it. I lament that the young men who roam Kal'ada these days have more thirst for blood than books."

The elder Mfundishi paused to catch his breath. After a few seconds, in which the men around the chamber waited patiently for their elder to speak again, he finally jerked his head up slightly as if he had just remembered he was addressing the Hall. With eyes that narrowed a fraction he nodded to himself. His voice took on an edge as it dropped low forcing everyone to lean toward him stretching to hear. "They were dark days. The reverberations of *The Wasting* still shook the Beautiful land. The Great Houses were only just being formed, even as the Shining Walls were just being raised, in the hopes that something could be saved. Mfundishi died faster than they could be *Raised*. I mean no disrespect when I say what I say next. But those men were harder than the ones who wear the black robes these days. And from time to time, a House needed an Mfundishi raised when there was no time for the proper rites. In those cases, the Mfunde was brought to the entrance of Kal'ada by the Baba of his House. If he made it to the Hall of Masters alive he was raised to the black robes."

There was stunned silence for several moments as the words of Gesi Aman were digested. One of the Masters, still seated, from a House Wen did not know spoke into the silence. His strong baritone echoed off the chamber walls. "How difficult could that be Gesi Aman? A man raised to the black robes for making a long walk?"

There was more murmuring, accompanied by a few uncomfortable bursts of laughter, as many others in the Hall nodded their agreement with the assessment of the Master who had spoken up. But Wen had caught the words that some of them had undoubtedly missed. Gesi Aman had said, *if he made it to the Hall of Masters alive*. Wen's blood ran cold as the elder Master spoke again. "Yassan N'delle, if you had listened more closely to me you would know that it was more than a long walk, much more in fact. The penitent had to arrive at the Hall *alive*. You see gaining the Will of the Hall meant that Mfundishi, present in Kal'ada, could stop the man along the way to Challenge him. It was a way of testing the man's skill. If, after loosing the yari, the Mfundishi was satisfied that the penitent showed the ability necessary to wear the black robes he would allow him to continue on to the Hall. And if he did not, he would either seriously wound the man, or kill him to keep him from succeeding."

With that, the elder Mfundishi bent slowly until he could once again ease himself into his seat. He leaned back in his chair, exhaling deeply from the exertion, while the Hall exploded with discussion. Men clamored for the floor while others argued with each other about what they had heard. Wen looked at Bantu who stood still. His face gave away nothing. She could not tell how he felt about what he had heard. After a few moments of allowing the Hall to continue in disarray Nduma motioned with his hand. The gong resounded with three sonorous notes. When he was sure all the talk had ended he leaned forward in his seat saying, "Far be it from me to disagree with a man who has sat along the Masters Wheel as long as the honorable Gesi Aman. But are we to fall back to ways so ancient that they have been nearly forgotten by the Mfundishi instead of holding to the way of things in the present Hall?"

Allazmakaz had been seated, refraining from speaking, as the elder Mfundishi spoke, but now he stood, replying to what Nduma had just said. "If I may, venerable Masters?" He paused a single beat before continuing. "It seems to me that this ancient Way, though harsh as those distant days made it, seems suitable to the task of meeting the burden of the Hall as well as the rights of Omorede. I call for the Masters Accord."

Wen turned to look at Nduma. The giant man had sat back in the large chair with a dark look on his face. For a moment it seemed as if a shadow fell across his features, but it was gone so quickly that Wen immediately began to doubt she had seen it at all. What struck her as odd though was the quick change in Nduma's disposition. The dark glowering look had been replaced by an even-tempered one. Already nodding his head, Nduma stood. When he rose, the Hall fell silent. Looking from one side of the Hall to the other, Nduma spoke, his deep resounding bass carrying the length of the chamber. "An Accord is not necessary, Son of Aassam. If the Son of Omorede wishes to accept the ancient Will of the Hall, then so be it." All eyes turned toward Bantu.

Without hesitation Bantu said, "I will."

Nduma said, "Then it is settled. Seven days from today Omorede will present its First Born before the First Wall to seek the Hall according to the ancient way." With a pointed look at Bantu he said, "And may the Ancient of Days have mercy on you -" The way he said it sent a chill up Wen's spine because she could almost hear what Nduma had left unsaid, *for we certainly will not*. With a dismissive wave of his hand Nduma turned as the gong sounded again. The Baba'a'funde walked out the way he had entered with the throng of N'kosi behind him. All around the Hall the other representatives of the Great Houses began to disperse. Wen watched as Bantu exchanged words with Mandisa and Allazmakaz, before turning to leave. Wen followed Bantu, along with the rest of Omorede, as they made their way out of the Hall of Masters along the same way they had entered. While they walked she asked one of the Omorede Mfundishi, who walked close to her, whose name she had not gotten, but did not think to ask, "Why did the Masters not vote? How could Nduma simply dictate what happened with Allazmakaz's offering to the Hall?"

Apparently, she was saying a number of things wrong because the man winced several times while she asked her questions. That did not stop him from politely answering her. Looking down at her with a smile, the kind you smile for children who do not yet understand what is obvious to you, he said, "My lady, Nduma is the Baba'a'funde. He is the

Father of Weapons, the Lion of the Corral, and among the Mfundade the Lion leads."

The man lengthened his stride walking on ahead of Wen. Soon, they were out of the central building in the Seventh Way, among the beautiful trees that surrounded it, on their way out of Kal'ada'abassa. When they exited the building the rest of Bantu's Honor Guard fell in behind them. *Seven days*, she thought, as they walked on. In seven days, they would return to watch men, some of the deadliest she had ever seen, try to kill Bantu.

The price of freedom is vigilance.

*~excerpt from The Precepts
Also known as the Book of
the Code of the Watchmen*

Wait until they sleep.

~General Agrabar Bellen
Commander of the Forces of the North
Just before sunset at the Battle of Bereneffe

CHAPTER TWENTY-FIVE

The hallowed place of horrors

Since leaving Gaul, hastily, in the middle of the night, their days had been long, though uneventful. That was how things really happened. In the great stories there was never a dull moment, or a lull in the adventure. Real life was very different. Days, even weeks, passed during which absolutely nothing happened. Cordovan, along with his two companions, the young, brooding Aubrey, followed by the older, more incessantly brooding, Dain Du'urdin, had been making their way to a particular valley, in the Black Hills, known to the former Inquisitor. After leaving Gaul their route took them north toward Marragen. Just shy of that border city they turned east, which pointed them toward the base of the Black Hills. Soon, Cordovan hoped, they would find Gaiden Colling. Not long after that they would have him kneeling before *Her*. Colling would be taken to Watchkeep. Once secured inside Watchkeep he would not be able to escape. The Ancient One help anyone who tried to break him out of the home of the Watch.

That morning they had put away their bedrolls, cleaned the campsite, and pulled themselves into the saddle. It had not been long before the doldrums of the past few days vanished into the crisp morning air. They caught sight of someone on their trail. It was the first sign of anyone they had seen since leaving Gaul in the dead of night. They quickly began trying to put some distance between themselves and whoever was following them. When they did they caught sight of another group of riders ahead of them. For days on end they had not seen anyone in the wooded lands of Northern Province. Now, seemingly out of nowhere, they were surrounded. Cordovan tried everything he knew to keep ahead of those behind them, while remaining behind those ahead of them. The nature of the landscape made that difficult. They spent most of the day exhausting every idea he could think up. He even asked Dain Du'urdin for suggestions. After employing Du'urdin's interesting suggestions they found that they were still trapped with the sun sinking behind the mountains.

Cordovan was about to try a tactic he had read in a book on military strategy when the party ahead of them disappeared. Turning to check their trail he calculated that the party behind them had begun to close the gap between them. In that instant Cordovan decided that he had better pick a defensible piece of ground. His hope was that they could defeat whoever was following them before whoever had been ahead of them attacked. Waving Aubrey and Dain Du'urdin into a stand of trees, Cordovan reined in the large black stallion he had picked up in Gaul. The trees grew closer together here. With sunlight quickly fading it was safer to stand their ground rather than race ahead. They could easily injure themselves or their horses riding hard in the dark. Just as he came abreast of Aubrey, who sat astride a white stallion, followed by Dain Du'urdin on a chestnut mare, the thicket of trees gave way to a clearing. Cordovan nearly cursed. They had fallen into a cleverly laid trap. The pursuers, who he thought had disappeared, were actually lying in wait for them. In minutes those pursuing from behind would be on top of them. The trap would snap shut neatly. There was only one thing to do. Digging his heels into the flanks of his mount Cordovan raced toward the men who stood waiting for them. The fading hope he clung to was to dispatch them before having to turn and face those who would be arriving from behind them in very short order.

†

The sun was beginning to disappear from the clear northern sky. Speckle's hooves thundered along the ground as he raced ahead at a full gallop, while Alla'mirridin tried looking everywhere at once. His voluminous black cloak flapped in the wind behind him pulling lightly at his neck. His brown stallion, white speckles dotting his broad chest, running down his powerful forelegs, and across his taut belly, raced along behind the Ki'gadi. Mino din' Darksbane leaned low across the back of his pale gray mare, which he called Whitemane. Beside him Zezza din' Nightblinder kept pace astride the golden stallion she called Sunchild. Alla'mirridin thanked the Ancient One that he had picked a well-bred stallion in Speckle who had, so far, been able to keep up with the Ki'gadi mounts that ran as though they were somehow enchanted.

They raced headlong through an open meadow along the northern-most edge of Province in the waning light of day. Off to their left rough, gray, snow-covered mountain peaks rose high into the skyline marking the end of the lands under Provincial Writ. Hundreds of yards off to their right, as well as a few miles ahead, the thick forest resumed. But for now their mounts had a little light left with some breathing room to run. So they took full advantage as they galloped, unrestrained, through knee high grass. The night had been uneventful. Breakfast had been a welcomed respite, a few moments of peace to enjoy some simple food washed down by strong choca. But not long after they had gotten in the saddle Zezza had performed her usual disappearing act. Scouting their trail had taken her a few miles ahead of them followed by a wide sweep several miles behind them. A few hours after midday, she had come galloping up to Mino with news that they had pursuers closing in on them. They had immediately begun putting distance between them and their would be hunters. Alla'mirridin prepared himself for another attack from dark things only thought to live in fairytales. Someone, it seemed, really wanted to kill the Ki'gadi. This would be the third attempt on their lives since Alla'mirridin had met them. Traveling with them had become a real danger to his health.

They made every effort to lose their pursuers without success. Alla'mirridin had watched the Ki'gadi use tricks he knew, even without the luxury of a memory, were quite ingenious. Whoever was on their trail was very good. It looked more likely, by the moment, that they were going to have to stop running and face them. Mino had shouted over the cacophony of galloping hooves, and jingling harnesses, that they would not fight on their hunters' terms. They would find a place of their own choosing to confront them. So, they hurtled along with the wind in their faces waiting for Mino to signal that he had chosen a spot. As they raced forward it occurred to Alla'mirridin that he never would have thought of Ki'gadi running from anything, even for the reasons Mino had given. In the stories told around latenight campfires the Ki'gadi never ran from anything.

Nearly another hour passed before they were forced to slow their pace to an easy canter. The sun had almost completely disappeared as they hit a gradual rise of earth where flat grassland became densely grown woods. It would be utterly foolish, even for the most experienced riders, to race through thick forest during twilight. That would be asking to injure your horse or yourself. After a few more minutes the gradual rise of ground leveled off. They broke through the trees into a clearing that was some thirty or so paces across. Mino, followed quickly by Zezza, leaped from their saddles in one graceful movement, slapping their mounts on their haunches as they landed so that they would trot off out of harms way. Alla'mirridin followed their example, sending Speckle off with a smack. Slowly, he made his way to where the Ki'gadi were standing. Positioning himself to Zezza's left, Alla'mirridin took note of how both Ki'gadi stood with a calm, eerie, stillness that belied the trouble they were in. Alla'mirridin envied them their detachment. The Ki'gadi's faces seemed to say that they were out for a walk in the woods to get a bit of fresh air. Alla'mirridin's mind was fixed on the fact that they might soon be dead. It bothered him that he might die without knowing who he was. There was no way of knowing how many were coming, who they were, or what they wanted. Given what he had already experienced in the company of the Ki'gadi, Alla'mirridin expected to see something out of nightmares, or maybe legend, come strolling into the clearing set to rend them limb from limb. The three of them simply stood in the fading light of dusk waiting.

It took a few more minutes but suddenly Alla'mirridin heard the sound of horses approaching. *Breathe*, he told himself. *Just breathe.* Forcing himself to ease his grip on the hilt of his sword, Alla'mirridin let his shoulders fall limp, releasing the tension he had allowed to take up residence there, while looking in the direction the sound was coming from. Slowly, he pulled in air letting it out even more slowly. The two Ki'gadi were to his right standing easily. Zezza had her hand on the hilt of her sword which, when drawn from its scabbard, looked more like a piece of art than a weapon. Its hilt was slightly curved, and intricately engraved, with tiny emeralds decorating it. There was no handguard. The blade had striated etchings running its length, which looked like patterned lace buried just beneath the surface of the steel. Her eyes were riveted to the spot where their pursuers would enter the clearing. Mino stood with his hands shoved deep into the recesses of the bell sleeves of his oversized brown robe absently looking around the clearing as if he had forgotten why they were there. Then they rode into the clearing.

Alla'mirridin crouched slightly as their pursuers entered the clearing. With a single look the man, who must have been the leader, kicked his mount into a full charge while drawing his sword. The others hesitated only a brief second before following his lead. Alla'mirridin kept his breathing even. He prepared to take the man to the immediate right of the one leading the charge. But just as their leader came into range he pulled up hard on the reigns of his horse shouting for his companions to halt. With weapons drawn and puzzled looks on their faces their pursuers followed the man's lead pulling their horses up short. Their leader looked from Mino to Zezza. After studying the two Ki'gadi for a moment the man, still holding his sword before him, cautiously, inclined his head briefly. When he raised his head he said, "Greetings Sages of the West. I must admit I am puzzled. I assume, by the hair that hangs to your shoulders, at least two of you are Ki'gadi. I don't know why Ki'gadi would pursue us or lay a trap for us, but I trust that it is something we may talk through rather than decide with steel. I am Cordovan del Allegressa, a Watchman of Alexandria. This is Aubrey Devilwind also of the Watch. Our other companion is Dain Du'urdin."

As the man spoke there was a momentary flutter in the deep darkness that was Alla'mirridin's memory. It was as if something the man had said should have been meaningful to him. While Alla'mirridin struggled to grab hold of the memory that seemed just out of his reach he turned to look at Mino. The senior Ki'gadi bowed his own head toward the leader of the other party saying, "And greetings to you Steel of the East. We know of the Watchmen of Alexandria. We honor your service to your Empress, long may She reign, but above all to justice and the Light. I am Mino din' Darksbane. This is my Had'wadai, Zezza din' Nightblinder. We are accompanied by, our companion, Alla'mirridin. If you will dismount, and put away your swords, I believe we can clear up what is apparently a grave misunderstanding."

At a slight tilt of Mino's head, Zezza slid her sword back into its scabbard. Alla'mirridin followed suit. The Watchmen, along with their companion, put away their own weapons before dismounting. When the six of them came to stand together in the center of the clearing, Mino continued, "I am afraid that we have all been fooled. We were not hunting you. In fact, we thought you were pursuing us. We made our way here in order to face the threat we thought you posed." Looking around him Mino considered the group, then the clearing. With an offhanded wave a small ball of blue flame appeared above his head casting light across half the clearing.

The lead Watchman looked at the floating ball of light without surprise. When Mino finished speaking he said, "We were under the impression that you were working with whomever has been following us most of the day in order to trap us. But if you are not working with them do you have any idea who they are?"

Mino shook his head. "No, Watchman. We were unaware that there were more pursuers following you. But it is my sense that whether they are tracking you or us they will not allow any of us to leave this clearing. How far behind you are they exactly?"

The Watchman looked at his companions briefly while he considered Mino's words. Then he said, "They will be here in moments. I propose we face the threat together."

Mino was nodding in agreement even as the Watchman finished, "Yes Watchman, I agree. Whatever is out there, it would be best if we faced it together." Alla'mirridin did not know if the Watchman caught that Mino had said *what*ever is out there rather than *whom*ever but he had. It sent a shiver up his spin.

Just as the two men finished speaking another unfamiliar voice sounded behind them. It was deep. The voice was too smooth by half. "Well, well. What do we have here? Two Whitehairs along with a handful of, what, minions you have duped into doing your bidding?" The first part was said as if it left a bad taste in the stranger's mouth. The Watchmen turned quickly, to see who was behind them, just as Alla'mirridin turned his own attention to the man confidently strolling into the clearing. He moved like he was out for a walk in the gardens. The man was about Alla'mirridin's height. He seemed well built beneath his black robes, which were embroidered with blood red thorns at the collar. Those embroidered thorns curled down his shoulder winding around the sleeves like a creeping vine. The robes were clearly made of a luxurious silk. His black boots shone with polish as if somehow charmed to ward off dust. A square jaw jutted out beneath a long, slender nose. Black eyes sparkled with the hint of something unpleasant. Shoulder-length hair hung perfectly straight. It seemed to glisten even blacker than his silk robes. The smile that clung to his face, as if it did not belong there, was bright, almost winning, against his sun-tanned skin. But what caught Alla'mirridin's eye, making his heart beat faster, was hanging at the man's waist. The slightly curving hilt, absent handguard, and small, artistic accents made the sword at the man's waist all too similar to what the Ki'gadi carried to be overlooked.

Alla'mirridin tried to rein in his thoughts. He heard Zezza to his immediate right hiss like a cornered cat with her back up. "Sicarri!" She said it like it was a curse. From the depths of the cloudy darkness that was Alla'mirridin's memory came a flood of successive thoughts, tumbling one after the other to the forefront of his mind. *Sicarri.* The word, in the Old Tongue, literally meant *graced* or *gifted*. It had belonged to a sect of gallant warriors who had died fighting the Darkness. But somewhere along the way the meaning had changed. It had come to mean *traitor* or *conspirator*. No one knew where those who now carried the name came from. Though most believed the Ki'gadi knew but would not say. The few who were said to have encountered the Sicarri, and lived, had claimed to see them perform frightening wonders. What was clear, from one tale to another, was that they serve the Darkness. Alla'mirridin swallowed hard. He watched the Sicarri standing easily with a smug smile on his face. He was looking them over as if wondering how best to end them.

Just then a young man strolled silently into the clearing behind the Sicarri looking from his left to his right. Standing a span taller than the older man, he walked with the kind of swagger only the young thought attractive. Not in robes, he wore calf-high boots, breeches, shirt and vest, with leather gloves, all of which were black. A swordhilt stuck up over his left shoulder. But there was a second swordhilt over his right. His shoulder-length, brown hair was tied back in a tail with a leather cord, revealing a slim, severe face. His dark eyes matched the unrelieved black of his clothing. It was all accented by a smile that turned up sharply on one side. The Sicarri half looked over his shoulder as the younger man approached. "Oh yes. I guess introductions are in order. I am Vesper Shadowell and this is my apprentice Hargin Hellsgate." Shadowell shifted his gaze, his dark eyes narrowing their focus to Zezza, as he said, "And we do not take kindly to that term, little Whitehair." Looking around at the rest of their small contingent he continued, "We are the Anointed, the *Da'shara*. We prepare the *Way* for *The One Who Is To Come*." Both men briefly inclined their heads but without lowering their eyes. As their heads came up Zezza spit out, "You are abominations, Darkling! You were given a chance at righteousness, but you chose damnation!"

Mino waved a hand saying, "Easy, my Had'wadai, easy. Do not allow the Sicarri the advantage of your anger."

Zezza bobbed her head once, sharply, at Mino's words, "Yes, my master." But her eyes never left the Sicarri as she bowed.

The senior Sicarri smiled broadly at Mino, "Well done, Master Sage. You have your pupil well in hand. We must be hard taskmasters if we are to make something out of our charges, hmm? I have given you our names, will you not introduce yourselves?"

Mino stood silently, calmly, simply watching the Sicarri. After a moment the man shrugged his shoulders. "Ah well. One would hope that even in circumstances such as these the niceties might still be observed." Taking a step closer to Mino the Sicarri continued, "Down to business then. I do not know what your little troop is up to Whitehair, but I am afraid you have wandered too far afield for me to allow you to continue. So, if you would be so kind as to lay down your weapons, you will live. Fail to do so and, I'm afraid, you will have to die."

Alla'mirridin nearly jumped when Mino burst out laughing. It was not a strained expression of amusement but a full-bellied chuckle. His warm voice echoed across the clearing. The Sicarri's face darkened slightly at the mocking sound. Mino said, "I am old, twisted one, but I am no fool. A Sicarri's word is like the slithering rattler sliding sideways across the ground. You take it to hand at your peril. Whatever you have planned we know that the likelihood of leaving this clearing alive has nothing to do with any promise that falls from your blackened lips."

The senior Sicarri turned up his lip in a sneer, "So be it. I have wasted enough of my precious time on you!"

At a motion from the Sicarri's hand shadows emerged from the dark places around the edge of the clearing, followed by things that looked like nightscreamers stretched to the size of men. All of them were being herded forward by a Graelim who sat astride a black stallion at the edge of the clearing. Draped in shadow, wrapped in its black cloak, the thing looked like something created to make the hearts of men fail. It only took a few heartbeats to see how badly their little band was outnumbered. Alla'mirridin looked from one side of the clearing to the other, as his mind raced, searching for alternatives. *There must be a way out*, he thought. Gaunts, followed by those tall, leathery creatures right out of a nightmare, slowly closed in on them while the Sicarri stood by watching. Alla'mirridin wracked his mind for some way out but nothing came. The only thought he could muster was that they would not go easily. They would take as many of their attackers with them into the darkness of the abyss as they could.

Just as the six of them put their backs to each other to face the threat as it closed in on them the sound of horses broke the eerie silence. Alla'mirridin looked up in time to see a group of soldiers come riding into the clearing behind the tightening circle of twisted things from the Pit. One of the men wore a green longcoat while the rest were in red and blue. From Alla'mirridin's left came the voice of the plump man called Dain Du'urdin. "Well dip me in horse draught and roll me in meal, if it isn't a Junior Inquisitor with a detachment of Legionnaires. Now that is unexpected." Then the portly man laughed, deeply. Both Sicarri turned to see the new arrivals just as the man to the Inquisitor's right, who must have been in charge of the detachment, laid eyes on the Gaunts, man-sized nightscreamers, and Graelim. Before anyone could say anything, he was shouting, "Twisted Ones! By the Creator, its Twisted Ones! Attack men, attack!" The Inquisitor was startled. He leaned forward as if he wanted to wave the soldiers off. But then he seemed to think better of the notion reigning his horse back out of their way as the men charged past him waving swords. The Legionnaires came rushing forward, crashing into the back line of the Twisted. Alla'mirridin realized the odds had changed significantly.

Before Alla'mirridin could pull his sword free, Mino had leaped across the distance between him and the senior Sicarri, landing blade to blade with the man. Tiny flashes of fire accompanied the meeting of their steel. A split second later Zezza was fighting for her life with the younger Sicarri who fell on her with a sword in each hand. Mino seemed ancient yet he constantly surprised Alla'mirridin with what he was able to do. But Alla'mirridin did not have time to watch the Ki'gadi battle the Sicarri or even to worry about whether Zezza could deal with her counterpart. In an eyeblink he found himself shoulder to shoulder with the younger Watchman. While he was young, much younger even than Alla'mirridin, it did not take long to see that he was skilled. Expressionless men who had lost their souls to the darkness, whom Alla'mirridin now knew as Gaunts, fell under their respective blades. Alla'mirridin caught glimpses of the other, older, Watchman through the jumble of bodies, who called himself Cordovan, just several feet away. The man was horrendously outnumbered, but somehow still alive. His sword seemed to dart everywhere at once. Their traveling companion, Dain Du'urdin, had taken to a tree. The portly, well-dressed man was hastily firing crossbow bolts at anyone or anything that came near him.

Then the soldiers in red and blue were among them. Some had been unhorsed, others were bleeding, but they were fighting for their lives against things the world thought long gone. In moments the Gaunts, who had besieged Alla'mirridin, began falling away. Those he had not killed were engaging the Legionnaires. In that moment a deep, inky blackness fell on the young Watchman. Before Alla'mirridin could go to his aid he found himself face to face with the Graelim who had, during the melee, made his way across the clearing.

In that instant the world narrowed. Alla'mirridin felt his heart quicken its pace while his throat tried to squeeze itself shut. A deep, overwhelming, fear clutched at him as if all hope had fled from the world. It was as if there was nothing left save despair. The sound of flames, steel on steel, even the shouting of men, seemed to fade into the background as the world at the edges of his vision blurred. The thing towered over him. His feet felt like they were buried in the ground up to his ankles. It moved like it was made of wind or water. Its face was a pale, pasty white, with hair just as white hanging down its back. The thing's face looked all the more haunting against the unrelieved black it wore. Even its eyes were so pale gray as to seem nearly white. A gleeful smile exposed sharp teeth as it bore down on him. Alla'mirridin stood frozen while the world erupted around him. The Graelim spun its long, black spear savagely slashing down at Alla'mirridin's head stopping a fingers-breadth from his neck. It took half a heartbeat for Alla'mirridin to realize that it was his own sword, in his own hands, that held the spear's curved, black blade at bay. The Graelim's gleeful smile changed as it pushed against his sword, becoming more feral, more blood curdling. Alla'mirridin thought he caught a flicker of surprise reflected in its eyes but then it was gone. As the thing pivoted, spinning around to attack from Alla'mirridin's left, he felt something stirring deep within him. The thing was an abomination. Something crafted in the Pit before being spewed out into the world to plunge it into darkness. Something made to catch the world unawares, while it slept. A twisted thing meant to instill fear, freezing the world in inaction, so that the servants of the Dark could have their way. Sliding under the spear's blade as it slashed at him from his left Alla'mirridin began to get angry. It was not an overwhelming, uncontrolled anger that washed away judgment. No, this was a cold, calculating anger that brought the world into keen focus, burning away everything else in its path.

The Graelim was fast, faster than anything had a right to be, not to mention strong. It was so fast that Alla'mirridin did not know how he kept up. It was so strong that it took all of his strength to keep his arms from buckling as his swordblade caught the blade of the spear turning it aside. A quick look around showed Alla'mirridin that he had been backed nearly to the edge of the clearing. With a reverse spin the Graelim caught Alla'mirridin on the right side of his head with the butt of its spear. A bright light flashed before his eyes. Letting his body fall to his left with the momentum from the blow he tucked his left shoulder as he hit the ground. Rolling on his shoulderblades, he came up a few feet to the Graelim's right. Gritting his teeth hard he shook his head trying to steady himself. The thing hissed at him like a serpent, "It is time to die."

The Graelim leaped. Its black cloak spread wide behind it as it rose into the air, blotting out the light from the Ki'gadi's glowing ball of blue flame, which still floated above the raging battle in the clearing. Shadows rose up from the ground around Alla'mirridin. He thought he could hear countless whispering voices rising up, getting louder, as the Graelim fell on him. In desperation he threw himself hard to his right. A scream erupted from somewhere like it was ripped from the person's throat. Then he realized that he was the one who had screamed. The blade of the Graelim's spear had cut down his left side. Alla'mirridin hit the ground hard. Straining for breath he scrambled along the ground in an attempt to stand. Behind him he heard the hissing of the thing. It would be on him in the blink of an eye. His hand struck the foot of a tree. Alla'mirridin hurriedly pushed himself up against the treetrunk. His side was a pulsing agony from chest to hip. His head still throbbed. The pain was so intense that he wavered on the edge of consciousness. The thing was right. Death had come calling. Blinking fiercely, his vision came into focus in time to see the Graelim move in on him. Alla'mirridin wrapped himself around that cold, calculating, anger still burning in him. Biting his lower lip, gripping his swordhilt hard with both hands, he launched himself off the treetrunk with a roar ripping open his mouth, not from rage but from the pain that shot up his side as he moved. His eyes watered up as he met the thing a few feet from the base of the tree. Then reason was gone, gobbled up by pain, anger, and a deep desire to live. Alla'mirridin wanted to live. So, *Leaf Catches the Breeze* became *Fox Rounds the Tree,* which was followed by *Sparrow Shakes the Branch.* Alla'mirridin twisted his sword around the spearblade grunting from the effort. With a half-hop backward, he slammed his blade against the side of the spearblade again. Without hesitation he made a reverse spin, which brought him under the Graelim's extended guard. Alla'mirridin finished the slashing spin, which brought him back around to face the Graelim. He dropped his guard. He just stood there breathing hard. It took a moment, but the look of ferocious perversity began fading from the Graelim's ashen face as its midsection opened up spilling its contents on the ground at its feet. The thing slumped to its knees. Its spear bounced to the ground. With one quick motion Alla'mirridin took its head off its shoulders. The body flopped around as it dissolved into a sulfurous cloud. The stink of it reached Alla'mirridin's nose just as darkness reached up to take him.

†

Someone was shaking him. He hated being awakened early. He especially hated having a very nice dream disturbed. *The woman's eyes were large, swallowing him whole with their beauty. The two of them were lying on a blanket next to a clear blue stream. She was on her side, leaning on him, feeding him plump, green grapes as he relished how her body felt against his and ....* someone was shaking him. Alla'mirridin tried to yell, *"Go away!"* but what came out of his mouth was a strangled cough. Blinking his eyes as they opened, on a blur of images, Alla'mirridin tried to focus. After a moment the blurry images came into sharp relief allowing Alla'mirridin to make out Mino and Zezza kneeling over him. A much larger ball of blue light hovered over the heads of the Ki'gadi. Dusk had become night. When he saw the two Ki'gadi his memory of the attack came flooding back, washing over him like a wave. Bracing for the pain that he knew was coming, he ran his left hand up his side but somehow the pain was gone. Bringing his hand up to his face Alla'mirridin saw the faint, glistening trace of ointment on his fingertips. He had seen Mino use an ointment on Zezza's wounds days ago. When there was time he would have to ask Mino what was in the ointment that allowed it to heal wounds so fast. When he sat up Mino said, "Take your time, my young friend. Your body has suffered a shock."

Sitting up, Alla'mirridin took a look around the clearing. There were bodies everywhere. The two Watchmen were dragging bodies to a pile in the center of the clearing. Dain Du'urdin had his crossbow trained on the older Sicarri who was on his knees. His nose was bloodied. But it was the odd-looking rope binding his arms to his sides that caught Alla'mirridin's attention. There was no sign of the Inquisitor in his green coat, or the younger Sicarri, but a closer look at Zezza showed more blood-stained rips in her shirt. Her lips were pressed tightly together decorating her beautiful face with a look of annoyance. Somehow the terse look did not detract from her loveliness. She must have already been attended to by Mino since there were no wounds that Alla'mirridin could see. Looking at the pile of bodies again Alla'mirridin could see as many red and blue uniforms as lifeless Twisted. The price of their little band's survival had been high. He wondered what would have happened if the Legionnaires had not shown up when they did and what exactly had brought them to the clearing in the first place. Pushing himself up, he got his feet under him. As he started to stand Zezza helped him up. Steadying himself he turned, flashing a broad smile at her. Zezza narrowed her eyes, adding that to already pressed lips, as she said, "You are a fool if I have ever seen one, *Approaching Storm*. Why you insist on attacking every Graelim who shows his face is beyond me. Keep it up and we will be burying you in these hills." With that she let go of him, turned, and stomped off. She always seemed to say the translation of his name with a hint of mockery. Alla'mirridin looked at Mino who shrugged his shoulders as if to say he could not help Alla'mirridin understand the woman who was his student. He was on his own. With Alla'mirridin on his feet Mino walked back to where the Sicarri was being held. Alla'mirridin, steadying himself as he went, followed the master sage.

Zezza had gone to help the Watchmen pile up bodies. Alla'mirridin joined Mino. The senior Ki'gadi was already leaning over the Sicarri checking his bonds. While he looked things over Alla'mirridin said, "How is it that you're able to restrain him Mino? Doesn't he have abilities similar to yours?" Mino grunted at that as he pulled lightly on the bonds that were wrapped around the man's arms. Then he said, "I have wrapped him in bonds made for the purpose. He cannot use his *abilities* as you call them, as long as he is bound so." Dain Du'urdin had a dubious look on his face as he nervously clutched his crossbow, which was still trained on their captive. The man looked like he would love to believe the Ki'gadi but did not.

Alla'mirridin leaned in examining the bonds more closely. They looked like ordinary rope at first glance. But as he got a closer look it became clear that they were anything but ordinary. The *rope* was made from strands of tiny links of gold wire twisted together to make a large cord. Looking even closer, he could see that there was something sparkling inside the individual strands. Leaning in, Alla'mirridin saw them. Connecting the small strands of gold links that made up the thick length of rope were tiny crystal shards pulsing with an inner light. Stepping back a bit Alla'mirridin was able to discern something else. The Sicarri was actually struggling against his bonds in an attempt to free himself. He must have also been trying to use his abilities because as he struggled the pulsing from the tiny crystal shards, all along the length of the golden cord, increased. When the Sicarri relaxed his efforts, the light dimmed. Alla'mirridin did not think, even without his memory, that he had ever seen anything like it. He was not sure he ever thought it possible to bind one of the *gifted*.

Crossing his arms, Alla'mirridin looked up from the Sicarri as the rest of their group joined them. In the back of his mind he thought it odd that the two Watchmen were not sweating from their exertion, but he let it go as a ridiculous notion. With the rest of the group standing around their captive Mino spoke to the man. "So, Sicarri. You will tell me why you were following us and why you attacked us."

The man laughed through a sneer that one could tell painted his features often. "You must be joking Whitehair. Surely you don't expect that I will divulge anything to you! You are incapable of doing what you would need to do in order to get the information you are seeking."

Mino stood with one arm across his chest propping up his other elbow with his chin resting on his hand as a finger tapped his lip. Just then the plump fellow with the crossbow spoke up. "I am Dain Du'urdin, Master Sage. While I would not reveal what I am about to share under normal circumstances, maybe, you should allow me to put your prisoner to the question. I was once an Inquisitor. If he knows something I will get it out of him."

An Inquisitor, Alla'mirridin thought. That was unexpected. Questions began to form in his mind. With what he could remember about Watchmen, he wondered how they came to be accompanied by an Inquisitor, even a former one. But he was stopped there in considering what he had just learned as Mino said, "No, Dain Du'urdin. While I do not question your abilities, this is my responsibility." Then Mino turned back to the Sicarri, his voice turning a shade colder as he said, "Besides, this Sicarri is wrong about what I am prepared to do to learn what I must." Turning from the kneeling man, Mino walked to where the horses, having apparently been retrieved from the woods while Alla'mirridin had been unconscious, were currently ground hitched. He made his way to his white-maned gray mare. Calling over his shoulder to his pupil he said, "Zezza, check our backtrail to be sure there are no more pursuers."

At Mino's words Zezza stiffened slightly. Her voice was a bit higher than usual when she said, "But Master, I am sure the threat has passed. And I wish to help you question this Sicarri."

Mino had made it to his horse. He was rifling through his saddlebags when his stern voice floated over the saddle, "You will obey me, Had'wadai."

Zezza paused for a moment, looking from Mino to the Sicarri. Then she walked toward her own horse. As she went the Sicarri yelled after her, "He does not want you to see him trample on your precious *Way*, Had'wadai. He knows that what he does next tarnishes your prized Ki'gadi principles!" Zezza was already trotting out of the clearing into the darkness, with her head held high and her back stiff, as the Sicarri shouted the last at her disappearing form. But even as Zezza left, the silence in their small group became deafening. Each of them looked around at the other. Mino returned quietly with something in his hands covered by a blue, silk length of cloth. His voice was even but with a slight edge. "Ordinarily Sicarri, you would be right about my not being able to do what was necessary. Though it is not a sufficient excuse, these are not ordinary times. I will ask you once more. Why were you following us?"

The Sicarri raised his head making a brief sniffing noise. It was clear that he was not going to answer. They all, including Alla'mirridin, looked at Mino. His face was like chiseled stone. With one hand he pulled back the silk cloth. Upon seeing what was in Mino's hand the Sicarri inhaled sharply. Looking around at their small group the man did something that shocked Alla'mirridin. He began to beg. "You, you must do something! One of you must do something! You must not allow this! He is Ki'gadi. It is an abomination to them!" The Sicarri's voice began to grow shrill as Mino stepped closer to him. "Please. Please. I was not going to hurt you. I was only going to turn you around! Someone, stop him!"

Alla'mirridin's heart was beating faster, but he looked closely at what Mino held in his hand. It surprised Alla'mirridin because it did not seem to be the least bit dangerous. Mino was holding a small necklace. It was a thick chain made of a black metal of some kind with barbed thorns all along its length. It was an ugly piece of jewelry. But innocuous as it seemed, the Sicarri was terrified by it. Mino placed the thing around the man's neck. Alla'mirridin looked at the others wondering if anyone would say anything. It was the senior Watchman who spoke up. Cordovan said, "With great respect, Master Sage. I'm troubled by this. While I am sure you have greater experience with his kind, and he knows how to weave a web of lies, I must ask, is this proper?"

Mino sighed heavily. "No, no, Master Watchman. You are well within your rights to ask. But this is my responsibility. If any of you do not have the stomach for it please leave, with my thanks." Without another word Mino turned back to his prisoner. What the Ki'gadi said next sent chills up Alla'mirridin's spine. "It is called a *Delvingdengadda*. Most came to call them *Tongue Thorns*. They were ugly things, made by the Twisted Ones, during the War of the Allgis-sein. It was thought that by the end of the war they had all been lost or destroyed. But one lay hidden in the stores at Palladawn until I found it. It took many years to discover its use. One must be very careful with Talismans from that Dark Age. But I came across a footnote in an ancient text on the history of the great conflict, which described the method the enemy used to extract information. You see once the Delver is placed around the neck it begins to inflict pain on the wearer. It is minor at first, nearly undetectable. But the longer it is worn the more excruciating the pain becomes until it is unbearable." Alla'mirridin, along with the rest of their party, turned to look at the Sicarri almost simultaneously. The man had begun to sweat. His face was beginning to look strained. While they watched the Sicarri Mino continued, "But the most pernicious aspect of the Tongue Thorn is that it somehow knows your limit. Those who wear it think they can hold out until they either pass out or die. But the Delver will not allow either to happen. It holds you on the very edge of consciousness while you scream, while you beg for blessed unconsciousness or death."

The Sicarri was breathing heavily now, sweat running down his forehead. Mino did not ask his questions again. He simply waited while the *Delvingdengadda* did its work. It began as low intermittent moans that seemed to escape from the man's lips unbidden. Then there were grunts emitted on purpose as he squirmed attempting to manage the building pain. He began to wail, through gritted teeth, hunching over as much as his bonds would allow. After a few more moments the man was howling, tears mixed in with sweat streaming down his cheeks. Falling over onto the ground he began to flail about. Just as Alla'mirridin was about to protest Mino bent down snatching the thing from around the man's neck. Alla'mirridin swallowed hard. He did not believe he had ever seen anything like it. Looking from face to face he saw the uneasiness of the rest of their party. The young Watchman, Alla'mirridin remembered that Aubrey was his name, was pale. Cordovan looked like he had eaten something bad. Dain Du'urdin was the only one of them who did not seem affected. Mino watched as the man sobbed for a few moments. After a brief interval he bent down helping the Sicarri back to his knees. The man's face was flush. There were tear tracks coated with dust along his cheeks. His eyes had a wild cast about them. Mino looked the Sicarri in his eyes as he said, "Answer my questions or we begin again."

The Sicarri looked around at each of his captors. When he did not see a single person ready to help him he opened his mouth. What he said made Alla'mirridin shiver. When Alla'mirridin looked at the senior Watchman he saw the man's face darken. There was a valley, a few miles north of the clearing, where the armies of the Dark were building up their forces. The Sicarri described nightmares that walked. One description in particular caused the Du'urdin fellow to whisper to the senior Watchman who nodded his head as the plump fellow spoke. According to the Darkling, soon their *Great and Glorious Lord* would return to lead them. The Glorious One's Hand would reach out from that place to claim the world. That dark, terrible, place had a name. *Dar'ken'thrall*. Mino translated for them. In the First Tongue it meant *the hallowed place of horrors.*

It is what you do not expect that makes life interesting.

> ~Keen Vellgell Chief Patriarch
> of the Fifth Estate at Millich
> Opening line of his address to
> incoming apprentices 478 C. E.

If you accept that things will always arise complicating your most earnestly prepared plans then you will have learned how to avoid disappointment. For the most unavoidable constant in all the world is that you will take nearly as many steps away from your prescribed path as you will ever take along it.

> ~excerpt form the Chai Langra
> The Fourth Book of Wisdom
> From the section entitled,
> On Disappointment

CHAPTER TWENTY-SIX

Sidesteps

Apparently, they were in no hurry. The Captain-Commander, Alec's Nsamsa, had set a leisurely pace since leaving Sanctuary. Onya Onoto rode a tall, deep-chested dun with well-shaped legs, at the head of their column. They were moving at a slow walk, an excruciatingly slow walk. It took days to leave behind all traces of Alexandria including the city's countryside, which was dotted with small cottages and large manors. They had passed everything from grain fields to cattle farms with time enough to watch the farmers work in their fields. Some had stopped long enough to gawk at the passing parade of soldiers with wide-eyed looks of apprehension from the adults, matched by wide-eyed looks of wonder from their children, before returning to pruning grapevines or picking select ears of corn to test for ripeness. Alec had always thought that when he finally retired from the Organization he was going to build a quaint, but sizable house somewhere in that beautiful, lush countryside. Maybe he still would.

Soon enough, after several days of travel, they were riding through the thick woods of the Westglenn on the Imperial Road. The Imperium, under the Sobrines, had come to be known for a number of things. One of those things was the building of roads. The notion that the empire should make one of its priorities construction, had begun with the sitting Empress' grandfather. The trend had continued with her father and had not ended with her. Great, smooth, stone roads, made from carefully quarried rock, expertly laid by the Mason's Guild, ran from Alexandria out to all parts of the empire. The network began as four broad roads leaving the capital city, stretching out in the four cardinal directions, before branching off into smaller roads, each flowing like tributaries from great rivers to every major city in the empire. The project's initial aim had been to make it possible for Imperial troops to be anywhere in the empire in short order. But it quickly became clear that there were ancillary benefits to such wide scale construction, namely that it made trade in the empire a more prosperous venture. Merchants could now virtually guarantee delivery of their goods in a safe, timely, manner. Furthermore, the empire was able to tax those goods, which in turn increased the size of the imperial coffers. One of the other things the Imperial Road did was to make travel in the empire convenient. So there they were, moving slowly, but easily, along the Imperial Road West on their way to a place called Saladon.

The Commander spent most of her time with the Arbiter. The two Ki'gadi were never far from her either. Alec had not yet been able to meet any of the iconic characters. He had never seen the Ki'gadi up close. The ancient order was something of a legend. Like most legends, Alec had heard a lot about them, but he had never had an opportunity to actually see one up close. Since leaving Alexandria he had been hoping for an opportunity to be around Onya while she was around them. That opportunity had not yet presented itself. Though Onya had the contingent moving slowly towards their destination she did not have the only Cadets in the party, namely his team, relaxing. She had said that their training would continue unabated for the duration of the trip and it had.

The evening had come, bringing with it cooler temperatures. While camp was being made for the night the Cadets were training.

A few hundred yards from the camp, in a small clearing surrounded by stands of Alwaysgreen, Finn and Tessa were firing Tink Crossbows at targets ranging from twenty to a hundred paces away. Sophie, the Team-Second, was debating strategy with one of their instructors as he ran her through her paces. They both sat hunched over a map, rolled out on a table, with small icons representing various armies engaged in a mock battle. Rex, the Team leader, was sparring hand-to-hand with another instructor on the opposite end of the clearing, his bright white shirt in stark contrast to his instructor's black. A small group of black-coated men and women stood a few feet from the match discussing the matter, periodically shouting instructions. Alec was standing, not far from Sophie, in full uniform, surrounded by seven members of the Company. The man in the center of that seven was his instructor from the Stone Hands, Lieutenant Hessle Drake. Short, black hair framed a strong face, from which looked cool, slate-gray eyes. The man seemed hard as stone in many ways, but Alec had come to know him as a decent, capable teacher. Alec respected the man in a way he had never respected members of the Organization. Those men had been hard in a different way. Hessle Drake was the kind of man you wanted guarding your back in a fight. Alec was coming to realize that he was starting to feel that way about a lot of the people in the Company. Drake's baritone rumbled deep in his throat. "Alec, with evening upon us, and deep woods around us, it seems like a good time to work on your evasion skills. You will find that getting out of a situation in which you or your primary is being held is the easiest part of a rescue. Success or failure will often depend on your ability to evade those sent to retrieve you. The seven of us will try to catch you. Your job is to evade us. This evolution will last for one hour. You will be given a three-minute head start. Prepare yourself." Drake pulled out his silver Tink timepiece from his coat. It hung on a silver chain that glinted in the last light of the day.

Alec was still at the early stages of learning one of the important skills taught by the Company. Being able to calm himself so that he could focus on the task at hand was first, understanding how his body would respond to the stress of a particular situation, and second, knowing how to mitigate that response. He began by deepening his breathing. Then he turned his mind toward thoughts that would be helpful in the coming task. He focused on his adversaries, going over in his mind what he knew about their abilities. Some of that knowledge had come from what he had experienced in training, while the rest had come from asking questions of his teammates. Compared to normal people the members of the Company were faster. They were also stronger. There were rumors among the cadets as to what happened when you were Called to the Black Coat. Somehow you were changed. What Alec knew was that three minutes was not going to help him much. The four men and three women who would be pursuing him were all Black Coats. They would likely have him in hand in ten minutes or less, but he was not going to come easily. *Focus*, he thought. *Breathe.*

Drake rumbled to the other six, "You see, that is what I like about him."

Then Alec realized he was grinning. His lips were pulled back from his teeth in a broad, dark, grin. He had decided to challenge them, and it was written all over his face. As Drake opened his mouth to say go, Alec was already running into the darkness. Drake's full-bellied laughter followed him into the trees. Drake shouted, "That's it Alec! You will be a Stone Hand one day! Make us fight for the victory. Make us fight!"

Drake's voice became a distant echo. Alec was running. He was running through the cloaked darkness of the forest. The first moonlight of the night was keeping the deepest part of the oncoming darkness at bay so that Alec could still see. Though he was running it was not at his top speed. That was another early lesson. You covered as much ground as you could but with strength in reserve for other things. He had gotten into good enough shape over the past several weeks that he could keep up the pace he had set for an extended period of time. But he knew that evading capture in the next hour would take more than speed. As he rounded a rock outcropping something slammed into the back of his head. Alec saw a flash of bright light. He watched the ground come leaping up toward him. In reality he knew something had sent him sprawling to the ground. But before he could recover hands had grabbed him roughly, trussing him up tightly with rope. Shaking his head, he tried to get his bearings. The back of his head throbbed violently. He could not seem to get his eyes to focus. Someone shoved him up against the cold base of a rock outcropping leaving him sitting there with his arms tied to his waist. As his vision began coming back into focus a familiar voice drifted down to him out of the darkness.

"I told you we would continue this later, eh?" A finger jabbed at his shoulder providing emphasis for what the man said next. "That you would do well to look over your shoulder, yes? But you did not do that did you Alec?"

With a sigh, followed by a grimace for his throbbing head, Alec said, "Why Pezzu, what brings you out here so early in the evening? If I knew you were coming I would have prepared a welcome for you."

A fist slammed into his jaw knocking Alec over. Pezzu said, "Sit him back up." Hands grabbed Alec roughly sitting him back up against the rock. With his jaw stinging, his head throbbing, and his mind racing Alec focused on remaining calm. Members of the Company would be there soon. He said, "How did you find me?"

The man was average height, his skin was a deep olive, and his curly, black, hair was cut short. His face was thin. It held a long nose, which hung under black eyes that bore down on Alec with unveiled hate as Pezzu played with a long knife. His high tenor was buoyed by a gloating tone. "It was not difficult Alec, just expensive. I paid men to watch Sanctuary night and day. I knew you would eventually have to leave. I thought it would take longer but, here we are, eh?"

Alec should not have said what came next, but he could not help himself. "Do you really think you will get away with this Pezzu? You were never a very good strategist. You should know the Company will not allow it."

Pezzu laughed darkly. "The last time we were together Alec, you had help. If I am such a poor strategist I would not have brought my own help this time, eh?" As Pezzu laughed again a tall, pale creature, draped in black, stepped out of the deep shadows among the trees. When it looked at Alec his blood seemed to freeze while his heart seized up in his chest.

A deep fear began to rise up in him like flooding waters reaching for a waterline. Nevermind that he was trusted up like a hog for slaughter by ropes, Alec knew that even if his arms had been untangled he still would not have been able to lift a finger. The thing towered over Pezzu, its face, eyes, and hair, were all white. Pezzu continued, "I was visited one night by my new associate who promised me assistance, in this matter, in exchange for other favors. You see Alec, this time I win, yes?"

It was then that Alec heard steel on steel, several yards back the way he had come, ringing out in the darkness. The tall nightmarish thing smiled wickedly at Alec, showing pointed teeth, as it hoisted a long, black spear ending in a nasty curving black blade. In an eye-blink it faded into the darkness. Alec opened his mouth to shout a warning, but something slammed into the side of his head. Darkness descended over him like a thick blanket.

†

Onya fought the anger that was attempting to rise up in her like a tidal wave, rolling in from the Macca Deep, crashing against the shoals of the cliff face beneath Sanctuary, as she made her rounds. She needed to remain calm. She kept reminding herself that there were important decisions to be made. It had only been minutes after darkness had fallen the night before that their encampment had been hit. Things that were rightly the subject of nightmares, things one did not believe actually existed, dark, twisted things, had come pouring out of the darkness of the deep wood. Some of them threw clouds of inky blackness coupled with fire. Others had been dark-draped men whose blank faces seemed to say they no longer had souls. All of them were led by a handful of towering, white-skinned creatures swathed in black that were incredibly difficult to kill. Those things, which the Ki'gadi had later named Graelim, had used abilities Onya thought relegated to the Sages of the West. Her contingent of Company members had been outnumbered, but thankfully because of their skill, the *gift*, and the assistance of the Ki'gadi, the casualties had been few. The clean up continued, as bodies were stacked together before being burned, while the camp was being struck. Onya had sent Windchasers to scout their surroundings while she saw to it that they would be ready to get underway in short order.

She finished her circuit of the camp. Her nose continued to search for air not tainted by the stink of sulfur. It had been difficult to enjoy a brief breakfast with the smell of dead Darkborn still hovering in the air. Onya pulled her mind away from those thoughts, along with the anger she was barely keeping at bay, at the sight of a harried looking Hessle Drake approaching her. Drake was followed by the single team of Cadets Onya had brought with them. Their white coats looked out of place in the presence of the vestiges of the carnage from the previous night. Drake snapped off a salute, as Onya looked him over. His face was dirty. Blood trickled from cuts on his right arm. He looked like he had been wrapped up into a ball then rolled around on the ground like a child's toy. Onya returned the Stone Hand's salute.

Drake's deep voice was tinged with concern. "Commander, I regret to report that Cadet Alexander sa' Salassian has been abducted."

The string of words that escaped from Onya's lips made Drake's face blanch. She could curse like a drunken sailor saddled with extra duty when she wanted. To his credit Drake did not take a step back as some were wont to do when Onya loosed her tongue. Looking over Drake's left shoulder Onya saw what she had missed earlier. The Cadets were obviously troubled. She could understand their feelings given that one of their team was missing. While Onya's own emotional state threatened to leap off into a chasm of deep concern for her Nsamsahdo her training took over immediately. She had already reconciled herself to the fact that there were important decisions to make in the wake of the attack, now they became grave decisions. "Drake. I understand your concern. I even share it. Alec is, after all my Nsamsahdo. Under normal circumstances I might be inclined to mobilize this entire contingent to chase after him. But, we have been witness to extraordinary events. Nightmares are walking, the likes of which, according to the Ki'gadi, have not been seen in an Age. Yet I have seen these twisted things twice in the span of several days. Something strange is happening. Given that, not to mention our current mission, I cannot rush off after one cadet."

Drake opened his mouth to protest but Onya forestalled his objections with a raised hand. "I will not be persuaded, Lieutenant." Drake clamped his mouth shut. Strangling whatever words had been on the tip of his tongue he waited for what Onya would say next. Looking over at the Cadets she turned her head to consider the rest of the camp. Onya made her decision. "Lieutenant, you will take the rest of these cadets in hand and return them to Sanctuary. I will assign two Stone Hands, along with a Windchaser, to retrieve Alexander sa' Salassian. Given what attacked us last night he may be dead already. Our priority is to make it to Saladon. That is all." Drake snapped off another salute. When Onya acknowledged it he went to take the Cadets in hand. Onya watched them go with a bitter taste in her mouth. Soldiers often desired to achieve a rank that would place them in command of others but far too many were blissfully unaware of what they were really seeking. There were burdens that came with command. Onya turned to go in search of two Stone Hands and a Windchaser in the hopes that Alec was still alive. If he were, then maybe he could be retrieved before it was too late. She was only sending three, but three of the Company could do much. *Please be alive Alec,* she thought as she made her way back through the camp. There was much to do but none of it was what she had planned.

†

Rex had been standing close enough to hear the Captain-Commander's orders to the Lieutenant. He listened carefully, while standing at attention, to the directions given to him by Lieutenant Drake before watching the man walk off into the camp to get his gear. As soon as he was out of earshot Sophie was at Rex's side. Her voice was not as high as most women, though she was of average height. But those were the only mundane things about her. Sophie was one of the youngest Team-Seconds in the entire Cadet Corps for good reason. Her mind for strategy was exceptional. One day she would command armies in battle, perhaps even the Company itself. Rex had no doubt in his mind about Sophie's talent or future. She was slim, but well rounded. Her skin was dark-brown like burnt cinnamon. Her long black hair, which she had woven into five or six thick braids, was placed around her head in a way that somehow suited her. High cheekbones were highlighted by big, black, smoldering eyes. All this complimented broad, but small, features. As Rex stood looking in the direction Hessle Drake had disappeared, Sophie spoke low so that only he could hear. "Rex, this is difficult for me to say, but we must leave now."

Rex took a moment to think, to weigh things in his mind. Disobeying a direct order was a very serious breach. They could all be drummed out of the Company for that kind of dereliction of their duty. So, without looking down at Sophie, Rex nodded. "Yes, I know Soph. I don't like it anymore than you do but the Captain-Commander has given her orders."

Sophie said, "No, Rex. You don't understand. Finn and Tessa have saddled our horses and grabbed our gear. We must leave now, before the Lieutenant returns."

Rex turned his head sharply, looking directly at his Second. "You want to disobey a direct order from the Captain-Commander? Have you lost your mind?"

Sophie had her face screwed up in that look Rex knew all too well. She had made up her mind, had dug in her heels. She was hoping she could convince him to go along with whatever scheme the rest of them had concocted. "Hear me out. First of all, they were not our orders, they were Drake's. Secondly, while I know three of the Company can do much, we should not leave Alec to those odds. He is *our* teammate. Bantu always says that our first duty is to the People. Alec is our responsibility. We should be the ones who go get him."

Rex put the period at the end of her statement by saying what she had not said, "And suffer the consequences later?"

Sophie looked at him but did not say a word, only waited, staring at him with those big, black eyes. Rex thought it through. Sophie's argument was slim, so slim that you could not slide a piece of parchment through it. It only worked as an immediate justification. It was not the kind of reasoning they would be able to stand on when they returned. They would all very likely be busted back down to Cadets of the Fourth rank and given extra duty for the rest of their lives, if they were lucky.

What was more likely to happen was being stripped of their rank, marched to the front gate of Sanctuary, given a sack of provisions, and told never to come back. You did not disobey orders in the Company without serious consequences. Yet even as he thought about the likely ramifications Rex knew he was avoiding the one credible point Sophie had made. Alec was their responsibility. As commander of Redhawk he was Rex's responsibility. Alec had been brought to Cadet House and placed on their team by the Captain-Commander, herself. He was new to the Company. What would he think if they abandoned him when he needed them most? What would it say about them? Rex sighed heavily as he nodded to himself. Looking around he knew Drake would be returning soon to take them in hand. If they were going it had to be now.

Looking at Sophie he said, "We will walk the horses past the treeline then ride like our lives depend on it."

The smile that broke through onto her face was almost reward enough. But then Rex was moving. If they did not leave immediately, under cover of the noise of the camp breaking, their departure would not go unnoticed. As they reached their teammates, quietly joining them in leading their horses slowly off toward the treeline, Rex thought to himself that this was the last thing he had envisioned doing when they had left Sanctuary on their way to Saladon. What was that old saying about the best-laid plans? He tried to remember it if only to keep his mind off the insanity he was leading his team into.

†

Lieutenant Hessle Drake sat quietly on his black stallion among the trees. He had bathed quickly before changing into a fresh uniform, packing his gear as he went. Now, he patted Whistle's neck while watching the cadets sneak through the treeline some thirty yards away. He had decided almost immediately that he could not disobey Onya's orders. But as he made his way to his tent a plan had begun to hatch in the back of his mind. Drake knew something about the team of cadets he had been helping to train on their way to Saladon. While they still had a lot to learn, they were very advanced even for Cadets. Drake had also come to learn something about them personally. It only took a few days to see how tightly knit the team was even considering that Alec was a new arrival. When Hessle saw the looks on their faces, as they heard Onya's orders, he had a hunch that they would not take it lying down. So, he decided to leave them alone while he went to retrieve his gear. He decided that it would take him a little more time than normal to accomplish that task. Besides, he had needed a bath.

When Hessle had finished he had gone directly to where his horse, with his packed gear, awaited him. Then he made his way to the treeline to find a hidden place to wait. Consequently, there was a smile on his face as he watched the cadets, who believed that they were escaping their chaperone, as they made their way into the deepwood. Hessle sat still giving them time to get ahead of him. After he felt a sufficient amount of time had passed he would go after them. After all, his orders were to take them in hand so that he could return them to Sanctuary. If he managed to get to them *after* they found Alec then he would be able to save his pupil as well as get them back to Sanctuary without disobeying his orders. Hessle Drake watched the sun climb a fraction in the sky as he waited. Smiling, he patted Whistle's neck.

†

Basil was amazed at how he could not really tell that he was on a ship at sea. The *P.S.S. Leviathan* dwarfed anything he had ever set foot on or even seen in the water. Not only was it enormous, *she,* he corrected himself, was a thing of beauty. The hall he was walking down was high enough, as well as wide enough, to have been located in a building on dry land. Not for the hundredth time did he thank the *Blessed One Who Watches* that Leviathan was large enough to actually avoid someone. Basil had been actively avoiding Macrina, along with her constant companion Anna, since setting foot on board. Somehow it had become a game that members of the crew were thoroughly enjoying. With winks, grunts, coughs, or outright warnings they had deftly, if humorously, helped him affect his escape from the women on several occasions. Basil had decided to leave the women's simmering ire to Bantu. His old friend would not be happy, but Basil would rather deal with Bantu's displeasure than the constant haranguing of those two women for the duration of the voyage. Basil had seen commanding officers hand out a dressing down to soldiers that left them looking for a hole to climb into but Macrina and Anna had tongues sharp enough to peel the skin off. Basil wanted to avoid that if possible. So, to the amusement of the crew, the game continued.

The floor he strolled along was golden hardwood, precisely laid, with a bright gloss finish, trimmed along each edge in a walnut so dark that it seemed black. The contrast of the golden birch with the dark walnut made for an elegant color scheme that ran through the main areas of the ship. The walls were covered by large, square panels of the same golden birch, two measures across by two measures high. Each square panel was separated by a slim length of dark walnut. Every ten paces or so the birch squares were interrupted by a long panel of dark walnut two measures across that ran floor to ceiling on each side of hallway. The wall, at these intervals, curved inward creating small recesses along the hall for tables upon which sat flowers or small carvings. The lighting was attached high up on those sections of dark wood. Curving brass sconces, holding glass globes, flickered with bright flames casting light from both sides of the hall.

Leviathan was so large that it had needed added design measures for getting from one part of the ship to the other. A central shaft ran through every deck at the very heart of the ship. The shaft held four *lifts*, which could carry you to every deck. As a nod to classic ship design every deck had a stairwell at either end. The polished, copper banisters curved gently upward to the next deck on their golden, wooden posts while the steps themselves were all dark walnut. Basil thought it again. *She is a beautiful ship*.

Darkness was fully upon them as they hurtled across the Deep. Though they had only put to sea a few days earlier they were already far out on the Macca Deep. Not only was the Leviathan large, she was fast. The waters through which they now sailed were not for small Coastcutters or Longboats, but were only for the larger, better made, vessels. Captain Nessera ela bin Stormcloud had been running Leviathan straight like an arrow flying toward its target. She was not flying the colors so the few ships they had seen had given them a wide birth. Leviathan must have looked otherworldly to them. Given her size, her speed, her lines, and the fact that she was not flying a single sail must have scared them to their very bones. Sailors were a superstitious lot so the word magic, or darkspawn, would likely be floating around the decks of those ships. Somehow Tink had found a way to power the ship without the need for the standard, billowing sails. Nessera had given Basil a tour their first day at sea. When they reached a room the crew were calling the *Sail Room*, a fellow with his sleeves rolled up, with a number of odd implements sticking out of the pockets of his vest, described what he called the *mechanism* that propelled Leviathan through the water.

The description had been very technical, mind numbingly so. While Basil loved knowledge, going so far as becoming a guest lecturer at the University in Alexandria, he was not overly fond of the dizzying descriptions of how Tinkcraft worked. What he came away with was that the giant, egg-shaped crystal, the kind used in other ways in Sanctuary, had been adapted to power giant, spinning, metal blades that propelled the ship through the water. When Basil mentioned that he had seen nothing of the like, the man had described the spinning blades to him. Apparently, they looked a bit like the great circular fans that captured the wind on windmills. As an aside he pointed out that windmills were where Tinker had gotten the idea in the first place. There was one set of these spinning blades on either side of the ship, extending out of the tail of the ship from the bottom of the hull, churning at great speed below the water. Basil had whistled long and low at that description. What would Tink think of next? Nessera had told Basil that the blades made Leviathan faster, as well as more maneuverable, than anything at sea. It was the reason they were so far out on the Deep so quickly.

Basil passed the curving staircase making his way down the length of the hall to the center of the deck. Placing his hand on a palm-sized, circular crystal, inset about chest-high on the wall, he watched it flare to glowing, blue life. He stepped back to wait for the lift to arrive. It only took a moment before the metal door slid open. Basil stepped into the square space, which could hold about seven people. Touching a matching crystal on the wall, inside the lift, to the right of the door, he said, "Command Deck." The door slid closed followed by the hum of the lift's movement upward. Soon the lift slowed, then stopped. The door slid open allowing Basil to step out. He walked down a hall that was nearly identical to the one he had just left except that here the flowers were different. There were yellow daffodils, white lilies, and orange roses, arranged in, overflowing bunches all along the hall. The variety was a nice thought. Several strides down the hall brought him to a door with a man on either side standing at attention. When Basil got to the door the man on the right opened it for him.

The giant room at the center of the first deck was called the *Bridge*. Sailors had a name for everything. The Bridge was large enough to hold about thirty people comfortably. There were ten distinct stations surrounding a single chair on a round, raised platform in the very center of the room. The chair faced a giant, glass window made from a single, thick pane, which covered most of the front wall. The window looked out on the foredeck of the ship along with the open waters ahead. Just below the window were two stations, each with a single person sitting at a kind of desk. Each desk had a small glass panel attached to its top tilting up so that the person sitting at the desk did not need to stare directly down at the top of the desk. The glass panels had writing made of colored light on the right side with various shapes on the left along with a glowing crystal the size of a fingertip in the bottom right corner. The attendants were touching those glass panels causing the writing displayed on the face of the glass to change. Basil stood quietly watching the crew at similar stations around the Bridge as they each performed the tasks, which made the ship function. Crew came and went from four other doors situated around the Bridge. Sitting at the center of this buzzing hive of activity was Nessera ela bin Stormcloud. She was leaning back in the large, plush chair, at the center of the room, looking at a glass panel of her own situated on a small table to the right of the chair. Every few seconds, she tapped the glass scanning through the writing that appeared there. The platform was high enough that everyone else on the

Bridge had to look up to see her, or speak to her, but Basil knew the true reason for the elevated position was so that the Captain could see everything that was happening. Periodically, crew approached her with information or questions. She doled out answers or orders as the need arose with the efficiency of a seasoned captain. This way of running ships had been Tink's unique creation. It had been put into practice on the earliest ships built for the Company. Though unique among sea going vessels the new way of commanding ships had served the Company well. The Company's sailors had grown accustomed to it years ago. So now they went about the business of sailing the ship in this manner without a second thought. Just as Basil was getting comfortable watching the activity from just inside the door a young Lieutenant noticed him, leaped to his feet, and barked, "Captain-Commander on deck!"

All around the Bridge the crew stopped what they were doing in order to stand, snapping to attention as they did. They did not salute, which was an old custom aboard ship. They would salute on land, but no one saluted at sea. That quaint practice had something to do with hands being needed for more important tasks aboard a ship than knuckling one's forehead. Looking to the chair at the center of the Bridge, Basil saw Nessera standing at attention as well. Basil spoke loud enough for everyone on the Bridge to hear, "At ease." Immediately the crew went back to work at their various stations. Basil made his way over to the platform at the center of the Bridge. He slowly climbed its two steps. Two more paces across the carpeted platform, which was a lovely lime green with blue blossoms curling around its edge, brought him to the chair that Nessera was standing next to instead of sitting in. As Basil came to stand in front of her she said, "I relinquish Command, sir."

As a Captain-Commander of the Company, Basil outranked her. Since he was Nessera's commanding officer he would have been well within his rights to take command of the ship if he wished. But Basil would not remove a Captain from command of their ship except for gross negligence or dire need. Neither of these were the case. Besides, Basil was not much of a sailor. Instead he said, "As you were Captain." With a brief nod Nessera ela bin Stormcloud stood at ease. Her smile was easy, her teeth seeming even brighter against the backdrop of her bronze skin. "What can I do for you on this fine evening Captain-Commander?"

Basil turned his attention back to the activity occurring all around him. "Actually Nessera, what I would like right now is a cup of choca."

Turning to her right, Nessera motioned to a young sailor who had been standing at attention to the right of the Captain's Chair the entire time. The young woman left her post, disappearing through one of the doors. Basil looked out the large window, which gave him a view of the front of the ship. Out there, glistening under the beaming moonlight, Basil could see the slightly rolling sea ahead of them. He could even see part of the night sky. The night was clear, even a bit bright, lit as it was by the heavenly bodies above, without a single cloud to hinder their celestial shine. Nessera turned to stand next to him, matching his gaze with her own. "A beautiful night isn't it sir?"

Continuing to look out the window Basil said, "Beautiful indeed Captain."

Nessera said, "If you would like, sir. I am about to step out into the air. We could have our choca on the Portico?" In response to Basil's raised eyebrow she said, "Follow me, sir. Lewellyn, you have the *C.O.N.*" The last was directed to a slim man with three, silver pips on the high collar of his vest. Two were full pips while the third was a pip that was hollowed out like a circle. He was a Lieutenant Commander. As Basil followed Nessera out one of the doors located around the Bridge he saw the man climb the platform and sit in the Captain's chair. He immediately began studying the glass panel to the right of the chair. Basil turned his attention back to Nessera just as a cool wind blew into his face bringing the salty scent of the sea with it. The door Nessera had opened led them directly out onto a small foredeck, apparently called a *portico*, which curved around the front of the Bridge. It was about ten paces wide, twenty across, with a copper rail curving around its edge. The deck was completely unadorned seeming to serve no other purpose than the one they were presently putting it to. Just as they made it to the rail looking out over the front half of the ship the young woman arrived with a silver tray. She quickly served them both choca in delicate, blue cups, trimmed in silver, with matching saucers. With a smile, matched by a nod, from Nessera the young woman flashed a brilliant smile of her own before disappearing back inside the Bridge.

Sipping from his cup Basil caught a hint of nutty flavor with a bold finish that meant the bean was probably from the South. Very good choca bean came from there. It was usually bolder flavors, which catered to a particular palate. It did not surprise Basil that sailors preferred it. Many probably took their choca without sugar or cream. His cup had a bit of both. Though he liked his with a little more cream, it was a very satisfactory cup. So, Basil stood at the copper rail of the Portico sipping his choca as the night air blew lightly over him. For a while he simply stood there sipping as he gazed out over the beauty of the Macca Deep while Leviathan cut her way through the great sea. He nearly forgot he was not alone. Without looking to his left where Nessera ela bin Stormcloud was standing sipping at her own cup he said, "Let me compliment you Captain. Many people find it difficult to refrain from talking, particularly when they have the ear of a superior officer."

Nessera placed her cup lightly on its saucer. "There is no need to compliment me sir. I am well aware of the need for silence from time to time. It is a rare delight especially on a ship. But I am thankful to Tinker, as well as the Shipwrights, for designing such a ship as this. On Leviathan space is less of a luxury than on any other ship at sea I have ever stood upon."

Basil finished his cup. He turned to look for a place to set it down. He was nearly startled when the young woman who had served him appeared again, almost out of nowhere, to take the cup from his hand. Clicking her boots together sharply, as she stood briefly at attention, she promptly disappeared again. With a wry half-smile Basil dug into his coat to retrieve his long-stemmed pipe. In a few moments he had the bowl filled. After lighting it he contented himself with puffing on it lightly while gazing out onto the wide, open, sea. A calm washed over Basil, one he had not felt for several days. Who could blame him given the difficulties the Company presently faced? But something about the sound of the Great Deep, the sweet saltiness of the air, and the glow of the starry night sky put him at ease. So much so that he felt like talking. "So, Captain. How do you feel about the new Flag Ship of the fleet?"

Nessera chuckled softly, "Well, sir. She is a beast, if you don't mind me saying. And when I say beast, I do not mean in a bad way. She displaces more water than anything I have ever seen but she still manages to be sleek. But more than that, she runs fast. Faster, in fact, than anything that has ever touched the deep. She is beautiful and frightening all at the same time. A ship like this, in the wrong hands, could do very bad things. I hope we are up to the task of sailing her."

Basil smiled around his pipe stem. Bantu had always said Nessera ela bin Stormcloud was two parts talent, three parts humility. She was a woman with every reason to boast but without the ability to do so. Basil said, "I am sure you and your crew will do the People proud." Just then a blast of fire erupted into the air in the distance. Before Basil could pull his pipe from his mouth Nessera's com-gem lit up. A voice said, "Captain to the Bridge!"

Nessera turned to look at Basil. It took him a second to realize she was waiting for him to dismiss her. With a nod from him she snapped to attention for a brief beat before stalking back through the door to the Bridge with Basil just behind her. As they re-entered the Bridge, making their way to the Captain's Chair, Nessera ela bin Stormcloud surprised Basil yet again. She did not shout or bark, but in a normal, steady, voice said, "Report."

When she reached the chair the slim man, who had taken command, stood. He moved to the side of the Captain's Chair as Nessera took her seat. While Nessera turned her attention to the glass panel the man, Lieutenant Commander Lewellyn, said, "We are too far out to get very much information, Captain, but we believe there is a ship out there under attack."

Nessera tapped her com-gem in a particular series, which caused all the com-gems aboard the ship, including Basil's, to light up. She said, "This is the Captain. All hands to battle stations." There was an immediate flurry of activity as people entered or exited the Bridge. Basil could only guess that there was similar activity all around the ship. The one thing that happened immediately was that the light that had made the Bridge bright dimmed to a low ebb. All around the Bridge the glass panels at the various stations were now more apparent in the lower general light. She said, "Helm, take us in."

The young man at the station directly below the large window on the left side responded, "Aye, Captain." He touched the glass panel in front of him. Basil could see, as he looked through the large window, that the ship turned toward the flames in the distance. As he stood on the command platform, just behind Nessera's chair, Basil thought to himself that this was not what he was supposed to be doing. They had been hurtling across the Deep on their way to retrieve their commander, but Basil was getting the feeling, as they moved closer to the flames in the distance, that they might not make it to their original destination. He clinched his jaw in order to keep himself from overriding Nessera's orders. In his mind, Basil thought of his old friend who would not have countenanced passing by whatever was happening out there in order to get to him. So, Bantu was going to be on his own. Basil thought to himself, *be careful my friend, we may not be there in time to help, so please be careful.*

Surprises are either sublime or dreadful and, on rare occasions, they are both.

*~Syndiene Issmis
on the occasion of meeting
the man she would marry*

Nightmares do not disturb a warrior's sleep, they are expected.

~An Mfundade saying

CHAPTER TWENTY-SEVEN

When visitors come calling

Wen crouched in the hall a few feet shy of the door. Her cup of juma was just shy of being too hot. She sipped at the dark, spicy liquid as wisps of steam rose from its surface. To be more precise, it was not actually a cup, at least it would not have been called a cup back in Alexandria. Juma was served in short, slender, intricately decorated glasses. The decorative touches were done in a white, glossy paint. Her cup had tiny stars, rushing from its base, circling halfway up its side, as if they were in a hurry to get somewhere. The cups were only ever filled halfway so that they could be held by their upper-half without burning your fingers. They were solid glass at their base making for a well-balanced piece of craftsmanship. While sipping on the spicy tea, which today tasted of lemon, Wen thought of how much time she had spent in this hallway. She felt like she could describe every inch of it blindfolded.

Six days had passed since returning to the Seat of Omorede from the Corral. While they had gotten to know more about the Commander's people she, along with the other Blossoms, had spent a lot of time in this hallway. On the other side of the tall, mahogany doubledoor was a large, empty, chamber with smooth, golden, hardwood flooring. The sounds of men exerting themselves, was a distant, muffled, constant that could be heard through the door. Upon his return to Omorede Bantu had immediately begun preparing himself. Everyday he was up at sunrise entering that room with the Mfundishi of his House to spend the day training. For hours they danced the forms, assailing Bantu relentlessly. Everyday those hardened men in black had left the chamber more humbled, more respectful, as Bantu showed them what he had learned in the Outlands. All the while the Blossoms had taken turns guarding him. Mostly that had meant crouching in the hallway outside what the Mfundishi called the *Doa* of the House. It literally meant *where steel is laid bare* but was more loosely thought of as *a place to train*. Wen had asked how the word could mean both. It had been explained to her that the Doa was the only place in the House where bare steel was allowed so the word had taken on a double meaning.

For the hundredth time, Wen looked over the hallway noticing the same hardwood floor, multi-colored wall tapestries, and silver oil lamps. The only things that changed were the flowers in the vases on the small tables situated along the hall. Today they were tiny blossoms in blue, white, and orange gathered from the flowerbeds all around the Great House. The hall smelled of jasmine with rose oil. The one oddity she continued to be amazed by was the weather. Al'akaz was relatively hot during the day but just as cool in the evening. Somehow the House managed to be the exact opposite. The sun had shown brightly all day, yet the hallway was comfortable, even in her Company uniform. Wen knew that evening was approaching because her stomach told her so. She was beginning to get hungry.

Seemingly on cue, Wen saw Isabelle coming down the hall. Her tall, lithe, form moved like a cat, as she rounded the corner. Isabelle's curly, black hair was laid back on the sides but sticking up in a kind of intertwining, wavy spike on top. Wen tugged lightly on one of her own long, thick braids. She had taken to braiding her hair that way with one braid hanging behind each ear. Looking at Isabelle she knew that she would look ridiculous with her hair done in such a way. But Isabelle made it look exotic, even comely. Her uniform was crisp. Her boots gleamed in the lamplight with fresh polish. They had all been offered robes in the colors of the House, but Bantu had declined on their behalf.

When asked about it he had told Wen that he did not want them mistaken for anything other than outsiders, guests in the House of Omorede. It made sense given that they were so unfamiliar with the many traditions of Al'akazian society. Bantu felt that their uniforms would keep their strangeness intact giving them some protection against the consequences of breaking customs they knew nothing about. Wen knew the Commander well enough to know that the explanation he had given them was only part of the reason. She suspected that the Commander wanted to make a statement about the life he had built away from Al'akaz, to remind his people that he did not return home begging, with his hat in his hand. Wen had made sure that her fellow Blossoms understood that unspoken notion. Since she had shared that explanation they had each gone out of their way to show the Commander's people, by the way they conducted themselves, that he had created something powerful, with real meaning. Spotless uniforms, matched by gleaming boots, were just the beginning of the idea they were trying to communicate.

As Wen watched Isabelle come prowling down the hallway she thought of how proud she was of the young Blossom. Isabelle had come close to being killed only a few days earlier but had bounced back. She was determined to remain unafraid. The Company taught that uncontrolled fear, fear that was not understood, would cripple a person. Fear had to be harnessed. When harnessed, fear could heighten one's sense of things, bringing focus to the moment, but it was never to be allowed to run amok. Fear, uncontrolled, would completely overshadow a person's judgment. As Isabelle came close Wen noticed that her smile was more exaggerated than usual.

Wen rose from her crouched position as Isabelle came to stand in front of her. The young woman's voice was not high but light with a bit of singsong in its tone. Her salute was a bit overly exuberant, which let Wen know that something was afoot. Wen returned the salute then put her right hand on her hip. She did not speak but simply raised an eyebrow at the young lieutenant. Isabelle coughed into her hand, looking down for a moment, then with a straight face, that she was struggling to maintain, said, "Commander, there is someone at the entrance to the House waiting to see you."

Wen gritted her teeth as she nearly cursed. She should have known that it was him, since Isabelle was having difficulty keeping her composure. Wen took her hand off her hip, passed the young woman her nearly empty cup, before starting off down the hall, leaving Isabelle on guard duty without another word. The almost imperceptible sound of strangled laughter followed Wen down the hall. Isabelle, along with Wen's sister Bella, thought the entire situation was hilarious. They had needled Wen with it since the day after they had arrived back at Omorede. Wen had gone from walking leisurely down the hall to stalking across the hardwood like a large cat on the prowl. She did not think it was funny at all. As she made her way toward the entryway Wen passed other women of the House. Apparently, her little problem had become fodder for the gossip among them. She passed the tall women without a word, all arrayed in beautifully bright shades of blue trimmed in white. Some of the women of House Omorede smiled, others covered their mouths to hide giggles, while one or two offered to accompany her in order to assist in the negotiations. When she made it clear that there were to be none, while politely declining their assistance, the women simply uttered what were clearly insincere acceptances of Wen's position. They nodded to her in that way that let you know your words were not being taken seriously. Sure, they understood that she did not need their assistance in this matter. But the words echoed down the hall unconvincingly. Their disbelief did nothing for her mood as her hurried pace brought her closer to the main entryway. Wen began sharpening the edge of her tongue with words that would put an end to the matter once and for all.

Rounding the corner at a near gallop Wen ran headlong into Jamila Ayo Na' Aassam, First Daughter of the Great House Aassam, and recent, perpetual, guest of House Omorede. They hit the hardwood floor, with a small thump, in a pile of arms and legs. After a few seconds rolling around on the floor, they began to untangle themselves. Finally, Wen was able to scramble to her feet, sputtering apologies, while jerking her coat into proper order. Wen could feel her face reddening with embarrassment while she straightened her swordbelt. Jamila Ayo Na' Aassam gathered herself more slowly, adjusting her robes as she rose to her feet with a quiet dignity. Her hands moved with the practiced elegance of a dancer moving to a set piece of music. She even had the self-possession to manage a chuckle as she steadied herself on her feet. Brushing at her sleeves, Jamila spoke, the rueful chuckle still deep in her throat. "Well, well, little sister. Is *Spearbreaker* chasing you through the halls of Omorede this fine evening?"

Spearbreaker, Wen had learned, was one of the names the people of Al'akaz had for the Betrayer. She had heard *Nightchaser, Stormbringer,* and one that puzzled her. Some of the women called the Betrayer *Shade.* Wen cleared her throat. "No, my Lady. I beg your pardon for running you over. It was clumsy of me."

Jamila laughed softly saying, "In the short time I have known you, *Mfundishi,* I have not known you to be clumsy. What could be so important that you would be rushing so?"

Wen caught that Jamila had called her Mfundishi. She also heard the emphasis Jamila had placed on the word as she said it. The First Daughter had grown tired of reminding the Blossoms to call her Jamila. When they did not call her by her given name she reminded them by calling them something other than their own name. Wen took the hint. "Jamila, I was on my way to handle a - a personal matter at the entrance to the House."

Jamila slid her hands into the ends of her flowing sleeves, nodding her head with an air of understanding. "Ah, yes. Now I understand. I will accompany you. And you must stop apologizing, I am as much at fault as you."

Wen turned on her heel starting off down the hall once more. In the few days she had known Jamila she had come to learn that the First Daughter of Aassam was difficult to argue with. So, with a deep sigh of resignation, Wen allowed the woman to fall into step with her. Jamila strolled along in flowing, silk robes of deep blue accented with bright green. A glance told Wen that the material was fine enough that Empress Natasha Sobrine herself would have worn it without a second thought. A deep, blue, slash of color ran down the very center of the robes, from neck to hem. A handspan from that center slash of vibrant color, the blue began blending slowly across the garment into bright green at the hem. It ran through every intermediate shade in between, along the way. Jamila's legs were long enough that she did not seem to hurry in order to keep pace with Wen. Glancing up at the woman from the corner of her eye, as they walked, Wen noticed that Jamila seemed to float along next to her. Wen also noticed the faintest hint of a grin on her face. The woman looked directly ahead as if Wen was not even there, as if the two of them just happened to be in the same hallway at the same time. Wen seemed to be the only person unhappy with the recent development.

As the two of them arrived at the main entrance to the House, a few Mfundishi, along with a handful of Mfunde, were milling about near the archway. Wen approached the archway. When she arrived one of the Mfundishi, his black robes shimmering in the last light of the day, stepped away from the others. He was a handsome man. Not for the first time since their arrival in Al'akaz Wen was taken aback at how the men of Omorede resembled the Commander. The man had the same medium-brown skin, as well as the same small, but broad, features. It all came together in a pleasant way. He had the Commander's light brown eyes, but this man had flecks of green in his. He was also a few measures taller than the Commander. His name was Gyasi, but Wen thought of him as Gyasi With the Big Smile. The man always seemed to be smiling. Today was no different. He intercepted her just before the archway. Gyasi smiled brightly, revealing nearly perfect white teeth. After a deep bow, acknowledging Jamila, he turned his attention to Wen. His voice was deep, but warm, as he spoke. "My Lady." The address came with a slight bow of the head. The men of Omorede had accepted the Blossoms as weapons, though they were women, on the word of the First of their House. But they could not bring themselves to speak to the Blossoms as they would to other men. Gyasi continued, his words formed with that pleasant way of speaking Al'akazians had as they wrapped their mouths around the entire word, pronouncing each syllable. Wen was growing accustomed to the music in the sound of their voices. He said, "I would entreat you again, my Lady, to allow me to act as your brother would in this matter. It is the least I can do as an Mfundishi of the House in which you are a guest."

Wen could not help but smile up at the giant of a man. Every day she had turned down his offer of assistance but after the third or fourth day she had begun to suspect that Gyasi stopped her at the entrance to the House to place a smile on her face before she could step outside. Though she tried to wipe the silly grin from her face she only partially succeeded. Waggling her first finger in the air at Gyasi, as if to tell him he was incorrigible, she walked past him toward the high archway that lead outside. All the while Gyasi maintained a straight face with the exception of the merest hint of a smile at the corners of his mouth.

Stepping out into the warm, waning, light of day Wen breathed deeply, taking in the smell of gardenia, lilac, and citrus. There was a lemon tree nearby laden with fruit nearly completely yellow, with only hints of green left in their skin. The cool breeze along with the wonderful smells did not help Wen in her attempts to maintain a sharp edge to her tongue. She cursed the incessant beauty of the place, silently, to herself. With Jamila a half step behind her, off to her right, Wen walked over to the small party that stood waiting.

He had come to the Seat of Omorede the day after they had returned from the Corral. Wen surmised that he must have seen her there while she had been accompanying the Commander. Everyday since, he had come, apparently according to custom, at least that was what the women of the House had told her. Tall as all the men of Al'akaz were, slim yet muscular, with medium-broad features on a narrow face framed by high cheekbones, he had the head-full of long braids that marked him an Mfunde of his House. The young warrior called himself Akikki. His robes were cotton, but woven well, in shades of the deepest blue slashed through with shimmering silver. His eyes were big. They were so light brown that they were almost golden, accentuated by skin that was just as light. According to the women of Omorede his House was called Osaze. While it was one of the smallest of the Great Houses they were quick to point out that Osaze had its honor. Osaze had even been an ally of Omorede from time to time. The women giggled among themselves when they told her that it was a well-known fact that Osaze had pretty men, very pretty men. Wen had to admit, as much as she hated to, that Akikki was no exception. He was young, tall, and very pretty. She shook her head quickly, saying to herself, *snap out of it, woman, this is neither the time nor place, there is important work to do. Be polite, but, send him on his way.*

When she approached Akikki's small contingent she opened her mouth to speak. But before she could get a word out he was very nearly yelling. His voice pitched to carry, the young man spoke so that half the House could hear him. "I am Akikki Sipho A' Osaze. I am, Mfunde." The last he said with the kind of emphasis that said it meant everything, said everything. Somehow, he managed to sound confident, not arrogant, which Wen liked. The man pointed to another Mfunde in the colors of his House holding a long scroll in his hands. "For all who wish to know what Honors I hold, Olegbah Thembi A' Osaze carries with him the record of my days." With a twirl and a twist Akikki pulled free his yari from its housing stabbing its blade deep into the ground before him. Stepping past the third man accompanying him, who carried a long pole with a small flag atop it, Akikki retrieved a handful of flowers from the only woman in the small party. The flag atop the pole, blue with white trim, the colors of Omorede, was the Osaze way of proclaiming that they were entering Omorede land in peace, according to custom. It, along with the make up of the group, according to those Wen had asked, allowed them safe passage in and out of Omorede land. Apparently, the flag, the woman with flowers, and the man with scroll in hand, was a regular sight in Al'akaz. The Omorede they passed would need only one look at the small assemblage to know them for what they were. They would be allowed to pass unhindered. Wen had wished a few times during the week that custom had required Akikki to fight his way to the entrance to the Seat of Omorede. But she had no such luck. Though custom allowed them access to Omorede it was not unchaperoned access. A fair number of strides off to the right were a handful of Omorede Mfunde who had followed the party, at a customary distance, on their way to the Seat of Omorede. When the Osaze party had finished their business, they would be followed out again.

Akikki, unarmed now, with a handful of the most beautiful bright green and purple, bell-shaped blossoms Wen had ever seen, approached her slowly. Wen crossed her arms over her chest, jutting her right hip out, as she tried to maintain a sour look on her face. Akikki towered over her but approached in such a gingerly manner that it made him seem smaller than he was. When he was a few steps away, he stopped moving. He bowed deeply before her. While continuing to bow, he held the flowers out in his hands with his arms extended. Wen had been told that the easiest way to get rid of Akikki would be to take whatever gift he offered, throw it to the ground, and turn her back to him. It would dishonor him deeply, but it would ensure that he would never return to court her. Some of the Omorede men she had asked said that it might even provoke him to fight whoever stood in the place of her closest male relative to save face. Wen looked around. She could see Jamila a couple of paces off to her right with a look of concern on her face. Several paces behind her a group of Omorede women stood silently watching, waiting to see what would happen. Squatting by the entrance to the House, Gyasi waited with his yari across his thighs looking ready to spring to action if the need arose. In that moment, Wen became all too aware of how much Akikki had extended himself by the offering he was making. Running her eyes across the small Osaze party Wen saw a rising concern on their faces as she took longer and longer to accept or reject their kinsman's offering. While she wanted nothing to do with the man, Wen did not want to hurt him either. He was bright, almost shining, in his beauty. She did not want to hurt him. Taking a deep breath, she reached out. In one smooth movement she snatched the flowers from Akikki's outstretched hands.

Behind her Wen could hear the women of Omorede begin murmuring excitedly amongst themselves. A self-satisfied grunt from Jamila made Wen's face begin to flush. Relief washed over the faces of the small party of the Osaze. Akikki rose from his bow to his full height, with a broad smile painting his features. Wen called up her best dressing-down tone. She pitched her voice low so that only Akikki could hear. Using the flowers in her hand she thrust them at him, statement by statement, for added emphasis. "Now you listen to me you overgrown ox. I am taking these flowers so that you may save face. But I do not want your attentions! You must stop this chasing after me! Do you understand?"

The smile never left his face. He said, "I thank you, my Lady, for your concern. I am indebted to you for such a kind gesture. Each time I see you I am amazed at your beauty and your grace. Your hair is like fire, your eyes like thunderclouds. I will go and meditate on what you have said. If you have need of me for any reason, please send to Osaze. I will come. I have done what I came for. I shall take my leave of you. The sun shine upon you, my Lady."

With that the man bowed deeply. Rising from the bow, he returned to his small party, sweeping them before him as he directed them to leave. After a minute or so the Omorede Mfunde, who had been standing off in the distance, fell in behind the Osaze at a respectful distance. Wen watched them all go. It was Jamila's voice that shook her out of her reverie. "You handled that very well, little sister. Men need a strong hand if they are to be of any use. Give them an inch and they will twist you around their small finger and have your head spinning. A man will have you so confused you won't know whether you are coming or going."

Wen looked up at Jamila with horror. "No, no Jamila. You have it wrong. I explained to him that I am not interested in him! I explained it in a very firm tone!" Wen nodded her head as if she had been nothing short of appropriate in her comments.

Jamila's face had a look of confusion on it as she spoke slowly. "Ah, little sister. You … accepted his offer of courtship. It is our custom to say something harsh to the man when we accept so that he knows we are strong, that we are not to be trifled with. If you were not interested, you should have thrown the flowers to the ground and stepped on them."

Wen nearly choked on her own words. "What do you mean accepted? I was only trying to help him save face, not encourage him!"

Jamila shook her head, clucking her tongue as she turned to go. "Little sister, you have just indicated to the Osaze and the House of Omorede that you will accept having Akikki Sipho A' Osaze court you. There could be worse things. After all, he is very pretty. Very pretty indeed." Jamila laughed softly as she made her way back into the House. The small gathering of Omorede women followed her inside clucking amongst themselves, like a brood of hens, leaving Wen standing by herself. Wen turned, stalking back toward the entrance, forgetting the large bouquet she clutched in her right hand. Her mind was spinning as she tried to figure out what she would do the next time she saw Akikki Osaze. Maybe if she tried to kill him he would leave her alone. But as she entered the house her last thought was that he *was* rather pretty. When she realized what she was thinking she growled so deeply that a young Omorede Mfunde standing by the entrance took three steps back while his eyes widened in alarm. Wen stalked off down the hall without even thinking about where she was headed.

†

Bantu flowed from one form to another. His mind was beyond thought, stilled by the *abundance,* which engulfed him. His body moved without conscious direction. It was only through that disciplined embrace that he was able to calm the throbbing in his head, which threatened to cripple him. Each day in Al'akaz the headaches had gotten worse. The nights had ended with a draught prepared by the Healers of the House to help him sleep while the mornings had become studies in discipline as he sought the embrace of the Abundance to keep the pain from being unbearable. At the moment the throbbing in his head was a distant thing he could almost see in the back of his mind waiting to leap forward so that it could engulf him. At the forefront of his mind was a cool nothingness that allowed the years of training to take over. The wisp of black cloth against skin, the faintest hint of dust being kicked up from the hardwood floor, the nearly imperceptible shift of air caused by yari slashing this way or that, these were the things his mind took in, allowing his body to adjust to each. *Sparrow Shakes the Branch* became *Serpent Slips the Noose. Eagle Leaves the Nest* flowed into *Dragon Breathes Fire.* Those were the names for the *forms,* as they were known across the Deep in the Outlands. It was an ancient way of teaching the sword found on both sides of the Deep. Those same forms were known by other names in Al'akaz.

Five Mfundishi, of House Omorede, circled him. Their faces were calm as an undisturbed pond in a forgotten meadow. They came at him relentlessly, their black robes swirling, their yari lunging, as they moved like wind whistling through trees. Again, and again, he turned them. They all held practice yari made of wood. They made a sharp *thwacking* sound as wooden blade met wooden blade. For nearly a week the best of the House had come to test him in the Doa. Tall, powerful men, with pride written all over them, had come. Their black robes, trimmed in gold embroidery, were covered in a kind of vanity. They had come to this large, circular room dedicated to the training of the weapons of the House. From morning to early evening, with a few breaks in between, the Mfundade of House Omorede had tested him. These hardened men, guardians of the honor of Omorede, had wanted to know for themselves whether the lost son of the House was worthy to wear the black. After all, they had not trained him. Who had? They wanted to know if his blade was sharp, his hand steady, his eyes clear? Would he embarrass himself, or the House, at the entrance to the Corral? Everyday they had come. They had not held back for fear of injuring the First of the House. Everyday Bantu had humbled them, one by one.

On the second day Mandisa had arrived at the Doa early, before the first session, with two women of the House in tow. They carried with them some of the most beautiful robes Bantu had ever seen. Made of the finest linen, they began as bright white at the neck passing into dark blue at the hem. Thick bars of various shades of blue ran parallel to the ground across the width of the robes. The cuffs and hem ended in thick gold cord. They were simply beautiful. The many shades of blue would mark him as the First of the House. There would be no other robes like them in all of Omorede. Other members of the House wore a single shade of sky blue trimmed in white. Bantu had accepted the gift graciously. He changed out of his uniform with the help of the young women of his House, who giggled softly at his apparent discomfort with undressing in front of them. Each morning he had found a new set of robes made from the same expensive cloth but with subtle changes in the pattern. There were always a number of shades of blue but sometimes the stripes were thick, and sometimes they were thin. There had been robes where the entire sleeve was white, or robes where the white was run through with gold. Today the stripes were thin lines of color meticulously woven together to create the cloth. Bantu was almost embarrassed to wear something that obviously took such an incredible amount of effort. But each day the Weavers of the House found a reason to walk past him at some point to see how he looked in their creations. Bantu made every effort to look as if he wore them with pride. Each day the women had left his presence with smiles on their faces. So, he bore the embarrassment of wearing such extravagance for the sake of the Weavers of his House.

Surprisingly, the robes did not hinder his movement as he danced from one form to another. The Weavers *Borjun,* their craft, had been practiced in the Beautiful Land for several thousand years. He should not have been surprised at how well they wove. His many shades of blue flowed brightly through the field of black made by the Mfundishi who danced the dance of death with him in the Doa. They were good. In fact, they were much better than good. While Omorede was not the largest of the Great Houses it had always produced some of the best weaponmasters in the Corral. Bantu had asked his father once about the reputation of the House in the Corral. His father had told him that the men who had first formed their House had been among the best in the Beautiful Land. The skill of those first Omorede had been passed from one generation to the next. The masters of the House, hard, deadly men that they were, pushed him, now, with that skill. Someone behind him grazed his shoulder. Bantu instinctively dove forward, rolling back up to his feet in one smooth motion as he brought his yari up to meet another Mfundishi's descending blow, which would have shaken the arms of another man. The man, Sowande was his name, had thought to catch him off guard as he came to his feet. Bantu spun sideways, passing his yari behind his back, as he slid under a sweeping midline attack from his left. When he completed the spin, making a full turn, he brought his yari up quickly to a high guard. It was the closest the Mfundishi had gotten all day. The members of his master's class back at Sanctuary had been trying for years. To their credit they had managed to touch him from time to time. It was a testament to how good the Mfundishi were.

From off to the right, by the entrance to the Doa, the sound of Mandisa clapping his hands loudly, three times, indicated an end to the session. The five Mfundishi lowered their guard, bowing deeply, to Bantu. When he returned their deep bows by a slight incline of his head they each put away their practice yari on racks along the wall. They left the Doa together, deeply involved in discussing certain aspects of the training session. Bantu caught sight of Sowande as he was leaving. The man inclined his head again, a broad smile spreading across his face, with features that made him look like he could have been Bantu's brother. They were all impressed by the skill of the First. There was a growing excitement among the Mfundade as he fought the best of them to a standstill. Not for the hundredth time that week Bantu wondered if it would be enough. What he was going to attempt at the Corral had not been done in a thousand years. Mandisa's voice brought Bantu back to the present.

"I think you are ready First." His voice seemed to be brimming with confidence.

Bantu nodded slowly as he walked to the wall, sliding his wooden yari into one of the racks. "We shall see Mandisa. We shall see." As he had each day Mandisa brought a towel for Bantu to wipe the sweat from his brow. He stopped his arm halfway to Bantu as he started to offer the towel realizing again that Bantu was not sweating. The man struggled to keep the look of perplexity from his face. Bantu knew Mandisa was wondering how it was possible that he could exert himself for such an extended period of time without a drop of sweat. Though he wanted desperately to ask it was not the way of the Mfundade to question a man about such a thing. For them it would have been considered too personal a question. Bantu ignored the question written plainly on Mandisa's face.

Mandisa said, "I think a good meal followed by a good night's sleep is all that is left to prepare you for what will come tomorrow."

At that moment Bantu realized that he was famished. "I think you are right cousin. I will retire to my rooms. Please have a bath prepared and some food sent to me. That will be all."

Mandisa bowed deeply as he said, "Yes, First. It is my honor to serve." Bantu only half heard the double doors to the Doa open then close. He stood in the Doa, alone now, for a few minutes more, letting himself cool down from the exertions of the past few hours. After a few more moments he decided to follow the dictates of his stomach. Leaving the Doa, he headed off to his rooms so that he could eat, bathe, and sleep. While he walked he rubbed at his temple. Now that he was finished training in the Doa, with the Mfundishi of his House, there were no distractions from the throbbing in his head. It was returning with a vengeance. Picking up his pace Bantu hurried to his rooms where he knew he would find food as well as the draught that would calm the throbbing in his head. After a good meal he would try to rest. Tomorrow, he would attempt the extraordinary.

†

The copper tub filled with hot water, sprinkled with jasmine bath salts, had done wonders for muscles that needed loosening. The tray of food had quieted a stomach that had been protesting. He could still taste the blued cheese mingled with the sauce on the redfish. It had been delicious. The draught that had been prepared had done its work, dulling the throbbing in his head. The elixir, in combination with his giant, soft bed made it possible for him to drift immediately off to sleep. Bantu was unaware of how much time passed before something pulled him forcefully awake. It made him sit up violently in the bed. Darkness shrouded the room. It only took seconds for him to realize what had brought him out of his deep slumber. His hands trembled, his body was soaked in sweat, and his stomach churned. There was only one explanation. Even in the darkness of his room he could still see the empty tray on a side table by the door. The thought of what must have occurred reached the surface of his mind. His stomach turned over violently. Leaning over the edge of the bed Bantu emptied the remaining contents of his stomach onto the floor. Throwing back the blankets that covered him like a shroud he slid unsteadily to the edge of the bed. He was supposed to be dead. The thought hit him like cold water being splashed in his face. His heart beat faster. Looking at the empty tray again, sitting innocuously next to the door, he thought he should be dead. Whoever had poisoned his meal did not know about the *gift*. It was the only reason he was not laying unmoving in his bed.

Lurching to his feet Bantu tried to steady himself. His vision was blurry, his legs were weak, while his stomach still rolled over on itself as it heaved trying to empty out contents that were no longer there. Bantu stood in the middle of his room with nothing on but his white smallclothes wrapped around his loins. Surprisingly, he was drenched in sweat from head to toe. The *gifted* never sweat. He shook. While he stood there shaking, as if the room were cold, his mind raced. Who? Who could have done this? It was not hard to guess who had wanted him dead but how had they managed to get someone in Omorede to do it? Maybe Bantu had seriously misjudged his House. He stumbled through the dark to another side table that held a pitcher of cool water. Ignoring the silver cup next to the pitcher Bantu turned it up with both hands gulping at the clear liquid. Dropping the silver pitcher back onto the table Bantu leaned on it heavily trying to mentally calm his stomach.

Without thought for his near nakedness he pushed open the doors to his rooms stumbling out into the hall. He took one step before stopping. Moving back into the room he grabbed the yari that had been his father's. Yari in hand, he stepped back into the hall. His eyes adjusted to the dim light of the hall. He caught sight of something moving in the shadows at the other end. *So*, he thought, *whoever wanted him dead wanted to be sure the job was done*. The thing flowed down the hall toward him like a serpent on sand. He had never seen its like. It was cloaked in darkness, its black cloak flowing like inky water behind it. Though it wore heavy black boots it made no sound as it drifted toward him in the dark. Sharp, white teeth sneered at him out of a sickly white face. Spikes of white hair stuck out from the black hood that covered its head. It was tall but still only managed to match Bantu's own height. The thing held a long, black spear with a wicked looking curved, black blade sprouting from its end. It smelled like death. It came toward him with the sound of icy whispers, whose words were just beyond making out, emanating from the inky blackness that surrounded it. Bantu stood just beyond his doorway. His vision was still blurred. His head was throbbing again, even as his body continued trembling. Death had come for him. Maybe his enemies' plan was going to work.

†

Wen bolted upright in her bed. She went from being sound asleep to wide-awake in a flash. A large bell was being hastily rung somewhere in the House. She leaped from beneath her blankets. She saw the other two Blossoms doing the same. Wen and Bella hastily pulled on breeches and boots, grabbing their swords as they hit the door to their room. They half-tucked their nightshirts into their breeches as they moved quickly into the hallway. Isabelle came flowing out of the room behind them with nothing but smallclothes wrapped around her chest and midsection. She carried her naked sword at the ready. The House was coming awake hastily. They made it halfway down the hall before two leathery beasts stepped out in front of them. Wen nearly gagged on the smell of sulphur. The things were tall enough to stand over even the men of Al'akaz. They had bulging eyes, fangs for teeth, long pointed ears, and brown leathery skin. Opening their mouths, they let out unearthly screeches. Wen took a step back as a slight grunt escaped her lips. It felt like something invisible had struck her. Looking down quickly she saw that she was untouched, but something had definitely hit her. She just did not know what. With a shout, she leaped forward with the other two Blossoms right behind her.

†

It had seemed like an eternity but finally it was over. Wen leaned on her scabbarded sword as she walked. She ignored the scratches that covered her. The creatures they had encountered outside their room had been incredibly hard to kill. They had not been the only dark things the Blossoms had fought through the night. Wen still had the smell of sulfur in her nose along with the memories of inky blackness wrapped in fire. The leathery creatures had not only been able to conjure clouds of blackness, but they could throw fire! The other Blossoms looked like Wen felt. Bella was limping. Her nightshirt had been singed by fire. Isabelle, still nearly naked, was bleeding from a gash along her forehead. The House was slowly returning to a semblance of order. There were dead bodies everywhere. There seemed to be as many Omorede bodies as things that had attacked them. Small parties of Mfunde, led by Mfundishi, roamed the House as well as the grounds around the House looking for any other enemies. But it seemed as if the attack had come to an end. Wen, followed by the Blossoms, made her way up a flight of stairs. They walked down two more hallways. Halfway through the attack it had occurred to Wen that only one thing had changed in Omorede that might have been the cause of the attack. The Commander had come home. They had fought desperately trying to make their way to him. Her heart was in her throat as they made their way to his rooms. Turning the last corner that would bring them to his hallway the three of them froze. At the end of the hall was a small pile of bodies next to the open door to the Commander's rooms. Wen ran to the end of the hall with Isabelle and Bella right behind her.

When they made it to the bodies Wen saw some of the Mfunde of the House had come to aid the Commander but now lay dead at his door. Their blue robes were stained red with blood. Some of the bodies were charred black by fire. There were five burn spots on the floor where the leathery beasts that had attacked them had died but no Commander. Slowly, Wen made her way around the bodies. When she walked into the main room of the Commander's quarters she saw two other burn spots in the room's center. There was blood everywhere. Dim shafts of moonlight poured into the room from the one window that had its curtains pulled back. Lying against the wall, just beneath the window, wrapped in shadow, was the Commander. Slumped over on his side he clutched at his yari with a bloody hand. His voice cracked when he said, "You look terrible."

Wen breathed a heavy sigh of relief as she raced to the window with the Blossoms on her heels. The three of them knelt down, crowding the Commander. Slowly, they helped him sit up. He was trembling slightly. He was also cut in several places. The Commander winced as they moved him. A bit of blood trickled from the corner of his mouth. But his eyes were bright as he looked the three of them over. Speaking softly, as if each word hurt a little bit to say, he said, "What have the three of you been doing? You look like someone balled you up and rolled you around in the dirt."

Wen smiled at him. "It has been a rough night Commander."

"Yes, yes it has." He said, his smile weak but intact. He continued, "The House?"

Wen's smile dimmed a bit when she said, "Many have been hurt, a number are dead, but the House is secure." Nodding as if he had expected no less Bantu said, "Help me up. I must check to see that things are as they should be."

Wen gritted her teeth as the other Blossoms looked at her. She was the ranking officer. Swallowing hard Wen said, "Forgive me Commander but you are in no condition to do anything but have your wounds tended. I wish there had been time to bring some of the Okoi with us, but since we do not have the luxury of the Water of Life, we will all have to heal the old-fashioned way." Wen knew that even healing the *old-fashioned way* would go much more quickly for the four of them. Even without the Water of Life they were still the beneficiaries of the *gift*. The Commander would heal quickly.

Bantu sat there for a moment with the moonlight shinning down on his face looking at the Blossoms. Then, with a slight nod he said, "Of course Wen, you are right. But one of you must see if Mandisa lives. Be sure that he reports to me that the House has truly been secured."

Wen nodded her head thankfully. "Yes sir. Now let us get you to the bed and send for the Healers of the House."

Gingerly, the Blossoms helped their Commander to the bed. Just as they pulled back the blankets members of the House began arriving to see about their First. It only took a few moments after the first Mfundishi arrived, poked his head through the doorway, and looked around the room, for women to begin arriving with buckets of hot water. They immediately set to cleaning the room as Mfunde arrived to carry away bodies, while other women came with bandages and ointments. In short order the Commander was cleaned up, bandaged, and sleeping. With the Commander taken care of the women of the House turned to bullying the Blossoms until they submitted to the same treatment. Wen did not want to leave the Commander for fear of another attack, but they were finally persuaded. It took the arrival of Mandisa with seven other Mfundishi in tow, all with faces like thunderclouds. The look of them with their yari bared was enough to assure Wen that no further harm would befall the Commander tonight. So, with the House on alert, the Blossoms made their way back to their room. It was not difficult for them to find sleep. As Wen drifted off she did not wonder who had brought walking nightmares down on Omorede, but what nightmares Omorede would conjure up in return. She also wondered what would happen when Bantu did not show up at the Corral in the morning to face the Challenge.

Character is easier to keep than to recover.

~an Al'akazian saying

Where there is no light, darkness reigns.

~a Griot saying

Chapter Twenty-Eight

Challenge

Wen awoke to a light prodding but did not open her eyes. Though she was no longer asleep she did not move. Someone was poking her. Her first thought was that the dangers of the previous night had returned. Tensing for whatever came next, she opened her eyes to see Isabelle, standing a few feet away, poking her with the tip of her sword's scabbard. Wen waved Isabelle off as she croaked, "I'm up. I'm up." Isabelle poked her one last time for good measure, sticking her tongue out as Wen glared at her. Ignoring Wen's displeasure at being awakened the tall woman went back to whatever she had been doing on the other side of the room. Bella sat at the long table, lounging in one of the large chairs, sipping what was likely a cup of juma. Her uniform looked crisp, as if it was freshly pressed. Their uniforms disappeared each night as soon as they took them off, only to be returned each morning perfectly clean. Wen noticed that when Bella shifted her weight in the chair she grimaced. Pulling back the blankets from her bed Wen pushed herself to its edge. She tried clearing her throat, but her voice still sounded like there were rocks at the back of her mouth. "Why did you wake me? You both should still be in bed recovering from last night."

Isabelle did not answer but continued pulling on her own clean uniform while nibbling on something from a bowl sitting on her bed.

Bella responded over the rim of her cup. "Sister, one of the Mfundishi arrived a short time ago to inform us that the Commander is awake and preparing to go to Kal'ada'abassa."

Wen jerked up even straighter on the edge of the bed as if someone had slapped her. Even with the benefits of the *gift*, the Commander would be in no condition to survive the Challenge. It was madness. Leaping to her feet, Wen stumbled to the neatly folded stack of clothes that was her uniform sitting on a chair at the foot of her bed. She hastily began throwing it on. Her mind raced. He could not go. He simply could not go. But how would she convince him. Pulling her freshly polished boots on Wen wrestled herself into her coat, as she rushed out of the room, with the other two Blossoms following. Isabelle chewed on a mouthful of whatever she was eating while she was belting on her sword. Bella was already in full regalia, including her sword, which was hanging from her black leather belt. But she carried her cup and saucer, contently sipping juma, as she trailed behind. The two Blossoms seemed resigned to whatever was happening. Wen could not be so calm. She was the ranking officer, which made her responsible for the Commander's safety. If he went to Kal'ada'abassa in his present condition the hardened men of the Corral would devour him like lions that had not eaten for a tenday. How could Wen return to Sanctuary with word that she had allowed the Commander to be butchered? Her mind raced as they made their way quickly toward his rooms. She hoped something had occurred to her by the time they reached him.

†

Bantu sat on the edge of his bed watching the sun come up through one of the windows in the main room of his quarters. The young Mfunde who had been left to stand guard at the door to his quarters had shaken him awake a few moments ago. The young man had not been happy about it. He had, apparently, been given instructions to let Bantu sleep. But after all the commotion had died down, and everyone had left him to go to their own beds, Bantu had pulled himself from his blankets in order to instruct the Mfunde to wake him at sunrise. Given the choice between the instructions he had been given versus a direct order from the First of the House the young man had no choice but to wake Bantu. The attack had come some time before midnight, so Bantu had still been able to get a good night's sleep. Though he was nowhere near fully recovered, he felt much better than he should have. The *gift* had done its job. The ointment used by the Healers of the House had also worked remarkably well. Cuts that had been an angry dark red the night before were already pink. He noticed that the trembling was gone as was most of the weakness.

Having sent for bath water, Bantu sat there thinking things over. Oddly enough, along with the other improvements in his condition, the constant throbbing of his head had completely disappeared. A hot bath, followed by some food, and he would be as well as could be expected. He was nowhere near his full strength but what strength he had would have to suffice. Breathing deeply, he centered himself. There would be objections when what he intended became known. So, he knew he needed to appear as if he was well enough to face it. A soft knock sounded from the double doors to his quarters. Bantu sat up straight as he said, "Enter." He had to speak slowly to ensure that his voice sounded firm.

The door opened emitting several women. Blue robes swirled around their curving bodies while their bare feet padded softly across the floor. The women carried a large copper tub. Others came in bearing buckets of hot water. Soon, he was fully immersed in the steaming liquid allowing the last remnants of the previous night to soak away. As the hot water did its work, one of the women applied the ointment to his head and face that would remove whatever hair was there. After waiting a few minutes to allow it to do its work, she took a soft cloth in her hand. Soaking the cloth in a bowl of water, she wrung it with both hands before using it to rinse the ointment away leaving smooth, hairless skin.

Just before the water in the copper tube began to cool, after the last woman left, Bantu washed thoroughly. Stepping out of the copper tub, he grabbed one of the heavy towels the women had left for him. Once he had dried off, he sat on the edge of the bed again applying some more of the healing ointment to his body. When he had finished he sat the jar aside. He quickly pulled on fresh linens followed by new robes. These robes had a broad panel of midnight blue across the shoulders, which faded into bright white at the hem like a color that was slowly being washed away by rain. The fading was precise making for a beautiful display of varying shades of blue running down the length of the fine linen. Bantu slid into black leather sandals that laced up to his knees.

Another soft knock announced the return of the women who served his quarters. Entering his room quietly, with their heads bowed, they carried off the tub leaving a tray of food, with an ornate jug of steaming juma, on the small table next to the double doors. The bread was dark. The cheese was sharp with a slight, pungent odor. There was a bowl of thick, cooked oats with honey, along with hot cakes covered in a mixture of berries with a dark, sweet sauce. The young woman who left the tray remained longer than the others to plead softly with the First to try to eat as much as he could. She also pledged to him that the food had been guarded from preparation to presentation. If he had doubts she had been instructed to taste the food in his presence. Bantu thanked her, assuring her that tasting his food would not be necessary. He also reassured her that he would try to eat as much as he could. He made her smile deeply by calling her little sister. The people of his House were a medium-brown complexion, so the young woman's blushing cheeks were hidden beneath her darkened complexion. When Bantu began to eat, he called for the young Mfunde at his door, giving him several messages to deliver. The young Mfunde bowed deeply assuring Bantu that he would have runners deliver the messages immediately. Bantu figured that he would be finished with his breakfast by the time his messages had been received. He was actually able to finish his breakfast, along with several cups of juma, before people began arriving at his door.

The first to arrive was Mandisa. After a short succession of knocks the young Mfunde pushed open the double doors allowing the *Baba* of the Mfundade of House Omorede to enter. Mandisa had apparently rounded up several Mfundishi to join him. They stood before Bantu's bed waiting quietly for the First to finish his juma. They looked like lions that smelled jackdaws in their territory and were waiting for the head of the Pride to release them to the hunt. All was not what it seemed however. While Bantu sipped from his delicate cup, he noticed clenched jaws, narrowed eyes, even fists, which gripped yari a fraction too tightly. They were agitated, maybe close to full on anger. The House had been invaded by dark things in the night. They had been things not seen since the founding of the Great Houses. The First had nearly been killed by, what the warriors of Al'akaz would consider, dishonorable means. Now, Bantu surmised from their grim visages, they thought he was preparing to throw away his life in the bargain. Bantu sat his empty cup on the tray that had held his breakfast, pushing it off to the side on his bed. Mandisa immediately jumped in.

"With respect, First. You must not go. I will send word of what has happened here to the Corral. I will also request that the Challenge be postponed. There will be no loss of honor."

The hard men standing behind Mandisa, swathed in black linen, silently nodded their assent. Bantu did not speak but stared out the window. Mandisa looked around as if puzzled by Bantu's lack of response but quickly regained control of himself. Setting the tip of his yari on the floor between his feet he leaned on it slightly. The First would respond when he was ready to respond. Bantu was not waiting to make a point with Mandisa or the other Mfundishi as they might have surmised. He simply continued staring out the window for a few moments more until it became apparent why he was waiting to respond.

The double doors, which had been closed again after emitting the Mfundishi, burst open without so much as a knuckle of warning. The short, red-haired woman in her black Company uniform came racing into the mainroom of Bantu's quarters with the other two Blossoms in tow. Isabelle was munching on something out of a bowl while Bella sipped what was likely juma from a cup. Wen's voice was slightly higher than normal. She immediatley protested. "Commander. Sir, you must not go. I am in charge of your safety, and as such, it is my duty to persuade you that you must not go. Not today, sir. I implore you. Please wait until you have regained your strength." It was at that moment the woman realized the room was full of Mfundishi. Wen was a native of Alexandria, so her complexion was very fair. It was apparent when her cheeks began to flush bright red. She looked from Bantu, to Mandisa, to the other Mfundishi, all of whom had the decency to appear as if they had not heard a word she had said, all of them except Mandisa.

Mandisa inclined his head briefly to Wen saying, "Outland Mfundishi. I have just put the same request before the First. It is also my hope that he will delay his trip to the Shinning Walls. I was awaiting his answer when you arrived."

Wen bowed her head slightly to Mandisa as she said, "I thank you Baba. We too await the Commander's response."

Bantu sat on the edge of his bed, still gazing out the nearest window, watching the darkness of early morning begin to brighten. He had waited to respond to Mandisa because he knew the Blossoms would be along to raise the same protest. Bantu wanted to respond to everyone's objections at the same time. The Blossoms had arrived just in time. Turning his gaze from the window to the gathering assembled before him Bantu said, "First things first. Mandisa, what has been discovered about the food that was delivered to me last night?"

Mandisa grimaced. Then, as if he was shamed by his failure to report on a matter so obviously important to the House, he said, "Yes, of course First. Forgive my negligence. The young woman who delivered your tray was found several hundred steps into the trees behind the House. Her throat had been ripped out as if by some animal. I had members of the staff from the kitchens brought to look upon her face. No one knew her. The search for answers in that matter continues. Someone must know who she was."

Discussion of Bantu's poisoning made the Mfundishi behind Mandisa shift around. They were uncomfortable with the idea that someone had tried to kill Bantu in such a fashion. In Al'akaz, if you wanted someone dead, you went to their House and challenged them. When they came out either you killed them or they you. You did not slink around in the darkness poisoning food. It was not honorable. What really troubled them was that most of them felt they knew who was behind the attempt on his life. If what they feared turned out to be true it would mean there were much more troubling things to be dealt with in the Corral. If it were true it would mean that there was corruption at the very top of the Mfundade. That thought had even these hardened men worried.

Nodding his head Bantu said, "Please continue your efforts in that matter Mandisa. The House needs answers. As for the objections to my plans for the Challenge, I thank each of you for your concern. I understand how you feel but consider a few things. I do not intend to allow another attempt on my life or attack on this House. I am recovered. I have waited a lifetime for this day to come. I know you are concerned for my safety, but I will not be deterred. Having said all that, I suggest you prepare yourselves. We leave within the hour. That is all."

They all stood around for a moment looking at each other before accepting that he was not going to say anything further on the matter. He had made up his mind. It was done. Mandisa was the first to bow. He left, taking the other Mfundishi with him. Wen stood there pouting at him for a moment longer before taking the other Blossoms with her into the hall to wait for him. They were apparently ready to go. The next half hour went very quickly. Responses to the other messages he had sent began to arrive. Mandisa returned with the contingent he had picked to accompany Bantu to Kal'ada. After reading through the responses Bantu checked the bundle he had wrapped, in blue linen, to be sure all its contents were there. When he entered the hallway, he placed the bundle in Isabelle's arms. Strolling down the hall, he did not need to look back to know that the Blossoms had fallen in directly behind him. They were followed by the rest of his escort. This time there would not be an entire host of members of the Mfundade of the House to accompany him. Aside from the Blossoms, he was followed by Mandisa who had chosen twelve hard-nosed Mfundishi. The Mfundishi of Omorede would be present to ensure that their First was given a fair testing. There would be no tricks or traps. They would see to it.

As they moved through the House, the halls became increasingly occupied by Omorede, who had lined up to watch the First's procession pass by. No one spoke. They simply bowed as he passed. The House was speaking in its, uniquely Al'akazian, way. *We are with you.* When Bantu reached the entrance to the House he was gratified to see that one of his final messages had been received. The small man stood just inside the archway absently gazing off into the distance. He was young with skin as dark as night. Long, woolly, black hair sprouted like a bundle of cotton all over his head. He smelled of sandalwood. Tattoos ran up the length of both arms. The left arm was covered in writing that only the Griot could read. The right arm had a colorful, four-legged serpent curling around it. It breathed golden fire up his shoulder as it clutched stars in its front claws. The tattoos marked the Griot in a particular way known only to other Griot. Those outside the Grammat knew only that novices had no tattoos while the eldest were covered in them. According to how this one was marked, they had sent neither a novice nor an elder. The only garment he wore was a bundle of many-colored cloth wrapped around his midsection. He wore black leather sandals with straps wrapped around his leg up to the knee. When Bantu approached him the young man came out of his reverie. He bowed deeply. "I bring you greetings from the Grammat, First Born. It is our pleasure to serve you. I am Asham' Urtu' Ulltuk. I will take you where you need to go."

Bantu bowed to the young Griot saying, "I greet you, Master Griot, on behalf of Omorede. I thank the Grammat for your service. I offer this token of our gratitude." Reaching behind him Bantu held out his hand. Mandisa placed a small red gemstone in his palm. Bantu turned back to the Griot holding out the payment. The young man bowed again, deeply this time. Rising he said, "I have been instructed by the Grand Tokatt' tel' luude to decline any form of gratitude from the House of Omorede on this day. Word has spread even to the steps of *Talis' tuk' tuu* of the Challenge brought by the Lost One. My master bids you speed and good hunting today, First Born. It has long been thought, among the Grammat, that jackdaws have taken over the lair where lions used to rule. Maybe you will run them out of Kal'ada and restore honor to the Shinning Walls."

Loud thumping sounded from behind Bantu as the Mfundishi who accompanied him drummed the ends of their yari on the floor. Bantu inclined his head again to the Griot. "I am without words Master Griot. I will do what I can. When you return to the Grammat tell the

Grandmaster that the Son of Omorede is honored by his words." The young man smiled broadly. "If the First is ready I will take him to his destination."

Bantu, followed by his escort, left the House. When they were far enough down the road, the young Griot spun his Woedom, calling forth the whirlwind, with its flashing lights, that would carry them far away. Bantu did not hesitate but stepped into the whirlwind followed by his escort. Though he did not seem to move he felt his insides twist sharply. In the blink of an eye they *shifted*. Bantu stepped out of the swirling wind into the thick woods of the Dagoonzu. He knew that a short walk would bring him to the rise overlooking Kal'ada'abassa. Moving forward, out of the way, he waited for the rest of his escort to exit the swirling vortex before making his way out of the great forest to the rise at its edge. Kal'ada's pristine walls shone brightly in the morning sun below. Though it was not his first time seeing the Corral from the bluff, the sight still took his breath away. Once the final members of his escort gathered behind him Bantu continued to stand there gazing down on the Shinning Walls. Old worries began to rise in his mind again. Was he really ready? Sure, he had trained unceasingly from the moment he boarded the ship that carried him away from Al'akaz. But would it be enough? These were the greatest warriors in the world. Was he really up to it?

Behind him, one of the Mfundishi spoke. The man's name was Sunduwesi. Speaking as if he had read Bantu's mind the man said, "It seems to me that maybe the First would care to hear a brief story before we descend on the Seven Walls?" Bantu turned to face his escort. They all stood in a small group encircling him. Sunduwesi was to his right. Bantu looked at the man whose features were so similar to his own he could have been his brother. "Yes, Mfundishi. We have a few moments. A good story is always welcome." With a broad, bright, smile the man began, "It was an age ago, when the Great Houses were young. It seemed as if they went to war almost daily. Zulumdebe had given some offense to Omorede, the exact nature of which is now lost to the far reaches of time. Having refused to apologize, as well as the service of a Keeper of the Peace, they found themselves arrayed on the plains of the Sedengatti. The morning was warm. The sun was shining. The burnt-gold robes, trimmed in blood red, of the Zulumdebe numbered in the thousands with a deep line of Mfundishi, arrayed in black, along its front edge. The drums of war sounded from deep within their tents."

Without so much as a nod to one another Sunduwesi stopped talking. Ollussuku continued in his place. His voice was a hair deeper but his smile was just as broad. "The ranks of the Omorede were far fewer than the Zulumdebe. The red and gold looked as if it would engulf the blue and white of our Fathers. But as the drums of war beat and the wood of the yari being struck together began to sound like thunder echoing across the plain, Yusunda Mballa As' Omorede walked out to the center of the plain between the yari of the two Houses. His black robes, trimmed in gold, billowed lightly from the morning breeze. Without a single word he loosed his yari from it's housing, barring his blade in the morning sun. He drew a single, thin line behind him, between himself and Omorede."

A third Mfundishi, Bantu thought his name was Gassim, picked up the tale. When he spoke, the others began humming an old tune that pulled at the distant memories of Bantu's childhood in Omorede. The hair on his forearms began to stand. Gassim spoke in a deep tenor. His smile was more a feral grin than anything else. He picked up where Ollusuku had left off. "It was clear to the yari of Zulumdebe what Mballa was about. It was the Challenge. From the earliest days of war among the Houses it had become custom for the yari of the Houses to test their skills against one another in single combat before the open warfare between those Houses began. Mballa's challenge did not go unanswered. As the sun began its climb in the sky, Mballa began a display of skill still talked about in whispers in the other Houses to this day. In moments, he cut down the first challenger. He spent the morning defeating every Zulumdebe Mfundishi that came against him. The bloodstained black robes of Zulumdebe piled up on the plains of the Sedengatti. The drums from their tents ceased. The sounds of their yari's striking one another fell silent. Not a single Zulumdebe challenger crossed the line Mballa had drawn on the ground.

The youngest of the Mfundishi accompanying Bantu took up the tale as Gassim's voice trailed off. Butundi said, "When the sun reached its peak in the heavens. The plains of the Sedengatti had grown silent and still. Only the ripple of black cloth in the wind could be heard. Mballa shouted at the top of his lungs at the Zulumdebe. *Challenge,* he shouted! *Challenge?* But there was no answer from the Zulumdebe. It was only when no other challenger stepped from the ranks of the Zulumdebe that Mballa collapsed where he stood. One hundred Mfundishi of the Zulumdebe had fallen at the hand of Mballa. Slowly, Neri Ossum A' Omorede walked to the line Mballa had drawn. Stepping over it, to stand where Mballa had stood, Neri cried out at the Zulumdebe. *Challenge!* He shouted. But no one came. One by one the House of Zulumdebe walked off the field of battle. Before nightfall a formal apology was delivered to Omorede from Zulumdebe for the offense that had been given. Mballa's skill had been so masterful that he had won that reputation for all of Omorede. To this day the yari of Omorede remains greatly respected in the Corral."

With a nod the young Mfundishi took a step back. The haunting tune the others had been humming came to an end. Bantu's heart was racing. He realized that he too was showing his teeth in that feral grin. Mandisa stepped forward. The other Mfundishi gave way to their Baba. With a respectful bow of his head to Bantu, Mandisa said, "First Born, many know the story of Mballa of the Omorede. What is not known outside the House is this: The offense the Zulumdebe gave was to say that Mballa's sister was unworthy to be courted by one of their House. Mballa had been raised to the black robes only a single day before the House went to war."

Bantu looked around the circle of the Mfundishi of his House. These hardened men, in their simple black robes, were not like the men of the Outlands who prided themselves on the number of their possessions. These men had not much more than the robes on their backs and the yari in their hands. They possessed what the House possessed. Outside of the House they had only their honor. As their First, who carried their honor, wrestled with doubt while standing above the Seven Walls, they had decided to remind him of who he came from. They were reminding him that he came from a great House, a House that had stood for more than a thousand years in the face of trial and adversity. He came from warriors who, though they stood in the face of great odds, had prevailed. They watched him closely, like great cats watching a cub, to see if their message had gotten through. Bantu looked each of them in the eye. Then, with that feral grin fully in place, he stalked down the hill toward Kal'ada'abassa. Crossing the bridge, he made his way to the entrance of the City of the Seven Walls with his escort in tow. The message he had sent to Kal'ada had been received. They were waiting for him.

Standing several feet in front of the first archway leading into Kal'ada was Nduma, surrounded by a small crowd of Mfundishi. A larger crowd of Mfunde, in the colors of various Great Houses, stretched out behind them. Beyond that group was a far larger gathering of men, women, and children who had come to see the spectacle. Bantu could see the colors of nearly every Great House in that crowd. The purple and gray of Gamba was matched by the red and gold of Zulumdebe, which seemed to brush up against the mud-brown and black of the Adari. The silver and bronze of Seseke was bright next to the dark green and gray of the Ossessi. It seemed that members of every House were present. The Bakari, Juumbai, and Bullotu made sure to be a good distance from the Tiku, Molombasa, and Fulani. The members of the Yaah and Nunsi stood so close together that one might have thought them of the same House, while the Ga and Ledelle, two of the smallest Houses, tried to look right through one another. The Umbara were way off to the left apart from the entire crowd while the Allaka walked from one part of the great gathering to another as if they were incapable of staying in one place. Since they were Allaka, the prickly, prideful Allaka, everyone gave them a wide berth. The one group that ignored the Allaka altogether was the suspiciously large number of N'kosi, which should not have surprised him. But Bantu took comfort in the presence of an even larger number of Aassam in their deep blue robes, which were accented with bright green. The Aassam was the one House that even the Allaka gave way to, knowing that Aassam was so large that it could feud with Allaka indefinitely without even noticing.

Though the gathering was large, it was silent. It was odd seeing so many people gathered without a single sound coming from them. Wind rustled the leaves in the trees along the river. The sounds of the waters of the Wadi-sanje tickled his ears as it rushed around both sides of the island Kal'ada sat upon. But the great crowd of people did not make a sound as they stood before the Shining Walls. Bantu came to stand before the assembly. He opened his mouth, speaking into that silence with a raised voice for all to hear. "I am Ossassande Bantu As' Omorede! In the Outlands I am known as Karshoon Deshar. This is the testimony of the numbering of my days. I am Shadow's Bain, the Hand that Reaches into the Dark, and the Light that Shines in the Abyss. I am the Thorn in Spearbreaker's paw and the First Born of Omorede. I have come to take my place along the Masters Wheel of Kal'ada'abassa. Let those who bar my way, beware!"

Bantu had never been one for boasting. But according to the message he had received from Baba Gesi Aman of the Solowetu, who had spoken so eloquently in the Masters Hall on his behalf, there were specific forms to be followed. In announcing his intentions, he had to provide a justification for Omorede's request that he be tested. His years as a commander of warriors could be used. His name of honor was also an important distinction as well as a probable justification. Maybe it was the fact that his House would go to war over it that mattered most. Behind him, the sound of yari being rapped against other yari, coming from his Omorede escort, echoed the agreement of his House, that his claim was just.

After another moment of silence, Nduma stepped forward, separating himself from the rest of the crowd. His deep bass reverberated across the distance separating him from Bantu. "I am Nduma Atwanda As' Nkosi and I am the Baba'a'funde." The giant man stopped allowing his words to echo across the crowd. In the Outlands Nduma would have been the equivalent of a powerful warlord, at the very least, or even a king. In Kal'ada'abassa he ruled. He was the Lion, and in the Corral the lion led. He continued, "According to ancient custom the Son of Omorede has the right to attempt the *Long Walk*. If he can enter the Hall of Masters, after passing through the Seven Ways, he will be found worthy to wear the black. Any Mfunde, or Mfundishi, who wishes to test his skill, along the way, may do so. I have been informed by the Baba of the Solowetu that only three challenges may be made in each Way. Once the Son of Omorede has defeated a member of a particular House no other member of that House may challenge. Any who challenge may withdraw at any time during the combat without loss of honor. A withdrawal will be considered an agreement that the Son of Omorede is worthy of the black. So, let it be done!"

Somewhere behind the first wall giant gongs were struck in quick succession. Nduma pointed at Bantu. Raising his voice to carry over the reverberating tones he said, "Son of Omorede, prepare yourself!" At that instruction, from somewhere at the back of the crowds, the drums of Kal'ada began a slow rhythmic cadence. It was a rhythm all members of the Mfundade knew. They had heard those heavy malleted drum beats their entire lives. It was the sound of the Challenge. Most Challenges happened outside the Shinning Walls, so they generally went unaccompanied by the drums. But any formal challenge that occurred within Kal'ada was subject to all the ceremony of the Corral.

According to instructions from Gesi Aman, at the sound of the drums Bantu shed his robes, sandals, and dropped his yari on the pile of well-made cloth. He took three steps forward and said, "I am ready!" By custom he was to come before the Shinning Walls as a child waiting to be born. So, he stood before the First Wall with nothing on but his smallclothes, woven from blue linen. He carried no weapon. According to the ancient tradition, if he were truly ready for the black robes, his body should be weapon enough.

Off to Bantu's right a man pushed through the crowd making his way toward Bantu. He wore the red, embroidered with white, of the N'kosi. The colors of his robes, coupled with the braids in his head, named him Mfunde. Bantu mentally pushed away the smile that tried to rush to his lips. N'duma wanted to see what he could do.

For years Bantu had thought about this moment. When he had begun training for the day he would return to Al'akaz for vengeance, he had thought only of his skill. He had pushed himself to become the deadliest man in the world. Those skills had come in handy over the years. But as he had come to be the man he was today, Bantu had learned something else along the way. He had learned that he would need more than skill. Even the greatest warrior, faced with the number of opponents he might have today, could easily falter. The Mfundade were possibly the most dangerous warriors the world had ever known. His skill, however prodigious, had to be coupled with something else. He had realized some years earlier, that if he were going to be successful, he was going to have to put fear of him in their hearts. Bantu had learned more than just skill, along the way, he had also learned theatricality. It was why the Company wore all black. Why they haunted the rooftops of Alexandria. It was the reason they learned to go *ghost*, to disappear almost right in front of an enemy's eyes. Bantu had not only worked hard to make the members of his Company skilled, but he had worked hard to cultivate their legend. The Peoples Company was respected for its skill but feared because of its legend.

Bantu breathed as the young man closed the distance between them. He did not move as the N'kosi Mfunde closed on him. When he was within striking distance the young man spun hard, twirling his arms as he loosed his yari. The blade came slicing around in a short, sharp, arc heading straight for Bantu's head. It was *Sussundande*, a particularly deadly yari form if used by someone who had mastered it. In Sussundande each stroke began with the yari in its sheathed form. The freeing of the yari from its housing through to the strike was a single continuous move which, when performed by a master, was as deadly as its name.

Bantu waited until the last possible instant. As the Mfunde's yari slashed in at his neck Bantu spun, arching his back, so the blade of the yari passed over his head rather than through his neck. With his back to the man, partway through his rotation, Bantu could actually watch the blade slash past his face. Bantu came out of his spin, which brought him face to face with the N'kosi Mfunde. He did not hesitate. There was a spot on the side of the head. It was between the eye and the ear just below the hairline. Struck with the proper amount of pressure it would render a person unconscious. Care had to be taken, though, because if it was struck too hard it could kill. Bantu slammed the inside ridge of his right hand, which he had straigthened into a knife-hand, into the man's temple. The N'kosi Mfunde collapsed in a heap like a puppet that had its strings cut. There was an audible gasp from the crowd. Bantu squatted down to make sure the Mfunde was still breathing. When it was clear that the man was, Bantu stood. Without a word he retrieved his yari, which was now his right to carry after defeating his first challenger. Bantu walked toward the entrance to the First Way in silence.

The secret, which evil keeps at all costs, is that it promises what it cannot deliver. The failing of evil, which is easy to see if one is looking, is that even when it can deliver a thing, it chooses not to.

~Kalic Severing Stormhaven
Ki'gadi

Love lights up the darkness.

~Solm Vendaban
Teacher to Pallem and main
character in his Dialogues, a
philosophical treatise on life
Atham B. C. E. 341

Chapter Twenty-Nine

Moh'di'ba

Bantu made it through the First Wall, into the First Way, before they fell on him. One after the other they came. Mfunde from Gamba, Fulani, Elazza, Ga, Nunsi, Yaah, and Bakari challenged him. It quickly became clear, as he engaged each of them in turn, that they wanted him dead. They did not simply want to humiliate him or force him to withdraw in shame. They wanted him dead. Actually - he mentally corrected himself - it must have been Nduma who wanted him dead. He knew Bantu would come for him once he made it through the *Long Walk*. The Baba'a'funde, First of House N'Kosi, the Lion of Kal'ada'abassa had apparently decided to take the opportunity presented by the Challenge to deal with Bantu before Bantu could get to him.

One by one, Bantu defeated them. With the morning sun warming his face, accompanied by the crisp smell of lilac, lavender, even burning jasmine incense that was drifting toward him from somewhere, the Molombasa, Tiku, Umbara, Ledelle, and Zulumdebe came against him.

From the First Way, to the entrance to the Fifth Wall, Bantu fought the Mfunde of thirteen different Houses to a standstill. Half of the Great Houses of Al'akaz were represented in the Mfunde who had come against him. Only with great difficulty had Bantu managed not to kill any of them. Colorfully robed men, their heads crowned with long braids, lay unconscious, or wounded beyond continuing, all along the path behind him. Bantu had decided on the trip to Kal'ada from Omorede that if he could, he would avoid killing those who came against him today. He had hoped to avoid causing any enmity to fall on Omorede by the time the day was done. The problem with his strategy was that avoiding killing someone who was trying to kill you was extremely difficult. The blood running down his left arm and right leg were indications of that difficulty. Though the wounds were far from superficial they were also not life threatening.

The Mfunde of Zulumdebe had just waved Bantu off. The young man withdrew just before slumping to the ground. He clutched his robe, at his waist, where the bloodstain spread slowly beneath his hand. He would live. Bantu had not gravely wounded him. But the battles were beginning to take their toll. Actually, it was all catching up to Bantu. The fact that he had only been partially recovered from the poisoning, as well as the fight for his life, the night before, was affecting him. All of that, mixed with the effort it had just taken to defeat the thirteen Mfunde he had already fought today, came crashing down on him. As Bantu walked through the Fifth Wall, into the Fifth Way, he forced his breathing to slow. Out of an abundance of caution he walked slowly. A light sheen of sweat had formed on his shaven head, something that was rare. It let him know that he was nearing his limits. The *gift* was a marvel but even members of the Company, with the *gift*, could push themselves too far.

Bantu had glanced at the Blossoms just before he entered the passage through the Fifth Wall. Noticing the worry written on their faces had been unavoidable. When he passed them, he had flashed them a brief smile. The men of Omorede walked behind him like an impenetrable wall. They cheered him on, rapping their yari together, while they whistled or chanted. Somewhere ahead of him the drums continued.

There had been some other indications of support along the way. Bantu had seen Mfunde from Seseke, Allaka, and Solowetu called down by stoic-faced Mfundishi of their own Houses when the younger men started to step forward to challenge him. There were those, even beyond Omorede, apparently, looking for him to succeed. The oddest intervention had come in the Fourth Way. After defeating a Ledelle Mfunde, just before locking yari with the Zulumdebe he had just beaten, a young, bright-eyed Mfunde of the Aassam had begun to step forward. But before the young man cleared the crowd he had walked past Jamila, the First Daughter of his House. When Jamila caught sight of the young man, in the blue and green of her House, on his way to face Bantu, her eyes had widened before quickly narrowing to slits. It had taken all of Bantu's flagging strength to keep from laughing out loud when Jamila latched onto the young man's ear. With a yelp, swallowed up by the sound of the drums, he was dragged by the First Daughter of his House to the back of the crowd. The young Aassam Mfunde had stood there, sheepishly rubbing at his ear, while Jamila gave him a tongue lashing that would have peeled skin from his body were her tongue made of steel. When she finished with the young man he had backed away, ducking his head as he went, until he was swept up by a band of fellow Mfunde from House Aassam. The group of young men had laughed loudly, cajoling, pushing, and roughhousing with him until he began laughing about it himself. With a withering look for all of the young Mfunde of her House, followed by a sharp nod to herself, as though her work was done, Jamila had returned to watching the spectacle.

Bantu strolled slowly, out of the passage in the Fifth Wall, into the Fifth Way. The bright light of the sun closing in on its zenith greeted him. It was a clear, cloudless day. The word *beautiful* came to mind. A light breeze blew across his face carrying a hint of the sweet smell of the starfire flower mixed with sandalwood. The crowd of spectators had already preceded him into the Fifth Way. Bantu was suddenly thirsty. Neither the *Challenge*, nor the *Long Walk*, made provision for taking a break, so Bantu licked his lips while trying to forget about it. The Omorede exited the passage behind Bantu. He looked ahead to see black robes blocking his way. The Mfundishi had decided it was time to join the Challenge. Bantu had known this was coming. The grandmasters of the Corral were not going to sit out the *Long Walk*. Where the Mfunde had simply drawn their yari this Mfundishi spoke.

"I am Usa Illomba A' Songhaa. Watching this ancient ritual has been entertaining, First Born. But it is time to put it to an end. You are skilled. There is no doubt of that. But you don't deserve to wear the black. Prepare yourself." The man was a hand taller than Bantu. He even looked a bit thicker. His shaven head seemed to come to a slight point at its crown. Oddly, in that moment, Bantu remembered that all of the Songhaa had that trait. Taking a deep breath, Bantu steeled himself. At some point his head had begun to throb again. This was where his fate would be decided. He had always felt he could survive the Mfunde. It had been the Mfundishi that had concerned him. They were death draped in black cloth. They were the men all the boys of Al'akaz wanted to grow up to be. It had been the Mfundishi he had thought about when he pushed himself while training. Bantu had always known that to get to Nduma he would have to go through the black-robed Masters of Kal'ada. Now it was time to find out whether he could or not.

Usa moved like the beating of a hummingbird's wings. It was almost over before it had even begun. Somehow, without thinking, Bantu had raised his yari to block the cut meant to take his head off at the neck. It happened so fast that the only thing that let him know he had blocked Usa's attack was the clear, singular note of steel ringing against steel that reverberated over the gathered assembly. Usa smiled a dark, sardonic smile at Bantu over their crossed blades. It had begun. The man was frighteningly fast. Bantu was immediately on the defensive dredging the reserves of his strength as he struggled to keep up. *Swan Skims the Lake* kept his leg from being taken off at the knee. *Eagle Leaves the Nest* saved him from being run through the gut. He scrambled to keep up with the Mfundishi of the Songhaa. Spinning like a whirlwind, the man slid under Bantu's guard. A backhanded slap lifted Bantu clean off his feet, spilling him onto the smooth stone of the Fifth Way like an overturned bucket of mop water. Somehow, he managed to keep a grip on his yari.

Bantu pushed himself hastily back to his feet. Laughter rang out behind him. Usa's laughter was filled to the brim with derision. Bantu turned to face the man. He saw disdain all over the Mfundishi's face. Silence had fallen on the crowd. Bantu did not look around him. He was afraid of what he would see. All of his attention was focused on Usa Illomba of the Songhaa. He stood there, near exhaustion, listening to Usa's laugh. Something deep within Bantu shifted. In that moment, he realized he had been afraid. He had been afraid that he wasn't up to the task, afraid of the Masters of Kal'ada, afraid that he was going to fail. He had been so afraid of failing that it had brought him to very brink of that failure. It had caused him to forget the death of his parents and all the years of training. But with his right cheek stinging from the backhanded slap, he felt his fear fall away. In fact, the entire world fell away. His fear, his fatigue, even the throbbing in his head became a distant concern. Everything fell away with the exception of Usa.

The Mfundishi of the Songhaa was still laughing at him as Bantu fell on the man. Calm washed over Bantu as the yari in his hand moved effortlessly. It was as though Bantu was watching himself from a distance. He felt fully grounded in the moment but at the same time somehow distant from what was happening. He moved with speed wedded to precision. He did not even think of the forms, he simply became them. It was as if everything he knew was right there at his fingertips. All the skill he had acquired over the many years of relentless preparation was there, available for the asking. *Scorpion Lashes its Tail* became *Willow Waves at the Moon*. *Sparrow Shakes the Branches* followed *Dragon Breathes Fire*. *Wind Trims the Sail* turned into *Cat Swats the Swallow*. Bantu danced. As he danced the dance of death Usa's visage changed. Laughter, mixed with disdain, faded from his features. It was replaced by fear. Bantu completely outclassed him. Usa could not touch him. It took all of the man's skill to keep Bantu at bay. For a moment, the idea of killing Usa Illomba A' Songhaa, crossed Bantu's mind. But then he remembered. *Theater.* Spinning to his right, Bantu stepped into Usa's left side, past his guard. He slapped the man with his open hand across the left side of Usa's face. Blocking two cuts of Usa's yari, Bantu slashed upward with his own yari throwing Usa's guard high, over his head.

Hopping a step forward, Bantu slapped Usa again, in the same spot. Dropping his yari across his body, over his left shoulder, Bantu blocked a high line attack as Usa tried to strike from his high guard. Turning his body left, back into Usa, he remained inside the man's guard. Bantu delivered a backhanded slap to Usa's opposite cheek. Usa reeled from it. Bantu fell on him like a rockslide down a mountainside. He struck at him from every angle with an avalanche of blows. Three different times, during the flurry, Bantu opened Usa's guard touching him lightly to show that he could kill him if he wanted. Finally, with a low to high back thrust he knocked Usa's yari from his hands. Bantu spun to a halt, in fifth position, with his yari's blade over his shoulder, waiting to deliver a final blow.

Usa collapsed to his knees with his arms covering his face. The sound of Usa's yari sliding across the smooth stone of the Fifth Way was the only sound that could be heard. Bantu just crouched there, standing over the Mfundishi, allowing the moment to wash over him. He gazed past Usa. He could see the crowd staring at him in amazement. Mouths hung open. Eyes were wide. Silence reigned in the Fifth Way.

Bantu held his stance for a few more seconds. He stared a hole in Usa until the man said, "I ... I yield, First Born."

But the man had said it so softly that even Bantu, who stood over him, barely heard it.

Bantu said, "Say it so that it may be heard Songhaa Mfundishi." Looking around with a shattered look on his face Usa found his voice.

He shouted, "I yield First Born!"

Sound rushed back into Bantu's awareness. The crowd erupted with a roar of cheers. Even the Mfundisihi standing off to the side nodded their heads in approval.

With a single motion, Bantu sheathed his yari, twisting the wood together. His exhaustion had rushed back in with the flood of sound. Without a word he turned toward the entrance into the Sixth Wall.

†

Bantu walked slowly. He had narrowed his focus to his feet. Fighting to keep the exhaustion at bay, he concentrated on putting one foot in front of the other. It was only when he noticed the pink and white blossoms of the blackwood trees in the Seventh Way that he realized he had not faced another Challenge. It hit him like a slap in the face. He jerked to a halt. Taking a deep breath, Bantu turned to look behind him. The crowd that had been with him since the entrance to the First Wall was still there, following him at a distance. They moved in complete silence. When they noticed he had stopped to look back at them they also stopped. The black-robed Mfundishi were in the front of the crowd. They stood there, unmoving, quietly reserved. Bantu looked down the row of Masters. None of them indicated any interest in moving to block his way. He looked down the line of lions of the Corral. He inadvertently caught the eye of Alazzmakaz. The First Son of the Aassam nodded briefly. It dawned on Bantu in that very moment. After watching Bantu utterly embarrass Usa they had decided. None of them wanted to face him. Standing a little taller, Bantu turned back toward the tower at the center of the Seventh Way. Breathing in the delicate scent from the blossoms of the sacred blackwood trees, he walked through them toward the tower entrance. The sacred trees, which were the only things populating the Seventh Way, surrounded the tower. They smelled like a light, sweet musk. Bantu let his mind dwell on that wonderful scent. Soon he would be raised to the Mfundishi. Then he could turn his attention to Nduma. But for now, he needed to make it to the Hall of Masters at the heart of the tower without falling over.

Taking his time, Bantu made his way to the tower. The Mfundishi who had been crouched at the door had risen at his approach. The man quietly stepped aside without comment. Bantu used his weight, leaning heavily on the large, black-lacquered doubledoors, as he turned the doorknob to open them. Using his yari as a walking stick, he made his way down the winding corridor of gray marble, streaked with white, while looking at the lines of color running along the floor's center. Finally, after what seemed like an interminably long walk, the doors leading to the Masters Hall came into view. The two Mfundishi, standing to either side of the double doors, looked shocked as he came around the curving corridor into view. But they remained silent as Bantu put a hand on the doorknob while pushing his shoulder against the carved lion halfway up the door's face. It opened without difficulty. With one long stride Bantu was finally standing in the Hall of Masters. He did not have the strength to smile but satisfaction welled up inside him. He made his way to Omorede's section around the Masters Wheel. Leaning on his yari, Bantu stood behind Omorede's chair with a swirl of blue etched into the gray stone beneath his feet. He had done it. The thought of success washed over him. He had completed the *Long Walk*. Soon he would be acknowledged as Mfundishi. Once that happened he would waste no time putting the Challenge to Nduma. Seven days should be plenty of time for him to recover. Then Nduma would pay. The man's deep baritone interrupted Bantu's thoughts.

"Well, well, First Born. You did it. Congratulations." Bantu looked up to see Nduma, followed only by black robes, entering the Hall. The surprise must have been written on his face. Nduma looked around him as he continued, "Oh, yes, yes. I apologize, First. You see only Mfundishi may be present at the *Raising*. It is custom. Since you completed the Long Walk, according to the ancient way, we must raise you to the Mfundishim. Only the grandmasters may be present as we bestow the black robes."

While Nduma spoke, the Mfundishi of the various Great Houses took their places around the Masters Wheel. Alazzmakaz smiled at Bantu when he took the seat of the Aassam. Mandisa bowed his head when he walked past Bantu to take the seat of the Omorede. It only took a few moments for the Hall of Masters to assemble itself. Somewhere a gong was struck. Nduma adjusted his silk robes. The golden lions around the cuff of his sleeves glistened in the lamplight. He sat in the only chair in the Hall with a back. The man was so large that the chair should have made a sound of protest. His deep voice followed the fading sound of the gong. "First of Omorede, Long Walker, please stand before the Masters of the Hall."

Following the motion of Nduma's arm, Bantu stepped into the center of the circle made by the chairs of the Masters of each Great House. He stepped slowly, even reverently, onto the swirling colors of the lion etched into the floor at the heart of the circle. It was the Masters Wheel. Around it, sitting in chairs set at the point of each Great Houses section, were some of the deadliest men in the world. Bantu stepped to the exact center, just behind the lion's great head. The Baba's of each Great House rose from those chairs. Alazzmakaz had an oversized, leather-covered book open in his arms. He began to read. "You were made from love for a purpose. Our forefathers and mothers were told that the Day would come. To this day we await the Darkness. Your House has offered you up as a sacrifice. To be a Yari thrown at the darkness when it comes. As a symbol of your willingness to raise a Yari against the evil that is to come will you wrap yourself in the black robes? Know that if you assent your life is no longer yours but Kal'ada'abassa's and your House. Know that when the Devouring Evil returns you will be called to face it. Know that no love, no fear, or doubt may come between you and this sacred duty. How say you son of Omorede? Will you don the black?"

It nearly took Bantu's breath away. He had known there were things only the initiates of the Corral knew, that there were secrets attached to being raised to the Mfundishim, but he had not been prepared to learn this. The black robes were a symbol of the Darkness? The Mfundade had been made to fight the Betrayer? Bantu suddenly realized that everyone in the Hall was waiting for him to answer. There would be time for questions later. With a clear, strong, voice Bantu said, "I will."

"Well said, First Born of Omorede. Well said indeed." Nduma's baritone rumbled off the walls of the still chamber. The giant man rose from his seat, adjusting his robes with a flourish. A few casual strides carried him to where Bantu stood at the center of the Masters Wheel. Bantu hated Nduma, but one would be a fool to underestimate him. The Lion of Kal'ada was among the tallest in Al'akaz. But he wasn't just tall. He had the heavy muscle to go with it. The Son of the N'kosi moved with the same deadly economy as the rest of the black-robed. Bantu barely had enough strength to grimace in distaste as the man came to hover over him. Lowering his voice so that only Bantu could hear him

Nduma leaned in conspiratorially to speak. "There is one more thing Omorede, before we can end the ceremony that will raise you to the black robes. Will you agree to forego a Challenge against me? There is a place here in Kal'ada at my right hand. With you and Alazzmakaz at my side we could accomplish a great deal. Think about it. They will sing of how we ruled in Kal'ada for a thousand years to come." Nduma paused to look at Bantu. No doubt he was gauging his reaction to what Nduma was offering. "I would also be willing to help you increase the influence of your House. Omorede should be as large an influential as Aassam and N'kosi. Just say the word Son of Omorede. We will begin again. All things will be new between us. Say yes, First Born."

It was a surprising offer. Bantu would be lying if he claimed he was beyond being tempted. But as Nduma's breath fell on his ear the desperate look of his mother's face rose up, unbidden, from somewhere deep in his mind. An image of her reaching for him, while his father held her back as the boat that carried him pushed away from the shore, filled his mind. It was as if he could almost see her in front of him. He had to stop himself from reaching out to her. That night had haunted Bantu's dreams for years. Now, the man responsible for that terrible night was standing in front of him. He was responsible for Bantu having spent his entire adult life away from his home and family. In spite of that, he thought he could placate Bantu with his offer of power. The only way Bantu could manage to speak was through gritted teeth. "Go to the Pit, Nduma." Had he not been in the sacred Hall of Kal'ada'abassa Bantu would have spit on the ground at Nduma's feet. That was a clear, concise, unmistakeable insult in Al'akaz. But Bantu refrained. Nduma simply nodded his head. Turning his back to Bantu he began walking back to his seat. As he went he said, "That's too bad Omorede. Though not unexpected." Raising his voice so that every Mfundishi in the Hall could hear him, Nduma said, "Kill him!"

Bantu froze. Had he heard right? Did Nduma just order the Masters of the Hall to kill him? He caught the eye of Alazzmakaz who had a bewildered look on his face. But as Bantu turned his head to glance around the Masters Wheel he saw black-robed men move. Had

Alazzmakaz been a fraction slower they might have killed Bantu. As it was the Son of Aassam had leaped to Bantu's side, deflecting the first attack, just before it sliced Bantu in half. Alazzmakaz stood to Bantu's right with his yari raised. Turning from Alazzmakz, Bantu saw Gesi Aman A' Solowetu had moved to guard his left side. Gesi Aman had been the Mfundishi who had initially raised the *Long Walk* as the solution to the problem of Bantu issuing the Challenge without the right to the black robes. The aged Baba of the Solowetu was apparently not under Nduma's control. What shocked Bantu even further was that Mandisa apparently was under his enemy's control. The man had his yari drawn but was not moving to help Bantu. Bantu took in the entire Hall. It seemed that nearly every Mfundishi present was under that man's control. Alazzmakaz's loud growl seemed to indicate that he had just come to the same realization. The First of Aassam was seething. "You vile jackdaws! You have betrayed everything we stand for by doing this. Everything! Any of you, who raise a hand against us, here in this sacred Hall, shows himself unworthy to wear the robes. Know this. I will kill every one of you. Every. Single. One of you!"

Bantu could almost feel the anger pouring from Alazzmakaz. He was, according to what he had heard since returning home, one of the most gifted Mfundishi in all of Al'akaz. He would need to be to survive this. On Bantu's left Gesi Aman remained silent. Maybe the elderly Mfundishi was marshalling what was left of his strength for what was to come. Some of the men surrounding them must have taken what Alazzmakaz had said to heart. Those who had been advancing on them had stopped. But Bantu was not feeling confident. They were three against a hall full of deadly warriors. He was so exhausted that he was going to be useless. Not only was he exhausted but, as Alazzmakaz had been venting his outrage, the pain in Bantu's head had become unbearable. He had bitten down hard on his teeth to keep from screaming out in pain. There had been times, as a boy, that the pain in his head had become nearly impossible to bear but it had never been this bad. His eyes watered as he heard Nduma command the Mfundishi again to kill him. *Kill all of them*, he yelled. Bantu dropped his yari to the floor. He grabbed the sides of his head as if his hands could keep it from splitting in half. They were going to die. The Mfundishi surrounding them closed to attack. When they moved Bantu heard a voice. *Hold on. I come.*

Dropping to his knees, Bantu screamed in pain. He knew his head was going to explode. Just then, the double doors to the Hall burst open. Bantu gasped as he saw, through watery eyes, what entered the Hall. It was as if the creature etched into the center of the floor in the Hall had come to life. It was a lion. But nothing like he had ever seen. The thing was twice the size it should be. Its mane was like spun gold with red and green streaked through it. Its eyes glowed with irises the size of gold coins. They were gold with bits of green, blue, brown, and red in them. The creature's fur was reddish-gold. Its paws were massive. Everyone in the Hall stood frozen. The enormous creature looked around the Hall until its eyes landed on Bantu. Its roar seemed to shake the room.

Nduma yelled something. The Mfundishi that had stood frozen at the great creature's entrance found their courage. They attacked. Bantu watched as they fell on him and his two-man guard. But within a few heartbeats something shocking occurred. A number of other lions trotted into the Hall from the doorway. Without hesitation, they turned on his attackers. It was pandemonium. All Bantu could do was try to hold his head together with his hands. He looked up to see the giant, unnatural looking, lion standing over him. *I am about to die*, he thought to himself. The voice he had heard earlier said, *No. We live.* A deafening roar was the last thing Bantu heard. His skin seemed to catch fire just as he was swallowed up by darkness. He lost his grasp on the world as he passed out.

†

Bantu could hear someone calling him. It was a woman's voice. But it sounded like she was in a tunnel. *Where was he? Who was interrupting his sleep?* He was lying face down, so he rolled over. *Why was the bed so hard?* He took a deep breath. He inhaled. The world came crashing in on him. The smell of blood was in the air. It was mixed with the musky scent of some kind of animal. Then there was a sharp scent, he could not place, that filled his nostrils even as it wrinkled his nose. He sniffed hard to try clearing it from his nose. A distant, but distinct, voice said, *Fear.* Bantu sat upright in the bed with a jerk. But he wasn't in bed. He was sitting on the hard, gray, marble floor of the Hall of Masters. He took another deep breath. He began to get his bearings. With a mental sigh of relief, he realized his head was not hurting anymore. Even the faint discomfort he had grown accustomed to, here in Al'akaz, of the pain simmering in the back of his mind had disappeared. It was gone completely. A relief he had not felt since arriving in Al'akaz settled on him. He rubbed his face, with both of his hands. He heard her voice calling him again. This time he recognized it. It was Wen.

"Commander! Wake. Up!" Bantu realized then that something was very wrong. He could hear it in her voice. Bantu turned his attention to the Hall. He really looked at his surroundings. What he saw took his breath away. There were dead bodies all around him. Black-robed Mfundishi lay unmoving everywhere. Then he saw the lions.

Standing slowly from where he had been sitting, Bantu gazed at the creatures nearest to him. The lions had made a protective circle around him. They were not letting anyone get close. Wen, the other Quiet Blossoms, Alazzmakaz, along with a number of the Mfundade of Omorede stood in a giant ring around the lions. Their blades were drawn but no one was moving. There were low growls emanating from the lions, aimed at the circle of people, warning them not to approach. Bantu looked across the crowd of Mfundade until he found Wen. Smiling at her he said, "Commander, what happened?"

The woman smiled as she shrugged her shoulders. "Quite honestly sir, I am not sure. We were waiting outside the Tower by the entrance to the Seventh Way when these lions came bounding in behind us. People scattered as they passed us but then we followed as they burst into the Tower. When we made it inside the Hall we joined the fight. Alazzmakaz shouted at us to fight the Mfundishi so we did. With the help of the lions we fought them. As for the rest, I have no idea how to explain what happened."

Wen finished but her words indicate that there was something else that Bantu needed to know. He looked around the Hall again. Over behind the great chair two Mfundishi held fast to Nduma. But the man kept glancing at the door along the wall behind him. Looking back at Wen he said, "Wen, what else is there?"

Wen opened her mouth then closed it again. Then she said, "A few of the Mfundishi got away through that door." With a dismissive wave of her hand Wen indicated the door Nduma kept glancing at. The man was likely wishing he had also managed to escape the same way. But Wen wasn't finished. Looking back at Bantu she said, "And then sir, there is that." Shrugging her shoulders as she spoke Wen just pointed at him. Bantu looked down at himself. He felt his mouth fall open. It had been a custom going back thousands of years. The Baba'a'funde, once raised to the First Seat, was named the Lion of Kal'ada'abassa. Custom dictated he be marked with a tattoo covering much of his upper body in the form of a lion that matched the lion carved into the floor of the Hall. While you could not see it while he wore his robes, Nduma had that tattoo. He was the Lion of Kal'ada, or at least he had been until today. But what Bantu could see made the markings worn by the Baba'a'funde's of the Mfundade pale in comparison. Down his arms he could see the reddish-gold forelegs of a lion. But they were more vibrant than any tattoo he had ever seen. He could see the life-like color running up his arms and across his shoulders. Looking up at Wen he found his voice, "Tell me."

Swallowing hard Wen said, "Sir, it runs down your back and halfway down your legs. The easiest way to describe it would be to say that it looks like that enormous lion jumped onto your back and melted into your skin. It's not like any tattoo I have ever seen. The colors look almost alive. It is the most beautiful thing I have ever seen."

Bantu turned his arm over as he stared in awe. This certainly was no tattoo done in his sleep. He had walked forward toward Wen without thinking. It was only when his leg brushed up against fur that he stopped. Looking down he saw that he had bumped into one of the female lions that encircled him. She turned her large head up to look at him. Before he could move she pushed her head up into his hand. Leaning against him as she nuzzled her head up into his hand she began to purr from deep within her chest. Bantu smiled as he rubbed her head with his hand.

Looking around the Hall at the rest of the big cats he somehow knew they would obey him. He made a rumbling sound in his throat that he did not know he was capable of making. When they heard it, the lions left their places around the circle they had formed. They all padded over to Bantu. Each nearly climbed over the other trying to get to him, so he could rub their heads. He laughed. After a moment, he clapped his hands. Bantu had no idea how he knew that would work but it did. They retreated to a corner of the Hall. After giving one last look at the people near Bantu they laid down. They began licking themselves as they lay against each other. In moments, they were studiously ignoring everything in the Hall. It was as if they were under a tree on the plain. Bantu gave them one more look before turning back to the people who had sheathed their blades. They were all standing around looking as puzzled as Bantu felt. It was a familiar voice, cracked with age, which provided an answer.

"We have not seen your like among the People for several thousand years." Bantu looked over to see Gesi Aman leaning on a younger Mfundi of his House. The man must have been wounded in the fighting. But Bantu smiled at the aged Mfundishi. He was glad the old man had survived.

Bantu said, "I don't understand Gesi Aman. What do you mean?"

The senior Mfundishi nodded his head. "During the war of the great powers of the heavens, the Allgis of the Light bound together animals and men to create soldiers that could stand against the Twisted Ones. It is said that the great cats were among the first in The Beautiful Land to agree to the bonding. These soldiers led the first of the Mfundade. They were called The *Moh'di'ba* in the First Tongue. We came to know them as *the lions that walk*."

It made Bantu's head spin. The questions began to pile up in his mind. But he knew he had some pressing matters to attend to first. Turning to the men who held Nduma, Bantu growled. "Release him." They pushed Nduma forward toward Bantu. He heard Wen behind him. She still had concern in her voice. "Commander, shouldn't you rest?" he waved her off. "No, Wen I am surprisingly fine. This will not take long."

Bantu took a step toward Nduma. The door the man had been constantly glancing at burst open. Nduma looked at Bantu with relieved triumph on his face. A strange looking man, in a green coat, with gray breeches stepped into the Hall. The smallish fellow plucked a square of silk from his sleeve. He looked around him raising the silk square to his nose. Bantu had seen his like among the Peerage of Alexandria. The silk square was often perfumed. The man was completely out of place in the Hall, but it did not seem to bother him. He had the look of a man used to getting his way.

The Son of N'kosi, wide-eyed, yelled something indecipherable. The man had a pale complexion, dark hair, and black eyes. He tilted his head turning to look directly at Nduma. His lips twisted into a dissatisfied grimace. He watched Nduma struggle in the grasp of the Mfindishi who held him fast. Disdain was clearly written across his features. But with an absent-minded wave of his hand, he motioned to the open door. At that signal *Twisted* things poured into the chamber like water from a faucet. Leathery things, throwing black inky darkness with one hand while flinging fire with the other, hobbled in. They were followed by giant, grayish-white, man-like creatures draped in black, wielding black-bladed spears. Behind them came a crowd of expressionless men in dark garb bearing black-bladed swords. It was as if the Pit had opened up right there in the Hall vomiting up its vile, twisted, contents.

Without warning the lions slammed into the oncoming horde. It took half a heartbeat for the warriors of Al'akaz, followed by the Quiet Blossoms, to join in the fray. Bantu rushed forward with a deep-throated growl. He nearly stumbled as he closed on one of the tall grayish-white creatures. He was moving faster than he was used to being able to move. The thing swung its foul looking spear down on him. He caught the black blade of the thing's spear on the blade of his yari. Instantly, he realized that he was also stronger. He pushed the thing's spear off his blade watching as the strength of it moved the creature back several steps. It looked at him with surprise. Barring its fangs, it looked around its immediate surroundings. Bantu realized it was looking for an escape. He grinned as he moved in. This was going to be fun.

†

It took Bantu a moment to realize it was over. He stood in the center of the Hall barely breathing. Even given the *gift*, he should feel like he had exerted himself, at least a little. But he did not. He felt like he could fight for days. But he had no one to fight. Looking around the Hall he realized all his enemies were vanquished. The fighting was over. Then he realized that people were staring at him. Bantu turned his head to see the Blossoms, along with a number of the Mfundishi, just looking at him. He looked down at himself. There was blood everywhere. He was covered in it. Taking a deep breath, he let his mind wander back over the last few moments. He had lost himself in it. After killing the first creature Bantu had given himself over to pure instinct. The lions in the Hall had flanked him. They fought alongside him. He had torn through the Twisted like they were, parchment covered, straw targets. He had lost himself in it. It wasn't blood lust. It had been something else. It was like thought was unnecessary. It was all smell, hearing, and moving. Now he stood in the center of the Hall with his companions staring at him. He saw it in their faces. They were worried.

The lions had returned to their corner. The Mfundishi were clearing away bodies. Someone had retrieved a number of buckets of hot water that were being used to wash away the blood. Bantu did not see Nduma or the odd little pale man who had ushered in the twisted. They must have escaped in the confusion of the battle. Gritting his teeth, Bantu thought to himself that he would hunt down Nduma if it was the last thing he did. Scanning the crowd, he looked over the black-robed Mfundishi until he found Alazzmakaz. "Son of Aassam, attend me." Alazzmakaz turned at the sound of Bantu's voice. He had been speaking with Gesi Aman. Bantu was glad to see the stubborn old man had still refused to die. His arm was being wrapped by one of the Mfundishi of his House. The elder Mfundishi nodded to Alazzmakaz as the younger man turned to stroll to where Bantu stood. To Bantu's amazement, as Alazzmakaz came to stand in front of him, the man dropped to one knee and said, "As you command, *Moh'di'ba*." It took Bantu aback. He just stood there looking down at Alazzmakaz who kneeled before him with his head bowed. After a few heartbeats Bantu found his voice. "Please stand Alazzmakaz. You have no need to kneel before me."

Alazzmakaz stood shaking his head. "I beg your pardon *Moh'di'ba*, but I do. I thought it only tales told to our children. Your kind has not walked among us for thousands of years. But you have returned. Gesi Aman is correct. You are the *Lion that Walks*. And as you well know, here in Kal'ada, among the Shinning Walls, *the Lion leads*." At that moment, all around the Hall, the Mfundishi of the Great Houses who had rushed into the Hall behind the lions to fight the Mfundishi who Nduma had turned, stopped what they were doing in order to take up Alazzmakaz's words. "The Lion leads." The words echoed across the Hall as, one by one, the warriors of the Great Houses of Al'akaz, did what they had never done in their lives. They bent down on one knee, bowing their heads, as they repeated the refrain, "The Lion leads." From the corner of the Hall where the Pride had settled the roars of lions filled the Hall.

One may never know what motivates another. It matters not. Their actions will tell you all you need to know.

> ~*Serris*
> *Philosopher*
> *From his writings*
> *entitled "The 28 b.c.e"*

I'll take my friends wherever I can get them.

~Overhead in a crowded bar in Verellan

CHAPTER THIRTY

Selene

Alec came awake in the way he had, only recently, been trained to. It took a bit of self-control to keep from wincing. His head throbbed as if a very large man was trying to, slowly, twist it off. The musty smell of moss mixed with fertile, black earth filled his nose. All along his jaw, he felt pain but he forced himself not to move. The metal-like taste of blood was still in his mouth. A glass of wine would not have gone amiss. Pushing thoughts of drink from his mind, he managed to keep his eyes closed while he continued breathing evenly. Anyone looking at him would assume he was still unconscious.

Pezzu had enjoyed beating on Alec. The man had not asked him as single question. The son of the Atazzi of Alexandria had discarded all pretenses. This was all about revenge for the death of his brother. Alec knew the initial beating was only the beginning. Before Pezzu was finished he was going to carve Alec into little pieces. He had a lot of experience with Pezzu. The man could be truly twisted when he put his mind to it. Having grown up in a ruthless family he had learned his lessons well. His father had likely blamed him for the death of his brother. So he had certainly put a lot of thought into what he was going to do to Alec when he caught up to him. Alec let that thought drift away without holding on to it. Another of the lessons he had already learned from his Stone Hand teachers. As he lay there on his side, tied up like a bale of hay, he just listened. They had drilled that into him during his training. *Listen and learn. Use whatever is readily available.* He did what his Stone Hand teachers had begun to teach him. Hopefully he could learn something useful.

Alec had already put some of that training to good use. While they were tying him up he had flexed his arms so that when they finished there was still a bit of play in the rope. While Pezzu beat on him he rolled with the punches, taking some of the power out of them. It was also an opportunity to use those movements. While Pezzu beat on him Alec worked at the play in his bonds, loosening the ropes even further. He would still be cut, even bruised, but moving with Pezzu's punches insured there wouldn't be any lasting damage. Alec knew how to take a punch long before joining the Peoples Company. So he lay there, breathing evenly, working his hands behind his back, while listening to his captors. Someone was coming. Pezzu had lain off beating on Alec because he had a meeting with someone important. Alec wondered who would come to a meeting with Pezzu this far out in the middle of nowhere. It wasn't long before he got his answer.

The sound of Pezzu's feet trampling on some of the undergrowth left in the clearing stopped. The handful of men Pezzu had brought with him fell silent. Alec heard Pezzu say, "Greetings. I am Pezzu of the Atazzi. It is an honor to meet you, yes?"

A silvery voice responded with an edge of contempt, "Is that a question Alexandrian?" Pezzu made an indeterminate noise, in the back of his throat, as if he were about to answer the man when he was cut off by that too-smooth voice. "Never mind, I am not here so that you may waste my time. You know why I have come. My present concern is *The List*. You have had your portion for months but what have you done? Nothing! You haven't removed a single name. It is vital that the two at the top of that list be eliminated!"

Alec heard the sound of twigs snapping under a booted foot. He could only imagine it was Pezzu taking a step backward. The man's tone told Alec he was right. "Yes, yes, I understand, my Lord. We have been working on ways to get to them. But it is difficult. It is very difficult! They are always well protected."

The unknown man's silvery voice hardened like steel being quenched in spring water. "I'm not interested in your excuses! You have no idea what is coming." The sound of Pezzu's voice bobbed up and down as if he were bowing. "Yes, yes, my Lord. Don't worry. We will hold up our end of *The Bargain*." The silky voice said, "We have given you the assistance you claimed you needed. We have also paid you handsomely. Finish the job we gave you or you will be dragged off to a place where you will beg for a death that will not come."

The threat seemed to end the conversation. Alec heard people moving around the clearing. What he heard next was unmistakable. Arrows whistled through the air into the clearing. It was enough to make Alec open his eyes. He looked up in time to see two of Pezzu's men fall with a thud, like large sacks of flour, with black arrows protruding from their chests. In the blink of an eye two more men fell to the ground with heavy grunts. Alec bent himself so that he could get his bound arms under his feet. He slid his arms up in front of him. He could not see who was firing arrows into the clearing. Whoever it was they were an incredibly good shot. Each arrow had killed its target instantly upon impact. The only ones left alive were Pezzu, the tall, grayish-white creature wrapped in black, and the mysterious man with the silvery voice.

Alec had begun to think members of the Peoples Company had come to rescue him when she walked into the clearing. It was clear she had been the one firing the arrows because she dropped the bow to the ground as she cleared the tree line. He should have been finishing the work of freeing his hands, but he could not take his eyes off her. The woman was a little taller than average. Her hair was as black as a crow's feathers. It was cut close to the scalp on the sides but flowed from the top of her head, down her back, like a river of ink. She was slim but curved, here and there, in a comely way. The double-breasted tunic she wore was black with rows of small, black buttons down the front like they were in a military formation. It folded over her chest and buttoned at the shoulder. A high, unadorned collar curved up to encircle her neck. The breeches were a matching black. They were tucked into black, suede, knee-high boots, which had a large ring of white fur around the top. They, somehow, appeared to lace up the back. Alec had to tell himself to breathe. She was stunning. Her face was all hard angles, which came together, in a breathtaking way, around full lips. He thought he could make out a thin scar running from her cheek to her forehead, while leaving her right eye untouched. There was certainly a story there. The woman sauntered, it was the only way to describe how she walked, into the clearing, to where the white creature, flanked by the two remaining men, still stood.

Pezzu slowly inched back behind the pale, otherworldly creature. The thing hissed at her approach. It was the strange man with the silvery voice who threw words at her like they were knives.

"Have you lost your mind woman? Who are you? I want to know your name before I kill you with my own hands!"

The woman's strange accent was like silk snapping in a staccato rhythm. It had the sound of the far northeast in it as she wrapped her mouth, almost delicately, around each word. "I am Selene Shadowhaven. Yes, that's right. I can see in your face that you recognize the given name of what most of the world call the *Sicarri*."

The man was still on the opposite side of the towering, white creature, draped in black, so Alec could not get a close look at him. But he continued to work on the rope tied around his wrists while he watched the exchange. The man's voice had changed now. "Well, Shadowhaven. Even if you are one of the *Anointed* you still have much to explain. I am Ersel Hopebreaker. Since I outrank you I demand you explain yourself before I crush you where you stand."

The woman looked around the clearing. Her gaze stopped on Alec for a brief moment before taking in the rest of her surroundings. When her eyes came to rest on the man who had identified himself as another Sicarri she exhaled as if a weight had been lifted from her shoulders. Alec was trying his best not to panic. *Two Sicarri! How, by the Pit, do I get myself in these situations?* He made himself breathe while focusing on the rope around his wrists. Two of the most evil, and powerful, beings in the world were only a few strides from him. He kept telling himself to *stay clam. Just breathe.* Another voice in the back of his mind was hysterical. It was screaming that he was going to die. Alec tried to focus on the rope around his wrists. But he was afraid. There was no doubt.

Though the woman's shoulders were relaxed her voice sounded like a hammer hitting the same spot over and over. "Hopebreaker. I have searched for you. For years I have searched for you. I actually managed to come close a few times. I missed you by a day in Bree. You'd been gone a week when I placed you in Antwimm. It took me years to prepare myself to find you. Once I was ready it still took even longer to run down your trail. But here you are, standing in front of me, finally." The woman grinned wryly as she continued. "Yes, I can see in your quizzical expression. Your memory escapes you. I know, I know, but don't worry. I will remind you. I will call your mind back to a small town in the northern most part of Province. Let your memories rise up to greet you, *Anointed One.*" She spat that title from her mouth like it was venom she had just sucked out of a snakebite. "Let the vision, of the night you came looking for a young girl with the *Talent* before the Ki'gadi could find her, come to the forefront of your thoughts. Recall the burning homes spewing black smoke, the butchered villagers left sprawled in the street, and the murdered family you left in your wake. You did all of that, all of it, because they would not voluntarily hand over a young girl to the Twisted."

Selene Shadowhaven seemed to fill up the clearing with her presence. She did not pace or sway, she just stood there letting the words pour out of her like a dam that had just burst. "Your precious *Coven* tried stripping all of that away from me as they trained me to use the *Talent*. They tried to reshape me into their image. I learned but I never forgot. I trained but I did not let the memories of that night, or who I was, get washed away in the Darkness of that harsh place. And when they finally let me off their leash, believing I was their trained, twisted thing I set out to find you. And look, here you are."

Ersel Hopebreaker took a step toward Selene Shadowhaven, allowing Alec to see him for the first time. The man was surprisingly average. Middling in height, with a round face, he was completely unremarkable. He had brown hair on top of that round face. Only two things about the man were worth noting. His voice seemed to belong to someone else entirely and his clothes were clearly expensive. The tunic was red with gold trim, which matched the red breeches. His turneddown boots were rust-colored leather. Their color matched his cape, which was secured at his shoulder by a large, ruby pendant that sparkled in the light. Hopebreaker flipped the right side of his cape over his shoulder. His voice took on a dangerous edge. "Well, well young one. Had I known you were looking so hard for me I would have made myself easier to find. You are very lovely, after all. I would say that I regret your loss, but I don't."

The woman spit on the ground. Alec wasn't sure if her disgust was at the crude suggestion or the man's lack of remorse. "No, Ersel Hopebreaker. I would say you are going to regret that I have finally caught up to you. But the truth is you will not live long enough." The woman slowly pulled a sword from over her shoulder. As the steel slid free of its scabbard it made a clear ringing sound. The pale creature standing alongside Hopebreaker hissed. It twirled its black-bladed spear in its hand as it brought it up to a defensive position. Pezzu stepped even further back. Ersel Hopebreaker spoke with a voice that was as hard as the ground in winter. "You should have stayed far, far, away from me youngling. I will split you open and suck the marrow from your bones. And then I will feed you to this Horror. It has not eaten in days."

Without warning Ersel Hopebreaker waved his hand, with a practiced motion, sending black tendrils of lightning streaking toward Selene Shadowhaven. The black, pulsating fingers trailed crackling power as they forked through the air leaving only the faintest afterglow behind. The woman twirled her sword in her right hand as she raised her left. The black lightning slammed into her palm. It exploded around her even as it passed to either side of her raised palm like a river rushes around a large stone. The force of the impact pushed her back several steps, throwing dirt into the air as she slid along the ground. It sounded like a whip being cracked as the lightning darted around her hand, striking the ground with a thunderclap. Without hesitating she leaped forward. Raising her sword high above her head, as she sailed through the air, higher than a person had a right to leap, Selene Shadowhaven brought her blade down in a smooth motion, striking at Hopebreaker's head. The man had pulled his own sword free in time to meet her stroke with a rising block. The clear sound of steel on steel filled the clearing. The male Sicarri managed to stop her blade from cleaving his head in two though his arms buckled with the effort. Red, green, and black flames erupted where their swords met. Alec had never seen anything like it. He could feel his heart pounding in his chest as he worked at his bonds. Even so, he kept watching the extraordinary display taking place a few strides from where he lay on the ground. Pezzu had disappeared altogether, but the *Horror*, as Hopebreaker had called it, was working its way around the edge of the clearing in order to get behind the woman. Alec reflexively ducked his head at the sound of green fire exploding around the two Sicarri. *The woman was throwing green fire!* Selene, using her free hand, was hurling head-sized balls of green fire at Hopebreaker. They exploded against a wall of swirling black mist hastily thrown up by a backhanded wave of the man's hand. The wall shuddered as each ball of green fire erupted against it. The clearing was quickly becoming littered with scorch marks, craters, small fires, and even burning trees. Though he had managed to block the green orbs of fire being hurled at him the man grimaced with each impact. Alec could see beads of sweat trickling down the man's face. Selene's face, on the other hand, remained smooth. There was a disaffected look about her as she floated around the clearing like a dancer on a stage. Alec saw hints of swordform in her movements. He thought he recognized *Serpent Slips the Noose*. Dodging more black tendrils of lightning, she twisted into what was almost *Widow Stirs the Pot*. Those crackling fingers of pulsating, black light couldn't have missed her by more than a hair as she spun around them. She flipped backwards into the air, sailing over the last tendril. As her feet passed over her head she threw more green fire. Landing lightly on her feet she took one hop before moving into what nearly mirrored *Leaf Catches the Breeze*.

Alec realized that the battle raging in front of him had frozen him in place. He had become mesmerized by what he had never seen before. Quickly, after shaking himself out of his reverie, he turned his attention back to the rope around his wrists. With a few more tugs his hands were free. In the span of a few more breaths the rope around his ankles was cast aside. He was free. But free for what? Should he run? *Yes, he should run.* As he stood to escape he saw the pale creature the man had called a Horror. It had quietly made its way around behind Selene. A quick glance made it clear that she had the upper hand against Ersel Hopebreaker. He was beginning to crumble under a barrage of arrowhead shaped darts made of black flame. A nearly invisible wall, which he was apparently holding in place with his palms facing Selene, was showing cracks as it shuddered under the barrage of black, flaming darts. Alec realized then that the man had simply been trying to survive her onslaught until the Horror could attack her from behind. A quick look at Selene told him she did not realize what was about to happen. She was engrossed in her eminent victory over the man she had tracked for years. This was a fight among his enemies. Alec should not have cared one way or the other what happened to these Sicarri or the Horror. The world would likely be a better place without any of their Dark-kind in it. He should take this chance to escape. These are the things he told himself as he watched the Horror get into position. But as Alec took one last look at Selene something in him knew he wasn't going to let her get hurt. Telling himself this was how he always got into trouble he moved.

The Horror leaped from its cover along the treeline. Had Selene been a fraction slower she would have lost her leg. She dived through the air, away from both of her enemies, managing to hit the ground rolling. It happened so fast that the Horror only managed a cut across her thigh. Selene came up out of the roll only to go down in a heap. In a blink the Horror was on top of her. Its spear rose as it stood over her. But before the creature could strike Alec slammed into the thing, at a dead run, causing them both to tumble away from her. The two of them landed in a tangle. Alec gagged at the smell of the thing. It was sulfur mixed with decay. They rolled around on the ground for what seemed like an eternity. The Horror was frighteningly strong. It only took a moment to realize it was too strong for him to handle. Alec tried to scramble away but the thing caught hold of his ankle. Its grip was like a blacksmith's vise. As it pulled him toward it he realized he was going to die. His last thought was what a fool he was. He had been given plenty of cover from the Sicarri's battle to escape. But instead he had decided to jump right in the middle of the fight. Now he was going to die for his trouble.

The thing pulled Alec back to it. Throwing him on his back, it climbed on top of him. All Alec could focus on were the white fangs that were about to rip out his throat and the smell. The thing hissed. When the thing's head went flying across the clearing it took a few heartbeats to realize what had happened. The headless body collapsed on top of Alec. That lovely voice, with its odd accent, drifted down to him. "The *Grealim* is about to burst into dark flame. If you don't want to be consumed along with it I suggest you move."

Alec pushed the headless thing off before rolling along the ground until he was several strides away from the *Graelim*. At least that was what she had called it. Just as he stopped rolling the thing did burst into reddish flames. The smell of sulfur filled the clearing. As it burned Alec just lay there, on his back, breathing. He almost couldn't believe he was still alive. *He was alive.* Resting his hands on his chest he just let himself lay there staring up at the sky. After a few moments the woman's head came into his field of view. She looked down at him. She stared at him for a bit before finally reaching out her hand to him. Alec slowly grasped her hand. It was a firm grip. She pulled him up without any apparent effort. As he steadied himself he looked at her. She stared back. He was a bit taller than her, so she had to tilt her head ever so slightly. Her head was titled, to the side, quizzically. Her eyes were slightly narrowed. What came next did not surprise him.

"Why did you help me?" Her voice was even, giving away no indications of sentiment. Alec could only detect genuine curiosity in her tone. He cleared his throat. "It seemed like the right thing to do." He tried to stop it, but he couldn't help it. A broad smile spread across his face. The woman's eyes narrowed even further as she said, "Why are you smiling?" Alec lied, "Because I am alive. For a moment, back there, I thought I was dead." The woman gave him a noncommittal grunt as if she didn't believe him. Nodding her head, to herself, she turned her attention to examining the clearing.

Alec also took a moment to gaze around the clearing. It only took a brief moment to realize that Ersel Hopebreaker was gone. Before he could stop himself, Alec said, "He's gone." Selene Shadowhaven's back stiffened a bit. Without turning to face him she said, "Yes. In the few moments when we were occupied with the Graelim he escaped. The man is an inveterate coward. I found him before, I will find him again." She said so matter-of-factly that Alec believed her. There was no doubt in her voice. In that instant something he had heard before she had attacked the men's meeting came back to him. Alec inhaled deeply. He did not even attempt to stop the sigh that followed. Rubbing his wrists to ease the rope burns he said what he had only just realized. "I have to go with you."

Selene Shadowhaven turned slowly to face him. There was nothing but hardness in her face as she gazed up at him. The word came out as if it was the first word ever spoken in the history of human beings. "No." She stared at him for the time it took to breathe in deeply as if she wanted it to sink in. Alec waited until she nodded to herself. When he spoke he could see her jaw clench. "I am sorry but it is unavoidable. It seems that I also have some important business with the man. I am not interested in getting in the way of whatever it is you need to do." He knew what she needed to do. She needed to kill him. But Alec thought it would have been indelicate to say it out loud. He continued, "But you must understand. Before you arrived, he was speaking with another man about something very important. I have to find Ersel Hopebreaker and question him about it. After that he is all yours."

Alec watched as Selene Shadowhaven stared at him as if she were the Ancient of Days weighing him on the *Scale of Life*. He could almost see the argument she was having with herself play out on her face. After a moment she grunted before saying, "I will allow it, only because you helped me with the Graelim. But mark me, if you get in my way, I will kill you myself. Do we have an understanding?"

Alec nodded. "Yes, Selene Shadowhaven, we have an agreement."

She gave her head a brief shake. "No, I do not carry that name anymore. I am Selene Ariella. You may call me Selene, I have neither the time nor the patience for pleasantries."

Alec inclined his head briefly as he said, "Selene, I am Alec sa' Salassian. You may call me Alec."

Glancing briefly at the night sky, Selene said, "Well Alec. We had best get moving. These men left horses and supplies in the treeline. We need to get you one of their horses, sort through their supplies, and find you something other than that ridiculous white coat to wear. When we are finished we can find somewhere a ways from here to camp for the night. In the morning we begin tracking Ersel Hopebreaker again." Without waiting for his reply Selene headed for the treeline. Alec looked down at his jacket. He brushed at his sleeve in an attempt to wipe off a bit of dirt. It was hard to keep clean, but Alec didn't like having her call it ridiculous. He took one more look around the clearing before following her into the treeline. In the back of his mind he tried not to think about how this night could have ended differently. What he did dwell on was unavoidable. Her name was Selene.

In nearly every battle there comes a moment when a sacrifice must be made.

~Commander Lewellen Verris
The Red Guard
The Fifth Legion

A fly in the jar will spoil the ointment.

~Overheard instructions to a customer
Jaibara's House of Healing
Purveyor of Medicinals, Potions, and Sundries

Chapter Thirty-One

Sacrifice

Night had begun to fall quickly. The last of the day's light leaked over the peaks of the Black Hills off to his left. High above his head, a nearly full moon, shone brightly as if it couldn't wait for the sun to fully disappear. The moon was so big in the sky Alla'mirridin imagined he could reach out and touch it. The air was brisk. It did not bother Alla'mirridin as he rode near the back wrapped in his voluminous cloak. He had, somehow, managed to end up just a few horse-lengths ahead of Zezza din' Nightblinder. The young Ki'gadi rode her gold-colored stallion, Sunchild, at the very rear of their small band in silence. Mino din' Darksbane had put her in charge of the prisoner. The Sicarri, or *Da'shara* as they called themselves, Vesper Shadowell was trussed up, like a slain deer, on the back of a horse under her watchful eye. Zezza had a rope in her hand leading the horse carrying Shadowell. She kept the horse beside her, on her right, rather than behind her as some might. As Alla'mirridin rode along, reigning in Speckle from time to time, in order to keep pace, he told himself he had picked this place, just in front of Zezza, at random. The brown stallion, with its white spots across his front quarter, wanted to run but they were only moving at a brisk walk.

Alla'mirridin had occupied himself with puffing on the slim cigar he had gotten from the plump fellow who had arrived with the Watchmen. Dain Du'urdin, though a little odd, was a pleasant enough fellow. The man had a large stash of cigars in his saddlebags. Alla'mirridin had smelled the sweet smoke as they rode. When the scent had drifted back to him a brief, brilliant, flash of memory had overcome him. Thoughts of a large, leather armchair and a strong drink, to chase the smoke of a mellow cigar, had overwhelmed him for a moment. When the memory began to fade back into the black well of clouded memories in his mind he decided to ask Dain Du'urdin if he had another cigar. The plump, small fellow had been more than happy to give Alla'mirridin a fistful of them. Though he had been obliged to ride alongside the man for a few hours while he rambled on about the various types of leaf, wrappers, and styles of rolling. Eventually he was able to settle back to his spot just in front of Zezza. He rode along quietly enjoying the mellow taste of the cigar. It had a nutty flavor with a hint of spice.

Up ahead of Alla'mirridin, rode the young Watchman, Aubrey Devilwind. Aubrey was young, but it had not taken Alla'mirridin much time at all to see that he was a handy fellow to have around. The small, plump, well-dressed Dain Du'urdin, with what Alla'mirridin thought was a ridiculous mustache, rode alongside Aubrey. Du'urdin continued talking non-stop about this or that. Alla'mirridin had stopped listening when the man had begun going on about the different rates at which varieties of candlewax burns. Aubrey seemed to listen patiently to the man but Alla'mirridin thought, surely, he must have been exhausted from Du'urdin holding forth on a mind-numbing array of topics. It became clear that Alla'mirridin was right when Aubrey spared a slightly withering look for Alla'mirridin, as he dropped back to his place in front of Zezza, leaving Aubrey as the sole focal point for Dain Du'urdin's rambling. Alla'mirridin had smiled at Aubrey, shrugging his shoulders apologetically, as he lit his cigar.

A few lengths ahead of where Du'urdin rode alongside Devilwind, the senior Watchman rode next to the older Ki'gadi. Alla'mirridin had not been riding close enough to hear that conversation even while Dain Du'urdin was handing him cigars. As he blew out a plume of heavy smoke he found himself hoping that the two men were in the process of coming up with a plan. He could see Cordovan del Allegressa, with that mythic, purple cloak spilling down his back. It was long enough to spill over the hindquarters of his black stallion. The Watchman was leading the conversation while Mino din' Darksbane nodded his head periodically. When their party had stopped to rest, or eat, the two of them had gone off from the rest with the bound Sicarri in tow. Zezza would disappear into the woods, ostensibly, to be on watch while their party made camp. It was an odd way to be on watch, but he kept that opinion to himself. Alla'mirridin assumed that the two leaders of their little band had been questioning the man further about their destination. They had been riding almost directly north for a few days. Their route had them traversing the thick woods that stretched from the foot of the Black Hills all the way south to the northern-most point of Province. This far north one only expected to run into bandits. But even that was unlikely this far out. After each of their private conversations with the Sicarri, Mino and Cordovan adjusted their route northward. It had been a very quiet few days.

As the last light of day gave way to the first rays of moonlight the trees of the forest melted away. They were suddenly at the foot of the Black Hills. A shiver ran down Alla'mirridin's spin. The mountain range ran for as far as he could see in either direction. It looked like an unending wall of jagged rock stretching up into the evening sky. He just sat there on Speckle looking up. Blowing cigar smoke into the darkening air, he looked around to see that everyone else was watching Mino and Cordovan. The two of them had dismounted and were leading the Sicarri toward a particular part of the rock face. The bound man looked around before indicating a direction with his head. Alla'mirridin puffed on his cigar as he watched the three of them approach the base of the mountain several hundred paces off to his right. The rest of their party sat their horses while quietly watching. It suddenly dawned on Alla'mirridin that he could hear nothing emanating from the forest directly behind him. It was eerie. Leaning back a bit in the saddle, he bent his ear toward the trees behind him, but there were no hoots or howls. He concentrated on listening but could not detect any buzzing, flapping, or rummaging. He could not detect any of the normal sounds that were a given in a forest at dusk. *Eerie*, he thought to himself. An odd stillness had settled on the world around them. It was as if life itself had deserted the area. Something about it did not feel right. Twice he had to reign in Speckle who seemed just as bothered by the place as Alla'mirridin was becoming.

Turning his attention back to the three men he watched as Cordovan made his way over to the rock face. Alla'mirridin watched Cordovan walk over to the rock face and disappear. Alla'mirridin leaned forward to make sure his eyes weren't playing tricks on him. As he did Zezza, off to his left, still astride Sunchild, said, "Your eyes do not deceive you, *Approaching Storm*." But before he could reply Cordovan had reappeared. The Watchman waved to them. One by one they nudged their horses forward. In a few moments they were all dismounted in front of an opening in the rock face that would go completely unnoticed unless you were right on top of it. They ground-hitched their mounts before walking over to it. Cordovan stood with Mino at the opening. The Ki'gadi had turned their captive Sicarri back over to Zezza. Both men had sober looks on their faces. Cordovan nodded to Mino.

The older Ki'gadi spoke to their entire party in grave tones. "According to our captive, this is just one of the ways into a valley where *Dar'ken'thrall* lies hidden from the world. We are about to enter a tunnel. The valley is on the other side. The exit should be as unguarded as this entrance, but we should not take that for granted. Our aim is simply to look around. We will gather as much information as we can. When we are finished we will return to this side so that we can decide what to do next. If Dar'ken'thrall is real, then the world must be made to know." No one spoke. They each nodded their heads. Mino looked around at each of their faces before nodding his own head. Alla'mirridin was thankful no one wanted to speak. He was not sure he could have spoken or what he would have said. His heart was beating in his chest so loudly that he was sure everyone else could hear it. With Mino in the lead, and Cordovan right behind the elder Ki'gadi, they all entered the tunnel, one by one. The tunnel was wide enough for several people to walk alongside one another. While it was dark, there seemed to be some light coming from somewhere. It was not bright, but it was enough to see by.

It did not take long for the smell to hit them. Alla'mirridin raised his arm to his face, sticking his nose in the crook of his elbow. The smell of sulfur filled the air. It got stronger the longer they walked. The tunnel wound around like a snake moving through high grass. After a while Alla'mirridin could feel the angle change. Suddenly they were moving downward. A few hundred paces more and Alla'mirridin began to see a dim light ahead. As they came around a final turn they could see out the opening in the end of the tunnel. Alla'mirridin caught a hint of night sky, what looked like liquid fire erupting from the earth, and black stone towers in the distance. But before he could see more the opening was blocked by moving shapes draped in shadow. Mino stopped. Everyone froze where they were with the exception of Cordovan who stepped up to stand beside Mino. Alla'mirridin could not see clearly what or who blocked the exit from the tunnel but when he spoke it became all too clear.

"Well, well, well, if it isn't the Whitehairs and their pets? You came all this way to return my Master?" Mino lifted his hand. A fist-sized ball of blue light appeared, floating up to the ceiling of the tunnel, illuminating the exit for everyone to see. Behind Alla'mirridin, Zezza let out a low growl that he thought only he heard. It was the young Sicarri they had fought with before capturing his Master. Zezza whispered, "Hargin Hellsgate." She managed to say his name like it dirtied her mouth to speak it. Without looking over his shoulder, as if reading his pupil's mind, Mino said, "Stay where you are Had'wadai."

Mocking Mino, the young man said, "Yes, *Had'wadai*. Stay where you are or I will give you another beating." Laughing softly, the young Sicarri stepped into the blue light created by the ball of flame hanging in the air. Alla'mirridin thought he could hear Zezza's teeth grinding behind him. But she did not move. Though she did mutter, "Yes, you beat me, with a lot of help, you coward." Alla'mirridin smiled to himself at her words. As the young Sicarri stepped closer Alla'mirridin remembered how tall he was. He looked down on Cordovan, who was not a small man. He towered over the much smaller Mino. The young Sicarri's shoulder-length, brown hair hung loose around his narrow face. A swordhilt stuck up over each shoulder. Alla'mirridin did remember the unrelieved black of boots, vest, breeches, and shirt. The young darkling had tucked his leather gloves behind his belt. As he came to stand in front of Mino, Alla'mirridin, for the first time, caught sight of what was behind the young Sicarri. They passed through the light, from shadow to shadow, as they flanked Hargin Hellsgate. There must have been a dozen of them. Tall, white *Horrors*, wrapped in black cloth, swarmed around the exit to the tunnel like a hive of disturbed wasps. Alla'mirridin thought he could hear hundreds of voices whispering, barely audible, at the edge of his range of hearing. They moved like liquid. Alla'mirridin blinked as he tried to keep track of their movement. Then he saw that there were other things just outside the exit to the tunnel. He could not make out what they were but there were other dark shapes out there waiting for them.

Hargin Hellsgate's voice brought Alla'mirridin's attention back to where the young Sicarri stood. "I'm not going to ask you to release my Master. It is unnecessary. We are going to take him. And all of you for that matter." Black tendrils of lightning leaped from the young Sicarri's fingers. Mino's left hand came up. The lightning exploded against the Ki'gadi's palm. Some of it slammed into the walls of the tunnel as it was reflected away from the older Ki'gadi. Rock exploded around them. Alla'mirridin reached for his sword but was struck hard in the back. He went down in a heap. More explosions ripped through the tunnel as he turned over to see that it was Zezza on top of him. Somehow Vesper Shadowell had shoved her into Alla'mirridin sending them both tumbling to the ground. The older Sicarri had run past them. He disappeared into the swirling mass of Horrors behind the younger Sicarri. As Alla'mirridin untangled himself from Zezza he looked back at the exit in time to see Hargin Hellsgate shout something unintelligible. It was a language he had never heard before. At the word from Hellsgate the Horrors surged forward. The blue ball of flame lighting the tunnel winked out as Mino brought both of his hands up. The Horrors, what Zezza had called *Graelim*, hit an invisible wall. Mino slid a step back as they pounded against the barrier he had thrown up. He had been a fraction too slow, however, because one of them had gotten through. Cordovan tumbled to the ground fighting for his life with the thing.

By the time Alla'mirridin had gotten to his feet Aubrey was already there. The young Watchman grabbed the Graelim. As if he did not know his own strength, he threw the creature off Cordovan, sending it flying through the air. Alla'mirridin caught a glimpse of the young Watchmen looking at his own hands as if he was astonished. Maybe he had not known how strong he was because when he had thrown the Graelim off Cordovan he inadvertently threw it into Mino. The senior Ki'gadi stumbled for the briefest instant. When he did his barrier came down. Before he could throw it back up three more Graelim came bounding through. There was no more time for thinking. Mino held the rest at bay as the other Graelim threw themselves, relentlessly, into his barrier. Hellsgate, now accompanied by his freed Master, approached the barrier hurling black lightning and green balls of fire from their hands. Alla'mirridin tried to ignore the amazing things he was seeing. He threw himself at one of the Graelim, which had gotten through the barrier. He also caught a glimpse of Mino trying not to buckle under the onslaught. In the next moment all thoughts of Mino were gone as Alla'mirridin careened into the Graelim standing before him. He spared no thought for Mino, Zezza, or anything else. In that darkened tunnel, lit by faint fire and exploding lightning, the world fell away. Dark, foul whispers tried to creep into his thoughts but they, too, fell away. All that remained was the thing trying to kill him. Alla'mirridin did not think, he did not try to manipulate the moment. He simply let the world come to him. It was a narrow, small world filled with only the twisted thing before him. He let it come. *Wind Trims the Sail* took him under the things black spearhead. Without a thought he pivoted into *Fox Rounds the Tree*. The pale thing slashed at him with its black-bladed spear, but it did not touch him. Nothing could touch him. This was his world. An errant thought flickered at the edge of his darkened memory, something about *The Master's Wheel*. But he did not entertain it. He let it flow past him. A few paces of dust-covered stone was his entire world, and it all belonged to him. Midway through *Serpent Slips the Noose* he twisted into *Sparrow Shakes the Branch*. The thing howled as it jumped backward. Its black cloak floated up revealing the missing arm. Alla'mirridin had taken it off at the elbow. But he did not stop. *Widow Stirs the Pot* flowed into *Scorpion Lashes its Tail*. The Horror spun, trying to recover. It flung up a pale, white, clawed hand. Something invisible hit Alla'mirridin. For the briefest moment fear gripped his heart threatening to freeze him in place. Sheer terror welled up in him like hot water exploding from a spring. Just as he froze in place a flash of heat hit him. The image of a woman, her hair trailing behind her to her feet, flashed before his eyes. When it did the fear left him. Alla'mirridin moved. The Horror was caught off guard. It thought he was frozen in place. *Willow Waves at the Moon* ended it. The things head bounced away down the tunnel as Alla'mirridin twirled his sword once over his head before bringing it back to Position One.

He watched as the thing burst into a sulfurous flame. A loud explosion of rock and flame brought him back to the world as it was. Zezza was screaming at him. He looked around him. Mino was on his knees, but his barrier was holding. Lighting, black tendrils of mist, along with green flames erupted violently against it. All the Graelim were dead. Zezza had dirt on her face but she seemed unhurt. The Watchmen were falling back. Dain Du'urdin was nowhere to be seen. Zezza shouted again. "Alla'mirridin! We must go! Now!"

The tunnel shook beneath his feet as an enormous explosion of black lightning pushed Mino, who had managed to get back to his feet, back a full stride. A third Sicarri had joined Hellsgate and Shadowell on the other side of Mino din' Darksbane's barrier. How powerful *was* Mino? It amazed Alla'mirridin to see it. All three were throwing dark lightning against the barrier. Mino was struggling to hold it, but he was holding it. Alla'mirridin looked into Zezza's eyes. What he saw there frightened him. He shouted above the din, "We can't leave him!"

Zezza flinched as if his words had hit her. Alla'mirridin regretted it as soon as he said it. A tear cut through the dirt on her face as it trickled down her cheek. He cut her off when she opened her mouth to speak.

"I'm sorry!" he yelled above the sounds of the explosions. "I'm sorry." He said it again as she nodded her head. Zezza pulled at his arm. When he started to move she let go, turned, and ran down the tunnel. Alla'mirridin looked at Mino one last time as he prepared to run. The two men looked eyes. Mino smiled. He mouthed a few words to him. Alla'mirridin nodded. The old man returned the nod. Then Alla'mirridin was running. It was too dark to see clearly but he ran. He brushed up against the wall of the tunnel, but he kept running. When he exited the tunnel at a full run a cloud of rocks and dust followed him out of the tunnel. He came to a halt. When he turned back to face the collapsed tunnel, Alla'mirridin did not realize he was screaming until Zezza grabbed his shoulder. He yelled, "No!" one last time.

Alla'mirridin just stood there for a moment. He just stared at the place where the entrance of the tunnel had been. He realized he was breathing heavily. His hands were clenched into fists. Mino was dead. Mino was dead saving them. It was not supposed to have happened like that. Zezza's voice broke a little when she spoke. Standing just behind him with her hand still on his shoulder the young Ki'gadi said, "Breathe Alla'mirridin. Breathe."

Alla'mirridin bobbed his head once. He did what she said letting himself breathe. Slowly, he began to calm down. His hands unclenched. He turned to see the others standing together in a small semi-circle. They were all covered with dirt, but no one seemed injured. Dain Du'urdin had the reigns of his horse in his hand. When Alla'mirridin joined them, he handed Speckle's to him. They stood there at the foot of the Black Hills. Night had fallen fully though the moon was full in the sky. Cordovan looked grim in the pale moonlight. Aubrey stood next to the senior Watchman looking even grimmer, if that was possible. Cordovan gave them a moment to catch their breath as he looked around their circle. After he met everyone's eyes he spoke. There was a hint of something in his voice that Alla'mirridin did not really want to identify.

"So, it is true. *Dar'ken'thrall* is real, as are the twisted things that protect it." Cordovan looked around their little circle again as each of them nodded their agreement. As he continued his voice got stronger. "The world is completely unprepared and unaware of what we have found. I will wager there is a dark, twisted army behind these peaks, hidden from view. Waiting for something. The world must know." Turning to look at Zezza he said, "Zezza din' Nightblinder, your *Shad'ha'dai* wanted Palladawn to know what we found here. I am not attempting to give you an order, Master Sage, but that was his wish." Zezza inclined her head sharply at the Watchman. Cordovan turned his head to look at Aubrey Devilwind. "Watchman, you will see it done. Help the Master Sage make it to Palladawn. Then report to Watchkeep. There are other ways in and out of this hidden valley according to the Sicarri we questioned so they will likely be coming for you. They will not want their secret known." Aubrey Devilwind nodded at the senior Watchman like a good soldier.

Cordovan looked over at Dain Du'urdin. "Old friend. I would be grateful if you got word of all of this to the Gallant Master of the Gate. Tell him in detail what has happened and what you have seen. He will know what to do." Dain Du'urdin, his hands shaking, managed to nod his head. The man was clearly unnerved by what he had seen. "Cordovan, I will make sure all of Alexandria knows what transpires here. Mark me, I will." Cordovan managed a smile for Dain Du'urdin. When the Watchman finally turned his attention to Alla'mirridin. Alla'mirridin said, "What are you going to do?"

Cordovan took a moment before answering as if he was steeling himself for what he was about to say. "I am going back for Mino." They each looked around their little circle at one another before looking back at him. Cordovan nodded as he said, "I know. I know. It is likely that Mino din' Darksbane, Master Sage of the Ki'gadi, is dead. But if he isn't I will not leave him to the likes of what we saw in that tunnel, or beyond it." Alla'mirridn said, "But how do you expect to save him by yourself?" Finally, Cordovan smiled as if remembering something. He said, "I am a member of the Watch." He spoke the words as if they said everything that needed saying. When Alla'mirridin did not challenge his assertion Cordovan said, "I think I can guess where you are going." Alla'mirridin said, "I am going to make sure Zezza gets to Palladawn."

Cordovan nodded as if it was nothing less than what he had expected to hear. Alla'mirridin did not share his reasons for going with Zezza. He simply let his statement stand as they mounted their horses. After a few words in the saddle and a quick grasp of hands, Dain Du'urdin turned his horse from Cordovan's. With a wave over his shoulder, he trotted off toward the south. Cordovan had a few private words with Aubrey Devilwind before turning his horse east. He rode off along the base of the mountain range looking for another way into the hidden valley. Alla'mirridin flanked Zezza, with Aubrey on her other side, as they headed west toward Palladawn. Alla'mirridin reflected on the words Mino din' Darksbane had mouthed to him just before he ran. In that brief moment he had mouthed, *keep her safe*. They had both known who he meant by *her*. As darkness settled across the mountains they raced west with a message for the world. He galloped Speckle on Zezza's left. *What would people do*, he began to wonder? What would they do when word came that twisted things from another age had returned? Alla'mirridin rode on. It was dangerous to ride in the darkness. But it could not be helped. They raced toward Palladawn even though night had fallen.

... it will be the beginning of the End of all things. When ... bright eyes have turned from their watching ... army, fit for darkness, will rise, awaiting ... Coming ... when fire will streak across the heavens. Nightmares will walk among us ... day will ... to never ending darkness ... night will fall ...

~*Translated by Pien iel den' Berric from the burned fragment* Codex 34 *found at the dig of Sepptis Corric' Dal, believed to be a page from* The Legacy, *concerning the Prophecy of the* One Who is to Come

The End of the First Book of *The Three Gifts*

ABOUT THE AUTHOR

Gerald L. Coleman is a Philosopher, Theologian, Poet, and Author residing in Atlanta. Born in Lexington, he did his undergraduate work in Philosophy and English at the University of Kentucky. He followed that by completing a degree in Religious Studies and concluding with a Master's degree in Theology at Trevecca Nazarene University in Nashville. His most recent work appears in, Pluck! The Journal of Affrilachian Arts & Culture, Drawn To Marvel: Poems From The Comic Books, Pine Mountain Sand & Gravel Vol. 18, Black Bone Anthology, the 10th Anniversary Issue of Diode Poetry Journal, and About Place Journal. He is a speculative fiction author with short stories published in the Science Fiction, Cyberfunk Anthology: *The City* and the Rococoa Anthology by Roaring Lion. He is the author of the Epic Fantasy novel saga, *The Three Gifts*, which includes *WHEN NIGHT FALLS: BOOK ONE* and *A PLAGUE OF SHADOWS: BOOK TWO*. He has appeared on panels at DragonCon, SOBSFCon, Atlanta Science Fiction & Fantasy Expo, the Outer Dark Symposium, and has been a Guest Author and panelist at JordonCon. He is a co-founder of the Affrilachian Poets and has recently released three collections of poetry entitled *the road is long*, *falling to earth*, and *microphone check*. You can find him at *geraldlcoleman.co*.

CPSIA information can be obtained
at www.ICGtesting.com
Printed in the USA
BVHW081444020919
557356BV00007B/97/P